THE TIME OF
TROUBLES I

Baen Books by HARRY TURTLEDOVE

The Time of Troubles I
The Time of Troubles II (forthcoming)

The War Between the Provinces series:
Sentry Peak
Marching Through Peachtree
Advance and Retreat

The Fox novels:
Wisdom of the Fox
Tale of the Fox

3 x T
The Case of the Toxic Spell Dump
Thessalonica
Alternate Generals, editor
Alternate Generals II, editor
Alternate Generals III, editor
The Enchanter Completed, editor
Down in the Bottomlands (with L. Sprague de Camp)

THE TIME OF TROUBLES I

HARRY TURTLEDOVE

A Baen Book

Baen Publishing Enterprises
P.O. Box 1403
Riverdale, NY 10471
www.baen.com

ISBN: 1-4165-0904-6

Cover art by Gary Ruddell
Map art by Christine Levis

First printing,in this format, June 2005

Library of Congress Cataloging-in-Publication Data

Turtledove, Harry.
    The time of troubles I / Harry Turtledove.
        p. cm.
    ISBN 1-4165-0904-6 (hc)
    1. Kings and rulers--Succession--Fiction. 2. Missing persons--
    Fiction. I. Title: Time of troubles 1. II. Title: Time of troubles
    one. III. Title.

    PS3570.U76T56 2005
    813'.54--dc22   2005005212

Distributed by Simon & Schuster
1230 Avenue of the Americas
New York, NY 10020

Production & design by Windhaven Press, Auburn, NH (www.windhaven.com)
Printed in the United States of Amcrica

10   9   8   7   6   5   4   3   2   1

CONTENTS

MAKURAN AND VIDESSOS AT THE START OF THE TIME OF TROUBLES

HALOGA LAND

Agder

KINGDOM OF AGDER

NORTHERN SEA

N

THATAGUSH

Y A

KHATRISH

ASTRIS RIVER

KUBRAT

IMBROS · PARISTRIAN MTS.

VIDESSOS

ACROSS

SYKEOTA

THE KEY

KALAVRIA

KASTAVALA

OPSIKION

GARSAVRA

KYSIKOS

GAVDOS

O F

VIDESSOS

SEA

Christine Levis

THE STOLEN THRONE

THE TIME OF TROUBLES,
VOL. 1

DEDICATION:

To the Redlines, father and son.

AUTHOR'S NOTE:

The events chronicled in the books of *The Time of Troubles* begin about 150 years before those described in *The Tale of Krispos* and thus about 650 years before those of *The Videssos Cycle*.

✦ **1**

From the battlements of the stronghold, Abivard looked north across the broad sweep of land his father, Godarz, held in the name of the King of Kings. Out beyond the village that surrounded the stronghold, most of what he saw was sere and brown from high summer; only near the Vek Rud River, and in the gardens nourished by the underground channels called *qanats*, did green defy the blazing sun.

Off to the east, the Videssians, Makuran's longtime foes, gave reverence to the sun as a symbol of their god. To Abivard, the sun was too unreliable for worship, roasting the highland plateau of Makuran in summertime and then all but disappearing during the short, cold days of winter.

He raised his left hand in a gesture of benediction familiar to his folk. In any case, the Videssian god was false. He was as certain of that as of his own name. *The* God had spoken to the Makuraners through the Prophets Four: Narseh, Gimillu, the lady Shivini, and Fraortish, eldest of all.

"Whom are you blessing there, son?" a gruff, raspy voice asked from behind him.

Abivard whirled. "I greet you, Father. I'm sorry; I didn't hear you come up."

"No harm, no harm." Godarz let loose a few syllables of laughter, as if he held only so much and didn't want to use it all up at once. Abivard sometimes thought his father was a mold into which he himself had been pressed not quite hard enough. They had the same long, rectangular faces; the same proud noses; the

3

same dark, hooded eyes under thick brows; the same swarthy skin and black hair; even, these past five years or so, the same full beards.

But Abivard's face still lacked the lines of character the years had etched across Godarz's features. The creases in his cheeks told of laughter and sorrow, the furrows in his forehead of thought. By comparison, Abivard seemed to himself a house not yet lived in to the fullest.

There was one furrow the years had not put in Godarz's face: the scar that seamed his left cheek came from the shamshir of a Khamorth raider. That mark vanished under his beard but, like a *qanat* traced by the greenery above it, a line of white hair showed its track. Abivard envied him that mark, too.

"Whom were you blessing?" Godarz asked again.

"No one in particular, Father," Abivard said. "I thought of the Four, so of course I made their sign."

"Good lad, good lad." Godarz was in the habit of repeating himself. Abivard's mother, Burzoe, and the *dihqan's* other wives teased him about it all the time. He always took it good-naturedly; once he had cracked, "The lot of you would be less happy if I hadn't cared to repeat my vows."

Abivard said, "If I asked the Four to ask the God to bless any part of this domain in particular, I suppose I should ask his favor for the flocks."

"You couldn't do better." Godarz thumped Abivard fondly on the shoulder. "We'd be poor—thieving nomads take *poor*, son; we'd be *dead*—without 'em."

"I know." Away from the river, away from the *qanats*, the land was too dry to support crops most years. That was true of most of the highland plateau. After the spring rains, though, grass and low shrubs carpeted the hills and valleys. Enough of the hardy plants lived on through the rest of the year to give fodder for sheep and cattle, horses, and camels. From those the *dihqans*—the lesser nobility—and all who depended on them made their livelihoods.

Godarz scratched at the puckered scar; though it was years old, it still sometimes itched. He said, "While you're about your prayers, you might do as I've done and beg the Four to give us another year of peace along the northern frontier. Maybe they'll harken to the two of us together; maybe they will." His expression grew harsh. "Or maybe they won't."

Abivard clicked his tongue between his teeth. "It's as bad as that?"

"Aye, it is," Godarz said. "I was out riding this morning, giving the new gelding some work, and I met a rider homeward bound toward Mashiz from the Degird River. The Khamorth are stirring again, he says."

"A messenger from the King of Kings?" Abivard said. "Why didn't you invite him to refresh himself at the stronghold?" *Then I'd have had a chance to talk with him, too, instead of getting my news secondhand,* he thought.

"I did, son, I did, but he said me nay," Godarz answered. "Said he grudged the time; he'd stop to rest only at night. The news for Peroz King of Kings was that urgent, he said, and when he gave it me, I could but bob my head up and down and wish him the God's protection on his road."

"Well?" Abivard practically hopped with impatience and excitement. Concern rode his voice, as well; not too many farsangs east of Godarz's domain, the little Vek Rud bent north and flowed into the Degird. The frontier and the steppe nomads who dwelt beyond it were close, close.

"He learned why the tribes are stirring," Godarz said portentously. After another pause that almost drove Abivard mad, the *dihqan* went on, "The tribes are stirring because, by the Four, Videssos is stirring them."

"Here?" Abivard exclaimed. "How could that be?"

Godarz's face went harsh; his scar, normally darker than the rest of his skin, turned pale: rage. But he held his voice under tight control. "The Pardrayan plain runs east almost forever. Videssos could send an embassy across it—not quickly, but it could. And, by all the signs, it has. The God, for reasons best known to Himself, has made Videssos rich in gold."

Abivard nodded. His father's treasure horde had more than a few fine Videssian goldpieces in it. Every nation in the world took those goldpieces and was glad to have them. The corruption and deviousness of the Empire of Videssos were bywords in Makuran, but the imperials kept their coinage honest. No matter which Avtokrator's face graced a coin's obverse, it would be pure gold, minted at seventy-two to the pound.

Makuran coined mostly in silver. Its arkets were good money, but money changers always took a premium above their face value when exchanging them for Videssian gold.

"I see I've no need to draw you a picture in the sand, no need at all," Godarz went on. "The cowardly men of the east, not having the kidneys to fight us as warriors against warriors, bribe the nomads to do their work for them."

"They are no fit warriors, then—they're no better than assassins," Abivard said hotly. "Surely the God will open a pit beneath their feet and drop them into the Void, to be nothing forevermore."

"May it be so." Godarz's left hand twisted in a gesture different from the one Abivard had used: one that condemned the wicked. The *dihqan* added, "Vicious dogs that they are, they know no caste."

Abivard copied the sign his father had used. To his way of thinking, Godarz could have pronounced no curse more deadly. Life in Makuran pivoted on its five castes: the King of Kings and the royal household; the priests and the Seven Clans of the high nobility; the lesser nobles like Godarz—Makuran's backbone, they called themselves; the merchants; and the peasants and herders who made up the bulk of the populace.

The Seven Clans and the *dihqans* fought for the King of Kings, sometimes under his own banner, sometimes under one of the high nobles. Abivard could no more imagine paying someone so he could evade that duty than he could think of taking a knife and cutting off his manhood. He would lose it no more one way than the other.

Well, if the Videssians were hucksters even at war, the nobles of the plateau would surely teach the nomads they had bought where true honor lay. Abivard said as much, loudly.

That brought back his father's smile. Godarz thumped him on the back and said, "When the red banner of war returns from Mashiz, blood of my blood, I think it likely you will ride with me against those who would despoil us."

"Yes," Abivard said, and then again, in a great shout: "*Yes!*" He had trained for war since he was a boy who barely reached Godarz's chest. He had learned to ride, to thrust with the lance, to bear the weight of armor, to wield a scimitar, to wield the bow.

But Makuran had been unwontedly peaceful of late. His lessons remained lessons only. Now at last he would have the chance to apply them against a real foe, and one who needed beating. If the nomads swarmed south over the Degird, as they had a way of doing every generation or two, they would kill, they would steal, and worst of all they would wreck *qanats* so people would go hungry until the underground channels were laboriously repaired.

Godarz's laugh was the small, happy one of a man well pleased with his son. "I can see you want to get into your mail shirt and clap on your helmet this very moment. It's a long way to Mashiz and back—we shan't be riding out tomorrow, or next week, either. Even after the red banner warns of war, it will be a while yet before the army reaches us and we join its ranks."

Abivard shifted restively from foot to foot. "Why doesn't the King of Kings have his palace in Makuran proper, not on the far side of the Dilbat Mountains overlooking the Thousand Cities?"

"Three reasons," Godarz said, sounding like a pedagogue though Abivard had only been venting spleen. "First, we of Makuran are most likely to be loyal to our lord, being of his blood, and hence require less oversight. Second, the land between the Tutub and the Tib, above which Mashiz sits, is full of riches: not just the famous Thousand Cities but also farmlands more fertile than any the plateau boasts. And third, Mashiz is a hundred farsangs closer to Videssos than the plateau, and Videssos is more important to us most times than our northwestern frontier."

"Most times, aye, but not today," Abivard said.

"No, today the Khamorth tribes are stirring, or so it's said," Godarz agreed. "But who set them in motion? Not their own chieftains."

"Videssos," Abivard said.

"Aye, Videssos. We are her great rival, as she is ours. One day, I think, only one of us will be left standing," Godarz said.

"And that one will rule the world," Abivard said. In his mind's eye, he saw the King of Kings' lion banner floating above the Videssian Avtokrator's palace in Videssos the city, saw priests of the Prophets Four praising the God in the High Temple to false Phos.

The setting for the capital of Videssos remained blurry to him, though. He knew the sea surrounded it on three sides, and he had never seen a sea, not even the inland Mylasa Sea into which the Degird River flowed. He pictured a sea as something like one of the salt lakes that dotted the Makuraner plateau, but bigger. Still, his imagination could not quite grasp a body of water too vast to see across.

Godarz smiled. "You're thinking we shall be the one, aren't you? As do I, son, as do I. The God grant it be so."

"Yes," Abivard said. "I was also thinking—if we conquer, Father, I'll see the sea. The sea around Videssos the city, I mean."

"I understood you," Godarz said. "That would be a sight, wouldn't it? I've not seen it, either, you know. But don't expect the day to come in your time, though. Their border has marched with ours for eight hundred years now, since the Tharpiya hillmen ruled Makuran. They've not smashed us yet, nor we them. One day, though—"

The *dihqan* nodded, as if very sure that day would come. Then, with a last grin at his son, he went on down the walkway, his striped caftan flapping around his ankles, every so often bending down to make sure a piece of golden sandstone was securely in place.

Abivard stayed up on the walk a few minutes more, then went down the stairs that led to the stronghold's inner courtyard. The stairs were only a couple of paces wide and had no railing; had a brick shifted under his feet, he could have dashed out his brains on the rock-hard dirt below. The bricks did not shift. Godarz was as careful and thoroughgoing in inspecting as he was with everything else.

Down in the courtyard, the sun beat at Abivard with redoubled force, for it reflected from the walls as well as descending directly. His sandals scuffed up dust as he hurried toward the shaded living quarters.

The stronghold was a rough triangle, taking advantage of the shape of the rocky knob on which it sat. The short wall on the eastern side ran north and south; the other two, which ran toward each other from its bottom and top, were longer and went northwest and southwest, respectively. The living quarters were tucked into the corner of the eastern wall and the one that went northwest. That gave them more shadow than they would have had anywhere else.

Abivard took a long, happy breath as he passed through the iron-faced wooden door—the living quarters, of course, doubled as citadel. The thick stone walls made the quarters much cooler than the blazing oven of the courtyard. They were also much gloomier: the windows, being designed for defense as well as—and ahead of—vision, were mere slits, with heavy shutters that could be slammed together at a moment's notice. Abivard needed a small stretch of time for his eyes to adjust to dimness.

He stepped carefully until they did. The living quarters were a busy place. Along with servants of the stronghold bustling back and forth, he had to be alert for merchants and peasants who, failing to find his father, would press their troubles on him. Hearing those troubles was one of his duties, but not one he felt like facing right now.

He also had to keep an eye out for children on the floor. His two full brothers, Varaz and Frada, were men grown, and his sister Denak had long since retreated to the women's chambers. But his half brothers ranged in age from Jahiz, who was older than Frada, down to a couple of brats who still sucked at their wet nurses' breasts. Half brothers—and half sisters under the age of twelve—brawled through the place, together with servants' children, shepherd boys, and whomever else they could drag into their games.

When they weren't in hot pursuit of dragons or evil enchanters or Khamorth bandits, they played Makuraners and Videssians. If Videssos had fallen as easily in reality as in their games, the domains of the King of Kings would have stretched east to the legendary Northern Sea centuries ago.

One of his half brothers, an eight-year-old named Parsuash, dodged around Abivard, thwarting another lad who pursued him. "Can't catch me, can't catch me!" Parsuash jeered. "See, I'm in my fortress and you can't catch me."

"Your fortress is going to the kitchens," Abivard said, and walked off. That gave Rodak, his other half brother, the chance to swoop down for the kill. Parsuash screeched in dismay.

In the kitchens, some flatbread just out of the oven lay cooling on its baking pan. Abivard tore off a chunk of it, then stuck slightly scorched fingers into his mouth. He walked over to a bubbling pot, used the piece of flatbread to scoop out some of the contents, and popped it into his mouth.

"Ground lamb balls and pomegranate seeds," he said happily after he swallowed. "I thought that was what I smelled. Father will be pleased—it's one of his favorites."

"And what would you have done had it been something else, son of the *dihqan*?" one of the cooks asked.

"Eaten it anyhow, I expect," Abivard answered. The cook laughed.

Abivard went on, "Since it is what it is, though—" He tore off another piece of flatbread, then raided the pot again. The cook laughed louder.

Still chewing, Abivard left the kitchens and went down the hall that led to his own room. Since he was eldest son of Godarz's principal wife, he had finally got one to himself, which led to envious sighs from his brothers and half brothers. To him, privacy seemed a mixed blessing. He enjoyed having a small place to himself, but had been so long without one that sometimes he felt achingly alone and longed for the warm, squabbling companionship he had known before.

Halfway down the hall, his left sandal started flapping against his foot. He peered down and discovered he had lost the bronze buckle that held a strap around his ankle. He looked around and even got down on his hands and knees, but didn't find it.

"It probably fell into the Void," he muttered under his breath. Moving with an awkward half-skating motion, he made it to his doorway, went into his room, and put on a new pair of sandals.

Then he went out again, damaged sandal in hand. One of Godarz's rules—which, to his credit, he scrupulously followed himself—was that anything that broke had to be set right at once. "Let one thing slide and soon two'll be gone, two lead to four, and four—well, there had better not be four, there had better not," he would say.

Had just a bit of leather fallen off the sandal, Abivard could have gotten some from the stables and made his own rough repair. But to replace a buckle, he had to visit the cobbler in the village that surrounded the stronghold.

Out into the heat again, then. The sun smote him like a club. Sweat sprang out on his face, rolled down his back under his baggy garment. He wished he'd had farther to go; he wouldn't have felt foolish about getting on his horse. But if his father had seen him, he would have made sarcastic noises about Abivard's riding in a sedan chair next time, as if he were a high noble, not just a *dihqan's* son. Abivard walked.

The gate guards pounded the butts of their spears against the hard ground as he went by. He dipped his head to return the salute. Then he left the stronghold and went into the village, an altogether different world.

Homes and shops straggled down to the base of the hill the stronghold topped and even for a little distance out onto the flat land below. Some were of stone, some of mud brick with widely overhanging thatched roofs to protect the walls from winter storms. Set beside the stronghold, they all seemed like toys.

The hill was steep, the streets winding and full of stones; if you tumbled, you were liable to end up at the bottom with a broken leg. Abivard had been navigating through town since he learned to toddle; he was as sure-footed as a mountain sheep.

Merchants cried their wares in the market square: chickpeas, dates, mutton buzzing with flies, utterances of the Prophets Four on parchment amulets—said to be sovereign against disease, both as prevention and cure; Abivard, whose education had included letters but not logic, failed to wonder why the second would be necessary if the first was efficacious. The calls rose from all around: knives, copper pots and clay ones, jewelry of glass beads and copper wire—those with finer stuff came to sell at the stronghold—and a hundred other things besides. The smells were as loud as the shouts.

A fellow was keeping a pot of baked quinces hot over a dung fire. Abivard haggled him down from five coppers to three; Godarz was not a man who let his sons grow up improvident. The quince *was* hot. Abivard quickly found a stick on the ground, poked it through the spicy fruit, and ate happily on his way down to the cobbler's shop.

The cobbler bowed low when Abivard came in; he was not near enough in rank to the *dihqan's* son to present his cheek for a ceremonial kiss, as a couple of the richer merchants might have done. Abivard returned a precise nod and explained what he required.

"Yes, yes," the cobbler said. "Let me see the good sandal, pray, that I may match the buckle as close as may be."

"I'm afraid I didn't bring it." Abivard felt foolish and annoyed with himself. Though Godarz was back in the stronghold, he felt his father's eye on him. "I'll have to go back and get it."

"Oh, never mind that, your Excellency. Just come here and pick out the one that nearest suits it. They're no two of 'em just alike, anyhow." The cobbler showed him a bowl half full of brass buckles. They jingled as Abivard sorted through them till he found the one he wanted.

The cobbler's fingers deftly fixed it to the sandal. Deft as they were, though, they bore the scars of awl and knife and needle and nail. "No trade is simple," Godarz would say, "though some seem so to simple men." Abivard wondered how much pain the cobbler had gone through to learn his business.

He didn't dicker so hard with the cobbler as he had with the fruit seller. The man's family had been in the village for generations, serving villagers and *dihqans* alike. He deserved his superiors' support.

Sandal repaired, Abivard could have gone straight back to the stronghold to escape the worst of the heat in the living quarters. Instead, he returned to the bazaar in the marketplace and bought himself another quince. He stood there taking little bites of it and doing his best to seem as if he were thinking about the goods offered for sale. What he was really doing was watching the young women who went from this stall to that dealer in search of what they needed.

Women of the merchant and peasant castes lived under fewer restrictions than those of the nobility. Oh, a few wealthy merchants locked their wives and daughters away in emulation of their betters, but most lower-caste women had to go out and about in the world to help feed their families.

Abivard was betrothed to Roshnani, a daughter of Papak, the *dihqan* whose stronghold lay a few farsangs south and west of Godarz's. Their parents having judged the match advantageous, they were bound to each other before either of them reached puberty. Abivard had never seen his fiancée. He wouldn't, not till the day they were wed.

When he got the chance, then, he watched girls—the serving women in the stronghold, the girls in the village square here. When one caught his eye, he imagined Roshnani looked like her. When he spotted one he did not find fair, he hoped his betrothed did not resemble her.

He finished nibbling the quince and licked his fingers. He thought about buying yet another one; that would give him an excuse to hang around in the square awhile longer. But he was sensitive to his own dignity and, whenever he forgot to be, Godarz made sure his memory didn't slip for long.

All the same, he still didn't feel like going back to the stronghold. He snapped his slightly sticky fingers in inspiration. Godarz had given him all kinds of interesting news. Why not find out what old Tanshar the fortune-teller made of his future?

An additional inducement to this course was that Tanshar's house lay alongside the market square. Abivard could see that the old man's shutters were thrown wide open. He could go in, have his fortune read, and keep right on eying the women hereabouts, all without doing anything in the least undignified.

The door to Tanshar's house was on the side opposite the square. Like the shutters, it gaped wide, both to show the fortune-teller was open for business and to give him the benefit of whatever breeze the God chose to send.

One thing Tanshar certainly had not done: he had not used the prophetic gift to get rich. His home was astringently neat and clean, but furnished only with a much-battered low table and a couple of wickerwork chairs. Abivard had the idea that he wouldn't have bothered with those had he not needed to keep his clients comfortable.

Only scattered hairs in Tanshar's beard were still black, giving it the look of snow lightly streaked with soot. A cataract clouded the fortune-teller's left eye. The right one, though, still saw clearly. Tanshar bowed low. "Your presence honors my house, son of the *dihqan*." He waved Abivard to the less disreputable chair, pressed upon him a cup of wine and date cakes sweet with honey and topped by pistachios. Not until Abivard had eaten and drunk did Tanshar ask, "How may I serve you?"

Abivard explained what he had heard from Godarz, then asked, "How shall this news affect my life?"

"Here; let us learn if the God will vouchsafe an answer." Tanshar pulled his own chair close to Abivard's. He pulled up the left sleeve of his caftan, drew off a silver armlet probably worth as much as his house and everything in it put together. He held it out to Abivard. "Take hold of one side whilst I keep a grasp on the other. We shall see whether the Prophets Four grant me a momentary portion of their power."

Busts of the Four Prophets adorned the armlet: young Narseh, his beard barely sprouted; Gimillu the warrior, a strong face seamed with scars; Shivini, who looked like everyone's mother; and Fraortish, eldest of all, his eyes inset with gleaming jet. Though the silver band had just come from Tanshar's arm, it was cool, almost cold, to the touch.

The fortune-teller looked up at the thatched roof of his little cottage. Abivard's gaze followed Tanshar's. All he saw was straw, but he got the odd impression that Tanshar peered straight through the roof and up to the God's home on the far side of the sky.

"Let me see," Tanshar murmured. "May it please you, let me see." His eyes went wide and staring, his body stiffened. Abivard's left hand, the one that held the armlet, tingled as if it had suddenly fallen asleep. He looked down. A little golden light jumped back and forth from one Prophet's image to the next. At last it settled on Fraortish, eldest of all, making his unblinking jet eyes seem for an instant alive as they stared back at Abivard.

In a rich, powerful voice nothing like his own, Tanshar said, "Son of the *dihqan*, I see a broad field that is not a field, a tower on a hill where honor shall be won and lost, and a silver shield shining across a narrow sea."

The light in the silver Fraortish's eyes faded. Tanshar slumped as he seemed to come back to himself. When Abivard judged the fortune-teller had fully returned to the world of rickety wicker chairs and the astounding range of smells from the bazaar, he asked, "What did that mean, what you just told me?"

Maybe Tanshar wasn't all the way back to the real world: his good eye looked as blank as the one that cataract clouded. "I have delivered the prophecy?" he asked, his voice small and uncertain.

"Yes, yes," Abivard said impatiently, repeating himself like his father. He gave Tanshar back the words he had uttered, doing his best to say them just as he had heard them.

The fortune-teller started to lean back in his chair, then thought better as it creaked and rustled under his weight. He took the armlet from Abivard and put it back on his parchment-skinned arm. That seemed to give him strength. Slowly he said, "Son of the *dihqan*, I remember nothing of this, nor did *I* speak to you. Someone—something—used me as an instrument." Despite the bake-oven heat, he shivered. "You will see I am no youth. In all my years of telling what might lay ahead, this has befallen me but twice before."

The little hairs prickled up on Abivard's arms and at the back of his neck. He felt caught up in something vastly bigger than he was. Cautiously he asked, "What happened those two times?"

"One was a skinny caravaneer, back around the time you were born," Tanshar said. "He was skinny because he was hungry. He told me I foresaw for him piles of silver and gems, and today he is rich in Mashiz."

"And the other?" Abivard asked.

For a moment, he didn't think Tanshar would answer. The fortune-teller's expression was directed inward, and he looked old, old. Then he said, "Once I was a lad myself, you know, a lad with a bride about to bear him his firstborn. She, too, asked me to look ahead."

So far as Abivard knew, Tanshar had always lived alone. "What did you see?" he asked, almost whispering.

"Nothing," Tanshar said. "I saw nothing." Again Abivard wondered if he would go on. At last he did: "She died in childbed four days later."

"The God give her peace." The words tasted empty in Abivard's mouth. He set a hand on Tanshar's bony knee. "Once for great good, once for great ill. And now me. What does your foretelling mean?"

"Son of the *dihqan*, I do not know," Tanshar answered. "I can say only that these things lie across your future. When and where and to what effect, I cannot guess and shall not lie to claim I can. You will discover them, or they you, as the God chooses to unwind the substance of the world."

Abivard took out three silver arkets and pressed them into the fortune-teller's hand. Tanshar rang them against one another, then shook his head and gave them back. "Offer these to the God, if that please you, but not to me. I did not speak these words, whether they came through me or not. I cannot accept your coin for them."

"Keep them, please," Abivard said, looking around the clean but barren little house. "To my mind, you stand more in need of them than the God."

But Tanshar again shook his head and refused to take the money. "They are not for me, I tell you. Had I read your future in the ordinary way, gauging what was to come by the motions of the Prophets' armlet between your hand and mine, I should be glad of the fee, for then I had earned it. For this—no."

One of the things Godarz had taught Abivard was to recognize a man's stubbornness and to know when to yield to it. "Let it be as you say, then." Abivard flung the arkets out the window. "Where they go now, and with whom, is in the God's hands."

Tanshar nodded. "That was well done. May the foretelling you heard through me mean only good for you."

"May it be so," Abivard said. When he rose from the chair, he bowed low to Tanshar, as he might have to one of the upper nobility. That seemed to distress the fortune-teller even more than the prophecy that had escaped its usual bounds. "Accept the salute, at least, for the God," Abivard told him, and, reluctantly, he did.

Abivard left the fortune-teller's house. He had thought to linger in the bazaar awhile longer, buying more small things he didn't really need so he could look at, maybe even talk with, the young women there. Not now, though.

He peered out over the sun-scorched land that ran out toward the Vek Rud River. Nothing much grew on it now, not at this season. Did that make it a broad field that was not a field? Prophecy had one problem: how to interpret it.

He turned and looked up the slope of the hill on which the stronghold perched. Was it the tower where honor would be won and lost? It didn't look like a tower to him, but who could judge how the God perceived things?

And what of the sea? Did Tanshar's words mean he would see it one day, as he hoped? Which sea had the fortune-teller meant? Who would shine a silver shield across it?

All questions—no answers. He wondered if he would have been happier with an ordinary foretelling. No, he decided. If nothing else, this surely meant he would be bound up in great events. "I don't want to watch my life slide by while I do nothing but count the days," he said aloud.

For all his father's teaching, he was still young.

In the days and weeks that followed, Abivard took to looking south and west from the walls. He knew what he was waiting to see. So did Godarz, who teased him about it every so often. But the *dihqan* spent a good deal of time at the corner where the eastern and the south-facing walls met, too.

Abivard felt justified in haunting that corner when he spied the rider approaching the stronghold. The horseman carried something out of the ordinary in his right hand. At first, Abivard saw only the wriggling motion. Then he recognized that a banner was making it. And then he saw the banner was red.

He let out a whoop that made heads turn his way all around the stronghold. "The war banner!" he cried. "The war banner comes forth from Mashiz!"

He didn't know where Godarz had been, but his father stood on the wall beside him in less than a minute. The *dihqan* also peered south. "Aye, that is the war banner, and no mistake," he said. "Let's go down and greet the messenger, shall we? Let's go."

The horseman who carried the token of war was worn and dusty. Godarz greeted him with all the proper courtesies, pressing wine and honey cakes on him before inquiring of his business. That question, though, was but a formality. The crimson banner, limp now that the messenger no longer rode at a fast trot, spoke for itself.

Still, Makuran was built on formality, and, just as Godarz had to ask the question, the messenger had to answer it. He raised the banner so the red silk fluttered again for a moment on its staff, then said, "Peroz King of Kings, having declared it the duty of every man of Makuran entitled to bear arms to band together to punish the Khamorth savages of the steppe for the depredations they have inflicted on his realm and for the connivance with Videssos the great enemy, now commands each high noble and *dihqan* to gather a suitable force to be joined to Peroz King of Kings' own armament, which shall progress toward and across the river Degird for the purpose of administering the aforesaid punishment."

Getting all that out in one breath was hard, thirsty work; when the messenger had finished, he took a long pull at the wine, then let out an even longer—and happier—sigh. Then he drank again.

Ever courteous, Godarz waited till he was comfortable before asking, "When will the armament of the King of Kings—may his years be many and his realm increase—reach the river Degird, pray?"

In effect, he was asking when it would reach the stronghold, which lay only a couple of days' journey south of the frontier. He was also asking—with perfect discretion—how serious the King of Kings was about going on campaign: the slower he and his army traveled, the less they were likely to accomplish.

The messenger answered, "Peroz King of Kings began mustering his forces the day news of the plainsmen's insolence reached him.

The red banner began its journey through the land that same day. The army should reach this neighborhood inside the month."

Abivard blinked to hear that. Godarz didn't, but he might as well have. "He is serious," the *dihqan* murmured. "Serious."

The word ran through the courtyard. Men's heads—swarthy, long-faced, bearded: basically cut from the same cloth as Godarz and Abivard—solemnly bobbed up and down. The King of Kings of Makuran had great power, and most often wielded it with ponderousness to match.

"Peroz King of Kings *does* want to punish the steppe nomads," Abivard said. He got more nods for that, from his father among others. Excitement blazed in him. He'd been a boy the last time the King of Kings—it had been Valash then, Peroz's father—campaigned against the Khamorth. He still remembered the glorious look of the army as it had fared north, bright with banners. Godarz had gone with it and come back with a bloody flux, recalling that took some shine off the remembered glory.

But still . . . *This time,* he thought, *I'll ride with them.*

Godarz asked the messenger, "Will you lay over with us tonight? We'll feast you as best we can, for your own sake and for the news you bring. We on the frontier know the danger from the plainsmen; we know it well." One hand went to the scar he bore; a forefinger tracked the white streak in his beard.

"The *dihqan* is gracious," the messenger replied, but he shook his head. "I fear I cannot take advantage of your generosity. I have far to travel yet today; all the domains must hear the proclamation of the King of Kings, and time, you will have gathered, is short."

"So it is," Godarz said. "So it is." He turned to one of the cooks, who stood in the courtyard with everyone else. "Go back to the kitchens, Sakkiz. Fetch pocket bread stuffed with smoked mutton and onions, aye, and a skin of good wine, as well. Let no man say we sent the mouth of the King of Kings away hungry."

"The *dihqan* is gracious," the messenger said, now sincerely rather than out of formal politeness. He had meant what he had said about his journey's being urgent: no sooner had Sakkiz brought him the food and wine than he was on his way again, urging his horse up into a trot. He held the war banner high, so it fluttered with the breeze of his motion.

Abivard had eyes only for the crimson banner until a bend in the road took it behind some of the village houses and out of sight. Then, as if awakening from a dream, he glanced toward his father.

Godarz had been looking at him, too. Abivard had trouble reading the expression on his face. The *dihqan* gestured to him. "Here, step aside with me. We have things to talk about, you and I."

Abivard stepped aside with Godarz. The folk of the stronghold stood back and gave them room to talk privately. Makuraners were a polite folk. Had they been Videssians, they probably would have crowded forward to hear better. So tales from the east said, at any rate. Abivard had never set eyes on a Videssian in his life.

"I suppose you expect to come with me on this campaign," Godarz said. "I suppose you do."

"Yes, Father. You said I would." Abivard gave Godarz an appalled stare. Could his father have been thinking of leaving him behind? How could he hope to hold his head up in the stronghold, in the village, if he was judged not enough of a man to fight to defend the domain?

"I can ill spare you here, son," Godarz said heavily. "The God only knows what would befall this place if one of us, at least, did not have his eyes on it."

Hearing that, Abivard felt his heart drop into his sandals. If his father didn't let him go, he would . . . He didn't know what he would do. He needed a gesture full of grand despair but couldn't think of one. What he felt like doing was bursting into tears, but that would only humiliate him further.

Godarz chuckled at his expression. "No need to look like that. I am taking you along, never fear—what I say I will do, I do. You should get a taste of war while you're still young."

"Thank you, Father!" Now Abivard wanted to caper like a colt. His heart returned to its proper place in his chest and began pounding loudly to remind him it was there. Of itself, his hand made slashing motions through the air, as if he were hacking a steppe nomad out of the saddle.

"The God grant you thank me after we come home once more," Godarz said. "Aye, the God grant that. One reason I want you to go to war, lad, is so you'll see it's not all the glory of which the pandoura players sing. It's a needful business at times, that it is, needful, but maiming and killing are never to be taken lightly, no matter how much they're needed. That's what I want you to see: there's nothing glorious about a man with his guts spilled out on the ground trying to slit his own throat because he hurts too bad to want to go on living."

The image was vivid enough to give Abivard a moment's pause. He knew you could die in battle. When he thought of that, though, he thought of an arrow in the chest, a moment's pain, and then eternity in the loving company of the God. A long, tormented end had never crossed his mind. Even now, he could not make himself believe it, not below the very surface of his mind.

"You think it can't happen," Godarz said, as if reading his thoughts. Abivard didn't answer. His father went on, "I see you think it can't happen. That is one of the reasons I want to take you to war: to show you it can. You'll be a better man for knowing that."

"Better how?" Abivard asked. What could an intimate acquaintance with war and brutality give him that he didn't already have?

"Better because you won't take war lightly," Godarz answered. "Men who don't know it have a way of getting into it too easily, before they think carefully on whether it answers their need. They kill themselves off that way, of course, but they also kill off too many excellent retainers bound to them by kinship and loyalty. When your day here comes, son, I'd not have you be that kind of *dihqan*."

"As you say." Abivard's voice was sober: Godarz's seriousness impressed him. He was a few years past the age when he would think anything his father said wrong, merely because his father said it. His brother Frada and some of his older half brothers were still caught up in that foolishness. Having come through it, Abivard had concluded that his father generally had a good idea of what he was talking about, even if he did repeat himself.

Godarz said, "I don't forget it's your first time, either. I just want you to go into it with your wits about you. Remember your first girl, all these years ago? You weren't the same afterward. You won't be the same after this, either, but it's not as much fun as your first woman, not unless you have a taste for butchery. I don't see that in you, no, I don't."

Abivard didn't see it in himself, either, nor did he look very hard. He remembered how exalted he had felt after he left a bit of silver at a certain widow's house down in the village. If he felt that way after a battle . . . Godarz's last few sentences undermined the lesson he had tried to get across.

Godarz ceremoniously inserted a long bronze key into the lock that held the door to the women's quarters of the stronghold sealed. He turned the key. Nothing happened. He scowled, pulled out the key, glowered at it, and inserted it once more. This time Abivard heard a satisfying click when the *dihqan* turned it. He raised the bar and pushed open the door.

A sigh ran through the men who gathered together at a respectful distance down the hallway. Abivard tried to remember the last time his female relatives and Godarz's secondary wives came forth from their seclusion. It had been years; he knew that.

As was her right, Burzoe led them. Abivard's mother had to be close to Godarz in age, but did not show her years. Her wavy hair remained black, with none of the suspicious sheen that would have pointed to the dyepot. Her face was a little broader than the Makuraner norm, and fairer, through being secluded and seldom getting the chance to go out into the sun kept well-bred women paler than their toiling sisters.

Burzoe walked out into the courtyard with a queen's pride. Behind her, another coin stamped from the same die, came Abivard's sister Denak. She grinned when she saw him, and stuck out her tongue. They had been born hardly more than a year apart, and stayed almost as close as twins until she became a woman and had to withdraw from the eyes of the world.

After Denak came the parade of Godarz's secondary wives and those of their daughters old enough to have gone into seclusion. The last couple of wives were no older than some of the daughters. Had it not been for the set order in which they came forth, Abivard would not have known into which group they fell.

The sun flashed from gold bracelets and rings, from rubies and topazes, as Burzoe raised her right hand to show she was about to speak. Silence at once fell over the courtyard. The *dihqan's* principal wife rarely appeared in public; she was, after all, a respectable Makuraner matron. But she was also a person of great consequence in the stronghold. Her body might be confined to the women's quarters, but through Godarz her influence extended to every corner of the domain.

"My husband, my sons, their brothers go off now to war," she said. "The army of the King of Kings is nigh; they shall add their strength to his host so he can cross into the plainsmen's country and punish them for the harm they have done us and the greater harm they plan."

Also, Abivard thought, *the sooner we join the King of Kings' army and the sooner that host moves on toward the frontier, the sooner they stop eating our domain out of house and home.* His mother had a glint in her eye that said she was thinking the same thing, but it was not something she could say out loud.

Burzoe went on, "Our clan has won distinction on the field times beyond counting. I know the coming campaign will be yet another such time. I pray to the God that she grant all the sons of this house come home safe."

"May it be so," the women intoned together. To them, the God was a woman; to Abivard and those of his sex, a man.

"Come home safe from the broad field beyond the river," Burzoe said.

"Safe," the women chorused. For a moment, Abivard listened to his mother going on. Then his head whipped around to stare at her. Was it coincidence that she used that phrase to describe the steppe country north of the Degird? Tanshar had seen a broad field in Abivard's future, too, though he had not known where it lay.

"Go swiftly; return with victory," Burzoe said, her voice rising to a shout. Everyone in the courtyard, men and women together, cheered loudly.

Godarz walked over, embraced his principal wife, and kissed her on the lips. Then he hugged Denak and moved down the line of women, hugging and kissing his wives, hugging his daughters.

Abivard and his younger brother Varaz, both of whom would accompany the *dihqan* to the camp of the King of Kings, embraced Burzoe and Denak. So did Frada, though he was sick-jealous of his brothers because Godarz would not let him go fight.

A couple of Abivard's half brothers were also joining the King of Kings' host. They hugged their mothers and sisters, too, as did their siblings who would stay behind in the stronghold. When the *dihqan's* women showed themselves in public, such greetings were permitted.

"As the wife of your father the *dihqan,* I tell the two of you to fight bravely, to make every warrior in the host admire your courage," Burzoe said to Abivard and Varaz. Her expression lost its sternness. "As your mother, I tell you both that every moment will seem like a year till you come back to me."

"We'll be back with victory, as you told us," Abivard answered. Beside him, Varaz nodded vigorously. His younger brother had something of the look of Burzoe, though his burgeoning beard helped hide that. He was wider through the shoulders than Abivard, a formidable wrestler and archer.

Denak said, "*I'm* wed to no *dihqan*, so I have no special pride to uphold. That means I can tell both of you to make sure you come back, and make sure Father does, too."

She spoke to both her brothers, but her eyes were chiefly on Abivard. He nodded solemnly. Though she had stayed behind the doors of the women's quarters since her courses began, some of the closeness she and Abivard had known as children still remained. He knew she chiefly relied on him to do what she had asked, and resolved not to fail her.

Varaz said, "They work gold well out on the plains. We'll bring back something new for the two of you to wear."

"I have gold," Burzoe said. "Even if I wanted more, I could get it easily enough. Sons, though, sons are few and precious. I would not exchange a one of them for all the gold in the world, let alone on the steppe."

Abivard hugged his mother again, so tightly that she let out a faint squeak. He said, "Have no fear, Mother. When the Khamorth see the armament we have brought against them, they will flee away in terror. More likely than not, our victory will be bloodless."

"May it be so, my son; may it be so," Burzoe said.

"Are you repeating yourself now?" Abivard asked her.

She smiled, looking almost as young as Denak beside her. But then she grew serious again, and time's mark showed in her concern. "War is seldom bloodless; I think you men would esteem its prizes less if they were more easily got. So I say again, take care." She raised her voice to speak to everyone, not just her sons: "Take care!"

As if that had been a signal—and so it may have been—Godarz's youngest and most recently married wife turned and walked slowly into the living quarters of the stronghold on her way back to the women's chambers. Behind her went the next most junior wife, then the next and her oldest daughter.

Denak squeezed Abivard's hands in hers. "It'll be my turn in a moment, mine and Mother's. Come back safe and soon. I love you."

"And I you, eldest sister. Everything will be all right; you'll see." Everyone was making such a fuss about coming home safe and avoiding disaster that he wanted to avert any possible bad omen.

As Denak had said, her turn to withdraw soon came. She and Burzoe walked with great dignity back toward the entrance to the living quarters. Godarz waited for them there, the key to the women's chambers in his right hand.

Burzoe said something to him, then, laughing, stood on tiptoe to brush his lips with hers. The *dihqan* laughed, too, and made as if to pat her on the backside. He stopped well before he completed the motion; had he gone through with it, the stronghold would have buzzed with scandal for weeks. That he even mimed it showed how close to the frontier his holding lay. Closer to Mashiz, manners were said to be more refined.

Denak went into the living quarters. A moment later, smiling still, so did Burzoe. Godarz followed them inside. After a couple of steps, they seemed to disappear into shadow. The doorway looked very dark and empty.

Abivard felt he had put on a bake oven, not his armor. Sweat ran down his face under the chainmail veil that hid his features from the eyes down. A similar mail hood attached to the rear of his tall, conical helmet protected the back of his neck and his shoulders.

And yet, compared to the rest of him, his head was well ventilated: the breeze could blow through the mail there and cool him a little. Under the leather backing for the rest of his armor, he wore cotton batting to keep a sword blow that iron might block from nonetheless breaking his bones.

Mail covered his rib cage, too; below it, two vertical rows of iron splints protected his belly and lower back. From the bottom of the lower splints depended a short mail skirt; his leather sleeves and trousers bore horizontal rings of laminated iron armor. So did his boots. Semicircular iron guards projected from the ends of his armored sleeves toward the backs of his hands; only his palms and fingers were free of armor.

His horse was armored, too, with a long scale-mail trapper open at the front and rear to let its legs move freely. A wrought-iron chamfron protected the animal's face. A ring at the top of the chamfron held several bright red streamers. A similar ring at the crown of his own helmet held others of the same shade.

He carried a stout lance in a boss on the right side of his saddle; a long, straight sword hung from his belt. The strength of Makuran lay in its heavy horse, armored to take punishment until they closed with the foe and gave it in return. Videssians fought mounted, too, but were more often archers than lancers. As for the steppe nomads...

"Half the plainsmen's way of fighting lies in running away," he said.

"That's so, but it's from necessity as well as fear," Godarz answered. The *dihqan* was armored much like his son, save that over his mail shirt he wore an iron plate bound to his breast with crisscross leather straps. He went on, "They ride ponies on the far side of the Degird: they haven't fodder enough to raise big horses like ours." He set an affectionate hand on the side of his gelding's neck, just behind the last strap that held the chamfron in place.

"We'll smash them, then, when we come together," Abivard said.

"Aye, if we can make them stand and fight. That's why they generally come to grief when they raid south of the Degird. we concentrate on them and force them to fight on our terms. Out on the steppe, it's not so easy—our army is like one dot of ink on a vast sheet of parchment."

The horses clattered out of the stronghold, Godarz first, then Abivard and Varaz, then their eldest half brother Jahiz, and then two other half brothers of different maternal lineages, Arshak and Uzav. Godarz's domain did not yield enough to support more than half a dozen fully armored riders. That made it a medium-sized fish in the pond that was Makuran.

The King of Kings' encampment had sprung up between the stronghold and the Vek Rud. Pointing to the sudden vast city of canvas and heavy silk, Abivard said, "*That* will be one dot of ink, Father? I cannot believe it."

Among the tents, men boiled like ants on spilled food. Some, maybe most, were warriors; the sun kept glinting off iron down there, although many soldiers, like Abivard and his kin, wore baggy caftans over their mail to keep themselves cooler. But along with the fighting men would be wagon drivers, cooks, merchants, body servants, and likely women as well, to keep Peroz King of Kings and his more prominent warriors happy of nights. More people milled in the camp than Abivard had imagined in Mashiz.

But Godarz laughed and said, "It's different on the far side of the Degird. You'll see, soon enough."

Abivard shook his head, disbelieving. Godarz laughed again. Varaz said, "I'm with you, brother mine. That's not an army; that's a country on the march."

Jahiz said, "Where are the villagers? I expected they'd cheer us on our way." Abivard had expected the same thing, but the narrow lanes were almost deserted. Getting a wave from a toothless old woman with a water jug balanced on her head was not the send-off he'd looked for.

"They have more important things to do than wave good-bye to us," Godarz said. "Everyone who's missing here is sure to be down at the camp, trying to squeeze arkets from the soldiers as if they were taking the seeds from a pomegranate. They won't have another chance at such riches for years to come, and they know it."

He sounded amused and pleased his subjects were making the most of their opportunity. Some *dihqans* would have turned a handsome profit themselves, by squeezing as much of their people's sudden wealth from them as they could. The motto Godarz had repeated until Abivard grew sick of hearing it was, *Take the fleece from the flock, not the hide.*

Down off the stronghold's knob rode Godarz and his five sons. Abivard's heart pounded nervously. All his life he had been something special, first son of the domain's *dihqan*. The nearer he got to the camp, the less that seemed to matter.

Banners marked the pavilions of the *marzbans* of the Seven Clans, who served as division commanders under Peroz King of Kings. Abivard's head went this way and that, searching for the woad-blue flags of Chishpish, in whose division he and his family were mustered. "There!" he exclaimed, pointing.

"Good for you, lad," Godarz said. "You spotted them before

any of us. Well, I suppose we'd best go pay our respects to his High and Mightiness, eh?" He urged his horse forward with the pressure of his heels against its barrel.

Behind Abivard, Jahiz let out a half-strangled cough. Abivard was a little scandalized himself, although he had heard his father speak slightingly of the high nobility before. As far as Godarz was concerned, the *dihqans* were the most important caste of Makuran.

The camp sprawled across a vast stretch of ground, with no order Abivard could see. Spotting Chishpish's banner from afar didn't mean he and his relatives could easily get to it. They had to pick their way around tents pitched at random and through groups of warriors and hangers-on intent on their own destinations.

At last, though, they stood before the entrance of the big silk pavilion. A pair of guards in armor fancier than Godarz's barred their way. "Who comes?" one of them asked as Godarz dismounted and tied his horse to a stake pounded into the rock-hard ground. The fellow spoke with a mincing southern accent, but Abivard would not have cared to have to fight him; he looked tougher than he sounded.

Godarz answered with flowery formality. "I am Godarz son of Abivard, *dihqan* of Vek Rud domain." He pointed back toward the stronghold. "I bring my five sons to kiss the feet of the *marzban* Chishpish, as we shall have the ineffable honor of fighting under his banner."

"If you fight as well as you speak, the *marzban* will be well served," the guard answered. Abivard sat up straight with pride. Godarz waved his hand to acknowledge the compliment, then turned to his sons. At his nod, they also got down from their horses and tethered them. The guard pulled up the tent flap, stuck his head in, and declared, "Godarz *dihqan* of Vek Rud and his sons."

"Let them enter," a voice from within said.

"Enter." The guard and his companion held the flaps apart so Godarz, Abivard, and the rest could easily pass within.

Abivard's first dazed thought was that Chishpish lived with more luxury in the field than Godarz did in his own stronghold. Light folding tables of fragrant sandalwood inlaid with ivory, silver bowls decorated in low relief and piled high with sweetmeats, a richly brocaded carpet that was to Abivard's mind far too fine to set on bare dirt, a small Videssian enamelwork icon of some Phos-worshiping holy man . . . it was as if the high noble had simply packed up his home and brought it with him on campaign.

He should have used the elephant for something more than its ivory, Abivard thought impolitely as he caught sight of his leader. *Riding, for instance.* Chishpish was heavy enough to strain any horse, that was certain. His flesh bulged against the fabric of his caftan, which sparkled with silver threads. His pilos, the bucket-shaped Makuraner headgear, had rings of bright colors broidered round it. He smelled of patchouli; the strong scent made Abivard want to sneeze.

For all his bulk, though, he had manners. He heaved him-self to his feet and offered a cheek for Godarz and his sons to kiss. Not all high nobles would have conceded that a *dihqan* and his scions were but a little lower in rank than his own exalted self; Abivard had expected literally to have to kiss the *marzban's* feet.

"I am sure you will fight bravely for the King of Kings, Godarz of the Vek Rud domain," Chishpish said. "Your sons are . . . ?"

"Abivard, Varaz, Jahiz, Arshak, and Uzav," Godarz answered.

The *marzban* repeated the names without a bobble, which impressed Abivard. The fat man did not look like a warrior—he looked more like two warriors—but he did not sound like a fool. Being Godarz's son, Abivard feared fools above all else.

Outside the tent, a trumpet blew a harsh fanfare. A herald bawled, "Eat dirt before the divine, the good, the pacific, the ancient Peroz, King of Kings, fortunate, pious, beneficent, to whom the God has given great fortune and great empire, giant of giants, formed in the image of the God. Eat dirt, for Peroz comes!" The fanfare blared out again, louder than before. Chishpish's guards flung the tent flap wide.

Abivard went down on his belly on Chishpish's fine carpet, his forehead pressed against the wool. His armor rattled and clanked as he prostrated himself. Around him, his siblings and father also went down into the posture of adoration. So did Chishpish, though his fat face reddened with the effort the sudden exertion cost him.

"Rise," Peroz said. Abivard's heart beat fast as he returned to his feet, not from having to stand while burdened with iron and leather but rather because he had never expected to encounter the King of Kings face to face.

Despite the herald's formal announcement, Peroz was not ancient, was not, in fact, much older than Godarz. His beard was mostly black; his mustaches, waxed stiff, stuck out like the horns of a bull. He wore his hair long, and bound with a fillet in back. His cheeks seemed unnaturally ruddy; after a moment, Abivard realized they were rouged.

"Chishpish of the Seven Clans, present to me these warriors whom I find in your tent," the King of Kings said.

"As your Majesty commands, so shall it be," Chishpish answered. "Here first we have the *dihqan* Godarz of Vek Rud domain, our present home. With him he brings the army his sons—" Again the high noble rattled off Abivard's name and the rest. His memory swallowed as much as his mouth—which, given his girth, was no mean feat.

"You are well equipped, and your sons, also," Peroz told Godarz. "Those are your horses outside the pavilion?" At Godarz's nod, Peroz went on, "Fine animals, as well. Makuran would be stronger if all domains contributed as yours does."

"Your Majesty is generous beyond my deserts," Godarz murmured. Abivard marveled that his father could speak at all; had the King of Kings addressed him, he was sure his tongue would have cloven to the roof of his mouth.

Peroz shook his head. "You are the generous one, offering yourself and your five stalwart sons that the kingdom may flourish. Which is your heir?"

"Abivard here," Godarz said, setting a hand on his eldest's armored shoulder.

"Abivard son of Godarz, look to your father as a symbol of loyalty," Peroz said.

"Aye, your Majesty; I do," Abivard said. He could talk, after all.

"Good," Peroz told him. "The God grant that you never need to put forth a like sacrifice. Should this campaign progress as I plan, that may come true. I aim to go straight at the nomads, force them to battle, and crush them like this." The King of Kings ground one fist against the palm of his other hand.

"May it be so, your Majesty," Abivard said—there, he had spoken twice now! All the same, he remembered what his father had said about the difficulties of fighting the plainsmen on their own ground. The wisdom of the King of Kings was an article of faith among Makuraners; the wisdom of Godarz, Abivard had seen with his own eyes and heard with his own ears.

Peroz turned back to Chishpish, whom he had truly come to see. "Chishpish of the Seven Clans, on you will fall much of the responsibility for bringing the Khatrishers to bay. Is all in readiness in that regard?"

"It is, your Majesty. We shall burn great swaths of steppeland, compelling the nomads either to face us or to lose their pasturage. Thousands of torches await in the wagons."

A torch, a bright one, flared inside Abivard's head. North of the Degird, the Khamorth lived by their flocks and herds. If those animals could not graze, the plainsmen would starve. They would have to fight to prevent that. He glanced over at Godarz. His father was slowly nodding. Abivard nodded, too, his faith in the wisdom of the King of Kings restored.

The broad, muddy Degird separated the farms and strongholds and towns of Makuran from the barbarians who lived on the far bank. No permanent bridges spanned the stream; any King of Kings who proposed erecting one would have had every *dihqan* in the northwestern part of the realm rise in revolt against him. The Khamorth managed to slip across the Degird too often as things were—no point in giving them a highway.

But the grand army of Peroz King of Kings could not go over the river by dribs and drabs. Nor could they wait for it to freeze solid, as the nomads often did. With the barrier of the Degird stretched out ahead of him, Abivard wondered how Peroz proposed to solve the problem.

Though he had yet to put his knowledge to much use, Abivard knew how to fight. He had some idea how to go about besieging a bandit's lair or other stronghold. Past that, his military knowledge stopped.

Over the next few days, it advanced several paces. The baggage train the army carried with it seemed preposterously large to him—until the engineers who had made the journey from Mashiz started driving two parallel rows of piles, about forty feet apart, into the bed of the Degird toward the northern bank.

The upstream piles tilted in the direction of the current; the downstream ones leaned against it. The engineers linked each upstream-downstream pair with a crossbeam whose fit the force of the current only improved as time went by.

Then the engineers ran trestles along each row of piles, from the south side of the Degird to the north. Across the trestles went planks, and over the planks poles and bundles of sticks. The army advanced from Makuran onto the plains of Pardraya less than a week after it reached the Degird.

It did not cross the river unobserved. Abivard had watched the Khamorth, tiny as horseflies on the far shore, watching the bridge march toward them. When the engineers got close enough, the plainsmen shot at them. Soldiers advanced down the growing bridge to shoot back and keep the nomads at a distance. The engineers took to carrying big wicker shields. Arrows pierced a few men anyhow, but the bridge and the army advanced regardless.

The hooves of Abivard's horse drummed over the bridge when his turn came to cross. The horse didn't care for that, or for the vibration of the timbers that came up through its feet from the motion of other animals and wagons on the bridge. The beast laid back its ears and tried to rear; Abivard fought it back down.

"So this is Pardraya," he said when he was back on solid ground. "It doesn't look much different from the land by the stronghold."

"No *qanats*," Varaz said beside him. "No cropland at all, come to that."

His younger brother was right. Grass and bushes, yellow-brown from summer heat, stretched ahead as far as the eye could see: that sereness was what had reminded Abivard of home. But he had always thought of the Pardrayan plain as being flat as a griddle. That wasn't so: it had rises and dips just like any other land.

The undulations reminded him of the waves of the sea. That, in turn, reminded him of the prophecy Tanshar had given. But no one could call this sea narrow.

Peroz King of Kings left behind a good-size garrison to protect the bridge, the army's lifeline back to Makuran. As he watched the chosen warriors begin to set up their encampment, Abivard spared them a moment's pity. Poor fellows, they had come all this way only to be denied the chance to help crush the Khamorth.

The main body of the army moved north across the plains. When Abivard turned around for another look at the bridge guards, he found they had disappeared in the great cloud of dust kicked up by thousands of horses and hundreds of wagons. The dust made his eyes water and gritted in every fold of skin he had. When he spat, he spat brown.

He looked up into the sky. The sun, at least, was still visible; the only clouds were the ones the army made. All the same, he said, "I wish it would rain."

Godarz's hand twisted in a gesture of aversion. "You don't know what you're saying, boy," he exclaimed. "A good downpour and all this turns to porridge, same as it does down by the stronghold. With one rider, it's a bloody nuisance. You try and get an army through it and you'll be weeks on a journey that should take days. Simple rule: dust is bad, mud is worse."

Abashed, Abivard said little after that till the army halted for the evening. He also realized that, if it rained, Peroz's plan to fire the plain would come to naught. Since he couldn't make himself be happy with the weather as it was but knew a change would be worse, he passed a discontented night.

Breakfast was hard rolls, dates preserved in honey, lamb sausage so salty and smoky it made Abivard's tongue want to shrivel up, and bad wine. After Varaz choked down his length of sausage, he made a dreadful face and said to Godarz, "You'd flog the cooks if they fed us like this back at the stronghold."

"I just might," Godarz said. "Aye, I just might." He finished his own sausage, then took a long swig of wine to wash away the taste. "But if we were going on a long journey, I'd flog them if they didn't pack us food like this. All of it will keep almost forever."

"The vermin can't stomach it, either," Abivard said. He meant it for a joke, and his siblings smiled, but Godarz nodded seriously, spoiling his fun.

The *dihqan* and his sons knocked down the tent they had shared, tied its wool panels and poles and their bedding aboard a packhorse, then armed themselves—each helping the others with clumsy catches—and rode north. One long, slow farsang followed another. Abivard's heart leapt once, when he spied a couple of bow-carrying men wearing only leather and mounted on unarmored horses, but they proved to be scouts riding in to report to their commanders.

"We can't all go rattling around in mail, or the Khamorth would ride rings around us and we'd never even know they were there," Godarz said. Abivard chewed on that and decided it made sense. The business of soldiering got more complicated every time he turned around.

The wind, what there was of it, came from the west. A little past noon, smoke and flames sprang up from the steppe, about half a farsang east of the army's line of travel. That was far enough to keep embers and smoke from spooking the warriors' horses, which moved on unconcerned. Trot, canter, walk, trot, canter, walk . . . the slowly changing rhythm filled Abivard's body.

As the armament of Peroz King of Kings moved north over the Pardrayan plain, his men set more fires, or rather extended the length of the first one. Every sudden gust gladdened Abivard, for it meant the flames were spreading over more of the nomads' pasturage.

He pointed east. "They can't let us do that for long, or they'll soon start to starve."

"That's the idea," Jahiz said. His handsome face—his mother was famous for her beauty—creased in a leer of anticipation. He reached for his upthrust lance. "Then they have to come to us."

For the rest of that day, though, and most of the following one, the advancing warriors saw no sign of the Khamorth through whose territory they rode. But for the fire that burned alongside them, they might have been alone on the steppe.

Late the next afternoon, the scouts brought in sheep and cattle they had captured north of the main body of the King of Kings' force. Abivard cheered as loud as anyone when he saw the animals. "We won't have to eat that beastly sausage tonight," he said.

"So we won't, so we won't," Godarz said. "But that's not all these captures tell me. They say we're getting very close, very close, I tell you, to the nomads themselves. Their herds are their lives; if we come across the beasts, the men who follow them across the plains must be close by."

Abivard looked this way and that. He saw his relatives, his comrades, the steppe, the fires the men from Makuran had set. Of the nomads there was no sign. Yet they were out there somewhere—probably not far. His father was bound to be right about that. The idea made Abivard uneasy, as if someone were peeking at him through a crack in his door back at the stronghold.

He looked around again, this time concentrating on the thousands of armored men who had come north with him from Makuran, their equally well protected mounts, the clever engineers who had bridged the Degird, and all the other appurtenances of a great and civilized host. Against such might, how could the plainsmen prevail?

When he said that aloud, Godarz let out a wry chuckle. "That's why we come here, son—to find out." Abivard must have looked stricken, for the *dihqan* continued, "Don't take it like that, for that's not how I meant it. I've seen a few armies in my day, aye, just a few, and this one's stronger than all the rest. I don't know how we can lose once the Khamorth decide they have to face us."

That eased Abivard's mind. If his father couldn't see any way for the plainsmen to win, he was willing to believe no such way existed. He said, "The King of Kings, may his years be many and his realm increase, strikes me as a man who will deal a hard blow when the time comes."

"He strikes me the same way," Godarz said. "If the lion banner isn't at the fore when at last we clash with the Khamorth, I'll be greatly surprised. Although I know of him only by repute, I've heard his son Sharbaraz is another of the same sort. He'd be your age, more or less."

"I've not seen his banner here," Abivard said.

"Nor will you," Godarz answered. "Peroz, may his years be long, left him back in Mashiz, as I left Frada back at the stronghold. Our reasons were different, though. I just didn't think Frada quite ready, not quite. Sharbaraz is a man grown, and I expect the King of Kings wants him to keep the eunuchs and nobles in line while Peroz goes off on campaign."

"Surely they'd not take advantage when the King of Kings was away . . ." Abivard faltered, very much aware of Godarz's cynical eye on him. He felt himself flush. "All right, maybe they would."

"No maybe to it, son, no maybe at all," Godarz said. "I just thank the God that's not something I have to worry about. I may be master of only a domain, not a realm, but I can rely on the people around me when my back is turned. In more ways than a few, I have the better half of that bargain."

"I think you do, too." Abivard could not imagine his father's servitors going against the *dihqan's* wishes. He had heard tales of corruption emanating from Mashiz but hadn't believed them. To learn they had some substance was a jolt. He said, "It must be that they're too close to the Videssian border, Father."

"Aye, that may have somewhat to do with it," Godarz allowed.

"I suspect they're too close to too much silver, as well. Having the coin you need to do what you must and a bit of what you like is pleasant, as wine can be. But a man who gets a rage for silver is as bad as one with a rage for wine, maybe worse. Aye, maybe worse."

Abivard chewed on that. He decided his father probably had a point, and admitted as much by nodding before he asked, "When do you think the plainsmen will stand at bay?"

Godarz scratched at his scar while he thought it over. "They won't wait more than another couple of days," he said at last. "They can't, else we'll have burned too much of the plain. Their herds need broad fields on which to graze."

That phrase again! Abivard had heard it twice now since Tanshar gave him his strange prophecy. What it meant, though, he still could not say. He wondered when he would find out.

When two days had passed, Abivard was ready to reckon his father a better fortune-teller than Tanshar. The first Khamorth fighters appeared in front of the Makuraner host the morning after the two of them had spoken. They shot a few arrows that did nothing in particular, then galloped away faster than their armored foes could pursue.

Such archers as the Makuraners had rode out in front of the main force to protect it from the plainsmen's hit-and-run raids. The rest of the warriors shook themselves out into real battle lines rather than the loose order in which they had been traveling before.

Under his veil of iron, Abivard's teeth skinned back in a fierce grin of excitement—at any moment, he might find himself in action. He glanced over at Varaz. He couldn't see much of his brother's face, but Varaz's flashing eyes said he, too, was eager to get in there and fight.

Godarz, on the other hand, just kept riding along at an easy canter. For all the ferocity and passion he displayed, the nearest Khamorth might have been a thousand farsangs away. Abivard decided his father was an old man after all.

A couple of hours later, more plainsmen appeared off the left flank of the army and plied it with arrows. Makuraner horsemen thundered out against them, raising even more dust than the host normally kicked up. They drove the nomads away, then returned to their comrades once more. The whole army raised a cheer for them.

"By the God, I wish the left were our station," Abivard exclaimed. "They have the first glory of the campaign."

"Where?" Godarz asked. "In chasing after the Khamorth? I didn't see them kill any. Before long, the nomads will come back and prick at us some more. That's how warfare works out here on the steppe."

Before long, Godarz's foretelling was again fulfilled. Not only did the Khamorth return to shadow the army's flanks, they began showing themselves in greater numbers, both on the left and at the front. A couple of men were fetched back to the healers' wagons, one limp, the other writhing and shrieking.

Abivard shivered. "The last time I heard a noise like that was when the old cook—what was his name, Father?—spilled the great kettle of soup and scalded himself to death. I was still small; Denak told me she had nightmares about that for years."

"His name was Pishinah, and you're right, he cried most piteously." Godarz lifted his helm off his head to wipe away sweat with a kerchief. He looked worried. "More nomads dogging us than I'd have guessed."

"But that's what we want, isn't it: to make them fight?" Abivard said, puzzled.

"Oh, aye." His father laughed sheepishly. "I get suspicious when the plainsmen give us what we want, even if we are forcing it from them."

"You predicted this, though, just the other day," Abivard protested. "Why are you unhappy now that what you foretold has come true?"

"It's not coming true the way I thought it would," Godarz answered. "I expected we'd force the Khamorth to battle, that they'd be desperate and afraid. Their archers out there don't have the manner of desperate men; they're moving to a plan of their own." He shrugged; his chain mail rattled about him. "Or, of course, maybe I'm just seeing evil spirits behind every bush and under every flat stone."

Jahiz said, "Couldn't the scriers scent out what the nomads intend?"

Godarz spat on the ground. "That for what the scriers can do. If you've lost a ring back at the stronghold, lad, a scrier will help you find it. But when it has to do with fighting, no. For one thing, men's passions make magic unreliable—that's why love philtres work so seldom, by the bye—and war is a hot-blooded business. For another, the plainsmen's shamans are using magic of their own to try to blind us. And for a third, we have to be busy to make sure the demon worshipers don't spy out what *we're* about. War is for iron, son; iron, not magic."

"A good thing, too," Abivard said. "If war were a matter for sorcerers, no one else would have the chance to join in it."

"Is that a good thing?" Godarz said. "I wonder, I do wonder."

"Why did you join the King of Kings' host, then?" Abivard asked him.

"For duty's sake, and because Peroz King of Kings—may his years be many and his realm increase—so bade me," Godarz answered. "Would you have me cast aside my honor and that of our clan?"

"By the God, no," Abivard exclaimed. Though he let it drop there, he wished his father sounded more as if his heart were in the campaign Peroz had undertaken.

At the head of the King of Kings' force, horns screamed the call Abivard had awaited since the crossing of the Degird: *the foe's army in sight.* The Makuraners had been advancing in battle array since the plainsmen began to harass them, but a hum of excitement ran through them all the same. Soon now they would have the chance to punish the Khamorth for the pinpricks they had dared inflict on the King of Kings' men.

Abivard rode to the top of a low swell of ground. Sure enough, there were the nomads, perhaps half a farsang to the north. They had mustered in two groups, a relatively small one in front and a larger one some little distance farther away.

"I think I see their scheme," Godarz said. "They'll try to keep us in play with their advance party while the rest of them spread out and flank us. Won't work—we'll smash the little band before the big one can deploy." He sounded more cheerful than he had before.

"Shouldn't we be at them, Father?" Abivard demanded. Finally seeing the Khamorth there waiting to be assailed made him want to set spurs to his horse and charge on the instant.

But Godarz shook his head. "Too far, as yet. We'd meet them with our animals blown from going so far at the gallop. We'll close to not far out of bowshot and pound home from there."

As if to echo Godarz, Chishpish, who rode not far away, bellowed to the horsemen under his command. "Anyone who goes after the plainsmen before the horns signal shall answer to me personally."

Varaz chuckled. "That's no great threat. He'd never catch up with anyone who disobeyed." And indeed, Chishpish's horse was as heavyset as the *marzban* himself, as it had to be to bear his weight. But Chishpish's threat, as every warrior who heard it knew full well, had nothing to do with physical chastisement. With the influence the high noble wielded, he could drop a man's reputation and hope for the future straight into the Void.

Abivard took his lance from its rest and hefted it in his hand. All through the ranks of the Makuraners, those iron-tipped lengths of wood were quivering as if a great wind swept through a forest. Abivard kept the lance upright, to avoid fouling his comrades; he would couch it only at the command.

Closer and closer the King of Kings' host drew to the foe. Peroz's banner fluttered ahead of Abivard; by Makuraner custom, he commanded from the right wing. The harsh war cries of the Khamorth floated faintly to Abivard's ears. He heard them without understanding; though the steppe tongue was cousin to his own, the plainsmen's shouts were so commingled that no separate words emerged from the din.

A horn cried, high and thin. As if with one voice, thousands of Makuraners hurled a battle cry back at the Khamorth: "Peroz!" Abivard yelled his throat raw, the better to terrify the enemy.

When the Makuraners closed nearly to within the range Godarz had specified, the small lead group of plainsmen spurred forward to meet them, screeching like wild things and shooting arrows into the massed armored ranks. A couple of lucky shots emptied saddles; a few more wrung cries of pain from men and horses. Most, as is the way of such things, either missed or were turned by the Makuraners' mail and plate and shields.

Just when Abivard wondered if the Khamorth would be mad enough to rush to close quarters with Peroz's vastly superior army, the nomads wheeled their little steppe ponies in a pretty piece of horsemanship and, almost in single file, galloped back toward their more distant comrades.

"Cowards!" Abivard screamed along with half the Makuraner host. "White-livered wretches, come back and fight!"

Beside him, Godarz said, "What *are* they doing?"

No one answered, for at that moment the horns rang out again, a call for which the whole host had waited: the charge. "Lower—lances!" Chishpish roared. The iron points glittered in the sun as they swung down to the horizontal. Even louder than before, Chishpish cried, "Forward!"

Already the banner of the King of Kings stood straight out from its staff as Peroz and his guards thundered toward the Khamorth. Abivard booted his own horse in the sides with iron-shod heels. Because the gelding was armored itself, it needed such strong signals to grasp what he required of it.

The ground flew by beneath him, slowly at first and then faster, fast enough for the wind of his passage to whip water from his eyes, fast enough for it to seem as if one more stride, one more bound, would propel him into the air in flight. The rumble of thousands, tens of thousands of hooves was like being caught in the middle of a thunderstorm. And thousands, tens of thousands of men charged with Abivard. He knew the great exaltation of being one small part of an enterprise vast and glorious. The God might have set a hand on his shoulder.

Then his horse stepped into a hole.

Maybe a rabbit had made it, maybe a badger. That didn't matter. What came of it did. Abivard felt the gelding stumble at the same instant he heard—amazingly distinct through the din around him—the bone break. Even as the horse screamed and fell, he kicked his feet out of the stirrups and threw himself clear.

He hit the ground with a crash and thud that made him glad for his mail. Even with it, he knew he would be a mass of bruises. His comrades thundered by; one horse sprang clean over him as he lay on the ground. How no one trampled him, he never knew.

He didn't care, either. Tears of mingled pain and frustration rolled down his cheeks. Here was what should have been the great moment of his life, ruined. Unhorsed, how could he close with the enemy and show his mettle? The answer was simple: he couldn't. His father and siblings would have the triumph all to themselves, and what about him? He would be the butt of jokes forever—Abivard, late for the fight.

The last Makuraners rode by, crying the name of the King of Kings. Abivard's horse cried, too, in anguish. He forced himself to his feet, staggered over to the thrashing animal, and cut its throat.

That done, he turned and started walking north—maybe, just maybe, the battle wouldn't be over when he got to it. Perhaps he could take the mount of someone who had fallen, or even ride a Khamorth steppe pony for a while, though it would not be pleased at supporting the weight of him and his armor.

Through swirling dust, he watched the proud banners that marked the front ranks of the Makuraner host. For a moment, he refused to believe his eyes when almost all of them went down at once.

The screams and shrieks of injured men and horses rose to the deaf, unfeeling sky. The men and horses themselves tumbled into the trench the Khamorth had dug across the plain and then cunningly concealed with sticks and dirt and grass. Only at the very center, where the nomads' advance party had withdrawn to their main force, could the Makuraners follow, and then in small numbers. Their foes set on them savagely, wolves tearing at a bear.

Abivard's shout of horror was drowned in the cries that went up from the overthrown Makuraner host. The King of Kings' banner was down. He could not see it anywhere. He moaned, deep in his throat. Nor were the frontmost ranks the only ones to fall in ruin. The warriors behind could not check their mounts in time and crashed into the ditch on top of its first victims.

"Father!" Abivard cried. Godarz was up there, somewhere in the middle of that catastrophe. So were Abivard's brother and half brothers. Clumsily, heavily he began to run in armor designed for fighting from horseback.

Even the Makuraners not caught by the plainsmen's ditch had to halt as best they could, any semblance of order lost. The Khamorth chose that moment to storm round both ends of the trench and begin to surround their foes.

"Not a broad field." Abivard groaned. "A trap!" Too late, the meaning of Tanshar's first vision came clear.

A trap it was. The Makuraners, the momentum of their charge

killed, their ranks thrown into confusion, were easy meat for the nomads. At short range, horn-reinforced bows could punch their shafts through mail. Two plainsmen could set on a single armored warrior, assail him from so many directions at once that sooner or later—most often sooner—he had to fall.

Abivard found himself outside the killing zone, one of a handful of Makuraners who were. At first his only thought was to keep on clumping ahead and die with his family and countrymen. Then he saw that riderless horses, mostly Makuraner stock but the occasional steppe pony as well, were getting out through the nomads' cordon.

They'll round them up later, he thought. *For now they reckon the men more important.* Had he been a nomad chieftain, he would have made the same choice.

Seeing the horses made him start to think again, not run blindly toward his doom like a moth flying into a torch flame. He could all but hear Godarz inside his head: *Don't be foolish, boy, don't be foolish. Save what you can.* A mounted demigod would have had a battle on his hands, smashing through the plainsmen to rescue the trapped warriors of Makuran. The chance of one horseless young man in his first fight managing it wasn't worth thinking about.

Abivard tried again to guess—no, to *work out;* Godarz didn't approve of guessing—what the Khamorth chiefs would do once their riders had finished slaughtering the Makuraners. The answer came back quick and clear: they would plunder the baggage train. Not till then would they start scouring the steppe for survivors.

"Which means I'd best get out of here while I can," he said aloud. A riderless horse, a steppe pony, had paused to graze less than a furlong from where he stood. He walked slowly toward it. It looked up, wary, as he approached, but then lowered its head and went back to cropping dry, yellow grass.

In a pouch on his belt he had some dried apricots, treats he had intended to give his gelding after the battle was won. Now the battle was lost, and the gelding, too. He dug out three or four apricots, put them in the palm of his hand, and walked up to the steppe pony.

"Here you are, boy," he said coaxingly; the pony was entire, with stones big for the size of the rest of it. It made a snuffling noise, half suspicion, half interest. Abivard held out his hand. The horse sniffed the apricots, delicately tasted one. It snuffled again, this time sounding pleased, and ate the rest of the fruit.

After that, it let Abivard come around alongside it and did no more than lay back its ears when he mounted it. At his urging, it trotted off toward the south. He found the ride uncomfortable; like a lot of nomads, the Khamorth who had owned it kept his stirrup leathers very short so he could rise in the saddle to use his bow. Bowless, Abivard perforce rode with his legs bent up.

Evidently he wasn't the first or only Makuraner to escape the disaster to the north; when he came up to it, the baggage train was boiling like a stomped anthill. He kept on riding. He had intended to give the alarm: he couldn't have faced himself had he simply fled. But he did not aim to be caught in the new catastrophe sure to come soon.

He could feel by the steppe pony's gait that carrying his armored self was more than it could easily handle. He knew he would have to shed the iron as soon as he could. If the pony foundered before he got back to the Degird, he was a dead man.

Perhaps half an hour later, he looked over his shoulder. A new column of smoke was rising into the sky. The men of Makuran hadn't set this one. The Khamorth were having their revenge.

The one good thing Abivard saw there was that it meant the plainsmen would be too occupied with their looting to comb the plain for fugitives for a while. He wasn't the only Makuraner to have escaped from the overthrow of the King of Kings' host; scattered over the steppe in front, behind, and off to the sides were riders traveling singly or in small groups. Some would be men fleeing from the baggage train; others warriors like Abivard who met with mischance before the trap closed on them; others, perhaps, men who had broken out of the ring of death the nomads had cast around the Makuraners.

Abivard thought hard about joining one of those small groups of retreating men from Makuran. In the end, he decided to keep clear and go his own way. For one thing, even all the fugitives he saw banded together lacked the numbers to stand up to the swarm of Khamorth who would soon be following. For another, bands traveling together were limited to the speed of their slowest member. He wanted to get as far away from the disastrous field that was not a field as he could.

Shock still dazed him. He had lost his father and four siblings.

Makuran had lost Peroz King of Kings and the flower of its manhood. The twin misfortunes echoed and reechoed inside his head, now one louder, now the other.

"What shall I do?" he moaned. "What will the kingdom do?"

Since he had no idea what the kingdom would do, he ended up concentrating on the first question. The first thing he had to do was get back over the bridge the King of Kings' engineers had thrown across the Degird. If he couldn't do that, he would be too dead to worry about anything thereafter.

If he did get back to the stronghold, he would be *dihqan*. He had known that would happen one day, but had thought *one day* lay years ahead. Now it was on top of him, a weight heavier on his shoulders than that of his armor on the steppe pony he rode.

"Speaking of which," he muttered, and reined in. He swung down off the horse, gave it a chance to graze and blow a little. He couldn't think just of the mad dash for escape, not when he was several days' ride north of the Degird. He had to keep the pony sound for the whole journey, even though every heartbeat he waited made him fidget as if taken by the flux.

He stopped again when he came to a small stream. He let the steppe pony drink, but not too much. It snapped at him when he pulled it away from the water. "Stupid thing," he said, and cuffed it on the muzzle. Horses would drink themselves sick or dead if you let them. They would eat too much, too, but that wasn't going to be a problem, not now.

How best to escape pursuit? At length, Abivard rode southwest, still toward the Degird but not as directly—and out of the line of march by which the host of Peroz King of Kings had approached disaster. Sure as sure, the Khamorth would ride down that line, sweeping away the warriors who had not the wit to avoid it.

By the time evening neared, Abivard no longer saw any of his fellow fugitives. That he took for a good omen: the nomads would not be likely now to spot him while chasing someone else.

When he came to another stream, he decided to stop for the night and let the steppe pony rest till morning. He dismounted, rubbed down the animal with a clump of dry grass for lack of anything better, then tied its reins to the biggest bush—almost a sapling—he could find.

After that, time came to shed his armor. He undid the catches at the side of his coat of mail and splints, and got out of it after unhooking the mail skirt that depended from it. He took off his iron-faced boots, then peeled down his iron-and-leather breeches.

The cuirass, the mail shirt, and the armored trousers he flung into the stream: no point in leaving them on dry land for some plainsman to take back to his tent as spoils. He stripped off the veil and hood from his helmet and threw them away, too. The helmet he kept, and the boots. They were heavy, but he feared he would hurt his feet if he did without them.

"You can stand that much weight, can't you, boy?" he said to the steppe pony. Its ears twitched to show it had heard, but of course it could not understand.

Wanting to keep the animal happy with him, he fed it another apricot from his dwindling supply. He ate one himself; he had had nothing but water since early that morning. Had a lizard skittered by, he would cheerfully have sliced it in two with his sword and eaten both pieces raw. But no lizard came.

Then he thumped his forehead with the heel of his hand and cursed his own foolishness. The steppe pony's saddle had saddlebags hanging from it. In them might be ... anything. He felt like shouting when he found strips of dried mutton. They were just about as hard as his own teeth and not much tastier, but they would keep him from starving for a while.

All he had on were thin linen drawers. He wished for his surcoat, then laughed. "Might as well wish for the army back while I'm at it," he said. With all that passion that was in him, he did wish for the army back, but he was too much Godarz's son not to know what such wishes were worth.

He passed a chilly, miserable night curled up on the ground like an animal, sword at his side so he could grab it in a hurry. He lost track of how many times he woke up to some tiny noise or a shift in the breeze or for no reason at all. Renewed sleep came harder and harder. At last, between dawn and sunrise, it stayed away for good. He gnawed more dried mutton and began to ride.

That day after the battle, he caught himself weeping again and again. Sometimes he mourned for his family, sometimes for his overthrown monarch and for Makuran at large, sometimes for himself: he felt guilty for living on when all he held dearest had perished.

That's nonsense, son. You have to go on, to set things right as best you can. So vividly did he seem to hear his father's voice that his head whipped around in sudden wild hope that the *dihqan* had somehow survived. But the steppe was empty as far as the eye could see, save for a crow that cawed harshly as it hopped into the air.

"Stupid bird, what are you doing here?" Abivard pointed over his shoulder. "The rich pickings are back that way."

Every so often, he saw rabbits lolloping across the plain. Just looking at them made him hungry, but hunting rabbits with a sword was like trying to knock flies out of the air with a switch, and he had no time to set a snare and linger. Once he spied a fox on a rabbit's heels. He wished the beast more luck than he had had himself.

Though he ate sparingly, he ran out of dried meat halfway through the third day. After that, his belly gnawed at him along with worry. He caught a couple of frogs by the side of a stream, gutted them with his dagger, and ate them raw. His only regret after he finished them was that he had thrown the offal into the water.

He looked for more frogs, or maybe a turtle or an incautious minnow the next time he stopped to water the steppe pony, but caught nothing.

Toward evening on the fourth day after the battle, he reached the Degird. He wanted to strip off his drawers, dive in, and swim across, but knew that, weak and worn as he was, he would probably drown before he reached the southern bank. Nor could he let the horse swim the stream and tow him with it, for it was in no finer fettle than he.

"Have to be the bridge, then," he said; he had talked to himself a lot lately, for lack of any other company. And if the bridge was down, or the Khamorth already across it . . . he tried not to think about such things.

Before night descended, he rode about half a farsang away from the river. Khamorth searching for fugitives still at large in their country were most likely to ride along the northern bank of the Degird, he reasoned. No point in making things easy for them. If they were already searching along the riverbank, the bridge was sure to be down, too, or in their hands, but he made himself not think about that, either.

Hunger woke him before the sun rose. He mounted the steppe pony, marveling at its stamina. A Makuraner horse could carry more weight, yes, and gallop faster for a little ways, but probably would have broken down on the long, grueling ride south. He had done his best to keep the pony rested but knew his best hadn't been good enough.

He rode into the morning sun, keeping the Degird in sight but not actually riding up to it unless he needed to water his horse or himself. He didn't know how far east he would have to ride to come on the bridge. "Only one way to learn," he said, and booted the pony up into a trot.

The sun climbed higher, burned off the early-morning chill, and grew hot. Abivard started to sweat, but he wasn't as uncomfortable as he might have been. A couple of weeks earlier, he had fared north in like weather armored from head to toe. He still had helm and iron-covered boots, but the drawers in between were far easier on his hide than mail and padding.

Was that the bridge up ahead? He thought he had seen it a couple of times already, only to find himself deceived by mudbanks in the river.

But no, not this time—that was the bridge, with riders in unmistakable Makuraner armor still in place on the Pardrayan plain: a gateway to a murdered dream of conquest. But even if the dream was dead, the bridge might keep Makuraner warriors—"Or at least one," Abivard told himself—alive.

He wrung the best pace he could from the tired steppe pony and waved like a man possessed to the garrison still loyally holding open the way back to freedom. A couple of the Makuraners broke away from their main body and came toward him at the trot, their lances couched and pointing at a spot about a hand's span above his navel. With a shock of fear, he realized they were ready to skewer him. He was, after all, riding a Khamorth horse.

"By the God, no!" he screamed hoarsely. Getting slaughtered by his own countrymen after escaping the nomads seemed a fate too bitterly ironic to bear.

The lances wavered when the riders heard him cry out in their own language. "Who are you, then?" one of them called, his face invisible and so all the more menacing behind his veil of mail.

"Abivard son of Godarz, *dihqan* of Vek Rud domain," Abivard answered, doing his best to sound like the real Makuraner he was rather than a plainsman trying to get across the Degird in disguise.

The two warriors looked at each other. The one who had spoken before asked, "D'you mean he's the *dihqan*, or are you?"

"He is," Abivard said automatically, and then had to correct himself: "He was. He's dead, along with my brother and three half brothers. That leaves me."

"So it does, and on a steppe pony, too," the lancer said, suspicious still. "How'd you stay alive through the fight if all your family perished?" *What sort of coward are you?* lurked under the words.

"My horse stepped in a hole and broke a leg as the charge was beginning," Abivard answered. "So I didn't go into the trench and I didn't get trapped when the cursed nomads sallied forth. I managed to get hold of this horse when it came out of the press, and I've ridden it ever since."

The Makuraners looked at each other again. The one who had been quiet till now said, "It could happen."

"Aye, it could," the other agreed. He turned back to Abivard. "Pass on, then. Makuran will need every man it can lay hands on, and we'd about given up on having any more get here—we were going to burn the bridge to make sure the nomads couldn't use it to swarm over the river."

"I'm surprised you haven't seen them yet," Abivard said.

"Why?" the talkier lancer asked. "When they wrecked the army, they ate the whole leg of mutton, and it filled 'em too full to bother with pan scraps like you."

The homely comparison made sense to Abivard. He nodded and rode on toward the bridge. The other warrior called after him, "Make your horse take it slow and easy as you cross. We've already doused it with rock oil, so it'll be slick as a melon rind. We'll torch it once we've all crossed."

Abivard nodded and waved to show he'd heard. The steppe pony's nostrils flared when it caught the stink of the rock oil; it snorted and shook its head. Abivard urged it on regardless. It stepped carefully through the black, smelly stuff poured onto the northern part of the bridge. In some parts of Makuran, they used rock oil in their lamps instead of butter or tallow. Abivard wondered how they put up with the smell.

About half a furlong in the center of the bridge was bare of the disgusting coating. The southern end, though, the part that touched the blessed soil of Makuran, also had rock oil poured over it.

Abivard halted his mount a few steps into Makuran. He turned around to watch the last of the garrison that had held the bridge come back over it. One final horseman remained on the planks. He carried a flickering torch. After pausing for a moment at the northern edge of the stretch that had no rock oil, the warrior tossed the torch into the stuff. Yellow-red flames and thick black smoke rose from a rapidly spreading fire. The Makuraner wheeled his horse and hurried across the bare patch and then through the oil that coated the southern end of the bridge.

"That was cleverly done," Abivard said. "The parts with the rock oil will burn quickly once flame reaches them, and the stretch in the middle without any made sure the fire wouldn't spread too fast and catch you still on the bridge."

"Just so," the fellow who had thrown the torch answered. "Have you worked with rock oil, then, to see this so quickly?"

Abivard shook his head. "No, never yet, though I thank you for the courteous words." Then his belly overrode everything else. "Sir, might a hungry man beg of you a bit of bread?"

"We haven't much ourself, for we've been feeding hungry men for a couple of days now, and our supply wagons left yesterday afternoon. But still—" He opened a saddle bag, drew out a chunk of flatbread wrapped around cracked bulgur wheat, and handed it to Abivard.

The food was stale, but Abivard didn't care. Only the memory of his father kept him from gulping it down like a starving wolf. He made himself eat slowly, deliberately, as a *dihqan* should, then bowed in the saddle to his benefactor. "I am in your debt, generous sir. If ever you have need, come to the domain of the Vek Rud and it shall be met."

"The God keep you and your domain safe," the warrior answered. The wind shifted and blew acrid, stinking smoke into his face and Abivard's. He coughed and rubbed his eyes with his knuckles. Then, glancing back toward the burning bridge and the Degird River, he added, "The God keep all Makuran safe, for if the nomads come in force, I don't know if we have the men left to save ourselves."

Abivard wanted to argue with him but could not.

✦   ✦   ✦

The bridge across the Vek Rud remained intact. When Abivard rode over it, he had food in his belly and a caftan over his dirty, ragged drawers, thanks to the kindness of folk he had met on the road. There ahead, crowning the hillock on which it stood, was the stronghold in which he had grown to manhood . . . his stronghold now.

The steppe pony snorted nervously as it picked its way through the village's winding streets; it wasn't used to buildings crowding so close on either side. But it kept going. Abivard, by now, figured it might keep going forever. He had never known a horse with such stamina.

A few people in the village recognized him and called his name. Others asked after his father in a way that said word of the full magnitude of the disaster on the steppe hadn't yet got here. He pretended not to hear those questions. People other than the villagers needed to hear their answers first.

The gates to the stronghold were closed. Someone knew—or feared—something, then. The sentry on the wall above let out a glad cry when he saw Abivard. The gates swung open. He rode in.

Frada stood waiting for him, panting a little—he must have come to the gateway at a dead run. Also panting was a black and tan dog at the heel of Abivard's younger brother. Frada's hands were greasy; maybe he had been feeding the dog scraps when the sentry's cry rang out.

"What became of your armor?" he asked Abivard. "For that matter, what became of your horse? Is the campaign ended so soon? Where are Father and our sibs? Will they come soon? All we have here is fourthhand tales, and I know how Father says they always grow in the telling."

"Not this time," Abivard answered. "All you've heard is true, I daresay, and worse besides. Peroz King of Kings is dead, slain, and most of the army with him—"

He had meant to plow straight ahead, but he couldn't. A low moan went up from the gathering crowd at that first grim sentence. Frada took a step backward, as if he had been slapped in the face. He was young enough to find disaster unimaginable. Whether he had imagined it or not, though, it was here. He did his best to rally, at least enough to ask the next question that had to be asked. "And Father, and Varaz, and Jahiz—"

Abivard cut him off before he named them all. "They charged bravely with the host. The God grant they took some plains-men into the Void before they died. Had I charged with them, I would have perished, too." He told again what had happened to his horse, and how the accident kept him from falling into the Khamorth trap with the rest of the Makuraner army. He had told the story several times now, often enough to make it feel almost as if he were talking about something that had happened to someone else.

"Then you are *dihqan* of this domain," Frada said slowly. He bowed low to Abivard. He had never done that before, save to Godarz. The salute reminded Abivard of how much had changed in bare days' time.

"Aye, I am the *dihqan*," he said, weariness tugging at him like an insistent child. "Whatever is piled up on the platter while I've been away will have to wait another day or two before I'm ready to look at it, though."

"What's the name of the new King of Kings?" someone called from the middle of the crowd.

"Sharbaraz," Abivard answered. "Peroz King of Kings left him behind in Mashiz to look after affairs while he himself fared forth against the plainsmen. Father said he was reckoned a likely young man."

"The God bless Sharbaraz King of Kings." That phrase rose to the sky too raggedly to be a chorus, but in the space of a few seconds everyone in the courtyard repeated it.

Frada said, "You'll have to tell Mother and the rest of Godarz's wives."

"I know," Abivard said heavily. He had thought about that more than once on the long ride south. Telling Burzoe and the other women would be only the barest beginning of his complications there. Along with the domain, the *dihqan's* wives passed under his control. They were *his* wives now, save only Burzoe who had borne him.

His thoughts had not been of sensual delights. For one thing, he had been afraid and half starved, a state anything but condu-cive to lickerish imaginings. For another, he had serious doubts about how well he would manage the women's quarters. Godarz had done pretty well, but Godarz had been older and added his women one at a time instead of inheriting them all at once.

He would worry about such things later. For now, he stuck to small, practical details. "The first thing I'll need to do is find a way into the quarters. Father certainly took the key and—" He stopped in confusion. "No, I'm a ninny. There must be a way in through the kitchens, not so?" So much for practicality.

"Aye, there is," one of the cooks said. "A serving girl can show you. We don't speak of it much, though." Makuraner formality dictated that noble women be separated from the world. Common sense dictated that the world needed to get to them. Common sense prevailed, but formality tried to pretend it didn't.

Abivard scanned the crowd for one of the women who served his mother and Godarz's other wives—no, Godarz's other widows. He pointed to the first one he spied. "Yasna, do you know this way?"

"Yes, lord," Yasna answered. Abivard shook his head like a man bedeviled by gnats. The title was his father's, or rather had been. Now he would have to get used to wearing it.

He followed her into the living quarters, through the kitchens, and into the larder. He had seen the plain door there a hundred times, and always assumed it led into another storage chamber. It didn't. It opened onto a long, narrow, dark hall. At the far end was another door, without a latch on this side but with a grillwork opening so those on the other side could see who came.

Yasna rapped on the door. She stood close by the grille, with Abivard behind her. After a moment, she rapped again. A woman's head obscured the light that came through the opening. "Ah, Yasna," the woman said. "Who is with you?"

"I bring the *dihqan*, lady Ardini," Yasna answered.

Ardini was one of Godarz's most junior wives, younger than Abivard. She let out a squeak, then cried, "The *dihqan* returns? Oh, the God be praised for bringing him home safe!" She unbarred the door and opened it wide.

As the door swung open, Abivard wondered if a man ever came this way and sneaked into the women's quarters. Some nobles kept eunuchs in the quarters to guard against such mishaps. Godarz had never bothered, saying "If you can't trust a woman, a guard will only make her sneaky, not honest."

At Ardini's cry, women came running up the hall. They were crying out, too. But when they recognized Abivard, they gave back in confusion. One of his half sisters said to Ardini, "You said the *dihqan* was here, not his son."

"That's what Yasna told me," Ardini answered sulkily. "Is it a crime that I believed her?"

"She told the truth," Abivard said, "though by the God I wish she'd lied. I am *dihqan* of this domain."

Some of the women stared at him, not understanding what he meant. Others, quicker, gasped and then began to shriek. The wails spread quickly as the rest realized their loss. Abivard wished he could cover his ears, but would not insult their grief so.

Even as they cried out, some of them eyed him with frank speculation. He could guess what was in their minds: *If I can but intoxicate him with my body, he may make me principal wife.* That meant riches, influence, and the chance to bear a son who would one day command the stronghold and rule Vek Rud domain.

He knew he would have to think of such things . . . but not now. Godarz had often gone to Burzoe for advice. That, from the wily *dihqan*, was recommendation enough for Abivard. He saw Burzoe at the back of the group of women, Denak beside her, and said, "I would have speech with my mother and sister first of all." If Godarz had trusted his principal wife's wits, Abivard respected those of his own sister.

Burzoe said, "Wait. Before you speak with us two, everyone who dwells in the women's quarters needs to hear what passed of our husband and sons who went off to war and who—who returned not." Her voice almost broke at the end; not only had she lost Godarz, but Varaz as well.

Abivard realized she was right. As quickly as he could, he went over the doomed campaign yet another time, taking it a further step from memory into tale. Spako and Mirud, mothers to Jahiz and Uzav, burst into fresh lamentation; Arshak's mother, a woman named Sarduri, was dead.

"And so I, and a few others, had the good fortune to escape the ambush, though I thought my fortune anything but good at the time," Abivard finished. "But the flower of the army fell, and times will be hard henceforward."

"Thank you, son . . . or should I say rather, thank you, lord," Burzoe said when he was done. She bowed deeply to him, as Frada had out in the heat of the courtyard. Holding her voice steady by what had to be force of will alone, she went on, "And now, if it is your pleasure to take counsel with Denak and me, follow and I shall lead you to a suitable chamber."

Godarz's widows and those of his daughters who had come into womanhood stepped back to make room for Abivard as he strode through their ranks. Some of the old *dihqan's* wives contrived not to step back quite far enough, so that he brushed against them walking by. He noted that without being stirred by it; grief and weariness smothered desire in him.

He looked curiously this way and that as Burzoe and Denak took him to the room they had in mind: he had not been in the women's quarters since he was little more than a babe. They struck him as lighter and airier than most of the living area in the stronghold, with splendid carpets underfoot and tapestries covering the bare stone of the walls, all products of the patient labor of generations of women who had made their homes here since the stronghold rose in the unremembered past.

"It's—pleasant here," he said.

"You needn't sound so surprised," Burzoe answered with quiet pride. "We are not mewed up here because we are guilty of some crime, but for our honor's sake. Should we live as if this were a prison?"

"Sometimes it has the feel of one," Denak said.

"Only if you let it," Burzoe said; Abivard got the feeling this was a running argument between mother and daughter. Burzoe went on, "No matter where your body stays, your mind can roam the whole domain—wider, if you let it."

"If you are a principal wife, if your husband deigns to listen to you, if you have learned—have been allowed to learn—your letters, then yes, perhaps," Denak said. "Otherwise you sit and gossip and ply your needle and work the loom."

"One thing you do not do, if you are wise, is air petty troubles before the *dihqan*," Burzoe said pointedly. She paused, waving Abivard into a sitting room spread with carpets and strewn with embroidered cushions. "Here we may speak without fear of disturbance."

"No one in Makuran can do anything without fear of disturbance, not today, not for months, maybe not for years," Abivard said. Nevertheless, he went in and folded himself into the tailor's seat on a carpet in the style of the steppes: it showed a great cat springing onto the back of a fleeing stag.

Burzoe and Denak also made themselves comfortable, reclining against big pillows. After a moment, the serving girl Yasna came in with a tray of wine and pistachios, which she set on a low table in front of Abivard. He poured for his mother and sister, offered them the bowl of nuts.

"We should serve you," Burzoe said. "You are the *dihqan*."

"If I am, then let me use my power by doing as I please here," Abivard said.

In spite of the dreadful news he had brought, that made Burzoe smile for a moment. She said, "You are very like your father, do you know that? He could always talk his way around anything he pleased."

"Not anything, not at the end," Abivard said, remembering horses crashing down into the trench the Khamorth had dug and others tumbling over one another as their riders tried desperately to bring them to a halt.

"No, not anything." The smile had already left Burzoe's face. "For the kingdom—is it as bad as that, truly?"

"Truly, Mother," Abivard said. "Only the river stands between us and the plainsmen; we have lost so many that if they do cross, we will be hard pressed to throw them back to their proper side once more."

"I have to remind myself to think in wider terms than this domain alone," Burzoe said with a shaky laugh. "We have lost so many, I find it hard to take in that the realm at large has suffered equally."

"Believe it," Abivard said. "It is true."

"So." His mother stretched the word into a long hiss. Her eyes were bright with tears, but they remained unshed. "For the sake of the domain, then, I can tell you two things that must be done."

Abivard leaned forward: this was what he had hoped to hear. "They are?"

"First," Burzoe said, "you must send to Papak's domain and ask that your wedding with Roshnani be celebrated as soon as is possible."

"What? Why?" Advice on making a marriage he had not expected.

"Two reasons," his mother said. "Do you know if Papak or any of those who fared forth with him survived the battle on the steppe?"

"I don't know. I would doubt it; few came forth alive. But I know nothing for a fact."

"If the *dihqan* and all his likeliest heirs fell fighting, those who find themselves in charge of the domain will be weak and will be looking round for any props they can find to bolster their hold on it. A strong brother-in-law is not the least of assets. And you will also have a claim on them if Vek Rud domain needs aid against the nomads. Do you see?"

"Mother, I do." Abivard inclined his head to Burzoe. He could admire such subtlety, but knew he was not yet capable of it himself. He said, "That's one reason. What's your other?"

"One that will benefit you more than the domain: when you bring Roshnani here, you can establish her as your principal wife with far less jealousy and hatred than if you were to choose one of Godarz's widows. The women here will understand why, for the sake of the domain, you have chosen someone not of their number. Were you to pick one of them, though, all but that one will think you have made a dreadful blunder and torment you and the lucky one without cease. Believe me, you do not want that. No *dihqan* can hope to accomplish anything with the women's quarters in turmoil."

"If Roshnani seems able to bear the burden, I shall do as you say," Abivard answered.

"She *will* bear the burden, because she must," Burzoe said.

Abivard let that go; his mother, he suspected, assumed all other women had her own strength of will. He said, "You've given me one thing I must do, then. What's the other?"

"What you would expect," Burzoe said. Abivard didn't know what he should expect but did his best not to let his face show that. Maybe it did and maybe it didn't; he couldn't tell. Burzoe went on, "It involves Denak, of course."

"Ah?" Now Abivard couldn't disguise that he was lost.

Burzoe sniffed in exasperation. Denak grinned; she knew what her mother was talking about. "You're not the only one in the family who was betrothed, you know."

"No, I didn't know," Abivard said, though on reflection he should have: a *dihqan's* eldest daughter by his principal wife was a valuable piece in the game of shifting power the nobles of Makuran played among themselves. He plucked at his beard. "To whom?" Now that *he* was *dihqan*, he would have to keep track of such things for all of Godarz's daughters.

"To Pradtak, eldest son of Urashtu," Denak answered.

"Ah," Abivard said. "Father made a fine match for you, then." Urashtu's domain lay southeast of the one Abivard unexpectedly found himself holding. Not only did it have good grazing land and hot springs that drew the wealthy infirm from all over Makuran, its stronghold perched on Nalgis Crag, an eminence so imposing that it made Vek Rud's castle seem to lie on flatlands by comparison.

Burzoe said, "As much as your match with Roshnani, we should pursue Denak's with Pradtak. If he survived the battle on the steppe, he will be eager to bring it to accomplishment for the same reasons we are; the God grant it be so. But if not, we can begin discussion with whoever now holds that domain."

Abivard looked over at Denak. Marriages were always chancy; family considerations counted for far more than passion. But at least in Pradtak Denak had the hope of a husband about her own age. If he had died in the Khamorth trap, she might find herself pledged to some wizened uncle who now held Nalgis Crag domain only because he had been too old to go out and fight. That seemed a dreadful fate to inflict on his sister.

Denak smiled back at him, but in a way that said, she, too, was worried about such things. She said, "No less than you, I will do what's best for the domain."

"Of course you will, child," Burzoe said; with her, there was no room for doubt. "Now we need solid allies, and marriage is the best way to come by them. It will be well enough. Have I not prospered here, though I never set eyes on Godarz till the day my hands were set in his?"

Prospered, Abivard noted. His mother had said nothing about being happy. If the idea entered her mind at all, it was less important to her than the other.

She went on in similar vein. "This domain shall prosper, too. You have your father's wits, Abivard; I know the God will help you use them as he did, for she loves the folk of Makuran more than those of any other land."

"As you say, Mother," Abivard answered. Not a word had Burzoe said of her outlining the course he was to follow. She had been the ideal *dihqan's* wife, always ready with ideas but content to let her husband, the public part of the pairing, take credit for them. Now she was doing the same for Abivard.

Maybe she thought to rule the domain as well as advise. With someone other than Godarz her husband, she might already have been doing that for years. Abivard was uncomfortably aware that, for the moment, she had more and better ideas than he did. If Vek Rud domain was to be his in fact as well as name, he would have to acquire wisdom and experience in a hurry.

A corner of his mouth quirked upward. Given the straits in which Makuran found itself, he would have plenty of chances.

✦ III

"A rider approaches!" a sentry bawled from the wall of the stronghold.

Down in the courtyard, everyone stopped what he was doing and looked up to see whence that cry had come. *The south-facing wall,* Abivard thought. The tension that knotted his stomach at every warning shout eased a little: Khamorth raiders would not come out of the south.

The sentry said, "He bears a red banner!"

"A messenger from the King of Kings," Abivard said to no one in particular. He walked over to the gate: making a royal messenger wait would have been as great an insult as delaying the King of Kings himself. As he walked, Abivard called for wine and fruit and meats, to show the horseman that everything in the domain was for his sovereign to command.

The lookout had spotted the rider well away from the stronghold, so the servitors had time to take their position behind Abivard with refreshments ready to hand when the fellow came through the gateway. He swung off his horse with a sigh of relief, swigged wine, and ran a wet towel over his face and head to cool down and wash away some of the dust of travel.

"Ahh," he said, a slow sigh of pleasure. "You are gracious to a man long in the saddle. In the name of the God, I thank you."

"The God enjoins us to meet the stranger's needs," Abivard replied. "Were not the Four wanderers themselves, seeking righteousness and truth among men?"

"You speak well; obviously you are as full of sound doctrine as

59

you are of courtesy to your guests," the messenger said, bowing to Abivard. He pulled a sheet of parchment from the pouch on his belt and glanced at it. "You would be—Godarz, *dihqan* of Vek Rud domain?" He spoke as if he doubted his own correctness.

He had reason to doubt, after the catastrophe in Pardraya. Gently Abivard answered, "No, I am Abivard son of Godarz, now *dihqan* of this domain."

The meaning of that was unmistakable. "The God grant your father peace and his companionship," the royal messenger replied. "If I may be permitted an opinion, his domain finds itself in good hands."

It was Abivard's turn to bow. "Thank you for your kindness."

"Not at all." The messenger took another sip of wine. "Because of the . . . sudden changes . . . we have undergone, I and others like me fare forth from one domain to the next, seeking oaths of allegiance to the new King of Kings, the God bless him and keep him, from nobles old and new alike."

"I would gladly swear allegiance to Sharbaraz son of Peroz, King of Kings of Makuran," Abivard said. "My father always spoke highly of him, and I am sure the kingdom will soon recover its glory under his rule."

Flattery was always more effective with truth stirred into the mix, or so Godarz had taught. Abivard waited for the royal messenger to give forth with more flowery phrases about his kindness or magnanimity or something else the fellow was equally unqualified to judge.

Instead, though, the messenger coughed delicately, as if to show he was willing to pretend he hadn't heard what Abivard said. After a moment he murmured, "Well, Vek Rud domain does lie hard by the frontier. I suppose I should not be surprised I am first to bring here news of the accession of Smerdis King of Kings, may his years be many and his realm increase."

Abivard felt that, instead of standing on solid ground, he found himself above the Void into which the God would cast all those who transgressed against his teaching. He said, "Truly, sir, I had not heard of Smerdis King of Kings. Perhaps you would be good enough to tell me more of him. I trust he is of the true royal line?"

"He is indeed," the messenger replied. "He is sister's son to the late Peroz's grandfather of the same name."

After a bit of thinking, Abivard realized that made Smerdis Peroz's second cousin and Sharbaraz's third: a member of the royal family, yes, but of the royal line? That, however, was not the issue. Abivard knew what the issue was: "Sir, before I speak further on this, I would have you tell me how it passed that Sharbaraz failed to succeed Peroz King of Kings."

"Naturally, I respect your caution in this matter," the messenger said. "The truth, however, is not difficult to set forth: Sharbaraz, feeling himself inadequate to hold the throne because of his youth, ignorance, and inexperience, stepped aside in favor of a man to whom years have given the wisdom Makuran needs in this time of trouble."

That sounded well enough, but if any great-aunt's son had presumed to tell Abivard how to run his domain, he would have sent the fellow packing, or maybe thrown him off the stronghold wall, depending on how importunate he got. And Abivard remembered the praise his father had given to Sharbaraz. If Peroz's son was anywhere near the man Godarz reckoned him to be, he would not tamely yield the throne to anyone, let alone some blueblood who had managed to remain invisible his whole life till now.

And yet Smerdis, by this messenger's account, ruled in Mashiz and reckoned himself entitled to the lion banner of Makuraner royalty. Abivard carefully studied the messenger's regalia. As far as he could tell, the man was genuine. He also knew he did not know and had no way of learning the reasons for everything that happened in Mashiz.

His answer, then, had to be submissive, if cautiously so: "Sir, do you swear by the God that what you have told me of the accession of Smerdis King of Kings is true?"

"By the God I swear it," the messenger answered, his voice deep and solemn, his face open and sincere—but if he lied, he would, had Smerdis a barleycorn of sense, have been chosen to lie well.

"Well, then, so long as your oath shall be shown to be true, I pledge myself the loyal subject of Smerdis King of Kings, and pray the God to grant him the wisdom he will need to rescue Makuran from the troubles ahead," Abivard said. "As you remarked, sir, we are close to the frontier here. We hear news from Mashiz but slowly. But from over the Degird we hear only too clear.

With so many of our warriors fallen, the borderlands are going to be ravaged."

"Smerdis King of Kings shall do everything in his power to prevent it," the messenger said. That Abivard was willing to believe. The question was, how much lay in his power? Not as much as had belonged to the King of Kings until Peroz threw away his army, that was certain.

Abivard glanced at the lengthening shadows. "Pass the night here," he told the messenger. "You'll reach no other stronghold before dusk overtakes you, that's certain."

The messenger gauged the shadows, too. He nodded. "Your hospitality leaves me in your debt."

"I am always pleased to serve the servants of the King of Kings." Abivard turned to his retainers and said, "See to the horse of—" He looked at the messenger. "Your name, sir?"

"I am called Ishkuza."

"See to the horse of Ishkuza the messenger of Smerdis King of Kings." That still seemed strange in Abivard's mouth. He wondered if his father had been wrong about Sharbaraz. Vek Rud domain was a long way from Mashiz. "Let us also see to his comfort. I know there's a leg of mutton cooking. We'll unstopper one of our finer jars of wine, as well."

Hospitality and upholding the reputation of his domain came first with Abivard. Not far behind them, though, ran the desire to ply Ishkuza with as much wine as he could drink in the hopes that it would loosen the messenger's tongue and let him learn more about the man who now controlled Makuran's destiny.

Ishkuza filled himself full of mutton and bulgur and flatbread and yogurt sweetened with honey; he drank horn after horn of wine, and praised it with the knowing air of a man who had tasted many vintages in his day. His face flushed. He grew merry and tried to pull a serving woman down onto his lap. When she evaded him, he laughed boisterously, not a bit out of temper.

But for all Abivard's questions—and he asked them freely, for who could blame a man for wanting to find out all he could about his new suzerain?—Ishkuza said remarkably little. He answered what he could on matters of fact. Of opinions or gossip he seemed entirely bereft.

So Abivard learned Smerdis was about sixty, which struck

him as elderly but not necessarily doddering. Of course he had served—"with distinction," Ishkuza added, though when speaking of a King of Kings it could have gone without saying—at the courts of Peroz and his predecessor, Valash.

"How did he serve there?" Abivard asked, wondering whether his duties had been purely ceremonial or if he had done some real work.

"For many years, he has overseen the operation of the mint," Ishkuza answered. Abivard nodded: not a post in which a man was liable to win great glory or repute, but not a sinecure, either. That made him feel a bit better about Smerdis: he had accomplished something in those sixty years, anyhow.

About the character and temperament of the new King of Kings, his messenger said nothing. Abivard accepted that: they were not likely to become a matter of intimate concern to a frontier *dihqan*, at any rate.

He was heartily glad Ishkuza had accepted his provisional oath of allegiance to this Smerdis King of Kings. Perhaps, if Makuran's new ruler had been dealing with the mint for many years, he had developed a calm and judicious temperament, one not like that of the usual noble.

Or, on the other hand, maybe Smerdis had enough troubles of his own to be content with any sort of allegiance he could get. Until Peroz's charger crashed down into the trench, Abivard hadn't imagined a King of Kings could have troubles like any other man. He knew better now.

The longer he thought about it, the likelier the second explanation felt.

A few days after Ishkuza rode out of the stronghold, another messenger rode in. This one brought more unambiguously welcome news: Abivard's request for an early wedding with Roshnani was accepted.

Yet even the sweet came stirred with bitter these days, for the *dihqan* acceding to the request was not Papak but his third son, Okhos. "No," the messenger said sadly, "he never came back from the steppe country, neither he nor his two eldest who rode with him."

"It was much the same with us," Abivard answered. "I lost my father, my full brother, and three half brothers, and only through what I thought to be misfortune did I escape the trap myself." He told how his horse's fall had led to his own survival.

"Truly the God watched over you," Okhos' messenger said. "As I told you, none of those from our stronghold returned; my new master carries but fifteen years."

"In times like these, youth must needs learn young," Abivard said, to which the rider, himself a stolid, middle-age fellow, nodded solemnly. Abivard wondered how much advice Papak's principal wife was putting into Okhos' ear, and how willing to listen to her a fifteen-year-old would be. Some, evidently, or perhaps Okhos had wit enough to see the sense in this offer on his own.

The messenger said, "By your leave, lord, the lady Roshnani and her wedding party will make for your domain the moment I get home. She and they might even have come in my place—gossip I hear says she wanted it so—but it was less than polite to show up at your gate without fair warning."

"Tell Okhos she and hers shall be most welcome, and the sooner the better," Abivard said; he already had preparations in train. He raised a forefinger. "Tell your master also to be certain her escort includes a good many full-armed men. These days they may find worse than brigands on the road."

"I'll give him your words, just as you've spoken them to me," the messenger promised, and repeated them back to show he could.

"Excellent," Abivard said. "May I put one more question to you?" At the fellow's nod, Abivard lowered his voice: "Is she pretty?"

"*Lord,* if I could tell you one way or the other, I would," the man answered. "But I can't. I never chanced to be in the court-yard when she came out of the women's quarters, so I just don't know. And I can't say I paid much attention back when she was a brat underfoot."

"Very well." Abivard sighed, reached into a pouch he wore on his belt and pulled out two silver arkets. "This for your honesty, at any rate."

The messenger sketched a salute. "You're generous to a man you've never seen. For your sake, I hope she's lovely. Her father and brothers, they aren't—or weren't—" his mouth twisted, "the worst-looking men the God ever made." With that limited reassurance, he rode back toward Papak's—no, Okhos' now—stronghold.

✦   ✦   ✦

The very next day, another rider came into the stronghold, this one sent out by Pradtak son of Urashtu. After the usual courtesies, the man said, "My master is now *dihqan* of Nalgis Crag domain and is pleased to accept your proposal to link our two holdings through his prompt marriage to your sister Denak."

"In that, you bring me good news," Abivard said, "though I grieve to learn his father has gone into the Void. Did he fare north into Pardraya?"

"He did," Pradtak's man replied. He said no more; after the disastrous end of Peroz's campaign, no more needed to be said.

"And your lord was lucky enough to come home safe?" Abivard asked. He was eager to learn of others who had survived the fight. Their numbers were not large.

And now Pradtak's messenger shook his head. "No, lord, for he did not go. Much to his chagrin, he broke an arm and an ankle in a fall from his horse during a game of mallet and ball not a week before he was to set out on campaign, and so had to remain at the stronghold. Now we say the God took a hand in preserving him."

"I understand what you mean," Abivard answered. "A fall from a horse kept me from disaster, too." He told his tale again, finishing, "I thought at the time the God had forsaken me, but I learned better all too soon. I wish he had watched over the whole army as he did over me."

"Aye, lord; you speak nothing but truth there." The messenger added, "It would greatly please Pradtak if you were to send your sister to his stronghold as quickly as you might, provided she be escorted well enough to see to her safety on the journey."

"Only one matter shall delay me," Abivard said. Without moving a muscle, Pradtak's man contrived to look unhappy; obviously, as far as he was concerned, no delay could be acceptable. Then Abivard explained: "My own bride will soon be traveling hither. After I am wed to her, I can accompany Denak to Nalgis Crag."

"Ah." The messenger had a mobile face; Abivard watched him concede the exception. "The God grant you and your wife great happiness, as he shall surely do with your sister and my master."

"May it be so," Abivard said. "And, speaking of my sister's happiness, I trust the *dihqan* Pradtak is healing well?" No matter what had been agreed when Denak was a little girl, Abivard did not intend to yoke her to a brooding cripple who might take out on her the resentment for his injuries.

But the messenger made a sign to turn aside evil suggestions. "Lord, by my head, by the God, in half a year no one shall know he was hurt. We have skilled bonesetters in our domain, and they have done their best for Pradtak. Oh, he may end up with the slightest limp, but he shall assuredly be a full and manly man for the ornament he receives from your women's quarters."

"Well enough, then. I shall hold you and him responsible for the truth of what you say." Abivard would have bet the fellow's expressive features would give him away if he lied. But they radiated candor. That reassured him.

Pradtak's man let out a couple of polite coughs, then spoke from behind the palm of his hand. "May I bring word to my lord of the beauty of your sister? I do not wish to see her—I ask nothing improper," he added hastily, "but you understand your word will help ease my master's mind."

Abivard almost burst out laughing; he had asked Okhos' man nearly the identical question. He thought before he answered; a man's word was as precious a gift as he could give. Was Denak beautiful? She was his sister; he did not look on her as he did on other women. But when he had gone into the women's quarters, she had not seemed out of place alongside Godarz's younger widows, who were quite lovely indeed.

"You may tell Pradtak that, in my humble opinion, he will not be disappointed in her appearance," he said at length.

The messenger beamed. "I shall do just as you say, lord. A last question and I depart: when shall we look for your presence to honor us at Nalgis Crag?"

"I expect my bride to reach this stronghold in a week's time, more or less. Add in another week for the wedding and the festivities that go with it, and the better part of another for traveling to your domain with an armed party and a woman. Say, three weeks in all. I shall send out a messenger on a fast horse two days before our wedding party departs, so that we do not take your master by surprise."

"You are thoughtfulness itself." Pradtak's man bowed deeply, then remounted his horse and rode back toward his own domain. Abivard nodded to himself. The position of the domain among its neighbors stood to be strengthened. Whether that would save it against the Khamorth remained to be seen.

Abivard's heart thumped as it had just before Chishpish ordered his warriors to couch their lances. He shook his head and twisted his fingers in a sign to turn aside the evil omen. Disaster had followed close on Chishpish's order; he prayed to the God and the Four to keep the same from happening in his marriage.

Soon now, he thought, peering out into the courtyard from a window close by the fortified door to the living quarters. There stood Okhos, shifting nervously from foot to foot, catching himself at it and stopping, then forgetting and starting to jiggle again.

And I reckoned taking over this domain hard, Abivard thought as he watched Okhos squirm. Not only had he been a man grown when Vek Rud domain landed on his shoulders, he had also been Godarz's chosen heir. But Okhos' beard was only dark down on his cheeks; he had been just another of Papak's sons . . . until Papak and everyone ahead of Okhos in the succession went off to Pardraya and did not come back. Now, for better or worse, Okhos had to cope with a *dihqan's* duties. Despite his own nervousness, Abivard spared him a moment's sympathy.

Next to Okhos stood the servant of the God, in the yellow robe that proclaimed his calling. His hair and beard were uncut and unkempt, to symbolize his devotion to things of the next world rather than this.

Abivard spared the God's servant only a passing glance. His gaze returned, as it had all morning long, to the gateway to the stronghold. There in the shade waited Roshnani. When she came out into the courtyard, it would also be his own time to advance.

"I wish he'd let me see her," Abivard muttered. Okhos and the wedding party had arrived the evening before. But the young *dihqan,* perhaps because he lacked the experience to know which customary practices he could safely omit, adhered rigidly to them all. And so, while Abivard had been able to greet his bride-to-be—and to learn her voice was pleasant enough—he still had not looked on her face; she wore a veil that must have left her nearly blind, and one that defeated all Abivard's efforts to learn what lay beneath it.

Out in the courtyard, one of Abivard's half brothers began to beat on a drum. On the fourth slow, deep reverberation, Roshnani stepped out from the shadows and began to walk slowly toward her brother and the holy man in yellow.

A younger half brother, Parsuash, gave Abivard a shove. "Go on," he squeaked. "It's time."

Roshnani's gown was bright as a beacon, orange-red silk twill decorated with a pattern of ornate, stylized baskets of fruit. Beneath its hem, the upturned toes of her red shoes peeked out. Her veil, this time, was of the same fabric as the gown, though not quite so opaque.

Parsuash shoved Abivard again. He took a deep breath and walked out into the courtyard. As when he had charged into battle, fear and exultation mingled.

When he came up to the people waiting for him, Okhos gave him a formal bow, which he returned. He bowed also to the servant of the God—who, having a higher master than Smerdis King of Kings, did not bow back—and last to Roshnani. Okhos returned that salute for his sister.

The servant of the God said, "In the names of Narseh, Gimillu, the lady Shivini, and Fraortish eldest of all, we are met here today to complete and accomplish what was set in motion years ago, the marriage of the *dihqan* Abivard to Roshnani, daughter of Papak the late *dihqan* and sister to the *dihqan* Okhos."

Okhos' face twisted. He looked as if he would have given anything to have Papak standing in his place. Abivard understood that; he longed to have Godarz standing strong behind him. But he was on his own, and so was Okhos.

His glance went over to the filigreed screens that covered the windows of the women's quarters. His mother would be behind one of those screens, his sister behind another. All the rest of Godarz's women—now *his* women—would be watching, too, watching as this stranger from another domain came into their world and likely eclipsed them all in status.

"The God grants his blessings, even in adversity," the holy man went on. "From him, as well as from men and women, springs each new generation, each new life. Is it your will, Abivard son of Godarz, that your betrothal be made into a true marriage this day?"

"It is my will," Abivard said as he had been coached. Not far away, Frada nodded slowly, as if making note of what to expect when his turn before the servant of the God came.

"Is it your will, Okhos son of Papak, that the betrothal of your sister agreed to by your father be made into a true marriage this day?"

"It is my will." Okhos' voice broke as he answered. He scowled and flushed. Abivard wanted to tell him not to worry, that it didn't matter, but the man in the yellow robe was already turning to Roshnani, who also had a say in this affair.

"Is it your will, Roshnani daughter of Papak, that your betrothal be made into a true marriage this day?"

"It is my will," she answered, so low Abivard could hardly hear her. No wonder she was nervous, he thought. He was but adding a new wife to several already in the women's quarters. If she turned out not to suit him, he had but to ignore her. But her whole life changed forever with her leaving the stronghold where she had been born . . . and it was so easy for the change to be catastrophically for the worse.

"In token of your wills, then—" The servant of the God handed Abivard and Roshnani each a date. She then gave hers to Abivard, he his to her. As he ate the one she had given him, he wondered if he would see her face as she put hers into her mouth. But no, she reached under the concealing veil and then again to take out the seed. She handed that seed back to the holy man, as Abivard did with his. The servant of the God said, "I shall plant these seeds side by side, that they may grow together as do the two of you."

Then he took Roshnani's hands and set them between Abivard's. That action completed and formalized the wedding ceremony. Cheers rang out in the courtyard and from some, though not all, the windows in the women's quarters. Frada pelted the new couple with wheat to remind the God to make them fertile.

Now that her hands rested in his, Abivard gained the right to lift Roshnani's veil. He had proved his own word and his faith in her father and brother by marrying her first. With that done, she passed from them to him.

The silk of the veil was slick against his fingers as he raised it. Roshnani tried to smile as he saw her for the first time. She was round-faced, pleasant-looking beneath her tension, with pretty eyes accented by kohl. She had painted a beauty mark on one side of her chin. Her cheeks were rouged—but not as heavily as Peroz's had been, that day in camp.

She was less than he had dreamed of, more than he had feared. As Godarz's son, he was plenty practical enough to make the best of that. "Welcome to Vek Rud domain, wife of mine," he said, smiling back at her. "The God grant you long years of happiness here."

"Thank you, husband of mine," she answered, her voice steadier— maybe she knew how to make the best of things, too. "May she be generous enough to grant you what you have wished me."

Frada threw another handful of wheat over them. Abivard took Roshnani's hand in his once more and led her through the crowd toward the living quarters of the stronghold. Retainers and kin all bowed low as they passed. Abivard paused for a moment as he went inside, to let his eyes adjust to the gloom.

Roshnani looked around curiously at people, wall hangings, and furniture. This was, after all, the first stronghold she had seen other than her own. "You've done well for yourselves here," she observed.

"So we have," Abivard said. "And now the domain has a fine new ornament in it." He smiled at her to show what he meant.

She had been properly brought up; she cast down her eyes with becoming modesty. "You are kind," she whispered. Her tone made Abivard wonder if she was saying what she meant or what she hoped.

"We go this way now," he said, and led her down the corridor that ended at the *dihqan's* bedchamber. He knew some trepidation in going that way himself. Since he had come home as lord of Vek Rud domain, he had kept on sleeping in the little room that had been his before the army plunged onto the steppe. He had slept alone every night, too, reasoning that he wanted to establish no favorites before Roshnani arrived.

Now, though, everything changed. He would have to occupy the chamber that had been his father's. Not only was its bed longer than the little pallet in his old room, but it had a door that connected to the women's quarters. After much searching, he had found a spare key to the lock on that door glued to the back of a frame that mounted a tapestry.

The outer door to the *dihqan's* bedchamber had a bar to it. When he shut the door, his siblings and retainers in the hallway behind him cheered and called out ribald advice. The cheers doubled when they heard the bar fall.

Abivard glanced over at Roshnani, who was looking at the bed, on which a serving woman had spread a square of white cotton cloth. She flushed when she noticed him watching her, then said, "By the God I swear I have known no man before, but—" She stopped in confusion.

"One of the things my father told me—" *One of the many useful things my father told me,* Abivard thought "—was that women don't always bleed the first time. If that proves so, there's a little pot of fowl's blood hidden in the chest of drawers, to make appearances proper."

"I think I may be luckier than I dared dream," Roshnani said quietly.

"I hope you go on thinking so," Abivard answered. "Meanwhile, though, whether you end up needing that pot of blood or not, we are here for a reason."

"A reason, yes." Roshnani turned her back on him. The gown had carved bone toggles all the way down. To undo some of them herself, she would have had to be a contortionist. He opened them one by one. His own hands grew less steady the farther he went. In a land where women concealed themselves, removing one from that concealment was intoxicatingly exciting.

Under the gown, Roshnani wore drawers of shimmering silk. She let Abivard slide those to the floor, too, then laughed nervously. "I feel I should cover myself from you, but I know that is not the way of what we do now."

"No," he said, a little hoarsely. Like her face, her body was, if not surpassingly beautiful, then plenty inviting enough. He pulled his caftan over his head, then hastily took off his own drawers. He was a little surprised to find Roshnani looking at him with even more curiosity than he had shown her. After a moment, the surprise vanished. She, after all, knew less of how men were made than he did of women.

He took her hand. It was cold in his. He led her over to the bed, saying "I will do my best not to hurt you, this being your first time."

"Thank you," she answered. "All of Papak's—Okhos', now—women have told me what to expect, but since no two of them say the same thing, my thought is that I shall have to find out for myself."

Even as he was about to draw her down onto the square of

cloth, he paused in admiration of her words rather than her body. "Do you know," he told her seriously, "my father would have said the very same thing, and he was the wisest man I ever knew." With that, he began to think she might have the makings of a principal wife after all.

Then they did lie down on the bed, which creaked and rustled under their weight. Abivard knew a certain nervousness himself; till this moment, the only virginity he had disposed of had been his own. Taking his bride's was another matter altogether.

He wondered if she even knew how to kiss. On making the experiment, he discovered she did. She let out a small giggle when their lips separated. "Your beard and mustache tickle," she said.

He had never thought of the act of love as a way to make the acquaintance of someone, but that was what it proved to be. He learned every time he touched her, every time his lips moved from here to there. And merely taking part in the act together joined them in a way nothing else could.

Some little while later came the time when he at last went into her. Her face twisted beneath him as he made his way through the gate no one had opened before. He did his best not to hurt her, but his urgency had its demands, too. He spent in a long, groaning rush of pleasure.

She wriggled a little after he gasped himself to completion. It wasn't a motion associated with arousal; it seemed more like *get off me—you're heavy.* He took his weight on his elbows, then slipped out of her.

He glanced down at himself and at Roshnani. "We won't have any need for the fowl's blood," he said.

She sat up, looking at the little driblet of blood from between her legs that stained the cloth. "So we won't."

"Are you all right?" he asked.

"Yes, I think so," she answered. "It hurt some, but I expected it to, so that wasn't so bad. I'm sure it will be easier next time, easier still the time after that."

"Did you—like it?" he asked hesitantly.

She gave the question serious consideration before she answered. He was getting the idea she generally thought before she spoke. That, to him, was a point in her favor. After a moment she said, "When it doesn't hurt any more, I think it will be pleasant enough, though I still may find your lips and tongue sweeter, as they can touch just the right spot." She looked at him anxiously. "Does that make you angry?"

"Why should a truthful answer make me angry?" Abivard said.

"I knew I shouldn't believe everything I heard in the women's quarters," his new bride answered, "They said a man was apt to be so proud of his prong—"

"Is *that* what they call it?" Abivard broke in, amused.

"Well, yes. Anyhow, they said he was apt to be so proud of it that he'd forget anything else. I'm glad to find they were wrong."

"Men aren't all the same, any more than women are, I suppose," he said. Roshnani nodded. Abivard wondered if she already knew the touch of lips and tongue. Stories said the inhabitants of the women's quarters, especially if their husband was old or infirm or had a great many wives and made love to each only rarely, sometimes sated one another's lust. He couldn't find any way to ask her. He didn't suppose it was properly his concern, anyway.

Roshnani said, "What you say stands to reason, but of men I must say I know little."

"I hope you will end up satisfied with this man, at least." Being young, Abivard was ready for a second round almost at once, but didn't take it from her, not when he had just made her bleed. Tomorrow would be another day. If she was to become his principal wife, he wanted her pleased with him in bed: they were more likely to be in accord thus on the proper running of the domain. Hurting her again wouldn't help that.

He got out of bed, pulled on his caftan, and picked up the bloodstained square of cloth. Roshnani started to put on her silk drawers, then shook her head. "I don't care to soil them," she said, and stepped back into her gown. "Fasten enough of the toggles to make me decent for the showing, will you please?"

Abivard did as she asked, then threw wide the door to the *dihqan's* chamber. The hallway outside was packed with eagerly—and curiously—waiting people. He held up the cloth with Roshnani's virgin blood on it. Everyone broke into loud cheers, as the proper sealing—or, in this case, unsealing—of a bargain. Roshnani faced the folk of Vek Rud domain with her head held high.

After the ritual showing, Abivard shut the door once more. From the hallway came ribald howls, but he had already decided against that second round. Instead of undoing the silk gown once more, he made sure all its toggles were closed in their proper loops. "We'll have you just as you should be before you go into the women's quarters," he said.

"I thank you for the care you show me." Roshnani looked and sounded as anxious now, in a different way, as she had when he had brought her to bed. And no wonder—she would live with these women for the rest of her days and, a newcomer, find her place among them.

Abivard took the key and used it to unlatch the door that led into the secluded part of the stronghold. Burzoe and Denak waited not far down that hall; he had expected them to be there. Leading Roshnani up to them, he said, "My mother, my sister, I present to you my wife."

The three women embraced one another. Burzoe said, "May you serve this domain as you did your father's. May you give us many fine heirs. May you be happy here." As usual, that came last with her.

"The God grant your wishes, mother of the *dihqan*," Roshnani said softly.

Denak said, "You must tell me everything of your journey here, and of the ceremony, and—" She, too, lowered her voice after a glance at Abivard "—other matters. I, too, am to be wed this season."

Roshnani turned her eyes toward Abivard. "I shall speak of whatever you wish—soon."

He could take a hint. Bowing to his wife, his mother, and his sister in turn, he said, "With your gracious permission, ladies, I shall take my leave. No doubt you will wish to discuss matters with which my merely male ears should not be profaned."

Roshnani, Burzoe, and Denak all laughed in a way that made him retreat even faster than he had planned. *No doubt you will wish to discuss matters with which my merely male ears would be scorched,* he thought. If Roshnani was going to tell Denak about his performance, he didn't want to be anywhere within fifty farsangs when she did it. Fleeing that far was impractical, but he could take himself out of earshot, and he did.

Frada let out a low whistle and pointed ahead to Nalgis Crag and the stronghold that sat atop it. "Will you look there?" he said.

"Any army could sit at the bottom of that pile of rock forever, but if it tried to go up—"

"It'd go back down again, and a lot faster, too," Abivard finished for his younger brother. Only one narrow, winding track led up to the stronghold of Nalgis Crag domain; even from a quarter of a farsang away, Abivard could see a dozen places where a handful of determined men could hold up the army Frada had mentioned.

"They have to have a way to get water, too, else the stronghold wouldn't have got the reputation it owns," Frada added, speaking with the tones of an aspiring general.

"I'll be pleased to get inside strong walls again," Abivard said. "I've felt half naked on the road." He gestured at himself. Like all the warriors in Denak's wedding party, he wore a helmet and carried sword and lance, as a proper Makuraner fighting man should. But the rest of his gear, and theirs, was leather hardened with melted wax, the same sort of light protection some of the Khamorth nomads used. The stronghold smiths were beginning to re-create the iron suits lost in the Pardrayan debacle, but even one of them would be awhile in the making.

Frada turned to Denak and said, "How fare you, sister?"

"I revel in being out of the women's quarters," she answered, "but I wish I did not have to travel veiled. I could see so much more of the countryside without this covering for my face."

"Till we got into the territory of Nalgis Crag domain this morning, there wasn't much to see," Abivard said. "Only desert and rocks between our lands and Pradtak's; save for patches of oasis, Makuran is less than fertile."

"When you've done nothing but look out windows these past ten years, even desert seems interesting," Denak said. As she usually did, she tried to look on the bright side of things: "Nalgis Crag stronghold is so high above the rest of the domain, I should have a broad view from the women's quarters."

Abivard had never worried much about the propriety of shutting high-born women away from the world as soon as they became women: it was the custom of his land, and he went along with it. He had not even worried about his sister being closed up in the women's quarters of the stronghold of Vek Rud domain. That had happened when he was scarcely more than a boy himself, and he had grown used to it. But to have her closed up in a women's quarters far away . . . that sent a pang through the core of him.

"I'll miss you, sister of mine," he said seriously.

"And I you," Denak answered. "We can, perhaps, write back and forth; I hope Pradtak won't mind." If Pradtak did mind, that would be the end of the idea, as they both knew. Denak went on, "What point to learning my letters, though, if I'm not allowed to use them?"

Abivard wondered why Godarz had decided to let Denak learn to read and write. Few Makuraner women could; he didn't think Burzoe knew how, for all her cleverness. His best guess was that Godarz, seeing ability, couldn't bear to let it lie fallow no matter how unusual the field. One thing his father had never been was wasteful.

High and thin in the distance, a horn call rang out from Nalgis Crag stronghold: the wedding party had been seen. "Come on!" Abivard shouted. "Let's give them all the swank we can, for the sake of our pride and the name of our domain." He wished the band could have ridden up Nalgis Crag and into the stronghold with armor jingling sweetly around them, but that could not be. At least Pradtak would understand and sympathize: few domains these days faced no such predicament.

The track that led up to the stronghold had been hacked into the side of the crag. As he rode up it, Abivard saw his earlier estimates had been wrong. At fifteen places on the narrow, twisting road, maybe even a score, a few determined men could have held up a host. Stones were heaped every furlong or less to rain down on the heads of attackers and tumble them to their doom.

At the end of the track, Nalgis Crag stronghold was no mean piece of fortcraft in and of itself. If any army somehow fought its way to the top of the crag, those frowning granite walls, cunningly made to hug every bit of high ground, would hold it at bay for a long time.

"Who comes?" a guard standing in the open gateway demanded fiercely, spear ready to bar the new arrivals' path.

"Abivard son of Godarz, *dihqan* of Vek Rud domain," Abivard answered formally. "With me comes my full sister Denak, intended bride of Pradtak son of Urashtu, the great and powerful *dihqan* of Nalgis Crag domain." He had no idea how great and powerful Pradtak was in person, but any *dihqan* who controlled this domain had access to power that would make some *marz-bans* jealous.

The guard performed a fancy flourish with the spear. "The God watch over you and your party as you enter Nalgis Crag stronghold, Abivard son of Godarz, and may your sister's union with our *dihqan* prove joyous and fruitful." He stepped aside so the wedding party could go ahead.

Now Abivard had to take the role young Okhos had played at Vek Rud stronghold. He helped Denak dismount; they stood in the shade of the gate while the rest of the wedding party had their horses seen to and took their places among the spectators from Pradtak's domain.

The servant of the God came out and stood waiting in the center of the courtyard, his yellow robe shining bright as the sun that beat down on him. Abivard turned to Denak, helping her off with the mantle that had kept her gown clean. "Are you ready?" he murmured. The veil hid her face, but she nodded. He took her hands—the only part of her visible—and led her toward the holy man.

The sun shimmered from the gown, too. It was a rich blue silk, patterned with back-to-back peacocks that shared a golden, jewel-decked nimbus. Above each pair floated a lily leaf; between pairs stood fancy columns with floral capitals.

"May the God and the Four bless you and keep you," the holy man said as they took their places by him. Abivard's eyes turned to the doorway to the stronghold's living quarters. It opened. Out came Pradtak, one arm in a sling, the other hand clutching a stick to help hold him upright. He took almost all his weight on his right leg. Pain cut through the grim determination on his face every time his left foot touched the ground.

Abivard studied him—was this man worthy of his sister? Pradtak was somewhere close to thirty, of a good height, with regular features and a beard trimmed more closely than most. He had courage, to walk on an ankle that so obviously had yet to heal. At first glance, he seemed suitable, though in his heart Abivard reckoned none but the King of Kings a suitable groom for Denak—and even that would not do, not now, not when a graybeard like Smerdis held the throne of Makuran.

The wedding ceremony began. Pradtak agreed it was his will that he marry Denak. The servant of the God turned to Abivard and said, "Is it your will, Abivard son of Godarz, that the betrothal of your sister agreed to by your father be made into a true marriage this day?"

"It is my will," Abivard declared, as firmly as he could. The servant of the God asked Denak if she also consented to the marriage. She put more voice into her answer than Roshnani had, but not much.

The holy man gave her and Pradtak the ritual dates they ate together in token of union and fertility. Denak handed hers to her new husband; he gave his to her. As Roshnani had, she contrived to eat the fruit without showing Pradtak her face. *Let him wait*, Abivard thought. *I had to.*

The servant of the God took the pits from the dates and put them in a pouch on his belt for later replanting. Then he set Denak's hands between Pradtak's. The folk of Nalgis Crag cheered and threw grain at the newlywed couple.

And then, as he now could with propriety, Pradtak lifted his bride's veil to see what manner of woman his father's bargain with Godarz all those years before had got him. Abivard needed an effort of will not to curl his hands into anxious fists. If Pradtak humiliated his sister . . . he didn't know what he would do, but it would be ugly. For Denak's sake, it would have to be.

But Pradtak smiled. He nodded to Abivard. "I find I am a fortunate man this day, my brother-in-law."

"May you and my sister be fortunate together for many years to come," Abivard answered, returning courtesy for courtesy. Then he said, "Now that we have been joined, my clan and yours, may I take the liberty of asking you one question that has nothing to do with this wedding?'

"A quick one," Pradtak said, his eyes full of Denak.

"Quick indeed; I would not delay you. Just this, then: have you yet sworn loyalty to Smerdis King of Kings?"

That made Pradtak think of something other than the nuptial bed. Cautiously, he answered, "Aye, I have. I found no compelling reason to do otherwise, as Sharbaraz has renounced the throne. And you?"

"The same," Abivard said, "and for the same reasons. Thank you, my brother-in-law."

"As you said, the question was quick," Pradtak said. "Now,

though, with my bride and my ankle, I have two good reasons to want to be off my feet."

"You may lean on me, if it eases you," Denak said. "Am I not to be your support in years to come?"

"You are," Pradtak admitted, "but not in public. This journey I shall make unaided, to feed my own pride. Walk beside me, if you will."

Denak's eyes flicked to Abivard—*maybe for the last time*, he thought with another stab of pain—asking him what she should do. Very slightly, he nodded. Robbing a man of his pride would not do, not on a wedding day, and, if Pradtak had managed to walk out here, he would probably make it back to the living quarters by himself.

So he did, albeit slowly, Denak at his side but not touching him. The crowd in the courtyard that would have surged after the newlyweds perforce came slowly instead, and jammed up at the entrance. Once inside, most of them turned to the left, toward the delicious smells coming from the kitchens. Others followed Pradtak and Denak rightward, toward the *dihqan's* bedchamber, baying the same sort of advice Abivard had heard not long before.

He went right himself, not out of lubricity but to show he had confidence in Denak and to deal with any difficulties that might arise. Should that square of cloth come out unbloodied, Pradtak could, if it suited him, declare the marriage void. Abivard did not expect that, but duty demanded that he be there in case of problems.

The door to the bedchamber closed. He heard the bar thud into place. After that, all was silent within. Some of the men speculated lewdly on what was going on. Abivard wanted to draw sword on them, but restrained himself: at a wedding, such jokes had their place. As minutes stretched, people got tired of waiting and drifted off toward the food.

Thump! In the bedchamber, someone removed the bar. The door opened. To cheers from the people still in the hallway, Abivard's not softest among them, Pradtak showed off a blood-stained square of cotton. "My brother-in-law indeed," he called to Abivard, removing any possible doubts.

Abivard bowed in return, then made his way to the kitchens, too. Denak would be going into the women's quarters, to emerge but seldom thereafter. It seemed imperfectly fair.

"Is all well?" Frada asked with his mouth full. He had pocket bread stuffed with mutton and pine nuts in one hand, a mug of wine in the other.

"All is well," Abivard said. "Did you expect otherwise?" He waited for Frada to shake his head, then went on, "Let me get some food, too; what you have there looks good. But after we've stayed long enough for politeness' sake, I want to leave for home as soon as we may."

"Why?" Concern etched Frada's face. "Did Pradtak offer offense to you or to our sister?" His hand slipped to the hilt of his sword. "If he did—"

"No, no," Abivard said quickly. "Nothing of the sort. All the same, this stronghold puts me out of spirit. The sooner I see Vek Rud domain once more, the gladder I shall be."

Here and there, Makuran was a spectacularly fertile land. Between here and there, it was desert. Not even lizards skittered across the gravel-strewn path from Pradtak's domain back to Abivard's.

He and his party set out at earliest dawn, to make as much distance as they could before the worst heat of the day. As the sun rose, it painted the hills north and west of Nalgis Crag in shadows of rose and coral, so that several men pointed to them and exclaimed over their loveliness.

But when the sun rose higher and its own rays lost the ruddiness of early morning, the hills revealed their true hues—dun brown and ashen gray. "They might as well be women," Frada said. "Take away their paint and they are beautiful no longer."

Most of the horsemen laughed heartily at that sally. Under other circumstances, Abivard would have joined them. But he was lost in thoughtful silence, wondering how Denak fared not only in Pradtak's arms but also in the women's quarters of the stronghold. For that matter, he wondered how Roshnani was faring back at Vek Rud domain. All had seemed well when he set out with Denak, but who could say what might have happened in the days since?

Frada asked him, "Do you think the smiths will have finished an armor by the time we get back to our stronghold? I know that first suit will be yours—you're *dihqan*, after all. But I'll wear the second."

"Don't be too eager to wear it, even once it's made," Abivard answered. "Had the domain boasted a seventh suit, you likely would have fared with us out onto the steppe, which meant you'd have been unlikely to come home safe again."

Frada only snorted. He didn't believe anything bad could ever happen to him. Abivard hadn't believed that, either, not until he saw the banner of Peroz King of Kings fall into the Khamorth trench. After that, he could not doubt misfortune fell on all, base and royal alike.

Out in the middle of the rocky, waterless plain, in stretches bare even of thorn bushes, a blue, shimmering mirage—a ghost lake, Godarz had always called it—gave the illusion of water in plenty. To make itself even more tantalizing, it kept pace with the travelers as they rode along, never letting them gain a foot on it. A thirsty man who did not know the lake for illusion would surely have perished pursuing it.

"By the God," Abivard said, "if the Khamorth do invade our land, may they seek to drink deep from a ghost lake and follow it to their ruin."

Frada said, "Perhaps they will remain on their own side of the Degird. If they were going to push into Makuran, would they not have done it already?"

"Who can say what's in a nomad's mind?" Abivard answered. "We and the steppe have warred since the days when heroes walked the earth. Now one side wins, now the other." Seldom, though, he thought, had victory been so absolute.

As day dwindled, the riders looked for a halting point. After unspoken consultation with men older and more experienced than himself, Abivard chose the tip of a low hillock that even boasted a few bushes and shrubs to fuel watch fires. He did not need advice in ordering sentries out in a triangle around the camp. Anyone, bandit or nomad, who wanted to surprise him in the darkness would have to work for it.

He never knew whether his precautions had anything to do with the peaceful night that followed, but he had no intention of neglecting them when evening twilight came again. After pancakes fried on a flat griddle and sour wine, the wedding party set out for Vek Rud domain once more.

Several days passed thus, and the stronghold grew ever nearer. Then, about an hour before noon, when Abivard was thinking of laying up for a while until the weather cooled, he spotted a group of men on horseback coming toward him and his followers.

"Not a caravan," Frada said, curiosity in his voice. "They're riding all the horses they have. I wonder what they're doing here." He shaded his eyes with the palm of his hand in hope of seeing better.

"No doubt they're wondering the same of us." Abivard made sure his sword was loose in its scabbard and his lance in its rest on the saddle. The men who approached might have been celebrants like the group he led. Or they might have been bandits, in which case they would sheer off soon: the numbers of the two parties were close to even, and bandits seldom relished odds like those.

Frada peered through heat haze again. "Miserable little horses they're on," he said. "They're no better than that steppe pony you brought back from—" He stopped, his mouth and eyes both opening wide.

Abivard knew what he was thinking; the same idea blazed in his own mind. "Khamorth!" he shouted, loud enough to startle himself. "Form line of battle. By the God, let's see if we can get ourselves a small measure of revenge."

His companions peeled off to either side of the road. They hadn't been trained to fight as a unit, but they knew what they had to do. When Abivard waved them forward, they booted their horses into a trot: no point to an all-out gallop till they drew closer to the foe.

"Stay in line," Abivard urged, eyes on the nomads ahead. They milled about in confusion for a moment, as if surprised at being recognized for what they were. But then they, too, shook themselves out into a fighting line more ragged than that of their Makuraner foes. They came on with as little hesitation as Abivard's men.

"Makuraaan!" Frada shouted. In an instant, the whole wedding party was screaming the war cry. No one, Abivard noted, yelled the name of Smerdis King of Kings. He remained too new on the throne to make much of a symbol for the land he ruled.

The Khamorth shouted, too, harshly. To Abivard, their unintelligible yells seemed like the bellows of wild beasts. Then, almost at the same instant, the nomads reached over their left shoulders for arrows, rose from their short stirrup leathers until they were all but standing, and let fly. Abivard flung up his shield. Buzzing like an angry wasp, an arrow flew past his head. One of his men let out a cry of pain, but no saddles emptied.

"Gallop!" Abivard cried, and spurred his horse forward.

The Khamorth broke off their own advance and fled back the way they had come, shooting arrows over their shoulders. But their aim was poorer that way, and the men pursuing them, though not armored in iron, still had some protection against glancing hits. And because the Makuraners were without their usual heavy mail and horse trappings, their big steeds ran faster than they would have otherwise. They quickly gained ground on the plainsmen.

The nomads realized that, too. They broke into several small groups and raced across the barren plain in different directions.

Abivard and Frada pounded side by side after a couple of Khamorth. One of the nomads yanked out his curved shamshir, but too late. Abivard's lance took him in the back, just below the left shoulder. He had never before felt the soft resistance flesh and bone gave to sharp-pointed iron. The Khamorth threw his arms wide; the sword flew from his hand. He let out a bubbling shriek and crumpled.

Blood gushed from the hole in the nomad's back when Abivard yanked the lance free. The point, which had gone in bright and shiny, came out dripping red, as did the last foot of the shaft. Abivard gulped. Talking about slaughtering Khamorth was all very well, but the harsh reality almost made him lose his breakfast.

"No time to be sick," he told himself aloud, and wheeled his horse to see how Frada was doing against his foe. His younger brother's lance thrust had missed; now he was using the long spear to hold at bay the plainsman he faced. Abivard spurred toward the battling pair. When the Khamorth turned his head to gauge the new threat, Frada punched the lancehead through his throat.

More blood spurted. Its iron stink filled Abivard's nostrils, as at the butchering of a sheep. He looked around to learn how the rest of the Makuraner wedding party fared.

Two big horses were down, and another galloped across the plain with an empty saddle. But the Khamorth had lost six or seven men, and the rest fled wildly from the Makuraners. The little battle hadn't lasted long but, such as it was, it brought victory to Abivard and his followers.

He expected them to burst into wild cheers, the cheers denied them when they had invaded the steppes. That didn't happen. He didn't feel like cheering himself, not now. Just savoring being alive sufficed.

He rode toward a shaggy-bearded man in the sueded leather of Pardraya who lay writhing on the ground. One of the Khamorth's legs twisted at an unnatural angle; both his hands were pressed to hold in his belly, trying without hope of success to keep the red tide of his life from ebbing away. Abivard speared him again, this time in the neck. The nomad thrashed a few times, then quit moving.

"Why did you do that?" Frada asked.

"He wasn't going to live, not with wounds like those," Abivard said, shrugging. "I don't have the stomach to torment him for the sport of it. What else would you have me do but put him out of his pain, then? I pray to the God someone would do the same for me, were I in such straits."

"Put that way, what you say makes sense." Frada sounded surprised even so, especially at the idea of having anything dreadful happen to him in battle. Abivard understood that. Up until a few weeks before, he had felt the same way. Not any more. He knew better now.

The Makuraners reassembled. Some of them dismounted to strip their fallen foes of bows and arrows, curved swords, and ornaments. "Look here," someone called, holding a gold brooch. "This is Makuraner work, surely plunder from the lost battle on the plains."

"Good and fitting that it return to its proper home, then," Abivard said. He looked around, seeing how his own men had come through the fight. Someone had just broken off an arrow and pulled it through Vidarnag's arm; the rag tied around the wound was turning red, but not too fast. Farnbag had a cut on his cheek through which Abivard could see several of his teeth. *Have to sew that up now,* he thought, *or it may be a hole for the rest of his days.* A couple of others had lesser hurts.

And Kambujiya and Dostan were missing. Half a furlong away lay a body with a lance beside it. The Makuraner's helm had fallen off, revealing a shiny bald pate. That was Dostan, then. And there sprawled Kambujiya, over in the other direction.

"The God grant them peace," Abivard said. He made some quick mental calculations. The wedding party was at most two days from Vek Rud domain. The very last part of the ride would be unpleasant, but . . . "We'll tie them onto a couple of pack-horses. Let them rest in the soil with their fathers."

"And let the jackals and ravens and buzzards squabble over the remains of the Khamorth," Frada added.

"Aye," Abivard said, "and may they find them sweet." He plucked at his bearded chin in a gesture he had picked up from his father. "Now what we have to find out is whether these plainsmen were on their own or if they're part of a bigger band. If they are . . ." He made a sour face. If they were, his assumption that the nomads would stay on their own side of the Degird had to go.

After the corpses of the two slain men had been picked up, the Makuraners started north and west again. Now they rode as if expecting battle at any time and from any direction, with one man a couple of furlongs ahead at point and another the same distance behind the main group to serve as rear guard.

They saw no more plainsmen for the rest of the day. When evening drew near, Abivard looked for a defensible campsite with even more care than he had before. Then he had worried about what might happen. Now he knew it could.

He finally found a steep hillock that might have been crowned with a stronghold had the land around it boasted any water. As he had before, he set out pickets in a triangle around it. He took his own turn at watch, too, replacing Frada for the middle-of-the-night stint.

"All quiet here," his brother reported, yawning. Lowering his voice, Frada added, "I would not say so in front of the men, but I mislike the omen we're bringing home."

"Aye, I had the same thought myself," Abivard answered, also quietly. "A wedding party's supposed to fetch back joy and hope. Instead, we'll hear women wailing when we get home to the stronghold." He spread his hands. "But what choice have we?"

"None I see," Frada said. "But all Makuran has heard too much of women wailing this season."

"Which does not mean we shall not hear more." Abivard slapped his brother on the back. "You fought well. Now go back up by the fire and get some rest."

Frada took a couple of steps, then stopped and turned back. "It's an uglier business than I thought—fighting, I mean. The blood, the stinks, the fear—" He hesitated before that last, as if afraid of being thought unmanly.

"Oh, yes," Abivard said. He couldn't see his brother's face; it was dark, and Frada stood between him and the embers of the fire, with his back to their glow. But he did see Godarz's younger son let his shoulders slump in relief.

Abivard paced back and forth on watch, not to be more vigilant but because he knew he was liable to fall back to sleep if he sat down in one place. But for the faint *scrape-scrape* of his boots on dirt and gravel, the night was eerily quiet. Once, a long way away, a fox yipped. After so much silence, the sound made Abivard start and grab for his sword.

He laughed at his own nerves as he began to pace again. Even to himself, though, the laughter seemed hollow. With the Khamorth loose in Makuran, every traveler who went beyond sight of his own stronghold would run risk of ambush. Some of those who failed to start at imaginary dangers would also fail to start at real ones.

The moon was down. The night was very black, stars glittering like tiny jewels set on velvet. The faint glimmer of what the Makuraners called the God's Robe stretched from horizon to horizon. Abivard never remembered seeing it clearer.

A shooting star flashed across the sky, then another. He whispered a prayer for the souls of Dostan and Kambujiya, carried through the Void on those stars. A third star fell. He couldn't believe it ferried the spirit of a Khamorth to the God. On the other hand, all too likely more Makuraners than his own two companions had fallen to the nomads today.

✦ IV

The rider took from his belt a tube of leather boiled in wax to make it impregnable to rain and river water. With a flourish, he undid the stopper and handed Abivard the rolled-up parchment inside. "Here you are, lord."

"Thank you." Abivard gave the fellow half a silver arket; people often cut coins to make change. The horseman bowed in the saddle, dug heels into his mount's sides, and rode away from Vek Rud stronghold.

Abivard unrolled the parchment. He had been sure the letter was from Denak; not only had he recognized the courier from his own trip to Nalgis Crag domain, but no one save his sister was likely to write him in any case. Still, seeing her carefully formed script always made him smile.

"'To the *dihqan* Abivard his loving sister Denak sends greetings,'" he read, murmuring the words aloud as if to call up her voice. "'I am gladder than I can say that you came home safe from the fight with the Khamorth. We have not seen any of the barbarians in this domain, and hope we do not. And, as you can see, Pradtak my husband has no objection to your writing to me or to my replying. I think he was surprised to learn I have my letters; I may be the only one in the women's quarters here who does.'"

Abivard frowned when he read that. Being singled out as different wouldn't make life in the women's quarters any easier for Denak. He read on: "'While caring greatly that his domain should prosper, Pradtak also enjoys the pleasures of the hunt. He still

87

cannot ride, and pines for the day when he will again be able to pursue the wild ass and the gazelle.'"

When he can stop worrying about the domain and go off and have fun, Abivard read between the lines. His father had occasionally had some pointed things to say about *dihqans* who put their own pleasures first. Denak would have heard them, too. Abivard wondered if she was trying to make her new husband see sense.

He looked down at the letter again. "'Because I read and write, he entrusts me day by day with more of the administration of the domain. Everything here is new to me, and I have more responsibilities than I am used to shouldering, but I try to decide what our father would have done in any given case. So far this seems to work well; the God grant it continue so. I pray to her to keep you well, and eagerly await next word from you.'"

So Father now runs two domains, even if not in the flesh. The thought made Abivard smile. He suspected it would have made Godarz smile, too. From Denak's letter, she was well on the way to becoming Pradtak's right hand, and probably three fingers of the left, as well.

He rolled up the letter again and put it back in its tube. Later he would read it to Burzoe, who no doubt would be proud of what her daughter was accomplishing. He wondered if he should read it to Roshnani. Maybe she would think it obligated her to try to run Vek Rud domain as Denak was taking over at Nalgis Crag. But Abivard was no Pradtak: he had his own ideas about how things should go.

For now, he would put guards out with his herdsmen, to protect them and their flocks from small Khamorth raiding parties. If a whole clan decided to try to settle on his grazing lands, guard detachments wouldn't be enough to hold them at bay, but he kept hoping that wouldn't happen. Of course, none of his hopes had come to much since he crossed into Pardraya.

"Well," he said to no one in particular, "everything that possibly could go wrong has already gone and done it. Things have to get better from here on out."

The cry from the battlements brought Abivard up the stairs at a dead run: "Soldiers! Soldiers under the lion banner of the King of Kings!"

Following a sentry's pointing finger, Abivard saw for himself the approaching detachment. It was bigger than he had expected, a couple of hundred men in bright surcoats over iron armor. If they hit the Khamorth, they could hit them hard. Abivard's heart leaped to see the sign of returning Makuraner might. "Open the gates," he shouted. "Let us make these heroes welcome."

While the gates swung slowly open, Abivard descended to greet the newcomers in person. All the doubts he had had about Smerdis King of Kings vanished like a brief rain shower into the soil of the desert. The new ruler was stretching forth his hand to protect his distant provinces.

Not all the riders could enter the courtyard together. Abivard ordered bread and wine sent to those who had to wait outside the walls. "You are blessed by the God for coming to the frontier in our hour of need," he told the commander of Smerdis' force, a tough-looking veteran with gray mustachios waxed into stiff spikes.

Even from a man who was nothing more than a soldier, he had expected a courteous reply; the folk of Makuran could swap compliments from morning till night. But the commander, instead of praising Abivard's hospitality or the site of his stronghold, suffered an untimely coughing fit. When at last he could speak again, he said, "You would be better advised, magnificent *dihqan*, to address your remarks to my colleague here, the famous Murghab."

Abivard had taken the famous Murghab to be the commander's scribe. He was a desiccated little man in a plain gray-brown caftan who looked uncomfortable on his horse. But if the soldier said he was a person of consequence, Abivard would greet him properly. Bowing low, he said, "How may I serve the splendid servant of Smerdis King of Kings, may his years be many and his lands increase?"

"Your attitude does you credit," Murghab said in a voice like rustling leaves. "I shall speak frankly: Smerdis King of Kings finds himself in need of silver and is levying a special assessment on each domain. We require from you payment of—" He pulled out a sheet of parchment and ran his finger down till he found the line he needed. "—eight thousand five hundred silver arkets, or their equivalent in kind. The assessment is due and payable forthwith."

Now Abivard coughed, or rather choked. He also felt like an

idiot. He could not possibly say no, not now, not after he had let so many of the King of Kings' warriors into Vek Rud stronghold. A dozen of them sat their horses between him and the doorway to the living quarters. They watched him with polite but careful attention, too—they were readier for trouble than he had been.

He gathered himself. He had that much silver in his treasury. If Smerdis was going to use it to defend the kingdom, it might even prove money well spent, however much he regretted parting with it. He said, "I hope Smerdis King of Kings is using my silver and what he gets from other *dihqans* to enroll new soldiers in his lists and to hire smiths to make armor and weapons for them."

The famous Murghab said not a word. Puzzled, Abivard looked to the military commander. The officer fidgeted in the saddle, waiting for Murghab to reply, but when he remained mute, the fellow said, "Smerdis King of Kings orders this silver collected so as to pay an enormous sum of tribute to the Khamorth, that they may withdraw over the Degird and stay on their side of the river henceforward."

"What?" Abivard howled, forgetting the disadvantage at which Smerdis' soldiers had him. "That's crazy!"

"So Smerdis King of Kings has ordained; so shall it be," Murghab intoned. "Who are you to question the will of the King of Kings?"

Put that way, Abivard was nobody, and he knew it. Instead of answering Murghab, he turned to the commander. "But don't you see, bold captain, that paying tribute when we're too weak to defend ourselves only invites the plainsmen back to collect a new pile of silver next year, and the year after that?"

"So Smerdis King of Kings has ordained; so shall it be," the officer said tonelessly. Though his words echoed Murghab's, his expression and manner argued he was less than delighted at the policy he had been ordered to uphold.

Murghab said, "The sum heretofore cited is due and payable now. Do not waste time even to scratch your head. Surely you would not wish to be construed as resisting the King of Kings?"

Had Abivard not let the foxes into the henhouse, he would have thought hard about resisting—as well throw his silver down a *qanat* as convey it to the Khamorth. As things were . . . Tasting gall, he said, "Bide here, O famous Murghab." He could not resist putting a sardonic twist on the man's honorific. "I shall bring you what you require, and may Smerdis King of Kings—and the Khamorth—have joy of it."

Godarz had been a methodical man. The silver in the stronghold's treasure room was stored in leather sacks, a thousand arkets to each. Abivard picked up two sacks, one in each hand, and, grunting a little, carried them through the halls and out of the living quarters to the courtyard, where he set them in front of Murghab's horse. He made the same trip three more times.

"Bide here a moment more, famous sir," he said when he had brought out eight thousand arkets. He went back into the treasury. Only three sacks of coins remained there, as well as some empty ones neatly piled to await filling. Abivard took one of those and dumped jingling silver coins into it till it weighed about as much as the sack from which he was taking the money. He sighed; this wasn't how Godarz had intended the sack to be used. He had wanted silver coming in, not going out. But Abivard could do nothing about that, not now. He carried out the half-filled sack and set it with the rest. "This may be twenty or thirty arkets too light, or it may be so much too heavy. Will you be satisfied, or must you have an exact count?"

Murghab pursed his lips. "The order of the King of Kings, may his years be long, calls for eight thousand five hundred, no more, certainly no less. Therefore I am of the opinion that—"

"It suffices, lord," the officer who led the detachment of royal soldiers broke in. "You have cooperated most graciously with our request."

What am I supposed to do, when you're already inside my stronghold? Abivard thought. Nonetheless, the soldier at least adhered to the courtesies Makuraners held dear. Abivard put the best face on extortion he could, saying with a bow, "It is a privilege for any subject to serve the King of Kings in any manner he requires. May I have your name, that I may commend you to him for the manner in which you perform your duties?"

"You honor me beyond my deserts," the soldier replied. Abivard shook his head. He wished he didn't know the famous Murghab's name. He couldn't say that aloud, but had the feeling the officer knew it. The fellow added, "Since you ask, lord, I am Zal."

"Zal," Abivard repeated, locking the name in his memory. He would not forget it. Nor would he forget Murghab, however much he tried. He asked, "May I serve you in any other way?"

"I think we are quits here." Zal sketched a salute to Abivard. At his order, a couple of men dismounted and loaded the silver from Vek Rud domain onto the patient back of a packhorse. Without apparent irony, Zal said, "May the God grant you continued prosperity."

Why? So you can come back and shear me again? Probably for that very reason, Abivard judged. But he could not afford such an outrageous payment again . . . and now he knew better than to open his gates to Smerdis' men. The next time they wanted silver for tribute, the would have to get it from him the hard way.

The *dihqan's* bedchamber had a window that faced east, giving its occupant the chance to look out over the domain. That window also let in early-morning sunbeams, to ensure that its occupant did not sleep too far into the day. Had the chamber not belonged to *dihqans* long before Godarz's time, Abivard would have guessed that was his father's scheme. Whosever idea it had been, back in the dim days when the stronghold was raised, it still worked.

One of those sunbeams pried his eyelids open. He sat up in bed and stretched. Roshnani was lying with her back to the sun, and so remained asleep. He smiled and set a gentle hand on the curve of her bare hip. His skin, toasted over years by the sun, was several shades darker than hers.

A dihqan's wife should be pale, he thought. *It shows she doesn't have to leave the women's quarters and work like some village woman.* Even after Smerdis' depredations, the domain was not so far gone as that.

Roshnani shifted on the down of the mattress. Abivard jerked his hand away; he hadn't wanted to waken her. But her squirming brought her face into the path of the sunbeam. She tried to twist away, but too late: her eyes came open.

She smiled when she saw Abivard. "Good morning, sun in my window," she said. "Maybe that last one started a boy in me." She set a hand on her belly, just above the midnight triangle between her legs.

"Maybe it did," he answered. "And if it didn't, we could always try again." He made as if to leap at her then and there. It was only play; he'd learned she wasn't in the mood for such things at daybreak. He did let his lips brush across hers. "Who would have thought a marriage where neither of us saw the other till after we were pledged could bring so much happiness with it?"

"I saw you," she corrected him. "Dimly and through the veil, but I did."

"And?" he prompted, probing for a compliment.

"I didn't flee," she answered. He poked her in the ribs. She squeaked and poked him back. He was ticklish, a weakness his father and brothers had exploited without mercy. He grabbed Roshnani to keep her from doing anything so perfidious again. One thing led to another, and presently he discovered she could be in the mood for an early-morning frolic after all.

Afterward, he said, "I'm greedy for you. I want to call you here again tonight."

"I'd like that, too," she said, running a fingertip down the middle of his chest, "but you might be wiser to choose another."

"Why?" He suspected his frown was closer to a pout. Having a great many lovely women at his disposal was a young man's fantasy. Reality, Abivard had discovered, was less than imagination had led him to believe. Oh, variety every once in a while was enjoyable, but he preferred Roshnani over the wives he had inherited from Godarz.

When he told her as much, she glowed like a freshly lighted lamp. All the same, she said, "You still might be better advised to choose someone else tonight. If you call only for me, I will be hated in the women's quarters—and so shall you."

"Has it come to that?" Abivard asked, alarmed.

"I don't believe so, not yet, but I've heard mutters around corners and from behind closed doors that make me fear such a thing is not far away," Roshnani answered. "Your lady mother might perhaps tell you more. But this I say: better to give up a little happiness now if in the giving you save a great deal later."

The words had the ring of sense Abivard was used to hearing from Burzoe, which to his mind meant Roshnani had the makings of as fine a principal wife as any *dihqan* could hope for.

"Do you know what you are?" he asked her. She shook her head. "A woman in ten thousand," he said. "No, by the God, in a hundred thousand."

That earned him a kiss, but when he tried for more this time, Roshnani pulled away. "You must be able to give your best to whomever you call tonight," she said.

He glowered in mock indignation. "Now you presume to question my manhood?" But since he had a pretty good notion of what he could do in that regard, he made no more than that mild protest—Roshnani was too likely to be right.

When evening came, he summoned Ardini instead of Roshnani. She came to his bedchamber in a silken gown so transparent he could see the two tiny moles she had just below her navel. That excited him, but she had drenched herself in rose water till she smelled stronger than a perfumer's. He almost sent her back to the women's quarters to scrub it off, but desisted: no point in embarrassing her. He regretted that later, for the bedchamber was redolent of roses for the next several days.

Abivard conscientiously summoned each of his wives from the women's quarters in turn. A couple of times, he had to pretend to himself that he was really making love with Roshnani, though he took special pains to make sure those partners never noticed. Thinking of what he did as a duty helped him get through it. He suspected that would have amused Godarz.

The duty done, though, he went back to spending most of his nights with Roshnani. Most of the times he summoned other women were at her urging. Some principal wives, he knew, would have grown arrogant if shown such favor. Roshnani did her best to act as if she were just one of many. That only inclined Abivard to favor her more.

One morning after sleeping alone—he had been drinking wine with Frada and some of his older half brothers, and came to bed too drunk to be much interested in female companionship—he woke with a headache so splitting, he didn't even feel like sitting up. Still flat on his belly, he reached down and blindly groped for his sandals. All he managed to do, though, was push them farther under the bed, beyond the reach of his sweeping arm.

"If I have to call a servant to bend down to get my shoes, everyone will know how bad I feel," he said aloud. Just hearing his own voice hurt, too. But even hung over, Abivard was dutiful. He got out of bed—actually, he came close to falling out of bed—and pulled out first one sandal, then the other.

Suffused in a warm glow of virtue that almost masked his crapulence, he was about to don the captured footgear when his bloodshot gaze fell on something else under the bed, something he didn't remember seeing there before—not that he spent a lot of time looking under the bed: a small, dark-gray, rectangular tablet.

Before he thought much about what he was doing, his hand snaked out and seized the tablet. His eyebrows rose as he pulled it out to where he could get a good look at it: it was heavier than he had expected. "Has to be lead," he said.

The upper side of the tablet was blank and smooth, but his fingers had felt marks on the thing, so he turned it over. Sure enough, the other side had words cut into the soft metal, perhaps with an iron needle. They were, at the moment, upside down.

Abivard turned it over. The words became clear. As he read them, his blood ran cold. *May this tablet and the image I make bind Abivard to me in cords of love. May he waste away from wanting me; may desire cling to him like a leech from the swamps. If he wants me not, may he burn with such pain that he would wish for the Void. But if he should die of desire for me, let him never look on the face of the God. So may it be.*

Moving as if in a bad dream, Abivard broke the curse tablet in two and spat on the pieces. Now his heart pounded as hard as his head. He had heard of women using magic to bind a man to them, but he had never imagined such a thing happening in the women's quarters of Vek Rud stronghold.

"Who?" he whispered. Roshnani? He couldn't believe that—but if she had ensorceled him, he wouldn't believe it, would he? Did she make him so happy because she had magically compelled him to fall in love with her?

It was possible. With cold rationality, he recognized that. He wondered how he would ever trust another woman if it proved to be so. But he also knew it didn't have to be so, not when he had had every one of his wives out of the women's quarters and into his bedchamber in the recent past.

He started to call for Burzoe, but then shook his head. He did not want even his mother to know of the curse tablet. If she let slip an unfortunate word, as even the wisest person, man or woman, might do, chaos would rule the women's quarters, with everyone suspecting everyone else. If he could find any way to prevent that, he would.

Whistling tunelessly between his teeth, he tossed the broken pieces of the tablet onto the down-filled mattress. When he had thrown on a caftan and buckled the sandals whose escape under the bed had led him to find the tablet, he put on his belt and stuck the two chunks of lead in one of the pouches that hung from it.

He was out the door and walking down the hall before he realized he had stopped noticing his headache. *Amazing what fear will do,* he thought. It was not a hangover cure he hoped to use again any time soon.

The normally savory cooking smells wafting through the living quarters only made his stomach churn: terror hadn't cured him after all. He hurried out into the courtyard and then down into the village that lay below the stronghold on its knob.

He knocked at the door of Tanshar the fortune-teller. The old man was as close to being a proper wizard as anyone in the domain—and that thought made Abivard wonder if Tanshar had prepared the curse tablet and whatever image went with it. But he could more easily imagine the sky turning brown and the land blue than Tanshar involving himself in something like this.

Tanshar awkwardly held a crust of bread and a cup of wine in one hand to free the other so he could open the door. His eyes, one clouded, the other clear, widened in surprise when he saw who had disturbed his breakfast. "Lord Abivard," he exclaimed. "Come in, of course; you honor my home. But what brings you to me so early in the day?" Tanshar made it sound more like curiosity than reproach.

Abivard waited till the old man had closed and barred the door behind him before he fished out the broken pieces of the tablet and held them in the palm of his hand so Tanshar could see them. "I found this curse under my bed when I arose this morning," he said in a flat voice.

The fortune-teller reached for them. "May I?" he asked. At Abivard's nod, he took the two flat pieces of lead, put them together, and held them out at arm's length so he could read them. When he was done muttering the words to himself, he clicked his tongue between his teeth several times. "Am I to infer one of your wives left it there, lord?"

"I can't see anyone else wanting to. Can you?"

"It seems unlikely," Tanshar admitted. "What would you now of me, lord? Have you felt yourself under the influence of this spell? Love magic, like that of the battlefield, is often chancy, because passion reduces the effectiveness of sorcery."

"I honestly don't know whether the magic has hold of me or not," Abivard said. "I won't be able to decide that until I learn who put the tablet there." If it was Roshnani, he didn't know what he would do . . . No, he did know, but didn't want to think about it. He forced himself to steadiness. "I know you're a scryer. Can you see who did set that thing under my bed?"

"Lord, I believe I could, but is that truly what you'd have of me?" Tanshar asked. "If I were to look into your bedchamber for the moment in which the tablet was placed there, I would likely find you and the woman who left it in, ah, an intimate moment. Is that your desire?"

"No," Abivard said at once; he was wary of his own privacy, and even more wary of that of the denizens of the women's quarters. He scowled as he thought, then raised a finger. "The tablet speaks of an image. Can you scry out where that image is hidden? That will help tell me who made it."

"The domain is lucky to have a man of your wit at its head," the fortune-teller said. "I shall do as you command."

He set the pieces of the curse tablet down on a stool, then went off into the back room of the little house. He returned a moment later with a water jug and a small, glittering bowl of almost transparent black obsidian. He put the bowl on top of the two pieces of lead and poured it half full of water.

"We must wait until the water grows altogether still," he told Abivard. "Then, without roiling its surface with our breath, we shall look into it together and, unless the God should will otherwise, we shall see what you seek to learn. When the time comes, remember to think on the image whose whereabouts you'd find."

"As you say." Abivard waited as patiently as he could. He glanced down into the bowl. The water there looked calm to him. But scrying was not his business. Tanshar did not presume to tell him how to run the domain, so he would not joggle the fortune-teller's elbow.

When Tanshar was satisfied, he said quietly, "Lay your hand on the edge of the bowl—gently, mind, so as to stir the water as little as you may—and set your thoughts on the God and the Four and what you would learn."

Abivard wondered how he was supposed to keep two different sets of thoughts in his head. He did his best. The obsidian was glassy smooth under his fingertips, but his touch disturbed the glassy smoothness of the water in the bowl. He glanced over at Tanshar. The fortune-teller nodded back; this, evidently, was expected.

When the water settled to stillness again, it showed not the reflection of the ceiling, or of Abivard and Tanshar peering down into it, but a little doll of wool and clay, almost hidden in shadows. Four strings were wrapped around it, at head, neck, heart, and loins. Each was made of four threads of different colors.

"That is a perversion of the reverence due the Four." Tanshar's voice was still low, but full of anger.

Abivard hissed in frustration. He could see the image, yes, but hardly anything else, so he had no idea where in the stronghold—if it was in the stronghold—it rested. But the thought itself was enough to give him a wider view. He saw the image lay enshadowed because it rested behind a chest of drawers in a chamber he recognized as Roshnani's.

He jerked his hand away from the bowl as if it burned his fingers. Instantly the scrying picture vanished from the water, which now gave back the reflections it should have. His own face, he saw without surprise, was twisted into a grimace of anguish.

"The news is bad?" Tanshar asked.

"The news could not be worse," Abivard answered. To think that what he had imagined to be joy was just sorcery! He still could not believe Roshnani capable of defiling him so. But what else was he to think? There lay the doll in her room of the women's quarters. Who else would have hidden it so?

When he said that aloud, Tanshar answered, "Would you not sooner learn than guess? The bowl and the water still await your view, if that be your will."

Almost, Abivard said no. Seeing Roshnani conceal the magic image, he thought, would cost him more pain than he could bear. But he had borne a great deal of pain lately, so down deep he knew that was only cowardice talking. "That is my will," he said harshly. "Let the thing be certain."

"Wait once more for the water to settle," Tanshar said. Abivard waited in grim silence. The fortune-teller nodded at last. Abivard brought his hand to the bowl again, then had to wait for the water to grow calm after his touch.

This time he expected to have to wait before a picture formed. When it did, it showed Roshnani's chamber once more, and

Roshnani herself sitting on a stool close by the chest behind which hid the image intended to bind Abivard in the ties of sorcerously induced love. She was bent over some embroidery, her pleasant face intent on the delicate needlework.

Abivard's glance flicked over to Tanshar. The fortune-teller's eyes were closed; he had the delicacy not to gaze upon his *dihqan's* woman. At the moment, Abivard did not care about that. He peered down into the quiet water, waiting for Roshnani to get up from the stool and conceal the image.

She looked up from the needlework and rose. Abivard forced himself to absolute stillness, lest he disturb the scrying medium. He stared at the simulacrum of his wife, wondering how far into the past Tanshar's magic reached.

Whenever it was, Roshnani did not go over to the chest, though it was but a couple of paces away. Instead, she smilingly greeted another woman who walked into the chamber. The newcomer pointed to the embroidery and said something. To Abivard, of course, her lips moved silently. Whatever her words were, they pleased Roshnani, for her smile got wider.

The other woman spoke again. Roshnani picked up the embroidery from the stool and sat back down. She started to work again, perhaps demonstrating the stitch she had been using. The other woman watched intently for a little while—Abivard wasn't sure time ran at the same rate in the scrying bowl as in the real world—then leaned back against the chest of drawers.

There! Her hand snaked to the rear edge of the chest, opened for an instant, and then was back at her side. Intent on the needlework, Roshnani never noticed.

"By the God," Abivard said softly. He took his hand away from the polished obsidian bowl. The scrying picture vanished as if it had never been.

Tanshar felt the motion of withdrawal and opened his eyes. "Lord, have you that which you require?" he asked.

"I do." Abivard opened the pouch at his belt, took out five silver arkets, and pressed them into Tanshar's hand. The fortune-teller tried to protest, but Abivard overrode him: "For some things I would not spend silver so, not after the way the famous Murghab robbed the domain in the name of the King of Kings. But for this, I reckon the price small, believe me."

"Are you then ensorceled, lord?" Tanshar asked. "If it be so,

I don't know if I am strong enough to free you from such a perverse enchantment."

But Abivard laughed and said, "No, I find I am not." He wondered why. Maybe his naturally conceived passion had been too strong for the artificial one to overcome; Tanshar had said love magic was a chancy business.

"I'm pleased to hear it," the fortune-teller said.

"I'm even more pleased to say it." Abivard bowed to Tanshar, then took the broken pieces of the lead tablet and headed up the dusty road to the stronghold. He stopped and stooped every few paces until he had picked up three black pebbles.

Roshnani looked up from her embroidery when Abivard stepped into the doorway. The smile she gave him reminded him of the one he had seen in the scrying bowl not long before. "What brings you here at this hour of the day?" she asked. Her smile grew mischievous as she thought of the obvious answer, then faded when she got a better look at his face. "Not that, surely."

"No, not that." Abivard turned to the serving woman who hovered behind him. "Fetch my lady mother and all my wives to this chamber at once. I know the hour is yet early, but I will have no excuses. Tell them as much."

"Just as you say, lord." The serving woman bobbed her head and hurried away. She knew something was wrong, but not what.

The same held for Roshnani. "What is it, husband of mine?" she asked. Now her voice held worry.

"Just wait," Abivard answered. "I'll tell the tale once for everyone."

Roshnani's chamber quickly grew crowded. Burzoe looked a question at her son as she came in, but he said nothing to her, either. Some of his wives grumbled at being so abruptly summoned from whatever they were doing, others because they had had no chance to gown themselves and apply their cosmetics. Most, though, simply sounded curious. A couple of Abivard's half sisters peered in from the corridor, also wondering what was going on.

Abivard brought the flat of his hand down onto the chest of drawers. The bang cut through the women's chatter and brought all eyes to him. He pulled out the two pieces of the curse tablet, held them high so everyone could see them. Quietly he asked, "Do you know what this is?"

Utter silence answered him, but the women's eyes spoke for them. Yes, they knew. Abivard dropped the pieces of lead onto the chest. They did not ring sweetly when they hit, as silver would have. The sound was flat, sullen.

He pushed a corner of the chest of drawers away from the wall and bent down to scoop up the image that went with the tablet. It was no longer than the last two joints of his middle finger, easy to conceal in the palm of a hand. He held it up, too. Someone—he didn't see who—gasped. Abivard removed the four cords that bound the image. Then he let it fall to the top of the chest. It broke in pieces.

He took out one of the black pebbles. He dropped it not onto the chest but onto the floor: the forms here had to be observed precisely. In a voice with no expression whatever in it, he said, "Ardini, I divorce you."

A sigh ran through the women, like wind through the branches of an almond grove. Ardini jerked as if he had stuck a sword in her. "Me!" she screeched. "I didn't do anything. This is Roshnani's room, not mine. If anyone's been in your bedchamber enough to try bewitching you, lord, she's the one, not me. You never want the rest of us, women who've been here for years. It's not right, it's not natural—"

"In a scrying bowl, I saw you hide the image here," he said, and dropped the second pebble. "Ardini, I divorce you."

"No, it wasn't me. It was somebody else. By the God I swear it. She—"

"Don't make your troubles in the next world worse by swearing a false oath." Formal and emotionless as a soldier making his report, Abivard told exactly what he had seen in the still water.

The women sighed again, all but Ardini. Roshnani said, "Yes, I remember that day. I was working on a bird with the bronze-brown thread."

"No, it's a lie. I didn't do it." Ardini's head twisted back and forth. Like so many people, she had figured out what her scheme's success would bring, but she had never stopped to think what would happen if she failed. Her voice sank to a whisper: "I didn't mean any harm." It might even have been true.

Abivard dropped the third pebble. "Ardini, I divorce you." It

was done. With the fall of the third pebble, with the third repetition before witnesses of the formula of divorce, his marriage
to her was dissolved. Ardini began to wail. Abivard clenched
his jaw tight. Casting loose even a wife who had betrayed him
was wrenchingly hard. So far as he knew, Godarz had never
had to divorce one of his women, and so had left him no
good advice on how to do it. He didn't think there could be
any easy way.

"Please—" Ardini cried. She stood alone; all the other women
had invisibly contrived to take a step away from her.

"I would be within my rights if I sent you forth from the
women's quarters, from this stronghold, from this domain, naked
and barefoot," Abivard said. "I will not do that. Take what you
wear, take from your chamber whatever you can carry in your
two hands, and be gone from here. The God grant we never see
each other again."

Burzoe said, "If you let her go back into her chamber, son,
send someone with her, to make sure she tries no more magic
against you."

"Yes, that would be wise, wouldn't it?" Abivard bowed to his
mother. "Would you please do that for me?" Burzoe nodded.

Ardini began screaming curses. Tears ran down her face, cutting through paint like streams of rainwater over dusty ground.
"You cast me out at your peril," she cried.

"I keep you here at my peril," Abivard answered. "Go now
and take what you would, or I will send you away as law and
custom allow."

He thought that would shut Ardini up, and it did. She cared
more for herself than anything else. Still weeping, she left Roshnani's
room, Burzoe with her to keep her from working mischief.

Roshnani waited until the other wives, several of them loudly
proclaiming undying loyalty to Abivard, had left her chamber. While
they, Abivard's half sisters, and the serving women exclaimed in the
hallway over the scandal, she told him, "Husband, I thank you for
not thinking I set that image when you saw it. I know something
of scrying; sometimes I can even make it work myself—"

"Can you?" Abivard said, interested. So much he still did not
know about this young woman who had become his wife . . .

"Yes, though far from always. In any case, I know you would
first have looked to find the image. When you saw it behind that

chest, it would have been easy for you to look no farther and cast me out with the three black pebbles."

Abivard did not tell her how close he had come to doing just that. She thought better of him because he hadn't, and that was what he wanted. He said, "Tanshar—the town fortune-teller and scryer—said love magic was never sure to work, because it depended on passion. And my passion seems to have turned long since away from Ardini."

Roshnani cast down her eyes at that, but her face glowed. "I'm very glad it has," she said quietly.

"So am I." Abivard sighed. "And by now, I think Ardini has had enough time to gather whatever she would, so I shall have the delightful task of escorting her out of the women's quarters and the stronghold and ordering her out of the domain. By the God, I wish she could have been content here."

"Beware lest she try to stab you or some such," Roshnani said.

"She wouldn't—" Abivard stopped. He would never have done anything so foolish. But Ardini might indeed think that, with her life ruined, she had nothing to lose. "I'll be careful," he promised Roshnani.

The women parted before him as he strode down the hall to Ardini's chamber. She looked up from the bulging knapsack she had filled. She wasn't crying any more; such hatred filled her face that Abivard almost made a sign to avert the evil eye. He covered his brief alarm with brusqueness, jerking a thumb toward the doorway that led out of the women's quarters.

Muttering under her breath, Ardini walked up the hall toward the bedchamber where she had left the lead tablet. Abivard thanked the God it was the last time she would ever go there. He did his best not to listen to whatever she was saying, for fear he would have to take formal notice of it.

All the same, he watched her while he relocked the door, letting his fingers do the work without help from his eyes: he wanted to make sure she placed no other curses in the chamber. She stood in the middle of the room for a moment, then spat at the bed. "You're not a quarter the man your father was," she hissed.

That stung. He wanted to hit her. Only the thought that she was deliberately baiting him made him hold back—he didn't care to do anything she wanted him to. As mildly as he could, he answered, "Praising my father will not gain you my forgiveness." The deliberate misunderstanding made Ardini snarl. Even so, it didn't satisfy Abivard; when he flung open the outer door to the bedchamber, he let it slam against the wall with a loud crash.

A servant in the hallway spun round in startlement. "Lord, you frightened me there," he said, smiling. "You—" He broke off when he saw Ardini beside Abivard. That was a bigger surprise, and one that could not be met with a few glib words. "Is all well, lord?"

"No," Abivard said. "I have pronounced divorcement against this woman, for she used sorcery to try to bind me to her. I cast her forth from the women's quarters, from the stronghold, from the domain."

The servant stared. He nodded jerkily, then retreated almost at a dead run. *He'll have gossip to drink wine on for the next fortnight,* Abivard thought. He turned to Ardini. "Come along, you."

Out to the doorway of the living quarters they went, and out through the courtyard. People stopped and gaped, then tried to pretend they had done no such thing. At the gateway, Ardini fell to her knees and clasped Abivard around the thighs. "Let me stay!" she wailed. "By the God, I swear to love you forever."

He shook his head and freed himself as gently as he could. "You are already forsworn, thanks to your magic," he said. "Get up; go. May you find a life of peace somewhere far from here."

She hissed a filthy curse at him as she rose, then stalked off down the steeply sloping road. He made a mental note to send word to all the villages in the domain that she had been divorced and expelled. He wondered where she would go; back to her family's stronghold, he supposed. He realized he did not even know who her father was. *Have to ask my mother,* he thought. What Burzoe did not know about the *dihqan's* women wasn't worth knowing.

Abivard sighed, wondering how much trouble the lying tales Ardini was sure to tell would cause him. He resolved to save the tablet, the fragments of the image, and the multicolored cords that had been tied around it, to prove he had indeed been sorcerously beset. Then he sighed again. Nothing ever seemed simple. He wished for once it was.

◆   ◆   ◆

"'To the *dihqan* Abivard his loving sister Denak sends greetings.'" Abivard smiled as he began the latest letter from Denak. Though he read it with his own voice, he could hear hers, too, and see the way her face would screw up in concentration as she dipped pen into jar of ink before committing words to parchment.

The letter went on, "'I rejoice that you escaped the wicked magic aimed your way, and grieve for the scandal to your women's quarters. When you wrote of it to me, I confess I guessed Ardini's name before I saw it on the parchment. I know she expected to be named your principal wife—though as far as I know she had no reason save her pride and ambition for that expectation—and did not take well to the affection that flowered between you and Roshnani even in the brief time I was there after your wedding.'"

Abivard nodded slowly to himself. Ardini was young and lovely and, as Denak had said, ambitious. She had thought that was plenty of reason for him to make her his chief wife. Unfortunately for her, he had had other things in mind.

"'I am well, and entrusted with ever greater management of this domain's affairs,'" Denak wrote. "'Pradtak says he reckons me as useful as a Videssian steward, and by the work he gives me, I believe it. Yet our lady mother could do as much, even without the advantage of her letters. Parni, one of the women in the quarters, is with child. I hope I may soon be, as well.'"

"I hope you are, too, sister of mine," Abivard murmured. Indignation grew in him—how could Pradtak prefer this Parni, whoever she was, to Denak? Abivard laughed at himself, knowing he was being foolish. Starting a child was as much a matter of luck as anything else. Roshnani, for instance, was not pregnant, either, though not from lack of enthusiastic effort on his part.

All the same, he worried. If Parni gave Pradtak a son, presumably his first since becoming *dihqan*, she was liable to rise in his estimation and Denak to fall. That would not be good.

He read on: "'My lord husband continues to recover from the bones he broke this summer. He no longer wears his arm in a sling, and can use it for most things, though it still lacks the strength of the other. He walks now with but a single stick, and can make several paces at a time without any aid whatever. He is also eager to return to horseback; he is in the habit of complaining how much he misses his games of mallet and ball, even if without them he would never have been hurt.'

"'Meanwhile,'" Denak wrote, "'aside from the pleasures of the women's quarters, he consoles himself with some scheme or other that he has not yet seen fit to impart to me—or to anyone, for if he had, word of it would surely have reached me through the serving women or his other wives. As I daresay you will have seen for yourself, the women's quarters hear gossip sometimes even before it is spoken.'"

"Isn't that the truth?" Abivard said aloud. He wondered what Pradtak was up to that even his principal wife couldn't know. Something foolish, was his guess: if it hadn't been, Pradtak would have let Denak in on it. Abivard hid nothing from Roshnani. How could he, if she was to give him all her aid in administering Vek Rud domain? Maybe Pradtak didn't see things that way; maybe Pradtak really was a fool.

Denak finished, "'I look forward to your next letter; the God grant it may hold better news than Khamorth raiders and a wife who could not be trusted. Every time I see your familiar hand, I return to the stronghold where I grew up. I am well enough here, but the place and its people are not those I knew so long and so well. I rely on you to keep them green in my heart. Remember always your loving sister.'"

Down in the village, a carpenter was making Abivard a frame of pigeonholes, twenty by twenty, so it would have in all four hundred openings. After he had stored that many letters from Denak, he supposed he could have the man turn out another frame. He rolled up the letter, retied it with the ribbon that had held it closed, and went off to set it in the drawer that served for such things until the pigeonhole frame was done.

No sooner had he taken care of that than a shout from the wall brought him out of the living quarters in a hurry: "A band of riders off in the distance, making for the flocks northwest of us!"

He sprinted for the stables. So did every other warrior who had heard the lookout's cry. He had taken to leaving his helmet and shield there. No time for more armor, not now. He clapped the helm on his head, snatched up his lance, and hurried for the stall where stable boys were saddling his horse. As soon as they had cinched the last strap tight, he set a foot in the stirrup and swung up into the saddle.

In the next stall over, Frada mounted at almost the same instant. Abivard grinned at him and said, "We have it easy. From what Father used to say, his grandsire remembered the days before we learned from the nomads to use stirrups."

"How'd great-grandfather stay on his horse, then?" Frada asked.

"Not very well, is my guess." Abivard looked round the stables. More and more men were horsed, enough to make bandits or nomads or whoever the riders proved to be think twice about running off his sheep and cattle. He raised his voice to cut through the din: "Let's go get back what's ours. The shout will be 'Godarz!'"

"Godarz!" the Makuraners yelled, loud enough to make his head ring. He used the pressure of his knees and the reins to urge his gelding out of the stall, out of the stable, and out of the stronghold.

Going down the knob atop which sat Vek Rud domain, he had to keep the pace slow, lest his horse stumble on the slope. But when he got to the flatlands, he urged the animal ahead at a trot he could kick up into a gallop whenever he found the need.

Behind him, someone shouted, "There they are, the cursed carrion eaters!"

There they were indeed, not far from the Vek Rud River, cutting out half a flock of sheep. "They're Khamorth—'ware archery," Abivard called as he got close enough to recognize the robbers. He wondered what had happened to the shepherd and the men guarding the flock with him. Nothing good, he feared.

"Godaaarz!" The war cry rang out again. This time the Khamorth heard it. All at once they stopped being thieves and turned back into warriors. To Abivard, their moves had an eerie familiarity. After a moment, he realized they were fighting like the band that had attacked the wedding party on the way back from Nalgis Crag domain.

Instead of making him afraid, that sparked a sudden burst of confidence. "We beat the plainsmen once before," he yelled. "We can beat them again." Only when the words had passed his lips did he remember that the nomads had beaten his countrymen, too, and far more disastrously than his retainers had hurt them.

The horsemen who galloped alongside him seemed to have forgotten that, too. They screamed like men possessed by demons. He had a decent number of archers with him today, too; he wouldn't have to come to close quarters to hurt the Khamorth.

The nomads started shooting at very long range. Abivard managed a scorn-filled laugh when an arrow kicked up dust a few yards away from his horse's hooves. "They think they can frighten us off with their bows," he said. "Will we let them?"

"No!" his men cried. Bowstrings thrummed to either side of him. One nomad's steppe pony slewed sideways and crashed to the ground. The Makuraners' shouts redoubled.

Then a shriek of pain cut through the war cries. Just to Abivard's left, a man slid off his galloping horse. He hit the ground limp as a sack of meal and did not move again. Now the plainsmen yelled in triumph.

With a deliberate effort of will, Abivard made himself not think about that. The Khamorth ahead grew from dots to dolls to men in what felt like a single heartbeat. He picked out a nomad, couched his lance, and bored in for the kill.

The Khamorth did not stick around to be stuck. In a fine bit of horsemanship, he made his animal wheel through a turn tighter than any Abivard would have imagined possible. As he galloped away, he shot back over his shoulder.

Abivard flung up his shield. The arrow ticked off its bronze-faced rim and tumbled away harmlessly. He knew a moment's relief, but only a moment's: the Khamorth shot again and again. He was not the finest archer the God had ever made, and shooting from a pounding horse at a moving target was anything but easy, anyhow. On the other hand, though, Abivard's horse was faster than his, which meant the range kept shortening.

"Aii!" Fire kissed the edge of Abivard's right leg. He looked down and saw he was bleeding. The shaft wasn't stuck in his leg; it had sliced his outer calf and flown on. Had he been wearing the lamellar armor the smiths were just now finishing, he might have escaped unwounded. No such luck, though.

Seeing he was about to be ridden down, the Khamorth drew his shamshir and slashed at Abivard's lance in the hope of chopping off its head. That did the nomad no good; the lancehead was joined to the shaft by a long iron ferrule. Abivard felt the blow in his shoulder but pressed on regardless.

At the last moment, the plainsman hacked at the lancehead again. He turned it enough to keep it from his own flesh, but it drove deep into the barrel of his horse. Appalled, Abivard yanked it back. The horse screamed louder and more piercingly—and with better reason—than Ardini ever had.

The Khamorth snarled a curse. His face, twisted in a grimace of hate, would stay in Abivard's memory forever: unkempt beard with threads of gray running through it, wide mouth shouting something perhaps a quarter comprehensible—two front teeth missing, a third black—beaky nose with a scar on the bridge, red-tracked eyes, lines on the forehead accented by ground-in smoke. The two men were close enough together that Abivard found himself trapped in the reek of ancient stale sweat and sour milk that hovered round the plainsman like a stinking cloud.

The steppe pony galloped wildly for perhaps a hundred yards, blood splashing the dry, dusty ground from the wound Abivard had made. Then, like a waterlogged ship at last slipping beneath the waves, it went down, slowly and gently enough for its rider to slip off and try to run.

The plainsman was slow and clumsy—his boots were not made for hard use on the ground. He had hung onto his bow; he had just wheeled around and was reaching for an arrow when Abivard's lance took him in the middle of the chest. The nomad grunted. The cry his horse let out had been much worse. A new stench joined the rest as the fellow folded up on himself.

Abivard jerked the lance free. He had to twist the head to clear it; it grated against the Khamorth's ribs as it came out. On the shaft, the plainsman's blood mingled with that of his horse. The new stains almost completely covered the older marks, now browned, where Abivard had first blooded the lance a few weeks before.

As in that first clash, he found that when he was engaged he could pay no attention to how the fight as a whole was going. When he looked around to get his bearings, he saw that most of the Khamorth had broken away and were galloping north for all they were worth.

Abivard and his men pounded after the nomads. The steppe ponies' hooves drummed on the timbers of the new bridge that spanned the Vek Rud. Three or four nomads reined in on the far side of the river and waited with nocked arrows for the Makuraners to try to force a passage.

"Hold!" Abivard flung up his hand. Shooting down the bridge

at men and horses who had to come straight toward them, the Khamorth could have taken a fearful toll, maybe even turned defeat into triumph.

"But they were running away," Frada protested.

"They're not running now," Abivard said. "Take a good look at them, brother. What do they want us to do? If you were a Khamorth chieftain on the other side of that river, what would you hope those stupid Makuraners on your tail would do?"

Frada was also Godarz's son: Confront him with an idea and he would worry it like a dog shaking a rat. "I expect I'd hope they threw themselves at me," he said.

"I expect the same thing," Abivard answered. "That's why we're going to stay right here until the plainsmen ride away. Then—" He scowled, but saw no help for it. "Then I'm going to burn that bridge."

Frada stared at him. "But it's stood since our great-grandfather's day, maybe longer."

"I know. Losing it will cost us commerce, too. But with the Khamorth loose in the realm, if I leave it whole I might as well paint 'ROB ME' in big letters on the outside of the stronghold wall." Abivard's laugh rang bitter. "See how the great tribute Smerdis King of Kings paid to the Khamorth is keeping them on their own side of the Degird."

"Aye, that thought had already crossed my mind. How much did the famous Murghab squeeze from us?"

"Eighty-five hundred mortal arkets," Abivard answered. "Years of patient saving gone in a day. And for what? For the nomads to fatten their coffers at the same time as they batten on our lands."

Frada pointed back to the downed ponies and plainsmen dotting the plain to the south. "They paid a price, too."

"They should," Abivard said. "They were trying to take what's ours. But we paid our heavy price at Smerdis' command and got nothing in return for it. Smerdis' messenger said Sharbaraz renounced the throne because he didn't have the experience he needed to rule. If this is what experience bought us, then I wouldn't mind a raw hand on the reins, by the God."

The farther he went there, the softer his voice got: he realized he was speaking treason, or at least lese majesty. But Frada nodded vigorously. "How could we do worse?"

Instead of cheering Abivard, that made him thoughtful. "The hurtful part is, we likely *could* do worse: every tribe on the steppe swarming down over the Degird, for instance, to try to take this land out of the realm forever. That was everyone's worst nightmare after Peroz King of Kings fell." The proud lion banner crashing into the trench—that dreadful image would stay with Abivard if he lived to be a hundred.

"Maybe we could at that," Frada said. "But the way things are is plenty bad enough. These little fights will drain us of men, too."

"Yes," Abivard said. Along with the plainsmen, three of his own followers were down, one lying still, the other two thrashing and crying their pain to the unheeding sky. *Maybe they'll heal,* he thought, and then, *Yes, but maybe they won't.* He made a fist and brought it down on his thigh. "You know, brother of mine, I wonder how bad things are elsewhere in the realm. What would Okhos say, for instance, if I wrote him and asked?"

"Does he have his letters?" Frada said.

"I don't know," Abivard admitted. He brightened. "Roshnani can tell me. Come to that, she's been after me to teach her to read and write. I think my getting letters from Denak showed her I didn't mind women learning such things."

"Are you teaching her?" Frada sounded as if Abivard had been talking not about letters but of some exotic, not quite reputable vice.

Abivard nodded anyhow. "Yes, and she seems to have the head for it. Father would have done the same, I'm certain; he let Denak learn, after all."

"So he did," Frada said thoughtfully. He, too, nodded. Even more than was true for Abivard, he used what Godarz would have done as a touchstone for right behavior.

Seeing that their foes would not obligingly impale themselves, the Khamorth rode north. The Makuraners moved over the field, finishing off wounded Khamorth, capturing steppe ponies, and doing their best to round up the scattered flock. That done and the wounded men hastily bandaged and splinted and tied onto horses, they headed back toward the stronghold. The skirmish with the plainsmen was, by every conventional sense of the word, a victory. But it had cost Abivard at least one man and maybe as many as three, and he doubted it had done anything to keep the Khamorth from raiding his lands again. He let his men cheer, but he didn't feel victorious.

"Aye, my brother has his letters, or he learned them, at any rate," Roshnani said. "How much use he has given them since the tutor left the stronghold, I could not say."

"Only one way to find out," Abivard said. "I'll write him and see what sort of answer I get. Just to be on the safe side, though, I'll have my rider memorize the message, too, to make sure it's understood. And I'll write to Pradtak, as well. I know he reads, for Denak remarked he was surprised to find out she could do likewise."

"Will you write the letters here in your bedchamber?" Roshnani said. "I want to watch you shape each word and see if I can figure out what it says."

"I know I have pen and ink here. Let's see if I can find a couple of scraps of parchment, too." Abivard kept a pot of ink and a reed pen in a drawer in a little chest by the bed, along with knives, a few coins, little strips of leather, and other oddments. He found himself rummaging through that drawer at least once a day; you never could tell when some piece of what looked like junk would come in handy.

He grunted in satisfaction when he came across a sheet of parchment as big as his hand. He used one of the knives to cut it neatly in half; each of the two pieces he made was plenty big enough for the notes he wanted to send.

He pulled the stopper from the ink pot and set it on the bedside chest. He put the first scrap of parchment on top of the chest, too, then inked his pen, leaned forward, and began to write. Roshnani sat beside him on the bed, so close that her breast brushed against his side. He ignored the pleasant distraction as best he could. *Plenty of time for sport later,* he told himself sternly. *Business now.*

Because he was not sure how well Okhos read, and because Roshnani was just learning letters herself, he took special pains to make his writing neater than the scrawl he usually turned out. "Okhos!" Roshnani exclaimed. "That's my brother's name you just wrote." A moment later she added, "And there's yours!" She almost bounced with excitement.

"You're right both times," he said, slipping his free arm around her waist. She leaned even closer, the scent of her hair filled his nostrils. He needed all his will to keep his mind on the letter. When he was done, he waited for the ink to dry, then handed it to her. "Can you read it?"

She did, one word at a time, more slowly than he had written it. When at last she had finished, she was sweating with effort but proud. "I understood it all," she said. "You want to know how much Smerdis took from Okhos to pay off the Khamorth and how badly they've raided his domain since."

"That's exactly right. You're doing very well," Abivard said. "I'm proud of you." To show how proud he was, he put both arms around her and kissed her. Whether by chance or by design—*whose?* he wondered later—she overbalanced and lay back on the bed. The letter to Pradtak got written rather later than he had planned.

Roshnani read that one aloud, too. Abivard paid less attention to her reading than he might have; neither of them had bothered dressing again, and this afternoon he was thinking about a second round. Roshnani, though, concentrated on what she was doing despite being bare. She said, "Except for the names, you used just the same words in this letter as in the one to Okhos. Why did you do that?"

"Hmm?" he said. Roshnani let out an irritated sniff and repeated herself. He thought about it for a moment, then answered, "Writing's not the easiest thing in the world for me, either. If the same words would serve me twice, I don't have to trouble myself thinking up new ones the second time around."

She considered that in her usual deliberate way. "Fair enough, I suppose," she said at last. "Okhos and Pradtak aren't likely to compare letters and discover you haven't been perfectly original."

"Original?" Abivard rolled his eyes. "If I'd known you'd turn critic when I taught you your letters, I might not have done it." She snorted. He said, "And I know something else that's just as good the second time as the first, even if done just the same way."

Roshnani still cast down her eyes as she had the day she first came to Vek Rud stronghold, but now more in play than in earnest. "Whatever might that be?" she asked, as if they were not naked together on the big bed.

Eventually the letters were sealed and dispatched. Okhos' reply came back in a bit more than a week. "'To the *dihqan* Abivard the *dihqan* Okhos his brother-in-law sends greetings,'" Abivard read, first with Frada peering over his shoulder and then, later, in the bedchamber with Roshnani. To Roshnani, he added, "See? He writes well enough after all." Okhos' hand was square and careful, perhaps not practiced but clear enough.

"Go on. What does he say?" Roshnani asked.

"'Yes, my brother-in-law, we have also been beset, both by Smerdis' men and the nomads. We lost five thousand arkets to the one, and sheep and cattle, horses and men to the other. We have hurt the nomads, too, but what good does it do to bat away one grain of sand when the wind lifts up the whole desert? We go on fighting as best we can. The God give you victory in your war, too.'"

"Is that all?" Roshnani asked when he paused to take a breath.

"No, there's one thing more," he said. "'Say to my sister who is your wife that her brother thinks of her often.'"

Roshnani smiled. "I shall write him a letter in return. Don't you think that will surprise him?"

"I'm sure it will," Abivard said. He wondered whether Okhos would be merely surprised or scandalized to boot. Well, if he was scandalized, that would be his own hard luck. It wasn't as if Abivard let his women wander around out of their quarters like a Videssian or allowed them something else that truly merited condemnation.

He had to wait longer for his reply from Pradtak. Not only did his letter to Denak's husband have a longer journey than the one to Okhos, but Pradtak also took his time before replying. Most of a month went by before a rider from Nalgis Crag domain rode up to the stronghold.

Abivard tipped the man half an arket for his travels. He might not have done so before the battle on the steppes, but any trip by a lone man was dangerous these days. Abivard knew that only too well—travel by large armed bands wasn't necessarily safe, either.

He opened the leather message tube and unrolled the parchment on which Pradtak had written his reply. After the polite formula of greeting, his brother-in-law's letter was but one sentence long: *I am loyal in all ways to Smerdis King of Kings.*

"Well, who ever said you weren't?" Abivard asked aloud, as if Pradtak were there to answer him.

"Lord?" the rider asked.

"Never mind." Abivard scratched his head, wondering why on earth his brother-in-law thought he suspected him.

✦ V

"**N**ow, this is more like it," Abivard said to the tired-looking man who swung down off his horse in the courtyard to Vek Rud stronghold. "No letter at all from Nalgis Crag domain for almost a month, and now two in the space of a week."

"Glad you're pleased, lord," the messenger said. Instead of a caftan, he wore leather trousers and a sheepskin jacket: winter hadn't started, but the air said it was coming. The man went on, "This one is from the lady your sister. That's what the serving woman who gave it to me said, anyhow. I've not read it myself, for it was sealed before it ever went into my tube here."

"Was it?" Abivard said; Denak hadn't bothered with such things before. He gave the rider a silver arket. "You deserve special thanks for getting it here to me safe, then, for you couldn't have told me what it said, had anything happened to it."

"You're kind to me, lord, but if anything had happened to that letter, likely something worse would have happened to me, if you know what I mean." The messenger from Nalgis Crag domain sketched a salute, then rode out of the stronghold to start his journey home.

The seal Denak had used was Pradtak's: a mounted lancer hunting a boar. Abivard broke it with his thumbnail, curious to find out what his sister hadn't wanted anyone to see. As usual, he read her words aloud: "'To the *dihqan* Abivard his loving sister Denak sends greetings.'" Her next sentence brought him up short.

116

"'It were wiser if you read what follows away from anyone who might overhear.'"

"I wonder what *that's* in aid of?" he muttered. But Denak had always struck him as having good sense, so he rolled up the parchment and carried it into the *dihqan's* bedchamber. *No one to listen to me here,* he thought. Then he glanced through the grillwork opening in the door that led to the women's quarters. He saw no one.

Satisfied, he unrolled the letter and began to read again. Denak wrote, "'Pradtak my husband recently walled off the chamber next to mine, which is close by the entrance to the women's quarters here, and had a separate doorway made for it alone. I wondered what his purpose was, but he spoke evasively when I asked him. This, I must confess, irked me no little.'"

Abivard did not blame his sister for her pique. The likeliest explanation he could find for Pradtak's behavior was installing another woman in the special room, though why he wouldn't simply admit her to the women's quarters baffled Abivard.

He read on. "'My temper vanished but my curiosity grew when, after I heard through the wall that the chamber was inhabited, I also heard it was inhabited by a man. Pradtak, I assure you, is not inclined to seek his pleasures in that direction.'"

"Well, what is he doing, then, putting a man into the women's quarters, even if the fellow is walled away from his wives?" Abivard asked, as if the letter would up and tell him and save him the trouble of reading further.

It didn't, of course. His eyes dropped back down to the parchment. "'With my door closed, I called quietly out my window,'" Denak wrote, "'not certain if the masons had sealed away the one in the adjacent room. I found they had not. The man in there was more than willing to give me his name. I now give it to you, and you will understand my caution with this letter: he is Sharbaraz son of Peroz and, he claims, rightful King of Kings of Makuran.'"

Abivard stared at that for most of a minute before he read on. If Sharbaraz had renounced the throne of his own free will, as Smerdis King of Kings claimed, why mure him up in a secret cell like a criminal awaiting the headsman's chopper? The only answer that came to him was stark in its simplicity: *Smerdis lies.*

Denak's next sentence might have been an echo of that thought:

" 'The first meal Sharbaraz ate after word of his father's overthrow reached Mashiz must have had a sleeping potion sprinkled over it, for when he awoke he found himself in a dark little room somewhere in the palace, with a knife to his throat and a written renunciation of the throne before him. Not wishing to perish on the spot, he signed it.' "

Someone let out a tuneless whistle. After a moment, Abivard realized it was himself. He had wondered that a young man of whom his father had expected so much should tamely yield the rule to an elder of no particular accomplishment. Now he learned Sharbaraz had not yielded tamely.

The letter went on, " 'Smerdis sent Sharbaraz here for safekeeping: Nalgis Crag stronghold is without a doubt the strongest fortress in all Makuran. The usurper pays Pradtak well to keep his rival beyond hope of escape or rescue. You may not be surprised to learn I read your latest letter to my husband; I grieve to hear how the Khamorth ravage my homeland in spite of the great tribute Smerdis handed over to them to stay north of the Degird. This tells me he whose fundament now befouls the throne has no notion of what the kingdom requires.' "

"It told me the same thing," Abivard said, as if Denak were there to hear him.

He had almost finished the letter. His sister wrote, " 'I do not think any army has a hope of rescuing Sharbaraz from the outside. But he may perhaps be spirited out of the fortress. I shall bend every effort toward finding out how that might be done. Since the area in front of Sharbaraz's cell remains formally within the women's quarters, and since I am trusted with affairs here, I may be able to see for myself exactly how he is guarded.' "

"Be careful," Abivard whispered, again as if Denak stood close by.

" 'I shall take every precaution I can think of,' " Denak wrote— *she might be answering me,* Abivard thought. " 'Be circumspect when you reply to this letter. Pradtak has not formed the habit of reading what you write to me, but any mistake here would mean disaster—for me, for Sharbaraz King of Kings, and, I think, for Makuran. May the God bless you and hold you in her arms.' "

Abivard started to put the letter with the others he'd had from Denak, but changed his mind almost at once. Some of his servitors could read, and this was a note they must not see. He hid it behind the wall hanging to whose frame Godarz had glued the spare key to the women's quarters.

That done, Abivard paced round the bedchamber as if he were a lion in a cage. *What to do?* echoed and reechoed in his mind, like the beat of a distant drum. *What to do?*

Suddenly he stood still. "As of this moment, I owe Smerdis miscalled King of Kings no allegiance," he declared as the realization crystallized within him. He had sworn loyalty to Smerdis on condition that Makuran's overlord had spoken truth about how he had come to power. Now that his words were shown to be lies, they held no more power over Abivard.

That, however, did not answer the question of what to do next. Even if all the *dihqans* and *marzbans* renounced Smerdis' suzerainty and marched on Nalgis Crag stronghold, they would be hard-pressed to take it—and would surely cause Sharbaraz to be killed to keep them from uniting behind him.

Then he thought of Tanshar's prophecy: a tower on a hill where honor was to be won and lost. Nalgis Crag stronghold was indeed a tower on a hill, and with the rightful King of Kings penned up there, plenty of honor waited to be won. But how would it be lost as well? That worried Abivard.

The trouble with prophecy, he thought as he read through Denak's letter again, was that what it foretold, while true, had a way of going unrecognized till it was past and could be seen, as it were, from behind. He wouldn't know if this was what Tanshar had predicted until after the honor was won and lost, if it was. Even then, he might not be sure.

"I have to talk with someone about this," he said; he sensed he needed another set of wits to look at the problem Denak had posed from a different angle. He started to call Frada, but hesitated. His brother was young, and too liable not to keep a secret. Word of Sharbaraz's imprisonment getting out could doom Peroz's son as readily as an army invading Nalgis Crag domain.

For the thousandth time, Abivard wished he could hash things out with Godarz. But if his father were alive, Peroz would probably still live, too, with Sharbaraz his accepted heir and Smerdis a functionary whose ambition, if he had had any before Peroz died, would be well concealed.

Abivard snapped his fingers. "I am a fool," he said. "This is an affair of the women's quarters, so who would know better what to do about it than the women here?"

He hesitated again before he went to Burzoe and Roshnani, wondering if they could keep so great a matter to themselves. Women's-quarter gossip was notorious all through Makuran. If a maidservant heard of this, she would surely spread word through the whole stronghold. But Burzoe had been Godarz's right hand for many years, something she couldn't have done without holding secrets close, and Roshnani did not seem one to talk out of turn. Abivard nodded, his mind made up.

He took the key and let himself into the women's quarters. He would have summoned his mother and principal wife to the bedchamber, but that struck him as more likely to alert others to something out of the ordinary.

Roshnani was embroidering in her chamber, much as she had been when Ardini hid the magical image behind her chest of drawers. She looked up from the work when Abivard tapped lightly on the open door. "My husband," she said, smiling. "What brings you here in the middle of the day?" The smile got wider, suggesting that she had her suspicions.

"No, not that," Abivard said, smiling, too. "That will have to wait for another time. Meanwhile, where's my lady mother? Something's come up on which I need your thoughts, and hers, as well."

"Do you want to talk here?" Roshnani asked. At his nod, she set aside the cloth on which she had been working. "I'll fetch her. I won't be but a moment." She hurried down the hall.

She was as good as her word. When she came back with Burzoe, Abivard shut the door to Roshnani's chamber. His mother raised an eyebrow at that. "What sort of secret has such earthshaking importance?" she asked, her tone doubting that any could.

Despite the closed door, Abivard answered in what was little more than a whisper. He summarized Denak's letter in three or four quick sentences, then finished, "What I want to do is find some way to rescue the rightful King of Kings. Not only is Smerdis forsworn, but his rule brings Makuran only more troubles."

Burzoe's eyes flicked to the door. "I owe you an apology, son," she said, speaking as quietly as Abivard had. "You were right—this is a secret that must not spread."

"Will Sharbaraz truly be better for Makuran than Smerdis is?" Roshnani asked.

"He could scarcely be worse," Abivard said. But that was not an answer, not really. He added, "My father thought he would make an able successor to Peroz, and his judgment in such things was usually good."

"That's so," Burzoe said. "Godarz spoke well of Sharbaraz several times in my hearing. And we paid Smerdis eighty-five hundred arkets at as near sword's point as makes no difference, and for what? He said he would spend them to keep the nomads from crossing the Degird, and we see how well he kept that promise. If Denak can rescue Sharbaraz, I think she should—and we must help all we can."

"But *can* she rescue him?" Abivard asked. "The two of you know more of the workings of a women's quarters than I could ever learn. That's why I brought this to you."

"It will depend on how Pradtak has rearranged things to make a cell there," Burzoe answered. "My guess is that he will have installed a guard—a man, whether his or Smerdis'—in front of Sharbaraz's cell, and walled off part of the corridor to keep the lustful fellow from sporting among the women. If Denak can get to the corridor in front of the cell, she may indeed accomplish something. If not, I know not what advice to give you: matters become more difficult."

"Perhaps she can offer to serve Sharbaraz—cook for him, or something of that sort," Roshnani said. "He may be a prisoner, but he is still of royal blood. And Smerdis, you said, is old. What if he dies tomorrow? Most likely, Sharbaraz gets his crown back—and he will remember, one way or the other, how Pradtak treated him at Nalgis Crag stronghold."

"A thought," Abivard agreed. "If Pradtak's principal wife were to wait upon him, Sharbaraz might see his captivity as honorable. Or so Denak could present the matter to Pradtak, at any rate."

"You are not without wit, child," Burzoe said to Roshnani, at which the younger woman blushed bright red. Pretending not to notice, Burzoe turned to Abivard. "The scheme has some merit. Much depends on how tightly Pradtak is used to controlling his women's quarters. If no man save he is ever allowed to see his wives' faces, he will not grant this to Denak. If on the other hand he learned an easier way from his father Urashtu, our chance for success looks better."

"Worth a try, anyway." Abivard bowed to his mother and his

principal wife. "Thank you for your wisdom. Whatever we do, we have to keep it secret. No word of this can get out, or we are ruined before we begin."

Roshnani and Burzoe looked at each other. Abivard watched amusement pass between them, and something else—something hidden in the way women had of hiding things from men. It made him feel perhaps seven years old again, in spite of his inches, his strength, and his thick black beard.

In a voice dry as the desert beyond the stronghold, Burzoe said, "See to it that you keep the secret as well as we. You may count on it that no one in the women's quarters will learn from us the reason you came here today."

Roshnani nodded. "Women love to spill secrets that do not truly matter—but then, so do men. And men, I think, are more likely to betray those that do."

Abivard hadn't thought about that. He shrugged, unsure if it was true or not. Then he opened the door and headed down the corridor that led out of the women's quarters.

Behind him, Burzoe's voice rose to a screech. "Wretch of a daughter-in-law, you bring embarrassment on us all when my son the *dihqan* notices how uneven the stitches of your embroidery are."

"They are no such thing," Roshnani retorted, just as hotly. "If you'd taught Abivard to recognize good work, he'd know it when he saw it."

The two women shouted even louder, both at once so Abivard couldn't understand a word they said. He almost ran back to Roshnani's chamber to break up the fight. Then he realized his principal wife and his mother were staging a quarrel based on something that would have given him a plausible reason for visiting them. The women's quarters might buzz with gossip for days, but it would be the right kind of gossip. He wanted to bow back toward the women in admiration, but that might have given away the game.

No one in the women's quarters came running to watch the fight. No one, as Abivard saw, affected to give it any special notice. But no one paid heed to what she was supposed to be doing, either. *Misdirection,* Abivard thought, *not concealment,* something worth remembering on the battlefield, too.

He went back to his bedchamber, locked the door that led into the women's quarters, and put the key into one of the pouches he wore on his belt. He flopped down onto the bed and thought hard.

"I can't even write back and tell Denak what to do, not in so many words," he muttered. "If Pradtak—if anyone—happens to set eyes on the letter, everything goes up in smoke."

Circumspection was not his strength. By Makuraner standards, he was blunt and straightforward. But Godarz had always said a man should be able to put his hand to anything. Like a lot of good advice, it sounded easier than it was liable to prove.

He thought awhile longer, then took out pen and parchment and began to write, a few careful words at a time: *To Denak, her loving brother the* dihqan *Abivard sends greetings. The news of which you write is, as always, fascinating, and gives me much to think about.*

Abivard snorted when he reread that. "By the God, nothing but truth there!" he exclaimed. He bent to his work again. Without his noticing, the tip of his tongue stuck out of one corner of his mouth, as it had in boyhood days when a scribe first taught him his letters.

He went on, *If you can help your neighbor, the God will surely smile upon you for your kindness. Perhaps he will look gladly on you if you make the approach.*

To someone who did not know what Abivard was talking about, that "he" would refer back to the God. Abivard hoped Denak would understand it meant Pradtak. He glowered at the parchment. Writing in code was hard work.

I am sure that, because of the bad temper your neighbor has shown to those placed over her, someone needs to keep an eye on her every minute. Perhaps you will be able to make friends with that woman or eunuch—however Pradtak sees fit to order his women's quarters—and so have a chance to improve your neighbor's nature.

He read that over. Denak should have no trouble following it. Most people who read it probably would not catch on. But if it fell into Pradtak's hands, the game was up. Abivard chewed on his lower lip. Denak had said her husband was not in the habit of reading the letters he sent them. Pradtak certainly didn't read her answers, or she would not have been able to write as frankly as she did. But he was liable to say something like "The gate guards tell me a letter came from your brother today. Show it to me, why don't you?" How could she say no?

To keep her from having to, Abivard got out another sheet of parchment and wrote a cheery letter about doings at Vek Rud stronghold that said never a word about imprisoned royalty. If Pradtak wanted to know what was in Abivard's mind—and keeping Sharbaraz prisoner in Nalgis Crag domain was liable to make him anxious even if he hadn't been before—Denak could show him the image of an empty-headed fellow full of chatter and not much else.

Abivard sighed as he put both sheets into a leather travel tube. Life would have been simpler—and perhaps more pleasant—if he could have lived the life he wore like a mask in that second letter.

He sighed again. "If the God had wanted life to be simple, he wouldn't have put Makuran next to the Khamorth—or to Videssos," he murmured, and set the stopper in the tube.

Tanshar opened the door, then blinked in surprise and bowed low. "Lord, you do me great honor by visiting my humble home," he said, stepping aside so Abivard could come in.

As always, the fortune-teller's dwelling was astringently neat—and almost bare of furnishings. Abivard took a few pistachios from the bowl Tanshar proffered but held the shells in his hand rather than tossing them onto the rammed earth on the floor. In some houses, they would have been invisible; here, they would have seemed a profanation.

Tanshar solved his dilemma by fetching in another, smaller bowl. As Abivard dropped the shells into it, the fortune-teller asked, "And how may I serve my lord the *dihqan* today?"

Abivard hesitated before beginning. Spreading the secret Denak had passed to him made him nervous. But if Denak was to get Sharbaraz free of Nalgis Crag stronghold, she would probably need magical aid: it stood a better chance of helping than an army, at any rate, or so Abivard judged. Cautiously he said, "What I tell you must spread to no one—no one, do you understand?"

"Aye, lord." In a wintry way, Tanshar looked amused. "And to whom would I be likely to retail it? To my numerous retainers?" He waved a hand, as if to conjure up servitors from empty air and bare walls. "To the townsfolk in the market square? That you might more easily believe, but if I gossiped like any old wife, who would trust me with his affairs?"

"Mock if you like," Abivard said. "The matter is important enough that I must remind you."

"Say on, lord," Tanshar said. "You've made me curious, if nothing else."

Even that worried Abivard; as he knew, Tanshar had ways of learning things not available to ordinary men. But he said, "Hear me, then, and judge for yourself." He told Tanshar what he'd learned from Denak.

The fortune-teller's eyes widened, both the good one and the one clouded by cataract. "The rightful King of Kings?" he murmured. "Truly, lord, I crave your pardon, for care here is indeed of the essence. You intend to free this man?"

"If it happens, Denak will have more to do with it than I," Abivard answered. The irony of that struck him like a blow. The men of Makuran shut away their women to keep power in their own hands, and now the fate of the realm would rest in the hands of a woman. He shook his head—nothing he could do about it but help his sister any way he could.

Tanshar nodded. "Aye, that makes sense; so it does. Your sister's husband—did you say his name was Pradtak?—would hardly give you the chance to storm his women's quarters with warriors, now would he?"

"It's not likely," Abivard said, which won him a slow smile from Tanshar. He went on, "Seems to me magic might manage more than men. That's why I've come to you: to see how you can help. Suppose I were to take you along with me on a visit to Nalgis Crag domain one of these days—"

"When would that be, lord?" Tanshar asked.

"Right now, the time lies in the hands of the God," Abivard said. "Much will depend on what—if anything—Denak can do from within. But if that proves possible, will you ride with me?"

"Gladly, lord—usurping the throne is surely an act of wickedness," Tanshar said. "How I can help, though, I do not yet clearly see."

"Nor I," Abivard said. "I came here now so we could look together for the best way." They talked quietly for the next couple of hours. By the time Abivard headed up to the stronghold again, he had the beginnings of a plan.

✦   ✦   ✦

Winter was another invader from the Pardrayan steppe. Though more regular in its incursions into Makuran than the nomads, it was hardly less to be feared. Snowstorms spread white over fields and plains. Herdsmen went out to tend their flocks in thick sheepskin coats that reached to their ankles. Some would freeze to death on bad nights anyhow. Abivard knew that—it happened every winter.

Smoke rose black from the stronghold, as if it had fallen in war. Makuran was not a land rich in timber; the woodchoppers had traveled far to lay in enough to get through the season. Abivard asked the God for mild days and got another blizzard. He did his best to shrug it off; prayers over weather were hardly ever answered.

What he could not shrug off was that winter also slowed travel to a crawl. He had sent his letter off to Denak, hoping the weather would hold long enough for him to get a quick reply. It didn't. He wanted to gnash his teeth.

Whenever one clear day followed another, he hoped it meant a lull long enough for a horseman to race from Nalgis Crag stronghold to Vek Rud domain. Whenever snow flew again afterward, he told himself he should have known better.

The horseman from Pradtak's domain reached Vek Rud stronghold a few days after the winter solstice, in the middle of the worst storm of the year. Children had been making snowmen in the stronghold courtyard and in the streets of the town below the walls. When the rider reached the gate, so much white clung to his coat and fur cap that he looked like a snowman himself, a snowman astride a snow horse.

Abivard ordered the half-frozen horse seen to, then put the rider in front of a blazing fire with a mug of hot spiced wine in his hand and a steaming bowl of mutton stew on a little round table beside him. "You were daft to travel," Abivard said, "but I'm glad you did."

"Wasn't so bad, lord *dihqan*," the man answered between avid swigs from the mug.

"No? Then why are your teeth still chattering?"

"Didn't say it was *warm* out there, mind you," the fellow answered. "But the serving woman who gave me the letter from the lady your sister said she wanted it to reach you as soon as might be, so I thought I'd try the journey. Here you are, lord *dihqan*." With a flourish, he presented a leather letter tube.

"I thank you." Abivard set the tube down on the stone floor beside him and reached into his belt pouch for a couple of silver arkets with which to reward the rider. Then he took a pull at his own wine; though he hadn't been on a horse in the snow, the inside of the stronghold was chilly, too.

"You're generous, lord *dihqan*." The man from Nalgis Crag domain stowed the silver in a pouch of his own. When he saw Abivard was making no move to unstopper the tube, he asked, "Aren't you going to read the letter now that it's here?"

"Alas, I should not, not here." Abivard had expected that question and trotted out the answer he had prepared: "Were I to read it in another man's hearing, it would be as if I exposed Pradtak's wife to another man's sight. With him generous enough to allow Denak my sister to correspond with me, I would not violate the privacy of his women's quarters."

"Ah." The messenger respectfully lowered his head. "You observe the usages with great care and watch over my lord's honor as if it were your own."

"I try my best." Abivard fought hard to hold his face stiff. Here he and Denak were plotting how to spirit a man out of Pradtak's women's quarters, and Pradtak's man reckoned them paragons of Makuraner virtue. That was what he had hoped the fellow would do, but he hadn't expected to be praised for it.

The man yawned. "Your pardon, lord," he said. "I fear I am not yet ready to head back to Nalgis Crag stronghold at once."

"I'm not surprised," Abivard answered. "Neither is your horse. Rest here as long as you like. We'll give you a room and a brazier and thick wool blankets."

"And maybe a wench to warm me under them?" the messenger said.

"If you find one willing, of course," Abivard said. "I'm not in the habit of making the serving women here sleep with men not of their choosing."

"Hmm." The rider looked as if he would grumble if he dared. Then he got to his feet. "In that case, lord, I shall have to see what I can do. The kitchens are that way?" At Abivard's nod, he swaggered off. Whatever his luck might prove, he didn't lack for confidence.

Abivard went in the other direction, toward his own bedchamber. As soon as he had barred the door behind him, he undid the stopper and took out Denak's letter. It was sealed, as the last one had been. He used his thumbnail to break the wax, unrolled the parchment, and began to read.

Even in the bedchamber, he kept his voice to a whisper. He wondered if one day, thanks to all this secrecy, he would be able to read without making any sound. That might prove useful.

After the usual greetings, Denak wrote, "'In the matter of Sharbaraz, I have done as you suggested. Much the same thought came to me before your latest letter, in fact. Pradtak has not objected. I do not know whether he thinks he is hedging his bets by letting me serve the rightful King of Kings, but if he does, he is mistaken; Sharbaraz seems to me a man who forgets neither friend nor foe.'"

"Good!" Abivard exclaimed, as if his sister were in the room with him. Feeling foolish, he returned to the letter.

"'Though Pradtak was willing to permit me to pass into the new hall that now holds Sharbaraz's cell—so long as I come and go when no one save he is in the bedchamber—the guards who came here with Sharbaraz have proved harder to persuade. They are Smerdis' men, not Pradtak's, and what the *dihqan* thinks matters little to them.'"

They would be, Abivard thought. He had hoped Smerdis would not have solidly loyal men behind him—he was, after all, a usurper. But if he did have any men who valued him above all others, standing watch on his rivals was the sensible place to put them. Too bad—he would have made matters much simpler if only he had been dumber.

Denak went on, "'I have, however, used every tool to persuade them—they are three in all, and watch in turn, one day, one evening, one dead of night—that their lives in Nalgis Crag stronghold will be happier if they let me do as Pradtak thinks best.'"

Abivard nodded vigorously. His sister was clever. A stronghold where everyone hated you, where your bread was moldy and your wine more nearly vinegar, could quickly come to seem like prison, even to a guard.

"'I pray to the God that my efforts here will be crowned with success,'" Denak wrote. "'Even if she grant that prayer, though, I do not see how I can hope to flee the stronghold with Sharbaraz.

If you have thoughts on that score, do let me know of them. I add, by the way, that you were wise to enclose the harmless sheet with the earlier letter you sent—I was able to show it to Pradtak without his being any the wiser that more important words came also in the tube. May your wisdom find a like way around this present difficulty.'"

Abivard went to the window. Clouds scudded across the sky, gray and ragged as freshly sheared wool. "When the weather clears—if the weather clears—I think I shall have to pay my brother-in-law a visit," he said.

"Who comes to Nalgis Crag stronghold?" The cry arose as Abivard was still a couple of furlongs before the stronghold itself.

He gave his name, then added, "Your lord should be expecting me; I wrote to say I was coming."

"Aye, you're a welcome guest here, Lord Abivard, and, as you say, looked for," the sentry answered. "Who's the old man with you, and what's his station? We'll guest him properly, as his rank warrants."

"My physician's name is Tanshar. He'll stay with me."

"However it pleases you, lord," the sentry said. "But did you think we have no healers here in Nalgis Crag domain? We're not Khamorth here, by the God." He sounded indignant.

"Tanshar has looked after me since I was a babe." Abivard spoke the lie with the ease of endless rehearsal on the road from Vek Rud stronghold. "I don't care to trust myself to anyone else."

The sentry yielded, repeating, "However it pleases you, of course. Come ahead. The gate is open."

Abivard urged his horse forward. Tanshar rode behind him on the narrow track up to the gateway. Situated as it was, Nalgis Crag stronghold could afford to leave the gate open almost all the time—a threatening army could not approach unobserved. In fact, a threatening army could hardly approach at all. Not for the first time, Abivard wished his own stronghold were as secure.

Pradtak came out of the living quarters to greet him in the courtyard. The *dihqan* of Nalgis Crag domain still walked with the help of a stick and was liable to limp for the rest of his life, but he moved far more easily than he had on the day of Denak's wedding.

"Fine to see you again, my brother-in-law," he said, advancing

with his hand outstretched. He looked from Abivard to Tanshar
to the pair of packhorses the latter led. "I would have expected
you to come with more men, especially with the barbarians loose
in the land."

"We managed," Abivard said with a shrug. "I didn't care to
detach many men from keeping the nomads off our flocks and
qanats. Let me present to you my physician Tanshar."

"Lord Pradtak," Tanshar said politely, bowing in the saddle.

Pradtak nodded back, then returned his attention to his social
equal, asking Abivard "What ails you, that you need to bring a
physician with you as you travel?"

"I have biting pains here—" Abivard ran his hand along the
right side of his belly. "—as well as a troublesome flux of the
bowels. Tanshar's potions and the hot fomentations he prepares
while we camp give me enough relief to stay in the saddle."

"However it pleases you," Pradtak said; Abivard wondered if the
sentry had borrowed the phrase from his master. The *dihqan* of
Nalgis Crag domain went on, "Come in, refresh yourselves. Then,
Abivard, you can speak to me more of the reasons for your visit.
Do not misunderstand me, you are most welcome, only your let-
ter was—you will forgive me?—rather vague."

"I forgive you most willingly," Abivard said as he walked with
Pradtak toward the stronghold's living quarters, "for I intended
to be vague. Some things should not be set down on parchment
in so many words, lest the wrong eyes light on them. I would
not have said even as much as I did, were I not sure of your
loyalty to Smerdis King of Kings, may his years be many and
his realm increase."

Pradtak looked sharply at him and more sharply at Tanshar.
"Should you say even so much, when we do not discuss this
matter in privacy?"

"What do you mean?" Abivard said. Then his eyes followed
Pradtak's to Tanshar. "Oh, the physician?" He laughed loud, long,
and a little foolishly. "He is a valued counselor, and has been since
my grandfather's day. Godarz my father even admitted him to the
women's quarters to treat his wives and daughters, Denak among
them. I'd sooner distrust the moon than Tanshar."

"Again I pray your forgiveness, but my father Urashtu sometimes wondered if Godarz was not too liberal for his own good,"
Pradtak said. "I speak not to offend, merely to inform. And I

must remind you I know this Tanshar not at all, only what you say of him. This makes me hesitant to rest on him the same trust you do."

Well it might, since I've been filling your ears with lies, Abivard thought. To Pradtak, however, he presented the picture of affronted dignity. Setting a hand on Tanshar's shoulder, he said, "Let us return to Vek Rud domain, my friend. If Pradtak cannot trust you, I see I cannot trust him." He took a couple of steps toward the stables, as if to reclaim his horse.

Tanshar had rehearsed, too. "But what of the news you bear for Denak, lord?" he cried. "Your lady mother's heart will surely break if you come home without delivering it."

"I don't care, not a fig," Abivard said, drawing himself up to his full height. "I will not stand by and let you be impugned. It reflects badly on me."

Pradtak stared from one of them to the other. *He's hooked,* Abivard thought, though he kept his face cold and haughty. "Perhaps I was hasty—" Pradtak began.

"Perhaps you were." Abivard took another step or two stableward.

"Wait," Pradtak said. "If you rely on this man so, he must deserve it. I apologize for any insult I may have accidentally given."

"The *dihqan* is gracious," Tanshar murmured.

Abivard let himself be persuaded by his retainer's acquiescence. "Since Tanshar feels no insult, none could have been given," he said, but kept his tone grudging. "And the matter, as I say, is of some importance. Very well, Pradtak, I overlook it; it never happened."

Pradtak still seemed pained. "I do not object to your seeing your sister, so long as I remain in the chamber, as well. A woman's close kin may view her without impropriety even after she has passed into the women's quarters of another man. But the physician—"

"Is a physician, and old, and blind in one eye," Abivard said firmly. "And he has seen Denak before. Do you believe he intends to fall on her and ravish her? Too, he would be the better choice to pass on some of what my lady mother said to me. The shock to my sister will perhaps be less, hearing it from someone outside the family."

"However it pleases you." Pradtak sounded sullen, but he yielded.

"Since you have come so far, your words must be important—and, from the dire hints you keep dropping, I am about to perish of curiosity. Tell me at once what you can, don't even pause to scratch your head."

"My throat is dry," Abivard said. "Even in winter, much of the road between my domain and yours is but a dusty track."

Pradtak twisted the head of his stick back and forth in his hand. Hospitality came first; so decreed custom binding as iron. And so, however much he fidgeted, he had to lead Abivard and Tanshar into the kitchens and do his best to make small talk while they drank wine and munched on pocket bread stuffed with grapes and onions and crumbly white cheese and chunks of mutton sprinkled with ground cardamom seeds. Whatever might be said against him, he set an excellent table.

At last Abivard said, "Perhaps you would be gracious enough to have more of this fine red wine brought to your chamber, lord *dihqan*, so we can wet our lips further while we discuss the concerns that brought us here."

"Of course, lord *dihqan*," Pradtak said with ill-concealed eagerness. "If you and your distinguished retainer will be so kind as to follow me—" He used a hand to help push himself upright from the table, but walked several steps before he remembered, almost as an afterthought, to let the tip of his stick touch the floor. As Denak had said, he was mending.

"You walk quite well," Abivard said. "Can you also ride these days?"

"Aye, and you have no idea how glad I am of it," Pradtak said; he, on the other hand, had no idea how glad Abivard was of it. Pradtak went on, "These past few weeks, I've been hunting a great deal to try to make up for all the time I lost while I was lamed."

"No man may do that." Tanshar's somber tones might have come from a servant of the God.

Pradtak looked at him with more respect than he had shown before. "I fear you are right, but I try nonetheless." To Abivard, with the air of a man making a concession, he added, "He has wisdom."

"So he does." Abivard hoped he didn't sound surprised. It wasn't that he reckoned Tanshar foolish; he wouldn't have brought him along if he had. But he hadn't expected the village fortune-teller to act so convincingly a role far above his true station. That made him wonder if Tanshar's station should perhaps be raised.

Before he had time to do more than note the thought, Pradtak said, "Let's take these discussions where we can pursue them more privately, as you yourself suggested." He tapped his stick impatiently on the stone floor.

"I am your servant." Abivard got up and followed him, Tanshar close behind as usual.

Abivard had been down the hall to Pradtak's bedchamber on Denak's wedding day, but then, of course, he had stopped short of the door. Now Pradtak unlocked it and held it open with his own hands, waving for his guests to precede him. "Go in, go in," he said. As soon as Abivard and Tanshar were inside, he barred the door behind them. "Now—"

But Abivard wasn't quite ready to start talking yet. He looked around in some curiosity: this was the first *dihqan's* bedchamber he had seen outside Vek Rud stronghold. In most regards, it was much like his own—a bed, a chest of drawers ornamented by some exceptionally fine cups, a little table. But, as Denak had said, it now had two doorways side by side in the far wall, one of them plainly of recent construction.

He pointed to them and pasted a leer on his face. "What's this? Do you put your pretty wives behind one door and the rest behind the other? How d'you keep 'em from quarreling?"

Pradtak blushed like a maiden brought to her wedding bed. "No. One of the doors leads to the apartment of a, ah, special guest."

"The bar is on this side," Tanshar noted.

"And what concern of yours is that?" Pradtak asked.

"Oh, none whatever, lord," the fortune-teller said cheerfully. "This is your domain, and you hold it as you think best. My mouth but said what my eyes—my good eye, anyhow—chanced to see."

Pradtak opened his own mouth, perhaps to warn Tanshar to watch his words more closely, but he shut it again without speaking and contented himself with a sharp, short nod. Into the silence, Abivard said, "Brother-in-law, could I trouble you for more wine? What I have to say comes so hard that I fear I need the grape to force my tongue to shape the words."

"However it pleases you," Pradtak said, but with a look that warned the matter was not as it pleased *him*. He limped back to the outer door and bawled for a servant. The fellow quickly returned with a jar big enough to get half a dozen men drunk. He dipped some up into the fine porcelain cups, then bobbed his head and vanished. Pradtak tossed back his own wine, then folded his arms across his chest. "Enough suspense," he growled. "Tell me at once of what you have been hinting at since you arrived here."

Abivard glanced at both inner doors. He lowered his voice; he did not want anyone behind either of them to hear. "I have word of a dangerous plot against Smerdis King of Kings, may his years be long and his realm increase. So many are involved in it that I fear the King of Kings may find himself in desperate straits if those of us who remain loyal to him do not do everything in our power to uphold him."

"I feared as much," Pradtak said heavily. "When you sent me that letter complaining of the payment his men had taken from you, I also feared you were part of the plot, seeking to draw me in: that is why I replied as I did. But Denak persuaded me you could not be disloyal."

"Good," Abivard said from the bottom of his heart: even before she had learned what Pradtak was up to, his sister had kept an eye out for the welfare of Vek Rud domain. He went on, "We received many complaints from those who had trouble giving to the treasury officials what Smerdis King of Kings demanded of them."

"I'd wager one of them was from your other new brother-in-law," Pradtak said. He was, in his way, shrewd. "He's but a lad, isn't he, not one to know the duties *dihqans* owe their sovereign."

"Many of the names would surprise you," Abivard answered. "Much of the northwest may rise with the coming of spring. Because you so plainly told me you were loyal to Smerdis King of Kings, I knew you would help me devise how best to stand against the rebels should they move."

"You did right to come to me," Pradtak said. "I have some small connection with the court of the King of Kings, and I—" He broke off. However much he wanted to brag, he had wit enough to realize that would be unwise. With hardly a pause, he went on, "Well, never mind. I am glad you came here, so we—"

He broke off again, this time because someone rapped on the door that led from the women's quarters. He stumped over to it, peered through the grillwork to see who was on the other side, then unbarred the door. Denak came through, carrying a silver tray.

"I crave your pardon, husband of mine," she began. "I did not know—" She brightened. "Abivard! And Doctor Tanshar with you."

Pradtak chuckled. "You mean word they were here had not reached you? I find that hard to believe. Be it as it may, though, I would have summoned you soon in any case, for your brother and the physician have news from your mother they say you must hear."

"From my mother? What could it be?" Denak said. Abivard was appalled at the way she looked. She seemed to have aged five years, maybe ten, in the few months she had dwelt at Nalgis Crag stronghold. Harsh lines bracketed either side of her mouth; dark circles lay under her eyes. Abivard wanted to shake Pradtak to force from him what he had done to her to have worked such a harsh change.

Pradtak said, "Why don't you take supper there in to our—guest? Then you can return free of your burden and learn this portentous news."

"However it pleases you," Denak answered—the phrase seemed to run all through Nalgis Crag domain.

Tanshar raised an eyebrow. "A guest splendid enough to be served by the *dihqan's* wife? Surely he deserves wine, then, to go with his supper." He picked up a cup from the chest of drawers, carried it over to the wine jar, and filled it.

"I thank you, good doctor, but two men wait behind that portal," Denak said.

"Then let them both have wine," Tanshar said grandly, and poured out another cupful. He set it on the tray as if he were a *dihqan* himself, tapping it once or twice with a forefinger as if to show how special it was.

Denak looked to Pradtak, who shrugged. He unbarred the newly built door. Denak passed through it. Pradtak shut it again behind her.

"More wine for you, as well, generous lord?" Tanshar plucked the cup from Pradtak's hand, now acting the conjurer instead of the noble. He gave it back to the *dihqan* full to the brim.

Pradtak sipped the wine. Abivard glanced to Tanshar, who

nodded slightly. Abivard raised his cup in a toast. "The God grant that we put an end to all conspiracies against the King of Kings, may his years be many and his realm increase." He drained the wine still in his cup. Tanshar, also, emptied his. And Pradtak followed his guests by drinking his cup dry, too.

He smacked his lips, frowning a little. "I hope that jar's not going bad," he said. He swayed on his feet. His mouth came open in an enormous yawn. "What's happening to me?" he asked in a blurry voice. His eyes rolled up in his head. He slid, boneless, to the floor. The lovely cup slipped from his hand and shattered. Abivard felt bad about that.

He turned to Tanshar and bowed with deep respect. "What was in that sleeping draft of yours, anyhow?" he asked.

"Elixir of the poppy, henbane, some other things I'd rather not name," Tanshar answered. "It took but a few drops in a cup. All I had to do was get between Pradtak and the wine so he wouldn't see me drug his share—and the one for the guard in there." He spoke in a near whisper as he pointed to the doorway through which Denak had gone.

Abivard slid his sword out of its sheath. If Denak had given the wrong cup to Sharbaraz's guard, or if the fellow hadn't drunk it straight off, he was going to have a fight on his hands. Fear ran through him—if by some horrid mischance she had given the drugged wine to Sharbaraz, all the careful planning they had done would fall straight into the Void.

He walked over to the door, unbarred it, and sprang into the hallway, ready to cut down the guard before the fellow could draw his own blade. To his vast relief, the man slumped against the wall, snoring. Another door at the end of the short hallway was barred on the outside. Abivard opened it. Out came Denak, and with her a broad-shouldered man a few years older than Abivard.

"Your Majesty," Abivard said. He started to go down on his belly.

"No time for that, not now," Sharbaraz snapped. His eyes flashed with excitement at getting out of his prison. "Unless I escape this stronghold, I'm no one's majesty. We'll deal with ceremony when we can."

He hurried past the drugged guard and out into Pradtak's bedchamber. Denak paused for a moment in the hallway. She kicked the guard in the belly, as hard as she could. He grunted and twisted but did not wake. Abivard stared at her. She glared back. "I'd do it to all three of them if I could—I'd do worse," she said, and burst into tears.

"Come," Tanshar said urgently. "We haven't time to waste, as his Majesty reminded us." Abivard went into the bedchamber. Denak followed him, still sobbing. When Tanshar saw her tears, he exclaimed, "My lady, you must be brave now. If they see you weeping, we fail."

"I—know." Denak bit her lip. She wiped her eyes on the brocaded silk of her robe, shuddered, and at last nodded to Tanshar. "Do what you must. I will not give away the illusion."

"Good," Tanshar said. Things were still moving too fast for Abivard to follow all that was going on, and they did not slow down. Tanshar beckoned to Sharbaraz. "Your Majesty, I need your aid now. Take Pradtak's hands in yours."

"As you say." Sharbaraz bent by the unconscious *dihqan*. Tanshar sprinkled both men with reddish powder—"Ground bloodstone," he explained—and began to chant. Abivard knew the sorcery was possible—any hope of escape from Nalgis Crag stronghold would have been impossible without it—but seeing it performed still raised awe in him. Before his eyes, Sharbaraz took on Pradtak's semblance, clothes and all, and the other way round.

When the change was complete, Abivard and Sharbaraz-who-seemed-Pradtak dragged the changed Pradtak into the cell that had held Sharbaraz, then barred the door. Tanshar said to Denak, "Now, my lady, to give you the appearance of the guard here, and then we're away."

Her eyes grew so wide, white showed all around her pupils. "I knew it would come to that, but how can I bear it?" she said. "Will I also see myself in his guise?"

"Lady, you will not." Sharbaraz held out a hand, looked at it. "To my own eyes, I remain myself." He sounded like Pradtak, though.

"That is the way of it," Tanshar agreed. "Your own essence remains undisturbed, and to you the change will be invisible."

Denak nodded jerkily. "I will do it, then, but must I touch him?"

Tanshar shook his head. "The ritual here is rather different, for the two of you will not exchange appearances; rather, you will borrow his. Stand there close by him, if you would."

Even that seemed more than Denak wanted, but she obeyed. Tanshar set a crystal disk between her and the guard; when he let go of it, it hung in the air by itself. He chanted again, to a different rhythm this time, and invoked the name of the Prophet Shivini, the lady, again and again. The crystal glowed for perhaps half a minute. When it faded, there might have been two guards, identical twins, in the hallway.

"Let me get away from him," Denak said, and her voice came out a man's harsh rasp.

Abivard closed the outer door to the hallway on the unconscious guard and barred it, again from the outside. He was grinning from ear to ear; things had gone better than he had dared hope. "Won't they be confused?" he said happily. "Not only will they *be* confused, in fact, they'll *stay* confused for—how long will the spells of seeming last, Tanshar?"

"A few days, if no magic is brought to bear against them." Tanshar sounded exhausted. "If a sorcerer should challenge them, though, he'll pierce them as an embroidery needle pierces silk. All the more reason to get away as fast as we can."

"Oh, I don't know," Sharbaraz said with Pradtak's voice. "When the *dihqan* stops looking like me and becomes himself again, they may still think him me, and using sorcery to try to escape. A lovely coil you've wound." He laughed with the joy of a man who has not laughed in a long time. "But the wise Tanshar is right—we should not test the magic overmuch." He trotted toward the outer door to the bedchamber.

"Your Majesty, uh, husband of mine for the moment—remember, you limp," Denak said. "Forget that and you may yet give the game away."

Sharbaraz bowed. "Lady, you are right," he said, though Denak's semblance was anything but ladylike. "I shall remember." He snatched up Pradtak's stick from where it lay on the floor and gave a convincing impression of a man with a bad ankle. "And now—away."

Sharbaraz made sure to close the newly installed bar outside Pradtak's bedchamber. Abivard nodded approvingly: now that the bedchamber was in effect the outer portion of the women's quarters, no *dihqan* would leave it open, lest the women somehow depart without his knowledge.

"Where now?" Sharbaraz asked in a low voice as the bar thudded home.

"The stables," Abivard answered, just as quietly. "Here, walk
beside me and make as if you're leading me and not the other
way round. Tanshar, Denak, you come behind: You're our retainers, after all."

Pradtak's household accepted the escaping fugitives as what
they seemed. Once reminded, Sharbaraz kept up his limp quite
well. He gave friendly greetings to Pradtak's kinsfolk and retainers; if he didn't address any of them by name, that was no flaw
in a brief conversation—and he made sure all the conversations
were brief.

At the stables, though, one of the grooms seeing to Abivard's
horses looked up in surprise. "You seldom come here without
bow and spear for the chase, lord," he said. "You are riding to
hunt, not so?"

Abivard froze, cursing himself for a fool. All that careful planning, to be undone by a moment's carelessness! But Sharbaraz
said calmly, "No, we're for the village of Gayy, east of here. Lord
Abivard was asking about the *qanat* network there because it
stretches so far from the Hyuja River, and he was hoping to do
the same along the Vek Rud. My thought was that showing him
would be easier than talking at him. What say you?"

"Me?' The groom looked startled, then grinned. "Lord, of making *qanats* I know nothing, so I have little to say." He looked to
Abivard. "You'll want your animal and your councilor's resaddled,
then?"

"Yes, and we'll take the packhorses, as well," Abivard answered,
vastly relieved Sharbaraz's wits were quicker than his own, and
also vastly impressed at Sharbaraz's intimate knowledge of Pradtak's
domain. He went on, "I may want to spend the night at, uh, Gayy
and look over the *qanats* some more in the morning."

"The town has a sarai, lord," the groom said in mild reproof.
Abivard folded his arms across his chest. The groom looked an
appeal to the man he thought to be Pradtak.

"However it pleases him," Sharbaraz said, just as Pradtak would
have. Abivard had all he could do to keep from laughing.

The groom nodded in resignation and turned to Denak. "You'll
be one of the gentlemen who rode in at night a ways back. I'm
sorry, sir, but I've not seen you much since, and I've forgotten

which of those horses was yours." He pointed down to three stalls at the end of the stable.

Before Denak could answer—or panic and not answer—Sharbaraz came to the rescue again. "It was the bay gelding with the scar on his flank, not so?"

"Yes, lord," Denak said in her sorcerously assumed man's voice.

The groom sent Sharbaraz a glance full of admiration. "Lord, no one will ever say you haven't an eye for horses." Sharbaraz made the image of Pradtak preen.

The horse that had belonged to Smerdis' man snorted a little when Denak mounted it. So did Pradtak's horse when Sharbaraz climbed aboard. The horses knew, even if men were fooled. Sharbaraz easily calmed his animal. Denak had more trouble; the only riding she had done since she became a woman was on her wedding journey to Nalgis Crag stronghold. But she managed, and the four riders started down the steep, winding trail to the bottom of Nalgis Crag.

"By the God, I think we've done it," Abivard breathed as the flat ground drew near. He called ahead to Sharbaraz, who as Pradtak was leading the procession. "Lord, uh, your Majesty, how did you come to know so much about the village of Gayy and its *qanats*? I'd not wager an arket that the real Pradtak could say as much of them."

"My father set me to studying the realm and its domains before my beard first sprouted, so I would come to know Makuran before I ruled it," Sharbaraz answered. His chuckle had more than a little edge to it. "I got to know Nalgis Crag domain, or its stronghold, better than I cared to."

"My father was right," Abivard said. "You will make a fine King of Kings for Makuran."

"Your father—he would be Godarz of Vek Rud domain?" Sharbaraz said, and answered himself: "Yes, of course, for you are Denak's brother. Godarz perished on the steppe with the rest of the host?"

"He did, your Majesty, with my brother and three half brothers."

Sharbaraz shook his head. "A victory in Pardraya would have been glorious. A loss like the one we suffered . . . better the campaign had never begun. But with a choice of strike or wait, my father always preferred to strike."

His horse reached the flat land then. He kicked the animal up into a fast, ground-eating trot. His companions imitated him: The farther from Nalgis Crag stronghold they got, the safer they would be.

Abivard said, "The confusion should be lovely back at the stronghold. When Pradtak wakes up in your shape, he'll insist he's himself, and the guards will just laugh at him. They'll say he's gone off to Gayy. And even when he does get his own appearance back, they'll think that's a trick, as you said."

"The only real problem will be that I won't return to the women's quarters," Denak said. "And the folk at the stronghold won't truly notice I'm missing for some time. Who pays any real attention to women, anyhow?" Her voice was deep and strange now, but the same old bitterness rode it.

Sharbaraz said, "Lady, a blind man would note your bravery, on a battlefield where no man would ever be likely to find himself. Do not make yourself less than you are, I pray you."

"How can I make myself less than nothing?" she said. When Abivard protested that, she turned her head away and would not speak further. He did not press her, but wondered what had passed at Nalgis Crag stronghold to make her hate herself so. His left hand, the one not holding the reins, curled into a fist. If he had thought Pradtak was abusing her, he would have served her husband as she had the guard who disgraced himself by helping to confine the rightful King of Kings.

The pale winter sun scurried toward the horizon. The weather, though cold, stayed clear. When the riders came to an almond grove not far from the edge of Pradtak's irrigated land, Abivard said, "Let's camp here. We'll have fuel for a fine fire."

When no one argued with him, he reined in, tethered his horse, and began scouring the ground for fallen branches and twigs. Sharbaraz joined him, saying "The God grant we don't have to damage the trees themselves. We should be able to glean enough to keep them intact."

Behind the two young men, Denak said to Tanshar, "Take your seeming off me this instant."

"My lady, truly I would sooner wait," Tanshar answered hesitantly. "Our safety might still ride on your keeping the guardsman's face."

"I would rather die than keep it." Denak began to cry again.

Tanshar's magic transmuted her sobs into the deep moaning of a man in anguish.

Abivard dumped a load of wood on the ground and dug in a pocket of his belt pouch for flint and steel. Tanshar sent him a look of appeal and asked, "Lord, what is your will? Shall I remove the enchantment?"

"If my sister hates it so, perhaps you had better," Abivard answered. "Why she should hate it—"

"She has reason, I assure you." Sharbaraz dropped more twigs and branches on top of the load Abivard had gathered.

His support, instead of cheering Denak, only made her cry harder than ever. Abivard looked up from the slow business of getting a fire going and nodded to Tanshar. The fortune-teller took out the crystal disk he had used to give Denak the appearance of Sharbaraz's guard. Again he suspended it in the air between them. This time his chant was different from before. Where the disk had briefly glowed, now it seemed to suck up darkness from the gathering night. When that darkness left it, Denak was herself again.

Abivard walked over to her and put his arms around her. "It's gone," he said. "You're you, no one else, just as you should be."

She shuddered under his touch, then twisted away. "I'll never be just as I should be, don't you understand?" she cried. "I left what I should be behind forever at Nalgis Crag stronghold."

"What, being Pradtak's wife?" Abivard said scornfully. "The cursed traitor doesn't deserve you."

"That's so," Sharbaraz agreed.

He started to say something more, but Denak cut him off with a sharp chopping motion of her right hand. "What you say of Pradtak is true, but not to the point. I left more than marriage behind in that stronghold. I lost my honor there, as well."

"Aiding the King of Kings against those who wrongfully imprisoned him is no dishonor," Abivard said. "You . . ." His voice trailed away as at last he found a reason why Denak might have kicked Sharbaraz's guard while he was unconscious, why donning his image was almost more than she could bear. He stared at her. "Did he . . . ? Did they . . . ?" He couldn't go on.

"He did. They all did," she answered bleakly. "It was the price they took from me for letting me in to serve the rightful King of Kings. They cared nothing that I had Pradtak's permission;

they were Smerdis' men, they said. And if I spoke a word of it to anyone, Sharbaraz would be dead in his cell one day. I knew, as you did, that he was Makuran's only hope, and so—I yielded myself to them."

"It's done. It's over." The words came flat and empty from Abivard's mouth. It might be done, but it would never be over. He felt sick inside. No matter why Denak had done what she did, how was he supposed to look at her after knowing of it?

She understood that, too. Shaking her head, she said, "All the way along the track down Nalgis Crag, I kept wishing I had the courage to throw myself over a cliff. Without my honor, what am I?"

Abivard found no answer. Nor did Tanshar, who sat by the fire, slumped and numb with fatigue. Nor did Sharbaraz, not at first; he got down on hands and knees and scratched in the dirt for several minutes. At last, with a grunt of triumph, he rose once more and showed what he held in his hands: three black pebbles.

"As rightful King of Kings, I have certain powers beyond those of ordinary men," he declared. He threw one of the black pebbles down onto the ground from which he'd grubbed it. "Denak, I divorce you from Pradtak." He repeated the formula twice more, making the divorce complete.

Denak remained disheartened. "I know you mean that kindly, your Majesty, but it does nothing for me. No doubt Pradtak, too, will cast the pebbles against me when he eventually gets free of your shape and your cell. But what good does it do me?"

"Lady, not even the King of Kings has the power—though some have claimed it—to ask the hand of a woman wed to another man," Sharbaraz said. "Thus I needed to free you from that union."

"But . . . your Majesty!" Denak's words stumbled out one and two at a time. "You—of all people—know how I . . . threw away my honor in the hall in front of your cell."

Sharbaraz shook his head. "I know you won great honor there, giving without concern for yourself that I, that Makuran, might go on. If you know nothing else of me, know I always aid those who aid me and punish those who do me wrong. When I sit on the throne in Mashiz once more, you shall sit beside me as my principal wife. By the God and the Four I swear it."

Abivard was never sure whether he or Denak first went down

into a prostration before Sharbaraz. His sister was sobbing still, but with a different note now, as if, against all expectation, the sacrifice and humiliation she had endured might have been of some worth after all.

"Honor lost is honor won," Sharbaraz said. "Rise, Denak, and you, Abivard. We have much to do before I return to my proper place in Mashiz."

"Aye, your Majesty." As Abivard got back to his feet, he glanced over at Tanshar, who was taking bread and dates from the saddlebag of a packhorse. The fortune-teller's second prophecy echoed within him: honor won and honor lost in a tall tower. He had seen that, sure enough, and more of each than Abivard had imagined.

Where, he wondered, would he find that flash of light across a narrow sea? And what would it bring with it?

✦ VI

odarz had taught Abivard many things: how to ride, how to rule a domain, how to think of next year instead of tomorrow. One thing he had not taught him was how to be a rebel. Abivard didn't think Godarz had ever dreamed—or had nightmares—of opposing Vek Rud domain to the power of the King of Kings in Mashiz.

Whatever he did, then, he had to do on his own, without his father's advice and warnings echoing in the back of his mind. He missed them. He had grown used to the idea that Godarz had an answer for everything and, could he but find it, all would be well. In the game he played now, that was not so.

Nor could he simply sit idle and let Sharbaraz bear the whole burden of the war against Smerdis. Not only would that have been unseemly for the King of Kings' brother-in-law—for Sharbaraz had kept his promise and wed Denak as soon as he came into Vek Rud stronghold—but Abivard knew most of the frontier *dihqans* better than his sovereign did.

"Old news," Sharbaraz complained one evening, munching bulgur wheat with pine nuts and mutton drenched in a sauce of yogurt and crushed mint leaves. "I know the domains, and I know of the lords they had before our army went into Pardraya, but how many of those lords still live? One here, one there. Mostly, though, it's their sons and grandsons and nephews who carry on for them, men whose ways I never studied. Whereas you—"

"Aye, I've hunted with some of them and played mallet and ball against others at festivals and the like, but I can't claim to know them well. Most of my dealings with them have been after I made my way back from Pardraya."

"Those are the important dealings, now," Sharbaraz said. "If we cannot bring the northwest to my banner, you might as well have left me mured up in Nalgis Crag stronghold, for that would prove Smerdis, curse him through the Void, will be the sure winner in our struggle."

Abivard rose from the bench in the kitchen and paced back and forth. "If we wrote out the lists of opposing forces on parchment, ours would be much smaller and weaker than Smerdis' even if all the northwestern *dihqans* went over to you," he said. "How do we go about overcoming that advantage?"

"If all the forces loyal to Smerdis today stay loyal to him, we're doomed," Sharbaraz answered. "I don't believe they will. I think most of them are with him because they believe I gave up the throne of my own free will. When they learn that isn't so, they'll flock to my banner."

They had better, Abivard thought. *Otherwise we'll see how bitter a death Smerdis can devise for us.* That, however, was not the sort of notion he could share with the man he reckoned his sovereign.

Sharbaraz looked up at him. Nothing about his dress proclaimed him King of Kings: he wore one of Abivard's woolen caftans, a good enough garment but hardly a royal robe. A bit of yogurt was stuck in his beard, just below one corner of his mouth. But when he spoke, confidence rang in his voice like a horn call: "When you rescued me from Pradtak's stronghold, you didn't stop to reckon up the cost or what would come afterward—you simply did what was right. We'll go on that way, and the God will surely smile on us."

"May it be so, your Majesty," Abivard answered.

"It *shall* be so," Sharbaraz said fiercely, slamming a fist down on the stone table in front of him. As they had before, his words set Abivard afire inside, made him want to leap onto his horse and charge down on Mashiz, sweeping everything before him by sheer force of will.

But however much he wanted to do that, the part of him that was Godarz's heritage warned him it would not be so easy. Peroz had charged down on the Khamorth—and look what it got him.

Frada came in then. One of the cooks handed him a pocket bread filled with the same mutton-and-bulgur mixture Abivard and Sharbaraz were eating. "Your Majesty," he murmured as he sat down beside Sharbaraz. His tone lay somewhere between admiration and hero worship; he had never expected to sit at meat with the King of Kings.

When he glanced toward Abivard, though, resentment congealed on his face. Abivard hadn't told him of the plan to rescue Sharbaraz; Abivard hadn't told anyone who did not absolutely have to know. He could see Frada wishing he had been along, too.

Sharbaraz also saw that. He said to Frada, "Secrets must be kept. You shall yet have the chance to show off your courage before me."

Frada preened like a peacock. Had he had tail feathers, he would have fanned them out in dazzling display. As things were, he had to be content with puffing out his chest, throwing back his head, and, in Abivard's opinion, looking very foolish.

But perhaps Frada wasn't so foolish after all. No less than Abivard, he was now brother-in-law to the rightful King of Kings. When Sharbaraz regained his capital, both Godarz's sons—and their younger half brothers, too—would be great men in Makuran. That hadn't fully occurred to Abivard till then.

For the moment, though, Frada was just his little brother. "Get out of here," he said, "before you stroll into the oven from not looking where you're going." The gesture Frada returned was emphatically not one of benediction, but he departed, chewing noisily.

Sharbaraz chuckled. "The two of you get on well," he said. His voice was wistful. "I grew up distrusting all my brothers, and they me."

"That happens in a fair number of domains, I've heard," Abivard said. "I can see how it would be worse in Mashiz, with the whole realm as a prize for the one who manages to inherit."

"Just so," Sharbaraz said. "When word came of my father's fall, I looked for one of my brothers to try to cast me down from the throne." He laughed a laugh full of self-mockery. "And so I paid no heed to my doddering cousin the mintmaster—and paid the price for that. I'd be paying it yet, without your sister and you."

Abivard dipped his head. Songs said a monarch's gratitude was like lowlands snow on a warm spring day, but he didn't think

Sharbaraz typical of the breed. With luck, the rightful King of Kings would remain a man among men even after he gained the throne.

"How do you and your brothers keep from quarreling?" Sharbaraz asked.

"Oh, we quarrel—like pups in a litter," Abivard answered. "But Father never let us turn it to feuds and knives in the back. 'The domain is bigger than any one of you, and big enough for all of you,' he'd say, and clout us now and again to make sure the lesson got through."

"My father used to say much the same thing." Sharbaraz shook his head. "He couldn't quite make us believe it. I wish he had."

"What do you suppose Smerdis will do when he learns of your escape?" Abivard thought it a good time to change the subject. "What would you do, were you in Mashiz and he a rebel in the provinces?"

"Were I on my throne, I would attack any rebel with as strong a force as I could mount, to make sure his men won no battles against forces too weak to do a proper job of rooting them out. That would only give them courage, the last thing I'd want rebel troops to have."

"Our thoughts travel the same track," Abivard said, nodding. "The next question is, does Smerdis think the same way we do?"

Sharbaraz stopped with a bite halfway to his mouth. "By the God, Abivard, I have more reason to bless the day I met you than that it was also the day I gained my freedom and claimed your sister as my bride. Do you know, that notion never occurred to me. I assumed Smerdis would set out from Mashiz with his whole host directly he heard I'd escaped, because I would have done as much in his place. But it may not be so."

"You must have known him at your father's court." Abivard thanked his father for drilling into him that there was commonly more than one way to look at a situation. "What feel do you have for the way he'll act? I've only met him, so to speak, when his men took my money to pay it to the Khamorth. From that, he doesn't strike me as a world-bestriding hero."

"I never reckoned him one, that's certain," Sharbaraz said, "but then, I hardly had him in my mind at all till he stole my throne from me. He was just a gray man with a gray beard, hardly worth noticing even when he spoke, and he didn't speak much. Who would have guessed such ambition hid behind that blank mask?"

"Maybe he didn't know it was there himself till he got the chance to let it out," Abivard said.

"That could be so." With the dainty manners of the royal court, Sharbaraz dabbed at his mouth with a square of cloth—a towel rather than a proper napkin, but as close as Vek Rud domain could come. When Abivard wiped his mouth, he used his sleeve. Setting the towel aside, Sharbaraz went on, "One thing is sure, though: he'll soon learn I'm loose, and then we'll find out what sort of man he is."

The rider from Nalgis Crag domain looked nervous as he waited for Abivard to approach. "Lord," he said, sooner than he should have, "I beg you to remember I am but a messenger here, bearing the words and intentions of Pradtak my *dihqan*. They are not my words or intentions, and I would not have you blame me for them."

"However it pleases you," Abivard said. The rider let out a long, smoky breath of relief, then gave Abivard a sharp look. Abivard carefully kept his own face innocent. He twisted his left hand in a gesture of benediction. "I pledge by the God that no harm will come to you because of the message you bring."

"You are gracious, lord. Pradtak bade me deliver these first of all." The rider unsealed a message tube. Instead of a letter, he let three black pebbles fall into the palm of his other hand. "These are the very pebbles he dropped before witnesses to pronounce divorcement from his former wife the lady Denak, your sister."

Abivard burst out laughing. Pradtak's messenger went from apprehensive to shocked in the space of a heartbeat. Whatever reaction he had expected—fury, most likely, or perhaps dismay—that wasn't it. Abivard said, "You may return the pebbles to your lord with my compliments. Tell him he's too late, that divorcement's already been pronounced."

"Lord, I do not understand," the messenger said carefully. "By custom and law both, you have not the power to end the marriage of your sister to my lord Pradtak."

"True," Abivard admitted. "But the King of Kings, may his years be many and his realm increase, does have that power."

"Smerdis King of Kings has not—" the rider began.

Abivard broke in. "Ah, but Sharbaraz King of Kings, son of Peroz and true ruler of Makuran, *has*."

"*Sharbaraz* King of Kings?" Pradtak's rider stared like a sturgeon netted out of the Vek Rud River. "Every man knows Sharbaraz renounced the throne."

"Evidently not everyone knows the renunciation was forced from him at knifepoint, and that he was locked away in Nalgis Crag stronghold for safekeeping," Abivard said. The rider's eyes got even wider. With relish, Abivard went on, "And not everyone knows my sister and I rescued him out of Nalgis Crag stronghold, and set your precious lord in the cell that had been his. How long did Pradtak take to get his own face back, anyhow?"

The messenger sputtered for close to a minute before he finally managed, "Lord, I know nothing of this. I am but a small man, and it is dangerous for such to meddle in the affairs of those stronger than they. I have here also a letter from my lord Pradtak for you." He handed Abivard another leather tube.

As Abivard opened it, he said, "You may not be powerful, but you must know whether your lord looked like himself or someone else for a while, eh?"

"I am not required to speak of this to you," the man said.

"So you're not." Abivard took out the scrap of parchment and unrolled it. The message was, if nothing else, to the point: *War to the knife*. Abivard showed it to the messenger. "You can tell Pradtak for me that the knife cuts both ways. If he chooses to support a usurper in place of the proper King of Kings, he'll find himself on the wrong end of it."

"I shall deliver your words, just as you say them," the rider answered.

"Do that. Think about them on the way back to Nalgis Crag stronghold, too. When you get there, tell your friends what's happened—and why. Some of them, I'd wager, will know what befell Pradtak when we rescued Sharbaraz. Before you go, though, take bread and wine and sit by the fire. Whatever Pradtak says, I'm not at war with you."

But the messenger shook his head. "No, lord, that wouldn't be right; I'm loyal to my own *dihqan*, I am, and I wouldn't make myself the guest of a man I'm liable to be fighting before long. I do thank you, though; you're generous to offer." He made small smacking noises, as if chewing on what Abivard had told him. His face was thoughtful.

"I wish your *dihqan* had shown the same loyalty to his rightful lord as you do to him," Abivard said. "Go in peace, if you feel you must. Maybe when you hear the whole story you'll change your mind. Maybe some of your friends will, too, when they learn it all."

Pradtak's rider did not answer. But as he turned his horse to start the journey back to Nalgis Crag domain, he sketched a salute. Abivard returned it. He had hopes that Pradtak had done his own cause more harm than good with those three pebbles and the accompanying letter of defiance. Let his men learn how he had betrayed Peroz's son, and Nalgis Crag stronghold, no matter how invulnerable to outside assault, might yet quake beneath his fundament.

The smithy was dark and sooty, lit mostly by the leaping red-gold flames of the furnace. It smelled of woodsmoke and hot iron and sweat. Ganzak the smith was the mightiest wrestler of Vek Rud domain; he had a chest and shoulders like a bull's, and his arms, worked constantly with blows of the heavy hammer, were thick as some men's legs.

"Lord, Majesty, you honor my hearth by your visit," he said when Abivard and Sharbaraz came in one wintry morning.

"Your fire's as welcome as your company," Abivard answered with a grin to show he was joking. Yet, as with many jests, his held a grain of truth. While snow lay in the stronghold's courtyard, Ganzak labored bare-chested, and heat as well as exertion left his skin wet and gleaming, almost as if oiled, in the firelight.

"How fares my armor?" Sharbaraz asked him. The rightful King of Kings was not one to waste time on anything when his vital interests were concerned. He went on, "The sooner I have it, the sooner I feel myself fully a man and a warrior again—and I aim to take the field as soon as I may."

"Majesty, I've told you before I do all I can, but armor, especially chain, is slow work," Ganzak said. "Splints are simple—just long, thin plates hammered out and punched at each end for attachment. But ring mail—"

Abivard had played through this discussion with the smith before. But Sharbaraz, being a scion of the royal family, had not learned much about how armor was made; perhaps his study of the domains and their leaders had kept him from paying much attention to such seemingly smaller matters. He said, "What's the trouble? You make the rings, you fit them together into mail, you fasten the mail to the leather backing, and there's your suit."

Ganzak exhaled through his nose. Had someone of less than Sharbaraz's exalted status spoken to him so, he might have given a more vehement reply, probably capped by chasing the luckless fellow out of the smithy with hammer upraised. As it was, he used what Abivard thought commendable restraint: "Your Majesty, it's not so simple. What are the rings made of?"

"Wire, of course," Sharbaraz said. "Iron wire, if that's what you mean."

"Iron wire it is," Ganzak agreed. "The best iron I can make, too. But wire doesn't grow on trees like pistachio nuts. By the God, I wish it did, but since it doesn't, I have to make it, too. That means I have to cut thin strips from a plate of iron, which is what I was doing when you and my lord the *dihqan* came in."

He pointed to several he had set aside. "Here they are. They're still not wire yet, you see—they're just strips of iron. To turn 'em into wire, I have to hammer 'em out thin and round."

Sharbaraz said, "I believe I may have spoken too soon."

But Ganzak, by then, was in full spate and not to be headed off by mere apology. "Then once I have the wire, I have to turn it into rings. They're all supposed to be the same size, right? So what I do is, I wrap the wire around this dowel here—" He showed Sharbaraz the wooden cylinder. "—and then cut 'em, one at a time. Then I have to pound the ends of each one flat and rivet 'em together to make rings, one at a time again. 'Course, they have to be linked to each other before I put the rivets in, on account of you can't put 'em together after they're finished rings. None of this stuff is quick, begging your pardon, Majesty."

"No, I see it wouldn't be. Forgive me, Ganzak; I spoke out of turn." Sharbaraz sounded humbler than a King of Kings usually had occasion to be. "Another lesson learned: know what something involves before you criticize."

Abivard said, "I've seen mail with every other row of rings punched from plate rather than turned out the way you describe. Wouldn't that be faster to make?"

"Aye, it is." Ganzak spat into the fire. "But that's what I give you for it. You can't link those punched rings one to another, only to the proper ones in the rows above and below 'em. That means the mail isn't near as strong for the same weight of metal. You want his Majesty to go to war in cheap, shoddy armor, find yourself another smith." He folded massive arms across even more massive chest.

Defeated, Abivard said, "When do you think this next armor will be finished?"

The smith considered. "Three weeks, lord, give or take a little."

"It will have to do," Sharbaraz said with a sigh. "In truth, I don't expect to be attacked before then, but I grudge every day without mail. I feel naked as a newborn babe."

"It's not so bad as that, your Majesty," Abivard said. "Hosts of warriors go and fight in leather. The Khamorth make a habit of it, their horses being smaller and less able to bear weight than ours, and I fought against them so while Ganzak was still at work on my suit of iron."

"No doubt," Sharbaraz said. "Necessity knows few laws, as you among others showed in freeing me from Nalgis Crag stronghold. But did you not reckon yourself a hero once more, not just a warrior, when the ring mail jingled sweetly on your shoulders?"

"I don't know about that," Abivard said. "I did reckon myself less likely to get killed, which is plenty to hearten a man in a fight."

"Lord, when I hear you talk plain sense, I can see your father standing there in your place," Ganzak said.

"I wish he were," Abivard answered quietly. Even so, he glowed with pride at the compliment.

Sharbaraz said, "At my father's court, I learned as much of war from minstrels as from soldiers. Good to have close by me someone who has seen it and speaks plainly of what it requires. Doing one's duty and staying alive through it, though not something to inspire songs, also has its place. Another lesson." He nodded, as if to impress it on his memory.

Abivard nodded, too. Sharbaraz was always learning. Abivard thought well of that: the very nature of his office was liable to make the King of Kings sure he already knew everything, for who dared tell him he did not?

Something else occurred to Abivard. Suppose one day Sharbaraz went wrong? As the King of Kings had said, he stood close by now. But how was he to tell Sharbaraz he was mistaken? He had no idea.

In the stronghold, Sharbaraz took for his own the chamber Abivard had used while Godarz still lived; Frada relinquished it with good grace. It lay down the hall from the *dihqan's* bedchamber; that convenience was a point in its favor.

Denak had returned to the women's quarters of Vek Rud stronghold when she, Abivard, Sharbaraz, and Tanshar came back to the domain. True to his vow, Sharbaraz had wed her as soon as a servant of the God could be brought to the stronghold. But though she was his wife, the women's quarters were not his. Had he gone in there to claim her whenever he sought her company, he would have created great scandal even though he was King of Kings.

The way round the seeming impasse created scandal, too, but not great scandal. The outer door to the *dihqan's* bedchamber became the effective boundary to the women's quarters—*just as it had at Nalgis Crag stronghold*, Abivard thought, and kept the thought to himself. Sharbaraz did not go inside. Abivard brought Denak to him there, and he escorted her to the room he was using. For her, that room was also part of the women's quarters.

So far, well and good. The trouble lay in the stretch of hall between the *dihqan's* bedchamber and Sharbaraz's room. No one in the stronghold was willing to consider a hallway part of the women's quarters, but nobody could see how Denak was supposed to join her husband without traversing it, either. Tongues wagged.

"Maybe Tanshar could magic me from my room to Sharbaraz's," Denak said one evening as Abivard walked her toward the controversial hall.

"I don't think so," he said doubtfully. "I just thank the God his strength sufficed for the uses to which we put it."

"Brother of mine, I meant that for a joke." Denak poked him in the ribs, which made him hop in the air. "It was the only answer I could think of that might stop the gossip about how we have to do things."

"Oh." Abivard tried it on for size. He decided to laugh. "It's good to have you back here."

"It's good to be back," she answered, turning serious again. "After what happened in Pradtak's women's quarters—" Her face twisted. "I wish I could have killed that guard. I wish I could have killed all three of them, a finger's breadth at a time. Escaping that place is not enough, but it will have to do."

He started to put an arm around her, but stopped with the gesture barely begun. She didn't want anyone but Sharbaraz touching her these days. Abivard wished she had killed the guard—all the guards—too, as slowly as she liked. He would have helped, and smiled as he did it.

She said, "In truth, it's just as well Tanshar can't sorcerously flick me about from chamber to chamber. No matter what others may say, walking down that stretch of hall makes me feel free, as if I had the run of the whole stronghold the way I did when I was a girl. Funny what twenty or thirty feet of stone floor and blank walls can do, isn't it?"

"I was thinking the same thing," Abivard said. "Do you know, Roshnani and some of my other wives are jealous of you?"

"I'm not surprised," Denak said as Abivard opened the inner door to the bedchamber for her to pass through. "To those with no freedom, even a tiny bit must look like a lot."

"Hmm." Abivard closed the door that led into the women's quarters, locked it, and walked with Denak to the outer door of the bedchamber. Sharbaraz stood waiting just outside. Abivard bowed to him. "Your Majesty, I bring you your wife."

Sharbaraz bowed in turn, first to Abivard and then to Denak. He held out his arm to her. "My lady, if you will come with me?" She crossed the threshold. Abivard turned away so that, formally speaking, he had not seen her walking down that much-too-public hall. Then he laughed at himself, and at the way he did his best to pretend custom hadn't been violated when he knew full well it had. He wondered whether custom wasn't more nearly the ruler of Makuran than the King of Kings was.

That evening, he brought Roshnani to the bedchamber. She looked wistfully toward the outer door. "I wish I could go through there, too," she said. "The women's quarters are bearable when you know everyone stays in them alike. When one can go farther—" She paused, perhaps swallowing some of what she had intended to say. "It's hard," she finished.

"I am sorry it troubles you," Abivard said. "I don't know what to do about it, though. I can't throw away untold years of tradition on a whim. Tradition didn't count on a King of Kings' having to take refuge in a back-country stronghold, or on his marrying the *dihqan's* sister."

"I know that," Roshnani said. "And please understand I do not hold Denak's luck against her. We get on famously; we might have been born sisters. I just wish my stretch of the world were wider, too. All I've seen of the world since I became a woman is two women's quarters and the land between the stronghold where I grew up and this one. It's not enough."

"You might have been born sisters with Denak," he agreed. "She's been saying much the same thing for as long as I can remember. I hadn't heard it from you till now."

"I didn't have any reason to think about it till now," she said, which made Abivard remember what Denak had said about a little freedom seeming a lot. Roshnani went on, "Does it anger you that I speak so? Few men, from what little I know, give their wives even so much rein." She looked anxiously at Abivard.

"It's all right," he said. "Smerdis, I'm sure, would have locked up Sharbaraz's thoughts along with—or ahead of—his body, if only he could. I don't see the sense in that. If you don't say what you think, how am I supposed to find out? I may not always think you're right—and even if I do, I may not be able to do anything about it—but I want to know."

Like the sun emerging and then going back behind the clouds, Roshnani's frown chased a quick smile off her face. She said, "If you think I'm right, why can't you do anything about it?"

He spread his hands. "We'll have nobles aplenty coming here to Vek Rud stronghold, sounding out Sharbaraz to see whether they should side with him or with Smerdis. Do you think he'd do his cause much good if he said he wanted all their wives and daughters out of the women's quarters? I don't think he does want that, but even if he did, saying so would cost him half his support, likely more."

"Not among the women," Roshnani said stubbornly.

"But the women aren't lancers."

Roshnani bit her lip. "Dreadful when a question of what's right and wrong collides with a question of what works well in the world."

"My father would have said that if it doesn't work well in the world, whether it's right or wrong doesn't matter. When Tanshar and I went to Pradtak's, I kept from having to talk too much too soon just by claiming hospitality. Pradtak had to serve me food and wine then, whether he wanted to or not. The women's quarters are the same way: because they're part of the way things have always been done, they won't disappear tomorrow even if Sharbaraz orders that they should."

Abivard watched Roshnani chew on that. By her expression, she didn't care for the flavor. "Maybe not," she admitted reluctantly. "But what about this, then: will you begin to ease the rules of the women's quarters after Sharbaraz wins the war and the assembled nobles of Makuran aren't all peering straight at your—our—stronghold?"

He started to answer, but stopped before any words crossed his lips. He had expected his logic to convince Roshnani—and so it had. But instead of convincing her he was right, it had just convinced her to accept delay in getting what she still wanted. It was, he thought uncomfortably, a very womanly way of arguing—she had conceded his point and turned it against him in the same breath.

So how was he supposed to reply? Every heartbeat he hesitated gave her more hope—and made his dashing that hope harder. At last he said, "I suppose we can try it; that probably won't make the world come to an end."

"If it doesn't work out, you can always go back to the old ways," she said encouragingly.

"That's rubbish, and you know it," he said. "Just as easy to put together the pieces of a butchered mutton carcass and say it's a live sheep again."

"Yes, I do know it," Roshnani admitted. "I was hoping you didn't."

"Devious wench."

"Of course," she said. "Caged away in the women's quarters as I am, what can I be but devious?" She stuck out her tongue at him, but quickly grew serious again. "Even knowing that you'll change the old way, you'd still let me—let us—out now and again?"

Abivard felt Godarz looking over his shoulder. He almost turned around to see what expression his father wore. His best guess was sardonic amusement at the predicament in which his son had landed himself. Break custom or make Roshnani—and his other wives when she was through with them—furious at him? Sighing, he said, "Yes, I suppose we can see how it goes."

Roshnani squeaked, jumped in the air, threw her arms around his neck, and kissed him. He would have called what happened next a molestation if he hadn't enjoyed it so much. Later, the watchful, thoughtful part of him wondered if he had been bribed. One of the nice things about Roshnani was that he could tease her with such without angering her.

"No," she answered. "You just made me very happy, that's all."

He looked at her. "I should make you happy more often."

"Well, why don't you?" she asked mischievously.

He flopped on the bed like a dead fish. "If I did it too often, I'm not sure I'd live through it." When she reached out to tickle him, he quickly added, "On the other hand, it might be interesting to find out."

"Royal soldiers!" a rider bawled as he drove his worn horse up the steep streets of the town toward Vek Rud stronghold. "Royal soldiers, riding this way!"

Ice that had nothing to do with winter ran up Abivard's back when he heard that cry. In one way, he had been expecting it since the moment he managed to get Sharbaraz out of Nalgis Crag stronghold. In another, though, as with battle or with women, all the anticipation in the world wasn't worth a copper when set against reality.

As soon as the horseman rode into the courtyard, Abivard shouted, "Shut the gates!" The men in charge of them hurried to obey. The iron-fronted timbers clanged as they closed. A great bar, thick as a man's leg, thudded down behind them. "How many?" Abivard asked the rider.

"Twenty or thirty, maybe, lord," the fellow answered. "Wasn't any huge host, that much I'll say."

"Do you think a huge host follows?" Abivard persisted.

The rider gave him an exasperated glare. "Lord, begging your pardon, but how should I know? If I'd been fool enough to hang around to try and find out, odds are the buggers would have spotted me."

Abivard sighed. "You're right, of course. Go into the kitchens and grab yourself some bread and wine. Then get your bow out of its case and take your place on the wall with the rest of us."

"Aye, lord." The horseman hurried away. Abivard went up the stairs two at a time as he climbed to the walkway atop the wall and peered south. The day was cloudy and gloomy, with enough snow pattering down to ruin visibility. He muttered under his breath. Smerdis' men weren't coming quickly. After the news his retainer had shouted, he craved action.

Sharbaraz came up on the wall beside him. "I heard the alarm raised," the rightful King of Kings said. "What's toward?"

"We're about to have visitors," Abivard answered. "Just when or how many I can't say, but they're not the welcome sort."

"We knew this would happen," Sharbaraz said, biting his lip. "But Smerdis is moving faster than we thought, curse him. I hadn't looked to be penned in this stronghold before I had an army of my own strong enough to oppose the usurper."

"Yes." Abivard's voice was distracted. He pointed. "Do you think that's them, or is it only a flock?"

Sharbaraz squinted as he looked down along Abivard's out-stretched arm. "Your eyes must be better than mine. No, wait, I see what you're pointing at. Those aren't cattle or sheep, I fear. Those are horsemen."

"I think so, too." Abivard would have been surer on a sunny day, with light sparking off lanceheads and horse trappings and chainmail. But the purposeful way the distant specks kept moving north told him all he needed to know.

"There aren't that many of them," Sharbaraz said after a bit.

"No. The rider who brought word said it was a small band," Abivard said. "Seems he was right." He looked toward the approaching troop. "I don't see any more behind them, either."

"Nor I." Sharbaraz sounded indignant, as if he thought Smerdis wasn't playing the game by the rules. "What can he hope to do by sending a boy—no, an unweaned babe—in place of a man?"

"If I knew, I would tell you," Abivard answered. "We'll find out within the half hour, though, I expect."

The royal soldier reined in at the base of the knob atop which Vek Rud stronghold perched. Some of the folk who lived in the town on the knob had fled up to the stronghold before Abivard ordered the gates closed. The rest did their best to pretend they were invisible.

One warrior rode up toward the stronghold with a whitewashed shield upraised as a sign of truce. He called in a loud voice, "Is it true Sharbaraz son of Peroz has taken up residence here?"

Abivard recognized the voice a moment before he recognized the face. "None of your affair, Zal," he called back. "Whether the answer is yea or nay, d'you think I'd let you in here again after the way you used me the last time you saw the courtyard?"

Zal's grin was wide and unashamed. "I just followed the orders I was given. But I think I have a token that will buy my way in."

"Do you? I'll believe that when I see it."

"Good thing the weather is so cold," Zal remarked as he reached back to open a saddlebag. "Otherwise this would stink a lot worse than it does." The comment made no sense to Abivard until the royal officer held up by the hair a severed head that, as he had said, was less than perfectly fresh but that had until recently without a doubt adorned the shoulders of the famous Murghab.

Gulping a little, Abivard said, "You're trying to convince me you're for Sharbaraz, not against him?"

Beside him, Sharbaraz whispered, "Whose head is that?"

"It belonged to Smerdis' tax collector, the one who extorted eighty-five hundred arkets from me as tribute for the Khamorth," Abivard whispered back. He raised his voice and called to Zal, "How say you?"

"Of course I'm for his Majesty," Zal cried. "I served Smerdis just as you did, thinking Sharbaraz had truly given up the throne. Then my men and I ran into a courier who had word from Nalgis Crag that his Majesty—his genuine Majesty, I mean—had escaped from imprisonment. That put a whole new light on things. I got rid of the courier and then I got rid of this thing—" He held Murghab's head a little higher. "—but I saved enough to maybe convince you I'm no assassin in the night."

"You ran into a courier, you say?" Abivard answered. "If that's so, you've taken your own sweet time getting here."

Zal shook his graying head. "Not so, youngster. I was a long way south, heading back toward Mashiz myself, when the fellow caught up with me. My best guess is that Smerdis Pimp of Pimps still hasn't heard the real King of Kings is loose."

Abivard and Sharbaraz looked at each other. If that was so . . . "It can't last forever," Abivard said.

"No," Sharbaraz agreed. "But the God would turn his back on us in disgust if we didn't make the best use of it we could."

"Are you two going to spend the whole day blathering up there?" Zal demanded impatiently. "Or will you open up so I can come in and we can talk without lowing at one another like cattle on the plains?"

"Open the gates," Abivard called to the men who served them. To Zal he said, "Come ahead—but you alone, for the time being. I still remember what happened the last time you got men in my stronghold."

"I wish I could give you back your silver, but this thing—" Zal raised Murghab's head. "—had already sent it on to the treasury. Only way for you to get repaid now is to fight and win that treasury for yourself."

He rode through the gates as they opened. Archers on the wall and in the courtyard covered him. Abivard shifted nervously from foot to foot. The soldiers down at the bottom of the knob were all cased in iron, and so were their horses; the King of Kings—even if he was now Pimp of Pimps, as Zal had called him—could afford to keep a great host of smiths busy turning iron strips into wire and wire into rings. If they galloped up for all they were worth, they might get in before the gates slammed, and if they got in, no telling how much damage they would do.

"Your Majesty, it were wiser for you to stay on the wall or on the stairs higher than a lance can reach," Abivard said.

"Wiser some ways, maybe, but not others." Without another word, Sharbaraz hurried down the stairway. He had said—and Abivard had seen, to his and Makuran's dismay—that his father Peroz had tended to strike first and ask questions later. By that standard, Sharbaraz was very much his father's son.

Zal swung down from his horse; though far from young, he was still smooth and limber. Careless of the slush in the courtyard, and of his coat and the armor under it, he went down onto his belly before Sharbaraz, knocking his forehead against the cobblestones.

"Get up, man," Sharbaraz told him. "You're Zal son of Sintrawk, one of the senior guard captains out of Mashiz?"

"Aye, that's me, Majesty." Zal sounded impressed and surprised that Sharbaraz should know of him. Abivard was also impressed, but less surprised. He had already seen Sharbaraz's mastery of detail.

Sharbaraz said, "When word I live does get out, how many other officers will also rally to my call?"

"A good number, Majesty, a good number." Zal went on, "The God willing, enough so all you'll have to do about Smerdis is hunt him down and lop off his head as I did with the famous Murghab. Only trouble is, I don't know whether the God will be *that* willing."

"Always an interesting question, isn't it?" Sharbaraz turned to Abivard. "This is your stronghold, lord *dihqan*; I would not presume to order you in its administration. But do you judge that Zal's men may safely be admitted here?"

The turn had offered Sharbaraz's back to Zal. At first, that alarmed Abivard: it struck him as a foolish chance to take. Then he realized Sharbaraz had done it on purpose. That left him no less alarmed, but he admired the nerve of the rightful King of Kings. Zal made no move to snatch out the sword or dagger that hung from his belt.

Seeing him pass that test, Abivard said, "Very well, Majesty." He asked Zal, "Would you sooner summon them yourself, or shall I do it?"

"Let me," Zal said. "They're less likely to think it's some kind of trap that way. In fact, given how far off they are, why don't I just ride back to them and let them know all's well?"

Abivard felt a whole new set of qualms: what was to keep Zal and his heavily armored fighters from heading back to Mashiz? Hunting them down would not be easy. He shook his head—if he had to reach that far for worries, they weren't worth the reach. He nodded to Zal. The guard captain got back onto his horse and headed down the knob.

Abivard glanced over to Sharbaraz. The rightful King of Kings was not as calm as he looked; he fidgeted most unregally. That made Abivard nervous again, too. He wanted to say something like *This was your idea,* but he couldn't, not to his sovereign.

Zal was too far away for anyone in the stronghold to hear what he said to his men. The cheer the squadron raised, though, rang sweet in Abivard's ears. He felt himself grinning like a fool. A broad, relieved smile stretched over Sharbaraz's face, too. "We got away with it," he said.

"Looks that way," Abivard agreed, doing his best to sound casual.

The horsemen rode up through the town, singing loudly and discordantly. Abivard needed a little while to recognize the tune: a song in praise of the King of Kings. Sharbaraz pumped an excited fist in the air. "The truth brings men to my side," he exclaimed, and Abivard nodded.

"Here comes someone else," Frada said, pointing out toward the southwest.

"I see him," Abivard answered. "If Smerdis chose to hit us now, he'd bag most of the *dihqans* from the northwestern part of the realm."

"If Smerdis chose to hit us now, his army would desert," his younger brother said confidently. "How could it be otherwise? Now that everyone knows he's but a usurper—and now that the rightful King of Kings is free—who could want to fight for him? He'll be cowering in the palace at Mashiz, waiting for Sharbaraz to come and put him out of his misery."

"The God grant that you're right." Though he didn't want to detail them before Frada, Abivard had his doubts. The last time he had been sure something would work perfectly, he had been riding north with Peroz to settle the Khamorth once and for all. That had indeed worked . . . but not the way Peroz intended.

"Who comes?" one of the men at the gate called to the approaching noble and his retinue.

"Digor son of Nadina, *dihqan* of Azarmidukht Hills domain," came the reply.

"Welcome to Vek Rud domain, Digor of the Azarmidukht Hills," the guard replied. "Know that Sharbaraz King of Kings has declared Vek Rud stronghold a truce ground. No matter that you be at feud with your neighbor; if you meet him here, you meet him as a friend. So Sharbaraz has ordered; so shall it be."

"So shall it be," Digor echoed. Abivard couldn't tell whether the order angered him; he kept his voice quiet and his face composed. Unlike a lot of the nobles gathering here, he was neither unusually young nor unusually old. Either he hadn't gone onto the Pardrayan steppe or he had come away safe again.

Abivard took out a scrap of parchment, a jar of ink, and a reed pen. He inked the pen, lined through Digor's name, and replaced the writing paraphernalia. Frada smiled. "Our father would have approved," he said.

"What, that I'm keeping a list?" Abivard smiled, too, then pointed down to the mass of men who milled about in the courtyard. "I'd never manage to have all of them straight without it."

"It took Sharbaraz's summons to bring them all here," Frada said, "and it's taking Sharbaraz's truce call to keep 'em from yanking out swords and going at one another. Some of the feuds here go back to the days of the Prophets Four."

"I know," Abivard said. "I'd hoped, with so many new men heading domains, some of them could have been forgotten, but it doesn't look that way. As long as they hate Smerdis worse than their neighbors, we should do well enough."

"I hope you're right," Frada said. "How many more nobles do we expect to come?"

"Three, I think." Abivard consulted his parchment. "Yes, three, that's right."

"I don't think his Majesty is in the mood to wait for them much longer." Frada pointed back to the living quarters, where Sharbaraz stared from a window. He had been pacing restlessly for the past three days, ever since the northwestern *dihqans* started flooding into Vek Rud domain in response to his summons.

"Just as well, too," Abivard answered. "They're eating us out of house and home, and who knows how long they'll keep honoring the truce here? One knife comes out and everyone will remember all the blood feuds—and drag us into them. Our line has mostly stayed clear of such, but a murder or two on the grounds of Vek Rud stronghold would be plenty to keep our great-grandchildren watching their neighbors out of the corner of the eye."

"You're right about that," Frada said. "Getting into a feud is easy. Getting out of one again—" He shook his head.

Sharbaraz evidently chose that moment to decide he would wait no more for the few remaining sluggards. He came out of the living quarters and strode through the crowd in the courtyard toward the speaking platform Abivard's carpenters had built for him. He had on no gorgeous robe like the one Peroz had worn even on campaign, just a plain caftan of heavy wool and a conical helm with a spray of feathers for a crest. Even so, he drew men's notice as a lodestone draws chunks of iron. The aimless milling in the courtyard became purposeful as the assembled nobles turned toward the platform to hear what he would say.

Abivard and Frada hurried down from their place atop the wall.

By the time they began jockeying for a place from which to listen to the rightful King of Kings, they would have had to commit an assault, or rather several, to get a good one. Abivard did not bother. Unlike the rest of the *dihqans*, he had had the pleasure of Sharbaraz's company for some weeks, so he already had a good notion of what the rightful King of Kings was likely to say.

Sharbaraz drew his sword and waved it overhead. "My friends!" he cried. "Are we going to stay enslaved to the Khamorth on the one hand and on the other to the bloodsucking worm in Mashiz who drains us dry to make the nomads fat? *Are* we?"

"No!" The roar from the crowd echoed and reechoed off the stronghold's stone walls, filling the courtyard with tumult. Abivard felt his ears assailed from every direction.

"Are we going to let some wizened clerk defile with his stinking backside the seat that properly belongs to true men?" Sharbaraz shouted. "Or shall we take back what's ours and teach a lesson that will leave would-be traitors and usurpers shivering and sniveling a thousand years from now?"

"Aye!" This time the roar was louder.

Sharbaraz said, "By now you've no doubt heard how the usurper stole the throne—drugs in my supper. And you've likely had him rob you, saying he'd pay the Khamorth to stay on their own side of the Degird. Tell me, lords, have the cursed plainsmen stayed on their side of the Degird?"

"No!" Now it wasn't a roar, but a harsh cry of anger. Few along the border had not suffered from the nomads' raids.

Warming to his theme now that he had stirred his listeners, Sharbaraz went on, "So, lords, my friends, will you leave on the throne this wretch who stole it by treachery and who lies with every breath he takes, whose own officers began to desert him the moment his lies became clear?"

"No!" the crowd cried once more.

Before Sharbaraz could go on, Zal shouted to everybody, "And I'm not the only one who'll flee him as if he were the plague, now that the truth comes out. What honest man could wish to serve a liar?"

"None!" the assembled *dihqans* yelled, again with that note of fury baying in their voices. When a noble of Makuran gave his word, a man was supposed to be able to rely on it. How much more did that apply to the King of Kings?

"So what say you, lords?" Sharbaraz asked. "Do we ride south when the weather turns fine? We'll sweep all before us, ride into Mashiz in triumph, and set Makuran back on its proper course. I'll not deny, we shan't be able to deal at once with the Khamorth as they deserve, but we can keep them out of our land. And, by the God, once I'm on the throne we can settle scores with Videssos. If the easterners, may the God pitch them into the Void, hadn't incited the nomads against us, our brave warriors, my bold father, would yet live. Are you with me, then, in taking vengeance against the Empire and its false god?"

"Aye!" Abivard yelled as loudly as he could. Settling Videssos' arrogance had ranked high with his father. If Sharbaraz chose to lead that way, he would follow.

By the cries that rose around him, most of the *dihqans* felt as he did. The Khamorth were close, but to any man of Makuran, Videssos was *the* enemy. The nomads' confederacies scattered like pomegranate seeds when the fruit was stamped underfoot, now dangerous, now harmless. Videssos endured.

Sharbaraz plunged into the crowd. Men swarmed toward him, to pound him on the back, clasp his hand, pledge loyalty forever, and boast of the mincemeat they would make of any of Smerdis' men misguided enough to stand against them.

Caught up in the moment, Abivard and Frada pushed through the nobles toward the rightful King of Kings along with everyone else. Working as a team, they made good progress. "You know, we're foolish to be doing this," Frada said after an exchange of elbows with some noble from a hundred farsangs west of Vek Rud domain. "The King of Kings has been here a long time, and he'll stay longer still."

"True, but what of afterward?" Abivard said. "When the war is won, he'll go live in Mashiz and never leave save to go on campaign, and we'll likely end up back here."

"That doesn't have to be so, not when he's wed to our sister," Frada said. "We have his ear on account of that; we could make our own place at the capital."

Abivard grunted dubiously. "What would become of the domain, then? The king's favor—any king's favor, be he ever so good—waxes and wanes like the moon. Land goes on forever, and this land is ours."

Frada laughed out loud. "I listen to you, and it's as if Father were still here to sound like a sage."

"Ha!" Abivard said, pleased at the compliment and worried he couldn't live up to it. Whatever other reply he might have made turned into a hissed exclamation of pain when a *dihqan* with a beard braided into three strands stomped on his foot and shoved him aside. Frada caught the fellow with an elbow in the belly that folded him up like a fan. The two brothers grinned at each other.

Only a few nobles stood between them and Sharbaraz. Around the rightful King of Kings, moving at all was hard, for those who had already spoken with him were trying to get away, while those who still wanted to gain his ear pushed in at them. A couple of *dihqans* squeezed out between Abivard and Frada—and incidentally almost knocked over the fellow who had trampled Abivard's instep—letting them gain another couple of steps toward their sovereign.

Men came at Sharbaraz from all directions. Just standing before him did not mean you could speak with him, for *dihqans* also shouted at him from behind and both sides. He kept turning his head and twisting about like a man playing mallet and ball—wary lest an opponent clout him, not the ball, with his mallet.

When Abivard caught his eye at last, Sharbaraz threw his arms wide, as if to encompass the whole packed courtyard. "They're mine!" he cried. "We'll sweep Smerdis Pimp of Pimps—" He had zestfully stolen Zal's mocking title for his rival. "—out of Mashiz like a servant woman getting the dust from a storeroom. Once that's done, we'll turn on Videssos and—"

"Duck, your Majesty!" Abivard and Frada cried together. Sharbaraz might not have seen battle, but he had a warrior's reflexes. Without gaping or asking questions, he started to throw himself flat. That saved his life. The knife the man behind him wielded cut his robe and scored a bleeding line across his shoulder, but did not slide between his ribs to find his heart.

"The God curse you, curse your house, straight to the Void," the *dihqan* cried, drawing back his arm for another stab. The fellow beside him, horror on his face, seized it before he could bring it forward again. Abivard and Frada both leapt on the would-be assassin and wrestled him to the ground.

He fought like a man possessed, even after the nobles forced the knife from his hand. Only the weight of men on top of him finally made him quit by crushing the air from his lungs. Since most of those men were on top of Abivard, too, he struggled for every breath he took.

"Haul him up," Sharbaraz said when the *dihqan* was subdued. One at a time, the nobles who had piled onto him got off. Abivard and Frada clutched him and yanked him to his feet. When he started to try to break free, someone hit him in the pit of the stomach. That made him double up and cost him the wind he had just regained.

Sharbaraz had his right hand clapped to his left shoulder. Blood stained his robe and trickled out between his fingers. But the wound was at the top of the shoulder, and his left arm and hand worked; he had that hand clenched into a tight fist against the pain. Abivard dared hope the wound less than serious.

The rightful King of Kings stared at his attacker. "What did I do to you, Prypat, to deserve your knife in my back?" Even after narrowly escaping death, he remembered his assailant's name.

Prypat's face twisted. "Why shouldn't I kill you?" he said in hitching gasps. "Thanks to your cursed sire, my own father, my grandfather, all my elder brothers are ravens' fodder and wolves' meat, their gear plunder for the plainsmen. Every man here holds blood debt against you, did he but have the wit to see it."

Sharbaraz shook his head, then grimaced; the motion must have hurt. "Not so," he replied, as if arguing in court rather than passing judgment on the man who had tried to murder him. "My father acted as he thought best for Makuran. No man is perfect; the God holds that for himself. But the campaign did not fail through malice, nor did the King of Kings murder your kin. I grieve that they fell; I grieve that so many from all the realm fell. But my house incurred no blood debt on account of it."

"Lie all you like—my kin still lie dead," Prypat said.

"And you'll join them," someone cried to him. The *dihqans* snarled like angry dogs. Fear wasn't the least part of that, Abivard judged. Here they had come to Vek Rud stronghold to join Sharbaraz against Smerdis. Had Prypat killed Sharbaraz, the revolt against Mashiz would have died with him; none of the northwestern men had the force of character to make a King of Kings. But when Smerdis learned they had assembled here, he would have taken vengeance just the same. No wonder they were so ready to condemn Prypat out of hand.

Sharbaraz asked him, "Have you any reason I shouldn't order your head stricken off?" That in itself was a mercy. Anyone who tried to slay the King of Kings was liable to death with as much pain and ingenuity as his torturers could devise. But here as everywhere else, Sharbaraz was straightforward, direct, averse to wasting time.

Prypat tried to spit on him, then knelt and bent his head. "I die proud, for I sought to restore my clan's pride."

"Knifing a man in the back is nothing to be proud of." Blood still welled between Sharbaraz's fingers. He raised his voice to call to the nobles: "Who carries a heavy sword?"

Abivard did, but he hesitated, not eager to speak up. Killing a man in battle was one thing, killing him in cold blood—even if he was passionately eager to die—another. While Abivard tried to nerve himself, Zal beat him to it. "I do, your Majesty, and practice using it for justice, as well."

"Strike, then," Sharbaraz said. So did Prypat, at the same time. That seemed to nonplus the rightful King of Kings, but he took his right hand off his wound for a moment to beckon Zal forward. Prypat waited without moving as the officer came up, drew the sword, swung it up with both hands on the hilt, and brought it down. The stroke was clean; Prypat's head sprang from his shoulders. His body convulsed. Blood fountained over the cobbles for the few seconds his heart needed to realize he was dead.

"Dispose of the carrion, if you please," Sharbaraz said to Abivard. He swayed where he stood.

Abivard rushed to support him. "Here, come with me, Majesty," he said, guiding Sharbaraz back toward the living quarters. "We'd best learn how badly you're hurt."

Servants exclaimed in dismay when they saw what had happened. At Abivard's barked orders, they arranged pillows in the hallway just inside the entrance. "Let's lay you down, Majesty," Abivard said to Sharbaraz, who half squatted, half toppled down onto the cushions.

Without Abivard's asking for them, a serving woman fetched him a bowl of water and some rags. He made the tear in Sharbaraz's robe bigger so he could get a good look at the wound. Sharbaraz tried to twist his neck and look down the side of his face so he could see it, too. He succeeded only in making himself hurt worse. "How is it?" he asked Abivard, his voice shaky now that he didn't have to keep up a front for the assembled *dihqans*.

"Not as bad as I thought," Abivard answered. "It's long, aye, but not deep. And it's bled freely, so it's less likely to fester." He turned and, as he had hoped, found the serving woman hovering behind him. He told her, "Fetch me the wound paint—you know the one I mean." She nodded and hurried away.

"Will it hurt?" Sharbaraz asked, anxious as a boy with a barked shin.

"Not too much, Majesty, I hope," Abivard answered. "It's wine and honey and fine-ground myrrh. After I put it on, I'll cover the wound with grease and bandage you up. You should be all right if you don't try to do too much with that arm for the next few days." *I hope*, he added to himself. In spite of medicines, you never could tell what would happen when a man got hurt.

The serving woman returned, handing Abivard a small pot. As he worked the stopper free, she said, "Lord, the lady your sister—your Majesty's wife," she added, working up the nerve to speak to Sharbaraz, "wants to know what befell and how the King of Kings fares."

"Tell her I'm fine," Sharbaraz said at once.

"Word travels fast. Tell her he got cut but I think he'll be fine," Abivard said, a qualified endorsement. He upended the pot above Sharbaraz's shoulder. The medicine slowly poured out. Sharbaraz hissed when it touched the wound. "Bring me some lard before you go speak with Denak," Abivard told the serving woman. Again, she rushed to obey.

When Abivard had treated the cut to his satisfaction, he put a bandage pad on top of it and tied the pad in place with a rag that went around Sharbaraz's shoulder and armpit. The rightful King of Kings sighed to have the ordeal done, then said, "I find myself in your debt yet again."

"Nonsense, your Majesty." Abivard poured a cupful of red wine. "Drink this. The magicians say it builds blood, being like blood itself."

"I've heard that myself. I don't know whether it's true, but I'll gladly drink the wine any which way." Sharbaraz fit action to word. "By the God, that's better going down my throat than splashed on my shoulder." He thrust the cup back at Abivard. "I think I may have lost enough to need more building."

As Abivard poured again, the serving woman returned once more and said, "Your Majesty, lord, may it please the both of you, the lady Denak says she wants to see you as soon as may be—and if that's not soonest, she'll come out to do it."

Sharbaraz looked at Abivard. They both knew Denak was capable of doing just that, and both knew the scandal it would create among the *dihqans* would not help the rightful King of Kings' cause. Sharbaraz said, "Lady, tell my wife I shall see her directly in my chamber."

The serving woman beamed at being treated as if of noble blood. She trotted out of the kitchens yet again. Sharbaraz set his jaw and got to his feet. "Here, your Majesty, lean on me," Abivard said. "You don't want to start yourself bleeding hard again by trying to do too much."

"I suppose not," Sharbaraz said, although he didn't sound quite sure. But he put his right arm on Abivard's shoulder and let the *dihqan* take a good deal of his weight as they made their way down the halls of the living quarters to the chamber he was using as his own.

"Wait here," Abivard said when they reached it. "I'll be back with Denak fast as I can." Sharbaraz nodded and sank onto the bed with a groan he did his best to stifle. In spite of the fortifying wine, he looked very pale.

Denak stood impatiently tapping her foot at the door between Abivard's bedchamber and the women's quarters. "Took you long enough," she said when Abivard opened that door. "No talking around it now—how is he?"

"Wounded," Abivard answered. "He can still use the arm. If he heals properly, he should be fine but for the scar."

Denak searched his face. "You wouldn't lie to me? No, you wouldn't, not when I'll see for myself as fast as we can walk there—and would you walk a little faster, please?" In spite of her brittle tone, something eased in her step, in the set of her shoulders, with every step she took. As much to herself as to Abivard, she went on, "Life wouldn't be worth living without him."

Abivard didn't answer. Again, he wanted to take his sister in his arms and hold her to try to make her feel better, but Denak went hard as stone if anyone save Sharbaraz, man or woman, tried to embrace her. Without Sharbaraz's quick thinking, she would have reckoned her honor altogether lost and, without her honor, Abivard didn't think she cared to live. He thanked the God that she had been able to piece together as much of her life as she had.

When she saw Sharbaraz flat on the bed, his face the color of parchment, she gasped and swayed before visibly gathering herself. "What happened?" she demanded of him. "I've already heard three different tales."

"I don't doubt that." Sharbaraz managed a smile that was less than half grimace. "One of the *dihqans* decided I was to blame for what his clan suffered out on the steppe and reckoned to avenge himself on me. He had courage; I've never seen nor heard of a man's dying better after he failed."

His detached attitude won him no points from Denak. "He might have murdered you, and you're talking about how brave he was? It's a good thing he's dead. If he'd done what he set out to do—" Her voice all but broke. "I don't know what I would have done."

Sharbaraz sat up on the bed. Abivard would have pushed him back down, but Denak beat him to it. The ease with which he flattened out again told of the wound he had suffered. Still, his second attempt at a smile came closer to the genuine article than the first one had. He said, "I can afford to be generous, since I'm alive. If I were dead and he still lived, I'd be less forgiving."

Denak stared at him, then let out a strangled snort. "Now I begin to believe you'll get better. No dying man could make such foolish jokes."

"Thank you, my dear." Sharbaraz sounded a bit stronger, but he didn't try to rise again. He went on, "Your brother here put me in his debt three more times: by shouting a warning, by helping to wrestle the knifeman to the ground, and for his excellent doctoring. If I do pull through, it will be because of him."

"Your Majesty is too kind," Abivard murmured.

"No, he's not," Denak said. "If you acted the proper hero, the world should know of it. The *dihqans* will take word back to their domains, but we ought to put a minstrel to singing your praises, too."

"Do you know what Father would say if he heard you talking of such things?" Abivard said, flushing. "First he'd laugh till he cried, then he'd paddle your backside for having the crust to even think of paying a minstrel to praise me for something it was my duty to do."

Invoking Godarz usually ended an argument as effectively as slamming a door. This time, though, Denak shook her head. "Father was a fine *dihqan*, Abivard, none better, but he never involved himself in the affairs of the realm as a whole. You've gone from being an ordinary *dihqan* like him to a man close to the throne. You rescued Sharbaraz and you became his brother-in-law, all in the space of a day. When he takes back his throne, you think some *dihqans* and most *marzbans* won't resent you for an upstart? The more you show you deserve your place at his right hand, the likelier you are to keep it. Nothing wrong with praising the courage you really did show to help you build your fame."

Denak set hands on hips and looked defiance at Abivard. Before he could reply, Sharbaraz said, "She's right. The court works like the women's quarters, though it may be worse. What you are is not nearly so important as what people think you are, and what people think the King of Kings thinks you are."

Godarz had said things like that, most often with a sardonic gleam in his eye. Abivard had never expected to have to worry about them. Now he was hearing them from his sister, and in a position where he had to pay attention to her even if—and partly because—she was a woman. He remembered the talk he'd had with Frada not long before Prypat tried to knife Sharbaraz. He might want to ignore the intrigues of Mashiz, but they would not ignore him.

Sharbaraz said, "Brother-in-law of mine, one thing has to happen before you start worrying about such things."

"What's that?" Abivard asked.

"We have to win."

✦ VII

Spring painted the fields around Vek Rud Stronghold with a green that, while it wouldn't last long, was lovely to look at for the time being. So Abivard found it most years, at any rate. Not now. Turning to Frada, he said, "By the God, I'll be glad when we ride south tomorrow. Another fortnight of feeding the fighters and their horses and our storehouses would be empty. Our own folk will need food, too, especially if the harvest isn't a good one."

"Aye." Frada took a couple of paces along the walkway, kicking at the stone under his feet. "I wish I were coming with you when you ride. All I ever do, it seems, is get left behind."

"Don't complain about that," Abivard said sharply. "If you hadn't been left behind last summer, odds are you wouldn't be alive to whine about it now. We've been over this ground a thousand times. I have to ride with Sharbaraz, and that means you have to stay here and protect the domain from whatever comes against it, be that Smerdis' men, or Pradtak's, or the Khamorth."

Frada still looked mutinous. "At the start of winter, you were saying land was most important because it lasted. If that's so, you ought to stay here to watch the land while I go out and fight."

"I hadn't thought through the politics then," Abivard said, reluctant to admit Denak had played a big part in making him change his mind. "Smerdis will know by now the part I played in freeing Sharbaraz from Nalgis Crag stronghold. For better or worse, I rise and fall with the rightful King of Kings. If I'm not at his side, people will say it's because I'm afraid. I can't have that."

"How can anyone say you're afraid of anything when they're probably singing that new song about you in Videssos by now?"

Abivard's ears got hot. "The song's about you, too," he said feebly.

"No, it's not. My name's in it a time or three, but it's *about* you." Much to Abivard's relief, Frada didn't sound jealous. Such things would have torn apart some clans, but Godarz had made jealousy among his sons a sin to rank with blasphemy. Frada went on, "It'll be your way, of course. How can I deny you know more about what's best than I do? I just wish I could shove a lance into Smerdis myself."

"When we ride against Videssos, you'll have your chance," Abivard said. Frada nodded. Everyone would ride against Makuran's great enemy.

"Look—Sharbaraz has come out," Frada said, sticking an elbow into Abivard's ribs. "You'd better go down into the courtyard with him; you know as well as I do that Mother will pitch a fit if the ceremony doesn't come off perfectly."

"Right you are." Abivard went down the stone stairs and took his place alongside the rightful King of Kings. The last time the women of Vek Rud stronghold had come forth from their quarters was the summer before, when he had stood with his father and brother and half brothers; of them all, only he had got home alive. And now his mother and sister and half sisters and wives had to wish him good fortune as he set out on another campaign. A woman's life was anything but easy.

The door to the living quarters opened. Denak and Burzoe came out together, as they had before. This time, though, Denak preceded her mother as they walked toward the waiting men: as principal wife to the King of Kings, she held higher ceremonial rank than anyone merely of Vek Rud domain.

She nodded to Abivard, then passed him to take her place by Sharbaraz. Burzoe stood in front of Abivard. Her face, which had seemed calm at first glance, showed deep and abiding anger when he looked more closely. He scratched his head; could his mother be offended because Denak took precedence over her? It seemed out of character.

Behind Burzoe came Roshnani. Like Burzoe's, her face appeared calm until Abivard got a good look at it. Where his mother hid anger, though, his principal wife was trying to conceal—mirth? Excitement? He couldn't quite tell, and wondered what new convulsion had shaken the women's quarters to set Burzoe at odds with Denak—and with Roshnani, too, he saw, for his mother's fury plainly included both of them. Not wanting to borrow trouble, he didn't ask. He might find out, or the trouble might blow over without his ever learning what had gone wrong. He hoped it would.

Whatever it was, the rest of his wives and his young half sisters didn't look to know anything about it. They stared and chattered quietly among themselves, enjoying the chance to see something wider than the halls of the women's quarters. For them, this was a pleasant outing, nothing more.

Burzoe turned toward Denak. Her lips tightened slightly as she did so; maybe she *was* angry her daughter had usurped her place at the head of the ceremony. Abivard clicked his tongue between his teeth; he hadn't thought her so petty.

Denak said, "We are met here today to bid our men safety and good fortune as they travel off to war." Burzoe stirred but did not speak. Fury seemed to radiate from her in waves; had it been heat, Ganzak might have set her in the smithy in place of his furnace. Denak went on, "We shall surely triumph, for the God stretches forth her arms to protect those whose cause is just, as ours is."

A stir of applause ran through the men and women who listened to her. Abivard joined it, though he was not so convinced by what she said as he would have been before the previous summer. How had the God protected those who followed Peroz into Pardraya? The short answer was *none too well.*

Denak took a step back, beckoned to Burzoe. With exquisite grace, her mother prostrated herself before Sharbaraz. "The God keep you safe, Majesty," she said, and rose. She embraced Abivard. "The God watch over you, as she did before."

Words, gestures—all unexceptionable. What lay behind them . . . Abivard wished he could disrupt the ceremony to inquire of Burzoe. But custom inhibited him no less than it had Pradtak back at Nalgis Crag stronghold.

In her turn, Burzoe stepped back and nodded to Roshnani. Polite as usual, Roshnani nodded back, but her gaze went to Denak. Their eyes met. Suddenly scenting conspiracy, Abivard wondered what his sister and principal wife had cooked up between them. Whatever it was, his mother didn't like it.

As Burzoe had, Roshnani gave the King of Kings his ceremonial due and wished him good fortune. Then she hugged Abivard, tighter than decorum called for. He didn't mind—on the contrary. She said, "The God keep you safe from all danger."

"What I'll think about most is coming home to you," he answered. For some reason, that seemed to startle his principal wife, but she managed a smile in return.

Abivard walked down the line of waiting women, accepting the best wishes of his other wives and half sisters. If the God listened to a tenth of their prayers, he would live forever and be richer than three Kings of Kings rolled together.

His youngest half sister started back toward the living quarters. The procession that had emerged withdrew in reverse order, those who had come out first going in last. Soon Burzoe's turn came. She let out a scornful sniff and, her back stiff with pride, stalked away toward the open door of the living quarters.

Roshnani and Denak still stood in the courtyard.

Abivard needed perhaps longer than he should have to realize they didn't intend to go back to the women's quarters. "What are you doing?" His voice came out a foolish squeak.

Roshnani and Denak looked at each other again. Sure enough, the two of them had come up with a plot together. Denak spoke for them both. "My brother, my husband—" She turned to Sharbaraz. "—we are going to come with you."

"What, to fight? Are you mad?" Sharbaraz said.

"No, not to fight, Majesty, may it please you," Roshnani answered. "We would fight for you, the God knows, but we have not the skill and training to do it well; we would be more liability than asset. But every army has its baggage train. The minstrels are not in the habit of singing of it—it lacks glamour, when set beside those whose only duty is to go into battle—but they say enough for us to know it exists, and know an army would starve or run out of arrows without one. And we know one more wagon, a wagon bearing the two of us, would not slow the host, nor endanger your cause."

The rightful King of Kings gaped. He hadn't expected reasoning as careful as that of a courtier who'd had a tutor from Videssos, but then he hadn't truly made Roshnani's acquaintance till this moment. He started to say something, then stopped and sent Abivard a look of appeal.

"It's against all custom," Abivard said, the best argument he could come up with on the spur of the moment. To himself, he added, *It's also getting ahead of the promise I made you of more freedom to move around after the war with Smerdis was over.* He couldn't say that aloud, because he didn't want to admit he had made the promise. He did add, "No wonder Mother is furious at the two of you." If anyone embodied Makuraner propriety, Burzoe was that woman.

Roshnani bore up under the charge with equanimity; Burzoe was but her mother-in-law, to be respected, yes, but not the guardian of proper behavior since childhood. The accusation hit Denak harder, but she was the one who answered: "It was against propriety for Smerdis to steal the throne from him to whom it rightfully belongs. It was against custom for me, a woman, to set his rescue in motion." She looked down at the ground. Of necessity, she had done other things that went against custom, too, things that ate at her still despite the honor Sharbaraz had shown her. She did not speak of them in public, but the people among whom the argument centered knew what they were.

Sharbaraz said, "What possible good could the two of you bring that would outweigh not only setting custom aside but also setting men aside to protect you when the fighting starts?" When the King of Kings retreated from absolute rejection, Abivard knew the war was lost.

But it still had to be played out "You value our counsel when we are in a stronghold," Roshnani said. "Do we suddenly lose our wits when we're in the field? Abivard planned with both Denak and me—aye, and with his mother, too—before he left to set your Majesty free."

"Having the two of you along would scandalize the *dihqans* who back me," Sharbaraz said.

"I already told Roshnani as much," Abivard agreed.

"Enough to make them head back to their domains?" Denak said. "Enough to make them go over to Smerdis? Do you really believe that?" Her tone said she didn't, not for a moment. It also said she didn't think Sharbaraz did, either. She might not have known him long, but she had come to know him well.

"What would you say if I forbid it?" he asked.

Had he simply forbid it, that would have been that. Making it a hypothetical question was to Abivard another sign he would yield. It probably was for Denak, too, but she gave no hint of that, saying in a meek voice most unlike the one she usually used, "I would obey your Majesty, of course."

"A likely story," Sharbaraz said; he had come to know Denak, too. He turned to Abivard. "Well, brother-in-law of mine, what shall we do with 'em?"

"You're asking *me?*" Abivard said, appalled. "As far as I'm concerned, we can give them both gilded corselets and style 'em generals. My guess is that they'd do a better job than three quarters of the men you might name."

"My guess is that you're right." Sharbaraz shook his head. "My father would pitch a fit at this—he took only tarts on campaign, and not many of them—but my father is dead. I'm going to say aye to your sister, Abivard. What will you say to your wife?"

If you want to be stern and stodgy, go ahead, he seemed to mean. Abivard knew he couldn't get away with it, not if he wanted peace in the women's quarters ever again. He chose the most graceful surrender he could find: "Where you lead, Majesty, I shall follow."

Roshnani's face lit up like the summer sun at noon. "Thank you," she said quietly. "A chance at seeing the world tempts me to do something most publicly indecorous to show how grateful I am."

"You and Denak have already been indecorous enough for any three dozen women I could think of," Abivard growled in his severest tones. His principal wife and sister hung their heads and looked abashed. Why not? They had won what they wanted.

Abivard started to scold them some more, but then got to wondering whether something publicly indecorous might not be privately enjoyable. That distracted him enough that the scolding never got delivered.

In the saddle and southbound . . . Abivard rode joyfully toward civil war. The rightful King of Kings rode at his side, on a horse from his stables. A good copy of the lion banner of Makuran floated at the fore of Sharbaraz's host.

Warriors rode by clan, each man most comfortable with comrades from the same domain. Abivard worried about how well they would fight as a unit, but reflected that Peroz's army, which had ridden forth against the Khamorth, was no more tightly organized, which meant Smerdis' troops weren't likely to be, either.

When he remarked on that, Sharbaraz said, "No, I don't expect them to be. If we were riding against Videssians, I'd worry about how loose-jointed our arrangements are, but they won't hurt us against our own countrymen."

"How are the Videssians different?" Abivard asked. "I've heard endless tales of them, but no two the same."

"My guess is that that's because of how different they are," Sharbaraz answered seriously. "They care nothing for clans when they fight, but go here and there in big blocks to the sound of their officers' horns and drums. They might as well be so many cups on the rim of a water wheel or some other piece of machinery. They take discipline better than our men, that's certain."

"Why don't they sweep everything before them, then?" Abivard asked; the picture Sharbaraz had painted was an intimidating one.

"Two main reasons," the rightful King of Kings answered. "First, they prefer the bow to the lance, which means a strong charge into their midst will often scatter 'em. And second and more important, they may have discipline, but they don't have our fire. They fight as if to win points in a game, not for the sake of it, and often they'll yield or flee where we might go on and win."

Abivard filed the lore away in his mind. He was building himself a picture of the foes he had never seen, against the day when Makuran's internal strife ended and Sharbaraz would begin to settle scores. Much of the Empire of Videssos bordered the sea. Abivard wondered if he would meet the third part of Tanshar's prophecy there.

No way to know that but to await the day. He glanced back toward the baggage train, where Tanshar rode with several other fortune-tellers and wizards their lords had brought with the warriors. Abivard wondered if the men could ward the army against the more polished magicians Smerdis might gather from Mashiz. He was glad to have Tanshar along; every familiar face was welcome.

Also traveling with the baggage train was a wagon that carried not wheat or smoked mutton or hay for the horses or arrows neatly tied in sheaves of twenty to fit into quivers and bowcases but his sister, his principal wife, and a couple of serving women from Vek Rud stronghold. He had nothing but misgivings about the venture, but hoped it would turn out well—or not too disastrously.

For the time being, the horses were not eating much of the fodder the army had brought along for them. In spring, even the dun land between oases and rivers took on a coat of green. Soon the sun would bake it dry again, but the animals could graze and nibble while it lasted.

That was as well, for Sharbaraz's host swelled with every new domain it approached. Horsemen flocked to his banner, calling down curses on Smerdis' usurping gray head. When yet another such contingent rode in, Abivard exclaimed to Sharbaraz, "Majesty, this is no campaign, just a triumphal procession."

"Good," Sharbaraz answered. "We threw away too many lives against the plainsmen last summer; we can't afford to squander more in civil war, lest winning prove near as costly as losing. We still need to protect ourselves from our foes and take vengeance on them. In fact, I've even sent a rider on ahead to Smerdis to tell him I'll spare his worthless life if he gives up the throne without a fight."

Abivard weighed that, nodding. "I think you did well. He never showed ambition till the once, and you'd watch him so close, he'd never get another chance."

"Wouldn't I?" Sharbaraz said. "He couldn't sit his arse down in the backhouse without an eye on him."

But before Sharbaraz formally heard from his rival for the throne, he got his answer another way. Off to the east, the snowcapped peaks of the Dilbat Mountains showed the way southward; the army would have to skirt them and then come back up on the far side of the range to approach Mashiz. Already the weather was noticeably hotter than Abivard would have expected so early in the season.

A scout came galloping back toward the main body of Sharbaraz's host, shouting "There's troopers up ahead looking for a fight. They shot enough arrows at me to make a good-size tree; the God's own mercy I wasn't pincushioned."

"Looking for a fight, are they?" Sharbaraz said grimly. "I think we shall oblige them."

Horns blared; drums thudded. From what Sharbaraz had

said to Abivard, that would have been plenty to move units of
a Videssian army as if they were pieces going from square to
square on a gameboard. Abivard wished his countrymen were
as smooth. Zal and his squadron of ironclad professionals came
forward front and center, to form the spearhead of the force.
Despite martial music and endless shouts both from their own
dihqans and from the officers Sharbaraz had appointed, most of
the rest of the warriors, at least to Abivard's jaundiced eye, did
more milling about than forming.

But by the time he saw dust ahead, the host had shaken itself
out into a battle line of sorts. Zal shouted frantically at anyone
who would listen. The only trouble was, next to nobody listened.
A raw army with raw officers wouldn't win battles by discipline
and maneuver. Courage and fury and numbers would have to
do instead.

Okhos rode by, his fuzz-bearded face alight with excitement.
He drew his sword and flourished it to Abivard; he almost cut
off the ear of the man next to him, but never noticed. Roshnani's
younger brother said, "We'll slaughter them all and wade in their
blood!"

Minstrels sang such verses when they wandered from stronghold
to stronghold, hoping to cadge a night's supper on the strength
of their songs. Grown men who knew war smiled at them and
enjoyed the poetry without taking it seriously. Trouble was, Okhos
wasn't a grown man; he had fewer summers behind him than
Frada. Minstrels' verses were all he knew of the battlefield, or
had been until the Khamorth started raiding his domain.

Then Abivard stopped worrying about how his brother-in-law
would fare and started worrying about himself. On across the flat
ground came Smerdis' army, growing closer faster than Abivard
would have thought possible. At their fore flew the lion banner
of Makuran. Beside Abivard, Sharbaraz murmured, "The curse of
civil war: both sides bearing the same emblem."

"Aye," Abivard said, though that was more philosophical than
he felt like being with battle fast approaching. "Well, if they don't
see for themselves that they picked the wrong man to follow,
we'll have to show them." The oncoming troops seemed resolute
enough. Abivard filled his lungs and shouted defiance at them:
"Sharbaraaaz!"

In an instant, the whole host took up the cry. It drowned in a cacophony of hatred whatever signals officers and musicians were trying to give. At last the nobles of the northwest and their retainers had a chance to come to grips with the man who had not only stolen the throne but stolen their money and given it to the barbarians who had killed their kin—without keeping those barbarians off their lands afterward as promised.

Inevitably, an answering cry came back: "Smerdis!" As inevitably, it sounded effete and puny to Abivard, who was less than an unbiased witness. He wondered how men could still lay their lives on the line for a ruler who had proved himself both thief and liar.

However they managed it, support Smerdis they did. Arrows began to fly; lanceheads came down in a glittering wave. Abivard picked a fellow in the opposite line as a target and spurred his horse into a full gallop. "Sharbaraz!" he yelled again.

The two armies collided with a great metallic clangor. Abivard's charge missed its man; he had swerved aside to fight someone else. A lance glanced off Abivard's shield. He felt the impact all the way up to his shoulder. Had the hit been squarer, it might have unhorsed him.

A lancer's main weapon was the force he could put behind his blow from the weight and speed of his charging horse. With that momentum spent after the first impact, the battle turned into a melee, with riders stabbing with lances, slashing with swords, and trying to use their horses to throw their foes' mounts—and their foes—off balance for easy destruction.

Sharbaraz fought in the middle of the press, laying about him with the broken stub of a lance. He clouted an enemy in the side of the head. The fellow was wearing a helm, but the blow stunned him even so. Sharbaraz hit him again, this time full in the face. Dripping blood, he slid out of the saddle, to be trampled if he still lived after those two blows. Sharbaraz shouted in triumph.

Abivard tried to fight his way toward his sovereign. If the rightful King of Kings went down, the battle, even if a victory, would still prove a final defeat. He had tried to talk Sharbaraz out of fighting in the front ranks—as well tell the moon not to go from new to full and back again as to have him listen.

An armored warrior who shouted "Smerdis!" got between Abivard and the King of Kings. The soldier must have lost his lance or had it break to pieces too small to be useful, for he hacked at the shaft of Abivard's lance with his sword. Sparks flew as the blade belled against the strip of iron that armored the shaft against such misfortune.

Abivard drew back the lance and thrust with it. The enemy ducked and cut at it again. By then they were almost breast to breast. Abivard tried to smash the fellow in the face with the spiked boss to his shield. A moment later he counted himself lucky not to get similarly smashed.

He and Smerdis' follower cursed and strained and struggled until someone—Abivard never knew who—slashed the other fellow's horse. When it screamed and reared, Abivard speared its rider. He screamed, too, and went on screaming after Abivard yanked out the lance. His cry of agony was all but lost among many others—and cries of triumph, and of hatred—that dinned over the battlefield.

"I wonder how this fight is going," Abivard muttered. He was too busy trying to stay alive to have much feel for the course of the action as a whole. Had he advanced since his charge ended, or had he and Sharbaraz's men given ground? He couldn't tell. Just getting back up with the rightful King of Kings seemed hard enough at the moment.

When he finally made it to the King of Kings' side, Sharbaraz shouted at him: "How fare we?"

"I hoped you knew," Abivard answered in some dismay.

Sharbaraz grimaced. "This isn't as easy as we hoped it would be. They aren't falling all over themselves to desert, are they?"

"What did you say, Majesty?" Abivard hadn't heard all of that; he had been busy fending off one of Smerdis' lancers. Only when the fellow sullenly drew back could he pay attention once more.

"Never mind," Sharbaraz told him. By now, the King of Kings' lance was long gone; his sword had blood on the blade. For one of the rare times since Abivard had known him, he looked unsure what to do next. The stubborn resistance Smerdis' men were putting up seemed to baffle him.

Then, just as he was starting to give orders for another push against the foe, wild, panic-filled shouts ripped through the left wing of Smerdis' army. Some men were crying "Treason!" but more yelled "Sharbaraz!" They turned on the warriors still loyal to Smerdis and attacked them along with Sharbaraz's soldiers.

With its left in chaos, Smerdis' army quickly unraveled. Men at the center and right, seeing their position turned, either threw down their weapons and surrendered or wheeled in flight. Here and there, stubborn rearguard bands threw themselves away to help their comrades escape.

"Press them!" Sharbaraz cried. "Don't let them get away." Now that striking hard had been rewarded, he was back in his element, urging on his warriors to make their victory as complete as they could.

For all his urging, though, a good part of Smerdis' army broke free and fled south. His own force had fought too hard through the morning to make the grinding pursuit that might have destroyed the enemy for good and all.

At last, he seemed to realize that and broke off the chase. "If I order them to do something they can't, next time they may not listen to me when I tell them to do something they can," he explained to Abivard.

"We did have a solid victory there," Abivard answered.

"It's not what I wanted," Sharbaraz said. "I had in mind to smash the usurper's men so thoroughly no one would think of standing against me after this. Just a victory isn't enough." Then he moderated his tone. "But it will have to do, and it's ever so much better than getting beat."

"Isn't that the truth?" Abivard said.

Sharbaraz said, "I want to question some of the men we caught who fought so hard against us: I want to learn how Smerdis managed to keep them loyal after they learned I hadn't given up my throne of my own free will. The sooner I find out, the sooner I can do something about it."

"Aye," Abivard said, but his voice was abstracted; he had only half heard the rightful King of Kings. He was looking over the field and discovering for the first time the hideous flotsam and jetsam a large battle leaves behind. He had not seen the aftermath of the fight on the Pardrayan steppe; he had fled to keep from becoming part of it. The other fights in which he had joined were only skirmishes. What came after them was like this in kind, but not in degree. The magnitude of suffering spread out over a farsang of ground appalled him.

Men with holes in them or faces hacked away or hands severed or entrails spilled lay in ungraceful death amid pools of blood already going from scarlet to black, with flies buzzing around them and ravens spiraling down from the sky to peck at their blindly staring eyes and other dainties. The battlefield smelled something like a slaughterhouse, something like a latrine.

The crumpled shapes of dead horses cropped up here and there amid the human wreckage. Abivard pitied them more than the soldiers; they hadn't had any idea why they died.

But worse than the killed, men or beasts, were the wounded. Hurt horses screamed with the terrible sopranos of women in agony. Men groaned and howled and cursed and wailed and wept and bled and tried to bandage themselves and begged for aid or their mothers or death or all three at once and crawled toward other men whom they hoped would help them. And other men, or jackals who walked on two legs, wandered over the field looking for whatever they could carry away and making sure that none of those they robbed would live to avenge themselves.

Still others, to their credit, did what they could for the injured, stitching, bandaging, and setting broken bones. A couple of the village wizards had healing among their talents. They could treat wounds that would have proved fatal save for their aid, but at terrible cost to themselves. One of them, his hands covered with the blood of a man he had just brought back from the brink of death, got up from the ground where he had knelt, took a couple of steps toward another wounded warrior, and pitched forward onto his face in a faint.

"Looking at this, I wish we hadn't brought our wives," Abivard said. "Even if they don't picture us among the fallen, they'll never be easy in their minds about the chances of war."

Sharbaraz looked back toward the baggage train, which lay well to the rear of the actual fighting. That distance seemed to ease his mind. "It will be all right," he said. "They can't have seen too much." Abivard hoped he was right.

The prisoner wore only ragged linen drawers. One of Sharbaraz's followers who had started the day in boiled leather—or perhaps in just his caftan—now had a fine suit of mail from the royal armories. The captured warrior held a dirty rag around a cut on his arm. He looked tired and frightened, his eyes enormous in a long, dark face.

Realizing who Sharbaraz was frightened him even more. Before the guards who had manhandled him into Sharbaraz's presence could cast him down to the ground, he prostrated himself of his own accord. "May your years be long and your realm increase, Majesty," he choked out.

Sharbaraz turned to Abivard. "He says that now," the rightful King of Kings observed. "This morning, though, he'd cheerfully have speared me out of the saddle."

"Amazing what a change a few hours can bring," Abivard agreed.

The prisoner ground his face into the dust. "Majesty, forgive!" he wailed.

"Why should I?" Sharbaraz growled. "Once you knew I'd not abandoned my throne of my own free will, how could you have the brass to fight against me?"

"Forgive!" the prisoner said. "Majesty, I am a poor man, and ignorant, and I know nothing save what my officers tell me. They said I give you their very words, by the God I swear it—they said you had indeed given up the throne of your own accord, and then wickedly changed your mind, like a woman who says 'I want my red shoes. No, my blue ones.' They said you could not go back on an oath you swore, that the God would not smile on Makuran if you seized the rule. Now, of course, I see this is not so, truly I do." He dared raise his face a couple of inches to peer anxiously at Sharbaraz.

"Take him away, back with the others," Sharbaraz told the guards. They hauled the prisoner to his feet and dragged him off. The rightful King of Kings let out a long, weary sigh and turned to Abivard. "Another one."

"Another one," Abivard echoed. "We've heard—what?—six now? They all sing the same song."

"So they do." Sharbaraz paced back and forth, kicking up dirt. "Smerdis, may he drop into the Void this instant, is more clever than I gave him credit for. This tale of my renouncing my oath of abdication may be a lie from top to bottom, but it gives those who believe it a reason to fight for him and against me. I thought his forces would crumble at the first touch, like salt sculptures in the rain, but it may prove harder than that."

"Aye," Abivard said mournfully. "If that one band hadn't gone over to you, we might still be fighting—or we might have lost."

"This had crossed my mind," Sharbaraz admitted, adding a moment later, "however much I wish it hadn't." He sighed again.

"I want pocket bread filled with raisins and cheese and onions, and I want a great huge cup of wine. Then I'll show myself to Denak, so she'll know I came through alive and well. But what I want most is a good night's sleep. I've never been so worn in my life; it must be the terror slowly leaking out of me."

"Your Majesty, those all strike me as excellent choices," Abivard said, "though I'd sooner have sausage than raisins with my onions and cheese."

"We may just be able to grant you so much leeway," Sharbaraz said. Both men laughed.

Roshnani said, "Almost I wish I'd stayed back at the stronghold. What war truly is doesn't look much like what the minstrels sing of." Her eyes, which looked larger than they were in the dim lamplight of Abivard's tent, filled with horror at what she had seen and heard. "So much anguish—"

I told you so, bubbled up in Abivard's mind. He left the words unsaid. They would have done no good in any case. He couldn't keep his principal wife from seeing what she had seen now that she was here, and he couldn't send her back to Vek Rud domain. Godarz would have said something like, *Now that you've mounted the horse, you'd better ride it.*

Since he couldn't twit her, he said, "I'm glad your brother only took a couple of small cuts. He'll be fine, I'm sure."

"Yes, so am I," Roshnani said, relief in her voice. "He was so proud of himself when he came back to see me yesterday after the battle, and he looked as if he'd enjoyed himself in the fighting." She shook her head. "I can't say I understand that."

"He's young yet," Abivard said. "I thought I'd surely live forever, right up till the moment things went wrong on the steppe last year."

Roshnani reached out to set a hand on his arm. "Women always know things can go wrong. We wonder sometimes at the folly of men."

"Looking back, I wonder at some of our folly, too," Abivard said. "Thinking Smerdis' men would give up or go over to us without much fight, for instance. The war will be harder than we reckoned on when we set out from the stronghold."

"That's not what I meant," Roshnani said in some exasperation. "The whole idea . . . Oh, what's the use? I just have to hope we win the fight and that you and Okhos and Sharbaraz come through it safe."

"Of course we will," Abivard said stoutly. The groans of the wounded that pierced the wool tent cloth like arrows piercing flesh turned his reassurances to the pious hopes they were.

Roshnani didn't say that, not with words. She was not one who sought to get her way by nagging her husband until he finally yielded. Abivard's will was as well warded against nagging as Nalgis Crag stronghold against siege. But something—he could not have said precisely what—changed in her face. Perhaps her eyes slipped from his for a moment at a particularly poignant cry of pain. If they did, he didn't notice, not with the top of his mind. But he did come to know he had done nothing to allay her fears.

He was irked to hear how defensive he sounded as he continued, "Any which way, what we stand to gain is worth the risk. Or would you sooner live under Smerdis and see all our arkets flow across the Degird to the nomads?"

"Of course not," she said at once; she was a *dihqan's* daughter. Now he recognized the expression she wore: calculation, the same sort he would have used in deciding if he wanted to pay a horsetrader's price for a four-year-old gelding. "If the three of you live and we win, then you're right. But if any of you falls, or if we lose, then you're not. And since you and Sharbaraz and Okhos are all right at the fore—"

"Would you have us hang back?" Abivard demanded, flicked on his pride.

"For my sake, for your own sake, indeed I would," Roshnani answered. Then she sighed. "If you did, though, that would make the army lose spirit, which would in turn make you likelier to be hurt. Finding the right thing to do isn't always easy."

"We chased that rabbit round the bush when we were talking about how—or if—you'd be able to come out of the women's quarters." Abivard laughed. "After a while, you quit chasing—you jumped over the bush and squashed poor bunny flat, or how else did you and Denak get to come along with the host?"

Roshnani laughed, too. "You take it with better will than I thought you would. Most men, I think, would still be angry at me."

"What's the point to that?" Abivard said. "It's done, you've won,

and now I try to make the best I can of it, just as I did when I
came back from the steppe last summer."

"Hmm," Roshnani said. "I don't think I fancy being compared
to the Khamorth. And you didn't lose a battle to me, because
you'd already said you were giving up the war."

"I should hope so," Abivard said. "You and Denak outgeneraled
me as neatly as the plainsmen bested Peroz."

"And what of it?" Roshnani asked. "Has the army gone to pieces
because of it? Has one *dihqan*, even one warrior with no armor,
no bow, and a spavined nag, gone over to Smerdis because Denak
and I are here? Have we turned the campaign into a disaster for
Sharbaraz?"

"No and no and no," Abivard admitted. "We might have done
better with the two of you commanding our right and left wings.
I don't think the officers we had out there distinguished themselves."

He waited for Roshnani to use the opening he had given her
to tax him about the iniquities and inequities of the women's
quarters and to get him to admit how unjust they were. She did
nothing of the kind, but asked instead about how the wounded
were faring. Only later did he stop to think that, if her arguments
sprang to life in his mind without her having to say a word, she
had already won a big part of the battle.

The farther south and east Sharbaraz's army advanced, the
more Abivard had the feeling he was not in the Makuran he had
always known. The new recruits who rallied to Sharbaraz's banner spoke with what he thought of as a lazy accent, wore caftans
that struck his eye as gaudy, and irked him further by seeming
to look down on the men who had originally favored the rightful
King of Kings as frontier bumpkins. That caused fights, and led
to the sudden demise of a couple of newcomers.

But when Abivard complained about the southerners' pretensions,
Sharbaraz laughed at him. "If you think these folk different, my
friend, wait till you make the acquaintance of those who dwell
between the Tutub and the Tib, in the river plain called the land
of the Thousand Cities."

"Oh, but they aren't Makuraners at all," Abivard said, "just our
subjects."

Sharbaraz raised an eyebrow. "So it may seem to a man whose

domain lies along the Degird. But Mashiz, remember, looks out over the Land of the Thousand Cities. The people who live down in the plain are not of our kind, true, but they help make the realm what it is. Many of our clerks and record keepers come from among them. Without such, we'd never know who owed what from one year to the next."

Abivard made a noise that said he was less than impressed. Had anyone but his sovereign extolled the virtues of such bureaucrats, he would have been a good deal cruder in his response.

Perhaps sensing that, Sharbaraz added, "They also give us useful infantry. You'll not have seen that, because they're of no use against the steppe nomads, so Kings of Kings don't take them up onto the plateau of Makuran proper. But they're numerous, they make good garrison troops, and they've given decent service against Videssos."

"For that I would forgive them quite a lot," Abivard said.

"Aye, it does make a difference," Sharbaraz agreed. "But I'll be less fond of them if they give decent service against me."

"Why would they do that?" Abivard asked. "You're the proper King of Kings. What on earth would make them want to fight for Smerdis and not for you?"

"If they believe the lie about my renouncing my renunciation, that might do it," Sharbaraz answered. "Or Smerdis might just promise more privileges and fewer taxes for the land of the Thousand Cities. That might be enough by itself. They've been under Makuran a long time, because we're better warriors, but they aren't truly *of* Makuran. Most of the time, that doesn't matter. Every once in a while, it jumps up and bites a King of Kings in the arse."

"What do we do about it?" Abivard knew he sounded worried. He had learned about some of what Sharbaraz had mentioned, but till this moment dust had lain thick over what he had studied. Now he saw it really mattered.

Sharbaraz reached out and set a hand on his shoulder. "I didn't mean to put you in a tizzy. I've sent men on to the valleys of the Tutub and the Tib. I can match whatever promises Smerdis makes, however much I'd rather not. And infantry is only so much good against horsemen. Men afoot move slowly. Often they don't get to where they're needed—and even if they do, you can usually find a way around them."

"I suppose so. I know about as much of the art of fighting against infantry as I do of the usages of Videssos' false priests."

"No, you wouldn't have the need, not growing up where you did." Sharbaraz chewed on his mustache. "By the God, I don't want the war against Smerdis to drag on and on. If the northwest frontier stays bare too long, the nomads *will* swarm across in force, and driving them back over the Degird will mean we can't give the Empire the time and attention it deserves."

Abivard didn't reply right away. It wasn't that he disagreed with anything Sharbaraz had said. But his concern with nomads over the border had little to do with what that would mean for the grand strategy of Makuran. He worried about what would happen to his domain: to the flocks and the folk who tended them, to the *qanats* and the farmers who used their waters to grow grain and nuts and vegetables, and most of all to Vek Rud stronghold and his brother and mother and wives, his half brothers and half sisters. Strongholds rarely fell to nomads—up in the northwest they were made strong not least to hold out the Khamorth—but it had happened. Being a worrier by nature, Abivard had no trouble imagining the worst.

Sharbaraz gave a squeeze with that hand on his shoulder. "Don't fret so, brother-in-law of mine. Frada strikes me as able and more than able. Vek Rud domain will still be yours when you go home wreathed in victory."

"You ease my mind," Abivard said, which was true. To him, Frada had seldom been more than a little brother, sometimes a pest, rarely anyone to take seriously. That had changed some after Frada's whiskers sprouted, and more after Abivard came back from the Pardrayan steppe. Still, hearing the rightful King of Kings praise his younger brother made him glow with pride.

But going home wreathed in victory? First there was Smerdis to beat, and then the Khamorth, and after them Videssos. And after Videssos had at last been punished as it deserved, who could say what new foes would have arisen, perhaps in the uttermost west, perhaps on the plains once more?

"Majesty," Abivard said with a laugh that sounded shaky even to him, "with so much fighting yet to do, only the God knows when I'll ever see home again."

"So long as we keep winning, you shall one day," Sharbaraz answered, with which Abivard had to be content.

He was doing his best not to think about the consequences of defeat when scouts came riding in with word of an army approaching from the south. Horns blared. Sharbaraz's forces, aided by officers who now had one battle's worth of experience more than they had enjoyed before, began the complicated business of shifting from line of march into line of battle.

Sharbaraz said, "If the usurper and his lackeys will not tamely yield, I shall have to rout them out. With comrades like you, Abivard, I know we'll succeed."

Such talk warmed Abivard—for a moment. After that, he was too busy to stay warm. His first automatic glance was toward the rear, to make sure the baggage train kept out of harm's way . . . and kept Roshnani and Denak safe with it. That taken care of, he started shouting orders of his own. One thing he had seen was that Sharbaraz did not care for close companions who were nothing but companions: the rightful King of Kings expected his followers to be able to lead, as well.

As he helped position Sharbaraz's riders, Abivard also scanned the southern skyline for the cloud of dust that would announce the coming of Smerdis' warriors. Soon enough—too soon to suit him—he spied it, a little farther east than he had expected from what the scouts had said. That gave him an idea.

He had to wait for Sharbaraz to stop barking orders of his own. When he gained his sovereign's ear, he pointed and said, "Suppose we position a band behind that high ground? By the direction from which the enemy approaches, they may not spot our men till too late."

Sharbaraz considered, working his jaws as he chewed on the notion as if it were so much flatbread. Then, with the abrupt decision that marked him, he nodded. "Let it be as you say. Take a regiment and wait there for the right moment. Two long horn calls and one short will be your signal."

"You want *me* to lead the regiment?" To his dismay, Abivard's voice rose in a startled squeak.

"Why not?" Sharbaraz answered impatiently. "The idea's yours, and it's a good one. You deserve the credit if it succeeds. And if you fought at my right hand in the last battle, you can lead a regiment on your own in this one."

Abivard gulped. The most men he had directly commanded at any one time was the couple of dozen he had led against

Khamorth raiders not long before he found out Pradtak was holding Sharbaraz captive. But to say that would be to lose face before the King of Kings. "Majesty, I'll do my best," he managed, and went off to gather his men.

Some of the officers he ordered to shift position gave him distinctly jaundiced looks. They were professionals who had left Smerdis' force for Sharbaraz's. As far as they were concerned, what was he but a frontier *dihqan* of uncertain but dubious quality? The answer to that, however, was that he was also the King of Kings' brother-in-law. So, however dubious they looked, they obeyed.

"We wait for the signal," Abivard told the troopers as he led them into the ambush position. "Then we burst out and take the usurper's men in flank. Why, the whole battle could turn on us."

The horsemen buzzed excitedly. Unlike their skeptical captains, they seemed eager to follow Abivard. Of course, a lot of them came out of northwestern domains, too. Those men weren't polished professionals; they were here because their *dihqans*—and they themselves—wanted to overthrow Smerdis and restore Sharbaraz to his rightful place. Did enthusiasm count for more than professionalism? Abivard hoped so.

He had taken his contingent well behind the low swell of ground he had spotted, the better to conceal it from Smerdis' advancing men. The only problem was, that also meant Abivard and his followers couldn't see the first stages of the fighting. He hadn't worried about that till it was too late to do anything about it without giving away his position.

He hoped sound would do what sight could not: show him how the battle was going. But that proved less easy to gauge than he had expected. He could tell by the racket where the fighting was heaviest, but not who had the advantage at any given spot. He shifted nervously in the saddle until his horse caught his unease and began snorting and pawing at the ground.

The men he led were just as anxious as the animal. "Let us go, Lord Abivard," one of them called. "Hurl us against the usurper!"

Others echoed that, but Abivard shook his head. "We wait for the signal," he repeated, thinking, *Or until I'm sure the battle's swung against us.* That would be time to do what he could. For the warriors, though, he added, "If we move too soon, we give away the advantage of the ambush."

He hoped that would hold them. They twitched every time a horn sounded—and so did he. Sooner or later, they would burst from cover no matter what he did to hold them back. He felt worthless—Sharbaraz would see he wasn't suited to command after all.

Blaaart. Blaaart. Blart. A shiver ran through Abivard. Now the waiting regiment could move, and he would still seem to be in control of it. "Forward!" he shouted. "We'll show Smerdis the proper punishment for trying to steal the throne. The cry is—"

"Sharbaraz!" burst from a thousand throats. Abivard dug his heels into his horse's sides. The beast squealed, half with rage at him and half with relief at being allowed to run at last. It went from walk to trot to gallop as fast as any animal Abivard had ever ridden. Even so, he was hard pressed to stay at the head of the regiment.

"Sharbaraz!" the riders cried again as they burst from concealment. Abivard stared, quickly sizing up the battle. On this wing, Smerdis' men had driven Sharbaraz back a couple of furlongs. Abivard couched his lance and thundered at the enemy.

It worked, he thought exultantly. Startled faces turned to stare at him in dismay while shouts of alarm rang out among Smerdis' followers. He had only moments in which to savor them. Then he speared from the saddle a soldier who had managed to turn only halfway toward him. That struck him as less than fair but most effective.

Sharbaraz's backers shouted, too, with fresh spirit. Abivard and his men rolled up the left wing of Smerdis' army. Its commander had savvy to spare: he pulled men from the center and right to stem the rout before everything was swept away. But a fight that had looked like a victory for the usurper suddenly turned into another stinging defeat.

Smerdis' host had trumpeters, too. Abivard recognized the call they blew: retreat. He screamed in delight: "Pursue! Pursue!" The shout rang through not only the regiment he led but from the rest of Sharbaraz's army, as well. Just as retreat made Smerdis' men lose heart, victory enspirited Sharbaraz's soldiers. They pressed the enemy hard, doing their best to keep him from re-forming his ranks.

The warrior who had urged Abivard to loose the regiment before the signal happened to ride close to him now. The fellow had a cut on his forehead from which blood spilled down over his face, but his grin was enormous. "Lord Abivard, you were right and I was wrong and I'm man enough to admit it," he declared. "We've smashed them to kindling—kindling, I tell you."

Another soldier, this one with more gray than black in his beard, caught Abivard's eye. "Lord, you'd better cherish that," he said. "You'll count the times your men own that you were smarter than them on the thumbs of one hand—and that's if you're lucky, mind."

"You're likely right, friend," Abivard said. Some of Smerdis' men staged a countercharge to buy their comrades time to get away. The fierce fighting that followed swept Abivard away from the cynical graybeard.

"To the Void with the renunciate! Smerdis King of Kings!" a lancer shouted as his mount pounded toward Abivard. Abivard dug heels into his own horse; the last thing he wanted was to receive an attack with no momentum of his own. He got his shield up just before they slammed together.

The enemy lance shattered on the shield. His own held, but Smerdis' horseman deflected it with his shield so it did him no harm. That left them at close quarters. Faster than Abivard had expected him to be, his foe hit him in the side of the head with the stump of his lance.

His iron helm kept his skull from caving in, but his head suddenly knew what a piece of iron caught between hammer and anvil felt like. His sight blurred; staying on his horse became all he could do. He noticed he didn't have his own lance any more but had no idea where he had dropped it.

The next thing he fully remembered was a tired, thin, worried-looking man holding a candle a couple of fingers'-breadths away from one eye. The fellow moved it to the other eye, then let out a long, wheezing breath. "The pupils are of different sizes," he said to someone—Abivard turned his head and saw Sharbaraz. "He's taken a blow to the head."

"That I have," Abivard said, all at once aware of a headache like a thousand years of hangovers all boiled down into a thick, sludgy gelatin of pain. That made him sad; he hadn't even had the fun of getting drunk. "Did we hold the victory? I lost track there after I got clouted." He found himself yawning.

"Majesty, he needs rest," the worried-looking man said; Abivard realized he was a physician.

"I know; I've seen cases like his," the King of Kings answered. To Abivard he said, "Aye, we won; we drive them still. I'm going to have Kakia here take you back to the wagon your wife and sister share; they'll be the best ones to nurse you for the next few days."

"Days?" Abivard tried to sound indignant. Instead, he sounded— and felt—sick. He gulped, trying to keep down what was in his belly. The ground swayed beneath his feet as if it had turned to sea.

Kakia put Abivard's arm over his own shoulder. "Lord, it's nothing to be ashamed of. You may not bleed, but you're wounded as sure as if you were cut. With your brains rattled around inside your skull like lentils in a gourd, you need some time to come back to yourself."

Abivard wanted to argue, but felt too weak and woozy. He let the physician guide him back toward the baggage train. The serving women who had accompanied Roshnani and Denak exclaimed in dismay when Kakia brought him to the wagon in which they traveled.

"I'm all right," he insisted, though the gong chiming in his head tolled out *Liar* with every beat of his heart.

"Should the God grant, which I think likely in this case, the lord will be right again in three or four days," Kakia said, which set off a fresh paroxysm of weeping from the women. With the curious disconnection the blow to the head had caused, Abivard wondered how they would have carried on had the physician told them he wouldn't be all right. Even louder, he suspected. They were quite loud enough as it was.

Climbing the steps up into the wagon took every bit of balance and strength he had left. Still twittering like upset birds, the women took charge of him and led him into the little cubicle Roshnani used as her own.

She started to smile when he walked—or rather staggered—in, but the expression congealed on her face like stiffening tallow when she saw the state he was in. "What happened?" she whispered.

"I got hit in the side of the head," he said; he was getting tired of explaining. "I'm—kind of addled, and they say I'm supposed to rest until I'm more myself. A day or two." If he told that to Roshnani, maybe he would believe it, too.

"What were you doing?" Roshnani demanded as he sank down to the mat on which she was sitting.

Even in his battered state, that struck him as a foolish question. "Fighting," he said.

She went on as if he hadn't spoken: "You could have been killed. Here, you just lie quiet; I'll take care of you. Would you like some wine?"

He started to shake his head but thought better of it, contenting himself with a simple, "No. I'm queasy. If I drink anything right now, I'll probably spew it up." *And if I try to heave right now, I'm sure the top of my head will fall off.* He rather wished it would.

"Here." Roshnani opened a little chest, took out a small pot, and undid the stopper. In a tone that brooked no argument, she said, "If you won't take wine, drink this. I don't think you'll give it back, and it will do you good."

Abivard was too woozy to quarrel. He gulped down whatever the little jar held, though he made a face at the strong, medicinal taste. After a while, the ache in his head faded from unbearable to merely painful. He yawned; the stuff had made him sleepier than he already was, too. "That's done some good," he admitted. "What was it?"

"You'll not be angry at the answer?" Roshnani asked.

"No," he said, puzzled. "Why should I be?"

Even in the dim light of the cubicle, he saw Roshnani flush. "Because it's a potion women sometimes take for painful courses," she answered. "It has poppy juice in it, and I thought that might ease you. But men, from all I've heard, have a way of being touchy about having to do with women's things."

"That's so." Abivard raised a languid hand, then let it fall on Roshnani's outstretched arm. "There. You may, if you like, consider that I've beaten you for your presumption."

She stared at him, then dissolved in giggles. Drugged and groggy though he was, Abivard knew the joke didn't rate such laughter. Maybe, he thought, relief had something to do with it.

Just then Denak came into the cubicle, stooping to get through the low entranceway. She looked from Roshnani to Abivard and back again. "Well!" she said. "Things can't be too bad, if I walk in on a scene like this."

"Things could be better," Abivard said. "If they were, one of Smerdis' rotten treacherous men wouldn't have tried using my head for a bell to see if he liked the tone. But if they were worse, he'd have smashed it like a dropped pot, so who am I to complain?" He yawned again; staying awake was becoming an enormous effort.

"The servants say the physician who brought him here thinks he'll get better," Roshnani said to Denak, as if Abivard were either already unconscious or part of the furniture. "But he'll need a few days' rest."

"This is the place for it," Denak said, an edge of wormwood in her voice. "It's as if we brought the women's quarters with us when we left Vek Rud stronghold. A women's quarters on four wheels—who would have imagined that? But we're just as caged here as we were back there."

"I didn't expect much different," Roshnani said; she was more patient, less impetuous than her sister-in-law. "That we are allowed out is the victory, and everything else will flow from it. Some years from now, many women will be free to move about as they please, and nobody will recall the terms we had to accept to get the avalanche rolling."

"The avalanche rolled over me," Abivard said.

"Two foolish jokes now—your brains can't be altogether smashed," Roshnani said.

Thus put in his place, Abivard listened to Denak say, "By the God, it's not right. We've escaped the women's quarters, and so we should also escape the strictures the quarters put on us. What point to leaving if we still dare not show our faces outside the wagon unless summoned to our husbands' tents?"

Roshnani surely made some reply, but Abivard never found out what it was; between them, the knock on the head and the poppy juice in the medicine she had given him sent him sliding down into sleep. The next time he opened his eyes, the inside of the cubicle was dark but for a single flickering lamp. The lamp oil had an odd odor; he couldn't remember where he had smelled it in the past. He fell asleep again before the memory surfaced.

When he woke the next morning, he needed a minute or so to figure out where he was; the shifting of the wagon as it rattled along and his pounding, muzzy head conspired to make him wonder whether he was getting up in the middle of an earthquake after a long night of drinking.

Then Roshnani sat up on the pallet by his. "How's the spot where you got hit?" she asked.

Memory returned. He gingerly set a finger to his temple. "Sore," he reported.

She nodded. "You have a great bruise there, I think, though your hair hides most of it. You're lucky the usurper's man didn't smash your skull."

"So I am." Abivard touched the side of his head again and winced. "He didn't miss by much, I don't think." Roshnani blew out the lamp. This time, Abivard recognized the smell. "It's burning that what-do-they-call-it? Rock oil, that's it. Peroz's engineers used it to fire the bridge over the Degird after the few stragglers came back from Pardraya. They said the southern folk put it in their lamps."

"I don't like it—it smells nasty," Roshnani said. "But we ran low on lighting oil, and one of the servants bought a jar of it. It does serve lamps well enough, I suppose, but I can't imagine that it would ever be good for anything else."

The serving women fixed Abivard a special breakfast: tongue, brains, and cow's foot, spiced hot with pepper. His head still ached, but his appetite had recovered; he didn't feel he was likely to puke up anything he put in his stomach. All the same, Roshnani wouldn't let him get up for any reason save to use the pot.

Sharbaraz came to see him around midmorning. "The God give you good day, Majesty," Abivard said. "As you see, I've already prostrated myself for you."

The rightful King of Kings chuckled. "You're healing, I'd say," he remarked, unconsciously echoing Roshnani. "I'm glad." Sentiment out of the way, he reminded Abivard he was Peroz's son with a blunt, "To business, then. The usurper's army has made good its withdrawal. We still have some horsemen shadowing us, but they can't interfere as we advance."

"Good news," Abivard said. "Nothing to keep us from getting south of the Dilbat Mountains and then turning north and east to move on Mashiz, eh?"

"On the surface, no," Sharbaraz said. "But what we ran into yesterday troubles me, and not a little, either. Aye, we won the fight, but not the way I'd hoped. Not a man, not a company, went over to us. We had to beat them, and when we did, they either fell back or, if they were cut off, surrendered. Not one of them turned on the others who back Smerdis."

"That is worrying." Abivard could feel he was slower and stupider than he should have been, which left him angry: Sharbaraz needed the best advice he could give. After a moment, he went on, "Seems to me the only thing we can do is press ahead, all the same. We can't very well give up just because things aren't as easy as we thought they'd be."

"I agree," Sharbaraz said. "As long as we keep winning, Smerdis falls sooner or later." He pounded a fist against his thigh, once, twice, three times. "But I was so sure the usurper would go down to ignominious defeat as soon as it was known I lived and hadn't abdicated on my own."

"One of the things my father always said was that the longer you lived, the more complicated life looked," Abivard said. "He said only boys and holy men were ever certain; men who had to live in the world got the idea it was bigger and more complicated than they could imagine."

"I think I've told you my father praised your father's good sense," Sharbaraz said. "The more I listen to Godarz through you, the more I think my father knew whereof he spoke."

"Your Majesty is gracious to my father's memory," Abivard said, warmed by the praise and wishing Godarz were there to hear it. "What do you plan to do next? Keep on with the straight-ahead drive toward the capital?"

"Aye, what else?" The rightful King of Kings frowned. "I know it's not subtle, but we have no other good choices. Smerdis has already had one army wrecked and another beaten; he'll hesitate to hazard a third. With luck, we'll be able to closely approach Mashiz before he tries fighting us head-on again. We win that fight and the city is ours—and if Smerdis wants to flee to Nalgis Crag stronghold, say, he'll learn we have the patience to starve him out." His eyes glowed with anticipation.

In the space of a few minutes, Sharbaraz had gone from gloom about the way Smerdis' backers declined to go over to him to excitement at the prospect of starving his rival into submission. Abivard wished he could lose his depressions as readily. But he, like Godarz before him, seemed a man who went through life without sinking deep into the valleys or climbing high on the peaks.

He said, "First things first, Majesty. Once we have Mashiz, assuming we don't bag Smerdis with it, then we can worry about hunting him down. Otherwise we're riding our horses before we bridle and saddle them." He laughed ruefully. "I have to say I'm just as well pleased we're not storming the capital tomorrow. I'd not be much use to you, even on a horse already bridled and saddled."

"You let yourself mend," Sharbaraz said, as if giving an order to some recalcitrant underling. "Thank the God we won't be doing much in the way of fighting till you're ready to play your proper part once more. You set me straight very smartly there when I let enthusiasm push me like a leaf on the breeze."

"Your Majesty is kind." Abivard was pleased with Sharbaraz. As long as the rightful King of Kings could recognize when he was letting his passion of the moment—whatever it might be—run away with him, he would do well. The question was, how long would that last after he won his civil war?

Sharbaraz reached out and touched him on the shoulder—gently, so as not to jostle his poor battered head. "I have to go off and see to the army. I expect I'll be back this evening, to visit you and Denak both. Rest easy till then."

"Your Majesty, what choice have I?" Abivard said. "Even if I wanted to be out and doing, Roshnani would flatten me should I try to get up without her leave. Men usually keep their wives shut up in women's quarters, but here she has me trapped."

Sharbaraz laughed loud and long at that, as if it hadn't been true. He ducked out of the cubicle; Abivard listened to him getting onto his horse and riding away. He was already shouting orders, as if he had forgotten all about the man he had just visited. Rationally, Abivard knew that wasn't so, but it irked him anyhow.

As a proper Makuraner wife should, Roshnani had stayed out of sight while another man visited her husband. She returned to the cubicle as soon as Sharbaraz was gone. "So I've trapped you here, have I?" she said.

"You were listening."

"How could I help it, when only curtains separate one part of the wagon from the next?" Looking innocent and mischievous at the same time, she pulled shut the curtain that opened onto the cubicle. "So you're trapped here, are you?" she repeated, and knelt beside him. "Trapped and flat on your back, are you?"

"What are you doing?" Abivard squawked as she hiked up his caftan. She didn't answer, not in words; her long black hair spilled over his belly and thighs. He did his best to rise to the occasion, and his best proved quite good enough.

✦ VIII

Where southern Makuran was a desert, it was barer than the wasteland around Vek Rud domain. Where it was fertile, it was far richer. "We tax the land here at twice the rate we use in the northwest," Sharbaraz said to Abivard, "and even then, some of the ministers think we are too lenient."

"Crops are very fine here," Abivard admitted. "What are the winters like?"

"You've driven the nail home," Sharbaraz said, nodding. "I'd read of winters on the steppe and close to it, but never lived through one till I was sent to Nalgis Crag stronghold and then went on to yours even closer to the frontier. Here they grow things the year around; they get snow only about one winter in two."

Remembering blizzards and snowdrifts and hail and ice three months of every year and sometimes four or five, Abivard laughed at that. He couldn't make up his mind whether to find it unnatural or one of the most wonderful things he had ever heard.

Before he decided, a scout rode back toward Sharbaraz. Saluting, the fellow said, "Majesty, a party of riders is approaching under shield of truce."

"Let them come to me," Sharbaraz said at once. "Tell them that if they're conveying Smerdis' surrender, I'll be happy to accept it." The scout laughed, wheeled his horse, and booted the animal up to a gallop as he went off to escort the newcomers to the rightful King of Kings. Sharbaraz turned back to Abivard and chuckled ruefully. "I'd be happy to accept Smerdis' surrender, aye, but I don't think I'm going to get it."

A few minutes later, a whole squadron of scouts came back
with Smerdis' delegation. Without being ordered to do so, they
placed themselves between Sharbaraz and Smerdis' men—no
assassinations here. The scout who had announced the coming
of the truce party said, "Majesty, here are the usurper's dogs."
Scorn harshened his voice.

A couple of Smerdis' followers stirred restlessly on their horses,
but none of them spoke. Sharbaraz did. Pointing to one of their
number, he said, "Ah, Inshushinak, so you've taken the old man's
silver, have you?"

Inshushinak was hardly in the first bloom of youth himself; he
was fat and gray-bearded and sat his horse as if he hadn't ridden
one in a long time. He nodded to Sharbaraz and said, "Son of
Peroz, his Majesty Smerdis King of Kings—"

He got no farther than that. Some of Sharbaraz's scouts reached
for their swords, while others swung down lances. One of them
growled, "Show proper respect for the King of Kings, curse
you."

Sharbaraz raised a hand. "Let him speak as he will. He comes
under shield of truce; the God hates those who violate it. I shall
remember, but then I already remember he has chosen to follow
the man who stole my throne. Say on, Inshushinak."

That did not make Inshushinak look much happier, but he
rallied and resumed: "Son of Peroz, his Majesty Smerdis King of
Kings, may his years be many and his realm increase, bade me
come with these my followers—" He waved to the half-dozen
men who rode with him: three soldiers, a couple of bureaucrats, and a skinny little fellow who could have been anything
at all, "—to seek to compose the differences that lie between
you and him."

"Inshushinak was my father's treasury minister," Sharbaraz murmured to Abivard. "Once Smerdis' superior; now, it seems, his
servant." He raised his voice and addressed the delegation from
Mashiz. "You may go back to the capital and tell my cousin that
if he casts aside the throne and recovers all the arkets he squan-
dered on the Khamorth and agrees to be confined for the rest
of his days as he confined me, I may perhaps consider granting
him his worthless life. Otherwise—"

"Son of Peroz, Smerdis King of Kings did not send me to you
in token of surrender." Inshushinak looked as if he wished Smerdis

had not sent him to Sharbaraz at all, but went on, "Would you care to hear the terms he proposes?"

"Not very much." But Sharbaraz relented: "Since you came to deliver them, you may as well."

"You are gracious." Even Inshushinak's years at court could not make that sound sincere. "In the interest of sparing the realm the torment of civil war, Smerdis King of Kings will confer upon you the title of King of the Northwest and will concede you autonomous rule there, subject to your paying him an annual sum to be determined by negotiation."

"Smerdis is generous," Sharbaraz said, and for a moment Inshushinak brightened. But Peroz's son continued, "How kind of him to concede to me a small piece of what I already hold, and to be willing to negotiate the sum I pay for the privilege. Since I can take all the realm, though, I shall not rest content to be given a part."

One of the soldierly men with Inshushinak said, "Be not so sure, son of Peroz. In most wars, unlike the one that overthrew your father last year, a single battle does not decide a campaign."

Sharbaraz bit his lip in anger but held his voice steady as he replied, "My best guess as to why you failed to go with my father, Hakhamanish, is that he reckoned you more a loss than a gain in the field. I'm not even angry at you for choosing Smerdis' side; measured against a real general, you're apter to hurt the usurper's cause than help it."

Hakhamanish's face went darker yet with angry blood. Abivard said, "Well struck, Majesty."

Inshushinak said, "Peroz's son, am I to infer from this that you reject the gracious offer of Smerdis King of Kings?"

"You need not infer it," Sharbaraz said. "I openly proclaim it. I give you leave to take my words back to Smerdis. Be wary of dining with him, though, lest you wake in a place you least expect." He paused. "And one more thing—if you fear to deliver my message out of worry over what he may do to you for reporting what I say, simply tell him I'll be in Mashiz soon enough, to give him the answer in person."

"Son of Peroz, arrogance will be your downfall, as it was your father's," Hakhamanish said. "You shall never approach Mashiz, much less reach it."

Inshushinak scowled at the officer. So did the nondescript little man, who, on any crowded street, would have become invisible as readily as a color-shifting gecko going yellow-brown when set on a slab of sandstone. Hakhamanish might have been on the point of saying more, but instead jerked hard at his horse's reins, made the unhappy animal rear and wheel, and rode away without so much as a farewell. The rest of Smerdis' party imitated his unceremonious departure, although Inshushinak rode off quite sedately: if his horse, an elderly gelding, had reared, no doubt he would have gone off over its tail.

Sharbaraz's eyes narrowed as he stared after Smerdis' backers. "They are more confident than they have any business being," he said to Abivard. "Smerdis, the God curse him, still thinks he can win this war, and he has no business thinking so, not on the way it's gone so far."

"Which means he knows, or thinks he knows, something we don't," Abivard said "Majesty, might it not be wise to follow this embassy and see if they're part of whatever he plans? Follow them at a discreet distance, of course."

"Not a bad thought." Sharbaraz rubbed his chin, then called to a couple of scouts and gave the orders, adding, "One of you report back to me at nightfall to tell me where they've camped and whether anyone's met with them. The other should watch them through the night as best he can."

The horsemen saluted and rode out after Inshushinak and his companions. Abivard said, "Mind you, Majesty, I don't expect they'll find out anything in particular, but—"

"Better to send them and learn nothing than not send them and not learn something we should have," Sharbaraz said. "I wouldn't think of arguing with you."

The army rode on. Off in the distance, the sun shimmered from a saltpan. A little closer, the illusion of water danced in the air. That happened up by the Vek Rud, too, though not so often. If you believed the water was really there and went after it, you could easily end up dying of thirst.

Evening came. Camp straggled over what seemed to Abivard like a farsang and a half. Had Smerdis had an army in the neighborhood, it could have struck Sharbaraz's scattered forces a deadly blow. The encampment of the grand army Peroz had led into Pardraya had been no better organized. Abivard wondered if something could be done about that.

Before he had the chance to think seriously about it, he all but bumped into Sharbaraz as the rightful King of Kings came back from a walk round the camp to make sure everything was running smoothly. "What word from the scouts, Majesty?" he asked. "Are Smerdis' henchmen planning to transform the lot of us into camels?"

Sharbaraz laughed, but quickly grew sober once more. "Do you know, brother-in-law of mine, I can't tell you, because that scout never came in."

Abivard glanced to the east. A fat moon, just past full, was climbing over the horizon and spilling pale-yellow light over the barren landscape. "Hard to lose the army, don't you think?"

The smile altogether vanished from Sharbaraz's face. "It is, wouldn't you say? Do you suppose Smerdis' men waylaid them?"

"Smerdis' men didn't look well mounted," Abivard demurred. "And if your scouts can't get away from the likes of the men we saw there, we've got the wrong people doing the job."

"You're right about that," Sharbaraz said. "But what does it leave? Accident? Possible, I suppose, but not very likely. As you say, scouts had better have a pretty good idea of what they're doing and how to get around."

"Magic, maybe." Abivard had meant it half as a joke, but the word seemed to hang in the air. He said, "Maybe we'd better not take any chances with magic, Majesty. Smerdis might well have sent out his men to see if he could buy you and, and if that failed—"

"—he'd turn a wizard loose on me," Sharbaraz finished. "Aye, that makes sense, and it fits the character—or rather, lack of character—Smerdis has shown all through his misbegotten, misnamed reign. What do we do to foil him?" He answered his own question: "We send out men to track down the embassy's camp, see what's going on there, and break it up if it's what we fear." He raised his voice and bawled for the scouts.

"Finding Smerdis' folk won't be easy, especially not at night," Abivard said. "And who knows how long the wizard—if there is a wizard—has been busy? You're going to need magical protection, just to keep you safe." He went out of Sharbaraz's tent, grabbed a man by the arm, and said, "D'you know where Tanshar the fortune-teller and the rest of those skilled in sorcery pitch their tents? Usually they're all close together, off to one side of the stores wagons."

"Aye, lord," the fellow answered. "I went to one of 'em—not Tanshar, I forget what his name was—the other night, and he looked at my palm and told me a big reward was coming my way soon."

"Get Tanshar and the rest of them back here to the King of Kings' tent as fast as you can and that fortune-teller's word will come true," Abivard said. The soldier blinked, scratched his head, then suddenly left at a dead run. He might have needed a moment to figure out what Abivard meant, but he wasted no time once he got it.

Abivard stared up at the moon. When you keep looking at it, he thought, it seemed to stand still in the sky—and if the moon didn't move, how could time pass? But the racket of the camp went right on, with a sudden addition when a troop of scouts resaddled and mounted their horses and rode off into the moonlight.

Inside the tent, Sharbaraz made a noise. It wasn't a word, nor yet a cry; it wasn't a noise quite like any Abivard had heard. He ducked back through the entry flap. As he straightened up, the camp bed in the tent, no finer than that which belonged to any other officer, went over with a crash.

Sharbaraz thrashed on the floor, wrestling with something he could see and Abivard could not. Abivard sprang to his aid. Guided by the motions of Sharbaraz's grasping hands, he tried to pull away the King of Kings' foe, even though that foe was invisible to him.

But his hands passed through the space between himself and Sharbaraz as if that space held only the empty air his eyes perceived. The same was manifestly not true for Sharbaraz. He writhed and twisted and kicked and punched, and when his blows landed, they sounded as if they struck flesh.

"By the God," Abivard cried, "what is this madness?"

When he spoke the God's name, he heard a groan that did not spring from his lips or Sharbaraz's, as if it pained the invisible attacker. That did not stop the thing, whatever it was, from keeping up its assault on Sharbaraz. It started to choke him; struggling like a madman, the rightful King of Kings tore its—hands?—from his throat.

"By the God," Abivard said again. This time he noted no effect, maybe because he was deliberately using the God's name as a weapon rather than invoking his deity out of need. Watching the King of Kings fight for his life and being unable to aid him brought back the dreadful helplessness Abivard had known when, afoot, he had watched Peroz and the flower of the Makuraner army tumble into the trench the Khamorth had dug.

"Lord Abivard? Your Majesty?"

Never had Abivard been so glad to hear an old man's quavering voice. "In here, Tanshar, and quickly!" he cried.

Tanshar burst into the King of Kings' tent, panting from having hurried from his own resting place. The fortune-teller stared at the spectacle of Sharbaraz struggling for his life against a foe imperceptible to others. He burst out with the same ejaculation Abivard had used, the same any Makuraner would have used: "By the God!"

Where the attacker had groaned when Abivard called on the God, he screamed now, as if beaten with red-hot pokers. He still grappled with Sharbaraz, but now, as they rolled over and over, the King of Kings was on top as often as his assailant.

Tanshar wasted no time with another invocation of the God. Instead, he snatched a vial of powder from the pouch he wore on his belt and sprinkled it over both Sharbaraz and whatever he was fighting with. No, not whatever—the powder let Abivard make out the faint outline of a naked, heavily muscled man.

"Strike!" Tanshar cried. "What you can see, you can slay."

Abivard jerked his sword from its scabbard and slashed at the still-misty figure Sharbaraz was fighting. This time he understood why the would-be assassin cried out with pain; the blood the fellow shed was plainly visible. He cut again and again; Sharbaraz got a grip on his opponent's throat. They knew they had slain their foe when, all at once, his body became fully visible to Abivard for the first time.

Sharbaraz stared down at the blood-splashed face of the man who had tried to assassinate him. Turning to Abivard, he said, "Wasn't he one of the warriors who rode with Inshushinak?"

"Majesty, I couldn't say for certain," Abivard answered. "A mail veil doesn't show much of a man's face—and besides, I paid most attention to the men who were talking. But if you say it, I wouldn't presume to disagree."

"You'd better not—I'm the King of Kings." Sharbaraz's laugh

was shaky. He felt at his neck. "The wretch was strong as a bear; I must be bruised. I never saw him, either, till he seized me by the throat."

"Nor I, Majesty." Abivard's face went hot with shame. "He must have walked past me and into your tent while I was outside sending for Tanshar here."

Sharbaraz shook his head, then winced; his neck *was* sore. "Don't blame yourself. Magic defeated your vigilance—how can you be expected to see through a mage's charm? Besides, what you say doesn't have to be true. For all we know, he could have been lurking here, pretending to be a piece of air like any other, until you went outside and he found the chance to strike."

"It could be so," Abivard agreed gratefully. "As long as he lived, only Tanshar's magic powder let me see him and fight him."

The fortune-teller's laugh ran raucous in the tent. "Your Majesty, lord, I used no magic powder, for I had none. That was just finely ground salt for my meat, nothing more."

Abivard stared. "Then how did we defeat the spell from Smerdis' sorcerer?"

"I have no idea whether you defeated the spell," Tanshar answered. "You defeated the man on whom it lay, and that sufficed."

"But—" Abivard struggled to put his thought into words. "When I called on the God, and then again when you did, this whoreson was plainly hurt. How do you explain that, if not by magic?"

"That probably was magic," Tanshar said. "When we called on the God, we disturbed the link—the evil link, evidently—through which Smerdis' mage controlled the sorcery he had set in motion. Perhaps we deformed the nature of the spell: not enough to destroy its effectiveness, but enough to cause this fellow pain as the mage regained or retained his power. I am but guessing, you must understand, for such magic is far beyond my power."

"Yet you helped defeat it, just as, against all odds, you helped me get free from Nalgis Crag stronghold," Sharbaraz said. "I think you give yourself too little credit. I shall not make the same mistake. When Mashiz is mine once more, you have but to name your reward."

"Majesty, you cannot give me back thirty years, nor yet the sight in this eye," Tanshar said, raising a finger to point at the one a cataract had dimmed. "I have no great needs, and I've seen enough years go by that I have no great desires, either."

"I wonder whether I should pity you or be bitterly jealous," Sharbaraz observed. "Have it as you will, then, but know that my ear is yours should you ever find any service I can perform for you."

Tanshar bowed. "Your Majesty is generous beyond my deserts. For now, if you will but grant me leave to return to my tent—" The fortune-teller waited for Sharbaraz to nod, then bowed again and slipped out into the night.

When he was gone, Sharbaraz abandoned some of the brave front he had kept up. Prodding the body of his assailant with one foot, he said, "Pour me some wine, brother-in-law of mine, if you'd be so kind. This son of a thousand fathers came far too close to killing me."

"Aye, Majesty." A jar and some cups sat on a folding table that somehow had not gone over during the fight. Abivard poured two cups full, handed one to the rightful King of Kings. The other he held high in salute. "To your safety."

"A good toast, and one I'll gladly drink to." Sharbaraz raised the cup to his lips. He winced when he swallowed. "That hurts. This cursed murderer—" He prodded the body again, "—was strong as a mule, and I think his hands were as hard as Ganzak the smith's."

Abivard had his doubts about that but held most of them from his reply: "The metal Ganzak pounds is harder than your neck."

"Can't argue with that." Sharbaraz drank again, more cautiously this time, but winced again anyhow. Wheezing a little, he said, "That's three times you've saved me now. But for you, Smerdis would be sitting comfortably on the throne, and I—I expect I'd be heading toward madness, locked up inside Nalgis Crag stronghold."

"To serve the King of Kings is an honor," Abivard said.

"You've earned honor, that's certain." Sharbaraz emptied the cup and held it out to Abivard. "Fill it up again, and drain your own so you can fill that, too. By the God, I've earned the right to drink deep tonight even if it sets my throat on fire, and I don't care to do it by myself."

"Let me drag this carrion out first." Abivard seized the assassin by the feet and hauled him out of the King of Kings' tent. The camp had quieted for the night; no one exclaimed at the sight of a corpse. Returning, Abivard said, "We can leave him there for the dogs and the crows to eat."

"A fine notion. Now pour me that wine, if you please."

The two of them were on their fourth or fifth cups—since Abivard was having trouble keeping track, probably their fifth—when riders came pounding into the camp. "Majesty! Majesty!" The cry rose above the thunder of hoofbeats and probably woke a good many men who had already gone to sleep.

Sharbaraz reached for his sword. "Have to—defend myself—if those aren't my scouts coming back." His speech was thick. Abivard suspected he would be more dangerous to himself with that blade than to any foes. He yanked out his own sword. He had already slain one would-be killer with it tonight. Why not another? The wine that made his movements slow and fumbling eloquently put forward its opinion.

Side by side, the King of Kings and Abivard went out to meet the approaching horsemen. In the moonlight, Abivard recognized the officer who had reported the arrival of Smerdis' embassy. The man saw Sharbaraz. "Majesty," he exclaimed, "we've rid you of a scorpion's nest of traitors."

Sharbaraz and Abivard exchanged glances. "That's—*hic!*—wonderful," the rightful King of Kings said. "Tell me at once what happened." To Abivard he whispered, "He'd better tell me at once; I have to piss fit to burst."

The scout, luckily, didn't hear that. He said, "We rode out until we found the camp where that Inshushinak, the God drop him into the Void, had paused with his henchmen for the night. Outside the camp, at a distance where they could watch and not be seen, we also found the two men you sent to keep an eye on the embassy."

"Why didn't one of them report back here as ordered?" Sharbaraz demanded.

A scout broke in. "Majesty, they was frozen stiff."

"Near enough," the officer agreed. "They were warm and breathing, but otherwise they might as well have been turned to stone. One of the men Inshushinak had with him, he must have been a wizard."

"We found that out for ourselves, as a matter of fact," Sharbaraz said dryly. "But this is your tale; pray go on with it."

"Aye, Majesty," the scout leader answered, curiosity in his voice.

"Well, when we got a good look at what the son of a serpent had done to poor Tyardut and Andegan, we were so angry we couldn't even see. We got back on our horses and charged straight for the camp. Some of us probably feared the wizard would do to us what he'd done to our friends, but not a man hung back, and that's a fact."

"Whether you know it or not, charging with rage in your hearts likely was the best thing you could have done," Abivard said. "Sorcery won't bite on a man who's full of passion; that's why love magic and battle magic are such chancy things." He knew he was giving back Tanshar's words, but if Tanshar didn't understand how sorcery worked, who did?

"However that may be, lord," the scout said. "Anyhow, we came down on the camp like wolves jumping on an antelope they've cut out of the herd. Nothing alive there now, just carrion. We had a couple of men hurt, neither one bad, it looks like. And hear this, too—when we started back, we found the scouts had come back to life. Killing that wizard must have broken the spell that held them."

Sharbaraz sighed. "Now Smerdis will curse me for having slain an embassy. And do you know what, brother-in-law of mine? I shan't lose a moment's sleep over it, not when he tried to slay me by sorcery under cover of that embassy."

"Majesty, the only thing concerning me there is that, while you know what you say is true, the rest of the realm may not know it," Abivard said.

Sharbaraz waved scornfully to show how little he cared for what the rest of the realm knew or didn't know. "Soon enough all Makuran will be mine. Then it will know what I wish it to know."

The peaks of the Dilbat Mountains petered out into low, rolling foothills after Sharbaraz's army rode south for another few days. Getting through the mountains then was no longer a matter of forcing a narrow, heavily defended pass but simply heading east and then turning north.

Abivard found the change disconcerting the very first day. "I'm used to watching the sun rise out of the mountains, not set behind them," he said.

"I've seen both," Sharbaraz said. "One's the same as the other, as far as I'm concerned. What I want to see is Mashiz." Restless hunger stalked along his voice.

"How long till we reach it?" Abivard asked. He wanted to see Mashiz, too, not just because entering the capital would mean victory but also because he was curious about what a real city was like. Some of the towns that sheltered under strongholds in the south of Makuran were a good deal larger and busier than the one in his own domain, but basically of the same type. He wanted to find out how different Mashiz would be.

"Ten or twelve days from here," Sharbaraz answered. "That's if we do nothing but ride, mind you. I expect we'll see some fighting, though. If Smerdis doesn't throw everything he has at me now, he loses."

"May he lose any which way," Abivard said, to which the King of Kings nodded. Neither of them spoke as much of Smerdis' men deserting as they had when the campaign was new and their enthusiasm unchallenged. Abivard had concluded that most of the men who followed Smerdis were going to keep right on following him. If Sharbaraz was to win, he would have to do it with the forces that had begun the fight on his side. That didn't make it impossible, but it didn't make things any easier, either.

"As long as we keep winning, we're fine," Sharbaraz said. Maybe he was trying not to think about the desertions that hadn't happened, too. Once his army left the northwest, he had stopped sweeping in whole strongholdsful of recruits. If he ousted Smerdis with what he had, Abivard expected the whole realm to acknowledge him as its ruler. If he didn't . . . Abivard tried not to think about that.

Three days after Sharbaraz's host turned north, they met another of Smerdis' armies. This time the scouts were laughing as they came back to bring the news to Sharbaraz. "Smerdis must be running out of horses, Majesty," one of them said, "for half his men are foot soldiers, maybe more."

"The men of the Thousand Cities," Abivard said.

Sharbaraz nodded. "Aye, no doubt. We'll smash straight through them and scatter them like chaff; one such lesson and they'll know better than to fight for the usurper ever again."

Peroz's son indeed, Abivard thought. Aloud he said, "Wouldn't we be wiser to try to flank them out of their position? We can move faster than they, and if we hit them while they're trying to shift to keep up with us, we stand a better chance of striking the deadly blow you want."

But the rightful King of Kings shook his head and waved to the east, saying, "That's still desert out there; we aren't yet up to the Tutub and the Tib. We'd have a hard time keeping ourselves in fodder for the animals and water for them and us both. Besides, I don't want to be seen as sidestepping Smerdis. I want to show the realm my men are bolder and fiercer than his."

"I hope that's so, Majesty," Abivard said, as close to direct criticism as he dared come. Sharbaraz glared at him, then shouted for Zal and his other captains and began giving orders for the direct assault. No one contradicted him or showed any misgivings.

At the end, he turned to Abivard and said, "Will you do us the honor of accompanying the attack?"

"Certainly, Majesty. May the God grant you success, and may he know I wish it for you," Abivard said. However much he tried to ignore it, Sharbaraz's sardonic question stung. He did not think his sovereign was making the right choice, but how was he supposed to tell that to Sharbaraz when he would not listen? He found no way. All that was left, then, was to go forward and hope the rightful King of Kings was right.

Martial music ordered the men into line of battle. Word that they were facing infantry raced up and down the line. They seemed confident, even contemptuous. "We'll squash 'em flat for you, lord," one of the horsemen said, and all the troopers around him nodded. Abivard's worries eased. Confidence counted a great deal in war. If the soldiers thought they couldn't be beaten, maybe they couldn't.

Smerdis' men came into sight. As the scout had said, they were infantry and cavalry both, the horse on the flanks, the foot in the center. Abivard shouted Sharbaraz's name. The war cry rose from the whole army. Smerdis' soldiers shouted back. A great din rose to the blue sky.

Horns belled the charge. Abivard swung down his lance and spurred his horse. The pound of the beast's hooves, and of all those around him, filled him like a quicker, stronger pulse. The enemy horsemen moved forward from their position on the wings to engage Sharbaraz's riders.

Smerdis' infantry held its ground. As Abivard drew nearer, he saw it sheltered behind a barricade of thorny brush. Through thundering hoofbeats, through the clamor of war cries, the clear, pure note of reed whistles rang out. Abivard scowled under his mail visor; that was no signal he knew. But it meant something to the infantry. In an instant, arrows filled the air, one flight, then another and another. They whistled, too, loud enough to drown out the call that had set them flying. Graceful as birds, they curved high into the sky—then fell on the charging horsemen.

Sharbaraz had archers, too, and they shot back at the foot soldiers, but not with so many arrows so steadily discharged. Men and horses crumpled, and when they fell they fouled others just behind them. The attack faltered.

An arrow slammed into Abivard's upraised shield and stood, thrumming. A palm's breadth to one side and it would have pierced his leg instead. The brush barricade was very close now. His horse pushed against it. The animal's body was armored, but the thorns on the brush still tore the tender skin of its legs. It hesitated, whinnying in protest.

Abivard kicked it in the ribs with his boots, inflicting worse pain to force it to obey his will. "Forward, the God curse you!" he yelled. The horse pushed forward, but hesitantly. Abivard got a good look at the foot soldiers on the far side of the barrier: dark, stocky men in leather jerkins, their long, black hair bound in a club at the nape of their necks. Some of them shouted insults in harshly accented Makuraner, others yelled what did not sound like pleasantries in their own guttural language. And all of them kept shooting arrows. Along with the quivers on their backs, they had others at their feet.

Had the brush been stiffened with stakes, it would have made a worse obstacle. As it was, the barrier broke here and there, letting trickles of Sharbaraz's men in among the enemy. They worked a fearful slaughter; but for their bows, the foot soldiers had only knives and clubs to defend themselves.

Abivard thrust his lance over the brush at an archer at the same instant the archer let fly at him. Maybe the two men frightened each other, for they both missed. They stared across the brush, the archer's face tired and worried, Abivard's hidden from the eyes down by chainmail. They both nodded, if not with joint respect, then at least with recognition of their joint humanity. By unspoken common consent, they chose other foes after that.

Pressure from behind forced Abivard's horse forward against

the thorns, no matter how little it cared to go. Branches scraped at the beast's armored sides and at the iron rings that protected Abivard's legs. Then he, too, was through the barricade, and a knot of Sharbaraz's warriors right behind him. Shouts of triumph rang in his ears, and cries of fear and dismay from Smerdis' infantry.

Some of the foot soldiers, recklessly brave, rushed toward the horses and tried to pull their riders from the saddle. Most of them were speared before they got close. Panic spread through the archers. Many threw away their bows to run the faster.

But they could not outrun horsemen. Abivard struck with his lance till it shivered; by then it was scarlet almost to the grip. He took out his sword and cut down more of the fleeing foe.

He never looked back on that part of the battle with pride—it always struck him afterward as more like murder than war. With their center broken, the cavalrymen Smerdis' generals had posted on either wing also had to give way, lest they be cut off and defeated in detail. The chase went on until nightfall forced Sharbaraz to break it off,

Abivard's stomach twisted as he rode back over the field. His horse had to pick its way carefully to keep from stepping on the bodies of fallen foot soldiers. Every few yards it would tread on one despite all its care, and snort in alarm as the corpse shifted under its hooves.

Then Abivard passed the broken barrier and saw what the archers had done to his own companions. He had pitied the hapless infantrymen as he had speared and hacked at them and afterward as he saw their bodies sprawled in death. Now he realized they were soldiers, too, in their own fashion. They had hurt Sharbaraz's followers worse than Smerdis' cavalry had managed in either of the earlier two fights.

He looked around for the banner of the rightful King of Kings. The fading light made it hard to spot, but when he found it he rode toward it. Sharbaraz had dismounted from his horse; he held out his arm for the physician Kakia's ministrations.

"You're wounded, Majesty!" Abivard exclaimed.

"An arrow, through my armor and through the meat," Sharbaraz answered. He shrugged, then winced, wishing he hadn't. He tried to make the best of it. "Not too bad. Your sister needn't worry that I need replacing."

Having done his utmost to make light of an injury of his own not long before, Abivard turned to Kakia for confirmation. The physician said, "His Majesty was fortunate in that the arrow pierced the biceps of the upper arm, and again in that the point came out the other side, so we did not have to draw it or force it through, causing him further pain. If the wound does not fester, it should heal well."

"And you'll make sure it doesn't fester, won't you?" Sharbaraz said.

"I have a decoction for that very purpose, yes," Kakia answered, taking a stoppered vial from a pouch on his belt. "Here we have verdigris and litharge, alum, pitch, and resin, stirred into a mixture of vinegar and oil. If your Majesty will undertake to hold the wounded member still—"

Sharbaraz tried valiantly to obey, but when Kakia poured the murky brownish lotion into the wound he hissed like red-hot iron with water poured into it. "By the God, you've set fire to my arm," he cried, biting his lip.

"No, Majesty, or if so but a small fire now to prevent the greater and more deadly fire of corruption later."

"That brew will prevent anything," Sharbaraz said feelingly as Kakia bandaged the arm. "Copper and lead and alum and pitch and resin—if I drank it instead of having it inflicted on me as you did, I'd be poisoned for certain."

"No doubt you would, Majesty, but the same holds true for many nostrums intended to go onto the body rather than within it," Kakia replied with some asperity. "For that matter, your caftan belongs around you, but would you swallow it chopped up with cucumbers? To everything its proper place and application."

With his arm paining him not only from the wound but also from the physician's treatment of it, Sharbaraz was not inclined to be philosophical. He turned to Abivard and said, "Well, brother-in-law of mine, you seem to have come through this fight with your brains unscrambled, for which I envy you."

"Aye, I was luckier this time. The day is ours." Abivard looked around at the grisly aftermath of battle. "Ours, aye, but dearly bought."

Sharbaraz suddenly looked exhausted as well as hurt. His skin stretched tight over his bones; Abivard was easily able to imagine how he would look as an old man—if he lived to grow old, which was never a good bet, most especially for a claimant to the throne of Makuran engaged in bruising civil war.

"Each fight is tougher," the rightful King of Kings said wearily. "I thought Smerdis' backers would collapse after the first battle, but they've given me two tougher ones since. How his officers keep their men in line I could not say—but they do. We'll have to fight again before we reach Mashiz, and if Smerdis is stronger then than now . . ." He didn't go on; he plainly didn't want to go on.

"You didn't expect him to offer battle till just in front of the capital." No sooner had he spoken than Abivard wished he could have his words back—no point to reminding Sharbaraz of past errors he couldn't correct now.

But Sharbaraz did not get angry; he only nodded. "My graybeard cousin has proved himself a man of more parts than I'd guessed, the God curse his thieving soul. It won't save him, but it makes our task harder."

Again Abivard envied the King of Kings for being able to haul himself out of swamps of gloom, apparently by sheer force of will. He asked, "How many more foot soldiers do you suppose he can bring against us? They hurt us worse than I would have dreamed such troops could."

"And I," Sharbaraz agreed. "Well, there's a lesson learned—I can't charge straight at archers with any sort of protection, not unless I want more of a butcher's bill than I fancy paying." He curled the hand on his wounded arm into a fist; Abivard was glad to see he could do that. "I hope the lesson wasn't too dearly bought."

"Aye," Abivard said. "Much will depend on the spirit of the men. If they decide this is another victory on our way to Mashiz, all will be well. We have to worry that they don't see it as a setback."

"Too true—if you think you're beaten, you probably are." Sharbaraz looked bleak. "I thought Smerdis would reckon himself beaten by now."

"Well, Majesty, if he doesn't, we'll just have to convince him," Abivard said, and hoped he sounded optimistic.

The land of the Thousand Cities was a revelation to Abivard. The land of his own domain wasn't rich enough to support one city, let alone a thousand. But in the river valleys, large towns squatted on little hillocks raised above the flat, muddy terrain.

When Abivard asked how those hillocks came to rise in the flatlands, Sharbaraz chuckled and said, "It's the cities' fault." Seeing that Abivard didn't follow, he explained: "Those cities have been there a long, long time, and they've been throwing out their rubbish just as long. When the street gets too much higher than your door, you knock down your house. It's not stone, only mud brick. Then you build a new one at the level the street has risen to. Do that for hundreds of years and pretty soon you're sitting on a hill."

From then on, Abivard looked at the hillocks in a whole new way: as pieces of time made visible. The idea awed him. The hill on which Vek Rud stronghold perched was purely natural—dig down a foot anywhere and you hit rock. That people could make their own hills had never occurred to him.

"Why shouldn't they?" Roshnani said when he spoke of that in her cubicle one evening. Her voice turned tart. "From all I've seen, this land is nothing but mud. Pile mud up and let it dry and you have a hill."

"Hmm," he said; his principal wife had a point, and one that diminished his wonder at what the dwellers in the Land of the Thousand Cities had done. He wasn't sure he wanted that wonder diminished: man-made hills seemed much more impressive than heaps of mud. "It takes a *lot* of mud to make one of those hills."

"As I said, there's a lot of mud here." Roshnani might have been sweet-natured, but she was also as tenacious in argument as a badger. Abivard changed the subject, tacitly conceding the skirmish to her.

Along with the mud went abundant moisture; irrigation canals spread the waters of the Tutub and the Tib over the plain between and alongside them. *Qanats* would have wasted less, but you couldn't drive *qanats* through mud, either.

Wherever it was watered, the plain grew abundantly: grain, dates, onions, melons, beans, and more. Farmers worked their fields wearing only cloths round their loins and straw hats against the pounding sun. Sweltering in his armor, Abivard most sincerely envied them. A few yards past the far ends of the canal, the land turned gray and dusty and held only thorn bushes, if those.

The folk of the Thousand Cities fled into their towns and took shelter behind their walls as Sharbaraz's army drew near. "How are we supposed to get them out?" Abivard asked at an officers' council.

"We don't," Zal answered. "If we besiege every one of these towns, we'll stay in the land of the Thousand Cities forever and we won't get to Mashiz. We just pass 'em by: take what we need from the fields and keep moving."

"They won't love us for that," Abivard observed.

"They don't love us now," Zal said, which, though cynical, was also undoubtedly true.

Abivard looked an appeal to Sharbaraz. "Zal is right," Sharbaraz said. "If we win the war with Smerdis, we'll hold the allegiance of the land of the Thousand Cities. And if we don't—what difference will it make?" He laughed bitterly. "So we take what we need."

Ten days after the battle with the archers Smerdis had mustered against them, Sharbaraz's men turned west again, away from the valleys of the Tutub and the Tib and toward the Dilbat Mountains once more. Ahead lay Mashiz.

Also ahead, and closer, lay the army Smerdis had gathered to hold his rival out of the capital. Smoke from its cook fires smudged the sky as Sharbaraz's forces drew near.

"He's making us come to him," the rightful King of Kings said as his own army encamped for the night. "There's only one broad, straight route into Mashiz. Caravans and such have other choices, but a handful of men can block those passes. I'll send scouts out to check, but I don't think Smerdis would have left them open for us."

"Can his men sally from any of them?" Abivard asked.

Zal did not sound happy when he answered: "It could happen, lord; we have a harder time keeping him away than he does us. But he hasn't shown much in the way of fighting push or trying to do more than one thing at a time with his armies up to now. Odds are good—not great, but good—things will go on that way."

"Since the odds of my ever being free to fight this war were long indeed, I am content and more than content with good odds," Sharbaraz declared. "The chief question ahead of us remains how best to win the main battle. There once more, I fear, we have little choice but to go straight at the foe."

He said *I fear*; the top of his mind still vividly remembered the tough fight when his men had attacked Smerdis' archers head-on.

But, despite his words, he sounded eager to go toe to toe with the enemy. Like his father before him, he had as his chief notion of strategy closing with whatever enemies opposed him and pounding them to pieces.

That worried Abivard, but he had to keep silent: he did not know the lay of the land in front of Mashiz and so could not offer an opinion on how best to fight there. Zal had served at the capital. The tough, gray-bearded officer said, "Aye, if they're going to stay there and wait for us, we don't have much choice but to try and hammer 'em out. If we try to outwait them, make them come down and attack us, it's just a gamble on where disease breaks out first, and since the water coming out of the Dilbats is cleaner than what we're drinking, it's a gamble we'd likely lose."

"Onward, then," Sharbaraz said with decision. "Once the capital is in our hands, all the realm will come to see who properly belongs at its head."

"Onward," his captains echoed, Abivard among them. As Zal had said, all other choices looked worse—and one more victory would give Sharbaraz Mashiz and all of Makuran. Viewed thus, chances looked good enough to bet on.

Mashiz! Till he had rescued Sharbaraz, Abivard had never imagined seeing the capital of the realm. He had been born on the frontier and expected to live out his life and die there. But now, tiny in the distance but still plain, his eyes picked out the spreading gray mass of the palace of the King of Kings, and not far from it the great shrine to the God: in all the world, only the High Temple in Videssos the city was said to be a match for it.

Seeing the wonders of Mashiz, though, was not the same as entering the city in triumph. Between those wonders and Abivard stood Smerdis' army in a position its leaders had chosen for making a stand. The closer Abivard got to that position, the more his stomach griped him, the more misgiving grew in his mind. By the look of things, no army made up of mere mortals was going to force its way through Smerdis' host. Yet the effort had to be made.

Horns blared. "Forward the archers!" officers cried. Heavy horse, usually the cream of a Makuraner force, could not play its normal role today, for Smerdis' captains, perhaps learning from their failure in the recent battle to the south, had posted unmounted bowmen behind a barrier of stones and dirt and timber. What the lancers could not reach, they could not overwhelm.

And so the horse archers, men wearing leather rather than costly mail and splint armor, rode ahead of the lancers to try to drive Smerdis' infantry back from its sheltering barricade. Shafts flew in both directions. Men and horses screamed as they were pierced. Mounted detachments brought fresh sheaves of arrows from the supply wagons to help the horsemen keep shooting.

Smerdis' barricade did not quite cover the entire width of the approach to Mashiz. The usurper's heavy cavalry waited at either wing. When Sharbaraz's archers were well involved in their duel with the foot soldiers, Smerdis' lancers thundered forth.

In that narrow space, the mounted archers could not stand against the charge of their ironclad foes. Some were speared out of the saddle; more fell back in confusion. But Sharbaraz had been waiting for that. "Forward the lancers!" he cried, a command echoed by his officers and the martial musicians in the army.

At last, the chance to fight, Abivard thought, with something between eagerness and dread. He swung down his lance, booting his horse in the side. The foe he struck never saw him coming; his lance went in just below the fellow's right shoulder. The luckless warrior gave a bubbling scream when Abivard jerked out the lancehead. Blood poured from the wound and from his nose and mouth as he slumped over his horse's neck.

The melee in front of the barricade became general. Smerdis' archers kept shooting into the milling crowd of warriors even though some of them were on their side. All of Smerdis' horsemen and horses in the fight were armored in iron, while many of Sharbaraz's were not, so their arrows remained more likely to hurt foe than friend.

Abivard was in the thick of the melee. "Sharbaraz!" he shouted again and again. Riders on both sides cried out the name of the King of Kings they favored; in such a mixed-up fight, that was the only way to tell Smerdis' backers from those who followed Sharbaraz.

A man yelling "Smerdis!" cut at Abivard. He took the blow on his shield, then returned it. Iron sparked against iron as their swords clanged against each other. They traded strokes until the tide of battle swept them apart.

Little by little, Smerdis' cavalry gave ground, retreating back toward either end of the barricade that sheltered the archers. Some of Sharbaraz's riders raised a cheer. Abivard yelled, too, until he took a good look around the field. Driving those horsemen back meant nothing. As long as the barrier kept Sharbaraz's men from breaking through and advancing on Mashiz, victory remained out of reach.

Sharbaraz's mounted archers went back to trading shafts with Smerdis' foot soldiers. That wouldn't do what needed doing if the battle went on for the next week. As long as those archers held their ground behind the barrier, Sharbaraz's men couldn't get close enough to tear it down. That was what had to happen for victory, but Abivard didn't see how it could.

Sharbaraz had another idea. Pointing to the left of the barrier, he cried, "We'll force our way through there—we have more lancers than Smerdis can throw against us. Then we can take those cursed bowmen in flank instead of banging our heads against their wall."

Horns and yelling officers slowly began to position Sharbaraz's army for the charge he had in mind. Abivard didn't know if it would work, but it held more promise than anything he had come up with himself. He swung almost out of the saddle to grab an unbroken lance that had fallen from someone's hands.

Smerdis' horsemen gathered themselves to withstand the assault. Before the charge was signaled, though, the horns on the right wing of Sharbaraz's host rang out in confused discord. Shouts of dismay and fear rose with the alarmed horn calls. "What's gone wrong now?" Abivard cried, twisting his head to see.

All at once, he understood why Smerdis' army had seemed so light in cavalry. It *was* light in cavalry, for the usurper's generals had divided it, sending part of the force to emerge from one of the narrow canyons and take Sharbaraz's men in the flank, much as Abivard had done against Smerdis' troops earlier in the civil war.

The results were much the same here, too. The right wing of Sharbaraz's army crumpled. Even Zal, who commanded there, could do little to stem the collapse. And with their enemy in disarray, Smerdis' men, who had been about to receive a charge, made one instead. They shouted with fresh confidence and fury.

Sharbaraz also shouted. Fury filled his voice, but not confidence. "Fall back!" he ordered, sounding as if he hated the words. "Fall back and regroup. Rally, by the God, rally! The day may yet be ours."

His men did not give way to panic or despair. Most of them were raw troops who had gone from victory to victory; Abivard had wondered how they would face defeat if ever it came. The answer was what he had hoped but hadn't dared expect—they kept fighting hard.

But fighting hard was not enough. With their line broken on the right, under simultaneous attack from flank and front, they had to retreat and keep retreating so they would not have whole bands of men cut off and captured or slain. After a while, retreat took on a momentum of its own.

Smerdis' men did not push the pursuit as hard as they might have. What point? They had the victory they had needed. Sharbaraz would not parade into Mashiz: Sharbaraz would not go into Mashiz at all, not now. And as soon as word of that spread through Makuran, many who had been sitting on the fence between the two rival Kings of Kings would decide in favor of the man who held the capital.

Three farsangs east of the battlefield, Sharbaraz ordered his men to halt for the night. The bulk of the army, or what was left of it, obeyed, but a flow of men, less than a flood but more than a trickle, kept on streaming east and south. "The first ticks dropping off the horse that fed 'em," Abivard said bitterly.

"Bad choice of metaphor," Sharbaraz answered with the air of someone criticizing a bard's work. "Ticks leave a horse when it's dead, and we still have life in us."

"Aye, Majesty," Abivard said. Inside, though, he wondered how much of Sharbaraz's defiance consisted of keeping up a brave front, maybe more for himself than for anyone else. A lot of it, he feared. A rebel needed win after win until power was his. Now the rightful King of Kings had to be wondering how to rally his men and turn his right to the throne into real possession of it.

"We'll renew the assault in the morning," Sharbaraz said, "making sure this time that we've covered the mouths to all the passes."

"Aye, Majesty," Abivard repeated dutifully, but he didn't believe it, not for a moment. Fraortish eldest of all, the most fiery of the Prophets Four, couldn't have rallied the army to a renewed assault if he had promised the God would come through the Void and fight alongside Sharbaraz's men.

Even Sharbaraz seemed to sense his words rang hollow. "Well, we'll see what seems best when morning comes," he said.

Abivard trudged wearily back to the baggage train. He breathed a silent prayer of thanks that Smerdis' men hadn't pressed the pursuit; if they had, they might have overrun the train and captured the wagon that carried Roshnani and Denak.

His principal wife and sister exclaimed in delight and relief when he went up into the wagon, and then again when he told them Sharbaraz remained hale. "But what happens next?" Roshnani asked. "With the way to Mashiz blocked, what do we do?"

"His Majesty spoke of a new attack tomorrow," Abivard said. Roshnani rolled her eyes and then tried to pretend she hadn't. Even Denak, who supported Sharbaraz as automatically as she breathed, didn't say anything to that. If Denak didn't believe the attack would come off, it was surely foredoomed.

Roshnani called to one of the serving women, who fetched Abivard a mug of wine. He drained it, sprawled out on the carpet in Roshnani's cubicle to relax for a moment, and fell asleep before he realized it.

Attack came the next morning, but Sharbaraz's men did not launch it. Perhaps emboldened by their victory, Smerdis' cavalry, some archers, the rest lancers, followed their foes through the night and struck just as dawn was breaking. Sharbaraz's followers outnumbered them. It did not help. They were demoralized from losing the day before and disorganized from camping hastily after a retreat they had not expected to have to make.

Some of them fought well; others broke and fled as soon as the first arrows hissed down among them. The army as a whole held its own till about midmorning. After that, men began falling back again in spite of desperate shouts from Sharbaraz and their officers. Scenting victory, Smerdis' men kept up the pressure, attacking wherever they saw weakness.

By the end of the day, Sharbaraz's army had returned to the land of the Thousand Cities, the floodplain of the Tutub and the Tib. The rightful King of Kings looked stunned, as if he had never imagined such a disaster overfalling him. Abivard hadn't imagined it, either, so he suspected he looked stunned, too.

"I don't think I can rally them straightaway," Sharbaraz said gloomily. "Best perhaps to fall back to country where the nobles and people back us with whole hearts, there to rebuild our strength to fight again another day."

Fall back to the northwest, he meant: essentially what Smerdis had offered him before the sorcerous attack, and what he had rejected with a sneer then. But at that point of the civil war, he had been winning battles and Smerdis losing. After a couple of losses of his own, he must have thought keeping some of the flock better than losing it all.

"Aye, Majesty, perhaps that would be for the best," Abivard said. Sharbaraz was right; the army he led had lost heart, and Smerdis' no doubt gained a corresponding amount. Under such circumstances, inviting battle also invited disaster. And, while a return to the northwest would seem like exile to the rightful King of Kings, to Abivard it would be going home. He wondered how his brother—and his domain—fared. He had heard not a word since he set out on campaign.

The next morning, Sharbaraz ordered his men to turn south, to skirt the Dilbat Mountains again so they could head north and west into territory friendlier to his cause than the Land of the Thousand Cities. Smerdis' men dogged their trail, not in such numbers as to invite attack, but always lurking, watching, reporting every movement back to their superiors.

Sharbaraz's soldiers had not ridden more than a farsang when they found canals broken open to spill out their water and flood the plain, making the way impassable. On the far side, more of Smerdis' soldiers sat their horses, watching with evident pleasure the discomfiture of their foes.

Abivard shook his fist at them. "Where now, Majesty?" he asked. "They've blocked the way homeward."

"I know." Sharbaraz looked as hunted as Abivard felt. "Here in the valleys of the Tutub and the Tib, we're like flies trying to get out of a spider's web. And the spider can push us to any piece of the web he likes before strolling over and sinking his fangs into the withered husk of our army."

"There's a pleasant picture." Abivard's stomach churned. "Have we any way to start moving by our own will rather than Smerdis'?"

"Perhaps if we strike north and get over one or two of the major canals before they can break the banks and open the sluices. The thing could be done; bridges of boats span the more important waterways."

The army tried. When they got to the canal Sharbaraz had wanted to cross, they found the boats drawn up on the far bank. More of Smerdis' men were strung out along the far bank, too, waiting to see if Sharbaraz would try to force a crossing. They quickly found the canal was too deep to ford.

Sharbaraz sighed. "We'd be asking to get massacred if I had the men swim across, with or without their horses. We can't go south, we can't go north, there's an army behind us to keep us from turning back to the west . . . even if the men would obey."

Sharbaraz thought in terms of strategy, Abivard in the more homely things he had had to worry about back at the domain. "They're herding us," he said.

"Aye, they are, and drop me into the Void if I can see what to do about it, either," Sharbaraz said. "I can't reach Smerdis' traitors there—" He pointed north across the canal. "—or to the south, and if I do make the army turn against the turncoats between us and Mashiz, they won't even deign to accept battle; I can see that already. They'll just fall back and open more canals to hold us up. They can wreck them faster than we can fix them."

"I fear you're right, Majesty," Abivard said. "We've already crossed the headwaters of the Tib. What happens if they force us across the Tutub, as well? What's on the far side of the Land of the Thousand Cities?"

"Scrub country, near desert, and then Videssos." Sharbaraz spat. "Nothing I want to visit, I assure you."

But in spite of what Sharbaraz wanted, the army had to keep moving east. They could not stay in one place more than a couple of days at a time; after that, they began to run low on food and fodder both. Smerdis' men and the canals they had opened blocked the way in other directions. The folk of the Thousand Cities shut themselves up behind their walls and would not treat with Sharbaraz.

"I might as well be leading Videssians," he fumed. "I'd pay the locals well, with money and later with exemptions, to aid me in setting the canals aright and free us up to maneuver . . . but they will not hear me."

Okhos chanced to be riding close to Sharbaraz when the rightful King of Kings loosed that blast. He said, "Majesty, when you sit on your throne as you should, surely you will take such vengeance on them as to make the bards sing and miscreants shudder a thousand years from now."

"Oh, a few city governors will find themselves short a head come the day—no doubt about that," Sharbaraz told Roshnani's brother. "But past that, what point to vengeance? Kill the peasants and craftsmen and where do the realm's taxes come from?"

Okhos stared; he was still new at running a domain, let alone the realm of Makuran. After a moment he asked, "Do taxes count for more than honor?"

"Sometimes," Sharbaraz answered, which made Okhos' eyes get wider. The rightful King of Kings went on, "Besides, the peasants and craftsmen are but obeying the command of their governors. How can I fault them for that when I would expect it of them were those governors mine? Massacre strikes me as wasteful. I'll have revenge, aye, but measured revenge."

Okhos considered that as he would have a lesson from a tutor. At last he said, "Your Majesty is wise."

"My Majesty is bloody tired," Sharbaraz said. "And if I were so wise, I'd be sitting in Mashiz right now, instead of slogging through the Land of the Thousand Cities." A bug landed on his cheek. He slapped at himself, but it flew away before his hand landed. "They ought to call these river valleys the land of the Ten Million Flies. It seems to have more of them than anything else."

"Oh, I don't know, Majesty," Abivard said. "In my humble opinion, it breeds more mosquitoes still." He scratched at a welt on his arm.

Sharbaraz snorted. His laugh was grim but a laugh, one of the few Abivard had heard from him since things went wrong in front of Mashiz. "Brother-in-law of mine, I admit it: you may be right."

Taking advantage of his sovereign's relatively good humor, Abivard said, "May I speak, Majesty?" At Sharbaraz's nod, he went on, "You may be wise to show yourself moderate in more things than vengeance on the Land of the Thousand Cities. Throwing an army headlong into battle cost your father everything and has badly hurt you as well."

The scowl he got from the rightful King of Kings neither surprised nor upset him; how often did Sharbaraz hear criticism? After a long pause, though, Sharbaraz slowly nodded. "Again, you may be right. I aim to do my foe as much harm as I can, as quickly as I can. That I sometimes do myself harm as well—how could I deny it?" His wave encompassed the hot floodplain across which his unhappy army perforce traveled.

Try as he would, he found no opportunity to break free of the network of flooded canals, hostile cities, and enemy forces that hemmed him in. Smerdis, by all appearances, cared nothing for the impetuous charge if he could get results without it. Hardly shooting an arrow, his men drove Sharbaraz's riders ever farther east.

"We'll be at the Tutub soon," Sharbaraz raged. "What then? Does he think we'll drown ourselves in it for his convenience?"

"I'm sure he wishes we would; that would be easiest for him," Abivard answered. "He makes war like a man who used to head the mint: he spends nothing more than he has to. That cheese-paring cost him west of the Dilbat Mountains, but it serves him well here."

Sharbaraz swore at him and rode off in a fury. Abivard wondered what would happen when they came to the Tutub. He was ready to bet the river would be too wide and deep and swift to ford. If Smerdis' men backed their foes against it, Sharbaraz would have no choice but to throw his army at that part of Smerdis' that looked to be most nearly accessible. Abivard didn't expect victory in such an effort, but he would follow without hesitation the man he had chosen as his sovereign. What were the odds Sharbaraz would have escaped from Nalgis Crag stronghold? If he had managed that, anything might happen.

The thought consoled Abivard until he realized how spiderweb-thin was the line that ran from *might* to *would*.

Pushed on, unable to make a stand because their worst enemies were hunger and broken canals rather than archers and lancers, Sharbaraz's men reached the Tutub three days later. Abivard fully expected to have to form up for a last stand of desperate battle. After backing Sharbaraz, he was not dead keen on falling into Smerdis' hands in any case.

He wished Roshnani and Denak hadn't persuaded Sharbaraz and him to let them accompany the campaign. Back at Vek Rud stronghold, they would have been safe enough, no matter what happened to their husbands. Here—

But, to his surprise, scouts who rode up and down the river came back with word that a bridge of boats still stretched across it. "We'll go over," Sharbaraz said at once. "On the far side of the Tutub, we'll be able to move as we please, less harassed by the troops who dog us."

Abivard's horse did not like the way the planks laid across the boats shifted under its feet. It snorted and sidestepped and did its best not to go forward until he booted it in the ribs hard enough to gain its undivided attention.

The far side of the Tutub seemed much like the near one. But as soon as Sharbaraz's army had crossed, Smerdis' men rode up and set fire to the bridge of boats. The rising smoke made Abivard wonder, too late, how many boats were left on the east bank of the river to aid Sharbaraz's army in returning to the fray. He didn't know, but he had the feeling the answer would be none.

✦ IX

"**W**e can't cross back and we can't stay here long," Abivard said to Roshnani that evening as the unhappy army made camp. "That leaves us little choice."

"If we had a choice, which would be better?" she asked.

"Even if we had a choice, neither would be much good," Abivard answered. "Back on the western side of the Tutub, we'd face all the problems that led to our getting trapped here in the first place. And even if we had all the livestock and grain and fruit in the world at our fingertips here, so what? Being King of Kings for the land east of the Tutub is like being Mobedhan-mobhed for the Khamorth. Not enough of them worship the God to make them need a chief servant for him, and this land is about enough to rate a *dihqan*, but not a sovereign."

"You will have seen more of it than I, since I'm closed up here in this wagon," Roshnani said. Denak would have sounded furious at that; Roshnani just stated it matter-of-factly, to let Abivard draw what conclusions from it he would. She went on, "Your point is well made. Both choices you named seem evil. What if we went east, then?"

Abivard shook his head, a gesture full of patience, love, and the desire to be as gentle with her naivete as he could. "East of here is scrub country, about as bad as the land between oases back in the northwest. It's no place for us to stay and regather our strength. And east of that lies—Videssos."

He spoke the name with a shudder; to him, as to any Makuraner warrior, Videssos was and could only be the enemy. But

233

Roshnani pounced on it like a cat leaping after a mouse that appeared from a hole it hadn't noticed: "Why don't we fare into Videssos, then? Their Avtokrator—do I rightly remember his name as Likinios?—could hardly do worse by us than Smerdis Pimp of Pimps, could he?" She brought out the contemptuous soldierly title with a fine curl of her lip.

Abivard opened his mouth to begin an automatic condemnation of the idea, but stopped with it unuttered. Put that way, it could not be dismissed out of hand. What he did say was, "I don't see much point in throwing myself on a Videssian's mercy when he's not likely to treat me any better than Smerdis would, either."

Once she got a notion, Roshnani was not one to abandon it before she had taken it as far as it would go. She said, "Why wouldn't he treat Sharbaraz better? Likinios is a King of Kings, too, of sorts. Does he take kindly to having a cousin steal a throne that ought to belong to a son? If he does, one fine day he may find a cousin stealing his own throne."

"That's—" Abivard started to say it was foolish and ridiculous, but it wasn't. If Smerdis had the gall to usurp the throne, why shouldn't a Videssian do likewise? By all accounts, Videssians were knavish and thieving by nature. If one of their Emperors left a throne lying around vacant, somebody to whom it didn't properly belong would try to abscond with it. "That's . . . not a bad idea," he finished in tones of wonder.

"My thought was simple: what have we to lose by going into Videssos?" Roshnani said.

While Abivard looked for an answer there, something else occurred to him: the third piece of Tanshar's prophecy. "Where am I likelier to find a narrow stretch of sea than in Videssos?" he said.

Roshnani's eyes got wide. "I hadn't thought of that," she said. "If the prophecy itself is urging us eastward—"

Denak stuck her head through the cloth curtain that screened off Roshnani's cubicle. She nodded to her brother, then said, "Eastward? How can we think of going eastward? Not only would we be fleeing, but there's nothing in that direction but scrub and desert, anyhow."

"There's also Videssos, beyond the scrub," Roshnani answered, which made Denak's eyes widen in turn. Speaking alternate sentences, almost like characters out of a traveling play about one of the Prophets Four, she and Abivard explained their reasons for wanting to take refuge in the Empire and seek aid from the Avtokrator.

When they had finished, Denak stared from one of them to the other. "I thought we were in a box," she said. "So did Sharbaraz. So, no doubt, did Smerdis—he has to be looking forward to finishing us off at his leisure. But if a box doesn't have to stay a box, if we can break down one of the sides and escape in a way no one imagined—"

Abivard raised a warning hand. "We have no guarantees if we try this," he reminded his sister. "The Videssians may prove as wicked and treacherous as the tales say they are, or they may take us for enemies and attack no matter what we do to show them we're friends. Or, for that matter, some of the men here may prefer Smerdis' mercy to what they think they'll find in Videssos. We'll lose more than a handful to desertion, I fear."

Roshnani laughed. "Here we are, reckoning up the good points and the bad to this move when we have not the power to order it."

Abivard took a deep breath. "Here I am, to say that having women along on this campaign may prove its salvation. I tell you now, I never would have thought of using Videssos for refuge if I lived to be a thousand. If it succeeds, the credit goes to Roshnani."

"Thank you, my husband," Roshnani said quietly, and cast down her eyes to the carpeted floor of the wagon as if she were an ordinary, deferential Makuraner wife who had never imagined setting foot outside the women's quarters of her stronghold.

"Thank you, Abivard," Denak said, "for being open enough to see that and honest enough to say it."

He shrugged. "Father always relied on Mother's wisdom—oh, not out in the open, but he made no great secret of it, either. And wasn't it you who said that if a woman's counsel was worth something back at the stronghold, it would be worth something on campaign, too?"

"I said it, yes," Denak answered. "Whether anyone listened to me is another matter. One of the things I found with Pradtak is that men often don't."

"Judging all men by Pradtak, I suspect, is like judging all women by Ardini," Abivard said, which made Denak frown angrily and

Roshnani, after a moment's hesitation, nod. He went on, "Do you expect Sharbaraz to, ah, attend you this evening?"

Still frowning, Denak said, "No, not really. He's come here less often since things went wrong. He'd sooner brood than try to make himself feel better."

"You're probably right." Abivard got to his feet; the top of his head brushed the canvas canopy of the wagon. "I'll go and take the idea to him, then. If he says no and I can't get him to change his mind, I'll send him hither. I hope you won't think less of me for saying wives have ways to persuade a man that brothers-in-law can't use."

"Think less of you? No," Denak said. "But I wish you'd not reminded me of things I did that I'd sooner forget."

"I'm sorry," Abivard said, and left in a hurry.

Sharbaraz's tent had guards round it now, and one of the army's sorcerers stood watch outside. Abivard doubted the need for that; now that Smerdis was winning the war by ordinary means, why would he bother with sorcery? The sentries saluted as he came up to the tent.

Inside, Sharbaraz sat on his camp bed, his head in his hands. "What word, brother-in-law of mine?" he asked dully. By his demeanor, he cared nothing for the answer.

But Abivard gave him a word he had not looked for: "Videssos."

"What of Videssos?" Now Sharbaraz showed interest, if no enthusiasm. "Has Likinios decided to cast his lot with Smerdis and join in crushing me? He would be wise if he did; Smerdis won't trouble Videssos for as long as he lives."

"You misunderstand, Majesty," Abivard said, and went on to explain Roshnani's idea. The longer he talked, the more animated Sharbaraz's features became; by the time he was through, the rightful King of Kings seemed more nearly himself than he had at any time since his army was forced across the Tutub.

"It might work; by the God, it just might," he said at last. "As you say, it will cost us men who refuse to follow. It will cost more than that, too; without a doubt, any aid we get from Likinios will have a price attached to it. But even so—"

"Aye, even so," Abivard said. Then he added, "I barely knew the Avtokrator's name before we set out on this campaign. I still know next to nothing about him. Has he sons of his own? If he wants to make sure the throne passes to one of them, he may be more inclined to take your side."

"He has four," Sharbaraz answered. "For a Videssian, that's a good number—they take but one wife apiece. He's been fighting a war with Kubrat, up north and east of Videssos the city. I daresay that's why he tried to set the Khamorth against us: to keep us from invading his western provinces while he was busy on the other frontier."

"It worked," Abivard said sorrowfully.

The rightful King of Kings snorted. "Yes, didn't it just?" He bowed very low to Abivard. "I would violate custom if I told the lady Roshnani how much in her debt I am. Therefore I rely on you to pass on to her my gratitude. I shall also convey the same message to your sister." He headed toward the tent flap, plainly intending to go out.

"You mean to visit her now?" Abivard asked.

"Indeed I do," Sharbaraz said, and vanished into the night. Abivard left the royal tent a moment later. He did not head back toward the wagon from which he had just come. But if Sharbaraz was going to call on Denak when he had stayed away since things began going wrong, that was a powerful argument that hope—among other things—had revived in him.

Sharbaraz's army, or the two thirds or so of it that was left, descended on the oasis like a pack of wolves tearing to bits a single chicken. With water, a small ring of fields, and a grove of date palms, the place was ideal for caravans crossing the badlands between Makuran and Videssos. Sharbaraz's men ate everything in sight, and he had to post armed guards around the water hole to keep them from fouling it.

When they rode out again two days later, men and beasts refreshed and water skins all filled, Abivard said, "We'd war with the Videssians more often, I think, if we could get at them more easily."

"Most armies, theirs and ours both, go by way of Vaspurakan," Sharbaraz answered. "The passes through the mountains there are the best invasion routes. But with things going against us, we couldn't hope to get there and get through and still have an army left when we were done."

"I wonder what the Videssians will think when we show up on

their border," Abivard said. "Maybe that we've started our own invasion." His smile held no humor. "One day—but not yet."

Abivard looked around. Even battered as it was from desertion and defeat, Sharbaraz's army numbered several thousand. If they threw themselves headlong against the Videssians and took mem by surprise, they could do a good deal of damage before they were overwhelmed. But, as he had said, that was not the plan . . . for now. If they were to regain Makuran, they needed Videssos' help.

Sharbaraz peered eastward. "If the charts and the guides don't lie, one more oasis, two days' ride from here, then a couple of more days of scrub, and then Serrhes—a different Empire, a different world."

"Do you speak Videssian, Majesty?" Abivard asked. He could follow the Khamorth dialects after a fashion, but they were cousins to his own language. Of Videssian he knew nothing.

But Sharbaraz rattled off several sentences in a smooth, purring tongue that rather reminded Abivard of wine gurgling out of a jar: glug, glug, glug. To his relief, the rightful King of Kings dropped back into Makuraner. "I was tutored in it, aye; my father thought it something I needed to know. A fair number of nobles and merchants speak it, especially in the east and south of the realm. Some of the Videssian grandees know Makuraner, too."

"That's a relief," Abivard said. "I was afraid I'd be the same as a deaf-mute all the time we were there."

"No, you'll manage," Sharbaraz told him. "And Videssian isn't that hard to pick up, though some of the sounds are hard for us to pronounce." He lisped and hissed to show what he meant, then went on, "But Videssians can't say *sh*, so it evens out. The language is very good for putting across delicate shades of meaning. I don't know whether that's because they use it so much to quarrel about the exact nature of their god Phos, or whether they quarrel the way they do because Videssian lets them. Which came first, the sheep or the lamb?"

"I don't know," Abivard answered. "I wasn't cut out to be a wise man; whenever I start thinking about complicated things, my wits seize up like a water wheel clogged with mud."

Sharbaraz laughed. "Most of the time, simple is better," he agreed. "If things were simple, I'd have taken my father's throne and that would have been that. But things aren't simple that way, and so we have to face the complications of Videssos."

Abivard pointed to a cloud of dust ahead, just at the edge of visibility. "We may have to face them sooner than we expected. What's that?"

"I don't know," Sharbaraz said in a hollow voice, "but it looks like an army to me." He slammed a fist down on his armored thigh. "How could they have learned we were coming? We can't put up much of a fight against a foe that's ready for us, not now."

Scouts were already riding forward to take the measure of the new threat. After a few minutes, one of them came galloping back toward the main body of the army. Abivard was shocked to see him laughing fit to burst.

Sharbaraz saw that, too, and purpled in fury. "Have you gone mad?" he shouted at the scout. "They're going to beat us like carpets, and you laugh?"

"Majesty, I crave your pardon," the scout said, but he didn't stop laughing. Tears of mirth cut clean tracks through the dust and grime on his cheeks. "That's no army up ahead, Majesty, just a big herd of wild asses raising a cloud, same as if they were cavalry."

Sharbaraz gaped, then laughed himself, a high, shrill cackle that seemed made up of concentrated essence of relief. "Asses, you say? By the God, they made asses out of us."

"Let's make them pay for their presumption," Abivard exclaimed. "They're fresh meat, after all, and we haven't seen much of that for a while. Hunting them would be fitting punishment for frightening us out of our wits."

"So ordered!" Sharbaraz said. Archers pounded after the animals, which fled across the scrubby ground. Watching the asses gallop away in terror made Abivard wish all foes could be so easily overcome.

Abivard was never quite sure just when the army crossed into Videssian territory, one stretch of arid landscape looked much like another. When the soldiers came to a village, though, all possible doubt disappeared: along with the scattered stone houses stood a larger building with a wooden spire topped by a gilded dome—a temple to Phos, the Videssian god of good.

The people had disappeared along with the doubt; dust trails in the distance showed the direction in which they had fled. "Nice to know we still look like a conquering army to someone," Abivard remarked.

Zal, who was riding close by, clicked his tongue between his teeth a couple of times. "This from the trusting young lord who let the tax collector into his stronghold without even checking how sharp his fangs were? Going off to war has coarsened you, lad." He grinned to show he meant no harm by the words.

"You're probably right," Abivard answered. "Once you watch your hopes bounce up and down a few times, you're not as sure things will all turn out for the best as you used to be."

"Isn't that the truth?" Zal said. "It's too cursed bad, but it's so."

From then on, Sharbaraz ordered the scouts to carry shields of truce so the Videssians would learn as quickly as might be that he had come as a supplicant, not an invader. That forethought soon proved its worth. Early the next morning, a scout came back not with the report of a herd of wild asses, but with a Videssian officer in tow.

Like a lot of Sharbaraz's men, Abivard stared curiously at the first Videssian he had ever seen. The fellow was mounted on a medium-good horse, with a medium-good mailshirt worn above leather trousers. He had a bow ready to grab, a quiver on his back, and a curved sword at his belt.

His helmet was halfway between the standard Makuraner cone pattern and a smooth round dome. No veil or iron links descended from it, so Abivard got a good look at his features. His skin was slightly paler than that of most Makuraners, his nose on the thin side, and his face nearly triangular, sloping down from a wide forehead to a chin of almost feminine delicacy. A fringe of beard outlined that chin and his jaw.

"Do you speak my language?" Sharbaraz asked in Makuraner.

"Aye, a bit," the Videssian answered. "Few on this frontier don't." He used Makuraner well enough, though his accent sometimes made him hard to understand. One of his eyebrows—so thin and smoothly curved that Abivard wondered if he plucked it into shape—rose. "But I ought to be the one asking the questions. For starters, who are you and what are you doing in my country with an army tagging along?" His quick, scornful glance up and down the line of riders said he saw better-looking armies every day of the week, and sometimes twice a day. He added, "Which side of your civil war were you on?"

"I am Sharbaraz, rightful King of Kings of Makuran, and I was on my own side," Sharbaraz proclaimed. Abivard had the satisfaction of watching the Videssian's mouth drop open like a toad's when it snapped at a fly. Sharbaraz went on, "I have come to Videssos to seek the Avtokrator Likinios' aid in restoring me to the throne that is properly mine. Surely he will understand the importance of preserving unbroken the legitimate line of succession."

The Videssian stayed silent for most of a minute before he replied. Later, when Abivard came to understand that Videssians rarely kept quiet for any reason, he would have a deeper appreciation of the depth of shock that conveyed. At last the fellow managed to put words together: "Uh, Lord Sarbaraz—"

As Sharbaraz had said, Videssians couldn't make the *sh* sound. But the officer's accent was not what offended Abivard. "Say 'your Majesty,' as you would for your own Emperor," he growled.

"Your Majesty," the Videssian said at once. "Your Majesty, I'm not the man to treat with you; the lord with the great and good mind knows that's so." His laugh came rueful. "I'm not the man to stop you, either. When the villagers rode into Serrhes screaming that all the soldiers in the world were heading that way, the *epoptes*—the city governor, you'd say—figured a pack of desert bandits had got bold; he sent me out to deal with them. I have fifty men back there, no more."

"Who will treat with me, then?" Sharbaraz asked. "Is this *epoptes* of yours a man of sufficient rank to discuss matters of state?"

"No," the Videssian said, then added, "your Majesty. But I hear tell Likinios' eldest son is traveling through the westlands, keeping things on an even keel here while the Avtokrator, Phos bless him, campaigns against the heathens of Kubrat. Hosios will be able to deal with you."

"Indeed." Sharbaraz regally inclined his head. "Will he come to the town of Serrhes? If so, when?"

"Drop me in the ice if I know," the officer said, apparently an oath but not one Abivard recognized. "If he wasn't planning to come there in his progress, though, I expect he'll change his mind when old Kalamos—sorry, your Majesty, that's the city governor—sends a letter off to wherever he is now, telling him you've come into the Empire."

"I suspect you may be right," Sharbaraz said. He and the Videssian soldier both laughed at the understatement.

Serrhes struck Abivard as being halfway between a stronghold
town and a real city. The whole perimeter was fortified, with a
wall higher and thicker than Vek Rud stronghold boasted. Inside,
on the highest ground in the place, stood a massive citadel where
warriors could retreat in case the outer wall was breached.

"Pretty strong fortress to stick out in the middle of nowhere,"
he remarked to Sharbaraz.

The rightful King of Kings chuckled. "The only reason the Videssians would site a fortress here is to protect their land from us."
Abivard thought about that, then nodded. Belonging to a people
who could inspire such precautions made him proud.

By the smooth way in which the *epoptes* took over the provi-
sioning of Sharbaraz's men, he might have had Makuraner armies
dropping in for a visit every other month. Some of the grain came
from the storerooms in the cellar of the citadel; soon pack animals
were fetching more from farther east. The spring that made the
town possible at all was barely adequate for the sudden influx.
Videssian guards made sure no one took more than his fair share.
They were stern but, Abivard had to admit, just.

Hosios arrived a bit more than two weeks after Sharbaraz's
shrunken host came to Serrhes. The *epoptes*, a plump little man,
went about his town in a transport of nervousness: if the protocol for the meeting between the Avtokrator's eldest son and the
claimant to the title of King of Kings of Makuran broke down,
the blame would all land on him, for both primary parties to
the meeting were of rank too exalted for any to stick to them.
Had Abivard been wearing Kalamos' boots, he would have been
nervous, too.

As a matter of fact, he *was* nervous, and for reasons related to
those of the city governor. Coming to Videssos had been Roshnani's idea, which he had sold to Sharbaraz; if it did not bring
the results for which he had hoped, Sharbaraz would remember.
Of course, if it didn't bring those results, Sharbaraz would not
be powerful enough to make his displeasure felt.

The ceremony the *epoptes* devised was as elaborately formal as
a wedding. Hosios rode out from the city, accompanied by Kalamos and a ceremonial guard of twenty men. At the same time,

Sharbaraz advanced from the tent city that had sprung up outside Serrhes, along with Abivard and twenty men of his own.

"Ah," Sharbaraz murmured as the Avtokrator's eldest son drew near, "he wears the red boots. Do you see, Abivard?"

"I see they *are* red," Abivard answered. "Does that mean something special?"

Sharbaraz nodded. "The Videssians have ceremonial usages of their own, as complicated as ours. Only an Avtokrator may wear boots all of red, without black stripes or something of the sort. Hosios is junior Emperor in his own right, in other words. I am treating with an equal, at least in theory."

Abivard didn't need that explained to him. In practice, Likinios made the decisions. Abivard said, "I'm glad Hosios speaks Makuraner. Otherwise I'd be as useful here as a fifth leg on a horse."

Sharbaraz waved him to silence; Hosios was drawing close enough to hear. He was about Abivard's age, with a narrow-chinned Videssian face made distinctive by a sword scar on one cheek and by eyes that gave the strong impression of having seen everything at least once. He wore a golden circlet that did not quite hide the fact that his hairline had begun to recede.

Because Sharbaraz had entered Videssos, he spoke first. "I, Sharbaraz, King of Kings, good and pacific, fortunate and pious, to whom the God has given great fortune and a great realm, a man formed in the image of the God, greet you, Hosios Avtokrator, my brother."

Hosios inclined his head; evidently he knew not only the Makuraner language but also the flowery rhetoric that flourished in Sharbaraz's realm. He said, "In the name of Likinios, Avtokrator of the Videssians, viceregent of Phos on earth, I, Hosios Avtokrator, greet you, Sharbaraz by right of birth King of Kings, my brother."

He held out his hand. Sharbaraz urged his horse forward a pace or two and clasped it, without hesitation but also without joy. Abivard understood that. The Videssians had flowery ceremonial language of their own, but he had caught the implications of *by right of birth King of Kings*. It sounded well, but promised nothing. If at some future time Likinios saw wisdom in recognizing Smerdis, he could do so with a clear conscience, for having the birthright of a King of Kings was not the same as actually being one.

Sharbaraz released Hosios' hand and introduced Abivard to him. Abivard bowed in the saddle, saying, "Your Majesty—"

"I am styled 'young Majesty,' to distinguish me from my father," Hosios broke in.

"Your pardon, young Majesty. I was about to say, I never expected to have the honor of meeting a Videssian Avtokrator, save perhaps on the battlefield—and then the introduction would have been edged with iron, not words."

"Aye—sharper than the one of us or the other would have liked, that's certain." Hosios sized up Abivard with the knowing eyes that, along with his scar, said he had been on a few battlefields in his time: perhaps against the Kubratoi, whoever they were: to Abivard, at any rate, no more than a name.

Sharbaraz said, "You will understand, Hosios—" With his rank, he was entitled to use the junior Avtokrator's name unadorned. "—I would sooner meet you as foe and outright enemy myself. You would know I was lying if I said otherwise. But since fate compels me to come before you as a beggar, I own that is what I am." He bowed his proud head to Hosios.

The junior Avtokrator reached out to set a hand on his shoulder. "No harm will come to you and yours in Videssos, Sharbaraz: may Phos the lord with the great and good mind damn me to the eternal ice if I lie. Whatever else befalls, I promise you a mansion in Videssos the city and estates in the countryside, with appropriate lodging throughout the Empire for the men who have followed you here."

"You are generous," Sharbaraz said, again with something less than a whole heart. Again, Abivard had no trouble figuring out why: Hosios proposed to dissolve the Makuraner army like a small spoonful of salt poured into a great tun of water. After a moment's pause to show he also grasped that point, Sharbaraz resumed: "But I did not come here seeking a new home for me and mine. I came to beseech your aid that I might return to Makuran, where I already have a home."

"I know that," Hosios answered calmly. "Were it in my power, you would have what you ask for on the instant. But my power, though large, does not reach so far. You will have to wait on my father's will."

Sharbaraz inclined his head once more. "Your father is well served in you. The God grant he realize it."

"In such ways as you can in your distress, you are generous to me," Hosios said, smiling. "One would have to be a very bold man indeed to contemplate going against my father's will. As with my power, my boldness is large, but does not extend so far."

Beside him, Kalamos the *epoptes* nodded vigorously. He had a good and healthy respect for the Avtokrator's power. Abivard approved of that. He wished a certain mintmaster back in Mashiz had shown similar respect for the power of the King of Kings.

"May I ask a question, Majesty?" he murmured to Sharbaraz. When his sovereign nodded, he turned to Hosios and said, "If Likinios has such power and boldness as you describe, young Majesty, what could keep him from coming to our aid?"

He didn't know what sort of answer he had expected, but it was not the blunt reply Hosios gave him: "Two things spring to mind, eminent sir. One, your principal there may not offer concessions substantial enough to make it worth our while to restore him to the throne. And two, related to one, the war against the Kubratoi has caused a hemorrhage in the treasury. Videssos may simply lack the funds to do as you desire, however much we might want to."

"We in Makuran speak of Videssos as a nation of merchants," Sharbaraz said. "I regret to say it seems to be so."

Hosios had his own kind of pride, not the haughty arrogance a Makuraner noble would have displayed, but a certainty all the more impressive for being understated. "If we were but a nation of merchants, Makuran would have conquered us long since. I would be impolite to remind you who seeks whose aid, and so I would never presume to do such a thing."

"Of course," Sharbaraz said sourly. Hosios' not-reminder could scarcely have hit any harder had the junior Avtokrator held up a sign.

"We are friends here, or at least not enemies," Hosios said. "I bid you to a feast this evening, to be held in the residence of the noble *epoptes* here. Bring a score of your chiefest captains with you, or even half again as many. And, since I am told you and your brother-in-law have your wives accompanying you, bring them, as well. Many of the leading citizens of Serrhes will have their ladies with them. My own wife is back in Videssos the city, or I would do the same."

"This is not our custom." Sharbaraz's voice was stiff. Abivard nodded.

Hosios ignored both of them. He said, "We have a proverb: 'When in Videssos the city, eat fish.' If you come to the Videssian Empire, should you not accommodate yourselves to our usages?"

Sharbaraz hesitated. As soon as he did, Abivard knew another fight was lost. This time, he resolved to get ahead of the rightful King of Kings. "Thank you for the invitation, young Majesty," he said to Hosios. "Roshnani will be honored to attend, especially since it's you who command it."

Hosios beamed and turned to Sharbaraz. The rightful King of Kings gave Abivard a so-you've-had-your-revenge look, then yielded with as much grace as he could muster: "Where Abivard's wife may go, how can his sister be left behind? Denak, too, will conform to your customs this evening."

"Excellent!" The junior Avtokrator carefully refrained from sounding smug or triumphant. "I shall see you at sunset this evening, then."

"At sunset." Sharbaraz carefully refrained from sounding enthusiastic.

"I'm so excited!" Roshnani squeaked as she walked through the streets of Serrhes toward the *epoptes'* residence. She stared at the golden dome atop a temple to Phos. "I never imagined I would see a Videssian city from the inside."

"I hoped I would, after taking it in war," Abivard said, "but not this way—never as guest to the Avtokrator's son."

A couple of paces ahead, Denak strode along beside Sharbaraz. By the casual glances she cast this way and that, she might have been born in Serrhes and come back to it after a few months' absence: she appeared interested but a long way from fascinated. Unlike her sister-in-law, she took the invitation to Hosios' supper as no more than her due.

The officers who trailed after Sharbaraz and Abivard imitated Denak in one respect: just as she did her best to seem unimpressed with the Videssian city, so they tried to pretend that she and Roshnani were not with their party. Their idea of society was rigidly masculine, and they aimed to keep it that way.

Kalamos' residence and Serrhes' main temple to Phos looked

at each across the market square below the hillock in which the citadel stood. The temple was impressive, with a large dome surmounting on pendentives walls thick enough to make another citadel in time of need. By contrast, the *epoptes'* residence was severely plain: whitewashed walls, slit windows, a red tile roof. If such a meager home was a perquisite of office, Abivard wondered how the Videssians managed to lure anyone into the job.

His perspective changed when he went inside. Videssians confined the loveliness of their homes to the interior, where only those so bidden could observe it. Mosaics of herding and hunting scenes brightened the floors, while tapestries made the walls seem to come alive. The residence was built around a courtyard. A fountain splashed there, in the middle of a formal garden. Torches did their brave best to turn evening to noontime.

Hosios and Kalamos greeted the Makuraner leaders as they arrived. Beside the *epoptes* stood his wife, a plump, pleasant-faced woman who seemed pleased to greet Roshnani and Denak and a trifle puzzled—though politeness masked most of that—the rest of the guests had no women with them. Other officials, as Hosios had said, also had their wives—and sometimes, along with their sons, their young and pretty daughters—at the supper. They all took that utterly for granted, which bemused even Abivard, who thought of himself as a liberal in such matters.

"It's what you're used to, I suppose," Sharbaraz said after accepting greetings from yet another highborn Videssian lady. "But, by the God, I'll need a while to get used to this."

Not all the Videssians spoke Makuraner, nor did all the Makuraners know Videssian. Those who had both languages interpreted for those who did not. Some from each group hung back, resolutely unsociable, suspicious of their longtime foes, or both.

No one hung back from the wine. Servants circulated with trays of already-filled cups. Some of the wine had a strong taste of resin. A Makuraner-speaking Videssian explained to Abivard, "We use pitch to seal the wine jars and to keep the precious stuff inside from turning to vinegar. I hadn't noticed the flavor for years, till you reminded me of it."

"It's what you're used to," Abivard said, echoing his sovereign.

The main course for the banquet was a pair of roasted kids. As the second highest-ranking Makuraner, Abivard was seated by

Kalamos. He turned to the *epoptes* and said, "I recognize garlic and cloves and the flavoring, but not the rest of the sauce."

"The oil is from the olive," Kalamos answered, "which I know is not common in Makuran. And the rest is garum, brought hither all the way from Videssos the city."

"Garum?" That was not a word Abivard knew. "What goes into it? It has a tang not quite like anything I've tasted." He smacked his lips, unsure whether he liked it or not.

"It's made from fish," the *epoptes* explained. If he had stopped there, everything would have been fine, but he went on, "They make it by salting down fish innards in pots open to the air. When the fish are fully ripe, a liquid forms above them, which is then drawn off and bottled. A great delicacy, don't you agree?"

Abivard needed a moment to realize that, when the helpful Videssian said *ripe*, he meant *putrid*. His stomach got the message before his head did. He gulped wine, hoping to quell the internal revolt before it was well begun. Then he shoved his plate away. "I find I'm full," he said.

"What was he saying about fish in the sauce?" asked Roshnani, who had been talking in very simple Makuraner with the *epoptes'* wife.

"Never mind," Abivard answered. "You don't want to know." He watched the Videssians downing their young goat with gusto, sauce and all. They really thought they were giving their guests the best they had. And in fact, the meal, while strange to his palate, hadn't tasted bad—but after he found out what garum was, he couldn't bring himself to eat another bite of kid.

Fruit candied in honey and cheese made safer choices. Minstrels played pipes and pandouras and sang songs that struck the ear pleasantly, even if Abivard couldn't understand the words. The sweets and wine helped drown the memory of fermented fish sauce.

Sharbaraz and Hosios had spent the banquet in earnest conversation, sometimes in the language of one, sometimes in that of the other. They seemed to get on well, which Abivard thought an advantage. It would have been a bigger one, though, had Hosios had authority to do anything much without Likinios' leave.

Sharbaraz bowed to his host as he stood to go. Abivard and the rest of the Makuraners imitated their sovereign. As they headed out of the *epoptes'* residence, a Videssian woman let out a short shriek and then exclaimed volubly in her own language.

"Oh, by the God!" Sharbaraz clapped a hand to his forehead. "She says Bardiya stuck his hand between her—well, felt of her where he shouldn't have. Get that fool out of here, the rest of you."

As some of the Makuraner officers manhandled Bardiya out into the night, he howled, "What is she complaining about? She must be a whore, or she wouldn't show herself to other men like that. She—" Somebody clapped a hand over his mouth, muffling whatever else he had to say.

"Forgive him, I beg you, kind lady, and you also, my generous hosts," Sharbaraz said rapidly. "He must have drunk too much wine, or he would not have been so rude and foolish." To Abivard, he muttered under his breath, "This is what comes of banquets run by customs other than our own."

Hosios said, "Perhaps it would be wiser if that man did not come into Serrhes again. One lapse is fairly easily forgiven. More than one—"

Sharbaraz bowed. "It shall be as you say, of course. Thank you for your gracious understanding."

Torchbearers lighted the Makuraners' way back to their encampment. Once they were out of earshot of the *epoptes'* residence, Abivard said, "That idiot might have ruined everything."

"Don't I know it," Sharbaraz answered. "Lucky Bardiya didn't try to drag her back among the flowers. That would have been a pretty picture, wouldn't it—a rape at a feast given us by our benefactors?"

"If he'd done that, he should have answered for it with his head," Denak said. "As it is, he ought to suffer more than just being hustled away in disgrace." Her voice had a brittle edge; Abivard remembered what she had endured from Sharbaraz's guards back at Nalgis Crag stronghold.

"What do you suggest?" Sharbaraz asked, though his tone gave no assurance he would heed what she said.

"Stripes, well laid on," Denak answered at once. "Use him to teach the lesson and it won't have to be taught again."

"Too harsh." Sharbaraz sounded like a man dickering over figs in the market square. "Here's what I'll do: come morning, I'll have him apologize to that lady as if she were Likinios' wife, right down to knocking his head on the floor. That may even humiliate him worse than a flogging, and it won't cost me as much goodwill in the army."

"It's not enough," Denak said darkly.

"It's better than nothing, and more than I expected you'd get," Roshnani said. Having her sister-in-law speak up for what Sharbaraz had proposed made Denak nod, too, a sharp, abrupt motion that showed consent without enthusiasm.

"We think of the Videssians as devious double-dealers," Sharbaraz said. "Like a coin that has two sides. In their poems and chronicles, they look on us as fierce and bloodthirsty. Most times, that's a good reputation for us to have. Now, though, we have to seem civilized enough by their standards to be worth helping. A formal apology should do the job."

"It's not enough," Denak repeated, but then she let the argument go.

Hosios conveyed his recommendations, whatever they were, to a courier to take to his father in the distant northeast of the Empire of Videssos. Not long after he did so, he, too, departed from Serrhes: he had other things to do besides attending to a ragtag band of Makuraners. After he was gone, the town seemed to shrink in on Abivard, as if the world outside had altogether forgotten him and his companions.

Summer turned to fall. The local farmers harvested their meager crops. Without the wagonloads of grain that came into Serrhes every day, its Makuraner guests would have starved.

Fall brought rain. Herders—much like their Makuraner counterparts—drove their cattle and sheep to the fields that showed the most new green. Soon the winds from out of the west—from Makuran—would bring snow instead of rain. The climate might be somewhere close to as harsh as that round Vek Rud stronghold . . . and tents were worse suited than castles to riding out winter blizzards.

Rain turned roads to mud. Even had Sharbaraz and his host wished to pull up stakes and go somewhere new, they would have been hard-pressed to move far or fast through the gluey, clinging ooze. Only when the first freeze turned the mud hard did travel cautiously begin again.

About a month after that first freeze, a courier came into Serrhes to report that the Avtokrator Likinios was little more than a day outside of town. The *epoptes* went into a cleaning fit, like a village woman who sees from her window her fussy mother-in-law approaching. As if by sorcery—and Abivard wasn't altogether sure Kalamos hadn't resorted to magecraft—wreaths and bunting appeared on the streets that led from the gates to the square below the citadel: just the streets Likinios was likeliest to travel.

Sharbaraz also did his best to bring order and cleanliness to his camp outside the wall. Even after that best was done, the camp still struck Abivard as a sad, ragged place: as if a broken dream had been badly animated and brought halfway to life. But he held his peace, for Likinios, should he choose, had the power to revitalize Sharbaraz's cause in full. Anything that might prompt him to do so was worth trying.

When Likinios did reach Serrhes, the ceremonial ordained for his meeting with Sharbaraz was similar to that which Hosios had employed. With Abivard and his honor guard, Sharbaraz rode out from his camp to greet the Avtokrator, who came forth from the city walls.

Abivard had looked for an older version of Hosios, just as Peroz, in both looks and style, had been an older version of Sharbaraz. But Likinios, although by his face he had plainly sired his eldest son, as plainly came from a different mold.

His features were individually like those of Hosios, but taken as a whole gave Abivard the impression that the Avtokrator was totting up how much the ceremony cost—and not caring for the answer he got. Likinios wore gilded armor, but on him it seemed more a costume than something he would don naturally.

"I welcome you to Videssos, your Majesty," he said in fair Makuraner. His voice was tightly controlled, not, Abivard thought, because he was using a language foreign to him but because that was the sort of man he was. The word that ran through Abivard's mind was *calculator*.

"I thank you for your kindness and generosity to me and my people, your Majesty," Sharbaraz replied.

"You have already dealt with the *epoptes* here, so I need not introduce him to you." Likinios sounded relieved at not having to spend any unnecessary words.

"Your Majesty, I have the honor to present to you my brother-in-law the lord Abivard, *dihqan* of Vek Rud domain," Sharbaraz said. Abivard bowed in the saddle to the Avtokrator.

Likinios grudged him a nod in return. "You're a long way from home, sir," he observed. Abivard stared at him. Could he know where in Makuran Vek Rud domain lay? Abivard would not have bet against it.

Sharbaraz said, "All my men in this your realm are a long way from home, your Majesty. With your gracious assistance, we shall return there one day in the not too distant future."

The Avtokrator studied him for a while before replying. Likinios' eyes didn't see just surfaces; Abivard had the feeling they measured like a cloth merchant checking the exact length of a bolt—and reckoned up cost with the same impersonal precision. At last Likinios said, "If you can show me how helping you is worth my while, I'll do it. Otherwise—" He let the word hang in the air.

"Your son was more forthcoming on this, your Majesty," Sharbaraz said. He did not presume to call Likinios by name, as he had Hosios.

"My son, as yet, is young." The Avtokrator made a sharp chopping gesture with his right hand. "He has no trouble deciding what he wants, but he has not yet learned that everything has its price."

"Surely having a King of Kings in Mashiz who was grateful for your generosity would be worth a pretty price," Sharbaraz said.

"Gratitude is worth its weight in gold," Likinios said. Abivard thought the Videssian ruler was agreeing with Sharbaraz until he realized words had no weight.

Sharbaraz also needed a moment to catch that. When he did, he frowned and said, "Surely honor and justice are not words without meaning to a man who has held the imperial throne for more than twenty years."

"No indeed," Likinios answered. "But other words also have meaning to me: risk and cost and reward not least among them. Putting you back on your throne won't be easy or cheap. If I decide to do it, I expect to be rewarded with more than gratitude, your Majesty." The way he aimed the honorific at Sharbaraz only emphasized that the rightful King of Kings would not be truly entitled to it without Videssian aid.

"If you fail to help me now, and I reclaim the throne even so—" Sharbaraz began.

"I'll take that chance," Likinios said, his voice flat.

Abivard leaned over to whisper to Sharbaraz: "Bluff and bluster will get you nowhere with this one, Majesty. All that's real to him is what he can see and touch and count. His son may be sentimental—his son might not even make a bad Makuraner, if it comes to that—but he's the cold-hearted Videssian in all our tales come to life."

"I fear you may be right," Sharbaraz whispered back. He raised his voice to address Likinios once more: "What could be more valuable to Videssos than quiet along your western frontier?"

"We have that now," the Avtokrator answered. "We're likely to keep it as long as Smerdis rules, too."

Sharbaraz grunted, as if kicked in the belly. Also as if kicked in the belly, he needed time to find the breath for a reply. "I had not looked for your Majesty to be so . . . blunt."

Likinios shrugged. "My father Hosios had me work in the treasury for a time before the throne came to me. Once you're around numbers for a while, you lose patience with twisting words around."

"That's not what Smerdis found," Sharbaraz said with a sour laugh. He pointed to Likinios. "You took the throne from your father, and you want your son to have it from you. But what if some treasury official not of your house takes courage from what Smerdis did in Mashiz and steals the throne that ought to belong to Hosios? If you encourage usurpers in Makuran, you encourage them in Videssos, too."

"There is the first argument of sense you've put forward," Likinios remarked. Abivard felt like hugging himself with glee. That wasn't Sharbaraz's argument, it was Roshnani's, at least in essence. How she would laugh—how she would brag!—when he told her what the Avtokrator of the Videssians had said about it.

"How much weight does it have?" Sharbaraz asked.

"By itself, not enough," Likinios said flatly. "Smerdis will give me peace in the west as well as you will. I need that peace for now, so I can properly deal with the Kubratoi once for all. Their horsemen raid all the way down to the suburbs of Videssos the city. A century and a half ago, the cursed savages forced their way south of the Istros River and set up their robbers' nest in land rightfully Videssian. I aim to take it back if it costs me every goldpiece in the treasury."

"This I understand, your Majesty," Abivard said. "We have our own trouble with nomads spilling south over the Degird." Videssos had subsidized those nomads, but he forbore to mention it. His sovereign needed Videssian aid.

Likinios' eyes swung away from Sharbaraz and onto him. They were red-tracked, pouchy, full of suspicion, but very wise—maybe dangerously wise. Had his father Godarz been filled with bitterness instead of calm, he might have had eyes like those. The Avtokrator said, "Then you will also understand why I say Videssos' aid has a price attached."

"And what price will you seek to extract from me?" Sharbaraz asked. "Whatever you ask of me, you may be fairly sure I will tell you aye. But you may also be sure I shall remember."

"And you, your Majesty, may be sure I am sure of both those things." Likinios' smile stretched his mouth wide but did not reach those disconcerting eyes. "A nice calculation, don't you think?—how much to demand so that I show a profit from the arrangement and yet keep from enraging you afterward." He shrugged. "We need not decide the matter now. After all, we have the whole winter ahead of us."

"You look forward to the dicker," Abivard blurted. Imagining a Videssian Avtokrator as devious was easy. Imagining him as a merchant in the bazaar was something else again.

But Likinios nodded. "Of course I do."

Snow swirled through the streets as Sharbaraz and Abivard rode toward the *epoptes'* residence. Abivard was beginning to pick up some Videssian. He laughed after he and the rightful King of Kings went past a couple of locals chatting with each other. Sharbaraz gave him a curious look. "What's so funny?"

"Didn't I understand them?" Abivard said. "Weren't they complaining about what a hard winter this is?"

"Oh, I see." His sovereign managed a smile, but a thin one. "I would have said the same thing till I saw what you endured every year."

In front of Kalamos' home, a servitor took charge of the Makuraners' horses. Another servitor, bowing deeply, admitted them to the residence, then made haste to shut the door behind them. Abivard heartily approved of that; ducts under the floor carried heat from a central fire to keep the *epoptes'* residence if not warm, then at least not cold.

That second servant led them to the chamber where Likinios awaited. They could have found the room without his help; they had been here a good many times before. The servant turned to

Abivard. "Shall I bring hot spiced wine, eminent sir?" he asked in Videssian—he knew Abivard was trying to learn his tongue.

"Yes, please, that be good," Abivard said. He wouldn't be writing Videssian poetry any time soon, but he was starting to be able to say things other people could follow.

Likinios bowed to Sharbaraz, then nodded to Abivard. When the formalities were done, the Avtokrator said, "Shall we go back to the map?"

He spoke of the square of parchment as Abivard might have of a fine horse, or Ganzak the smith of a well-made sword: it was his passion, the place where his interest centered. In most circumstances, Abivard would have judged that a spiritless thing to have as a controlling interest. But not now. In the duel Likinios waged with his Makuraner guests, maps were tools of war no less than horses and swords.

As he always did, Abivard admired the Videssians' lucid cartography. His own people didn't worry so much about portraying every inch of ground, perhaps because so much of the ground in Makuran held little worth portraying. But Likinios had detailed pictures of land Videssos didn't even own—yet.

"I knew we would come down to haggling over valleys in Vaspurakan," Sharbaraz said gloomily.

"You'd not have the wit to be King of Kings if you didn't know it," the Avtokrator retorted. He pointed to the map again. The mountain valleys of Vaspurakan ran east and west between Videssos and Makuran, up to the north of Serrhes. They offered the best trade routes—which also meant the best invasion routes—between the two lands. These days most of those routes lay in Makuraner hands.

Sharbaraz said, "Along with the lay of the land, Vaspurakan grows good fighting men. I hate even to think of giving them up."

"Caught between your realm and mine, they have to be good fighting men," Likinios said, which drew a startled chuckle from Abivard; he hadn't thought the Avtokrator a man to crack any jokes, even small ones. Likinios continued, "The Vaspurakaners also worship Phos. Videssos grieves to see them under the dominion of those who will spend eternity in Skotos' ice for their misbelief."

"I think Videssos grieves more over that than the Vaspurakaners do," Sharbaraz answered. "They think you worship your god the wrong way, and complain that you try to make them follow your errors."

"Our usages are not errors," Likinios said stiffly, "and no matter what they are, you, your Majesty, are in a poor position to point them out to me."

Sharbaraz sighed. "That's true, I fear." Reluctantly, he walked over to the map. "Show me again what you propose to wring from me in exchange for your aid."

Likinios ran his finger down a zigzagging line from north to south. He was not modest in his demands. At the moment, Makuran held about four fifths of Vaspurakan. Were Sharbaraz to accept what Likinios wanted, that holding would shrink to less than half the disputed country.

Abivard said, "Tell him no, your Majesty. What he asks is robbery, no other word for it."

"That is not true," Likinios said. "It is a price for a service rendered. If you do not wish the service, your Majesty, you need not pay the price."

"It is still too high a price," Sharbaraz said. "As I warned you when we first met, did I pay it, I should feel honor-bound to try to recover it when my strength allowed. I tell you this again, your Majesty, so you may be forewarned."

"You'd start that war of revenge for this, eh?" Likinios frowned and paced back and forth. "It could be so."

"It is so," Sharbaraz answered. "I pledge my word on it, and the word of a Makuraner noble—unless he be Smerdis—is to be trusted. If you insist, I will pay this price, but we shall have war afterward."

"I cannot afford more war now," Likinios said irritably, spitting out *afford* as if it were a curse. "However much I should like a friendly King of Kings in Mashiz, you tempt me to think an ineffectual one will serve as well."

Abivard studied the map once more. He also listened again in his mind to the way Likinios had spoken. He pointed to a symbol in one of the valleys Likinios sought to claim. "These crossed picks represent a mine, not so?" Likinios nodded. Abivard continued, "What would your Majesty say to a boundary that marched more like this?" He drew his own zigzag line, this one taking in several valleys with mines but not the great stretch of territory to which the Avtokrator wanted to lay claim.

"It still gives away too much," Sharbaraz said.

At the same time Likinios said, "This is not enough."

The two men of royal blood looked at each other. Abivard took advantage of their hesitation: "Your Majesties, isn't a plan that leaves both of you less than happy better than one that satisfies Videssos too well and Makuran not at all, or the other way round?"

"Ah, but if I am not satisfied, I have only to withhold aid and my life goes on anyway, much as it would have without these talks," Likinios said.

"While that's true, your Majesty, if you don't give me aid, you lose the chance to put a King of Kings beholden to you on the throne in Mashiz, and you leave a usurper there as a temptation to every ambitious man in Videssos," Sharbaraz said. "And if you think Smerdis will be grateful to you for not backing me, remember how he treated me."

Likinios scowled and studied the map again. Encouraged because he did not reject the proposal out of hand, Abivard said, "If the precise border I suggested fails to please you, your Majesty, perhaps you will propose one along similar lines. Or perhaps my master the King of Kings, may his years be many and his realm increase, might offer one of his own?"

"How do you speak of the realm's increasing in one breath and ask me to take away a great slice of Vaspurakan in the next?" Sharbaraz asked. But, to Abivard's relief, he did not sound angry. Instead, he walked over and gave the map a long, hard look himself.

Abivard thought serious talk, as opposed to posturing, began then between the King of Kings of Makuran and the Avtokrator of the Videssians. The next time he tried to suggest something to move the talks along, both men stared at him as if he were a drooling idiot. He felt humiliated, but not for long: two days later, they reached an agreement not very far from the one he had outlined on the map with his finger.

Tanshar bowed low to Abivard. "May it please you, lord," the fortune-teller said, "you are being spoken of—complimented, to make myself clear—by our people and the Videssians alike." He bowed. "Always an honor to serve you, and doubly now. What is your wish?"

"Were I to suggest what I propose to you in aid of a King of Kings rather than an Avtokrator, I should be guilty of treason," Abivard answered.

The fortune-teller nodded, unsurprised. "You want me to learn what I can of the Videssian royal house?"

"Just so," Abivard said. "I want you to scry out, if you can, how long Likinios will remain on the throne and how long Hosios will rule after him."

"I shall try, lord, but I make no guarantees as to the results," Tanshar answered. "As you say, you would be committing treason if you sought to learn these things about the royal house of Makuran. Not only that, you would have a hard time learning them even if you had no fear of treason: the King of Kings will normally surround himself with spells that make divining his future as difficult as possible, in my judgment a sensible measure of self-preservation. I would be most surprised if the Avtokrator did not similarly ward himself."

"I hadn't thought of that," Abivard said unhappily, "but yes, you're likely to be right. Do your best all the same. Perhaps you will have better luck than a Videssian mage might, for I'd guess the Avtokrator would be best protected against the kind of sorcery usual in his own country."

"No doubt that's so, lord," Tanshar agreed, "but we, plainly, are the next greatest magical threat to the Avtokrator's well-being, so his future may be shielded against our magecraft, as well."

"I understand," Abivard said. "If you fail, we're no worse off than we would be otherwise. But if you succeed, we'll have learned something important about how far we can rely on the Videssians. Do the best you can; that's all I can say."

"Fair enough," Tanshar said. "I appreciate your not expecting the impossible of me. What I can do, I shall do. When do you want me to make the attempt?"

"As soon as may be."

"Of course, lord," Tanshar said, "although you may not find it exciting to watch. The charms involved have little drama to them, I confess, and I may have to go through several of them to find one that works—if, indeed, any of them succeeds. As I said, I have no assurance of success in this undertaking. But if you like, I will begin trying this evening after you return from the latest talks between his Majesty and the Avtokrator Likinios."

"That will be fine," Abivard said. Having haggled over what Sharbaraz would yield in exchange for aid, the two men were now dickering over how much aid he would get; Likinios would indeed have made a marvelous rug seller. In the end, Abivard suspected Sharbaraz would make most of the concessions once more. Having the royal blood without ruling Makuran ate at him.

When Abivard went back to Tanshar's tent, he found the fortune-teller waiting for him. "I have assembled a number of means for looking into what may be," Tanshar said. "The God willing, one will pierce not only the veil of future time, but whatever the Videssians may have thrown up around their Avtokrator."

He tried scrying with water, as he had when Abivard brought him Ardini's curse tablet. Since Abivard had touched and dealt with Likinios, Tanshar reckoned him an appropriate link to the Avtokrator of the Videssians. But no matter how still the water in the scrying bowl became, it never gave the fortune-teller and Abivard any picture of what Likinios was doing or how long he might go on doing it.

"I might have known," Tanshar said. "Scrying with water is the simplest way of looking into the future. If the Videssians warded against any of our styles of divination, that would be the one."

He tried again with a clear, faceted crystal in place of the bowl of water. The crystal turned foggy. Abivard did not need to ask anything of the fortune-teller to realize that meant his magical efforts were being blocked. Tanshar replaced the clear crystal with one of chalcedony. "This is a Videssian-style divination," he said. "Perhaps it will have more success."

But it didn't. As he had guessed, the Videssians warded the Avtokrator against their own methods of seeing what lay ahead, too. Next he tried a divination that was in large measure an invocation of the God. Abivard had high hopes for that one: surely the God was stronger than the false deities of good and evil in whom the Videssians believed.

The invocation, though, failed as utterly as had the earlier divinations. "How can that be?" Abivard demanded. "I will not imagine for a moment that the Videssians worship correctly and we do not."

"Nor need you imagine that," Tanshar answered. "The truth is more simple and less dismaying: while the God of course outstrips Phos and Skotos in power, so, also, must the Videssian wizards charged with protecting their ruler surpass me. Together, they and their gods—" He curled his lip in scorn, "—suffice to block my efforts. Had we a stronger Makuraner mage here—"

"Like the one who tried to slay Sharbaraz?" Abivard broke in. "Thank you, but no. I'm sure you will use whatever you find in the service of the rightful King of Kings, not against him."

Tanshar bowed. "You are kind to an old man who never looked to be drawn into the quarrels of the great." His clouded eye but made the smile he donned more rueful. "I wish I could live up to the confidence you place in me."

"You shall. I have no doubt of it," Abivard declared.

"I wish I didn't." Tanshar rummaged in a leather pouch he wore on his belt and came up with a lump of coal that left black smears on his hands. "Perhaps divination by opposites will evade the Videssians' wards," he said. "Few things are more opaque than coal; Likinios' future, however, seems at the moment to be one of them."

He poured the water out of the scrying bowl and set the coal in its place. The dialect of Makuraner in which he murmured his summons to the God was so archaic, Abivard could hardly understand it. He wondered what would happen if the scrying succeeded. Would the lump of coal become transparent, as his clear crystal had grown murky?

With a *snap*! almost like a small bolt of lightning, the coal burst into flame. Tanshar jerked his head away just in time to keep his mustache and bushy eyebrows from getting singed. A pillar of greasy black smoke rose to the roof of his tent.

"Does that tell you anything?" Abivard asked.

"One thing, and that most clearly," Tanshar answered in a shaken voice. "I am not likely to learn how long Likinios will remain Avtokrator, not with any sorcery I have under my control."

Abivard bowed his head, accepting that. But he was the sort who, when thwarted in one direction, would turn to another to gain his ends. "All right, then," he said. "Let's see how long Hosios will reign once he succeeds his father."

Tanshar waited till the coal had burned out, then swept the ashes from the scrying bowl. He swung a small censer full of bitterly aromatic myrrh over the bowl. "I want to purify it before my next attempt," he explained. "No trace of that previous magic may remain."

He began anew with the simplest scrying tool: plain water in the bowl. Together he and Abivard waited for stillness, then touched the bowl and waited again.

Abivard had not placed much faith in this try. He gasped when the water roiled and bubbled, then gasped again when, instead of showing him a scene that would answer his question, it turned thick and red. "Blood!" he said, choking a little.

"You see that, too?" Tanshar said.

"Yes. What does it mean?"

"Unless I'm much mistaken," Tanshar said, sounding sure he was not, "it means Hosios shall not live to wear the Avtokrator's crown and red boots, for, by that conjuration, the blood was surely his."

X

Spring came to Serrhes a couple of weeks earlier than it would have in Vek Rud domain. By the time rain replaced snow and closed the roads for a spell, though, Likinios had brought in a good-sized force of cavalry to join Sharbaraz's men against Smerdis.

At the head of the cavalry regiments was a general who reminded Abivard of a fatter version of Zal: a tough fellow in his fifties, not long on polish but liable to be very good in the field. His name was Maniakes. In spite of that, he didn't look like a Videssian; he was blocky, square-featured, with a truly impressive fleshy promontory of a nose and a tangled gray beard that hung halfway down the front of his mail shirt.

"I'm Videssian enough, thanks," he answered when Abivard asked him about it, "even if all four of my grandparents came out of Vaspurakan."

"But—" Abivard scratched his head. "Don't you worship differently from the Videssians?"

"I do, aye, but my son was raised in Videssos' faith," the officer answered. "From what my grandfathers said, that's a smaller change to make than worshiping the God whom you Makuraners were trying to ram down the throat of Vaspurakan."

"Oh." Abivard wondered if the Makuraner overlords of Vaspurakan still behaved as they had in the days of Maniakes' grandfather. He hoped not. If they did, the folk of that land might be more ready to welcome Videssos than Sharbaraz thought.

With the cavalry came a regiment of engineers with wagons full of carefully sawn timbers and lengths of thick rope and fittings of iron and bronze. The men seemed more like mechanics than soldiers. They practiced assembling engines and putting together bridges much more than they went out with bow and spear. In his campaign against Smerdis the year before, Sharbaraz had enjoyed no such aid. That had cost him in the maneuverings between the Tutub and the Tib. It would not cost him this time.

"When do we move out?" Abivard asked the rightful King of Kings after a morning of mock cavalry charges.

"We're ready. The Videssians are ready—and so is their Vaspurakaner general." Sharbaraz made a sour face. He had found out about Maniakes, then. "The trouble is, the Tutub and the Tib aren't ready. This is their flood time. The engineers don't want everything swept away if the flood proves worse than usual—and there's no way to gauge that till it happens."

"The Vek Rud and the Degird wouldn't come into flood so soon," Abivard said. After a moment he went on musingly, "Of course, the snow wouldn't be melting so early in the season up in my part of the world, either." He shrugged, prepared to make the best of it. "More time to spend with Roshnani."

Sharbaraz laughed at him. "Having but one wife along has turned you uxorious. What will the rest of your women think when you go back to your stronghold?"

"They knew she was my favorite before she set out on campaign with us," Abivard said. "I do begin to understand now, as I didn't before, how the Videssians, even the grandees among 'em, make do with but one wife each."

"Some truth to that," Sharbaraz agreed. "Having the wife in question be as clever and lovely as the lady your sister does add to the compensation, I must say."

"You are gracious, Majesty."

"I'm yearning to return to my country," Sharbaraz said. "I wonder what Smerdis is expecting. He'll know we fled to Videssos, of course, and he'll know some of what's been going on here from caravans and single traders. But whether he knows we'll have an imperial army with us when we head west again—that we'll have to find out."

"If he does, he'll be using it to whip up hatred against you," Abivard said. "He'll be calling you things like traitor and renegade."

"All he can call himself is thief and usurper," Sharbaraz answered. "Next to that, he can't do much of a job with the tar brush on me. But you're right—he'll try. Let him." The rightful King of Kings folded his hands into fists. "I'm looking forward to renewing our acquaintance."

Abivard had always reckoned his own folk pious. He believed in the God and the Prophets Four, he invoked them frequently, and he would not have thought of undertaking anything major without first praying; the same held true for any Makuraner.

But the Videssians were not merely pious, they were ostentatiously pious in a way that was new to him. When their army prepared to sally forth with that of Sharbaraz, the chief prelate of Serrhes came out to bless them in a robe of cloth-of-gold and seed pearls with a blue velvet circle over his heart. Behind him marched a couple of younger men, almost as gorgeously robed, who swung golden censers that distributed puffs of incense widely enough for even Abivard's heathen nostrils to twitch. And behind them came a double line of priests in plain blue robes with cloth-of-gold circles on their breasts. They sang a hymn of praise to Phos. Abivard could not understand all of it, but the music was strong and stirring, a good tune with which to march into battle.

Among all the holy men, the farewell from Kalamos almost got lost in the shuffle. The *epoptes* made his little speech, the Videssian cavalrymen near enough to hear it clapped their hands a couple of times, and he went back to his residence to sign parchments, stamp seals, and probably do his best to forget that the Makuraners had ever disturbed his nearly vegetative peace.

Sharbaraz made his own speech. Pointing to the gold sunburst on blue that fluttered at the head of the Videssian ranks, he said, "Today the lion of Makuran and Videssos' sun go forth together for justice. The God grant we find it soon."

His men cheered, a roar that dwarfed the spatter of applause the Videssians had deigned to dole out to Kalamos. One thing Sharbaraz knew was how to play to a crowd. He waved, made his horse rear, and then turned it toward the west, toward Makuran and home.

His lancers followed. After them came his baggage train, refurbished and supplemented by the Videssians. Their army did not ride directly behind Sharbaraz's, but on a parallel track. That was not just to keep from having to swallow their new allies' dust—it also served to remind Sharbaraz and those who traveled with him that the Videssians were a force in their own right.

Before long, they rubbed that in even more unmistakably. Videssian scouts trotted up to ride alongside the lead detachments of Sharbaraz's force. That did not sit well with Abivard; he pointed to them as they went past and said, "Don't they trust us to keep a proper watch on what lies ahead?"

Sharbaraz sighed. For the first time since he had learned Likinios would aid him, even if at a price, he seemed almost like the hopeless, despairing self he had shown when things went wrong the summer before. He said, "The short answer is, no. The Videssians will do as they please, and we're in no position to call them on any of it."

"You're in overall command of this army," Abivard insisted. "Likinios agreed to that without a murmur, as he was in honor bound to do."

Now Sharbaraz smiled, but the expression seemed more one of pity than amusement. "Every so often, brother-in-law of mine, you remind me that the world of a *dihqan* along the Vek Rud differs from that of Mashiz—or of Videssos the city." He held up a hand before Abivard could get angry. "No, I mean no offense. Your way is surely simpler and more honest. But let me ask you one question: If Maniakes declines to obey an order I give, how am I to compel him?"

Abivard bit down on that like a man breaking a tooth on a pebble in his bowl of mutton stew. As many Videssians were riding west as Makuraners, maybe more. Maniakes could more easily force Sharbaraz to do his bidding than the other way round. If he withdrew, Sharbaraz's Makuraners could not beat Smerdis by themselves. They had proved that the year before.

"I begin to think running a realm may be a deeper sorcery than many over which the mages crow," Abivard said at last. "You have to keep so many things in mind to hope to do it properly—and you have to see them to be able to keep them in mind. That one never occurred to me; maybe I am the innocent you say I am."

Sharbaraz leaned over and set a hand on his arm. "You do fine. Better not to have to look for serpents under every cushion before you sit down."

"If they're there, you'd better look for them," Abivard said.

"Oh, indeed, but I wish they weren't there," Sharbaraz replied. "By the God, when I take Mashiz and the throne, I'll kill every one I find."

"That would be splendid, Majesty; may the day come soon." Abivard rode along for a while in silence. Then he said, "In a way, though, I am sorry to be leaving Videssos so soon."

"What? Why?" Sharbaraz asked sharply. "Has your own realm lost its savor after half a year in another?"

"No, of course not." Abivard's fingers twitched in a gesture of rejection. He went on, "It's just that, because Videssos has around it so many seas, I thought Tanshar's prophecy of something shining across a narrow one might come to pass here. I've already seen fulfilled the other two he gave me."

"If that's your reason, I forgive you," Sharbaraz said, nodding. "But prophecy is a risky business."

"That's so." Abivard remembered he hadn't told his sovereign of the scrying he had had Tanshar do of Hosios' future. He described how the water in the scrying bowl had taken on the semblance of blood.

"Now that's . . . intriguing," Sharbaraz said slowly. "Had Likinios refused me aid, I might have used it against him to claim he, like my father, ran the risk of being the last of his line. But since the Videssians do ride with us, I don't know quite what to make of it or how to employ it. Best simply to bear it in mind, I suppose, till the time comes when it proves of value to me." He paused. "I wonder if Likinios' wizards made similar inquiries into my future, and what they learned if they did."

That was something else that hadn't occurred to Abivard. He bowed in the saddle to the rightful King of Kings. "Majesty, henceforward I leave all the searches for serpents and scorpions to your sharp eyes."

"I'd be more flattered at that if I'd spotted Smerdis," Sharbaraz said. Abivard spread his hands, conceding the point. Every pace their horses took moved them farther west.

Roshnani said, "I'm sorry we're leaving Videssos."

"That's odd." Abivard sat up in her little cubicle in the wagon she shared with Denak. The sudden motion stirred the air and made the lamp's flame flicker. "I said the same thing to the King of Kings earlier today. What are your reasons?"

"Can't you guess?" she asked. "Women there live as your sister and I would."

"Oh." Abivard chewed on that for a little while, then said, "And they also suffer outrages they never would in Makuran. Look what happened to that Videssian lady when Bardiya took her for a woman of no virtue."

"But Bardiya is from Makuran," Roshnani said. "I dare hope, at least, that Videssian men, used to the freedom of their women and not thinking it wrong or sinful, would never behave so."

"I didn't see them doing so, or hear tales of it," Abivard admitted. "But, being a man, I know somewhat of men. If men find themselves around such free women all the time, a good number of them will surely become smooth, practiced seducers of a sort we also do not know in Makuran."

Roshnani bit her lip. "I suppose that is possible," she said. Abivard admired her honesty for admitting it. She went on, "On the other hand, I doubt the Videssians are troubled by problems like the one Ardini caused in your women's quarters last year."

"You're probably right there," he said.

Now she smiled. He did, too, understanding her well. Neither of them was one to deny the other could have a point. Lowering her voice to a whisper, Roshnani said, "Unlike your sister, I don't claim giving women freedom from their quarters will solve all their old problems without causing any new ones. That's not how the world works. But I do think the problems that come will be smaller than the ones that go."

Abivard said, "Do you suppose some women, once freed as you say, might turn into seducers themselves?"

Denak would have got angry at such a suggestion. Roshnani considered it with her usual care. "Very likely some would," she said. "As with men, some are more lecherous than others, and some also less happy with their husbands than they might be." She ran a hand down along his bare chest and belly. "There I proved very lucky."

"And I." He stroked her cheek. He thought of what he had said to Sharbaraz earlier in the day. "With you, I think I'd have no trouble holding to the Videssian custom of having but one wife. My father would laugh at that, I'm sure, but after all, we've been together on this campaign for most of a year, and I've never felt the need for variety." He sighed. "Somehow I doubt, though, that all men are so fortunate."

"Or all women," Roshnani said.

He took her hand in his and guided it a little lower yet. "And what shall we do about that?"

"Again? So soon?" But she was not complaining.

Even the badlands that lay between Videssos' western outposts and the Land of the Thousand Cities donned a ragged cloak of green in springtime. Bees buzzed among flowers that would soon wilt and crumble, not to be seen again till the following year. Horses pulled plants from the sandy ground as they trotted west, saving some of the fodder the army had brought with it.

Maniakes rode up to Sharbaraz and Abivard. With him came a young man, hardly more than a youth, who was his image but for a beard that showed no sign of gray and features thinner and less scarred. He said, "The worst thing Smerdis could do to us would be to poison the wells along the way. We'd have Skotos' own time making it to the Tutub without stopping for water along the way, even at this time of year when the stream beds may yet hold some."

"He won't," Sharbaraz said confidently.

Maniakes raised a bushy eyebrow. "What makes you so sure?" he wondered. Abivard wondered the same thing, but couldn't have been so blunt about asking it.

Sharbaraz said, "The first thing Smerdis thinks of is money. If he poisons the wells, caravans can't cross between Videssos and Makuran, and he can't tax them. Sooner than that, he'll try to find some other way to deal with us."

"It could be so. You know Smerdis better than I do; nobody in Videssos knows much of him at all." Maniakes kept his voice neutral. He turned to the young man who looked like him and asked, "What do you think?"

In slow Makuraner, the young man replied, "I would not give away a soldierly advantage, sir, to gain money later. But some might. As Smerdis was mintmaster, money may matter much to him."

"Well reasoned," Sharbaraz said.

"Indeed," Abivard said. To Videssians, who loved logic-chopping, that was higher praise than it would have been for a Makuraner; he wondered if the same held true for Vaspurakaners who had adopted Videssian ways. In case it didn't, he nodded to the younger man—who was a few years younger than he—and asked Maniakes, "Your son?"

Maniakes bowed in the saddle—Abivard *had* pleased him. He said, "Aye, my eldest. Eminent sir," he said, rendering the Videssian title literally into Makuraner, "and your Majesty, allow me to present to you Maniakes the younger."

"Unfair," Sharbaraz said. "Makuran and Videssos are usually foes, not friends, and one of you on Videssos' side is trouble enough for us. Two seems excessive."

The elder Maniakes chuckled. The younger one murmured, "Your Majesty does me too much credit, to rank me with my father so soon."

Abivard noted the qualification of his modesty. He said, "May I ask a question?" After waiting for the two Maniakai to nod, he went on, "How is it that you both share a name? In Makuran, it's against custom to name a child after a living relative; we fear death may get confused and take the wrong one by mistake."

"The Videssians share that rule with us, I think," Sharbaraz put in.

The elder Maniakes rumbled laughter. "Just goes to show that, even if my line follows Videssian orthodoxy, we're still Vaspurakaners under the skin. Phos made us first of all peoples, and we trust him to know one of us from another, no matter what name we bear. Isn't that so, son?"

"Aye," the younger Maniakes answered, but he said no more and looked uncomfortable at having said so much. Abivard suspected he was less Vaspurakaner under the skin than his father thought. After a while, if a family lived among people different from them, wouldn't that family take on more and more of its neighbors' ways?

Spurred by that thought, he asked the elder Maniakes, "Have you any grandchildren, eminent sir?" He used the same non-Makuraner honorific the general had applied to him.

"No, none yet," Maniakes answered, "though a couple of my boys have wed, as will my namesake here if the girl's father ever stops pretending she's made of gold and pearls rather than flesh and blood."

Even though his own father hadn't so much as named the lady to whom he would—or rather, might—be married, the younger Maniakes got a soft, dreamy look in his eyes. Abivard recognized that look; he wore it whenever he thought of Roshnani. From that he concluded that the younger Maniakes not only knew but had already fallen in love with his not-quite-betrothed. That was yet another way the Videssians differed from his own people, among whom bride and groom seldom set eyes on each other before their wedding day.

Or so things worked among the nobility, at any rate. Rules for the common folk were looser, though arranged marriages were most common among them, too. Abivard wondered how lax things were for Videssian commoners, and if they had any rules at all.

The elder Maniakes turned the conversation back toward the business at hand: "Your Majesty, what do we do if the wells are fouled?"

"Either fall back into Videssos or press on toward the Tutub," Sharbaraz answered, "depending on how far we've come and how much water we have with us. I won't lead us across the waste to die of thirst, if that's what you're asking."

"If you try, I won't follow you," the elder Maniakes answered bluntly. "But aye, you talked straight with me, and you'll seldom hear a Vaspurakaner prince—which means any Vaspurakaner, just so you know—complain about that." He snorted. "Sometimes you can go for days before you get a Videssian to come out and tell you what he means."

Again, Abivard glanced toward the general's son. The younger Maniakes didn't say anything but didn't look as if he fully agreed with his father. Abivard chuckled to himself. Aye, Videssos had its hooks deeper in the son than in the father. Knowing that might prove useful one day, though he couldn't guess how.

Sharbaraz pointed ahead. "There's the first oasis, unless my eyes are playing tricks on me. We'll soon find out what Smerdis has been up to here."

Smerdis had not poisoned the wells. Both armies had their wizards and healers test the water at each stop on the journey west toward Makuran, and used a few horses to drink several hours before the men and the rest of the animals refreshed themselves, just in case the wizards and healers were wrong.

With the last oasis past, nothing but scrub—now rapidly going from green to its more usual brown—lay between the armies and the Tutub. But before they reached the river that marked the eastern boundary of the land of the Thousand Cities, Smerdis sent forth an embassy not to Sharbaraz but to the elder Maniakes.

Abivard had feared that. Smerdis' best hope now was to split the Videssians away from the rightful King of Kings. He had a way to do that, too: by offering more concessions to Likinios than Sharbaraz had. The Videssians were a devious people. For all Abivard knew, Maniakes might have accompanied Sharbaraz precisely to extort those concessions from Smerdis. If he got them, would he turn on Sharbaraz? Or would he simply order his horsemen to turn around and ride for home? That would be disastrous enough by itself.

Scouts had reported to Sharbaraz the arrival of the embassy. Had Sharbaraz been dismounted, he would have paced back and forth. Abivard understood that. When Zal's men had in essence seized his stronghold to force Smerdis' tax levy from him, his fate was taken out of his hands. Now Sharbaraz had to wait for others to decide his destiny.

"If he sells us out, I'll kill him," Sharbaraz snarled, one slow word at a time. "I don't care what happens to me afterward. Better I should fall slaying Videssians than at Smerdis' hands."

"I'll be beside you, Majesty," Abivard answered. Sharbaraz nodded, pleased at the pledge, but his face stayed grim.

Then the elder Maniakes, accompanied by his son, rode toward the rightful King of Kings. Trailing the two Videssian officers came a handful of unhappy-looking Makuraners. The elder Maniakes jerked a thumb back toward them. "They were inquiring into the price of having us switch sides," he remarked.

"Were they?" Sharbaraz fixed Smerdis' envoys with a smile that might have belonged on the face of a wolf. "The God give you good day, Paktyes. So you serve the traitor now, do you?"

One of the envoys—presumably Paktyes—looked even more uncomfortable than he had before. "S-son of Peroz, I serve the authorities in Mashiz," he said.

"By which he means he'll lick any arse that's shoved in his face," Abivard said, his voice greasy with scorn. "I never thought I'd see anything worse than a traitor, but now I have: a man who just doesn't care."

"He is disgusting, isn't he?" Sharbaraz remarked. Talking about Paktyes as if he weren't there was nicely calculated to make the ambassador all the more miserable. Ignoring him again, the rightful

King of Kings turned to the elder Maniakes and asked, "Well, my friend, how much is the Pimp of Pimps offering?"

The Videssian general blinked, then guffawed till he coughed. When the coughs subsided to wheezes, he answered, "Oh, these fellows here say he'll give up the whole of Vaspurakan, along with enough silver for a man to walk dryshod from the westlands across to Videssos the city if he poured it into the Cattle Crossing—that's the strait between 'em."

A narrow sea, Abivard thought. Maybe that was what Tanshar had meant. But how likely was he to cross all the wide westlands and come in sight of Videssos' fabled capital?

Thinking of his personal concerns made him miss for a moment the way Sharbaraz stiffened. "That is a considerable offer, and one more, ah, generous than I would care to make," Sharbaraz said carefully. "How have you replied?"

"I haven't, till now," the elder Maniakes answered. "I wanted you to hear it first."

"Why? To make me match it? If Likinios needs silver so badly—"

"Likinios always needs silver," Maniakes interrupted. "And even if he didn't, he'd think he did. I'm sorry, your Majesty—you were saying?"

"If he needs silver, I can pay him some once I regain the throne," Sharbaraz said. "If he must have all of Vaspurakan—" The rightful King of Kings bent his head back, exposing his throat. "Strike now. He shall not have it from me."

"There, do you see?" Paktyes cried. "My master offers you better terms!"

"But *my* master doesn't care," the elder Maniakes said. "He doesn't like the idea of people stealing thrones that don't belong to them. He'd sooner have an honest man ruling Makuran than a thief, you see. Can you blame him? Whoever's on the throne in Mashiz, Likinios is going to have to live with him, and honest men make better neighbors."

"Very well, then," Paktyes said. He did his best to seem fierce but succeeded only in sounding liverish. Still snapping, he went on, "The brave armies of the King of Kings, may his years be long and his realm increase, have routed the renunciate once. They can surely do it again, even if he has treacherously gained aid from our ancient foes in Videssos."

He and his delegation rode back toward the west. The elder Maniakes turned to Sharbaraz and said, "If he's the best your rival can send out, this campaign will be a walkover. That would be nice, wouldn't it?"

"Aye, it would," the rightful King of Kings answered. "But I thought my campaign last spring would be a walkover, too. And so it was—for a while. The longer it went on, though, the tougher Smerdis' men got."

Maniakes chuckled. "I know how to fix that: beat him good early so he doesn't have time to get better late." Sketching a salute, he kicked his horse in the ribs and went off to his own army.

"There's a relief," Abivard said. "The Videssians could easily have sold us out, and they didn't."

He thought Sharbaraz would also be pleased, but the rightful King of Kings replied, "So far as we know they didn't. Paktyes and Maniakes could have said anything at all before they came to us. I have no idea how good a mime Maniakes is, but any general needs some of that if he's to adapt himself to the things that can go wrong in war. As for Paktyes, I know for a fact that deceit's in his blood. How could it be otherwise, when he swings this way or that like a bronze weathervane on a farmer's roof, always turning whichever way the wind of influence blows."

"Your Majesty, you are right." Abivard looked over his right shoulder at the elder Maniakes, who had almost rejoined his men. For a few minutes, he had been elated at the idea of the Videssians' probity being assured. Now he saw it was not so. The world remained full of ambiguity.

Sharbaraz said, "The only way to be certain the Videssians stay on our side is to have them actually fight against Smerdis. Even then we won't be absolutely sure until after the last fight is won: any sooner than that and they could be dissembling, building our confidence and trust so as to make betrayal the more devastating when it comes."

Abivard sighed. With every day that passed, he was gladder his brother-in-law was the rightful King of Kings and not himself. Sharbaraz saw and took precautions against treachery in places where Abivard didn't even see the places. He had let down his guard for one moment against his elderly cousin, and that lapse might yet forever cost him his throne. Abivard wondered if Sharbaraz would ever let down his guard for anyone again.

He said, "If the Videssians do betray us, what can we do about it?"

Sharbaraz gave him a very bleak look. "Nothing."

Even so early in the season, mirages danced and sparkled across the badlands that lay between Serrhes and the land of the Thousand Cities. Abivard had grown used to them, and as used to ignoring them. When he saw water ahead, then, he discounted it as just another illusion.

But this water did not seem to stay the same unchanging, tantalizing distance ahead of him no matter how far he traveled. The farther west he rode, the closer it looked. Before long he could make out the greenery it supported. A murmur ran through the army: "The Tutub. We've come back to the Tutub."

How many of them, when they had left the easternmost river of Makuran and struck out across the desert for Videssos, had really believed they would return—and return with a good chance of restoring Sharbaraz to the throne? Not many was Abivard's guess. He had had doubts himself, and the move had been his own wife's idea. What must the rank-and-file soldiers—those who hadn't deserted the rightful King of Kings—have thought?

The murmur grew to a great roar: "The river! The river!" Men cheered and wept and pounded one another on the back. Makuran lay ahead of them. No, so many had never expected to see this day. Abivard's eyes filled with tears. No matter how little the land of the Thousand Cities resembled Vek Rud domain, he, too, was coming home.

As he drew nearer, he saw horsemen waiting on the far side of the Tutub. They probably had not looked for Sharbaraz's return, either, and had to be less than delighted to see it now. Some held their places; others rode off to the west, no doubt to warn of Sharbaraz's arrival.

Green and growing things covered both banks of the river. So soon after the spring flood, the greenery extended a long way out from the Tutub. Canals guided every precious drop to plants that would perish without the lifegiving water.

Sharbaraz sent riders up and down the Tutub, a couple of farsangs north and south, to see if Smerdis' men had left behind a bridge of boats on which they could cross. Abivard was unsurprised when they found none.

He had watched the engineers of Peroz King of Kings throw a bridge across the Degird River. That had taken days. Now he saw the Videssian engineers in action. The structure they put together was a lot less impressive than the bridge the Makuraners had run up, but they built it a lot faster. They anchored thick, heavily greased chains to the shore at one end and to a wooden pontoon at the other. Then they rowed out to the pontoon in a tiny boat, anchored a new set of chains to its far side, and hitched them to another pontoon farther out in the Tutub.

They had long planks to reach from pontoon to pontoon and, incidentally, to reduce the distance each newly placed pontoon could drift downstream from its predecessor. They had shorter planks to lay across the long ones. And, in an amazingly short time, they had themselves a bridge.

At first, Smerdis' men on the west bank of the Tutub didn't seem to realize the Videssian engineers were creating a structure on which Sharbaraz's army could cross to attack them. Only when the western end of the bridge was well within bowshot did they send a few arrows toward the laboring engineers. The Khamorth on the north bank of the Degird had harassed Peroz's artisans much more effectively.

As Peroz's men had, the Videssians used soldiers with big shields to hold off most of the arrows. They also brought archers of their own forward along the growing bridge to shoot back at their foes. Before long the bridge was anchored to the west bank of the Tutub as well as the east. Riders began to cross—first Videssians, for the elder Maniakes made his own men use the bridge before he risked Makuraners on it, then Sharbaraz's lancers, and last of all the wagons of the Videssian engineers and the rest of the baggage train.

As soon as the last wagon rolled onto the west bank of the Tutub, the engineers began disassembling the pontoon bridge. Watching, Abivard thought they might have used a magic to aid them in the deconstruction; just as the bridge had grown from the east bank of the Tutub to the west, so now it shrank in the same direction. The engineers rolled up the last heavy, greasy chain, stowed it in the wagon from which it had come, and shouted in Videssian that they were ready to move on.

The elder Maniakes rode up to Abivard and Sharbaraz. Coughing a little, he said, "You understand, I hope, it won't be this easy all the time."

"Oh, indeed," Sharbaraz said. "We caught them by surprise. They'll be more ready to fight back, next crossing we have to force. But being back in Makuran, in my own realm, feels so fine in and of itself that I won't worry about the future till I bump into it."

"The Land of the Thousand Cities isn't much like Vek Rud domain," Abivard said. "I was thinking that a little while ago. Serrhes reminded me a lot more of home: dust and heat—aye, and cold through the winter—and a healthy fear for enemies from over the border."

"You mean us," Sharbaraz said, grinning.

"So I do." Abivard smiled, too. "But I got to thinking what I would have done if an important Khamorth chief crossed the Degird with his clan and came to my stronghold asking for Makuraner help to get him back his grazing lands. What should I do there? Probably about what Kalamos did: act as friendly as I could while I sent a messenger hotfooting it to the capital to find out how I was really supposed to act."

"You couldn't go far wrong doing something like that," Sharbaraz agreed. "Such things have happened now and again, too. Sometimes we'd aid the nomads, sometimes we wouldn't, depending on what looked advantageous."

Abivard thought of Likinios and his beloved map. Yes, the Avtokrator had settled for fewer concessions from Sharbaraz than he had demanded at first, but he had taken a bite out of Makuran just the same. Suppose Sharbaraz had refused to yield that bite. Where would he and his followers be now?

Abivard saw two answers. The first was the one Hosios had promised: the army broken up, with each man getting land according to his rank. In that case, Abivard's grandchildren would likely have ended up as Videssian as the younger Maniakes. Not the worst of fates, but not the best, either.

Given the way Likinios looked at the world, though, the second picture that sprang into being in Abivard's mind struck him as much more likely. What better use for the Avtokrator of the Videssians to get out of a host of Makuraner refugees than to take them to the northeast and hurl them against the Kubratoi? Every nomad horseman they killed would help Videssos, while they did the Emperor no harm even if they died.

The scheme was devious, underhanded, and economical . . .

Likinios to the core. Abivard was glad the Avtokrator had not had the chance to think of it.

Sharbaraz said, "This whole realm is mine, the land of the Thousand Cities no less than any other part of it. Perhaps it helps that I grew up looking out on it from Mashiz and that I visited some of the cities down here on the flood plain. It's not alien to me, though I admit I prefer the highlands. I am a true Makuraner by blood, after all."

"Of that, Majesty, no one had any doubt." Abivard waved to the flat, green landscape ahead. "Where I have doubts is wondering how we're to move here in any direction save the ones Smerdis dictates. Are the Videssian engineers good enough to let us do that?"

"My father always had the greatest respect for them," Sharbaraz said, invoking Peroz as Abivard was wont to invoke Godarz. "Never having fought against them nor seen them in action, I cannot speak from firsthand knowledge. I will say this, though: they'd better be."

As they had before, the cities of the land of the Thousand Cities closed themselves to Sharbaraz's army. As he had before, the rightful King of Kings bypassed them and kept moving. If he beat Smerdis, they would fall to him. If he didn't . . . Abivard saw no point in worrying about that.

Smerdis did not have a large force between the valleys of the Tutub and the Tib. His men shadowed Sharbaraz's host and the accompanying Videssian army but made no effort to attack. "Cowardice." Sharbaraz snorted. "He thinks he'll stay on the throne if he can outwait me."

"Strategy," the elder Maniakes insisted. "He's holding back to hurt as much as he can, at a time of his choosing."

Being the two men of highest rank in the army, they had trouble finding an arbiter to choose between them, but before long they settled on Abivard. He said, "May it please your Majesty, I think the eminent sir is right. Smerdis isn't quite the fool you made him out to be; if he were, we'd never have needed aid from Videssos."

"He's a thief and a liar," Sharbaraz said.

"No doubt he is, your Majesty," the elder Maniakes agreed politely. "However wicked those qualities are in most walks of life, though, they often come in very handy in war."

Two days later Smerdis' men broke down the eastern bank of one of the larger canals that stitched together the Land of the Thousand Cities. The Videssian engineers quickly repaired the breach and ended the flood, but that did nothing to deal with the furlongs of black, smelly mud the waters left in their wake.

"Now we see if they earn their silver," Abivard declared.

The engineers earned not only Makuraner silver but also Videssian gold. They used the same planks that had paved the pontoon bridge over the Tutub to lay down a roadway that let the army advance through the flooded zone and up to the canal. They also recovered the planks—except for a few that had been trampled deep into the mud—so they could use them again in either bridge or roadway.

"Now I understand," Sharbaraz said as the engineers matter-of-factly went about bridging the canal. "They let the Videssian army go wherever it wants to. You can't just make a flood or build field fortifications and think you're safe from the imperials: they'll be inside your tent before you even know they're around."

"They are good," Abivard admitted grudgingly. "I haven't had a lot to do with them, but just watching them go about their business, seeing them talking and gambling around campfires of evenings, makes them seem more like ordinary men than they ever did before. Our tales always make Videssians out to be either wicked or ferocious or underhanded or—I don't know what all, but none of it good. And they're just . . . people. It's very strange."

"You take any one man from anywhere and he's apt to be a pretty good fellow," Abivard said. "Even a Khamorth will probably love his children—"

"Or his sheep," Abivard put in.

The rightful King of Kings snorted. "It's rude to interrupt your sovereign when he's waxing philosophical. I don't do it much; maybe it comes from being around Videssians, since they're finer logic-choppers than anyone else. As I was saying, your plainsman will love his children, he won't beat his wife more than she deserves, and he'll care for his horses as well as any groom in Makuran. Put him in the company of a couple of hundred of his clansmates and let him overrun a Makuraner village, though, and he'll do things that will give you nightmares for years afterward."

"But we have a lot more than a couple of hundred Videssians

here, and they're still behaving well," Abivard said. "That's what surprises me."

"Part of that, I suppose, is that they're aligned with us: if they act like a pack of demons, they'll make the people here hate them and us both, and so hurt our cause," Sharbaraz said. "And they're more like us than the Khamorth are. When they aren't soldiering, they're farmers or millers or artisans. They don't destroy canals for the fun of watching other farmers starve."

Abivard plucked at his beard. "That makes sense, Majesty. Maybe you should—what did you call it?—wax philosophic more often."

"No, thank you," Sharbaraz answered. "There's also one other thing I didn't tell you: I asked the elder Maniakes to make sure his priests stuck to their own and didn't go about trying to get honest Makuraners to worship their false god. The blue-robes who follow Phos are better organized than our servants of the God, and they go after converts like flies diving into honey."

"They have been quiet," Abivard said. "I didn't realize this isn't the way they usually behave."

"It isn't," Sharbaraz assured him. "They're as certain of the truth of their Phos as we are about the God. And since they think they have the only true god, they're sure anyone who doesn't worship him—or who doesn't worship him the right way—will spend eternity in ice, just as we know misbelievers vanish into the Void and are gone forever. They think they have a duty to get people to worship as they do. Getting Maniakes to muzzle them hasn't been easy."

"Why not?" Abivard asked, puzzled. "If a noble gives an order, those who serve under him had better obey."

Sharbaraz laughed raucously. Abivard looked offended. The rightful King of Kings said, "Brother-in-law of mine, you're not used to dealing with Videssians. From all I've seen, from all I've heard, those blue-robed priests are so drunk with their god, they don't care to take orders from any mere noble. Even the Avtokrator sometimes has trouble getting them to do his bidding."

"We don't do things so untidily in Makuran," Abivard said. "Northerwesterner though I am, I know that much. If the Mobedhan-mobhed ever presumed to displease the King of Kings in any way—"

"—there'd be a new Mobedhan-mobhed inside the hour,"

Sharbaraz finished for him. "After all, the King of Kings is the sovereign. No one has any business displeasing him." He laughed again, this time at himself. "I've been nothing but displeased since the throne came—or should have come—into my hands. When it's truly mine at last, that won't happen any more."

His voice held great certainty. At first, that pleased Abivard: Sharbaraz needed confidence that he would be restored. Then Abivard wondered if the rightful King of Kings simply meant he would refuse to listen to anything distasteful once he ruled in Mashiz. That worried him. Even a King of Kings might need to be reminded from time to time of how the world worked.

Something had changed. Abivard knew it as soon as he climbed up into the wagon Roshnani and Denak shared, even before he set eyes on his wife. The serving woman who bowed to him said not a word out of the ordinary, but her voice had a timbre to it he hadn't heard before.

"My husband," Roshnani said as he stepped into her small cubicle. Again, the words were everyday but the tone was not. Then she added, "Close the curtain. It helps keep out some of the mosquitoes that plague this land." That sounded like her.

Abivard obeyed. As he did, he studied Roshnani. She looked—like herself, if a little more tired than usual. He scratched his head, wondering if his imagination was running away with him. "Is anything wrong?" he asked as she tilted her face up for a kiss.

"Wrong? Whatever makes you think that?" She laughed at him, then went on, "Unless I'm very much mistaken, though, I am going to have a baby."

"I'm glad everything's all ri—" Abivard said before what Roshnani had told him got from his ears to his mind. His mouth fell open. When he shut it again, he said, "How did that happen?"

If Roshnani had laughed before, now she chortled, great ringing peals of mirth that left her hiccuping when she finally brought herself back under control. "Unless I'm very much mistaken," she said, deliberately echoing herself, "it happened in the usual way. We've been wed for going on two years now. I was beginning to wonder if I was barren."

Abivard's fingers twisted in a sign to turn aside words of evil omen. "The God prevent it," he said. Then he blinked. "The God has prevented it, hasn't he?"

"Yes, she has," Roshnani said. They both smiled; when a man and a woman talked about the God in back-to-back sentences, the effect could be odd on the ear. Roshnani went on, "May I give you a son."

"May it be so." Abivard sobered. "I wish my father were here, so I could set his first grandchild in his arms. If that child were heir to Vek Rud domain, all the better." He thought of something else, lowered his voice. "I might even wish it weren't Father's first grandchild. Have you told Denak you're with child?"

Roshnani nodded. "I told her this morning; this is the first day I've been sure enough to speak to anyone. She hugged me. I understand what you mean, though: how wonderful it would be if a first grandchild were also heir to the throne of the King of Kings."

"Of course, if Father were alive, Peroz King of Kings would likely also still live, and Denak wouldn't be wed to Sharbaraz King of Kings," Abivard mused. "The more you look at things, the more complicated they get." He spoke quietly again. "I'm glad she's not jealous you've conceived when she hasn't."

"I think perhaps she is, a little," Roshnani said, almost whispering herself. "But then, she's also a little jealous that you visit me more often than the King of Kings comes to see her."

"Is she? Do I?" Abivard knew he wasn't altogether coherent, but he had never before been told he was going to be a father. None of the serving women and occasional courtesans he had bedded had made that claim on him, and they would have with even the slightest suspicion he had put a child in them: as a *dihqan's* son, he would have been obligated to make sure their babes were well cared for. And none of his other wives had quickened before he left with Sharbaraz. Perhaps he should have fretted over the strength of his seed.

"Yes and yes," Roshnani answered. Everything he said this evening seemed to amuse her. She called to the serving woman for a jar of wine and two cups. The jar was a squat one from the land of the Thousand Cities; when she tilted it to pour, the wine slithered out slowly. She made a wry face. "Not only is it made from dates, the people here seem to think they ought to be able to poke a knife in it and bring it to their mouths that way."

"It doesn't matter, not for this." Abivard took one of the cups from her and raised it in salute. "To our child. May the God grant him—and you—long years, health, and happiness." He drank. So did Roshnani. Not only was the wine thick as molasses, it was nearly as sweet, too. He almost felt the need to chew to get it down.

It did what wine was supposed to do, though. By the time he had finished the cup, the world seemed a more cheerful place. Roshnani poured it full again. As he sipped, the words of his toast came back, and so did worry. Women could die giving birth, or of childbed fever afterwards. The possibility loomed too large to be ignored, but the idea of commending young and vital Roshnani to the God because her span was cruelly cut short sent fear through him.

To keep from thinking about it, he gulped down the second cup of sweet date wine. When he had finished it, he said, "May Denak and Sharbaraz soon know this same happiness." He *was* happy, despite the worry. He would worry about his sister, too, but he would also be glad for her and her husband.

Roshnani nodded. "Not only will it be good for them, it will be good for the realm as well, especially if it proves to be a boy. Having an heir to the throne can only help settle the realm."

"It should help settle the realm, you mean," Abivard said. "Peroz King of Kings had an heir, too, if you'll recall."

"I recall it perfectly well," Roshnani said. "If Smerdis had recalled it, too, we'd all be better off—except for Smerdis, which, I daresay, was all he thought about."

"Too true." Abivard sighed. "When I was growing up at Vek Rud stronghold, I thought about seeing the land of the Thousand Cities and Videssos, aye, but I expected to go to war against Videssos for the King of Kings, not with Videssian allies against a man who calls himself the King of Kings. Civil war is a strange business."

"When I was growing up, I never thought about seeing anything except the stretch of road between my father's stronghold and yours," Roshnani answered. "I'd known only the stronghold and later only the women's quarters in it. Next to that, my bridal journey seemed travel enough to last me a lifetime." She laughed. "We can't always guess what's to come, can we?"

"No," Abivard said, thinking of Tanshar. "And even if we do learn what's to come, we don't know when or where or how."

"The only thing left for us is to go on as best we can," Roshnani said. "Come to think of it, that's what we'd be doing even if we knew just what all the prophecies meant."

"So it is." Abivard looked at her sidelong. "The best way to go on after finding out you've a child in your belly that I can think of is—"

Roshnani might have had the same thought at the same time. The date wine made Abivard's fingers a little clumsy as he unfastened the wooden toggles at the back of her dress, but after that everything went fine.

Smerdis' men did their best to delay and misdirect Sharbaraz's army and his Videssian allies by opening canals between the Tib and the Tutub, but their best was not good enough, not when the Videssian engineers could repair holes in the canal banks and plank roads as fast as the enemy damaged them.

"When we cross the Tib, they're ours," Sharbaraz said.

"Aye, Majesty," Abivard answered, though he could not help thinking that Sharbaraz had shown the same confidence the summer before, only to have it prove to be overconfidence.

But perhaps Smerdis came to the same conclusion as his rival. As Sharbaraz's men neared the Tib, their foes drew up in battle array to try to stop them from crossing a major canal. Prominent in the ranks of Smerdis' men were the dismounted archers who had brought such grief to Sharbaraz's forces as they had advanced from the south against Mashiz the previous year.

The elder Maniakes looked down his formidable nose at the bowmen. "If we ever close with them, their souls will be falling down to Skotos' ice quick enough after that," he said.

"Oh, indeed," Sharbaraz answered. "The same holds true for my lancers. But I don't relish trying to force a crossing in the face of all the archery they can bring to bear on us."

He's learning, Abivard thought with something approaching joy. The summer before, Sharbaraz would have chosen the most straightforward way to cross the canal and get at his foes, and would have worried about casualties later, if at all.

"Your Majesty, may I make a suggestion?" the elder Maniakes asked.

"I wish you would," Sharbaraz said. The Videssian commander spoke for several minutes. When he was through, Sharbaraz whistled softly. "You must have a demon lurking in you, to come up with a scheme like that. No wonder Makuran seldom profits as much as it should in its wars against Videssos."

"You're too kind to an old man," the elder Maniakes said, considerably exaggerating his decrepitude. "You would have seen it yourself in a moment, had you but noticed the little hill that town there rests on."

"You'll want us to sit tight through the night and start the attack in the morning, then, won't you, eminent sir?" Abivard said.

"We'll have better hope for success that way, surely," the Videssian general answered. He beamed at Abivard. "You do see what needs doing, eminent sir, and that's a fact. Can't complain about that, and I wouldn't think of trying." He plucked at his gray beard. "Hmm, now that I think on it, 'eminent sir' is probably too low a title for you, what with you being brother to his Majesty's wife, but I mean no harm by it, I promise you."

"I took no offense," Abivard said, "and even if I had, I wouldn't have shown it, not after that lovely plan you came up with."

The elder Maniakes beamed. "The only reason I thought of it was to give my son some glory. I'll have him lead the interesting half."

Sharbaraz turned to Abivard. "The time to trust Videssians least is when they're being modest. Of course, that isn't something you'll run into often enough to have to worry about it much."

"Your Majesty, I am wounded to the quick!" The elder Maniakes clapped both hands over his heart, as if hit by an arrow. "You do me a great injustice."

"The biggest injustice I could do you would be to underestimate you," the rightful King of Kings answered. "You will forgive me, I pray—you're not so young, you're plump, you're droll when you want to be. And you're as dangerous a man as I've ever seen, not least because you don't seem so."

"What do I say about that?" the elder Maniakes wondered aloud. "Only that if you've seen through the act, it isn't as good as it should be, and I'll have to put more work into it." He sounded genuinely chagrined.

The next morning dawned clear and hot, as did almost every morning in late spring, summer, and early fall in the land of the Thousand Cities. The Videssian engineers had enough pontoons and chains and planks to bridge the Tib and Tutub—plenty to bridge an irrigation canal many times over. As soon as it was light, they started throwing a good many bridges across the canal that held them apart from Smerdis' men.

To Abivard's dismay, scouts from Smerdis' army were alert. No sooner had the bridges started to snake across the oily-looking water than the unmounted archers came rushing up from their camp and began shooting at the engineers. As at the crossing of the Tutub, some of the Videssians held big shields to protect the rest from the rain of arrows. As the bridges moved forward, Videssian horse archers rode out onto them and started shooting back at Smerdis' men.

They were badly outnumbered, but did damage to the foe all the same: few of Smerdis' bowmen wore any sort of armor. The heavy cavalry with the foot soldiers gathered in knots in front of the growing bridges to fight off any of Sharbaraz's men who managed to cross.

Sharbaraz's own armored lancers assembled near their end of a bridge that grew ever nearer the west bank of the canal. Abivard sat his horse at their head, wondering how, if the men he led charged over the bridge in one direction while Smerdis' followers charged in the other, the Videssian engineers would keep from getting squashed between them.

He found out: as soon as the engineers got the last planks in place, they dove into the canal and started swimming through the turbid water back toward the eastern bank. No sooner had they splashed down into the water than Abivard cried, "Sharbaraz!" and booted his horse forward.

The bridge swayed, as if in an earthquake, under the galloping hooves of dozens of horses. Abivard met his first foe not quite two thirds of the way toward the west bank of the canal—he might have started a heartbeat sooner than Smerdis' man, and perhaps he was better mounted, too.

He twisted his body away from the questing point of the foe's lance. At the same time, he struck with his own. The blow caught Smerdis' soldier in the chest and pitched him off over his horse's tail. Abivard's mount, a trained warhorse, lashed out at the fallen lancer with iron-shod hooves. Abivard spurred the horse ahead toward the next enemy.

The bridge was not wide. More splashes, some of them big ones, marked men and horses falling or getting pushed into the canal. In their heavy iron armor, most of them did not come up again.

"Sharbaraz!" Abivard cried again. He and the backers of the rightful King of Kings slowly pushed Smerdis' men toward their own end of the bridge. Not one of Sharbaraz's followers, though, had yet set foot on the muddy western bank of the canal. Smerdis' troopers yelled the name of their candidate for the throne as loudly as Sharbaraz's warriors extolled him.

Then, from the north, a new cry rang out along the canal's western bank: "Sarbaraz!" Abivard whooped gleefully. Even if the Videssians couldn't pronounce the *sh* sound, they were not only good soldiers but subtle planners. The elder Maniakes had predicted Smerdis' soldiers would be so busy fighting the warriors they saw that they would pay no attention to anything else. Some of his engineers had taken advantage of the cover offered by the hillock the Videssian general had mentioned to run one more floating bridge across the canal. A large force of Videssian mounted archers proceeded to cross with no opposition whatever.

They shot up Smerdis' unarmored foot soldiers, then, crying "Sarbaraz!" once more, they charged them, swinging sabers and thrusting with light spears. They weren't quite so deadly as Makuraner lancers would have been, but they were more than enough to rout the dismounted archers, who were useful when they could ply a foe with arrows without being directly assailed in return, but whose clubs and knives offered next to no defense in close quarters.

Smerdis' heavy cavalry had to break off the fight at the bridge-heads to swing back against the Videssians and keep themselves from being surrounded and altogether destroyed. But that let Abivard and his men reach the west bank of the canal, just as the flight of the bowmen let the Videssian engineers finish more bridges so more of Sharbaraz's lancers could cross.

The officer who led the Videssian flanking force had a nice sense of what was essential. He let the archers run and concentrated on Smerdis' horsemen. His own troopers were more heavily armed than nonnoble Makuraner warriors, though they didn't wear iron from head to toe and their horses bore only quilted cloth protection. They could hurt Smerdis' men if those men didn't assail them with everything they had, and could stand up well enough against an all-out charge to ensure that Smerdis' lancers couldn't smash through them and escape from Sharbaraz's men.

Smerdis' lancers were quick to realize that. They began throwing down their long spears and swords. Some cried, "Mercy!" Others shouted Sharbaraz's name. Some fought on. Most of those went down, but a few managed to break away and run.

The Videssian commander—it was the younger Maniakes, Abivard remembered—was not content with victory, but sent his own horsemen after Smerdis' fleeing lancers. They brought down quite a few more before returning to their comrades.

"A cheer for the Maniakai, father and son," Abivard shouted. "The one planned the victory, the other made it real." The Makuraners he had led yelled themselves hoarse. Any of them who happened to be near Videssians pounded their allies on the back, bawled in their ears, and offered them wine from the skins they wore on their belts. For that moment, at least, the ancient enemies could not have been closer friends.

Abivard rode toward the younger Maniakes. "Well done," he said. "You're younger than I am; I envy you your cool head."

The younger man smiled. He had a small cut on his left cheek and a dent and a sparkling line on the bar nasal of his helmet; without the nasal, he would have taken a bad wound. He said, "You did well yourself, eminent sir; if you hadn't pressed them so hard, they might have punched through us and got away in a body."

"That's what I was trying to stop, all right," Abivard said, nodding. "There'll be a great wailing and gnashing of teeth in Mashiz when word of this fight gets back to Smerdis Pimp of Pimps."

"Good," the younger Maniakes said, grinning. "That was the idea, after all. And there'll be a great wailing and gnashing of teeth in the land of the Thousand Cities, too. We used those unmounted archers hard, and anyone with an eye in his head to see with can figure out that we would have used them harder if we hadn't had more important things to do. The folk hereabouts may want to think twice before they back Smerdis over Sar—*Shar*baraz." He pumped his fist in the air in triumph at correctly pronouncing the Makuraner sound.

"We beat those archers once and fought them again, but it didn't make the Thousand Cities change their mind," Abivard said. "Maybe this time it will, though. I hope so."

"This fight happened in the middle of the Land of the Thousand Cities, not off in the southern desert," the younger Maniakes said. "And Smerdis' army looks to have broken up, to boot. Every man who gets away alive will go home, and every man who gets home will spread the tale of how we smashed Smerdis' general. That can't do Smerdis' cause any good."

"So it can't." Abivard eyed the Videssian commander's son with new respect. "Not just a fighter, eh? You like to think about the way things work, too; I can see that."

The younger Maniakes had an impressively luxuriant beard for a man of his few years, a trait that, Abivard had learned, testified to his Vaspurakaner blood. In spite of that beard, which reached up almost to his eyes, Abivard saw him flush. He said, "You are generous to a man who, after all, is more likely to be your enemy than your friend."

"I hadn't forgotten that," Abivard assured him. "But maybe, just maybe, the help Likinios Avtokrator is giving to Sharbaraz will bring our two realms a long peace. The God knows we both could use it."

"Phos grant that it be so," the younger Maniakes said. Impulsively, he stuck out his hand. Abivard took it. They squeezed with all their strength and let go, smarting, after a draw.

"All I truly want to do is get back to my domain in the northwest and make sure the Khamorth haven't ravaged my lands too badly—or punish the plainsmen if they have," Abivard said. "Peace with Videssos will ensure that I can do that."

"Peace with Makuran will let the Avtokrator Likinios finish punishing the Kubratoi, too," the younger Maniakes said. "A peace both sides can use is more likely to last than any other kind I can think of."

"Aye." Abivard had agreed before he remembered that Videssian gold had stirred up the Khamorth tribes north of the Degird River against Makuran in the first place. Without that incitement, Peroz King of Kings might never have campaigned against the nomads, which meant Smerdis wouldn't have stolen the throne from Sharbaraz, which meant in turn that Videssos and Makuran wouldn't have joined together against the usurper. Abivard shook his head. Indeed, the more you looked at the world, the more complex it got.

Something else crossed his mind: the more you looked at the

world, the more you could learn. Videssos would never directly threaten his domain; the Empire's reach wasn't long enough. But the Khamorth were causing endless trouble in the northwest of Makuran, and that worked to Videssos' advantage. If Makuran ever needed to put similar pressure on Videssos, who could guess what a subsidy to Kubrat might yield?

Abivard stuck the idea away in the back of his mind. Neither he nor any Makuraner could use it now. Makuran had to put its own house in order before worrying about upsetting those of its neighbors. But one of these days...

He glanced toward the younger Maniakes. For all his obvious cleverness, the Videssian officer hadn't noticed Abivard was thinking about enmity rather than friendship. *Good,* Abivard thought. As he had said, he wouldn't mind a spell of peace, even a long one, with Videssos. But certain debts would remain outstanding no matter how long the peace lasted.

The younger Maniakes said, "Do you think they'll try to stop us again this side of the Tib?"

"I doubt it," Abivard answered. "We smashed Smerdis' cavalry, and you were the one who noted that those unmounted bowmen are likelier to make for home than to come back together again. What does that leave?"

"Not bloody much, eminent sir," the younger Maniakes said cheerfully. "That's how I read things, too, but this isn't my realm, and I wondered if I was overlooking something."

"If you are, I'm overlooking it, too," Abivard said. "No, as I see it, we have one fight left to win: the one in front of Mashiz." He had thought as much the summer before, too, but Sharbaraz hadn't won that fight.

After the victory, Sharbaraz's forces and their Videssian allies pushed hard toward the Tib. Smerdis' men broke the banks of canals on their route; the Videssian engineers repaired the damage and the armies kept moving. Smerdis' troops did attempt one stand, along the western bank of a canal wider than the one they had used as a barrier before the battle. Abivard worried when he saw how strong the enemy's position was. So, loudly, did Sharbaraz.

The elder Maniakes remained unperturbed. As the sun was setting on the day the army came up against Smerdis' force, he ostentatiously sent a detachment of engineers and a good many of his horse archers north along the east bank of the canal. Inky darkness fell before they had gone a quarter of a farsang.

When morning came, Smerdis' soldiers were gone.

"You are a demon, eminent sir," Sharbaraz exclaimed, slapping the Videssian general on the back.

"We'd hurt 'em once with that trick," the elder Maniakes replied. "They weren't going to give us a chance to do it again." He chuckled wheezily. "So, by threatening that trick, we won with a different one." The army crossed the canal unopposed and resumed its advance.

After that, city governors from the land of the Thousand Cities began trickling in to Sharbaraz's camp, something they had never done the summer before. They prostrated themselves before him, eating dirt to proclaim their loyalty to him as rightful King of Kings. Not yet in a position where he could avenge himself on them for having stayed loyal to Smerdis so long, he accepted them as if they had never backed his rival. But Abivard watched his eyes. He remembered every slight, sure enough.

Abivard wondered if Smerdis' men would contest the crossing of the Tib. Though the flood season had passed, the river was still wide and swift-flowing. Determined opposition could have made getting across anything but easy. But the west bank was bare of troops when Sharbaraz and his allies reached it. The engineers extended their bridge, one pontoon at a time. The army crossed and moved west again.

✦ XI

Abivard eyed the approaches to Mashiz with suspicion. Sharbaraz's troops had come to grief there once before, and the army the rightful King of Kings commanded now was smaller than the one he had led the previous summer. One more victory, though, would redeem usurpation and defeat and exile. The Makuraners who had suffered so much for Sharbaraz's cause were grimly determined to achieve that victory.

The Videssians who had accompanied them and made victory possible had no such personal stake in the war. Abivard wondered how they could fight so well without that kind of stake. He asked the younger Maniakes, with whom he had become more and more friendly after the battle in the land of the Thousand Cities,

The Videssian commander's son rolled his eyes. "From what my father says, you've met Likinios Avtokrator. How would you like to go home and explain to him that you hadn't done quite all you could?'

At first, the prospect didn't seem too daunting. Likinios hadn't struck Abivard as a man who flew into a murderous rage without warning, as some memorable Kings of Kings of Makuran had been in the habit of doing. Then he thought of the Videssian Emperor's coldly calculating mind. Likinios wouldn't kill you because he was angry; he would quietly order you slain because he judged you deserved it. But you would end up just as dead either way.

"I take your point," he told the younger Maniakes. The Videssian ruler's style might be coldblooded and alien to the Makuraner way of doing things, but it had its own kind of effectiveness.

Sharbaraz's force advanced through the wreckage of the failed campaign of the year before: skeletons of horses and mules, some with mummified skin still clinging here and there; the burned-out remains of overturned supply wagons; and unburied human bones, as well. The rightful King of Kings surveyed the near ruin of his hopes with an expression thoroughly grim. "Not this time," he declared. "Not this time."

But taking the capital of the realm would not be easy. Where before Smerdis' men had built a temporary barricade across most of the one wide way into Mashiz, now permanent fortifications protected the city from attack. Getting past them looked like a formidable undertaking.

"Don't worry about it," the elder Maniakes said when Abivard did just that. "We'll manage, never you fear."

Promises, even from one who had shown he delivered on them, left Abivard cold. When the Videssian engineers began taking wood and ropes and specialized parts of bronze and iron from their wagons and assembling them into large, complicated contraptions, however, he felt oddly reassured. What they did with such things wasn't magic in any true sense of the word, but it struck him as every bit as marvelous as a lot of the things sorcerers achieved.

"They're very good," Sharbaraz agreed when he said that aloud. "I think the ones who went north over the Degird with my father could have matched them, though. But most of my father's engineers are dead with the rest of his army, and I don't think Smerdis has many of those who are left alive working for him, either. Were things different, the lack could hurt Makuran badly; we'll have to train up a new team of such folk as soon as may be. But for now having engineers, when our foes don't, works for us."

The timbers the Videssians had used to make the flooring for their pontoon bridges and to corduroy roads through the muck left by flooded canals also proved to be the right size for constructing the frames of the engines they were erecting. At first, Abivard thought that an amazing coincidence. Then he realized it wasn't a coincidence at all. The sophisticated planning inherent in that deeply impressed him.

The engines went up at the front and on the right of the northern flank—the one on which Smerdis' men had gained success the summer before—well out of range of archers sheltered by the works the usurper had thrown up. Sharbaraz asked, "Will they be enough to let us pass by the fortress without losing so many men as to ruin us?"

"Provided we beat the men they have outside the walls, the engines will keep those within too busy to do much to us," the elder Maniakes replied.

Abivard said, "What about men issuing forth from one of the narrow ways into Mashiz? That flank attack ruined us last year, and we don't have the men to plug all those routes, not if we want to do real fighting, too."

"The trick of the trade is getting what you want with as little fighting—especially the messy, expensive hand-to-hand you mean— as you can," the Videssian general said. He pointed over to the bank of dart-throwers going up on the northern flank. "Skotos hold my soul in the ice forever if those don't make any charging lancer ever born the most thoughtful man you know."

"May it be so," Sharbaraz said. "My men are eager for the attack. When will all this hammering and spiking be done?"

"We'll be through by evening," the elder Maniakes replied. "Smerdis' men could have given us a deal of grief if they'd come sneaking around trying to wreck the engines or burn 'em down, but they didn't. Maybe they didn't think of it, or maybe they just didn't think it'd work." He shook his head to show his opinion of that. "You always try. Every once in a while, you end up surprising yourself with what you can do."

"I agree," Sharbaraz said. "If I didn't, I never would have fled into Videssos last year."

If Roshnani hadn't thought of it, you'd never have fled into Videssos, Abivard thought. That brought a surge of pride in his wife. It also brought the realization that Denak had been right all along: women's counsel could be as valuable on campaign as back in the women's quarters of the stronghold. Abivard wondered if Sharbaraz had figured that out yet.

He didn't get long to contemplate the notion. The elder Maniakes said, "True enough, your Majesty, but we're on the point of bringing you back home now."

Dawn brought the promise of a day to steam a man in armor. Abivard was sweating even before he donned the leather-lined shirt of mail and splints, the mail skirt, and the trousers of iron rings. By the time he had affixed his ring-mail veil and aventail and settled his helmet on his head, he felt ready to go into the oven and come forth as cooked meat.

Perhaps, in spite of everything, Smerdis still had spies in Sharbaraz's camp, or perhaps his officers were just good at piecing together what they saw from the works he had built in front of Mashiz. In any case, his soldiers came forth from their camps behind those works and filled the gaps between their walls and the nearly impassable badlands to either side. No, getting into Mashiz was not going to be the triumphal parade Abivard and Sharbaraz had imagined when they set out from Vek Rud stronghold.

The elder Maniakes took charge of proceedings at the outset. Collaring Abivard, he said, "I want you and your best men in front of the siege engines to protect them."

"What?" Abivard said indignantly. "You'd ask me and our best lancers to forgo the charge?"

If the Videssian general noticed his ire, he ignored it. "That's just what I'd ask, for the beginning of the fight, anyhow," he answered. "If we're to win this battle, that's what we need to do. You'll get enough fighting to satisfy the most picky honor later on, I promise you."

He spoke as if honor were something worth only a couple of coppers. *You make war like a merchant, and your son is twice the man you'll ever be,* Abivard thought. But he could not insult an ally by saying such things to his face. If he took the question to Sharbaraz . . . He shook his head. He couldn't do that. If he did, the elder Maniakes would lose prestige, or else he would lose some himself. Either way, the alliance would suffer.

That left him only one choice. "Very well, eminent sir," he said icily. "I shall rely on your promise."

The elder Maniakes paid no more attention to ice than he had to indignation. "Good, good," he said, as if he had taken Abivard's compliance for granted. "Now do get moving, if you'd be so kind. We can't put on our little show until you do."

Still fuming, Abivard rounded up Zal's regiment of lancers. Zal and many of his riders grumbled when Abivard told them they weren't going to sweep gloriously down on the enemy. He said, "You'll do real fighting later in the day. By the God I swear it." He had to hope he wasn't giving them a false oath.

Grumbling still, the lancers took their places in front of the siege engines the Videssians had built. Made with muddy timbers, the engines looked like frameworks for houses abandoned after a flood. The engineers loaded heavy stones into some and large, stoppered jars with greasy rags sticking out of the stoppers into others.

Abivard twisted in the saddle so he could watch the Videssians touch torches to those greasy rags. At the command of their captains, the engineers discharged the creations. The engines jumped and kicked, as if they were wild asses like those that had given Sharbaraz's followers such a fright the autumn before.

The stones and jars described graceful arcs through the air. As their captains cursed them to ever greater efforts, the Videssians turned windlasses to rewind the engines' ropes and ready them to shoot again. Abivard paid scant heed to that. He watched the stones smash into Smerdis' works. Some fell short, some crashed against the wall, some flew over it to land within. He wouldn't have wanted to be under one of those stones when it came down, any more than he would have cared to be a cockroach stepped on by a lancer's armored boot.

The jars trailed smoke as they flew. Even from a couple of furlongs, even through the shouts of Smerdis' soldiers inside their fortress, he heard pottery smashing. Columns of black, greasy smoke started rising from within the fortifications.

Abivard turned in the saddle again. "Any of you speak my language?" he asked the engineers behind him. When one of them nodded, he went on, "What's in that stuff you're flinging there?"

The Videssian grunted. "Rock oil, sir, and sulfur," he said in fair Makuraner, "and some other things I don't want to tell you what they is. Burns good, don't it?"

"Yes," Abivard said. One of the pillars of smoke was growing rapidly; he guessed the inflammable liquid had splattered over wood or canvas. The engines bucked again, this time in a more ragged salvo. Ragged or not, though, it sent another round of stones and jars flying against the fortress.

"By the God," Zal said, "I'd not like to have to go out in that kind of rain." His gaze sharpened. "And if that kind of rain keeps falling on the fortress for very long, the folk there won't be worth much. They'll be too squashed or toasted to do anything to speak of in the way of fighting."

"That's the idea," Abivard said, also suddenly figuring out why the elder Maniakes had said defending the engines would be a crucial role to play. Sooner or later, Smerdis' generals would realize they had to stop the Videssians from rendering their fort useless. They couldn't do it with archers; the engines were out of range of any bowman. They would have to charge down on them instead.

Sure enough, the charge came, but not from the warriors gathered directly in front of Mashiz. Instead, Smerdis' generals loosed a flanking force of the sort that had brought Sharbaraz such grief in his last attack on the capital. Shouting Smerdis' name, the horsemen thundered down out of the narrow way to the north, as they had the year before.

They got a different reception from the one they had had then, though. The engines on the army's right flank went into action. Some of them threw stones that smashed men and horses alike. No armor could stop the yard-long darts others shot. They pinned soldiers to their mounts and sent them crashing to the ground to foul the troops behind them.

Smerdis' men were brave enough. They kept coming in spite of the toll the engines took. Videssian horsemen rode out to keep them away from those engines and from the main body of Sharbaraz's force.

That was the sideshow, the distraction. The chief action remained at the front. The Videssian engines there kept on pounding the fortress Smerdis had erected. Its wall, which could have stood forever against mere lancers, began to look like a man with bad teeth as it got knocked to pieces. Behind the wall, flames leapt high. Smoke rose higher. It made Abivard cough, and must have been twenty, a hundred times worse for Smerdis' soldiers in the fort, those lucky enough not to have been cooked.

The Videssian captain of engineers shouted more orders in his own language. His men swung the engines slightly off to one side. Then they started shooting again, this time at Smerdis' lancers gathered by the fortress.

Zal grinned a wicked, carnivorous grin. "What a nasty choice that leaves them," he said. "Withdraw out of range and open the way for us or come out and fight and open it anyhow if they lose."

Horns rang out in Smerdis' battered army. Lanceheads glittered in the sun as riders couched their weapons. "Here they come," Abivard said. Smerdis might have been a treacherous usurper, but the troops who had stuck by him had courage enough and to spare.

Abivard swung down his own lance till it pointed straight at the onrushing horsemen. "Sharbaraz!" he cried, and booted his horse in its armored sides to get it going. It sprang forward, seemingly glad to run. Zal echoed his war cry. So did the rest of the soldiers. They had waited far too long to suit them. Now they would have the straight-up fight they had craved.

Someone screeching "Smerdis!" spurred straight for Abivard. Above the fellow's chainmail veil, he caught a brief glimpse of hard, intent eyes. His foe was as glad to be fighting at last as he was. Smerdis' men hadn't just had to wait. They had also watched their comrades in the fortress bombarded and then taken a bombardment themselves.

By the way he sat his horse, the fellow boring in on Abivard knew exactly what he was doing. Instead of aiming for the larger target of Abivard's torso, at the last moment he flicked the point of his lance up at his face.

Fear turned the inside of Abivard's mouth dry and rough. He barely turned the stroke with his shield. His own went wide. He didn't care. He was just glad to be alive to fight someone else who wouldn't unfurl quite so many lethal tricks.

As cavalry battles have a way of doing once the initial impetus of the charge is lost, this one turned into a melee, with men milling about and cursing at the top of their lungs when they weren't shouting their chosen sovereign's name to keep their friends from trying to kill them. They thrust with lances and slashed with swords; their horses, many of them stallions, joined in the fight with bared teeth and flailing hooves that could dash the brains out of a man on the ground.

Somehow one of Smerdis' men had got turned around so he faced back toward the burning fortress. Abivard thought him an ally till he yelled the usurper's name. Then he speared the fellow in the back, thrusting with all his strength to force the lance point through the warrior's armor.

The fellow screamed and threw his arms wide; his sword went spinning through the air. The soldier screamed again. He crumpled, blood pouring from a hole somewhere between his left kidney and his spine. He hadn't known Abivard was there till the lance went into him. Abivard felt more like a murderer than a warrior until someone tried to blindside him. After that, he bore in mind that in battle there was precious little difference between the two.

Little by little, Sharbaraz's men forced their foes back toward the fortress. Videssian horsemen and light-armed Makuraner cavalry, more nimble than either side's lancers, tried to nip in behind Smerdis' horse and cut them off, clearing the way for Sharbaraz's lancers to burst through and storm for Mashiz.

A few archers up on the battered walls of the fortress shot at them. Hundreds would have been up there but for the pounding the siege engines had given the place. But many now were dead, many more hurt, and others fighting the fires the pots of oil had started.

"Onward!" That voice, some yards ahead of him, made Abivard jerk his head up. Sure enough, there was Sharbaraz, laying about him with his sword and spurring his horse on toward the gap that led to Mashiz.

Abivard couldn't imagine how the rightful King of Kings had pushed so far forward in the fighting, but Sharbaraz would have been a dangerous warrior no matter what his station. The only trouble was that, if he fell now, everyone else's exertions would be for nothing.

"Onward!" Abivard cried, and pointed to his sovereign. Now he did not call out Sharbaraz's name, for fear of drawing the enemy's notice to the rightful King of Kings. He pointed to him, though, and waved his arm to urge on his own followers. Not all of them understood his gestures, but enough did to give Sharbaraz a respectable force of protectors in a few minutes.

But Sharbaraz did not want protectors—he seemed to want to be the first man into Mashiz. He plunged into the press once more. His ferocity made those of Smerdis' men who were not in deadly earnest draw back from him. His own men pushed forward to fill the gap and to guard him from the foes who remained full of fight.

A tiny lull in the battle gave Abivard a moment to look around at more than sword's length from him. He realized with surprise and sudden and growing triumph that Smerdis' fortress was no longer in front of him and the rest of the leaders of Sharbaraz's forces—instead, it lay to their right. Sharbaraz had lost this fight the summer before, but he was winning it now.

"Come on!" Abivard yelled, waving again. "One more push and we have them. Once we get past the walls here, the way opens out again, and drop me into the Void if Smerdis' lancers can hold us out of Mashiz then."

Smerdis' soldiers saw that as clearly as he did. They rallied, fighting desperately. But Sharbaraz's men were desperate, too, knowing what another defeat in front of the capital would mean. And their Videssian allies, even without personal stake in the battle, fought as bravely as anyone. They plied Smerdis' men with arrows and pressed the fight at close quarters with sabers and spears. Sharbaraz had worried about betrayal, but the men from the east stayed not only loyal but ferocious.

The counterattack from Smerdis' lancers faltered. Yard by yard, they began giving ground once more. Then, all at once, the way the fortifications had narrowed grew wide again. "To Mashiz!" shouted Sharbaraz, still at the van.

Not only the capital of Makuran loomed ahead. Closer and perhaps more tempting were the tents that marked the encampment of Smerdis' men. "I'll castrate anybody who thinks of loot before victory," Abivard said. "First we win, then we plunder."

As far as he was concerned, the prospect of entering Mashiz was worth more than any booty he could pull from the camp. Other, poorer men, though, were liable to think of silver before victory.

Smerdis' army, the last army that could hold Sharbaraz out of his capital, began to break up. Here and there knots of determined men still fought on, although they had to know victory was hopeless. But others fled, some back toward Mashiz, others over the badlands, hoping their foes would be too busy to pursue them. And still others, as they had between the Tib and the Tutub, threw away their weapons and gave up the fight.

Abivard shouted for some Videssians to take charge of the prisoners. "That's well done," Sharbaraz said, recognizing his voice.

"Thank you, Majesty," he answered. "My thought was that they won't be as hot for revenge as our men." He rode closer to the rightful King of Kings before quietly adding, "And the fewer of them who go into Mashiz with our men, the better."

"Aye, that's just right," Sharbaraz agreed. "They've been all we could ask for as allies—more than I looked for them to be, the God knows. But Mashiz is *ours*; we can reclaim it on our own." Bitterness crossed his face for a moment. "The Videssians have sacked Mashiz a couple of times, while we've never made our way into Videssos the city. What I wouldn't give to be the King of Kings who changed *that.*"

"Oh, indeed," Abivard said, quietly still. "Not tomorrow, though."

"No." Sharbaraz nodded at that. "But I'm willing to bet Videssos will give us the chance before too many years go by, however well we work with father and son of the Maniakes clan. As you say, first things first." He booted his horse in the ribs, wanting to lead his army into Mashiz. The capital lay less than a quarter of a farsang—a quarter hour's ride—to the west.

Abivard kicked his own mount up to a fast trot to keep pace with his sovereign. "Will we have more fighting to do inside the city?" he asked.

"I hope not," Sharbaraz said. "With any sort of luck, his army will have gone to pieces. But the palace is a formidable place. If he has men willing to fight for him, he could hold out a long time there."

"The Videssians and their siege engines—" Abivard began.

Sharbaraz shook his head. "No, by the God," he said harshly. "If they pound the usurper's men or the works he threw up against me, well and good. But the palace doesn't belong to Smerdis—it's mine, just as Mashiz is ours. I don't want it wrecked if I can find any way around that; I want to live in it after I take Mashiz, as I did before Smerdis stole the throne."

"Very well, Majesty," Abivard said, humbled. To him, the palace was just another military target. To Sharbaraz, it was home.

On they rode. The closer they got, the bigger Mashiz looked to Abivard. It dwarfed Serrhes, which was the only city into which he had ever gone. The towns of the land of the Thousand Cities might well have been as crowded, but they weren't large, not with each one sitting atop a mound made from generations of its own rubble. Mashiz sprawled over the foothills of the Dilbat Mountains. At the eastern edge of the city was a marketplace big enough all by itself to swallow Serrhes. Now it boiled like an anthill knocked down by a small boy. All the merchants who had never imagined Sharbaraz's troopers could enter the capital—and there seemed to be quite a few of them—now were trying to hide their goods, and often themselves, too.

"Too late for that," Sharbaraz said, pointing ahead. "I wonder how big an indemnity to set on them for doing business as usual under my thief of a cousin." His laugh held a predatory note. "They're wondering the same thing, too."

"We can worry about that later, though, surely, Majesty," Abivard said. "First we need to take the palace and lay hold of Smerdis Pimp of Pimps."

"Aye," Sharbaraz said, predatory still.

He knew the way through Mashiz's maze of streets. Though the palace was an imposing structure of gray stone, other, lesser buildings kept blocking it from view, so Abivard might have taken hours to find his way to it down streets that twisted back on themselves like snakes, as if in a deliberate effort to keep newcomers from going anywhere on them.

The palace had an outwall formidable enough to make Abivard think once more of having to batter it down, but no soldiers paced upon it or shouted defiance down at the rightful King of Kings. All the gates, their timbers shod in iron, looked formidable, but they all stood open.

"He's yielded," Sharbaraz said in tones of mixed wonder and suspicion. He urged his horse across the open area in front of the wall. Abivard went ahead with him. So did the soldiers who had accompanied them through the city.

Abivard was about halfway across the open area when everything went black.

It did not feel as if he had been stricken blind. Rather, night—moonless, starless, lightless—seemed to have fallen on Mashiz. His horse snorted and stopped dead. In an odd way, that reassured him: if the animal was dumbfounded, too, the trouble did not lie inside his own eyes.

"Majesty?" he called to Sharbaraz a few feet away.

"Abivard?" the rightful King of Kings replied. "Is that you? I can hear your voice, but I can't see you."

"I can't see anything," Abivard said. "Can you?"

"Now that you mention it, no." Sharbaraz raised his voice to call to his soldiers. "Can anyone see anything?"

Several people said no. Several others were shouting things that weren't answers but that also meant no. Abivard stared through the darkness that filled his eyes, seeking without success to find light. He also stared with his ears, trying to have them serve for the sense that had failed him. With them he had better luck. Shouts and screams came not only from near but also from as far as he could hear.

"The whole city's gone black," he exclaimed.

"You're right, I think," Sharbaraz said a few moments later, as if he had first paused to listen and to weigh what he was hearing. "Smerdis must have made the court magicians cast this gloom down upon us for his own purposes."

"Battle magic—" Abivard began, but then stopped—it wasn't battle magic, not really, for it seemed to have fallen on all of Mashiz's inhabitants—even on the animals—and not just on combatants. In battle, magic rarely bit on a man; his passions were too likely to be inflamed for it to be effective. Now, though, Sharbaraz's soldiers, victory already in their hands, had eased away from the peak of life-or-death excitement, and so . . .

"I pray the gloom does extend over the whole of Mashiz," Sharbaraz said. "If Smerdis' men can see while our eyes stay swaddled in darkness—" Abivard admired him for laughing, but he did not sound amused. "In that case, Smerdis Pimp of Pimps will enjoy a longer reign than I'd thought."

There was a thought to put fear in a man. Abivard wondered what he would do—what he could do—if horns suddenly blared and horses clattered across the cobbles at him. Swing his sword wildly in all directions until a lance he never saw skewered him? Better to yank off his helm and draw that sword across his own throat. That, at least, would be quick.

But no horns belled out a blast of triumph. All he heard around him was chaos. Slowly the fear of sudden attack faded. But fear did not flee—it merely changed its shape. Smiths at their forges, tavernkeepers with torches to light up their taprooms, cooks at hearths and braziers . . . how long before one of them started a fire impossible to fight?

If that happened, he didn't know what he could do about it, save to bake like a round of pocket bread in the oven. You couldn't flee fire any more than foe, not if you couldn't see which way to run.

"What do we do?" Sharbaraz asked. By his voice, thoughts like Abivard's had been running through his mind.

"Majesty, I don't know," Abivard answered. "What *can* we do? All I can think of is to stay as calm as we can and hope the light returns."

"Believe me, brother-in-law of mine, I have no better ideas." Sharbaraz raised his voice, called out his name and Abivard's suggestion, and added, "Pass my words on to those too far away to hear them straight from my lips. Say also that our sorcerers will soon overcome the darkness Smerdis Pimp of Pimps has raised against us." In a muttered aside to Abivard, he said, "They'd better."

"Aye," Abivard said. "I wonder how far out from the palace—or out from Mashiz—this blackness reaches." As soon as he spoke the words, he wished he hadn't. They made him imagine not just the magicians groping in darkness but the whole world so afflicted.

From the noise wrenched out of Sharbaraz, the rightful King of Kings—the veritable King of Kings, if light ever returned—didn't care to think about that, either. After a moment, he found words: "I'm going to ride forward very slowly until I fetch up against the wall. Then I'll know exactly where I am—and I'll have something at my back."

"I'm with you, Majesty," Abivard said at once; having something at his back suddenly seemed precious as emeralds. Foes might still come at him then, but from only one direction.

Sharbaraz's horse clip-clopped across the cobbles, one cautious step after another. Abivard didn't know how—or if—his own mount would respond when he urged it ahead. But it obeyed, as if relieved to find that the human atop it knew what he was doing after all. Abivard hoped the animal wasn't paying him too great a compliment.

He heard a faint thump from ahead, followed a moment later by an indignant snort. "Ah—I've found the wall," Sharbaraz said.

"Found it the hard way, unless I'm wrong," Abivard said, and Sharbaraz did not tell him he was. He eased back on the reins, slowing his horse even more in an effort to keep from imitating his sovereign. He didn't succeed, though; his horse fetched up against the wall before he knew it was there. In the absence of eyes, the other senses hadn't given either him or the animal warning enough to stop in time.

The horse let out the same sort of irritated snort Sharbaraz's beast had used. It turned its body till it was parallel to the wall, in the process scraping Abivard's leg against the stones. It snorted again, this time in satisfaction, as if assured it had taken its revenge. For his part, he was glad of the armor he wore.

"Is that you, brother-in-law of mine?" Sharbaraz asked.

"Yes, Majesty," Abivard said. "I wonder how long we'll have to wait till the light returns." What he really wondered, but would not say, was whether the light would ever return. When he got thirsty and hungry, how would he find his way out of Mashiz if he couldn't see where he was going?

"Those are all fascinating questions," Sharbaraz said when he posed them aloud. "I'm sure they're occurring to other people about now, too. I wish I could truthfully say I had so little concern that they'd never occurred to me, but I can't." He sighed. "I wish I had answers for them, too."

Time stretched. Since Abivard could see neither sun nor moon nor stars, he couldn't tell how much of it was passing. To give him some sense of duration, he sang and hummed and hummed and sang. That helped, but not enough. His ears told him other men were doing the same, and doubtless for the same reason.

Eventually he had to make water. When he dismounted, he was careful to hold onto the horse's reins, for fear of getting turned around and never finding the animal again if he let go of them. That meant he had to take down his armored breeches little better than one-handed and, worse, pull them up again the same way. "Amazing what you can do when you try," he remarked to the blackness around him.

Out of the blackness, Sharbaraz answered, "So it must be. I'm going to have to try to imitate you before too long. If I manage to lose myself, call my name and I'll come to the sound of your voice."

"As you say, Majesty. If I'd dropped the reins there, I would have asked the same of you."

"I wonder what happened to Smerdis' men," Sharbaraz said. "It's as if the God scooped us all into the Void."

Abivard drew in a sharp, frightened breath at that. The comparison was only too apt—Abivard wondered if it wasn't literal truth rather than comparison. Why the God should choose to do such a thing at a moment when righteousness was about to triumph, he could not imagine—but the God did not have to justify himself to a mere mortal, either.

Through the confused and often panic-stricken hubbub, through the ragged snatches of song that calmer men used to keep themselves enspirited, came a more purposeful chant, sung by many men at once. At first Abivard just noted the strong, calm music of it, which lifted his own spirit. Then he realized it was not in his own tongue, but in Videssian.

The chanters came closer. As they approached, he made out more and more words. He had heard the hymn before, back in Serrhes; it was a song of praise to Phos, the Videssian god of good—and, Abivard remembered, of light. Whether he believed in Phos or not, light was what he and all of Mashiz needed most at the moment.

His ears said the Videssians were entering the square around the palace. Their joyous song rang out, glorifying not only their god but also the sun, Phos' chiefest symbol, marked by the golden domes atop the spires of their temples and by the cloth-of-gold circles Videssian priests wore on the breasts of their blue robes, just above their hearts.

Then he saw the Videssian priests. For a moment, they were all he did see, striding through the blackness, all around them as if unaware of its existence. After that moment, his sight cleared altogether, and he saw the whole square. When it blurred in his sight, alarm ran through him, but he did not need long to realize tears of relief accounted for that.

Sharbaraz gave the Videssians one of their own salutes, his right fist over his heart. "My friends. I am very glad to see you," he said in Videssian, then dropped into his own language to add, "and you may take that however you wish."

One of the Videssian priests bowed in return. The late-afternoon sun gleamed from his shaven pate as if it were one of the gilded domes that topped his faith's temples. Seeing how close to the mountain peaks the sun had slid gave Abivard an idea of how long he had been without sight—quite a while longer than he had thought.

In fair Makuraner, the priest said, "Your Majesty, we are sorry we did not come sooner to your aid. This was a strong magic, and needed all our strength to overcome. Also, you Makuraners have a way of working wizardry different from ours, so we had trouble devising counterspells to deal with what had been done."

"However you did what you did, I'm glad you did it," Sharbaraz said. "Now we can enter the palace and cast down Smerdis once for all."

"Happy to be of service, your Majesty," the priest said, and bowed again.

With light restored, servitors began straggling out of the palace compound. Some of them recognized Sharbaraz. They went to their bellies, eating dirt before the King of Kings. "Now you come into your own, Majesty," Abivard said softly.

"Not quite yet," Sharbaraz said. "Not until the usurper is in my hands."

But none of the palace functionaries, for all their loud protestations of loyalty to Sharbaraz, admitted to knowing where Smerdis was. Sharbaraz sent soldiers through the palace. He sent eunuchs into the women's quarters, where soldiers could not go. No one found a trace of his elderly cousin.

Before long, though, some of the soldiers brought him three men whom he recognized. "Ah, the royal wizards," he said, while the Videssians and his own men bristled. "I take it you worthies are to blame for the recent events?"

Abivard admired his sangfroid. The wizards knocked their heads on the cobblestones. "Majesty, forgive!" one of them wailed. "Your rival compelled us to do his bidding, holding our families hostage to ensure that we did as he demanded. Forgive!" he repeated, and the other two echoed him.

"Perhaps I shall. Then again, perhaps I shan't," Sharbaraz said. "Tell me more, Khuranzim—tell me the purpose of a magic that darkened everyone's sight, for instance."

"Why, to allow Smerdis to escape unseen, of course," answered the wizard who had spoken before—presumably Khuranzim. "Over him the spell held no power. He tried to make us extend that over his soldiers, as well, but we told him truthfully that such was impossible: attempt to employ this cantrip as battle magic and you throw it away, for the spleen of men assailed by unseen foes would be so roused that in moments it would hold no sway over them."

Beside Sharbaraz, Abivard let out a long sigh of relief. The nightmare he and the King of Kings had feared could not have come true—although no small number of men would have died before the rest awoke from that nightmare.

He thought of something else. "Wizard, you say Smerdis had

you cast this large and complicated spell just to let him get away?"

"Yes, uh, lord," Khuranzim answered cautiously. Sharbaraz he knew. He had never seen Abivard before and could not gauge how high in the affection of the King of Kings he stood. High enough to merit a soft answer, at any rate.

Abivard said, "By the God, why didn't he simply have you change his face, so he could sneak out of Mashiz with no one the wiser?"

"Lord, your words make it evident you are a man of sense," Khuranzim said, bowing. His lip curled. "The same cannot be said of Smerdis. To him, how large and showy a magic was counted for more than its mere effectiveness. When I suggested to him the very plan you named, he said he would cut the throat of my eldest son, give my principal wife over to his guardsmen . . . I am a potent mage, lord, given time to prepare my charms. Edged iron can be too quick for me."

"Can you track him now, to learn where he's fled?" Sharbaraz asked.

"Possibly, your Majesty," Khuranzim said, cautious again. "But some of the shielding spells laid on a King of Kings do not require frequent renewal, so detecting him by such means will not be easy."

Sharbaraz made a sour face, but then his expression lightened. "Never mind. Search your best, but whether you find him or not, my men will." His voice flamed with anticipation.

"Lord Abivard?" One of the serving women who had accompanied Roshnani and Denak from Vek Rud stronghold waited for Abivard to notice her, then went on, "The lady your sister would speak with you, if you have the time."

"Denak? Of course I'll see her," he said, though he suspected he sounded surprised. She had sometimes come to talk with him when he visited Roshnani, but he couldn't remember the last time she had asked him to come herself. "Lead me to her."

The wagon that had taken his sister and his principal wife through so much remained with the rest of the baggage train just outside of Mashiz. The serving woman went up and into it ahead of Abivard. After a moment, she beckoned at the entrance for him to follow.

Denak waited in her little cubicle, which was on the other side of the wagon from Roshnani's and fitted out in mirror image to hers, which made it familiar and disconcerting at the same time for Abivard. After he hugged his sister, he sat down crosslegged on the carpet and said, "What is it? How can I help you?"

"You probably can't," Denak answered bleakly. She sat down, too, leaning against the outer wall of the wagon with her hands on her belly. "I'm with child, and I'm going into the royal women's quarters tomorrow."

"You're going to have a baby, with luck an heir to the throne? That's wonderful!" Abivard exclaimed. Then he really heard the rest of what Denak had said. "Where else would you stay but in the women's quarters?"

"Staying there is one thing," Denak said. "Whether I ever come out again before they bury me is something else again." Her eyes flicked back and forth, like those of an animal caught in a trap. "I might have borne it before, when I knew no better. But I've been free—well, freer—awhile now, and the thought of being caged up again . . . I don't think I can."

"Why should you be? Trapped, I mean?" Abivard said. "The King of Kings let you travel with him, we all dined in Serrhes together . . . He's been good about keeping the promise he made back at our stronghold."

"Not as good as he might have been, but on the whole, yes, you're right." All the same, Denak looked at Abivard as if he had proved himself a blockhead. As if teaching a small boy his letters, she went on, "I am going into the women's quarters tomorrow. My husband will ride out in pursuit of Smerdis the same day. Until he gets back, do you think I shall be able to poke so much as the tip of my nose outside the women's quarters?"

"Oh," Abivard said, and tasted the emptiness of the word. He did his best to look on the bright side: "He's already sent riders after the usurper. The God willing, he'll be back in Mashiz very soon."

"The God willing, yes, but what if he's gone for months? Even if I'm resigned to spending some time in the women's quarters here, will he remember his promise—will he honor it?—when he gets back after he's gone for a long time?"

"I don't know," Abivard admitted. "I will say, though, that he strikes me as careful in matters that touch his honor. From the little I saw of Peroz King of Kings, his father was the same way."

"May you be right," Denak said. "The other thing I worry about is what will become of *me* in the women's quarters. I'll be a white crow there, not just because I'm the daughter of a frontier *dihqan* and not a princess from one of the Seven Clans, but also because I've been out in the world and seen things and done things. What will they think of me?"

"If they have any sense, they'll be jealous," Abivard said. "When Sharbaraz does come back, why don't you try to get him to give his other wives the same privileges he's granted you? If that works, how can they help but be grateful to you?"

"Knowing what goes on in women's quarters, I suspect they'd find a way," Denak said. But she leaned forward and kissed Abivard on the cheek, just above the line where his beard stopped. "It is a good idea. I'll try it; the worst he can tell me is no." She seemed to change the subject. "You'll be riding with Sharbaraz, won't you?"

"Yes, of course," Abivard answered.

Denak sighed, then lowered her voice. "And you'll be taking Roshnani with you, naturally—even though Smerdis fled south, away from Vek Rud domain, that's still the way around the mountains and back toward home." She sighed again. "How I envy her those extra weeks of freedom."

"It will be all right, Denak." Abivard summoned up courage of a kind different from what he had needed to face foes lance to lance on the field and said, "Surely it will be better than what you would have known at Nalgis Crag domain, even had Sharbaraz never ended up there."

Denak stared at him. Since she and Sharbaraz had escaped from Nalgis Crag stronghold, Abivard had hardly ever mentioned it. That he did so now, deliberately, made her stop and think. "Aye, it will be better than that," she said, but her voice was grudging. "Better, though, is not good."

"I didn't say it was," Abivard answered at once. "But nothing happens all at once, no matter how we wish it would. And if you work to make 'better' better still, your daughter—or her daughter—may think her life is . . . good."

"Maybe." At first Denak did not seem convinced, but after a moment she slowly nodded.

◆   ◆   ◆

The pursuit of Smerdis went south, as Denak had said. Every day Abivard expected the hard-riding scouts at the head of Sharbaraz's pack to run his cousin to earth like an exhausted antelope. Every day, though, the hunt went on. The Dilbat Mountains were dwindling into desert foothills. Soon, if he so desired, Smerdis would be able to swing north and west.

"I wonder what Likinios would have done if he'd fled to Videssos," Abivard said as they encamped east of those foothills.

Sharbaraz looked at him like a man staring at a cockroach cooked into his bowl of lentils. "Now there's an . . . interesting . . . thought," he said after a pause in which he seemed to discard several more pungent descriptions. "I don't suppose he'd put him at the head of a new Videssian army—that would be too raw. More likely, he'd keep him in luxury at Videssos the city for as long as he lived, just to remind me I'd better behave myself unless I wanted trouble from the east. That's what I'd do in his boots, anyway."

Abivard nodded. "That's about what I was thinking, Majesty. Now I want us to be able to do something to Smerdis."

"So do I," Sharbaraz said. "If he'd yield himself up, I'd be grateful enough that I'd strike off his head and have done. I wouldn't even bother hauling him back to Mashiz to see how ingenious the executioners could be."

"Fair enough," Abivard said, then kicked at the dirt in frustration. "Where has he gone to, anyway?"

"Drop me into the Void if I know," the King of Kings answered. "When I set out on this chase, I thought it would be over soon. Now—" He stamped his foot, too. Abivard thought of what Denak had said. Before he could speak, though, the King of Kings went on, "I'm glad we brought the regiment of Videssian engineers with us after all. If he's managed to hide himself in a stronghold somewhere, they'll help us winkle him out."

"What with their baggage train, they slow us down," Abivard said in oblique disagreement. "Even the scouts can't get too far ahead of our main body, for Smerdis has scraped up enough followers to treat a small band roughly."

"I'm not worried about that. We'll run him to earth pretty soon, come what may," Sharbaraz said. "He's an old man, after all, and he was a mintmaster, not a horseman. He'll wilt in the saddle like greens in the stewpot."

He stood tall and proud and young and confident, every inch a proper King of Kings of Makuran. Seeing that kingly arrogance—all of it deserved, no doubt—Abivard had to remind himself that Sharbaraz had underestimated Smerdis before.

"I don't believe it," Sharbaraz said in disgust.

"I don't believe it," Abivard said in sympathy.

"I don't believe it," the commander of the Videssian engineers said in awe. Ypsilantes was a lean, dour, sun-baked man who would have been on the quiet side even for a Makuraner; for a Videssian, he was astonishingly taciturn. But when he stared up and up at the stronghold atop Nalgis Crag, he was as impressed as any Makuraner would have been.

Sharbaraz treated him with respect, perhaps more than he might have given to a Makuraner in the same position. He said, "Having seen what your men accomplished between the Tutub and the Tib, I refuse to believe anything beyond your powers. Surely you'll devise some ingenious way to force Smerdis to come down."

"Damn me to the ice if I know what, your Majesty," Ypsilantes answered. His quiet had nothing to do with the way he spoke Makuraner; he was quite fluent. He was simply one of those uncommon people who say only what's necessary and not a word more.

The King of Kings scowled. "Starving Nalgis Crag stronghold into submission would take years." Ypsilantes just nodded, which did nothing to improve Sharbaraz's temper. He clenched his fists. Abivard knew he would have liked nothing better than to see Nalgis Crag stronghold torn down stone by stone. But getting up to the stronghold, let alone tearing it down, would be the next thing to impossible.

Abivard said, "Majesty, it strikes me that the stronghold does have one weakness after all."

Ypsilantes grunted and shook his head; he got more meaning into that than some men would have with an oration. Sharbaraz freighted his voice with sarcasm: "Enlighten us, O sage of the military art. The distinguished engineer sees a perfect fortification. I must confess I see a perfect fortification. How gratifying, then, that you've found a weakness which evades us. And that weakness is?"

"Pradtak son of Artapan," Abivard answered at once. "The fortress itself could be all of adamant, not just stone and iron. With Pradtak leading it, it might yet fall. You've had some dealing with him, Majesty. Am I right or am I wrong?"

Sharbaraz did not reply at once. His eyes got a faraway look that had nothing to do with staring up and up to the fortress that crowned Nalgis Crag. Till that moment, he had been considering only the fortress, not the men inside it. He made small clicking noises as he thought. At last he said, "Brother-in-law of mine, it could be so."

"Knowing the man you fight is better than knowing the fort he fights from," Ypsilantes said—a very Videssian notion, when you got down to it. He turned to Abivard. "What of this Pradtak, eminent sir?"

Now Abivard hesitated. How to characterize his former brother-in-law? "He's . . . weak," he said after a moment. "He's not a coward, nothing like that, but he has a crust of bluster, if you know what I mean. Crack that and he's soft underneath."

"Like an oyster," Ypsilantes said. Abivard knew the word, though he had never tasted one. He nodded. The engineer rubbed his chin. "How to crack the shell, then?"

"Tell him what will happen to him when Nalgis Crag stronghold does fall at last—and fall it shall," Sharbaraz said, anticipation in his voice. "Not only do I owe him for giving Smerdis refuge, but also for the delightful accommodations he granted me year before last. Put enough fear in him and he'll do what we want. He must know what the executioners back in Mashiz can make him suffer before they finally let him die."

But Abivard shook his head. "Forgive me, Majesty, but I don't think you can put him in fear for himself, not that way. Even if we do take Nalgis Crag stronghold—" He was too polite to contradict the King of Kings directly, but he still doubted it could be done, "—how do you propose to take Pradtak himself? A step off the wall and he's cheated the executioners." He shivered a little. From the walls of Nalgis Crag stronghold, it was a *long* way down. What would you think about, the wind whipping at you, till the moment of blackness?

Sharbaraz glared at him. But Ypsilantes said, "Good sense," in a way that would have made Sharbaraz seem petulant, even to himself, if he disagreed.

"What then?" the King of Kings snapped. "If we can't even reach Pradtak, how are we to put him in fear enough to make him want to hand over Smerdis?" He meant it as a rhetorical question, and it was certainly one for which Abivard had no good answer. Clenching his fists, Sharbaraz went on, "Outrageous that a single *dihqan* should be able to defy the entire realm."

Had Abivard not defied the entire realm, Sharbaraz rather than Smerdis would have been mured up in Nalgis Crag stronghold. He thought it impolitic to mention that. But the complaint from the King of Kings sparked a thought in him. "Majesty, you're right: all the realm is yours, while Pradtak holds but the one domain here. If you were to begin to wreck it, most methodically, leaving him with the prospect of holding nothing but the stronghold once you were through—"

With an engineer's practicality, Ypsilantes said, "He is up high. He can see a long, long way. Every village that burned—"

Sharbaraz didn't answer right away. Abivard had learned better than to push him too hard, especially now that he was coming into full awareness of his power. He waited to hear what the King of Kings would say. "We'll try it," Sharbaraz declared at last. "First, though, we shall warn Pradtak of exactly what we intend. If he chooses to sacrifice his domain for Smerdis Pimp of Pimps, let the blame rest on his head."

"As you say, Majesty." Abivard nodded. "The God willing, he'll yield to the threat alone and not make us carry it out"

"He will if he cares a fig for his domain," Sharbaraz said. "And I know the perfect envoy from this force to put our terms to him, too."

"Who's that, Majesty?" After getting his idea, Abivard hadn't taken it any farther.

Sharbaraz clicked his tongue between his teeth, as if to say Abivard had disappointed him. He stabbed out a forefinger. "You."

Abivard held the truce shield high as he rode the narrow, winding track up toward Nalgis Crag stronghold. He wished he had a surefooted mule or donkey under him rather than his horse. Prestige forbade it, of course. If his horse slipped and he fell, he would die of prestige. That was far from the most common cause of death in Makuran, but it was also far from unknown.

He felt very much alone. If Pradtak wanted to seize him, too, and hold him as a hostage to try to twist Sharbaraz's will, he could. Abivard didn't think that would have any effect on the King of Kings, and didn't care to think about the effect it would have on him.

He had already passed several of the garrisons on the lower, less steep parts of Nalgis Crag. Sharbaraz's army could conceivably have driven them out of their positions, though it would have hurt itself badly in the driving. As for the barrier ahead and the men who stood guard beyond it . . .

A warrior scrambled over the stones. "What would you?"

Abivard flourished the shield of truce. "I come with a warning from Sharbaraz King of Kings, may his years be many and his realm increase, as to what will befall Nalgis Crag domain if the *dihqan* Pradtak fails to yield up the rebel Smerdis to him. I am ordered to deliver this warning to Pradtak personally."

"You wait here," the man said. "Who are you, that I may give your name to my lord the *dihqan*?"

"Abivard son of Godarz, once his brother-in-law," Abivard answered.

Pradtak's man stiffened, as if unexpectedly stung by a wasp. Abivard stiffened, too. He had dreaded that question. Pradtak was liable to have left orders that he be killed out of hand. But evidently not; the warrior said, "I shall take the *dihqan* your words. Wait." Rather jerkily, he climbed back over the stones that could rain down on attackers and hurried toward the stronghold.

Abivard dismounted, fed his horse some dates, and brushed down the animal. He did his best to ignore the men watching him from behind the heaped stones—and the ones he had already passed, the ones who could block him from returning to friends and safety. It wasn't easy, and grew harder as time crawled by.

He looked up the ever steeper slope toward the stronghold. His patience was at last rewarded when he caught sight of two men riding slowly in his direction. After a few minutes, he knew one of them was the officer who had gone up to tell Pradtak he would come. Then he recognized Pradtak, too.

His former brother-in-law scrambled over the stony barrier between them and approached. Behind the barrier, Pradtak's men waited with drawn bows. If Abivard thought to try anything, he would be pincushioned before he could. Since he didn't, he bowed to Pradtak and said, "The God give you good day. You're moving very well; I'm glad the ankle has healed as it should."

"It doesn't trouble me much any more, not so far as moving goes," Pradtak answered. "But when rain or bad weather is coming, I always know it a day before anyone else in the stronghold." He fixed Abivard with a suspicious stare. "You didn't ride up here to talk about the state of my leg."

"That's true," Abivard said. "I came up here to demand in the name of Sharbaraz King of Kings, may his years be many and his realm increase, who is my brother-in-law through my sister Denak whom you will no doubt recall, the person of the usurper Smerdis."

"I don't give a moldy date for what Sharbaraz demands," Pradtak said, snapping his fingers in contempt. "He's nothing but a renunciate, and Smerdis the proper King of Kings. And I don't give a moldy date about *you*, either. The sooner you drop into the Void, the happier I'll be. Have you forgotten it's war to the knife between us? Only your truce shield and my generosity keep me from ordering you slain this instant."

He puffed out his chest, obviously sure he had made Abivard afraid. Having seen him bluster before, though, Abivard was less than impressed. He said, "Sharbaraz King of Kings will spare you even though you imprisoned him, providing you yield up the usurper. If you don't, your domain will pay the price for it—and so will you, once he starves you out."

Pradtak snapped his fingers again. "That for Sharbaraz and his threats, and you may tell him I said so. If he proposes to take Nalgis Crag stronghold, I wish him joy of the attempt."

"But Nalgis Crag stronghold is not all of Nalgis Crag domain," Abivard answered. He told Pradtak what he and Sharbaraz had worked out, adding, "By the time we're through with your lands, a crow that flies across them will have to carry its own provisions. I warn you, heed what I say."

Pradtak's face darkened with fury. Now Abivard knew fear, fear that Pradtak would be enraged enough to forget the shield of truce and the generosity he had averred only moments before. "I shall not give Smerdis up," Pradtak said thickly. "He has my oath of loyalty, which I honor yet."

"He lied as to the terms under which you swore it," Abivard

said, "for Sharbaraz King of Kings did not give up the throne of his own free will. Thus the oath has no true hold on you."

"You might as well be a Videssian, like the ones to whom Sharbaraz sold his soul for a chance to steal the realm," Pradtak said. "I don't care what you claim—I shall not surrender Smerdis to you."

"Your domain will pay the price for your stubbornness, and so will you, when eventually you yield to the King of Kings," Abivard warned. "Think twice, think three times, on what you do today, Pradtak."

He didn't want to push his former brother-in-law too far, lest he push Pradtak into a place from which he could not extricate himself. Thus he spoke as softly as he could, within the limits Sharbaraz had set him. But it was not soft enough. Pradtak shouted, "Go down to your master and tell him I'll never wear his livery."

Abivard could not resist a parting shot. "Why should that worry you, when you wore his seeming for a couple of days?" He wheeled his horse and rode down Nalgis Crag, away from the curses Pradtak hurled after him.

Sharbaraz looked gloomy when Abivard returned emptyhanded. He said, "If that pompous fool thinks I'm bluffing, I'll have to show him how wrong he is. I hate it—his subjects are my subjects, too—but I will have Smerdis from him, come what may."

Abivard rode with the party that fired the village at the base of Nalgis Crag. The people there had been warned of what was coming; most of them were already on the road, carrying such belongings and treasures as they could, when the soldiers came into their village. A few stragglers still remained behind, though. One of them, an old woman, shook her fist at the jingling horsemen. "The God and the Four curse you for harming us who never harmed you," she cried, her voice mushy because she had no teeth.

"Go on, grandmother, take yourself out of here," Abivard said. His left hand twisted to turn aside the curse. "Blame your lord, for not giving Sharbaraz King of Kings the fugitive who is his by rights."

"If you blame Lord Pradtak, burn Lord Pradtak," the old woman retorted. But Sharbaraz's army could not do that, not with the *dihqan* impregnable inside Nalgis Crag stronghold, so Pradtak's subjects would have to suffer in his stead. Still cursing and bemoaning her fate, the woman shouldered a blanket wrapped around her few meager possessions and trudged after the rest of the villagers.

"I don't envy these folk," Abivard said. "If Pradtak holds to his purpose, we may have to burn them out again and again."

One of the horsemen passed out torches. Another got a fire going in the center of the market square. When flames crackled there, Abivard thrust the head of his torch into them, then waved it in the air to bring it to full life. He touched it to the thatched roof of a nearby house. The dry straw caught almost at once. Flames ran toward the crown of the roof; burning straw fell down into the building to ignite whatever was inside.

A couple of dogs sat in the square, not far from the fire the trooper had set. They howled disconsolately, breaking off only to sneeze and snort now and again as the smoke grew thicker. Abivard watched the soldiers torch the village. Some of them went at it with real enjoyment, ducking into houses to emerge with jars of wine or with trinkets for camp followers, then burning with whoops of glee the places they had just looted. Others simply set a fire, went on to another building, and did it again.

In the end, Abivard couldn't see that it mattered much one way or the other. The village burned.

Coughing, his eyes streaming from the smoke, he rode with the rest of the incendiary party back to camp. The black column of smoke that rose from the village's funeral pyre climbed higher than the summit of Nalgis Crag. The wind whipped it and frayed it and eventually dissipated it, but the smell of the burning must surely have reached the stronghold.

Pradtak, though, made no move to surrender Smerdis.

When morning came, Sharbaraz sent Abivard out with another troop of horsemen to burn down the village next nearest to Nalgis Crag—about a farsang off to the north. A shower of arrows greeted them when they arrived. A couple of men and a horse were wounded. "Forward!" Abivard cried. The troopers rode into town full of grim determination. More arrows fell among them, wounding another horse. In this kind of fight, horses were not much use. Armored men were. Once they knocked down a few doors and killed the defenders inside, the fight went out of the rest of the people in the village.

Abivard barely kept his soldiers from slaughtering them just the same. "They had a right to fight," he insisted. "No one warned them there'd be a massacre afterward if they did. Next time, though—"

He drove the villagers out of their homes with only the clothes on their backs and a chunk of pocket bread and a wine jar each. After that, the smoke rose into the air again, a pillar even thicker and darker than the one that had gone up the day before. The troopers went about their business with a single-mindedness they hadn't shown in the other village; they wasted no time on horseplay here.

Sharbaraz nodded when Abivard told him what he had done. "That was just right, brother-in-law of mine. Tomorrow, if we need to go out tomorrow, we'll tell them they may leave with what they can carry if they offer no resistance. Otherwise, we'll treat it as war in all ways." He looked up toward Nalgis Crag stronghold. "With any luck at all, Pradtak will see he'll have no domain left if he keeps the usurper much longer."

But a village to the south went up in smoke the next day. The people there left sullenly but without fighting the King of Kings' lancers, who went out in greater force. The day after that, villagers in a fourth hamlet had to be overcome in battle—and were.

Along with the houses, vines and pistachio trees also burned. Sharbaraz had meant what he said: Pradtak might keep Nalgis Crag stronghold for a long time, but nothing in the domain except for the stronghold would be worth having once the soldiers and their torches were done.

On the fifth day, the village of Gayy, the one Sharbaraz had known of and exploited during his escape from the stronghold, was given over to the flames. Sighing, he said, "Whatever I learned about the town will have to be rewritten."

His incendiaries were about to ride out for their sixth day of devastation when a man bearing a shield of truce came down from Nalgis Crag and prostrated himself before him. After the ritual eating of dirt, the fellow said, "Majesty, may your years be many and your realm increase. If Lord Pradtak surrenders to you the person of your cousin Smerdis, will you forgive him whatever transgressions he may in your mind have committed, leave off destroying his domain, and confirm not only his safety but his tenure as *dihqan* here?"

"I hate to give him so much," Sharbaraz said. But when he glanced at Abivard, Abivard nodded. Sharbaraz frowned, irresolute, but finally said, "Very well. For the sake of ending this civil war, I will. Let the usurper be brought to me before noon today and all shall be as Pradtak says." The *dihqan's* envoy rode back toward Nalgis Crag at a gallop. Sharbaraz turned back to Abivard and said, "I may forgive, but drop me into the Void if I forget."

Abivard took that to mean Pradtak would be wise to stay up in Nalgis Crag stronghold the rest of his mortal days unless he wanted those days abruptly curtailed. The thought slid out of his mind almost as soon as it formed, overwhelmed by surging relief that the long struggle which had torn Makuran apart soon would at last be over.

He was also consumed with curiosity to learn—finally—what the man who had taken Sharbaraz's throne looked like. Long before the sun reached its high point in the sky, three men rode down from Nalgis Crag: two warriors leading a graybeard who had been tied onto a mule. Once Smerdis was in Sharbaraz's hands, the soldiers didn't wait around to learn what sort of reception they would get from the King of Kings. Like Pradtak's earlier spokesman, they galloped back toward safety.

Though Smerdis was unkempt and wearing only a dirty caftan, the family link among him, Peroz, and Sharbaraz was easy to see. He did his best to hide the fear he had to feel.

"Well, cousin, what have you to say for yourself?" Sharbaraz asked him.

"Only that I should have taken your head along with your throne," Smerdis answered. His voice was almost as mushy as that of the old woman in the village; he had lost a good many teeth.

"A mistake I will not imitate," Sharbaraz said. "But you have more spirit than I credited to you. I'll just shorten you and have done."

Smerdis nodded. Sharbaraz's officers gathered round to witness the execution. One of his men cut Smerdis' bonds and helped him off the mule. He got down on all fours and stretched out his neck for the sword. It bit. His body convulsed briefly. Had he lived as well as he died, he might have made a worthy King of Kings.

"It's over," Sharbaraz said.

✦ XII

Along with the wagon that carried Roshnani, the surviving horsemen who had come from Vek Rud domain, and Tanshar the fortune-teller, Abivard rode back toward his home with a company of troops from the army that had besieged Nalgis Crag stronghold. "Call them my parting gift," Sharbaraz said as he took his leave. "You may run into plainsmen along the road to your domain."

"That's so." Abivard clasped the hand of the King of Kings. The rest of Sharbaraz's army was breaking camp, too, some of the northwestern contingents to return to their home domains, some to go south to Mashiz with the King of Kings, and Ypsilantes' Videssian engineers to fare back to their native land. Abivard went on, "Majesty, I'll miss you more than I can say. After so long—"

Sharbaraz snorted. "I named these men here a parting gift, brother-in-law of mine, not a farewell gift. You have to make sure your own house is in order; I understand that. But before too long I'll want you at my side again. You know what my plans are."

Abivard glanced over toward the Videssians. None of them was in earshot. Even so, he lowered his voice: "We owe them a debt, Majesty." That was as close as he felt like coming to reproving the King of Kings.

"I know," Sharbaraz answered calmly. "A debt is exactly what it is, as if I'd had to borrow ten thousand arkets from a money-lender. I'll pay it back as I can. And once I have, do you think such a stickler as Likinios will give me no excuse to get back Makuran's own?"

"Put that way, no," Abivard said. Likinios was a very able ruler; he had seen that. But Sharbaraz was right: in trying to calculate everything beforehand, the Videssian Avtokrator left scant room for anything outside his calculations. And no man, however wise, was wise enough to foresee everything. That was for the God alone.

Sharbaraz clapped him on the back. "The God grant that all's well with your domain and your family."

"Thank you, Majesty." Abivard hesitated, then said, "Majesty, if you see your way clear to giving my sister some freedom from the women's quarters, it would mean a great deal to her."

"I know that, too," Sharbaraz said. "You need not worry there. I owe Denak far more than I owe Likinios. I shall attend to it." He laughed. "I may even make it the fashion for men to be seen with their wives. What a scandal that will be for the graybeards!" He sounded as if he relished the prospect.

"Majesty, I thank you," Abivard said.

"Go on home, tend to your business—and, in a while, it will be time to tend to mine," Sharbaraz said.

The last time Abivard had traveled from Nalgis Crag stronghold back to Vek Rud domain, he had made the trip as fast as he could without killing the horses he, Sharbaraz, Tanshar, and Denak were riding. Till he got back onto his own land, he had feared Pradtak's warriors were one ridge behind him, riding hard to recapture the fugitive King of Kings.

Now he could make the journey at an easier pace. Not only did he no longer fear enemies at his back, he had enough men with him to overawe almost any band of Khamorth. Turning to Tanshar, who rode beside him, he said, "The nomads missed their chance to take big chunks of the northwest and turn them into an extension of the Pardrayan steppe."

"So they did," the fortune-teller said, nodding. "They all joined together against us when Peroz King of Kings crossed the Degird in arms, but they're clans, not a nation. If they started squabbling among themselves once their victory was won, they wouldn't have had the chance to do as you said. I don't know that's what happened, mind you, but it could have been."

Abivard laughed. "Odd to hear a fortune-teller say he doesn't know what happened. You're supposed to know such things."

"Lord, when as many years pile onto you as weigh my shoulders down, you'll find out that one of the biggest things you know is just how little you know," Tanshar answered. "Oh, if I was ordered and if I could get past the tribal shamans' magic, I might be able to learn why the Khamorth didn't swarm over the Degird as we feared, but who cares about the why after the fact? That they didn't is what matters."

"Mmm." Abivard chewed on that; he found a hard core of sense there. "I see what you're saying. But don't go parading your own ignorance. You accomplished more on that campaign than—than—" He stopped, not sure how to go on without insulting Tanshar, which was the last thing he wanted to do.

"More than you'd expected from a village fortune-teller, do you mean?" Tanshar asked gently. Abivard felt his ears heat but had to nod. Smiling, Tanshar went on, "I've lived in the village under Vek Rud stronghold all my days, and what came to me were village-size concerns. I do not complain, mind; I was as content as a man without a good wife can be. There must be many men like me, in all walks of life, through the whole of Makuran. Most of them stay in their villages their whole lives long and never have the chance to show what they might do on a larger stage. Thanks to you, I had that chance, and I took it."

The fortune-teller's quiet words gave Abivard a good deal to think about. Was what Tanshar said true? Could any man, if opportunity came his way, do more than he had ever dreamed of? If so, how many common folk were wasting lives of potential excellence just in the round of making a daily living on farms and in villages throughout the realm? If Tanshar was right, would it pay the King of Kings to seek them out? How would he find them, without some crisis in which they could display their talents? Abivard didn't know the answers, but thought the questions worth sending on to Sharbaraz.

He also found another question to put to Tanshar: "When darkness came on Mashiz, the Videssian priests were the ones who raised it. What happened to you and the rest of the Makuraner wizards Sharbaraz King of Kings had with him?"

"What happened to us, lord?" The fortune-teller's laugh was full of self-deprecation. "What happened shows the limits of what I said before, for against that magic we were all helpless as children; we had neither the training nor the skill to raise it.

Till this past year I never heard anything good about Videssos, but I thank the God the Videssians were there. Without them, Mashiz might be dark yet."

"Now there's a thought—a nasty one," Abivard said. The idea of blundering through the streets trying to escape the spell, of being essentially blind, sent cold chills through him even though the possibility had evaporated weeks before.

The party rattled on toward Vek Rud domain. High summer lay heavy on the land, burning spring greenery yellow-brown and the ground itself gray. Without the fodder and the jars of water in the supply wagons, Abivard wouldn't have cared to make the trip through the desert at that season.

Little spiral winds kicked up dust and danced across the flat, baked ground. Abivard took them for granted. Some of the soldiers in the company Sharbaraz had given him, though, claimed the little whirlwinds were the outward manifestation of mischievous demons. One of the men shot an arrow through a whirlwind, which promptly collapsed. He turned in triumph to Abivard. "You see, lord?"

"Hmm," was all Abivard said, though he wondered if the fellow might not have been right.

The next day, strong winds threw sand and grit at the travelers from sunup to sundown. It wasn't one of the disastrous sandstorms that could change the whole look of the landscape and bury a caravan in blowing dust, but it was quite bad enough. When, toward evening, the wind eased at last, Abivard issued a stern decree: "No more shooting at whirlwinds." He didn't know whether the archery could have had anything to do with the storm, and he didn't care to repeat the experiment.

That evening, when he went into the wagon to see Roshnani, he found her green around the gills. "Morning sickness," the serving woman said. "I wish lemons were in season; sucking on one would help ease it."

"Given the choice between those two, I think I'd sooner have morning sickness," Abivard said.

Roshnani wanly shook her head. "You don't know what you're talking about," she said. Since that was literally true, he spread his hands and yielded the point. She said, "At my father's stronghold, some of the women would be sick all the way through their time, while others would have no trouble at all. I seem to be in the middle. Some days I'm fine, but others—" She made a horrible gagging noise. "Today was one of those."

"I hope tomorrow will be a good day for you." Abivard patted her hand. "Just a few days more and we'll be home again at last."

From outside Roshnani's cubicle, the serving woman asked, "My lady, would you care for some mutton broth and flatbread? That should sit well in your stomach."

"Maybe later," Roshnani said, gulping.

"You should eat," Abivard said reprovingly.

"I know I should," she answered. "But if I ate anything now, I'd just give it back, and that wouldn't do me any good." She hugged herself, carefully. "My insides are sore enough as is."

"Very well," Abivard said. Since he knew next to nothing about how pregnancy worked—not that a man could know much anyhow—he was willing to trust his wife's estimate of the state of her stomach. From what he had seen of Roshnani these past couple of years, her estimates of most matters deserved trust.

She laughed a little. He raised a questioning eyebrow. She said, "Forgive me, but I still have trouble thinking of Vek Rud stronghold as 'home.' I've spent more time in this wagon than I did in your women's quarters, and we've been gone for more than a year, so it hardly seems real to me."

"I can understand that," Abivard said. "I've seen more of the world since we set out on campaign than I ever imagined I would."

"You!" Roshnani exclaimed. "What of me? I don't have quite the same fear Denak did of being caged forever, but staying in one place, seeing only rooms and walls and always the same landscape out the windows, will seem very strange."

She stopped there, but sent Abivard an anxious look. He knew what it meant: now that he was coming home in triumph, would he forget the promise he had made to let her out of the women's quarters now and again? He said, "Don't worry. You'll be able to go round the stronghold and see things from all sides."

"Thank you," she said quietly. "After so much travel, even that will seem little enough, but thank you."

Abivard thought of the conversation he'd had with Tanshar. If men in large numbers never got to do all they might because they stayed on farms or in villages and never met the wider world, what of women confined to their own quarters from the onset of womanhood to death? If his fellow *dihqans* didn't ostracize him for the scandalous favoritism he had shown Roshnani, he might quietly accomplish more for the realm simply by his example than by most things he had done during the civil war.

When he musingly said as much aloud, Roshnani cocked her head to one side and studied him for a few seconds, as she had a way of doing. "Well, of course," she said.

Traveling with a large force and the supply wagons needed to keep it fed and watered meant a slow journey back to Vek Rud domain. To compensate for that, it gave Abivard the luxury of posting van- and rear guards, as well as scouting parties out to either side of the track that ran through the wasteland. He availed himself of that luxury. Had Peroz King of Kings done the same, Sharbaraz might still have been a prince back in Mashiz and Smerdis mintmaster there. Now the one was King of Kings and the other, no doubt, would serve as an object lesson of execration to minstrels and chroniclers for generations to come.

A couple of days before Abivard expected to enter his own territory once more, a rider from the vanguard came pelting back toward the main body of the force, which traveled with the wagons. "Lord, there's plainsmen and their flocks up ahead," he said. "Don't know how many of them and how many of their beasts, but enough to stir up a deal of dust, that's certain."

Abivard ran a hand down the front of his caftan. In the summer heat, without expectation of a fight, neither he nor his horse wore armor. The same held true for his entire band. *No help for it now,* he thought. He and his followers could quickly don helmets and grab shields, at any rate. That would be plenty to put them on a par with the Khamorth.

Before he started talking, he spent a little while in thought. Though nearly two years had passed since the disastrous battle on the Pardrayan steppe, he could still hear his father as if Godarz stood beside him: "Your brains are smarter than your mouth, son, if you give them the chance to be."

When he gave his orders, they came in crisp succession. He sent riders galloping out to recall the scouting parties on either wing. He sent another man back down the road they had just traveled to bring up the rear guard to protect the wagons. Meanwhile, like him, the soldiers of the main body were grabbing helms and targets and checking to make sure their bowstrings were sound and their quivers full. When everyone had come in and prepared, he waved his arm and shouted, "Forward!"

Crying his name and that of Sharbaraz, his men rode forward. But he kept a wide line of scouts out a couple of furlongs ahead of the main band. He had no reason to expect the Khamorth might have set a trap. As far as he could tell, this was but a chance encounter. But he had no interest in repeating the tragedy of Peroz on a smaller scale.

A man nearby pointed ahead. Abivard saw not only the cloud of dust the nomads and their animals kicked up but also the animals themselves: sheep. He clucked thoughtfully. Maybe sheep could find enough forage to get through summer in the badlands, but he wouldn't have wanted to try it. Cattle would already have starved.

Instead of giving him the fight for which he had nerved himself, the nomads fled in wild disorder. They numbered somewhere between a double handful and a score; when they saw more than a hundred Makuraners bearing down on them, they did the only thing that might have saved their lives. In their stirrups, Abivard would have acted the same way.

Some of his men pursued the Khamorth and knocked a couple of them out of the saddle with good archery. The nomads shot back over their shoulders as they fled, and scored one or two hits on troopers from the company Sharbaraz had lent to Abivard. The Khamorth steppe ponies were little and ugly, but they could run. After perhaps half a farsang's chase, the Makuraners gave up and went back to rejoin their comrades.

Abivard set the men to work rounding up the sheep, which had done their best to scatter in the confusion. "Fresh mutton tonight!" he shouted, which raised cheers—everyone was tired of smoked meat, yogurt, pocket bread, and other travelers' foods. He added, "The sheep we don't butcher, we'll bring home to my domain. Here's a fight against the nomads where we turn a profit."

That brought fresh cheers from the soldiers. Only after he had said it did he stop to think that he sounded more like a Videssian than a proper Makuraner noble. *Too bad,* he thought. Winning fights was better than losing them, no matter how you phrased it.

✦   ✦   ✦

The Khamorth had let their flock range wide over the desert floor so the sheep could take advantage of whatever dry grass and water they happened to find. The nomads let the animals set their direction, and they followed. Unlike them, Abivard was going somewhere in particular and bringing the sheep along. If the forage happened to be bad alongside the track that led to his domain, he preferred losing a few beasts to turning aside to let them fatten up.

When he and his followers approached the most southeasterly village in his domain, the villagers saw the flock and began to flee, thinking the sheep heralded the arrival of a band of plainsmen. On discovering they were wrong, they returned to their homes with glad cries, greeting Abivard as warmly as if he were King of Kings himself.

News was slow trickling into the northwest of the realm; the villagers had yet to hear that Sharbaraz had vanquished Smerdis. The report sent them into fresh transports of delight, although Abivard had trouble seeing how it would change their lives much one way or the other.

By way of experiment, he brought Roshnani down from the wagon in which she had traveled so far and announced his hope that she was carrying the heir to the domain. Some of the people in the village—the older ones, mostly, and a couple of well-off merchants who probably kept their own wives secluded in imitation of the nobility—seemed startled to see her out in public, but most cheered that as one more bit of good news for the day.

Emboldened by those cheers, Roshnani leaned over and kissed Abivard on the cheek. That startled him with its boldness, but the raucous yells of approval it drew from the crowd declared the people weren't shocked. Beaming, Roshnani said, "There, you see—no one really cares if a noble's wife turns out to be a human being like any other."

"Most people don't seem to," he admitted. "I must say, I expected it to cause a bigger stir. But I can tell you one person who will care very much: my mother."

Roshnani's face fell; she had been away from the formidable presence of Burzoe for more than a year, and flourished like a flower transplanted from shady ground into bright sun. After a moment's pause to collect her thoughts—and perhaps to hold back something biting—she said, "If living her life in the women's quarters suits her, I would never be so rude as to try to make her do anything different. Why can't she extend me the same privilege?"

"Because her way of life has been customary for so long, she thinks the God ordained it," Abivard said, only half joking. "But you have one weapon in the fight that I don't think she'll be able to resist."

"What?" Roshnani suddenly giggled. "Oh." She interlaced her fingers and put both hands over the child growing, as yet invisibly, in her belly.

"That's right." Abivard nodded. "Not many mothers, from all I've heard, can resist the idea of becoming grandmothers." He paused thoughtfully. "Of course, we've been traveling long enough that Frada may have taken care of that already. He's fond of a pretty face; no reason he couldn't have sired a bastard or two in all this time. But that's not the same as fathering—or carrying—the heir to the domain . . . if it's a boy, of course."

"If it's a boy," Roshnani echoed. "Just how much that would matter never struck me till now." She gave Abivard a worried look. "Will you be very angry at me if it turns out to be a girl?"

"Me? Of course not. I'd just want to try again as soon as we could. Eventually, I expect, we'd get it right. But Mother might be upset. I've heard that she apologized to Father when Denak was born because she was a daughter, not a son."

"No wonder Denak wants so much to be free of the women's quarters," Roshnani exclaimed.

"I hadn't thought of it that way, but you're probably right," Abivard said.

"Of course you hadn't thought about it that way—you're a man," Roshnani said. "Men don't have to worry about such things. Women do."

Abivard spread his hands, not having any reply he thought adequate. When Denak had said things like that, she sounded angry. Roshnani just said them, as if remarking that the mutton wasn't cooked with enough mint. Somehow, that made coming up with an answer even harder.

Sensibly, he changed the subject. "If it is a boy, we ought to know that, so we can tell my mother right away." He snapped his fingers. "Tanshar should be able to tell us."

"Are you that curious?" she asked. When he nodded, her face lit up. "Good. I am, too. Let's go find him."

The village boasted a couple of taverns, but the fortune-teller wasn't in either of them. Nor was he still feasting with the soldiers and villagers. They finally came upon him rubbing down his horse. When Abivard had explained what they wanted of him, he smiled. "Aye, I believe I can do that, lord, lady. The village women ask it of me often enough. Only—"

"There, you see?" Abivard said triumphantly. Then he noticed he had interrupted the fortune-teller. "Only what?"

Tanshar coughed delicately. "The magic requires a single hair plucked from, ah, the private place of the woman who is with child. As soon as the spell is complete, the hair is burned, but if the noble lady objects to providing it, of course I shall understand." He seemed a little uneasy in Roshnani's presence.

Again, though for a very different reason this time, Abivard didn't know how to respond. His face warmer than summer alone could be blamed for, he looked to Roshnani. She said, "If the women in the village can do this, I can, too. I see you have your saddlebags there, Tanshar. Do you have what you'll need for the spell in them?"

"Let me think, lady," the fortune-teller said. After a few seconds, he nodded. "Yes, I'm sure I do. Are you certain that . . . ?"

Before he could answer the question, she turned her back and walked off toward her wagon. When she came back, she was holding something—presumably the hair—between thumb and forefinger. She made a wry face. "That stung," she said.

"Er—yes." Tanshar didn't quite know what to make of such cooperation. "If you will just keep that for a bit while I ready the spell—"

He fumbled through one of the saddlebags until he found his scrying bowl. Instead of filling it with water, though, he kept on rummaging until at last he turned up a small, shapely glass jar with a cork stopper. He held it up with a grunt of satisfaction.

"That looks like Videssian work," Abivard said.

"It is," Tanshar answered. "It's full of olive oil. Often a wizard will attempt this spell with melted fat. Then, if he's not most careful, the sex of the animal that provided the medium will affect the magic. Choosing a vegetable oil should reduce the chances of that."

"Rock oil would be even better," Roshnani said.

"In that particular way, yes, but not in others: Since it comes from the ground rather than from a living creature, it is not the medium to be preferred for detecting new life," the fortune-teller said.

"You know best, I'm sure," Roshnani said.

"Yes," Tanshar agreed absently. He poured oil into the bowl, then held it out to her. "If you would be so kind as to put in the hair, my lady . . ." When she had done so, he turned to Abivard and said, "You see, lord, that I have not and shall not touch the hair myself."

"So you haven't," Abivard said. From the fuss the fortune-teller made, it was as if he was assuring Abivard he hadn't and wouldn't touch the place whence that hair had come. Abivard suddenly sobered. Magic dealt with just such equivalences. Perhaps the assurance was more than polite formality after all.

Tanshar set the bowl on the ground, then squatted by it. "Lord, lady, I daresay you will want to observe this for yourselves," he remarked, so Abivard and Roshnani squatted, too. Tanshar began a slow, nasal chant that frequently invoked Fraortish eldest of all and the lady Shivini, using two of the Prophets Four, one of each gender, to seek from the God the information he desired.

The short, curly black hair quivered in the bowl of olive oil, then all at once stretched out perfectly straight. "What does that mean?" Roshnani asked.

"My lady, it means you have a boy child growing inside you," Tanshar answered. "May he prove as brave and clever and handsome as his father."

Roshnani and Abivard stood up and hugged each other. "That's splendid news," Abivard said. He dug in the pouch at his belt, took out a jingling handful of silver arkets, and gave them to Tanshar. When the fortune-teller tried to protest, he ignored him. Then curiosity got the better of him, and he asked, "Were it a girl, what would the sign have been?"

"Instead of straightening so, the hair would have twisted into the form of a circle," Tanshar said. He pulled flint and steel from the saddlebag, then a clay lamp, which he filled from the jar of olive oil. He also took out a small leather pouch filled with crushed dry leaves, dry grass, and small twigs. He made a small pile of the tinder, striking flint and steel over it till it caught. When he had a small fire going, he lit a twig at it and used the twig to set the lamp alight. Pointing at the scrying bowl, he told Roshnani, "Take out the hair and burn it in the lamp's flame. Since it's been used once for magic, it becomes more vulnerable to being used so again unless consumed."

She did as he bade her. The oil that coated the hair made the flame flare hot and bright for a moment. Roshnani had got her fingers oily, too; she jerked them away to keep from being burned.

"A boy," Abivard said softly after he and Roshnani made their good-byes to Tanshar. "You're going to have a boy." It seemed real to him for the first time. Women know intimately what it is to be with child. Men have trouble taking it in until their wives' bellies swell, or sometimes until they hold the babes in their arms.

"Your mother will be pleased," Roshnani said.

"I wasn't thinking about that, not in the slightest," he replied. They smiled at each other and, ignoring centuries of encrusted custom, walked back to her wagon hand in hand.

After Nalgis Crag, the rocky knob on which Vek Rud stronghold sat seemed to Abivard hardly more than a pimple on the face of the earth. But the familiar bulk of the almost triangular fortress raised a lump in his throat. So much had changed for him in the year and more he had been away, but the stronghold, his home, remained the same. *As it should,* he thought.

Actually, that wasn't quite true. Banners flew from the walls. As he drew closer, he saw they bore the red lion of Makuran. Considering why he had set out on campaign, that felt fitting and proper.

The village below the fortress was also decked out in festival garb, bright with banners and garlands and with everyone dressed in holiday finery. Abivard turned to the commander of the company Sharbaraz had lent him. "You're welcome to revel with us for as long as you like, but feel free to make for your own homes whenever you care to."

"Thank you, lord," the captain said, grinning. "By your gracious leave, I'll take you up on both halves of that."

Tanshar rode up to Abivard. "Lord, with your kind consent, I'll go start cleaning out my house. The women here will have taken care of it for me, no doubt, but no one's hand is ever as right as your own."

Abivard pointed up toward the stronghold. "You're welcome to come and stay with me, you know. You're not just a village fortune-teller any more; as you yourself said, you've shown your talents are greater than that."

"That may be, but my place is here," Tanshar answered. He sounded so determined, Abivard did not try to argue with him. The fortune-teller headed for his neat little home by the marketplace.

The gates to the stronghold were open. Frada stood there waiting for Abivard. The two brothers waved to each other, one on horseback, the other afoot. "By the God, it's good to see you," Frada called.

"By the God, it's good to see everyone and everything here," Abivard answered, which raised a cheer from all who stood close enough to hear him. He went on, "Roshnani's back there—" He pointed to the wagon. "—and carrying, Tanshar says, a boy. And Denak, back in Mashiz, will bear the child of the King of Kings."

That news also brought cheers, though not quite so many as he had expected. He rode past Frada into the courtyard and looked toward the doorway of the living quarters, wondering if his brother had arranged a procession of his mother and wives and half sisters. The occasion was surely solemn enough. But no women came forth from that iron-shod door; he supposed Frada hadn't cared to usurp a prerogative he might have reckoned exclusively his own, and concluded that Frada had more delicacy than he had suspected.

He got another cheer, a loud one, when he swung down off his horse and set foot on the cobbles of Vek Rud stronghold once more. Roshnani's wagon rattled through the gates and into the fortress. He walked over to it and called to her to come forth. She did, to loud applause. No one thought he was violating custom by showing her off now, not when he and she were returning in triumph.

"I give my last command before turning the domain back to Abivard my brother," Frada shouted. "Let everyone feast and drink and make merry!" The yell that went up after that dwarfed any Abivard had got, but he didn't care. Had Frada not given that command, he would have.

He hugged his brother. "It is so good to be home," he said.

"As may be, but here I am jealous of you again," Frada said. "You get all the glory, and I stay behind."

"I told you two years ago, there's less glory to war than you think," Abivard answered. "Whatever there is, though, you'll get your share. With Sharbaraz on the throne, may his years be many and his realm increase, there's not doubt of that."

"May you be right," Frada said. "I'm glad you're home, too, though." His face clouded. As if continuing the same sentence, he went on, "Mother wants to see you as soon as you can spare even a moment."

"I want to see her too, of course," Abivard said.

"I really think you should do it as soon as you can," Frada said, still sounding unhappy. "Maybe even now—what with the feasting, no one will particularly notice if you're away from the middle of things for a bit."

Roshnani caught what Abivard was missing. "Something's gone wrong in the women's quarters, hasn't it?"

Frada seemed uneasy at the prospect of speaking to his brother's wife, but he nodded. Abivard clapped a hand to his forehead. Battle was clean and simple; you could tell at a glance who had won and who had lost, and often have a good idea about why. None of that held true for disputes in the women's quarters. Having but one wife with him, he had been free of such tangles the past year and more, an advantage of monogamy he hadn't considered till now. He said, "All right, I'll see her this instant."

Relief blossomed on Frada's face. "Come with me, then." He gestured to include Roshnani in the invitation but still did not say anything directly to her.

As Abivard walked toward the doorway into the inhabited part of the stronghold, eyes watched from the windows of the women's quarters. What were his wives, or perhaps his half sisters, thinking in there? What had gone wrong past the power of his mother and brother to fix?

Inside the entranceway, the savory smells of fresh pocket bread and roasting mutton, the bouquet of sweet wine, made his nose twitch and his stomach rumble. No less than anyone else, he wanted to feast and drink and rejoice. But he turned away from the kitchens and went with Frada and Roshnani down the hall that led to the *dihqan's* bedchamber. Frada stopped at the door. "I've gone into this room, brother, to meet with our mother. By the God, I swear I have not gone past it and into the women's quarters proper since you set out with Sharbaraz to reclaim his throne."

"Just telling me would suffice," Abivard said. "You needn't take on about such a matter as that. If I didn't trust you, would I have left you in charge of the stronghold?"

Frada didn't answer, nor did he seem eager even to enter the bedchamber now that Abivard was back at Vek Rud stronghold. His scruples seemed excessive, but Abivard shrugged and went into the chamber with Roshnani alone. As he closed and barred the door, Frada's footfalls rapidly receded down the corridor. Abivard shrugged again.

He had carried a key to the door of the women's quarters all the way to Videssos and back. Now he used it to open that door. He was anything but surprised to find his mother waiting for him on the other side. He took her in his arms, kissing her cheek. "It's so good to be back," he told her, as he had Frada.

Burzoe accepted his affection as her due, as she did Roshnani's more formal greeting. To Roshnani she said, "If you think I approve of your breaking our ancient customs, you are mistaken. If you think I am not delighted to learn you are carrying a son and heir, you are even more mistaken. I welcome you back to the domain and your proper place in it, principal wife of my son."

"I may not always stay in what you think my proper place, mother of my husband," Roshnani answered. Abivard would have had trouble imagining her impolite, but that did not mean she would abandon the greater freedom she sought.

"We shall speak of this again," Burzoe said, retreating not a barleycorn's width from her position, "but now is not the proper moment." She turned to Abivard. "Come with me to my chamber—the two of you may as well come, now that I think on it. The decision here, though, must be yours, my son."

"What is this in aid of, Mother?" Abivard asked as they walked down the hall. "Frada told me something was amiss, but would say no more than that."

"He acted properly," Burzoe said. She stood aside to let Abivard precede her into the chamber, then went in ahead of Roshnani. A serving woman appeared at the doorway, as if conjured up by magic. Burzoe fixed her with a baleful glare. "Bring Kishmar and Onnophre here. They know what they need to bring."

"Yes, mistress." The woman hurried away. Her face was pale and frightened.

Wives, not half sisters, at any rate, Abivard thought. In a way, that was a relief. He had bedded both the women a few times for form's sake, but that was about all. They were pretty enough, but no great spark had flared in him, nor, he thought, in either of them.

The serving woman returned. Behind her came Kishmar and Onnophre. Their appearance startled Abivard: both were heavier, softer, than he remembered, and both had dark, tired circles under their eyes. The reason for that was easy enough to understand, though—each of them carried a baby wrapped in a soft wool blanket. Abivard did not know a great deal about babies, but someone who knew much less than he would have known these two were far too small to have been conceived while he was at Vek Rud stronghold.

He stared at his mother. She nodded grimly. "Oh, dear," he said.

She rounded on his junior wives, her voice fierce. "The *dihqan* has returned to his domain. What have you to say for yourselves, whores?"

Onnophre and Kishmar both began to wail, producing a hideous discord that grated on Abivard's ears. "Forgive!" Onnophre cried, a heartbeat before Kishmar bawled out the same word. They started telling their stories at the same time, too, so he sometimes had trouble figuring out which one he was listening to. It didn't matter. Both stories were about the same. They had been bored, they had been lonely, they had feared he was never coming back from wherever he had gone—neither woman seemed quite clear on that—and so they had managed to find a way to amuse themselves . . . and paid an all too common price for that amusement.

He looked at them. "By the way things seem, you didn't wait any too long before you found yourselves, ah, friends." That set his wives wailing again. Ignoring the racket, he turned back to Burzoe. "Are there any others with bulging bellies?"

She shook her head. "There should not have been these two. The blame for them is mine; I failed to keep proper watch on the women's quarters. But the fate of these two sluts and their worthless brats lies in your hands."

"Oh, dear," Abivard said again. If he felt like slaughtering the women and the babies, he would have been within his rights. Many a *dihqan* would have whipped out his sword without a second thought. Many a *dihqan* wouldn't have waited to hear what the miscreant wives had to say; he would have slain them as soon as he saw the babes in their arms.

"What will you do with those who have brought cuckoo's eggs into your nest?" Burzoe demanded. Her eyes expected blood.

Roshnani stood silent. This choice was Abivard's, not hers. All the same, he looked at her. He could not read her face. He sighed. "I make a decent soldier," he said wearily, "but I find I haven't it in me to be a butcher. I shall find black pebbles and divorce them and send them far away. Too many in Makuran have died this past year. Four more will not help."

"It is not enough!" Burzoe cried, and Abivard was reminded overwhelmingly of Denak's dismay at anything that smacked of half measures. *Father and son, mother and daughter,* he thought.

Kishmar and Onnophre babbled out thanks and blessings. Onnophre took a step forward, as if to embrace him, then checked herself, which was one of the wiser things she had done. Abivard said, "If I didn't put Ardini to the sword, how can I kill these two? They weren't so much wicked as foolish. They can sew; they can spin. They'll make their way in the world."

"Cast them out at once then," Burzoe said. "Every day they stay in the women's quarters adds to their shame—and to my own."

Abivard suspected the latter concern weighed more heavily in his mother's mind than the former. He said, "Since the scandal has been here for months, one more day to settle it won't matter. I've been away for more than a year. Today I aim to enjoy my return."

Burzoe's upraised eyebrows spoke eloquently of disagreement, but all she said was, "You are the *dihqan* of Vek Rud domain and the master of the women's quarters. It shall be as you ordain."

Abivard's soon-to-be-former wives showered him with benedictions. They could have faced the sword like Smerdis, with their babes left out on the hillside for dogs and ravens, and well they knew it. No doubt it hadn't seemed real to them while he was away on campaign. He might not have come back at all, in which case their adulteries stood a chance of going unpunished. Having him before them suddenly put matters in a different light.

"Be still," he said, in a voice he might have used to order his lancers to charge. Onnophre and Kishmar stared at him. No one, plainly, had ever spoken to them so. If someone had, perhaps they might not have found themselves in their present predicament. He went on, "I do not forgive you. I merely spare you. If the God grant that you find other husbands, use them better than you did me." The women started to talk. He overrode them: "You've said too much, you've done too much already. Take your bastard babes and get out of my sight. Tomorrow I will find the black pebbles and send you forth."

They fled out of Burzoe's chamber. Burzoe looked at him with a small, grudging hint of approval. "That was well done," she said.

"Was it?" Abivard felt weak and sick inside, as if he had just been through a battle in which he almost died. "Tomorrow it will be over. They can go off and be stupid at someone else's expense, not mine."

"It won't be easy for them, even so," Roshnani said. "Yes, they can earn their bread, but they'll have hard lessons in living outside the women's quarters. How to deal with butchers and merchants, how to speak to men—"

"That they know already," Burzoe said savagely.

"What would you have had me do?" Abivard asked Roshnani.

She sighed. "What you could do, you did. As you said, this should be a day of joy. I'm glad you chose not to stain your hands with blood here."

Burzoe shook her head. "He was soft. Mercy now will only encourage others to act as those sluts did."

"Mother of my husband, we do not agree." Roshnani's voice was quiet. She did not offer Burzoe argument, but she did not back away from her own view, either.

Burzoe did not seem to know what to make of that. Roshnani had been properly deferential, as a daughter-in-law should have, but had not yielded, as most daughters-in-law would have. The combination was disconcerting. She took refuge in a common complaint: "You young people have no respect for the way things should be done. If I'd gone gallivanting off to the ends of the world the way you and Denak did, I don't know—and I don't want to think about—what would have happened to my reputation."

"Nothing happened to Denak's reputation," Roshnani said with the same quiet determination to get her point across that she had shown before, "save that she got to bear a child who, with luck, will be King of Kings far earlier than she could have if she'd stayed behind here till the war was won."

"If Roshnani hadn't come with us, the war likely would have been lost, not won," Abivard told his mother, and explained how it had been his principal wife who had the idea to take refuge in Videssos. He added, "If they'd stayed, you probably never would have had a grandchild with a chance to be King of Kings."

"Custom—" Burzoe said, but she let it go as that. The prospect of a King of Kings or royal princess as a grandchild did have considerable allure.

Abivard said, "Nor will the world end if Roshnani, who after all has already traveled far, sometimes comes out of the women's quarters to see the rest of the stronghold. Sharbaraz King of Kings has promised to allow Denak the same liberty in the palace at Mashiz, and how can following what the King of Kings does be wrong?"

"I don't know the answer to that—you'd have to ask Smerdis," his mother replied tartly. Abivard felt his ears heat. Roshnani sucked in her breath with a sudden sharp sound—Burzoe could still be formidable. But she went on, "You will do as you will do and take no special notice of me in the doing. So life goes, however the old try to make it otherwise. But if you think you will make me love the changes you work, please think again."

Greatly daring, Abivard went over to her and put an arm around her shoulder. She had always been the one to console him, never the other way round—till now. He said, "By the God, Mother, I shall let no dishonor come to Vek Rud stronghold, nor to any who dwell here."

"I thought the same," Burzoe said, "and look what came of it."

"It will be all right," Abivard said with the confidence of youth. Roshnani nodded vigorously.

Now it was Burzoe who did not agree but forbore to argue. She said, "It will be as it is, however that may prove. But I know, son, that you would sooner be feasting than dealing with the troubles of the women's quarters—or with me. Go on, then. Perhaps the lady your wife will spend a little while here and regale us with tales of the far-off lands she's seen."

"Of course I will," Roshnani said at once. Abivard could read her thoughts: the more women heard of the outside world, the less content they would be with separation from it.

Maybe Burzoe saw that, maybe she didn't. In either case, having made the invitation, she could scarcely withdraw it. Abivard took leave of them both. He locked the door to the women's quarters behind him—not that that had mattered much to Onnophre and Kishmar. He wondered who had fathered their children. If he ever found out, Vek Rud stronghold would have a couple of more folk leaving it.

Frada still waited in the hallway not far from the *dihqan's* bedchamber. "You heard?" he demanded. Abivard nodded. His brother went on, "What will you do?"

"I'll divorce them both tomorrow and send them out of here," Abivard answered. "That will do. I've seen too much blood spilled this past year to want more on my hands."

His brother's shoulders slumped with relief. "I told Mother your answer would be something like that. She was all for taking their heads the minute their bellies started bulging." He rolled his eyes. "We went round and round on that one like peasant women in a ring dance. Finally I got her to wait for your word."

"What was it Father would say? 'Easier to do something now than undo it later if it happens to be wrong.' Something like that, anyhow. I'd have been upset if I got home to find two of my wives had gone on the chopping block like a couple of pullets."

"That's what I thought," Frada answered. "You're more tender-hearted than Father was, or you put up with more nonsense, anyway. Women promenading all over the landscape—" His snort showed what he thought of that. "But you're the *dihqan* now, and the stronghold runs by how you think we ought to do things."

"Am I?" Abivard said. "More tenderhearted, I mean." He wondered what Godarz would have done had a wife of his borne a child he could not have sired. Something interesting and memorable, he had no doubt. "Well, maybe I am. Every now and then, the world does change."

"Maybe so." Almost like Roshnani, Frada acknowledged without necessarily agreeing. Then he clapped his brother on the back. "However that may be, there's a feast waiting for us down the hall. If you'd stayed closeted much longer, my nose and my belly would have dragged me off to it."

"I expect I'd have forgiven you," Abivard said. "Let's go."

Somehow, word of what he had decided in the women's quarters got out to the rest of the stronghold faster than he did. Some people praised his mercy; others plainly thought he had been too soft. But everyone knew what the verdict had been. He drank two quick cups of wine to try to dull the edge of his bemusement.s

In the kitchen, a cook gave him a plate of lamb and herbs and chickpeas all mashed together, and a bowl of lamb broth with toasted chunks of pocket bread floating in it as an accompaniment. He dug in with a silver spoon. "That's good," he said blissfully. "Now in truth I start to feel at home."

"Didn't they make it at Mashiz?" Frada asked,

"They did, yes, but with different spices—too much garlic and not enough mint, if you ask me," Abivard answered. "This is the way it's supposed to taste, the way it's tasted ever since I was a boy."

"The way it's tasted as long as Abalish has commanded in the kitchens, you mean," Frada said, and Abivard nodded. His brother went on, "And what did they eat in Videssos? That must have been interesting."

"They generally bake their bread in loaves, not in pockets," Abivard said, thinking back. "They eat lamb and kid and beef, much as we do; they're even more fond of garlic than the folk around Mashiz. And—" He broke off suddenly, remembering the fermented fish sauce.

"What is it?" Frada asked eagerly. Abivard told him. He looked revolted, though not as revolted as Abivard had felt. "You're making that up." Abivard shook his head. Frada said, "I hope you didn't eat any of the horrible stuff."

"I did till they told me what it was." Abivard spooned up some broth to drive away the memory. When that didn't work, he drank some wine.

"What . . . did it taste like?" Frada asked, like one small boy querying another who had just swallowed a bug.

Abivard had trouble recalling. After he had learned the sauce was made from rotten fish, horror overwhelmed whatever flavor it might have had. At last he said, "It wasn't as bad as it might have been—more cheesy than anything else."

"Better you than me, brother of mine, that's all I have to say." Frada waved to a halt a woman with a tray of boiled mutton tongues, sweetbreads, and eyes. He filled the plate he had emptied of mashed lamb. "Now here's proper fare."

"You're right, of course," Abivard said. "Here, Mandane, let me have some of those, too." When his plate was full, he took out his belt knife and attacked the savory spread with gusto.

Presently, full to the point of bursting and drunk to the point where he seemed to float a hand's breadth above the stones of the floor, he made his way back toward the bedchamber. Only then did it occur to him that he ought to summon one of his wives to bed with him, and one other than Roshnani. She had had him all to herself for a year and more, which had to have stirred up savage jealousy in the women's quarters. He hoped that jealousy wouldn't manifest itself as it had with Ardini.

But whom should he choose? Whichever wife he first bedded on his return would also be an object of jealousy. The other relevant issue was that he was so laden with food and drink that he did not want a woman and had doubts he could do one justice. Such fine points spun slowly through his mind as he went into the bedchamber and, after a couple of fumbles, let down the bar.

He took off his sandals. Trying to work the buckles was harder than barring the door had been. At last he managed. With a sigh of relief, he lay down to think about which wife he should call. The next thing he knew, it was morning.

For the first time since he had become *dihqan*, Abivard had the chance to run his domain in something approaching peace. From time to time, small bands of Khamorth would cross the Degird and trickle south to his lands, sometimes with their flocks, sometimes as mere raiders, but he and his horsemen always managed to drive them off. The great eruption of plainsmen into Makuran everyone had feared after the disaster on the Pardrayan steppe did not come.

"Much as I hate to say it, maybe the tribute Smerdis paid the nomads did some good," Abivard remarked.

Frada spat on the walkway of the stronghold wall they paced together. "That for Smerdis and his tribute both. Stinking usurper. How could you speak any good of a man against whom you spent most of two years at war? If it weren't for you, he'd likely still be King of Kings. Aren't you glad he's gone?"

"That I am. As you say, I went through too much getting rid

of him to wish he were still here." A little voice inside Abivard,
though, asked how much difference having Sharbaraz on the throne
rather than Smerdis would mean for Makuran in the long run.
Was changing the ruler worth all the blood and treasure spilled
to accomplish the job?

Fiercely, he told the little voice to shut up. In any case, whatever the civil war had done for Makuran as a whole, it had
surely made his fortune—and his clan's. Without it, he would
never have become brother-in-law to the King of Kings, nor
possibly uncle to Sharbaraz's successor. He would have stayed
just a frontier *dihqan*, rarely worrying about what happened
outside his domain.

Would that have been so bad? the little voice asked. He ignored
it.

Roshnani came out of the door to the living quarters and
strolled across the courtyard. She saw him up on the wall and
waved to him. He waved back. The stablemen and smith's helpers
and serving women in the courtyard took no special notice of
her, which Abivard reckoned progress. The first few times she had
ventured out of the women's quarters, people had either stared
popeyed or turned their backs and pretended she wasn't there,
which struck Abivard as even worse.

From the women's quarters, eyes avidly followed Roshnani as
she walked about. Because of what Kishmar and Onnophre had
done, Abivard hesitated to give his other wives and half sisters
the freedom Roshnani enjoyed. He would willingly have granted
it to his mother, but Burzoe did not want it. If one of the faces
behind the narrow windows was hers, he was sure her mouth
was set in a thin line of disapproval.

Frada nodded down to Roshnani and said, "That hasn't worked
out as badly as I expected."

"There's the most praise I've yet heard from you about the
idea," Abivard said.

"It's not meant as praise," Frada answered. "It's meant as something less than complete hatred of the notion, which is the place
from which I began."

"Anything less than complete hatred is the most praise I've
heard from you," Abivard insisted.

Frada made a horrible face at him and mimed throwing a
punch in his direction. Then, hesitantly, he said, "I hope you

don't mind my telling you that I've talked to the lady Roshnani a few times."

Abivard understood his hesitation; if by Makuraner custom a noble was the only man who with propriety could look at his wife, he was even more emphatically the only man who could with propriety speak to her. Abivard said, "Don't fret yourself about it. I knew such things would happen when I gave her leave to come out of the women's quarters. I didn't see how it could be otherwise: if she came out and no one would speak to her, that might be even worse in her mind than staying confined in there."

"Doesn't it bother you?" Frada demanded. "You've stood more customs on their heads—"

"I'm not the only one," Abivard reminded him. "Sharbaraz King of Kings is doing with our sister what I'm doing with my wife. And a lot of customs got overthrown summer before last, along with our army. I've tried to keep the changes small and sensible. Really, I don't think Father would have disapproved."

Frada pondered that. At last, he gave a grudging nod. "You may be right. Father . . . I won't say he often broke custom, but he never seemed to take it as seriously as, say, Mother does."

"Well put." Abivard nodded in turn. "He'd work within custom whenever he could, but I don't think he'd let it bind him if he needed to accomplish something."

"Hmm. If you put it that way, brother of mine, what do you *accomplish* by letting Roshnani out of the women's quarters?" Frada looked smug, as if sure he had come up with a question Abivard couldn't answer.

But Abivard did answer: "I get the benefit of her advice more readily, which served me—and Makuran—well on campaign. And her advice is apt to be better if she sees things for herself than if she hears about them secondhand. And, on top of all that, I make her happy, which, as you'll discover when you marry, is not the least important thing in the world." He sent Frada a challenging stare.

His brother said, "If it's not the least important thing in the world, why did you set it at the foot of your list of arguments, not at their head? No, don't answer. I know why: to make the others seem bigger."

"Well, what if I did?" Abivard said, laughing. He set a hand on his brother's shoulder. "You've grown up, this past year. When I went off to war, you'd never have noticed the way an argument was made."

"I've heard enough of them since, wearing your sandals while you were away." Frada rolled his eyes. "By the God, I've had more people try to sneak lies past me than I ever imagined. Some folk have no shame whatever; they'll say anything if they think they see an arket in it."

"I won't say you're wrong, because I don't think you are. What made Smerdis do what he did, except that he thought he saw an arket in it?"

"Rather more than one," Frada said.

"Well, yes," Abivard said. "But the idea behind his greed and everyone else's is the same." He gave Frada a sidelong look. "And how many lies got past you?"

"Drop me in the Void if I know—I couldn't very well notice the ones that got past me, now could I?" Frada answered. He paused for a moment, then resumed. "Fewer and few as the months went by, I do hope."

"Yes, that's something worth aiming at," Abivard agreed.

He looked out over the battlements toward the Vek Rud River to the north. Ripening crops watered by *qanats* made the land close to the river a carpet of gold and green; herds grazed on the scrub farther away. He let out a long sigh.

"What is it?" Frada asked.

"I was standing just here, near enough, and peering out toward the river two years ago, when Father came up on the wall and told me the Videssians had been spreading gold around among the Khamorth to make them want to fight us," Abivard said. "Everything that followed sprang from that."

"It's a different world now," Frada said.

"It certainly is. I didn't expect to be *dihqan* for another twenty years—the same for Okhos and for Pradtak, too, I suppose," Abivard said. "Sharbaraz didn't expect to be King of Kings for a long time, either—and Smerdis, I daresay, never expected to be King of Kings at all."

Frada looked out at the domain, too. "Lords come and lords go," he said. "The land goes on forever."

"Truth again," Abivard said. "I give thanks to the God that the nomads contented themselves with going after our flocks and herds and didn't seriously try to wreck our croplands. Repairing *qanats* once they're broken isn't a matter for a season; it takes years."

"We fought a couple of skirmishes with them last year near the edge of the irrigated land; they wanted to pasture their flocks in the wheat and the beans," Frada said. "But when they found out we had enough warriors left to keep that from being an easy job, they gave it up—the God and the Four be praised." He wiped his forehead. "I'd be lying if I said I wasn't worried; for a while, I feared you'd hardly have a domain to come home to."

"That's all right," Abivard said. "For a while, I didn't think I was coming home, anyway. Smerdis had us by the neck—pushed out across the Tutub, away from the land of the Thousand Cities, with the desert at our backs . . . If it hadn't been for Roshnani, I expect we'd have perished there."

Frada glanced down at Roshnani, who was talking with a leatherworker. He still hesitated to look directly at her for more than a moment, but let his eyes slide across her and then back. Even so he said, "Well, considering what she did, maybe she does deserve to be out and about."

Since that was as close to a concession as he would get from his brother, Abivard clapped Frada on the back. "I thank you," he said. "Do remember, this is new for me, too. I expect it will grow easier for both of us—and maybe for Roshnani, as well—as time goes by. The Videssians let their women out freely, and so do our common folk. I don't think we'll fall into the Void if we do the same."

"I notice you haven't turned your other wives loose," Frada said.

"I would have, if Kishmar and Onnophre had kept their legs closed while I was away," Abivard answered irritably. "You'll notice they both got themselves with child while they were supposed to be locked away in the women's quarters, too; they could hardly have done more if they were selling themselves in the market square down in the village. But rewarding the others right after that would have been too much."

"What about our half sisters?" Frada asked.

"You're full of impossible questions today, aren't you?" Abivard said. He thought that one over, then sighed. "I probably won't let them out, not right away, anyhow. Having them known for wandering about outside the women's quarters wouldn't do their chances for a proper marriage match any good."

"That makes good sense," Frada allowed. "I give you credit for seeing the potholes and ruts in the road you're traveling."

"I'm glad of that," Abivard said. "Sometimes I don't think you see the road in the potholes and ruts I'm traveling." Both brothers laughed. Abivard said, "By the God, I did miss you. Sharbaraz King of Kings is a fine man and a good friend, but he's not an easy fellow to be foolish with."

"Nice to know I'm good for something," Frada said. "If all's well up here, as it looks to be, shall we go down and find out how Ganzak is doing with the latest armor? If he stays as busy as he has been, we'll be able to outfit a formidable band of lancers before long." His grin turned predatory. "All the neighboring *dihqans* will fear us."

"There are worse things," Abivard said. "Aye, let's go." Together, they descended from the wall and hurried across the courtyard to Ganzak's smithy. In winter, the smithy had been a welcome refuge against the cold. With fall still some ways away, sweat started on Abivard's brow as soon as he went into the fire-filled chamber.

Ganzak labored naked to the waist; his forehead and broad, hairy chest gleamed with sweat. Its odor filled the smith, along with woodsmoke and the almost-blood smell of hot iron. When Abivard and Frada came in, Ganzak was working not on armor but on a sword blade. His muscles rippled as he brought a hammer down on the iron bar he held to the anvil with a pair of tongs. Metal clashed against metal; sparks flew.

The smith plunged the blade-to-be into a barrel by the anvil. The hiss that rose might have come from the throat of a great venomous snake. Ganzak lifted the blade out of the quenching bath, examined it with a critical eye, and set it aside. He laid the tongs down on the anvil with a clank. "The God give you good day, lord," he said, nodding to Abivard.

"And to you," Abivard answered. Then he blurted, "How do you stand the heat in here?"

Ganzak threw back his head and laughed, loudly and gustily. "Lord, this chamber is my home. When I come out of it, I sometimes think I'm about to start shivering, I'm so used to it here."

Abivard and Frada exchanged glances. Frada said, "What I

think is that you ought to go down into the village and have Tanshar or one of the old wives brew you up a potion, for it's plain you're not a well man."

The smith laughed again. He was always good-natured, which, given his size and strength, was fortunate. Now he stretched, and the molten motion of the muscles under his sweat-shiny skin was like those under a lion's pelt. "Do I look infirm to you?" he demanded.

"No, no," Frada said hastily. However good-natured Ganzak was, only a foolish man would undertake to argue with him.

Abivard said, "We came to see how you were faring with the armors the domain needs."

"I should finish the eighth suit before the moon is new again," the smith answered. "That's gear for man and horse both, you understand, and puts us two equipages ahead of where we were before Peroz King of Kings led the army up into Pardraya. We're also ahead in helms and shields both, and I've had men ask for mail shirts, too: they're a long way from full armor, I'll not deny, but better than leather dipped in boiling wax."

"I know where they got the idea, unless I'm much mistaken," Abivard said. "Are they men who rode with Sharbaraz King of Kings?"

Ganzak's brow furrowed. "Now that you mention it, lord, they are. How did you know that?" Before Abivard could answer, the smith snapped his fingers. "Wait! I have it. You think they filched the notion from the Videssians, don't you?"

"I certainly do," Abivard said. "The Videssians wore armor enough to dominate our light-armed horse archers and even to confront our lancers, but they were a lot more mobile than heavy cavalry. Their way of doing things had merit, I thought, and from what you say, I wasn't the only one."

"Mm—I wouldn't quarrel with you," Ganzak said. "They turned out to be men of more parts than I'd expected, I will say that for 'em. I figured they'd be all gold and sneakery and no guts, and they weren't like that at all." His jaw worked, as if he were chewing on something whose flavor he didn't quite fancy. "I don't know but what I'd sooner have had 'em be more like the tales tell. They'd be less dangerous, I think."

"I think you're right," Abivard said. Ganzak showed clear understanding. He was a good smith, no doubt about that. Abivard wondered what sort of *dihqan* he would have made, had he been born to the nobility. A good one, was his guess. The realm needed smiths, yes, but it also needed good leaders. As Tanshar had asked, what was it losing because so many men never got to display the things of which they were capable?

Frada looked frustrated to the point of bursting. "Everyone chatters on about the Videssians and how they're this and how they're not that," he cried, "and here I've never been within a thousand farsangs of one."

"Don't let it bother you, brother of mine," Abivard said. "You'll have your chance against them, too."

"When?" Frada asked. "When I'm old and gray like Smerdis? I won't be able to do any good against them then. What with Sharbaraz King of Kings all friendly with Likinios Avtokrator, we're liable to have peace for the next generation." He spoke as if that were one of the worst things that could happen, but then, he had never been to war.

"I don't think you'll have to wait so long," Abivard said. "Sharbaraz King of Kings is a man of honor; he wouldn't pick a fight with Likinios without good reason. But Likinios is liable to give him reason. He took a chunk of Vaspurakan from us, remember, as the price for his aid. He's the kind who's always reaching out for his own advantage. One day he may well overreach himself, and then you'll have your wish."

Frada bent his arm, as if to couch a lance in the crook of his elbow. "It can't come soon enough."

Abivard laughed at him. "I said one day, brother of mine, not tomorrow or even next year."

"I heard what you said," Frada answered. "I just didn't listen to you."

✦ XIII

The winter before, Abivard had passed his time in chilly exile at Serrhes in the Empire of Videssos. The winter before that had been filled with excitement and frantic preparations for revolt, with Sharbaraz a fugitive and Smerdis holding most of Makuran in the hollow of his hand.

This winter was different. It wasn't the near hibernation Abivard had known in his younger days. He was *dihqan* now, not Godarz, and on his shoulders rested responsibility for solving the squabbles in his domain and for making sure supplies would stretch till spring. But the harvest had been good—better than he had expected—and the storehouses held enough wheat and nuts and fruit to ensure that the domain would not go hungry before warmth returned.

He got the chance to relax a little, the first time he'd had that chance for two and a half years. He made the most of it, sleeping through long winter nights, drinking hot spiced wine to fight the chill of snowstorms and icy breezes, taking advantage of the good harvest to eat until he had to fasten his sword belt one notch closer to the end than he had before.

Some crops grew despite the beastly weather. Roshnani's belly swelled, which she regarded with a mixture of pride and wry amusement. As her pregnancy advanced, her ankles also swelled when she was on her feet for any length of time. That limited her trips outside the women's quarters, much to her annoyance.

Abivard kept calling her to his bed even after she had grown quite round. That irked his other wives; one of them complained,

"Why don't you summon me more often? Aren't I prettier than she is?"

"If you have to ask the question, the answer is always no," Abivard answered, "because just letting it cross your lips makes you ugly."

The woman stared at him in bafflement. "I don't understand," she said.

"I know," he answered, sighing. "That's part of the problem."

Little by little, he began to let his other wives make excursions outside the women's quarters. He remained unconvinced that was a good idea but found no way around it. Before he let any of his wives out to explore the rest of the stronghold, he offered such freedom to his mother. Burzoe rejected it, as she had before. He had expected as much, but it still saddened him. Others were moving in new directions, but her path through life remained fixed.

"What are we going to do with her?" he asked Roshnani one chilly night when the two of them huddled together in the bed in the *dihqan's* bedchamber as much for warmth as from affection. "If those others go out and see things and do things she doesn't, how will she keep the lead in the women's quarters?"

"She probably won't," Roshnani answered. "It will pass to someone else." Since she was the present *dihqan's* principal wife, when she said "someone else" she undoubtedly meant herself, but she was characteristically self-effacing.

She was also sure to be right. Abivard realized that change would have to come anyway, sooner or later: Burzoe was, after all, only the widow of the former *dihqan.* But she had been undisputed mistress of the feminine side of the stronghold for longer than he had been alive; the idea of that power slipping out of her hands was as upsetting as an earthquake. He shook his head in bemusement.

Roshnani felt the motion and asked, "What is it?"

He explained, then said, "I was thinking of all the changes that have happened lately, but here's one I hadn't looked for: maybe that's what makes it so upsetting."

"As you said, though, it's a change that's coming because she refuses to change," Roshnani reminded him. "And more changes are yet to come." She took his hand and set it on her belly. The skin there was stretched tight over her growing womb.

The baby inside her kicked and squirmed, then pushed something hard and round against Abivard's palm. "That's the head," he said in delight. "That has to be his head."

Her hand joined his. "I think you're right," she said, just before, like some magical island that could rise out of the water and then vanish once more, it sank away from them as the baby shifted position.

Abivard hugged Roshnani to him. As he did so, the baby kicked vigorously. They both laughed. "Someone's doing his best to come between us," he said.

Roshnani turned serious. "That will happen for a while, you know," she said. "I'll need some time to recover after the baby's born, and he'll need me for a while, too, in spite of servants and wet nurses."

"I do know that," Abivard said. "I expect it will be all right. I'm just waiting to see which of us he favors. If he looks like your brother Okhos, he'll have all the maidens sighing for him."

"I've no reason to complain of the looks on your side of the family," Roshnani said, which made Abivard hug her again and also made the baby wiggle in her belly—or perhaps the baby would have wiggled anyhow. Roshnani went on, "And what shall we call him, once he comes out?"

"I'd like to name him Varaz, after my brother who perished up on the Pardrayan plain," Abivard answered. "Do you mind? You lost your father and brothers on the steppe, as well."

"He'll be of Vek Rud domain, and heir to it, so he should have a name that goes with it," Roshnani said after a little thought. "We'll have others to remember my kin—and your father, too. I'd thought you might want to name the boy Godarz, in fact. Why don't you?"

"Because my father's memory will stay green for years to come in the hearts and minds of everyone who knew him," Abivard said; he had thought about that, too. "He was *dihqan*, and a good one; he touched people's lives. That's a better monument than a baby's name. But Varaz was cut down before he had the chance to show everything he could do in life. He deserves to be remembered, too, and for him I think this is a good way."

"Ah." Roshnani nodded against his chest. "Every so often, you've accused me of being sensible. Husband of mine, I have to say I'm not the only one here with that affliction."

"Accused? Affliction?" Abivard snorted. "You make it sound as if something's wrong with common sense. The only thing wrong with it I can think of is that not enough people have any of it . . . Some of my former wives spring to mind," he added with a touch of malice.

Roshnani refused to let the last gibe distract her. "What could be more wrong with it than that?" she asked, and, as she had a way of doing, left Abivard groping for an answer.

Winter solstice came and went. The year before, in Serrhes, the Videssians had celebrated the day with raucous, sometimes rowdy rites. Here it passed quietly, almost unnoticed. In a way, that felt good and normal. In another way, Abivard missed the excitement of the Videssian festival.

Snowstorms rolled down from the north one after another: invaders from the steppe as dangerous as the Khamorth and, unlike the nomads, impossible to repel. The storms killed beasts and occasionally herdsmen; like everyone in the stronghold and the village below, Abivard worried that the fuel carefully gathered during the warm season would not last through the cold. Every icy blast that shook the shutters on the window to his bedchamber made him fret more.

Then, one day when the year's reckoning said the equinox was approaching but the snow-covered ground seemed certain winter would last forever, such mere pragmatic concerns as fuel vanished from his mind, for a maidservant came out of the women's quarters and, wrapped in thick sheepskins, hurried down to the village. She soon returned with the midwife, a gray-haired woman named Farigis.

Abivard met the midwife in the courtyard, just inside the main gate. She bowed politely, then said, "Your pardon, lord, but I would sooner not stand about here making polite chitchat. Your wife has more need of me than you do right now."

"Of course," Abivard said, stepping aside to let her pass. She swept by him without a backward glance, her long coat trailing in the snow. Far from being offended, Abivard was relieved: to his way of thinking, anyone who put business ahead of conversation was likely to know that business.

He did not follow Farigis into the women's quarters. For one thing, he suspected she would have thrown him out, and in such matters her word, not his, was law. And for another, childbirth was a women's mystery that frightened him worse than any of the armored lancers he had faced during the civil war: this was a battlefield on which he could not contend.

As he paced the hall outside his bedchamber, he murmured, "Lady Shivini, if you'll hear the prayer of a mere man, help bring my lady through her ordeal." That done, he went back to pacing. He wanted to send the prayer up again and again but refrained, fearing he would anger the prophet if he seemed to nag.

After a while Frada took him by the arm, led him into the kitchens, sat him down, and set a mug of wine in front of him. He drank mechanically, hardly aware of what he was doing.

"This is taking a very long time," he said presently.

"It can do that, you know," Frada answered, although he knew less about the matter than Abivard did, which, given the level of Abivard's ignorance, was not easy. He picked up Abivard's empty mug and carried it away, returning a moment later with it full and a matching one for himself in his other hand.

Every time a serving woman came into the kitchens, Abivard jumped, thinking either that she was Farigis or that she brought word from the midwife. But the sun had set and darkness settled over the stronghold like a cloak before Farigis came forth. Abivard sprang to his feet. The smile on the midwife's face told him everything he needed to know, but he stammered out his questions anyhow. "Is she . . . ? Is the baby . . . ?"

"Both well, and you have a son, as I gather Tanshar told you that you would," Farigis answered. "A good-size lad, and he cries as loud as any I've heard, which is good, though your lady won't think so when he wakes up howling a few weeks from now. She says you'll name him for your brother. The God grant him a long and healthy life."

"May I see her?" Abivard asked, and then, correcting himself, "May I see them?"

"Aye, though she's very tired," the midwife said. "I don't know how long she'll want to see you, and this once, lord, you'd do well to let your wife's wishes prevail, not your own."

"My wife's wishes prevail more often than you think," Abivard told her. She didn't seem much impressed; Abivard got the feeling she was anything but easy to impress. The sweet jingle of the silver arkets with which he paid her fee, though, definitely gained her complete, undivided, and approving attention.

"Congratulations, lord!" The call followed Abivard through the stronghold to the door of his bedchamber, then picked up again, higher-pitched, in the women's quarters.

Roshnani looked up when he came into her room. Farigis had warned him she was weary, but the exhaustion she showed shocked him. Beneath her naturally swarthy cast of skin, she was dead pale. The room smelled of stale sweat, as if she had labored in the fields rather than in childbed.

"Are you all right?" he asked, alarmed.

The corners of her mouth turned upward in what would have looked more like a smile had it come with less obvious effort. She said, "If I could sleep for the next week, I might be well enough after that, but I doubt Varaz here will give me the chance." She shifted the blanket-covered bundle she held in the crook of her left elbow.

"Let me see him," Abivard said, and Roshnani lifted the soft lamb's wool from his son's face.

Again he was shocked, and again did his best not to show it. Varaz looked like nothing so much as a wizened little red monkey with an absurd fringe of hair like a bald old man's. His eyes were shut tight enough to pull his whole face into a grimace. He breathed in little snorting grunts and occasionally twitched for no reason at all.

"He's a handsome boy," Abivard declared, the most sincere lie he had ever told.

"Isn't he?" Roshnani said proudly. Either she was lying, too, or mother love—or possibly the rigors of childbirth—had left her blind.

Abivard would have bet on the latter—the longer he stared at Varaz, the better the baby looked. "May I hold him?" he asked, gulping a little. He knew how to hold newborn pups, but babies— especially this baby, his own baby—were something else again.

"Here." Roshnani held the wrapped bundle out to him. "Keep one hand under his head, mind you—he can't hold it up for himself."

"I don't blame him, poor chap," Abivard answered. "It's much the biggest part of him." Varaz squirmed as the transfer was made and threw out his arms and legs without waking up. Abivard carefully supported his head. "Once I was this small, with my father holding me. Could it be possible?"

"If you'd been born the size you are now, your poor mother would have been . . . upset is hardly the word," Roshnani returned. "Bringing forth even a baby is quite hard enough, thank you."

Abivard blinked, then laughed. "If you can joke, you'll get over it sooner than you think."

"May you be right." Roshnani yawned and said, "Set him in the cradle, would you? I'd like to sleep as long as he'll let me."

As if Varaz were made of parchment-thin glass, Abivard laid him down. When the corner of the baby's mouth brushed the blanket that lined the cradle, he made little sucking noises. Abivard kissed Roshnani and said, "Do rest. I hope he gives you plenty of chances."

"So do I," Roshnani said, "but that's in his hands, not mine." She yawned again. "Whatever chances he gives me, I'll take."

When Abivard had walked to his bedchamber the night he had come back to Vek Rud stronghold, too much wine had made him feel his feet were floating above the ground. He had drunk some wine waiting nervously while Roshnani delivered Varaz, but was for all practical purposes sober. Nevertheless, he floated much higher now than he had then.

Winter yielded to spring in its usual grudging, curmudgeonly way. Varaz thrived as if he were an early spring flower himself. Everyone exclaimed at his size, at his looks, at how enthusiastically he nursed. He quickly learned to smile. He had had Abivard's heart before, but with that he captured his father all over again.

The first crops were beginning to sprout when a dusty, muddy horseman made his way up the knob to Vek Rud stronghold, asking after Abivard. Men hurried to fetch the *dihqan*, for the rider bore word from Sharbaraz King of Kings.

He bowed when Abivard came before him and said, "Lord, I am bidden to deliver two messages to you. First is that your sister, the lady Denak, was before I departed for this domain delivered of a daughter, the princess Jarireh. She and the little one were both well when I left Mashiz."

"This for your good news," Abivard said, giving him a couple of arkets. He hoped Denak hadn't apologized to Sharbaraz for bearing a girl. He would have reckoned the news better still if she had had a boy, but as long as she had come through birth all right, she would have more chances for that later. He asked the horseman, "What is the King of Kings' other message?"

"Lord, it may not please you." The rider nervously licked his lips. "Sharbaraz King of Kings orders you to come to Mashiz as fast as you may."

"What?" Abivard said. "Does he say why?"

"He does not," the messenger said. "But there you are bidden. Would you presume to disobey the King of Kings?"

"Of course not," Abivard replied at once. He suddenly realized that being Sharbaraz's brother-in-law could bring him danger as well as privilege. If he didn't obey the King of Kings, even in the smallest particular, he ran the risk of being suspected of treachery or undue ambition—not that the two would look much different from Sharbaraz's point of view. If an obscure cousin could aspire to the throne, what of a less obscure brother-in-law?

Abivard had no more desire to become King of Kings than he did to climb up on the stronghold wall and jump off. He also had the feeling that the more he tried to convince Sharbaraz of that, the less Sharbaraz would believe him. He asked the messenger, "Does his Majesty want me to leave for Mashiz today?"

"Indeed he does, lord," the fellow answered. "I am to accompany you on the journey, and to make it as quick as may be." He pulled a pair of parchments from a message tube on his belt. "Here is his written order, which I have just delivered. And here is a command enabling us to draw on the stables of all the domains on the way back to the capital, thus speeding us on our way."

"He's in earnest, then," Abivard said, nodding. Only half in jest he added, "Have I your leave to make farewells before we set out?"

"Lord, I am your servant," the messenger said. "But we are both servants of Sharbaraz King of Kings, may his days be long and his realm increase."

"Well said," Abivard answered. "Here, come to the kitchens, take food and drink. I shall attend you as soon as I can." He called to one of his men to take the rider into the living quarters of the stronghold, then went looking for Frada.

His brother's eyes snapped with excitement when Abivard gave him the news. "What do you suppose it means?" Frada asked. "Do you think we're at war with Videssos already?"

"I don't see how we could be," Abivard said. "Sharbaraz wouldn't attack Likinios without good reason, and Likinios went to too much trouble too recently to put Sharbaraz on the throne to give him a good reason so soon."

Frada made a clucking noise. "I'd argue with you, but I don't see how I can. But off you go again, and leave me behind to watch over the stronghold. It hardly seems fair." He laughed at Abivard's expression. "No, no, don't look like that. I'm just giving you a rough time. Whatever Sharbaraz wants, I expect I'll find out if there's a place in it for me. Maybe it's something to do with Denak."

"There's a thought," Abivard agreed. "You could be right—that might account for his not telling the messenger much." Now he knew he looked worried. "I hope it's nothing bad. But no, it could hardly be, not with the other word the fellow brought."

"You'll know fairly soon," Frada said. "Mashiz is a long way from here, but you won't have to fight any battles to get there, not this year."

"I'd better not!" Abivard exclaimed, laughing. He quickly grew serious once more. "That leaves you in charge of the domain again, brother of mine. I know you can run it—you've had more chance to show that than I have. Only one place where I'll tell you anything at all—"

"The women's quarters, I hope," Frada said.

"Why did I guess you were going to say that?" Abivard's chuckle was rueful. "As a matter of fact, though, you're right. Let my wives keep the privileges I've given them, but grant no new ones. If you need advice, you could do far worse than going to either Mother or Roshnani, or to both of them. If they agree, they're almost sure to be right. If they don't, you'll have to use your own judgment. Myself, I'm more inclined to think along with Roshnani."

Frada nodded. "I'll bear all that in mind. But it's not what I'm really worried about. That's simple: what do I do if one of your wives has a belly that starts to bulge?"

"I'll take care of *that*, by the God," Abivard said grimly. He hunted in the dirt of the courtyard till he found three black pebbles, then rounded up three witnesses. He chose men of unquestioned probity, among them Ganzak the smith, whom no one would have thought of doubting. With the witnesses watching, Abivard passed Frada the pebbles, saying, "To my brother I commit these, and give him my proxy to use them to divorce any wife of mine who adulterously gets herself with child while I am gone from the stronghold."

"I shall keep these pebbles safe against a day I hope never comes," Frada said, his voice solemn.

"We have seen your purpose, lord, and will speak of it should there be need," Ganzak said. "I also hope that day does not come." The heads of the other witnesses bobbed up and down.

"So do I," Abivard said. "But what I hope and what will be . . ." He let that hang. His brother and the witnesses all knew whereof he spoke.

By the time he went into the women's quarters, the messenger's news had already got there. He did not warn his wives he had left the pebbles with Frada; he doubted threats of that sort would keep them on the straight and narrow path if they were inclined to stray. And if they could not figure out that he might do such a thing, they were too foolish to belong in the women's quarters even as ornaments.

Roshnani said, "You won't have me nagging you to come along this time, husband of mine, not with Varaz still so small. I'll pray to the God that she bring you home quick and safe."

"I'll offer him the same prayer," Abivard answered.

Roshnani started to say something, closed her mouth on it, then cautiously tried again: "Will your other wives and I be confined to the women's quarters while you're away from the stronghold?"

"No," Abivard answered. "I've told Frada that your privileges are to remain the same."

That got him a hug fervent enough to squeeze the breath from him and to make him wish Sharbaraz's messenger wasn't waiting impatiently in the kitchens. Roshnani said, "Truly the God has been kind enough to grant me the most generous, most forbearing husband in all the world. I bless her for it and love him for it."

Abivard had intended to go on with something commonplace and fatuous about not abusing the privileges that would continue. Instead he stopped and stared. He and Roshnani had been man and wife for close to three years now; in all that time, he didn't think either of them had mentioned love. Marriages were made to bind families together. If you were lucky, you got on well with your wife, you could rely on her, and she gave good advice—to

say nothing of an heir. All those things he had had with Roshnani. Anything more . . .

She was watching him warily, perhaps wondering if she had
said too much. After a moment, he observed thoughtfully, "Do
you know, wife of mine, until you named the name I didn't
realize we had the thing it describes. That's a magic worthy of
Tanshar at his best. And do you know what else? I'm angry at
you because of it."

"You are? Why?" Roshnani asked, puzzled.

"Because now I'll be even sorrier to go away from you, and
even more begrudging of every day till I'm home again." He
squeezed her as hard as she had him.

"Those days will be empty for me, too," Roshnani said. But
then, because she was a practical person, she laughed at her poetic
pretension and said, "Well, not quite empty, not with Varaz filling
them so. But I'll miss you more than I know how to say."

"I understand, because I feel the same way," he said, and
then, cautiously: "I love you, too." He hugged her again. "And
now I have to leave." He kissed her, then made his way quickly
toward the door to the women's quarters. Because those steps
were so hard to take, he made himself hurry them, lest he find
he could not.

Sharbaraz's man was finishing his wine when Abivard walked
into the kitchens. He got up from the bench on which he sat.
"Let us be off, lord," he said. "If you will be so kind as to show
me to the stables—"

"Certainly, although I would like the chance to ready a packhorse before we set out," Abivard answered. "Strongholds, even
villages, are few and far between up here in the northwest, and
the land from one to the next often bad. If anything should go
wrong, which the God prevent, I'd sooner not be stuck in the
desert without any supplies at all. That's how vultures grow fat."

The messenger muttered under his breath but had to nod.
Servants carried sacks of pocket bread and lamb sausage rich
with garlic and mint and cardamom and skins of rough-edged
red wine out to the stables, where grooms lashed them aboard a
big gelding with good endurance.

A couple of hours before sunset, Sharbaraz's man swung up
onto his horse with very visible relief. Abivard mounted, too, and
put the packhorse on a long leather lead. With the messenger,

he rode out of Vek Rud stronghold, down the knob on which it sat, and away toward the southeast.

As Abivard had predicted, the journey to Mashiz went far more smoothly than it had when he had set out for the capital with Sharbaraz two years before. Not only did no one take up arms against him as he traveled, but lesser nobles went out of their way to offer hospitality as extravagant as they could afford. Being brother-in-law to the King of Kings had its advantages.

So did the warrant Sharbaraz's man flourished whenever occasion arose. Not only did it entitle him and Abivard to fresh horses at their stops, but to victuals on demand. The bread and meat and wine Abivard had packed back at Vek Rud stronghold stayed all but untouched.

"I don't care," he said when the messenger remarked on that. "Who knows what might have happened if we didn't have them with us?"

"Something to that," the fellow admitted. "Things you get ready for have a way of not going wrong. It's the ones you don't look for that give you trouble."

Sharbaraz's rebellious army had swung south around the Dilbat Mountains and then up through the desert toward Mashiz. Because the realm was at peace and the season approaching summer, Abivard and Sharbaraz's man traversed the passes through the mountains instead.

Abivard had thought he was used to high country. He had grown up atop a knob, after all, and he had scaled Nalgis Crag, which was a most impressive piece of stone all by itself. But looking up to steep mountains on either side of him reminded him of his insignificance in the grand scheme of things more forcefully even than the immense emptiness of the Pardrayan plain.

Fortresses in the passes could have held up an army indefinitely, both by their own strength and with the avalanches they could have unleashed against hostile troops. Seeing the gray stone piles and the heaped boulders, Abivard understood why Sharbaraz had never once considered forcing his way through the shorter route. He would not have reached Mashiz.

As things were, though, the officers who commanded the forts vied with one another to honor the brother-in-law of the King of Kings. The men struck him as being as much courtiers as soldiers, but the garrisons they commanded looked like good troops.

And then, early one morning, he and the messenger came round a last bend in the road and there, laid out before them as if through some great artist's brush, sat Mashiz, with the river valleys of the land of the Thousand Cities serving as distant backdrop. Abivard studied the scene for a long time. He had seen and even entered Mashiz from the east, but the capital of the realm took on a whole new aspect when viewed from the other direction.

"This is how it must have looked to our ancestors the God only knows how many years ago, when they first came off the high plateau of Makuran and saw the land they would make their own," he said.

The messenger shrugged. "I don't know anything about that, lord. I'm glad to see Mashiz again because I'm coming home to my wife and son."

"You took me away from mine," Abivard said, although not in real reproof: the man was but obeying the command of Sharbaraz King of Kings. "Lead me to the palace now, so I can learn the King of Kings' wishes and go back to my home once more."

In many ways, this was the first good look he had had at Mashiz. When he had entered it with Sharbaraz, he had been too busy fighting for his life to pay much attention to his surroundings, and then, just as he reached the palace, sorcerous darkness had swallowed the city. Now he took it all in: merchants and whores, servants of the God and horse traders, drunkards and servitors, farmers selling lettuces, farmers buying copper trinkets, singers, dancers, beggars, two men with picks stolidly knocking down a mud-brick wall, women hawking caged songbirds, and a thousand more besides. The noise was overwhelming, both in volume and variety.

Without the messenger to guide him, he would soon have been hopelessly lost. Streets writhed and twisted and doubled back on themselves, but Sharbaraz's man unerringly picked his way through the maze and toward the palace. At the gates, he turned Abivard over to a plump, beardless flunky and rode away.

At first Abivard thought the functionary was a man, although he had never seen a man without a beard. Then he thought the person was a woman, for the voice with which he was addressed seemed too high and smooth to belong to a man. But he had trouble imagining a woman in such a prominent position at the court of the King of Kings.

Then he realized he was dealing with a eunuch. He felt like a country bumpkin, unused to the sophisticated ways of the capital. As the courtier guided him to the throne room, though, he wondered what the fellow thought of his own state. Sophistication had its prices, too.

"Great and magnificent lord, I shall be beside you as you are presented to Sharbaraz King of Kings, may his years be many and his realm increase," the eunuch said. "At my signal, thus—" He touched Abivard on the arm. "—you are to prostrate yourself before him."

"As you say," Abivard agreed. Being brother-in-law to the King of Kings did not excuse him from any of the formalities of court ceremonial. If anything, it made his punctiliousness in observing those formalities more important than it would have been for someone of less exalted rank.

His feet glided soundlessly over thick wool carpets beautifully dyed and elaborately woven: carpets too fine to be walked upon anywhere save in the palace of the King of Kings. The torches that lit the hallways were of sandalwood; their sweet smoke filled the air. He had put on his best caftan to enter Mashiz, but felt woefully underdressed all the same.

"We approach the throne room," the eunuch murmured in his strange, sexually ambiguous voice. "Walk beside me, as I told you, and be ready for my signal."

Courtiers, ministers, generals, and high nobles from the Seven Clans filled the throne room. Abivard felt their eyes on him and did his best to bear up under the scrutiny. He looked straight ahead and tried not to notice the grandees staring at him, studying him, taking his measure. They had to be wondering, *What is this backwoods noble like?*

Holding his own eyes on the throne helped him keep his composure. It was not, he saw, a single seat, but two. There sat Sharbaraz, unmistakable in his gorgeous robes and crown, but who was that beside him? The throne room was very long. Abivard had advanced halfway toward the high seats when he suddenly grinned an enormous grin and felt all his nervousness fall away—Denak sat next to her husband.

Now he looked around at the important personages who

packed the throne room, to see how they liked the idea of having a woman—and not just any woman, but his sister!—in the company of the King of Kings. If they didn't like it, they didn't let on. That was as he had expected.

No one but Sharbaraz's guards stood closer than about five paces from the throne. The eunuch halted there. Like a well-trained horse, Abivard halted, too. The eunuch unobtrusively tapped him on the arm. He prostrated himself before the monarch of Makuran.

The carpet had stopped a few paces before. The stone to which Abivard pressed his forehead was worn smooth and shiny. He wondered how many prostrations had been performed just there over the centuries. He also noticed a thin, tiny seam that separated the stone on which he crouched from the one just ahead, and tried without any luck to figure out what it might mean.

"Rise, brother-in-law of mine, and advance to receive my favor," Sharbaraz said.

Abivard got to his feet and walked up to the throne. The guards stood aside to let him pass, but did not leave off watching him. Sharbaraz also rose, took two steps toward him, embraced him, and offered him a cheek to kiss, suggesting the two of them differed only slightly in rank. Tiny murmurs ran through the throne room as the courtiers, used to reading such subtle signs, drew their own conclusions. Denak beamed proudly.

"I have come to Mashiz in obedience to your command, Majesty," Abivard said, hoping Sharbaraz would give him some clue as to why he had been summoned.

But the King of Kings merely said, "That is as it should be. We have much to discuss, you and I, of great import to the realm." Again Abivard's ear caught those little ripples of whispering, this time, he thought, with an excited undertone to them. The assembled grandees knew what Sharbaraz was talking about, even if Abivard didn't. But, he thought proudly, the King of Kings wanted to confer with him, not with them.

After that formal greeting, Sharbaraz gave him back into the keeping of the eunuch, who led him into a little chamber of such perfect elegance that he guessed it had to be a waiting room for the King of Kings. A servant brought in roasted pistachios, little cakes savory with almond paste, and a wine sweet as honey, smooth as silk, and warming as the sun on a fine spring day.

Abivard refreshed himself, then piled some cushions high and leaned back against them to await his sovereign. Sure enough, Sharbaraz came in after a little while, Denak a pace behind him. When Abivard rose and began another prostration, Sharbaraz waved him to a halt. "You've finished the ceremony," he said. "Now we do business."

"May I see my niece first, Majesty?" Abivard asked.

"I'll go fetch her," Denak said, and hurried away.

"I have someone else I want you to meet, but I'll introduce him to you presently," Sharbaraz said. He took a pistachio, cracked the thin shell between thumb and forefinger, and popped the nut into his mouth.

Denak came back. She pressed a tiny bundle into Abivard's arms and smiled when he automatically held the baby so as to support her head. "That's right, you have a son of your own," she said, as if reminding herself. Was that jealousy in her voice? Maybe a little, he judged. She went on, "Hard to remember I'm an aunt, just as you're an uncle."

"She's a pretty baby," he said, looking down at Jarireh. Not only was she pretty, she was, for the moment, being quiet; that, as he had learned, was a virtue of considerable magnitude. "I'm trying to decide which of you she favors."

"She looks like a baby," Denak said, as if that explained everything.

Sharbaraz impatiently shifted from foot to foot. "I thought you were eager to hear why I summoned you across the length and breadth of the realm."

"I am, Majesty. It's only—" Abivard held up Jarireh. "May I use your daughter as my excuse?"

"You'd have trouble finding a better one," Sharbaraz said with a laugh. "But hear me all the same: Likinios Avtokrator is dead."

Ice ran through Abivard. "How did it happen?" he whispered. "Are you on decent terms with Hosios his son, or does the war begin now?"

"Hosios is dead, too, as Tanshar foretold," Sharbaraz said. Abivard could only gape at the King of Kings, who went on, "Hear the tale, as it came to me with the beginning of spring. You know Likinios Avtokrator was a pinchpenny; we saw that when we were in Serrhes. And you know also that the Empire of Videssos was at war with the nomads of Kubrat, up north and east of Videssos the city."

Abivard held his niece out to the King of Kings to show how confused he was. "What you say is true, Majesty, but what has one of these things to do with the other?"

"As it turns out, everything," Sharbaraz answered. "Likinios won a string of victories against the Kubratoi last year and hoped to ruin them for good and all, maybe even conquer them altogether. He didn't care to pull his army back into his own country and have to start over again this spring, so he ordered them to winter north of the Istros River, out on the edge of the steppe, and to support themselves by foraging. That way he wouldn't have to pay for feeding them through the winter, you see. He was already behind with their silver; no, I take it back, Videssians pay—or, in his case, don't pay—in gold."

"By the God," Abivard said softly. He tried to imagine a Makuraner army ordered to winter north of the Degird. Troops would, to put it mildly, not be happy about that. He had to ask the next question: "What happened then?"

"Just what you'd expect," Sharbaraz answered. "I can see that in your eyes. Aye, they mutinied, killed a couple of generals—"

"Not the Maniakai, I hope," Abivard exclaimed, and then remembered whom he had interrupted. "Forgive me, Majesty."

"It's all right," the King of Kings said. "This news is enough to make anyone jumpy. No, the Maniakai, father and son, had nothing to do with it. When they got back to Videssos, Likinios named the elder one governor of some island on the edge of nowhere and sent the younger there, too, to command the garrison. It was supposed to be a reward for a job well done, but I think the Avtokrator was just putting someone who might be a rival out of the way. Now, where was I with the main story?"

"The mutiny," Abivard and Denak said together.

"Ah, that's right. Likinios' army rebelled, as I say, killed some high-ranking officers, and named a fellow called Genesios as Avtokrator. The God only knows why; he was nothing more than a cavalry captain, a commander of a hundred. But they made some red boots, put 'em on him, and marched for Videssos the city."

"With that kind of leader against him, you'd think Likinios would have won easily," Abivard said.

"If they fought wars on parchment, you'd be right," Sharbaraz said, "but as soon as Likinios had a rival, any sort of rival, everyone stopped paying attention to him. This wasn't the first time he'd fallen behind with soldiers' pay, and everybody just got sick of him. He ordered troops out against Genesios. They left Videssos the city, sure enough, but then they went over to the rebel. That city could stand siege forever, I think, but the men at the gates opened them for Genesios' soldiers."

"Likinios should have fled," Abivard said. "He must have known you'd have received him well here, just for what he did for us in Serrhes."

"None of the sailors would take him and his sons across the little strait to the westlands," Sharbaraz said; the words tolled like doom through the little private chamber. Abivard picked up a pistachio, then put it back in its silver bowl—he had lost his appetite. The King of Kings went on, "In the end, he tried to get across in a boat he and his sons would row themselves. Too late: Genesios' men were already in the city. They caught him."

"And killed him, and Hosios, as you already told me," Abivard said.

"They did worse than that," Denak said; she had heard this tale of horror before. "They slew each of Likinios' sons before his eyes, Hosios his eldest last of all, and then they slew Likinios, too, a little bit at a time." She shuddered. "Filthy." Maybe because she had just had a baby herself, she seemed to find the idea of slaying anyone's child, particularly in front of him, especially dreadful.

"And that is how Genesios Avtokrator took the throne in Videssos," Sharbaraz said. "Part of it I've pieced together through the tales of travelers and merchants, and the rest from the embassy Genesios sent me to announce his accession as Avtokrator of the Videssians. Once he'd murdered his way into the palace, he decided he would start observing the forms, you see."

"What did you tell the envoys?" Abivard asked.

"I told them to leave the realm and be thankful I didn't clap them into the dungeons under the palace here," Sharbaraz answered. "I said I would not treat with men who served a ruler who had murdered my benefactor." His eyes flashed; thinking of Likinios' terrible end infuriated him. But he shook his head before going on, "I might have served my purpose better if I'd kept my temper and given them a soft answer. As things stand, Genesios knows I am his foe and can prepare accordingly."

"Do the Videssians all recognize him as Avtokrator?"

Sharbaraz shook his head again. "Videssos writhes like a snake with a broken back, seethes like a soup pot left too long over the fire. Some in the Empire support the usurper, some proclaim they are still loyal to the house of Likinios even though that house has been destroyed to the foundations, and I've heard rumors that another general, or maybe other generals, have proclaimed themselves Avtokrator in opposition to Genesios." He rubbed his hands together. "It is indeed a lovely mess."

"Aye, it is," Abivard breathed. "We had our civil war over these past years. Now it's the Videssians' turn, and from what you say, they have the disease worse than we did. What will you do, Majesty?"

"Let them stew in their own juice this year, I think, unless they fall altogether to pieces," Sharbaraz replied. "But I will take back all the stretch of Vaspurakan Likinios made me cede to him, and I will do it in the name of avenging him." He rubbed his hands again, plainly savoring the irony there. His voice turned dreamy. "But I want more than that, much more. And I have a key to open the lock. I'll show it to you." He hurried out of the chamber.

"What does he mean?" Abivard asked Denak.

She smiled. "I know, but I won't tell you, not when you'll see in a moment. That would spoil the surprise."

The King of Kings returned then, in the company of a young man gorgeous in Videssian imperial robes and shod with scarlet boots. He had a Videssian cast of feature, too, narrow and more delicate through the lower part of the face than most Makuraners. To Abivard he said, "It is good to see you again, eminent sir." He spoke with a strong Videssian accent.

"Forgive me, sir, but I do not believe we've met," Abivard told him. Then he turned to the King of Kings. "Majesty, who is this fellow? I've never set eyes on him in my life."

"What?" Sharbaraz played startled confusion too melodramatically to be quite convincing. "Can you tell me you've been so quick to forget the face of Hosios son of Likinios, legitimate Avtokrator of the Videssians?"

"He's not Hosios," Abivard blurted. "I've seen Hosios and talked with him. I know what he looks like, and he . . ." His voice trailed away. He stared from Sharbaraz to the man who was not Hosios and back again. "I know what Hosios looks like, and you, Majesty, you know what Hosios looks like, but how many Videssians really know what Hosios looks like?"

"You see my thought perfectly," Sharbaraz said in a tone of voice that suggested anything less would have disappointed him. "As our armies move into Videssos, how better than if we come to restore the murdered rightful Avtokrator's son and heir? If the God grant that we reach Videssos the city than to install Hosios here—" He spoke the name with a perfectly straight face, "—in the imperial palace there?"

"No better way," Abivard said. He looked over to the fellow in the Videssian imperial costume. "Who are you really?"

The man glanced nervously at Sharbaraz. "Eminent sir, I am only and have always been Hosios son of Likinios. If I am not he, who that walks the earth is?"

Abivard thought it over, then slowly nodded. "When you put it that way, I suppose no one has a better claim to the name than you do."

"Just so." With justice, Sharbaraz sounded proud of his own cleverness. "Here we'll have the King of Kings and the Avtokrator leagued together against the vile usurper, just as we did against Smerdis. How can anyone hope to stand against us?"

"I see no way," Abivard said loyally. He knew, though, that ways he did not see might exist. That was why you went to war: to find out how well the plans you had made meshed with the real world.

He let his eyes slip to "Hosios" once more. Whoever he was— most likely a trader who happened to have been in Mashiz when Sharbaraz learned of Likinios' murder, or perhaps a renegade Videssian soldier—he had to be anxious, though he hid it fairly well. He was disposable, and was a fool to boot if he didn't know it. The first time he made Sharbaraz unhappy with him, he was only too likely to suffer a tragic accident . . . or maybe he would just disappear, and someone else styled "Hosios" would end up wearing the imperial raiment.

Sharbaraz said, "We understand each other well, Hosios and I."

"That's as it should be, Majesty," Abivard said. He glanced at the man who was now the only Hosios there was. Taking Videssos the city would be splendid; no King of Kings had ever done it, not in all the years of warfare between Makuran and the Empire of Videssos. But if Sharbaraz succeeded in capturing the imperial capital and put "Hosios" here on the throne, how long before the fellow forgot he was a puppet and remembered he was a Videssian? *Not long enough* was Abivard's guess.

"It was a pleasure to renew my acquaintance with the eminent sir, Majesty, but now—" "Hosios" paused.

"I know you have urgent business of your own," Sharbaraz said, again without obvious irony. "I shan't keep you here any longer."

"Hosios" bowed to him as equal to equal, though that rang as false as the King of Kings' ostentatious politeness toward him. The pretender nodded to Abivard, one sovereign to another's close companion, then left the small private chamber. Sharbaraz poured himself another cup of wine and looked a question to Abivard, who nodded. Sharbaraz poured one for him, too, and one for Denak.

Abivard raised his cup—not plain clay, as it would have been back at Vek Rud stronghold, but milky alabaster, bored out so thin he could see the wine through it. "I salute you, Majesty," he said. "I can't think of a better way for us to take vengeance on Videssos." He drank.

So did Sharbaraz and Denak. The King of Kings said, "And do you know what the best of it is, brother-in-law of mine? Not only are the Videssians themselves up in arms against this Genesios, but, from the word that filters through Vaspurakan and across the wasteland, the man would make the late unlamented Smerdis seem a paragon of statesmanship beside him."

"Have a care, there," Abivard said. "You almost made me choke on my wine. How could anyone make Smerdis look like a statesman?"

"Genesios manages, or so it's said," Sharbaraz answered. "Smerdis had some notion of keeping his enemies quiet: the tribute he paid to the Khamorth, for instance. The only thing Genesios seems to know how to do is murder. Killing Likinios and his sons made sense enough—"

"Not the way he did it," Denak broke in. "That was brutal and cruel."

"By all accounts, Genesios *is* brutal and cruel," Sharbaraz said, "and terror the only tool he turns to in ruling. He's meted out torture, blindings, and mutilation to all of Likinios' cronies he could catch, and each new tale that comes in is more revolting than the last. Part of that may spring from the nature of tales, but when you smell something bad, you're probably riding past a dung heap."

Thoughtfully Abivard said, "He'll frighten some folk into following him with ways like those, but most of them will be men who would have favored him anyway. He won't cow the ones he really aims to terrify, the ones with true spirit. They'll just hate him more than they do already."

"Just so," Sharbaraz agreed. "The more he tries to break their spirits, the more they'll do battle against him. But he holds Videssos the city, and if ever there was one, it's Videssos' Nalgis Crag, all but impossible to take without treachery." His grin was quite broad. "Our best course, I think, is to let it be known we have 'Hosios' here, wait while Videssos falls farther into chaos—and, by all appearances, it will—and then move in. If Genesios is as bad as latest rumors paint him, we truly will be welcomed as liberators."

"Isn't that a lovely thought?" Abivard said dreamily. "You said the two Maniakai were sent off to some distant island?"

"Aye. Likinios did that, not Genesios," Sharbaraz said.

"Either way, it's just as well. They'll be safe off at the edge of the world, where Genesios' eye can't fall on them. They're good men, the father and the son, and they did quite a lot for us. I don't want to see them come to harm."

"No?" Sharbaraz said. "I'd send up a loud, long prayer of thanks to the God and the Prophets Four if I heard Genesios had ordered both their heads to go up on the Milestone in Videssos the city. They'd be in good company, by all accounts; the Milestone's supposed to be a crowded place these days."

"Majesty!" Abivard said, as reproachfully as one could speak to the King of Kings. Denak nodded, agreeing with her brother rather than her husband.

Sharbaraz refused to apologize. "I meant what I said. Brother-in-law of mine, you said the Maniakai were good men, and you were right. But that's not the point—no, it is, but only a small part of it. The true rub is that the father and son are both of them *able* men. The more like that Genesios murders, the weaker Videssos will be when we move against her."

Abivard pondered his sovereign's words. At last, he bowed. "Spoken like a King of Kings."

Sharbaraz preened, ever so slightly. But Abivard hadn't altogether meant it as a compliment. A King of Kings had to do things for reasons of state and to look at them from his realm's viewpoint rather than his own. Thus far, well and good. When you began to forget your viewpoint as a man, though, and were willing, even eager, to celebrate the deaths of loyal friends, you became something rather frightening. That, to Abivard's way of thinking, was different from, and much worse than, recognizing that those deaths would be to your advantage while mourning them nonetheless.

He opened his mouth to try to explain that to Sharbaraz, then shut it again with the words unspoken. As he had discovered, what even a brother-in-law could tell the King of Kings had limits. The office Sharbaraz held, the robes he wore, worked toward stifling criticism of any sort. Oh, Abivard's head wouldn't answer for such an indiscretion; Sharbaraz would even listen politely—he owed Abivard that much, and did not think him a potential enemy . . . or Abivard hoped he didn't, at any rate. But while he would listen, he would not *hear*.

Sharbaraz said, "Your brother or his designee will be running Vek Rud domain for some time to come, brother-in-law of mine. I'll want you here at my right hand, readying our forces for the move against Videssos. We'll begin next year, I expect, and not just as raiders. What I take, I intend to keep."

"May it be so, Majesty," Abivard said. "I think I'll have to write to Frada to give him leave to appoint a designee and join the campaign himself. Otherwise, my guess is that he'd appoint one without my leave and come just the same. He's missed two chances already; he won't stand it a third time. Sometimes you need to know when to yield."

"A point," Sharbaraz said, though the only time he had yielded, so far as Abivard knew, was when Smerdis' minions held a knife to his throat. Abivard shook his head No, the King of Kings had also given in when Likinios demanded territory in exchange for aid. In the face of necessity that dire, he could retreat.

"A good point," Denak said, and Abivard remembered that Sharbaraz had also yielded to her in a variety of ways, from letting her accompany him on campaign to allowing her to show herself in public here in the palace. No, he had done more than merely allow that: he had adjusted court ceremonial to accommodate it. Abivard revised his previous opinion—Sharbaraz could make concessions, after all.

Turning to his sister, Abivard asked, "How does it feel, living in the palace here at the capital instead of back at our domain?"

She considered that with almost the care Roshnani might have given it before answering. "There are good things here I could never have had in the stronghold." She glanced down at the sleeping Jarireh—remembering Kishmar and Onnophre, Abivard knew Denak could have had a baby in the women's quarters, but he kept quiet—then over to Sharbaraz. The King of Kings smiled as his eyes met hers; the two of them seemed well enough content with each other.

Denak went on, "But, at times, it's harder here. I often feel very much a stranger, which of course would never have happened back home. Some of the women in the women's quarters openly resent me for being principal wife when my blood's not of the highest."

"I've told them they'd better not," Sharbaraz said sharply. "When they've rendered a hundredth part of the service you have, then they may begin to complain."

"Oh, I don't much mind that," Denak said. "If I were in their slippers, I should probably resent me, too. The ones who frighten me, though, are those who spread on sweetness as if it were mutton fat on a chunk of pocket bread, when in their eyes I see them wishing I'd tread on a viper. You'd not see that sort of dissembling back at Vek Rud stronghold."

"No?" Abivard said. "You were already at Nalgis Crag when Ardini tried to bespell me, but you must have heard about it when you came home again."

"That's true; I did," Denak said in a small voice. "I'd forgotten." She laughed, perhaps in embarrassment, perhaps nervously. "Memory always makes the things you've left behind seem better than they really were, doesn't it?"

"Sometimes it can make bad things seem better than they were," Sharbaraz said. "Then it's a blessing from the God."

"And other times, when you sit and brood . . ." Denak didn't go on. She shook her head, angry at herself. "I try to forget, I truly do. But sometimes things swim up, all unbidden. It doesn't happen as often now as it did before."

"Good," Sharbaraz said. "If the God is kind, we have many

years ahead of us in this world. Before the time your span is done, my principal wife, I pray your troubles will have vanished altogether from your mind."

"May it be so," Denak said. Abivard echoed her.

Sharbaraz turned to him. "Now you know part of why I summoned you here. As I told you, I'll want you to stay in Mashiz. You showed in the battles of the past two years that you're fit to be one of my great captains. You've hoped to lead an army against Videssos; now that hope comes true."

Abivard bowed. "Majesty, you could do me no greater honor."

Sharbaraz laughed. "That's not honor, brother-in-law of mine: That's because I need you. The other part of the reason I ordered you here to Mashiz was to do you honor. I shall lay on a great feast tonight, and summon courtiers and soldiers to see what sort of man has a sister fit for the King of Kings."

Now Abivard laughed nervously. "One with a northwestern accent and rustic ways, one from the lesser nobility rather than the Seven Clans—"

"One who makes too little of himself," Sharbaraz interrupted. "Remember, the purpose of the feast is to honor you, and I delight in doing so. Everyone there, no matter how high his blood, will be hoping you offer him a cheek to kiss; and for all of them, the choice will be yours."

"The prospect is . . . dizzying, Majesty," Abivard said. "That grandees from all over Makuran will be noting what I do, what I say . . . almost I wouldn't mind going back to obscurity, just for the sake of escaping that."

"If you hadn't said 'almost,' I would be angry with you," Sharbaraz answered. "I know you traveled here quickly, I know you're worn, and I know you'll want to be properly decked out to meet the court: clothes are armor of a sort. Sleep for a bit, if you care to; when you wake, or when we wake you, we'll see to it that you're properly bathed and groomed and dressed."

Sharbaraz and Denak left the little room. Abivard stretched out among the pillows on the floor and did fall asleep. A eunuch presently woke him and led him to a steaming chamber where he soaked in deliciously warm water, then rubbed scented oil on himself and scraped it off with a strigil, Videssian-style. A barber curled his hair and beard with hot irons, then waxed the tip of that beard and his mustachios to disciplined stiffness. He had to admire the image he made in a polished bronze mirror the barber handed him.

The caftan the eunuch brought him was of saffron silk shot through with silver threads. He knew it must have come from the closet of the King of Kings and tried to protest, but the eunuch was gently implacable. Along with the caftan came a bucket-shaped *pilos*, also covered in saffron silk, for Abivard's head and a pair of sandals with heavy silver buckles. The sandals fit perfectly, which impressed him all over again, for his feet were smaller than Sharbaraz's.

When he was properly turned out, the eunuch conducted him to the dining hall. He hoped a servitor would conduct him back when the feast was done; he had doubts about finding his way around the immense palace without help.

A man with a big, deep voice called out his name when he entered the dining hall. Immediately he found himself under siege, for the courtiers and generals of Makuran converged on him to introduce themselves, to put forward their schemes, and to take his measure.

From what they said, every word that fell from his lips was a perfect pearl of wisdom. Until that evening, he had thought he knew what flattery meant. Listening to such fulsome praise was seductive, like having a sloe-eyed dancer sway before you while the tambours and pandouras poured forth a passionate tune. But, just as the dancer might take you to bed more in hope of a gold bracelet than for yourself, so the courtiers' fulsome words were also plainly self-seeking.

At last Abivard said, "Gentlemen, were I as wise as you make me out to be, which for a mortal man not of the Four seems scarcely possible, would I not see that you are interested in me as brother-in-law to Sharbaraz King of Kings, may his years be many and his realm increase, rather than as Abivard son of Godarz, who otherwise would scarcely draw your notice?"

That produced a sudden, thoughtful silence. The crush around him drew back a little. He hoped he hadn't offended the grandees of Makuran—but if he had, he would bear up under it.

Sharbaraz came in just then, with Denak on his arm. The arrival of the King of Kings cast all lesser luminaries, Abivard included, into the shade. The eunuchs presently began moving people to their proper places. Abivard was surprised to note that a couple of men had, like Sharbaraz, brought their wives with them to the feast. There as in other matters, the royal pleasure counted for a great deal.

Abivard took his place at Sharbaraz's right hand. Servitors fetched in wine, a sherbet of quinces and lemon juice, and another of rhubarb sweetened with honey. For the opening toast, everyone filled his cup with wine. Sharbaraz proclaimed, "Let us drink to Abivard, whom the King of Kings delights to honor!"

In return, Abivard rose and said, "Let us drink to the King of Kings, to the Makuran he rules, and to vengeance for Likinios Avtokrator!"

A storm of applause washed over him. "Hosios," who sat at the same table, clapped loud and long. Abivard wondered if his ambitions were for Sharbaraz and Makuran or for himself.

Then the waiters brought in tureens of soup, and Abivard stopped worrying about anything but his appetite. The soup was a simple one—yogurt thinned with water, finely chopped cucumber, and ground onions, with raisins sprinkled over the top. Salt was the only spice Abivard could taste. A peasant might have served the dish's like. Of its kind, though, it was as good as any Abivard had ever had.

After the soup came bowls of buttered rice topped with slices of mutton spiced with cloves, cinnamon, cardamom, and ground rosebuds. More yogurt and raw eggs accompanied the dish. Abivard spooned yogurt into his bowl, then broke two raw eggs and stirred them into the rice, too.

He didn't remember eating raw eggs in Videssos, and glanced over at "Hosios." The man who would take the place of Likinios' murdered son mixed eggs into his rice without a qualm. Abivard caught his eye and said, "You have a taste for Makuraner food, I see."

"So I do, eminent sir," "Hosios" answered. "I've eaten it a great many times, and find it tasty." Maybe he had been a merchant, then, and in the habit of going back and forth between Videssos and Makuran.

The servants cleared away the bowls after the feasters had emptied them. This time they set plates before the grandees: gleaming copper for those tables farthest from the King of Kings, silver for those closer, and gold for his table. Abivard stared at his platter.

With such wealth as this at his command, Smerdis had chosen to squeeze his nobles to find money to pay the Khamorth! Truly the man had been a fool.

On the plates the servitors set pieces of braised duck cooked in a sweet-and-sour sauce of onions fired in sesame oil, pomegranate syrup, lemon juice, honey, pepper, and pistachios ground to powder. More pistachios, these chopped coarsely, were sprinkled over the duck. Abivard worried meat from the bones with knife and fingers, then dipped his hands into a bowl of rose-scented water and dried them on a square of pure white linen.

Talk and wine and sherbets occupied the meal. By the time he got down the last bite of fat-rich duck, Abivard was convinced, as he had been on the day he returned to Vek Rud stronghold, he would never need to eat again. He had been wrong then; he supposed he might be wrong now.

He soon found he was. From the kitchen came goblets filled with a compote of melon balls and peach slices in a syrup of honey, lime juice, and rose water. As a special treat, they were topped with snow brought down from the peaks of the Dilbat Mountains.

Abivard got to his feet. "Behold the power of the King of Kings, who brings snow to Mashiz in summer!" he called.

Again the nobles cheered—this time, he reckoned, for him and Sharbaraz both. Sharbaraz beamed. Abivard sat quickly down to enjoy the wonder; not all the power of the King of Kings could long keep snow from melting here at this season.

The snow glittered in the light of lamps and torches. That gleam called to mind Tanshar's last prophecy: a silver shield shining across a narrow sea. The sea, Abivard was suddenly certain, would be the strip of salt water that separated the Videssian westlands from Videssos the city, the great imperial capital. But who would make the shield shine, and why?

Abivard dug his spoon into the compote. When Sharbaraz moved against Videssos, he would find out.

HAMMER AND ANVIL

THE TIME OF TROUBLES, VOL. 2

✦ I

When the younger Maniakes looked west from the governor's residence—a polite name for a fortress—in Kastavala, he could see only ocean. Even so, staring out at that ocean did not bother him unduly: he knew that beyond it lay the town of Opsikion, and beyond Opsikion the rest of the Empire of Videssos.

He and his father, from whom he drew his name, had lived on the island of Kalavria half a dozen years now. It was exile, but polite, honorable exile: the elder Maniakes was governor of the island. The Avtokrator Likinios had named him to the post, and Genesios, after murdering Likinios and all his sons and seizing the imperial throne for himself, had seen fit to leave him undisturbed. In his day, the elder Maniakes had been a soldier to reckon with; Genesios was no doubt just as glad to keep him busy far, far away from Videssos the city, the great capital of the Empire.

The younger Maniakes stirred restlessly. He knew just how far Kalavria was removed from the center of the imperial stage. In his six years here, he had ridden over almost every inch of the island. He had camped by a fire on the eastern shore and looked out to where the Sailors' Sea ran on . . . forever, as far as anyone knew. The view east shouldn't have looked different from the view west, but somehow it did. Realizing you had your back to everything you would ever know seemed to change the way your eyes worked.

A voice came from behind him: "Woolgathering again, I see."

"Father! I didn't hear you come up," the younger Maniakes said.

"Proves my point, doesn't it?" The elder Maniakes chuckled raspily. He was a solidly made man in his middle sixties. A great fleshy beak of a nose dominated the rest of his features. He had aged about as well as he could for a man of his years. He still had most of his teeth, and his eyes and ears worked well enough. Along with his big, thick, bushy beard, his hair was white, but he had most of it, too. His wits, if anything, were sharper than they had ever been.

"I wasn't woolgathering," the younger Maniakes insisted, though his voice rose a little in embarrassment. "I was thinking." He had fewer than half his father's years, but most of the same features, including the impressive nose and the heavy beard that grew up almost to his eyes. Both were signs of the Vaspurakaner blood the two Maniakai shared: the elder Maniakes' father had left the land of the princes to take service with Videssos, and his scions had prospered there.

Now the elder Maniakes laughed out loud. "And what were you thinking that was so all-fired important you didn't even notice me?"

The younger Maniakes looked around, and listened, too. No, no servants were in earshot. You couldn't be too careful these days. Lowering his voice, he said, "About Genesios."

That got his father's attention. "Were you?" the elder Maniakes said, also quietly. He strode forward to stand by his son and look west with him. The governor's residence stood on a height above the town of Kastavala proper. From it, the red tile roofs of houses and shops and the golden spheres that topped Phos' temples seemed spread out as if on a chart of parchment.

Beyond the houses, beyond the temples, lay the harbor that was Kastavala's true reason for being. By the sea squatted sun-bleached wooden warehouses and fish-drying sheds. When the wind blew out of the west, as it did more often than not, everyone in Kastavala was reminded of those sheds without any need to see them.

Wooden piers jutted into the sea. Most of the vessels tied up at them were fishing boats. The men who took them out day after day brought back the mackerel and squid that helped feed Kastavala. The merchant ships that came from Opsikion and sometimes even from Videssos the city loomed over them like bulls over calves.

At the base of one of those piers stood a spear, its butt jammed into the sand. Suspended from the point of the spear was a skull. A little skin, a little hair still clung to it. At Genesios' command, that spear and its burden had stood in place there for more than five years. When it came to Kastavala, the skull had been a head: the head of Hosios, eldest son and heir to the overthrown Avtokrator Likinios.

Softly still, the younger Maniakes said, "Genesios Avtokrator hasn't done all the things he might have for Videssos."

Beside him, his father snorted. "Tell the truth, son. As far as I can see, Genesios Avtokrator hasn't done *any* of the things he might have for Videssos." Scorn filled his voice. Even so, he did not raise it. One thing Genesios was good at: scenting treason growing and rooting it out before it came to flower.

The younger Maniakes said, "Between the civil war, the Kubratoi, and the Makuraners, I wonder if there will be anything left of Videssos after a few more years. Here on this island, we're away from trouble, too."

"If it hadn't been for the Kubratoi, Likinios would still be Emperor today, or Hosios after him," the elder Maniakes said with a sigh. "Better he should have lost against the nomads than won a victory that made him think he could win more by ordering his troops to stay north of the Astris River through the winter and live off the land." He shivered at the thought of it "If I'd been in that army, I might have rebelled, too."

His son shook his head, not believing it for a moment. The elder Maniakes had the grace to look abashed. Duty ran deep in him. He might complain about the onerous parts of a soldier's life, but he would never shirk them.

The younger Maniakes said, "Since Likinios fell, it hasn't been just the Kubratoi running wild up in the northeast." He stopped, bemused by a perspective based on the view from Videssos the city. Kubrat lay north of Kalavria, but also west, not east. But then, from Kalavria just about everything lay to the west. He went on, "The men of Makuran have caused the Empire even more grief, I think."

"And whose fault is that?" The elder Maniakes pointed first at his son, then at himself. "Ours, no one else's."

"No, Likinios', too," the younger Maniakes said. "If he hadn't ordered us to help Sharbaraz—" In Videssian fashion, he pronounced the name of the Makuraner King of Kings as if it were *Sarbaraz*. "—get his throne back from that usurper, Makuran would be in no position to fight a war against Videssos. They'd have their own troubles to deal with, out there in the far west."

"Likinios Avtokrator may have ordered it, but we accomplished it, you and I," his father answered. "Sharbaraz was properly grateful, too; I'll say so much for him. And now he uses gratitude as an excuse to avenge his benefactor—and swallow up as much of the Videssian westlands as he can."

The younger Maniakes turned and stared out the window again. At this distance, the standing spearshaft and the skull on it were invisible, but he knew where they stood. Half to himself, he said, "I wonder if the Hosios Sharbaraz claims to have with him might actually be Likinios' son."

"No." The elder Maniakes' voice was hard and flat. "Whatever else Genesios Avtokrator may be, he is an effective butcher. If he claims he massacred Likinios' whole clan, you may rely on him to speak the truth there—even if nowhere else. And I recognized that head when it still had flesh on it. Didn't you?"

"Yes," the younger Maniakes admitted unwillingly. "But still—"

"—You wish we had some legitimate choice besides Genesios and his endless murders and betrayals," his father finished for him. "By Phos the lord with the great and good mind, so do I. But with Genesios holding Videssos the city, we don't, so what point even to thinking about it?"

The younger Maniakes left the window. His sandals clicked over the mosaic tiles of a hunting scene as he walked to the doorway. He looked out into the hall. It was empty in both directions. All the same, he closed the door before he went back to his father. When he spoke, it was in a whisper. "We could go into rebellion."

"No, by the good god," the elder Maniakes said, almost as quietly. "Do you know how many rebels' heads adorn the Milestone in the plaza of Palamas these days? A couple of dozen, maybe more. If an Avtokrator who holds the capital is even slightly awake to the world around him, a revolt in the provinces—especially in a Phos-forsaken province like Kalavria—is foredoomed to failure. Videssos the city is too hard a nut to crack."

"Yes, Father." The younger Maniakes sighed. They had this discussion about twice a year, or whenever word of some new disaster of Genesios' came into Kastavala, whichever was more frequent. By now, they both knew all the steps in it as well as a standard opening sequence in the Videssian board game.

But now, like a skilled player trying a variation on one of those sequences, the elder Maniakes said, "Or are you still pining for that fiancée of yours back in Videssos the city?"

Swarthy though he was, the younger Maniakes knew he was flushing. "You know bloody well it's not that," he said. He had been engaged to Niphone, the daughter of Likinios' logothete of the treasury, and assotted of her, as well. But when Likinios named his father governor of Kalavria and packed both Maniakai off to the island, they had had to leave in too much haste for a wedding. The younger Maniakes had wept bitter tears most of the way to Kastavala.

"I didn't think that was it," his father said with a twinkle in his eye, "but I did want to check. I'm sure Rotrude will be glad to hear it."

The younger Maniakes flushed again. Rotrude had been his leman for four years now. She had stayed behind in Kastavala when her husband, a trader in furs and amber from up in cold Halogaland, died of a flux of the bowels. Her exotic good looks had caught the younger Maniakes' eye: almost no Videssians had golden hair and eyes the green-blue color of the sea.

"Hard to believe Atalarikhos will be three soon," he said. He gave the boy's name the Videssian pronunciation and ending. Rotrude had wanted to name her son after her dead husband, and in the Haloga fashion simply called him Athalaric.

"He's a likely enough lad, but one of these days you should get yourself a legitimate heir," the elder Maniakes said.

His son turned that one against him like a board-game player bringing a captured piece back into action on his own side. "By the good god, where am I to find a girl of proper noble birth here on Kalavria?"

"A point." The elder Maniakes conceded that it was a good one by dipping his head and changing the subject. He pointed out to sea and said, "Isn't that a sail coming in from the west?"

"By Phos, I think it is," the younger Maniakes answered. "Nothing wrong with your eyes, Father, that's plain enough."

"Nothing wrong for looking out over the ocean, anyhow. When I try to read, it's another matter. I have to hold everything at arm's length, and then, half the time, the letters are too small to make out."

"That's a good-sized ship," the younger Maniakes said, gauging it against a fishing boat bobbing in the chop not far away. "I think I'll go down to the pier and see what cargo it brings." Watching a merchantman unload was more interesting than most things that happened in Kastavala.

"Pick up the news from the mainland, too," his father said. "It won't be good—it never is any more—but we should have it."

"I'll do as you say, Father."

The younger Maniakes hurried downstairs. At the doorway that opened onto the path leading down into town, he almost ran into his cousin Rhegorios. The two of them looked enough alike to be brothers: not surprising, since Rhegorios' father Symvatios, the elder Maniakes' younger brother, could almost have been his twin.

"Where away in such a hurry?" Rhegorios asked.

"Down to the harbor. I was on the top floor and saw a merchantman coming in," the younger Maniakes said. "Want to come along?"

"Why not?" his cousin answered. "Wait here a moment—let me get my swordbelt." He trotted down the hall toward his chamber.

Maniakes was already wearing his sword, belted on over a robe of brocaded silk. When winter came and snowstorms rolled across the sea and into Kastavala, he changed to tunic and trousers and thick sheepskin jacket, as did everyone else in town. Many men, maybe most, wore tunic and trousers the year around, but nobles were expected to be respectably conservative.

Rhegorios hurried back, still closing the heavy gold buckle on his swordbelt. He liked display better than Maniakes did. But then, he'd seen less fighting than his cousin: a fancy-decked soldier only made a juicier target for his foes.

A servant came up to bar the door behind Maniakes and Rhegorios. The wind was rising, and from out of the west. Maniakes coughed a little—it threw the reek of the fish-drying sheds full in his face. Rhegorios laughed, understanding him. "Think on the bright side, cousin," he said. "It stinks, aye, but it brings that ship in faster."

"True enough," Maniakes said. The slope of the rise lengthened his strides and sped his pace into town. He knew the slog back would be long, but was young enough not to worry about that till he had to do it.

Kastavala had no wall. Danger here came from the sea, not from the island. Soon Maniakes and Rhegorios were in among houses, most presenting to the world only whitewashed fronts with narrow, shuttered windows and stout doors; taverns and inns and brothels that catered to sailors; eateries smelling of fried fish; and shops of all sorts, most with trades connected to the sea—sailweavers, ropemakers, carpenters, coopers, with here and there a silversmith or a jeweler: a good many sailors carried their wealth on them.

Sailors and artisans, merchants and farmers from the hinterland crowded Kastavala's narrow, winding streets. Only the road that led from the harbor up to the governor's residence was cobbled; dust rose from the others in a hovering, eye-stinging cloud. Maniakes and Rhegorios picked their way through the crowd, now and then dodging a wagon heading up from the quays with a rattle of iron-clad wheels and horseshoes on cobbles and the hideous squeak of ungreased axles.

In dodging, Maniakes almost bumped into a priest. "Your pardon, holy sir," he said.

"No harm done. Phos bless you, young man." The priest sketched the good god's sun-circle above his left breast He wore a gold-embroidered circle there on an otherwise plain robe of sky-blue wool. That garb, his shaven pate, and an untrimmed beard normal for a Vaspurakaner but unusual among all Videssians save clerics were the badges of his office.

Maniakes and Rhegorios returned the gesture and pressed on. A moment later, Maniakes glanced around and saw his cousin was no longer with him. He whirled around. There stood Rhegorios, ogling a pretty girl. By her plain linen tunic and disordered hair, she was probably a laundress or cook rather than a tart seeking to draw men's eyes.

"Come on," Maniakes called.

Rhegorios came, still looking back over his shoulder. "I want to see which shop she goes into," he said. The road bent. He sighed. "She's gone—lost forever." He clapped a melodramatic hand over his heart.

Maniakes let out a snort. "You can take a pandoura into a tavern here and sing of your vanished love. Bring a sailor's cap along and you'll cadge enough coppers for a night's worth of wine. Meanwhile, watch where you're going. You almost stepped into a pile of horse turds there, and didn't even know it."

"You're a cruel, hard man, cousin of mine." Rhegorios staggered, as if wounded.

"What are you miming—being pierced by the arrow of common sense?" Maniakes asked. Rhegorios poked him in the ribs with an elbow. They half wrestled their way down to the piers.

Aboard the approaching merchantman, the sailors had put sweeps into the oarlocks fore and aft and were using them to guide the ship toward a good-sized open space on one of the quays. "Pull, lads, pull!" the captain called, his voice easily audible across a narrowing gap of water. "A little to port on the steering oars . . . a little more. Now—back water!" The ship stopped smoothly by the quay. Sailors jumped across to hold it in place with lines.

Rhegorios pointed to a knot of well-dressed men who stood close by the ship's near rail. "Not the usual sort of crowd you find at sea," he remarked. "Wonder what it means that they're here?"

"It means trouble," Maniakes replied. "You see that one in the saffron robe with the red and black brocade?" Without waiting for his cousin to nod, he went on, "That's Kourikos, the logothete of the treasury."

"Your fiancée's father." Rhegorios' eyes widened.

"That's right," Maniakes answered grimly. "Him I'd know anywhere. The others—it's been six years, but I recognize half of them, maybe more. All the ones I do recognize are men who ran things back in Videssos the city before Genesios overthrew Likinios. The ones I don't know have the same look to them, too; I'd bet they're Genesios' appointees to fill the jobs of men he's killed. But your question was the right one: what are they doing *here*?"

Rhegorios drew his sword. He held it with the point down by his right foot, but seemed ready to raise it and strike at any provocation—or none. "You gave it the right answer, cousin: they're bringing trouble."

A little more slowly than Maniakes had spotted him, Kourikos recognized his daughter's betrothed. He waved frantically at

Maniakes, then turned and said something to his companions. In an instant, they, too, were waving like men possessed. At the captain's orders, a couple of sailors extended a gangplank from the ship to the pier. The richly dressed men almost fought one another to be first across it; Maniakes was surprised no one fell—or got elbowed—off the plank and into the sea.

Kourikos in the lead, the nobles and government ministers rushed toward Maniakes and Rhegorios. "Eminent, most noble Maniakes!" his fiancée's father cried, bowing low before him. "Take us at once to the dwelling of your wise and heroic father, that we may pour out for him our tale of the woe and horror and despair that have fallen on the city, the queen of cities—" He meant the imperial capital but, like many Videssian nobles, preferred talking around something to coming right out and saying it. "—and have overwhelmed the Empire!"

One of the other men—Maniakes thought his name was Triphylles—said, "Only your father can rescue Videssos from our present calamity!" Everyone else nodded emphatically.

"What's gone and fallen to the Makuraners now?" Rhegorios asked.

"The Makuraners?" Now Kourikos, evidently spokesman by virtue of his relationship to the younger Maniakes, shook his head. "The Makuraners outside the city do dreadful things, too, seizing our land and carrying off prisoners innumerable, but that murderous Genesios does worse than they within."

Triphylles tapped him on the arm and said, "Eminent Kourikos, if you go through the whole tale of woe here, it will delay us in reaching the elder Maniakes, whereupon we shall just have to retail it over again."

"What you say is true, excellent sir," Kourikos answered. He turned back to the younger Maniakes. "Phos grant that you forgive my cutting short intercourse with you here, that we may speak to your magnificent father as soon as is practicable."

"Yes, certainly," Maniakes said after a moment—he was no longer used to the flowery language in vogue among the upper classes at the capital and had to make sure he knew what Kourikos meant. But instead of leading the delegation of grandees straight back toward the governor's residence, he held up a hand. "First you must tell me whether Niphone is safe and well."

"She was well when I left Videssos the city," Kourikos answered, "and as safe as she could make herself: she and her mother have both entered the convent dedicated to the holy Phostina. We all pray that even the monster Genesios will hesitate before dragging out anyone, female or male, who has taken service with the good god."

"May it be so," Maniakes said, and sketched Phos' sun-circle over his heart. With any Avtokrator he had ever heard of, the safety of those mured up in monasteries or convents would have been a given. If Kourikos still worried about what Genesios would do, then Genesios probably was a monster. Maniakes took a step toward the base of the pier. "Come with me, excellent sirs, eminent sirs." He pointed toward the mansion on the high ground in back of town. "There dwells my father. He will hear you with great attention, I am sure."

Together, he and Rhegorios led the nobles from Videssos the city back through Kastavala. The Kastavalans stared curiously at the newcomers, who stood out not only because they were strangers but also by virtue of their rich and splendid robes. Seeing such obvious wealth, a couple of tarts called sweet-voiced invitations. The nobles took no notice; they were undoubtedly used to better.

By the way they looked at Kastavala, that attitude applied to more than just the easy women of the town. Next to the capital, Kastavala was small and drab and dirty and smelly. Maniakes knew that perfectly well. But the same applied to any provincial center. He had seen a great many such towns, all through the Empire of Videssos; Kastavala was typical of the breed. After a while, he realized some of the grandees hadn't seen anything outside Videssos the city save perhaps their country estates and hunting lodges. For them, a provincial town had to be something of a shock.

"Coming out!" somebody called from a second-story balcony, and emptied a jar of slops, *splat!* in the middle of the street. Kourikos and the rest jumped back in alarm and disgust, tugging at the hems of their robes to makes sure the stinking stuff didn't splash them.

"That woman should be clapped in irons," the logothete of the treasury declared.

"Why?" Maniakes asked. "She warned us before she let fly."

Kourikos stared at him in horror that only grew when he

realized his prospective son-in-law was serious. Most of the houses and blocks of flats in Videssos the city had drains that connected them to underground sewers. That was an unimagined luxury in Kastavala.

Several of the grandees from the capital were puffing and red in the face by the time they reached the governor's residence. Maniakes didn't need to open the door and usher them inside: someone had seen them coming, and quite a crowd had gathered in front of the residence to greet them and learn what word they brought.

Voice doubtful, Kourikos asked, "Eminent Maniakes, is that your father there?"

Maniakes didn't blame him for being wrong; the resemblances was striking. "No, that's my uncle Symvatios, father to Rhegorios here. He and my father have always been like as two peas in the pod. And that's his daughter there beside him—my cousin Lysia."

Lysia was still too far away to have heard him speak her name, but chose that moment to wave to him. He waved back, smiling as he did so. He had hardly known her before Symvatios and his family sailed with the Maniakai to the island of Kalavria, but the two of them had grown close since: so close that Rotrude had teased him about it once or twice. He hadn't risen to the teasing as he usually did; it left him nervous.

As Maniakes and the nobles drew near, Lysia called, "What interesting people you've brought us, cousin! Phos' blessing on you for that." Symvatios nodded vigorously. So did more than a few of the grooms and cooks and serving women who had come out with their masters. The prospect of fresh faces and fresh news piqued everyone's curiosity.

Maniakes pointed to a servant. "Aplakes, go fetch my father at once. The eminent Kourikos here and these other excellent sirs and eminent sirs have come from Videssos the city to confer with him on an urgent matter."

Aplakes dashed back into the mansion. Everyone else started buzzing. The grandees looked like important people. Hearing just how important they were set tongues wagging. Lysia stared at Maniakes, her eyes shining in a face slightly rounder and less craggy than that of her brother Rhegorios. Better than the servants, she could guess one reason why the nobles might have come from the capital to Kastavala.

Aplakes hadn't bothered closing the entry door after him. He soon emerged, the elder Maniakes a pace behind. As soon as the elder Maniakes appeared, Kourikos and his companions, instead of bowing as the younger Maniakes had expected, dropped first to their knees and then to their bellies, touching their foreheads to the dirt in the full proskynesis normally reserved for honoring the Avtokrator of the Videssians alone.

The younger Maniakes simply gaped. His father's bushy white eyebrows climbed toward his hairline. He spat on the ground, as if in rejection of the dark god Skotos. "Get up, the lot of you," he growled, anger and fear in his voice. "If you think you'll trick me thus into treason against Genesios Avtokrator, you can bloody well think again."

As the grandees rose, they looked at one another with mixed horror and dismay. "Most noble Maniakes, you misunderstand," Kourikos said, a quaver in his voice. "We are the ones guilty of treason, at least in Genesios' eyes. We have fled here from Videssos the city to beg you to take the crown and save the Empire. Without you, it will surely fall, either from the ravages of the Makuraners or simply from the insane excesses of the tyrant whose bloodstained backside now defiles the imperial throne."

The two Maniakai exchanged glances. Not long before the ship that had brought Kourikos and his comrades to Kastavala came into sight, they had talked about rebellion against Genesios. The elder Maniakes had rejected it then. Now—now he looked thoughtfully at the group of nobles and asked, "What has Genesios done to turn you against him after you followed him like dogs these past half-dozen years?"

Several of the grandees hung their heads. Kourikos had more spirit—or perhaps more desperation—than most; he said, "If you speak of following like dogs, Lord Maniakes, I noticed you've not taken poor Hosios' head down off its pike in all these years. D'you bark with the rest of us, then?"

"Mm, put that way, maybe I do." The elder Maniakes stroked his beard. "Very well, eminent sir, say on: why would you sooner see my backside on the throne than Genesios'?"

"Why?" Kourikos clapped a dramatic—and possibly rehearsed—hand to his forehead. "Were Skotos to come up to Videssos from his hell of ice—" He spat as the elder Maniakes had. "—he could hardly serve it worse than Genesios the poxed, the madman, the butcher, the blundering, bungling idiot who is about to cast centuries of imperial splendor onto the dungheap forever."

The elder Maniakes bowed slightly. "You can curse with any man, eminent sir. But what has Genesios actually *done*?"

Kourikos took a deep breath, "Let us leave to one side the disasters against Makuran and the misfortunes against Kubrat. You surely know of those already. Not long ago, Genesios spoke to the city mob in the Amphitheater, currying favor with them because he knew everyone else hated him. But some of their leaders jeered him because of his many failings. He sent soldiers in among the seats, seized a dozen men, maybe more, ordered them stripped naked, and put them to the sword in front of the crowd.

"When the general Sphrantzes failed against the Makuraners—and how could he do otherwise, with neither men nor money enough to fight?—Genesios whipped him to death with leather lashes. Elpidios the prefect of the city exchanged letters with Tzikaste, Likinios' widow. Genesios cut off his hands and feet and then his head. Then he slew Tzikaste herself and both her daughters at the same spot where he'd murdered Likinios Avtokrator and his sons. At this rate, not a man nor woman will be left alive in Videssos the city by the time winter comes, save only the tyrant and his toadies. Save us, save Videssos, I beg you, most noble Maniakes!"

"Save us!" the rest of the nobles chorused.

"Eminent sirs, excellent sirs, if you expect me to jump into your ship and sail back to Videssos the city with you, I'm afraid I'm going to leave you disappointed," the elder Maniakes said. "But I'll not deny you've given me much to think on." He peered down toward the harbor. "Will your servants be fetching your baggage here to the residence?"

"Most eminent Maniakes, we found the opportunity to flee, and we took it," Kourikos answered. "We brought no servants; the more who knew of our plan, the likelier we were to be betrayed to the monster. As for baggage, what you see is what we have."

The elder Maniakes' eyebrows rose again. For Videssian nobles to travel without baggage was a truer measure of desperation than any woeful tale, no matter how heartrending. The revelation startled the younger Maniakes, too. He did notice the grandees had fat leather pouches at their belts, pouches that might well be filled with goldpieces. They might have come as fugitives, but they probably weren't beggars.

"Well, well," the elder Maniakes said. "In that case, come in and be welcome. I shan't turn you over to Genesios; that much I promise you. If he has a ship on your heels, you can flee into the countryside and escape. For now, though, more gladsome things: Aplakes and the other servants will show you to chambers. We have room and to spare, that we do, by Phos. And at supper in the courtyard this evening, we'll speak further on these matters. Meanwhile . . ." He used his eyes to gather up his son, Rhegorios, and Symvatios.

The servants led the nobles into the governor's residence. As the younger Maniakes went up to his father, Lysia set a hand on his arm. "Isn't it marvelous!" she exclaimed, her black eyes flashing with excitement. "At last, Phos willing, Genesios will get what he's long deserved. And then—"

"And then," Symvatios broke in, his voice almost eerily like that of the elder Maniakes, "we have to figure out what to do next, if we decide to do anything at all. Are you going to plot with us here?"

Lysia made a face at her father. "I would if you'd let me, but I don't suppose you will." Symvatios slowly shook his head. His daughter made another face. She stood on tiptoe to kiss the younger Maniakes on the end of his nose—he was used to that; because his beard was so thick and full, she did it a lot—then went into the residence herself.

The two older brothers and their sons put their heads together. Rhegorios said, "Uncle, they aim to set you on the throne." His eyes snapped with the same high spirits that had filled Lysia's.

"I know that," the elder Maniakes answered matter-of-factly. "What I don't know is whether I want to sit there. Way things look to me now, I have my doubts, and big ones."

His son, brother, and nephew all gaped in amazement. In the middle of their gaping, the door to the mansion opened. The cook came out. He sent the elder Maniakes a dirty look and headed down the slope toward the markets of Kastavala almost at a run. Symvatios laughed. "That's what you get for inviting a whole raft of people to supper on short notice," he said, resting a hand on his paunch for a moment; he was heavier than his brother.

"If a glare is all I get, I'll count myself lucky." The elder Maniakes chuckled. "I just hope it's not nightshade in the soup, or some such." He sobered. "Back to it. Look at me, all of you. I'm an old man. I've done nothing but fight since I was fifteen years old, except these past few years here in Kalavria. I hated Likinios when he sent me here, but do you know what? I've come to like this place and to enjoy the easy life. I don't want to fight any more, and I don't care to sit on a throne and know half the people watching me are trying to figure out how to throw me off it. What do you think of that?" He looked defiantly at his kinsmen.

"Let it all be as you say, Father," the younger Maniakes answered. "Can we sit out here on this island and watch the Empire get dragged down to the ice? If Genesios is as bad as this, even Videssos the city may fall to the Makuraners—or to the Kubratoi. One day a fleet may sail for Kalavria with the red lion of the King of Kings of Makuran painted on the sails."

The elder Maniakes chuckled again, but without humor. "And wouldn't that be strange, when the two of us led the Videssian army that helped put Sharbaraz back on his throne? But you're right. If he saw the chance, he wouldn't hesitate, not even for a heartbeat."

"Well, then," the younger Maniakes and Rhegorios said together.

"Well, then—what?" the elder Maniakes answered.

"You have to take the throne," his son explained, as if the necessity were as obvious as a geometric proof.

"Nonsense," the elder Maniakes said. "I don't have to do any such thing. What's more, the more I think about it, the less I want to do any such thing. I'm perfectly content to rusticate, and, as best as I can recall, I've never been perfectly content before. Governor of Kalavria suits me fine. If you think the Empire needs saving, son, *you* save it."

Symvatios and Rhegorios looked from the elder Maniakes to the younger. For a moment, he didn't understand why they were looking at him as they were. Then he did, and ice and fire might have coursed together through his veins. "Father," he said slowly, "if I go, will you help me?"

Now it was the elder Maniakes' turn to hesitate before he replied. "You mean this," he said. It was not quite a question. The younger Maniakes nodded. The elder sucked in a long breath, then folded his son into an embrace that still had a good deal of strength in it. "Of course. The whole clan will." His eyes swung to his brother and nephew.

"Aye," Symvatios said at once.

"Aye," Rhegorios agreed. "If Maniakes here hadn't spoken up, I would have myself." Now the younger Maniakes stared at his cousin. He was far from Avtokrator as yet, but did he already have a rival?

"We shall essay it, then," the elder Maniakes said. That should have been a ringing declaration. Instead, as had his earlier words, it came out almost as a query. A moment later, he showed the reason for his doubt: "If we fail, we die. The whole clan dies, all the kinsfolk we have whom Genesios can reach. We had best not fail. We don't need to move on Videssos the city tomorrow, and we'd be mad if we did. We think it through before we try it."

"Yes," the younger Maniakes said. Beside him, Rhegorios twisted like a restive horse. He didn't want to wait. He wanted to charge right at Genesios. The younger Maniakes remarked, "Sometimes the straightest way is not the shortest one."

"My boy!" his father said, now full of pride. "You've learned something after all." He hugged the younger Maniakes again.

Symvatios said, "Now that we know we are going to do this thing, let's go in and get ready for supper. I want to see Kourikos' face when he finds out he's going to be father-in-law to an Avtokrator right away."

The elder Maniakes chuckled, but the younger said, "Genesios will find that out, too. I hope it doesn't put Niphone in any danger; Kourikos said she was in a convent in Videssos the city."

"One more thing to worry about," the elder Maniakes said. "On campaign, you'll add something to your list a hundred times a day. But for now, Symvatios is right. We've done what we can for the time being. Let's get ready for supper."

One more thing to worry about, the younger Maniakes thought as he walked toward the tables and chairs that had been hastily set up among the flowers of the courtyard. Rotrude was on his arm, with Atalarikhos walking along holding his mother's hand. How Kourikos would react on seeing his soon-to-be-son-in-law with not only a leman but also a bastard boy was liable to be . . . interesting.

By rights, the logothete of the treasury had no cause for

complaint. He could hardly have expected Maniakes to have stayed celibate as a monk when he had been far away from his intended bride all these years. He might have expected Maniakes not to show his woman here so openly. Maniakes had thought about that. If he had left Rotrude behind, it would have said he was ashamed of her, which not only wasn't true but would have infuriated her had it so much as crossed her mind.

Most of the nobles fled from the capital were already in the courtyard, talking among themselves, drinking wine, and pretending to admire the plants. The younger Maniakes knew they were politely insincere there; the formal gardens of Videssos the city outshone this one as the sun did a dim star.

Talk of the garden ceased when they saw Rotrude. Few women of the Halogai came into the Empire. Her golden hair drew a Videssian man's eye like a lodestone. Once you stopped staring at that, you noticed the eyes, the strong chin, thrusting cheekbones, and short straight nose, the sheer size of her—she was almost as tall as the younger Maniakes, who was not short—and her shape, womanly despite her inches.

The grandees' stares gave him a certain amount of pride. They irked her. Turning to him, she said, "I am not one of the big beasts from the Hot Lands, the ones with snakes for snouts." Her Videssian was clear but slow, with the half-drawled accent of her homeland.

"They're admiring you," Maniakes said. "If you'd been born in the Empire, you'd be preening for them."

"If I had been born in the Empire, I would have the same seeming as they and you, so they would not need to gape." She reached down and ruffled Atalarikhos' hair. "So your son does."

"Mostly," Maniakes said. The hair through which Rotrude ran her fingers was as black as his own, but straight, not wavy like Maniakes'. But Atalarikhos had some of his mother's coloring: Maniakes was slightly swarthier than the average Videssian, his son slightly fairer. The shape of his face was more like Rotrude's, too, though even at less than three he gave signs of developing a nose of impressive proportions.

Kourikos strode toward Maniakes and his companions. Behind the logothete, the other nobles grew suddenly quiet, watching to see what he would do. Kourikos bowed to Maniakes. "Good to see you again, eminent sir," the grandee said, his voice politely neutral. "Will you be so kind as to perform the introductions here?"

"Of course," Maniakes said, matching his courtesy. "Eminent Kourikos, I present to you my lady Rotrude and her son—our son—Atalarikhos." There. The truth was out. Let Kourikos make of it what he would.

"Your—lady," Kourikos said carefully. "Not, I take it, your lady wife?"

"No, eminent sir," Maniakes answered. "How could that be, when I am affianced to your daughter?" Rotrude knew about his engagement to Niphone. She had a fierce, direct way of looking at the world; keeping things of importance *from* her was unwise. Up till now, the engagement had never bothered her; a woman far away in Videssos the city remained quite nicely hypothetical. But if Kourikos was real, that made his daughter realer, too.

As if Rotrude were not standing before him, the logothete of the treasury said, "Of course you will put your—lady—aside when your father is anointed and crowned Avtokrator of the Videssians."

Rotrude looked not at Kourikos but through him. He might have abruptly ceased to exist. Dodging part of the question, the younger Maniakes said, "It's not for me to discuss my father's plans. He is more than able to do that for himself—and here he comes now."

Kourikos and the rest of the nobles cried, "Thou conquerest, Maniakes Avtokrator!"—the traditional acclamation of a Videssian Emperor. They began to prostrate themselves, as they had in front of the governor's mansion.

"Stop that!" the elder Maniakes said testily. "I'm not Avtokrator and I don't intend to become Avtokrator, so stop treating me as if I were. If you think you can flatter me into donning the red boots, you can bloody well think again."

Kourikos' expression said the elder Maniakes might have just taken an image of Phos from the iconostasis of a temple and set a torch to it. The rest of the grandees looked similarly downcast. Triphylles said, "But your maj—uh, most eminent sir—"

"All I'm going to say now is that you won't get left in the lurch." The elder Maniakes waved to the servitors behind him. "First we sup. Then we talk."

Sulkily, the nobles from Videssos the city took the places

to which Aplakes led them. They kept on murmuring among themselves. The younger Maniakes watched their eyes flick this way and that. Sometimes those glances rested lightly on him, sometimes on his father, sometimes on Symvatios and Rhegorios. Whenever you caught a noble staring, his gaze would flit away like a frightened fly.

From down the table, Lysia caught the younger Maniakes' eye. Her eyes gleamed; her father or brother must have told her what they had decided. Maniakes smiled at her, glad to find someone who could look his way without seeming guilty about it.

The cook might have been dismayed at the prospect of having to serve a flock of unexpected guests of high rank, but he acquitted himself well. His first course was a salad, carrots and parsnips lightly cooked in olive oil and cumin, then served with salted olives and hard-cooked eggs on a bed of endive. Atalarikhos devoured his egg and the olives and started to cry when Rotrude tried to make him eat some carrots.

"Don't force him, not tonight," the younger Maniakes told her. "Let's keep him quiet if we can."

She sucked in her underlip, as she did when she disapproved. "He needs to eat to grow strong," she said. Then she sighed. "I yield. One night's food does not matter—much."

After the salad came an earthenware casserole full of leeks and fava beans stewed in broth and then wrapped in cabbage leaves. At the sight of that, Atalarikhos said something in the Haloga language he had learned from his mother. The younger Maniakes was glad none of the grandees from the imperial city understood enough of that speech to realize he had called the casserole a big chamber pot.

For the main course, the servants brought from the kitchen trays of steamed young mackerel stuffed with a mixture of mint leaves, pepper, chopped almonds, and honey. Atalarikhos enthusiastically ate up his stuffing but wanted no part of the fish in which it was contained. Now it was the younger Maniakes who avoided Rotrude's probing eye.

The sweet was apple slices, apricots, and grapes, candied together in honey. Atalarikhos swept his own bowl clean, then started stealing grapes from his mother. Rotrude sighed. "He is not starving," she said, as if reminding herself.

Servants swept away dishes, knives, and spoons while supper

guests licked their fingers clean. More servants lit torches all around the courtyard. The sky above darkened from bright blue toward black. The first stars began to glisten.

Grunting a little and patting his belly, the elder Maniakes got to his feet. The nobles stared expectantly at him. He swigged from his cup of wine, set the silver vessel down with a clang, and cleared his throat. "I'm not much for speechmaking," he said, which was a crashing lie; his son had never seen anyone better at rousing troops to go forward even when some of them were sure to die. But the lie served its purpose here: it let him say what he wanted without having to festoon it with curlicues of rhetoric. He went on, "You are gracious enough to say you wanted me to wear the crown. Very well, lords, I shall give you a Maniakes Avtokrator."

"Thou conquerest, Maniakes!" Kourikos shouted. In an instant, all his companions took up the cry. So did some of the servants, their voices rising in excitement. Maybe they dreamt of escaping Kastavala for the fabled splendor of Videssos the city.

The elder Maniakes held up a hand. He coughed once or twice, a habit of his when he thought he had outsmarted someone. "I told you this afternoon, lords, I wasn't sure I cared to be Avtokrator. I've spent the day thinking on it and, as I said before we sat down to sup, I have to tell you I've decided I don't. But I won't deny this carbuncle on the arse of Videssos named Genesios needs casting down. And so, my friends, I give you—Maniakes Avtokrator." He pointed to his son.

As the elder Maniakes sat down, the younger rose. He had known this moment was coming, but knowing that and living it were not one and the same. The grandees studied him now, their glances sharp as swords. They were older than he, and more experienced. Some of them would want to rule him, or rule through him—probably the ones who least looked like it, for they would be the most accomplished dissemblers.

He would sooner have gone into battle against the fearsome cavalry of Makuran, its men and horses glittering alike in armor of iron, than face these cagey, devious lords. But if he could not master them, how was he to hope to rule Videssos?

He said, "If Phos has not altogether despaired of the Empire, he will give Videssos a ruler who can end the civil strife that has so long consumed us, who can reclaim from the King of Kings the cities and provinces Makuran has stolen from us, and who can hold in check the ferocious horsemen of Kubrat. Doing any one of those things will be hard. Doing all three at once . . . I wish the lord with the great and good mind had not brought Videssos to such a pass. But since he has, I shall do all I can do to rescue the Empire from those who threaten it, whether on the borders or in Videssos the city itself."

It wasn't the sort of speech to send men rushing into battle, throats full of cheers, swords held high. The Empire's problems were too great for the younger Maniakes even to think about making a speech like that. If he could win the throne, he knew what he wanted to do. How he would do it, unfortunately, was another question altogether.

The grandees courteously heard him out. He was not surprised when Kourikos was again first to cry out "Thou conquerest, Maniakes Avtokrator!"—his prospective father-in-law naturally hoped to use his accession for himself. But all the nobles acclaimed him, their voices fulsome if not necessarily sincere.

The younger Maniakes raised his goblet high. "To Videssos!" he shouted, and drank.

"To Videssos!" shouted his family, the servants, and the grandees, all together. The younger Maniakes wondered for how many that toast actually meant, *To me!*

A single lamp burned on the night table next to Rotrude's bed. Atalarikhos slept in the next room, with an unbarred connecting door between them. Once or twice, that had proved embarrassing for the younger Maniakes. He hadn't been used to a little boy wandering in at an awkward moment, needing to piddle or to be comforted after a bad dream.

Rotrude took such interruption in stride. From what she had said, in Halogaland several families often lived together in one big room under the same roof. Privacy was a Videssian notion to which she had had to acclimate herself.

Now she sat at the edge of the bed, brushing out her long, golden hair. Maniakes watched the lamplight play off it. Shadows filled and magnified little lines at the corners of her mouth and by her eyes; she hadn't many fewer years than he.

She tossed the bone-handled brush onto the night table. The flame from the lamp jumped for a moment, then steadied. Her face still full of the intent concentration it had held while she was brushing, she turned to Maniakes and said, "If you win your fight for the city, you will marry the maiden Kourikos sired?"

He bit his lip. He hadn't thought she would put it so bluntly. But the men and women of Halogaland, from what he had seen of them in the capital and here in Kastavala, were a straighter-spoken folk than most Videssians. Rotrude simply sat, awaiting his reply. He sighed. "Yes, I suppose I shall," he said. "Before I came here, as I've told you, I was very much in love with her."

"And her father stands high among the Emperor's counselors," Rotrude said, "and would have reason for wrath were she cast aside."

"That also," Maniakes agreed soberly.

Rotrude bit down on the nub of it "And so what of me? And so what of our son, child of our flesh?"

Again, Maniakes had hoped that question would not come so soon, or would have been phrased to give him more room to talk around it. None of the answers he came up with struck him as good enough. He did the best he could: "Come what may, both of you will always be dear to me. If you want to stay on Kalavria, you will want for nothing—by Phos I swear it." He sketched the sun-circle over his heart.

Rotrude shrugged. She didn't mock Phos, but she didn't worship him, either; her reverence belonged to the gloomy, bloodthirsty gods of her homeland. "And if we fare forth to Halogaland once more, what then?" she asked.

"I wish you would promise not to do that," Maniakes said slowly. The thought of how much mischief a Haloga chieftain could work with an Avtokrator's bastard for a tool made his blood run cold. "So long as you stay, you can have anything here you wish."

"What I wish here mostly is you," she answered. He hung his head. Most Videssian women, just then, would either have dissolved in tears or started throwing things. Rotrude did neither; she measured him with her eyes as a warrior might have over the top of his shield. "What if I were to find another man who suited me?"

"If you wanted to wed him, and if I thought he would treat you and our son well, you would have my blessing," Maniakes said.

Rotrude studied him again. "I wonder if you tell me this because you care for me not at all or because you care for me very much," she said, perhaps half to herself, and then went on, "You have said what will be, and not wrapped lies in honey to make them sound sweet. For so much I give you credit. Not all men of my folk would have done as much, and few of you southrons, from what I have seen. So I shall choose to believe you. You are one who counts the needs of your folk before those of yourself, is it not so?"

"I hope I am, at any rate," Maniakes answered. It gave him an easier escape than he had looked for. If he wasn't that sort of man, he thought, now would be a good time to try to become such.

"You shall not sail on tomorrow's tide," Rotrude said. "To ready a rebellion to topple the tyrant, you will need to think before you do. What shall become of us before you wander west from Kastavala, from Kalavria?"

Maniakes said, "I leave that up to you. If you find you want nothing more to do with me now that you know I'm going to fight Genesios—" That seemed a better way to put it than *now that you know I'm going to leave you.* "—I can hardly blame you. I won't force myself where I'm not wanted." He would have felt more virtuous about that speech had he not known any number of women would throw themselves into an Avtokrator's bed, some simply because power drew them, others in the hope of the advantage they might wring from it.

Rotrude glanced down at her robe. "This sleeve has a seam that wants fixing," she remarked. Instead of reaching for needle and thread—sewing, like reading, was best done by daylight—she got to her feet and pulled the robe off over her head. She stood a moment in her linen drawers, then slid them down over her legs and kicked them aside. Almost defiantly naked, she stared a challenge at Maniakes.

Her body was thicker than those of most Videssian women, but shapely in its own way. Where the sun never saw it, her skin was so pale and fair, it seemed to glow in the lamplight. Even after she had nursed Atalarikhos for close to two years, her nipples were a delicate pink, hardly darker than the full, heavy breasts they topped. The triangle of golden hair at the joining of her legs matched the long locks that fell over her shoulders.

Maniakes' mouth went dry as he looked at her. If he tore a seam getting out of his own robe, he never noticed. Only when he yanked down his drawers did he realize he was still wearing sandals. He pulled out his feet without unfastening the catches, and threw the shoes against the wall. That was foolish; it might have wakened Atalarikhos. This time, luck went with him.

The coupling reminded him as much of battle as of lovemaking. When Rotrude bit the strip of flesh between his shoulder and neck, he wondered if she had drawn blood. His hands roamed rough over her body, squeezing, demanding. Their kisses smashed lips hard against teeth.

At last, both of them afire, she straddled him. When she impaled herself on him, she groaned as if pierced by a veritable lance rather than one that would presently lose its hardness. Something like triumph was on her face as she slowly began to move. "You will never forget me," she whispered, her breath warm and moist against Maniakes' cheek. "Never."

For a moment, even through growing ecstasy, he knew alarm, wondering if she was trying to bewitch him. They had wizards and witches in Halogaland, even if their magic was different from that of Videssos. Then she lowered her head to kiss him again. Her breasts brushed against the thick mat of hair on his chest. His arms tightened around her back, pulling her down to him. Women could work magic even when they used no spells.

Their lips were joined once more when she moaned and quivered above him, and a moment later when he, too, cried out. The bedchamber was not warm—even summer in Kastavala was mild, and summer nights often cool and foggy—but sweat soaked both of them.

He ran a hand along the slick curve of her back. "I will never forget you," he said, "but you're heavy on top of me." He laughed. "You've told me that, often enough."

"That's so," she admitted, and got up on her elbows and knees. Their skins made small, wet, squelching noises as they separated. Her hair spilled down onto his face. Through the strands, he saw her intently looking at him. "You are a warrior," she said at last. From a woman of the Halogai, he could expect no higher praise.

"On the battlefield, one side or the other must lose," he said. "This fight, we both won."

She stretched out beside him. "Also true," she said. "And here, we can quickly struggle again." She let a hand rest on his chest for a moment, then teased his nipple with thumb and forefinger, as he had with her a little before. Her hand wandered down, closed on him. "For as long as you are here by me, I shall be greedy of you, and take all you can give."

"Whether I can give again so soon—" Maniakes shrugged. When his beard was newly sprouted, he had been as randy as a he-goat. He remained proud of what he could do, but thirty wasn't seventeen, no matter how he wished it could be. His lance needed longer now to regain its temper.

But rise again he did. He and Rotrude joined with something close to the desperation they had shown in their first round. They were both worn and gasping when they finished. After such frenzy, Maniakes wondered what sort of appetite he would be able to conjure up for his promised bride if all went well and he cast Genesios down from the imperial throne.

He didn't wonder for long. Sleep swallowed him before he could raise his head to blow out the bedside lamp.

The two Maniakai, Symvatios, and Rhegorios strode along the beach north of the harbor of Kastavala. The younger Maniakes looked back toward the town and toward the governor's residence on the rise beyond it. He and his kinsmen had come too far for him to see the grandees up on the wall there, but he knew they were staring out toward him as he peered their way.

Symvatios half turned back toward the residence, too, but only for a moment. He made a slashing, contemptuous gesture with his left hand. "They have their gall," he said scornfully. "This is family business now, and they can bloody well keep their beaks out of it."

"Beaks indeed," the elder Maniakes said, chuckling. He set a hand on his own great nose. "They've lived in Videssos the city all their lives is their trouble; they think it gives them the right to give orders anywhere in the Empire. Not a proper soldier among 'em, either, which is too bad. Help worth having we could have used."

"They help us," Maniakes said. "If his own chiefest men can stomach Genesios no more, Videssos the city may drop into our hands like a ripe orange falling off a tree." He sighed. He missed oranges. They would not grow on Kalavria: summers did not get hot enough for them to flourish.

"If the orange doesn't fall from the tree, we'll cut it off." Rhegorios drew his sword and slashed at the air.

"If we think this fight will be easy, we are doomed before we begin," the elder Maniakes said. "How many rebels have thought the city would fall to them?" He opened and closed his hands several times to answer his own question. "And of that great flock, how many have seized the throne so?" He held up one hand, the fingers curled in a fist, none showing. "The usual way for an Avtokrator to lose the throne is by treachery within Videssos the city itself."

"Well, what of Likinios?" Rhegorios said. "Genesios took the city from without."

"Only because his own men wouldn't fight for him," the elder Maniakes answered. "If I'm keeping the accounts, that also goes down as treachery from within."

"By all the stories, Genesios' men hate him, too," the younger Maniakes said. Rhegorios nodded vigorously. He made more cut-and-thrust motions. His impulse was always to go straight at a foe.

"Not all of them," the elder Maniakes answered. "If enough of them hated him, his head would go up on the Milestone, not those of all the rivals he's slain." He set a hand on his son's shoulder. "I don't want to see your head there, lad. When we move against Genesios, that's not something we can take back if it's not going as we'd like. We have only the one chance."

The younger Maniakes nodded. He had been through enough battles, and had enough years on him, to know things could go wrong. You did what you could to keep that from happening, but not everything you did was going to work.

Symvatios said, "What the fleet on the Key does will be the key to whether we rise or fall."

No one misunderstood him. The island called the Key lay south and east of Videssos the city and was indeed often the key to the city's fate. Its fleet was next in power after that based at the capital itself. With it, the rebels would stand a fair chance of success. Without it . . .

"You have spoken truth," the elder Maniakes said to his brother. "And it is a truth that worries me. I have—we all have—connections wide and deep within Videssos' army. Some we've not used in a while, but they're there. I expect we can take advantage of them.

But few men of Vaspurakaner blood have taken to sea. The grand drungarios of the fleet and his captains have no reason to back us."

"Save that Genesios is a beast," Rhegorios said.

"Genesios has been a beast for some time," the elder Maniakes replied. "He has also been an enthroned beast for some time."

Thoughtfully, the younger Maniakes said, "Perhaps some of our, ah, guests back at the residence have relations serving in the fleet. We should look into that."

"A good notion," his father agreed. "We shall look into that. We'll also have to gather ships and fighting men from all around Kalavria to make the core of our force. We'll have enough ships to get the men and horses across to the mainland, I expect: we need a decent-sized fleet hereabouts to put down the pirates who drip into Videssian waters."

"We sail for Opsikion, I suppose," Symvatios said. "There's a fine highway from there to take the soldiers straight west to Videssos the city. If we leave them at Opsikion, they can attack by land while the fleet sails around the cape and then up to invest the sea walls."

"See what the clan can do when we put our heads together?" the elder Maniakes said. "Seems to me that's the only way to take Videssos the city, if it can be done at all: assail it from all sides at once, stretch the defenders too thin to guard everything, and pray all the powerful mages are either dead or fled from Genesios like the grandees. If we have to sit for weeks outside the city's walls, some deviltry will land on us, sure as Genesios is bound for Skotos' ice."

Rhegorios looked at the younger Maniakes. "You'll command the fleet, I suppose. That will be our striking arm and probably reach the city before the overland forces can. Give me leave to lead the infantry and cavalry, then. I'll get them across from Opsikion as fast as I can. Phos willing, I'll bring plenty of troops from the garrisons along the way, too."

Symvatios coughed. "I'd thought to play that role myself, son." Rhegorios looked stricken. Symvatios coughed again. "It may be that you're right, though." He patted his belly. "I may be too old and too round to push ahead as hard as would suit us best. Have it your way."

Rhegorios whooped and sprang in the air. The elder Maniakes

slipped an arm round his brother. "I'm not going, either, Symvatios," he said. "Better the young, strong ones come to power now than that we seize it and have them hating us and counting the hours till we die. Having your sons sitting around hoping your eyes will roll up in your head and you'll fall down dead off the throne—that's no way to rule. Worrying whether your sons might give you something to make your eyes roll up in your head—that's worse."

"We'd never do such a thing!" the younger Maniakes cried. Again Rhegorios nodded.

"You say so now," the elder Maniakes answered, "but you're liable to find never is a long time. Suppose *I* seized the throne now—just suppose. And suppose I live another fifteen years or more, till I'm past eighty. It could happen, you know—nothing's killed me yet." He chuckled wheezily. "You'd be pushing on toward fifty by then, son. Would you be getting impatient, waiting for your turn? Suppose I found some pretty little chit in the city, too, and got a son on her. His beard would be starting to sprout. Would you peer at him out of the corner of your eye and wonder if he'd get the prize you'd wanted so long? What do you think? Answer me true now."

Rhegorios and the younger Maniakes looked at each other. Neither of them felt like meeting the elder Maniakes' eye. The younger Maniakes did not care for what he feared he saw in his own heart. His father was right: he hadn't looked far enough ahead when he shouted out his protest.

The elder Maniakes laughed again, this time long and deep. "And that's why Symvatios and I, we'll stay back here on the island and give the two of you good advice while you're doing the hard, dirty work it'll take to throw down Genesios."

"How many men and ships can we realize from the island?' his son asked; like the elder Maniakes, the younger yielded points by changing the subject.

"In terms of numbers, I can't begin to guess until I go through the records and see just what's spread out in the harbor and garrisons," the elder Maniakes answered. "In terms of what we can do with what we have, my guess is that it amounts to this: we'll get enough here to begin the job but not enough to finish it. If all the top soldiers and sailors in the Empire decide they'd rather see Genesios on the throne than you, you're a dead man. We're all dead men."

"From the news that trickles out to Kalavria, Videssos is liable to be a dead empire if they decide that," the younger Maniakes said.

"Which doesn't mean it won't happen," his father told him. "If men weren't fools so often, the world would be a different place—maybe even a better one. But Skotos pulls on us no less than Phos. Sometimes I wonder if the Balancer heretics of Khatrish and Thatagush don't have a point—how can you be *sure* Phos will triumph in the end?" He held out his arms, the palms of his hands out before him, as if fending off his kinsmen. "I'm sorry I brought that up. Don't start arguing dogma with me now like so many theology-mad Videssians, or we'll never get back to the residence."

Rhegorios said, "I don't know whether our generals and ship captains are fools, but I can name two men who aren't: Sharbaraz King of Kings and his brother-in-law Abivard, his chief general."

"That's true," the two Maniakai said in the same breath. The elder went on, "And it was thanks to the infinite wisdom of Likinios that we helped put Sharbaraz back on the throne of Mashiz and gave Abivard the chance to show what he could do: do to us, I should say."

"No, the two of them aren't fools," the younger Maniakes agreed. "That means just one thing: if we're going to keep them from swallowing up all the westlands—maybe even keep them from swallowing up all the Empire of Videssos—we'd better not be fools, either."

✦ 11

Lysia strode rapidly through the courtyard, now going almost to one of the doors that led to the mansion, now coming straight back to the younger Maniakes. At last she stopped in front of him and burst out, "I wish I were going with you."

He took his first cousin's hands in his. "I wish you were, too," he said. "I'll miss you. Nothing like living in each other's belt pouches for the last half-dozen years to make us friends, is there?"

She shook her head. "I'm sick-jealous of my brother, do you know that?" All at once, she hugged Maniakes. "And I'm worried more than I can say for you. Do you know *that*?"

His arms went around her back. "It will work out all right, I think," he said. "We have a good chance of winning, else we'd not so much as try." As he spoke, he noticed, maybe for the first time with the top part of his mind, that not all his feelings for Lysia were chaste and cousinly. She was, without any possibility of doubt, a woman in his arms.

Lysia's eyes widened slightly. Had his arms around her tightened more than they usually did? He didn't think so. Was she feeling some of the same things he was? He didn't know, or know how to ask. If she was, was this the first time for her? He couldn't begin to guess.

In a small, shaken voice, she said, "Phos grant that it be as you wish. May your bride be safe in Videssos the city, and may the two of you pass many glad years together." She pulled away from him; with a forefinger, she drew the good god's sun-sign over her heart.

408

Maniakes imitated the gesture. "May it be so," he said. He made a wry face. "If I don't go down to the ships now, they're liable to sail without me." He laughed to show that was a joke. Down at the harbor, his father would have had liquid fire flung at any ships that proposed to sail without him, not that any would have.

Lysia nodded and turned away. If she was crying, Maniakes told himself, he didn't want to see. He turned, walked out of the courtyard, and headed for the doorway that led out of the governor's mansion.

He had already said his good-byes to Rotrude and Atalarikhos. He was not surprised, though, when he found her waiting by the door with their son. He was fond of the boy; he scooped him up, kissed him, mashed him in a hug, and set him down. Then he embraced Rotrude and kissed her for what would probably be the last time. Atalarikhos grabbed them both by the legs. If there was going to be any hugging going on, he wanted to be included in it.

"Be bold," Rotrude said. "Be bold and you will be safe. If you think too much of safety, it will escape you."

She spoke matter-of-factly; Maniakes wondered if he was entitled to draw omens from her words. Haloga magic was often so low-key that a Videssian, used to showier sorcery, would hardly notice it was there. Omen or not, he thought she had given him good advice, and said so.

"Though you leave me, though you go to another, still I wish you well, and I have no thought of revenge," she answered. From one of Haloga blood, that was as great a concession as a Videssian's yielding a doctrinal point

He nodded to show he understood. "I'll miss you," he said. He rumpled Atalarikhos' hair, dark like his own but straight like Rotrude's. "I'll miss both of you. Now I have to go."

Rotrude nodded. She kept her face very still; Haloga women reckoned public tears as great a disgrace as did the northern men. If she cried after he was gone, no one would know but her pillow.

Maniakes opened the door, closed it after him. One book of his life had just ended. As he took his first steps down toward the harbor, he began to unroll the papyrus of a brand-new book.

Ships filled the harbor. Almost every warship Kalavria boasted was tied up alongside one of the piers. Only a handful of vessels remained in the north to defend against piratical inroads from Khatrish or Thatagush or Agder or even distant Halogaland. With all the Empire of Videssos at stake, Kalavria would have to fend for itself at the moment.

With warships jamming the docks, the fishing boats that normally moored there had been forced aside. Most of them were out to sea now, trying to feed not only Kastavala's usual populace but also the influx of sailors and soldiers who had come into town with the ships. When evening came and the fishing boats returned to harbor, they had to beach themselves. If a big storm blew in, Kastavala would go hungry—and Genesios would no longer need to fear rebellion from out of the east.

Maniakes walked down from the governor's residence toward the harbor. Only a few weeks before, he and Rhegorios had made that same walk, to see what news the incoming merchantman might bring. Neither dreamed the news would pitch them headlong into a revolt that just moments before the elder Maniakes had dismissed as hopeless.

People stared at the younger Maniakes as he strode through the streets of Kastavala. He had had to endure a certain amount of that for years; the townsfolk were always curious about what the governor's son was doing. But he was no longer merely governor's son. "Thou conquerest, Maniakes Avtokrator!" someone called to him.

He waved acknowledgment. That call came again and again. It was premature, as he knew full well. Only after the ecumenical patriarch had anointed him and crowned him at the High Temple in Videssos the city would he formally become Avtokrator of the Videssians. But he did not fret his well-wishers with formalism. If he did not soon become Avtokrator, he would die. He had no middle ground left, not anymore.

The streets no longer swarmed with sailors, as they had since the Maniakai summoned to Kastavala such might as Kalavria possessed. Now the seamen were down by the ships. If the wind held, they would sail later today. Nothing would be easy. The younger Maniakes had assumed that. Easier to adjust for things going better than planned than for worse.

For the first time in more than five years, the spear that had held up Hosios' head as a warning to those who would oppose Genesios no longer stood at the harbor. Maniakes had ordered it brought aboard his flagship. Not everyone had loved Likinios and his clan, but they gained virtue by comparison with what had replaced them. Maniakes could and would claim to be avenging the house of Likinios.

He kicked at the dirt. From Makuran, Sharbaraz King of Kings trumpeted the same claim. Even Maniakes, who knew better, had wondered whether the Videssian in imperial raiment whom Sharbaraz kept in his retinue might somehow miraculously be Hosios son of Likinios. He might have accepted the pretender as genuine simply to rid Videssos of Genesios. Now, Phos be praised, he did not have to worry about that dreadful choice.

He had renamed the strongest warship in the fleet the *Renewal*, in hope of what he would bring to Videssos the city. In the fleet at the Key, though, the *Renewal* would have been no more than a middling vessel, and in the fleet at Videssos the city less than that. He and all his kinsmen knew their revolt would fail if the Empire's naval forces did not join them.

Maniakes refused to let himself think of failure. He strode toward the *Renewal*, acknowledging salutes as he came. The hierarch of Kastavala, gorgeous in a robe of cloth-of-gold with a blue circle indicating Phos' sun, stood on the dock by the long, lean craft, chanting prayers to the good god to bring it safely through the upcoming fight. Behind him, two lesser clerics in plainer robes swung censers, perfuming the air with sweet cinnamon and sharp, almost bitter myrrh.

"Good day, holy sir," Maniakes said, bowing to the hierarch.

"Good day, your Majesty." The spiritual leader of the town was a skinny, elderly man named Gregoras, whose shaved scalp made him look even more skeletal than he would have otherwise. His words were proper, but his tone left something to be desired. So did the suspicious stare he sent Maniakes.

Maniakes sighed. He had seen that stare from Gregoras before. The hierarch had doubts about his orthodoxy. His father still worshiped Phos after the manner of the Vaspurakaners, believing the good god had shaped Vaspur, the first man, ahead of all others, and that all Vaspurakaners were to be reckoned princes on account of their descent from him.

In Videssian eyes, that was heresy. The younger Maniakes had grown up taking it for granted, but he had also grown up among Videssians who were as passionately sure it was wrong as his father was convinced of its truth. Now he was certain of only one thing: if he wanted to wear the Avtokrator's red boots and rule Videssos, he would have to satisfy not just the ecumenical patriarch but also the people of his orthodoxy. He could not afford to have Genesios scream from the housetops that he was a heretic.

He stretched his hands up toward the sun and recited, "We bless thee, Phos, lord with the great and good mind, by thy grace our protector, watchful beforehand that the great test of life be decided in our favor."

Gregoras repeated the creed of Phos' cult. So did the lesser priests, and everyone who heard Maniakes' prayer. That did not stop the hierarch from giving him another suspicious glower. Vaspurakaners recited the creed in the same way as those who followed what the Videssians called orthodoxy.

But, grudgingly, Gregoras decided not to make an issue of it. He stretched up his hands once more, saying "May the lord with the great and good mind bless you and all the men who sail with you. May you travel in victory, and may you restore to Videssos the glory of which she has been too long deprived. So may it be."

"So may it be," Maniakes echoed. "Thank you, holy sir." Even a prelate as sternly orthodox as Gregoras was willing not to inquire too closely into the younger Maniakes' beliefs, for that simple reason that Genesios, while also orthodox, was vile enough to embarrass those who agreed with him no less than those who did not.

Maniakes walked over the gangplank from the pier to the deck of the *Renewal*. The men at the oars and the rest of the sailors raised a cheer for him. So did Kourikos and Triphylles. At his father's suggestion, Maniakes had split the grandees from the capital among several ships. He had told them he didn't want them all lost in one disaster, which had some truth in it. More important, though, he did not want them plotting among themselves.

A sailor with a long, straight bronze trumpet strode up to Maniakes and waited expectantly. He looked around the harbor. As far as he could see, all the ships were ready. He nodded to the trumpeter. The man took a deep breath and raised the horn to his lips. His cheeks puffed out like the throat sac of a chirping frog. The blast he blew meant only one thing: *we begin*.

Sailors undid lines from the docks, then jumped back into

their vessels. Oarmasters shouted out the stroke. Grunting, the big-shouldered, hard-handed men at the oars rose from their benches, stroked, sat again. The seats of their breeches were lined with leather to keep them from wearing through to the flesh in short order.

The *Renewal* pulled away from the dock. She pitched slightly in the light chop. Maniakes hadn't done much sailing since his journey to Kalavria. Having the deck shift under his feet made him nervous; it put him in mind of the queasy way the ground shook during an earthquake. But an earthquake soon stopped, while this went on and on. He did what he had done when Likinios sent his clan into their genteel exile: he pretended he was not standing, but on horseback. That helped keep his stomach happy.

They had hardly got out of bowshot of the pier when a sailor dashed to the rail and hung onto it for dear life, his head thrust far out over the side. His comrades jeered at him. Maniakes would have thought him too busy puking to notice, but when he came up he said, "There, that's done. Now, Phos willing, I'm good for the rest of the voyage."

To keep their stroke, the rowers began a raucous song. Maniakes grinned in recognition. Foot soldiers sang about the little bird with the yellow bill while they were marching, oarsmen while they were rowing. He wondered if accountants used the same ditty to help them keep their records straight down to the last copper.

The song seemed to have as many verses as it did singers. The rowers' version included a good many Maniakes hadn't heard before. Like those the foot soldiers sang, though, a lot of them had the little bird doing some very salty things indeed.

Glancing over at Kourikos, Maniakes decided accountants didn't sing about the little bird while they pushed pens over parchment. The logothete of the treasury plainly had never imagined, let alone been subjected to, singing like this. Beneath its swarthiness, his face was almost as green as that of the sailor who had vomited when the *Renewal* was leaving its berth at the pier.

He walked up to Kourikos and said, "The men are in high spirits today, don't you think, eminent sir?"

"Er—yes, your Majesty," the logothete answered, as bravely as he could. He was a spindly little man, so much so that the loud, lewd words of the song almost had him literally staggering. "Most, uh, exuberant."

His effort to show enthusiasm left Maniakes ashamed of teasing him. He turned to face the bow of the *Renewal*. The wind blew out of the west, running its fingers through his beard and flipping his hair back from his forehead. He said, "They won't stay exuberant if the wind's against us all the way to Opsikion. That's a long, hard pull across the open sea."

"It can be done, though?" Kourikos sounded anxious.

"Oh, yes," Maniakes said. "Even a—" He shut up. *Even a lubber like me knows that much,* he had started to say. Kourikos exhaled sharply. He might not know much about sailing, but he had had no trouble supplying the words Maniakes had omitted. Scowling at himself far more than at his prospective father-in-law, Maniakes looked back over his shoulder at Kalavria receding in the distance.

The harbor and town of Kastavala passed out of view before the governor's residence on the height in back of them. Idly, Maniakes wondered why that was so. The mages at the Sorcerers' Collegium in Videssos the city had all sorts of arcane knowledge. Maybe, if he took the city, he would ask them. *No, when I take the city,* he corrected himself. *When.*

Above Maniakes' head, the wool sail flapped and billowed in the fitful breeze. The wind had swung round from west to south, letting the fleet from Kalavria sail at a reach. By now, Maniakes took no notice of the sail's noise. All that mattered to him was the dark green line that divided sky from sea in the west: the highlands above Opsikion.

As Kalavria had vanished over the horizon, so the mainland appeared above it. The first Maniakes saw of Opsikion itself was the sun glittering off the gilded globes of its temples. That flash told any incoming seaman he was approaching a town of the Videssian Empire.

Next to Videssos the city, Opsikion was unimpressive. Next to Kastavala, it was a metropolis. Unlike Kastavala, a formidable stone wall ringed it round. The wild Khamorth horsemen had raided farther south than this, back in the days a century and a half before when they spilled off the Pardrayan plain and overran great stretches of the Videssian eastlands. Towns hereabouts needed walls.

These days, the Khamorth had formed themselves into three

groups that functioned more or less as nations: Khatrish, nearest Opsikion and aptest at aping Videssian ways; Thatagush, to the north of Khatrish, whose borders did not march with those of Videssos; and Kubrat, south of the Astris and touching the Videssian Sea. The Kubratoi, whatever deficiencies they had from the standpoint of civilization, were monstrously good at war—and alarmingly close to Videssos the city.

Maniakes watched the commotion in the harbor of Opsikion as lookouts spied the approaching fleet. All the ships from Kalavria flew the Videssian banner, a gold sunburst on blue, but he did not blame the soldiers and marines for showing alarm even so. For one thing, pirates could mimic the Videssian emblem and seek to use it to approach with impunity. For another, a fleet's being Videssian, these days, did not have to mean it was friendly. If Opsikion's own fleet held its loyalty to Genesios, then Maniakes' galleys and transports were anything but friendly.

The captain of the *Renewal* was a middle-aged man named Thrax. He was striking to look at: he had gone gray young, and the sun had bleached that gray to glistening silver while baking his skin brown as bread. Coming up to Maniakes, he asked, "Your Majesty, shall we lower the mast and ready for combat? Shall we signal the rest of the fleet to do likewise?" As commander of the flagship, he was in effect drungarios of the fleet.

Maniakes considered, then shook his head. He pointed in toward the harbor. "They don't look to be sallying everything they have against us." In fact, only a couple of small craft, neither one a match for the *Renewal*, were putting to sea. "Signal our vessels to have all in readiness to brail sails and lower masts, but not to do it until I give the order or until the *Renewal* is attacked. As for what we do here, we go forward and parley. Show the white-painted truce shield at the bow."

"Aye, your Majesty." Thrax looked incompletely happy, but turned and loudly relayed Maniakes' commands to the crew.

The *Renewal* glided forward over the gray-green water. The small ships from out of Opsikion approached startlingly fast. Thin across the sea came a questioning hail: "Who comes to Opsikion with such a fleet, and for what purpose?"

Maniakes hurried to the bow. Standing by the truce shield, he cupped both hands in front of his mouth and shouted: "I come, Maniakes son of Maniakes, Avtokrator of the Videssians, for the purpose of casting the murderous, infamous, bloodthirsty wild beast Genesios down from the throne he has drenched with the gore of slaughtered innocents." There. It was done. If the officers on Opsikion had been unaware rebellion was brewing on Kalavria, they were no more. Maniakes added, "With whom do I speak?"

For a couple of minutes, no one answered him from either of the ships. Then a man resplendent in a gleaming chainmail shirt came to the bow of one of them. Wearing armor at sea was a risky business; if you went over the side, you drowned. The fellow said, "I am Domentziolos, tourmarkhos here."

The garrison commander, Maniakes thought. He must have been down by the waterfront, to have boarded ship so quickly. "What say you, Domentziolos?" Maniakes demanded.

"Thou conquerest, Maniakes Avtokrator!" Domentziolos shouted in a great voice. The men aboard his vessel erupted in cheers. So did those aboard the other small ship. And so did those aboard the *Renewal.*

Maniakes felt giddy, almost drunk, with relief. His force was not large. A fight at Opsikion could have ruined him even if he won: it would have given Genesios' retainers the idea that Maniakes could be vulnerable. Ideas like that had a way of becoming self-fulfilling prophecies. If, on the other hand, everyone joined him against Genesios . . .

"Use our harbor, use our city, as your own," Domentziolos said. "We'd heard rumors this day might come, but knew not how much faith to put in them. Praise the lord with the great and good mind they prove true."

Maniakes hadn't wanted anyone hearing rumors. He supposed fishermen sailing out of Kastavala or one of the other Kalavrian towns from which he had pulled men and ships had met their counterparts from Opsikion on the sea. They wouldn't have kept quiet, not when they were carrying that kind of news. But if Opsikion had heard rumors, the odds were good that rumors had gone on to Videssos the city, and to the ear of Genesios.

"Will the hypasteos of the town grant us the same welcome you have, excellent Domentziolos?" Maniakes asked. Civil officials outranked soldiers in the administrative hierarchy, not least to make rebellions by provincial commanders harder. Likinios had sent the elder Maniakes, a general, to govern Kalavria, but Kalavria was both far from the heart of the Empire and subject to attack by pirates: divided authority there would have been dangerous. In any normal circumstances, an Avtokrator had little reason to fear revolt from Kalavria. If Likinios or Hosios still lived, the Maniakai would have lived out their days on the island.

"Old Samosates? He's over there in the other ship, yelling for you fit to burst." Domentziolos pointed. His vessel had drawn close enough to the *Renewal* for Maniakes to see his teeth skin back in a shark's grin. "Besides, if he weren't for you, your Majesty, we'd soon fix that, the lads and I."

In normal times, a local commander did not casually talk about disposing of the town administrator appointed by the Emperor. Civil war, though, changed all the rules. Maniakes wasn't shocked, as he would have been in peacetime. He was delighted.

"Splendid, excellent Domentziolos," he said. He had no idea whether Domentziolos deserved to be called excellent, and didn't care. If the officer wasn't a noble but performed well in the fighting ahead, he would earn the title with which Maniakes was honoring him now. Maniakes went on, "We'll land infantry and cavalry here, to move overland against Genesios while the fleet, along with your own flotilla, sails round the cape and up toward the Key."

He waited to see how Domentziolos would take that. If the captain was dissembling, he would not want Opsikion to yield tamely to Maniakes' men. He might suddenly decide to fight, or he might cast about for excuses to delay the entry of Maniakes' force into the town or to have the soldiers camp outside.

But he said, "By the good god, your Majesty, come at the usurper every way you can. I've sent up enough prayers that someone worthwhile would rise against him. If you want 'em, you'll have hundreds of men from the soldiery here who'd love to march with you."

"Not with me," Maniakes answered. "I lead the fleet; my cousin Rhegorios will command the soldiers."

That made Domentziolos grin all over again. "Who would have thought a man of Vaspurakaner blood anything but a land soldier? Yet you have the right of it, your Majesty; your fight will be won or lost on the sea."

"My thought exactly." Maniakes turned toward the other ship. "Eminent Samosates!"

A man who was as gray as Maniakes' father and bald to boot

came to the bow of the vessel. "Aye, your Majesty?" he called. "How may I serve you?" His voice was not only wary but mushy as well; he couldn't have had many teeth left.

"By yielding up your city and all its supplies to me," Maniakes answered. "Since you've named me your sovereign, you cannot object to that."

Samosates was perfectly capable of objecting, and Maniakes knew it full well. A recalcitrant hypasteos, or even a reluctant one, would make his stay here more difficult. The bureaucrats of Opsikion would take their cue from their leader and could make nuisances of themselves by nothing more than obstructing supplies. Separating malice from simple incompetence was never easy.

But Samosates seemed suddenly to catch fire. "The city and everything within it are yours," he cried. "Dig up Genesios' bones! To the ice with the usurper! May his head, filled only with thoughts of blood, go up on the Milestone." The hypasteos bowed to Maniakes. "I am your man."

He certainly was. After he had publicly reviled Genesios, the only thing he could expect from the Avtokrator now sitting in Videssos the city was the headsman's sword. He had made his choice, and he had made it plain. For a bureaucrat, that was a miracle of decisiveness.

Maniakes turned to Thrax. "Make signal to the fleet that we are to tie up in the harbor of Opsikion."

"Aye, your Majesty," Thrax said, and gave the order to his trumpeter. Notes rang across the water. The trumpeters in the nearest ships picked them up and relayed them to those positioned farther out on the wings. Thrax spoke two other words, and the trumpeter relayed them, too: "Maintain caution."

"Excellent." Maniakes thumped Thrax on the back. "If they have something nasty in mind—" He shook his head. "You don't get old in this business taking people for granted."

But the Opsikianoi all seemed as delighted as Domentziolos and Samosates to welcome Maniakes and his sailors and soldiers. Of course, taverners threw their doors wide and tarts promenaded in their skimpiest and filmiest outfits: they had profits to make. But carpenters and cobblers, farmers and fishermen, vied with one another to greet the newcomers, to buy them a glass of wine or bread smeared with sea-urchin paste and crushed garlic.

To Maniakes, that said one thing: everybody hated Genesios.

Had everyone admired the ruler in the capital, he would have had to fight his way into the town. Had feelings been mixed, he might have got into Opsikion without a fight, but houses and shops would have stayed shuttered against his men. As things were, he worried only that his men would be so taken by the place that they wouldn't care to leave.

Samosates put him, Rhegorios, and the grandees from Videssos the city up in his own residence in the center of town, not far from the chief temple to Phos. The red-tiled building housed not only him but several hundred years of the records of Opsikion; servants hastily carried wooden boxes stuffed with old scrolls out of bedchambers to make room for the noble guests. That affected Maniakes himself not at all; he got the chief guest suite, with Rhegorios installed alongside him.

Supper was tuna and squid and mussels, much as it might have been back in Kastavala. The wine was better here. When Samosates noticed Maniakes thought well of it, he made sure his servitors kept the would-be Emperor's cup full. As more servants cleared away the supper dishes, the hypasteos asked, "How long will you stay in Opsikion, your Majesty?"

Maniakes had drunk himself happy, but he hadn't drunk himself foolish. "A few days, to ready the land forces to move west and to join your local ships here to our fleet," he answered. "How many 'a few' may be, I don't quite know." And if he had known, he wouldn't have told Samosates. The fewer people who were privy to his plans, the fewer who could pass those plans to Genesios.

But Samosates said, "I quite understand, your Majesty. I was just thinking that, since rumor of your rebellion, to which Phos grant success, had reached us here, it might well have traveled on to Videssos the city. That being so, you would be well advised to look to your own safety while you are here."

"D'you think Genesios could have sent assassins out so soon?" Maniakes asked; he, too, had worried about rumors spread west from Opsikion.

"Your own valiant strength, your Majesty, should be protection and to spare against mere assassins," Samosates said. Maniakes knew that was polite nonsense; he wondered if the hypasteos did, too. Evidently so, for Samosates went on, "I was not thinking so much of knives in the night as of wizardry from afar. Have you brought with you accomplished mages to ward against such danger?"

"I've brought a couple of men from Kastavala, the best the island of Kalavria can boast," Maniakes answered. He knew he sounded uneasy; against the best of Videssos the city, those wizards might be a couple of coppers matched against gold-pieces. "I'd not expected to need much in the way of sorcerous protection until I reached the Key, if then." He turned to the grandees fled from the capital. "How say you, eminent sirs, excellent sirs? Has Genesios still strong sorcerers who will do his bidding?"

Triphylles said, "Your Majesty, I fear he does. Just this past spring, Philetos the mintmaster died of a wasting sickness that shrank him from fat man to skeleton in half a month's time. Bare days before he'd taken ill, he'd called Genesios a bloodthirsty fool outside the mint. Someone must have overheard and taken word back to the tyrant."

"He has mages, or at least one," Maniakes agreed. "Eminent Samosates, what sort of wizards does Opsikion possess?"

"Our best is a man who commonly calls himself Alvinos, for fear his true name would ring harshly in Videssian ears," the hypasteos replied. "He was, however, given at birth the appellation Bagdasares."

"A Vaspurakaner, by the good god!" Maniakes exclaimed happily. "Send for him this instant."

Samosates called to a retainer. The man hurried away. Maniakes sipped more wine and waited for the wizard to arrive. The nobles from Videssos the city kept up a desultory conversation with Samosates. They tried to act as if they thought him their equal, but could not quite manage to seem convincing. Better they hadn't bothered pretending, Maniakes thought.

After about half an hour, the servitor returned with Bagdasares, sometimes called Alvinos. Sure enough, he had the stocky build and heavy features common in those who sprang from Vaspurakan. He was younger than Maniakes had expected, probably younger than Maniakes himself.

"Your Majesty!" he cried, and went down in a full proskynesis. When he returned to his feet, he rattled off several sentences in the throaty Vaspurakaner language.

That left Maniakes embarrassed. "Slowly, please, I beg," he said, his own words halting. "I have little of this tongue, I fear. My father and mother spoke it when they did not want me to understand what they said. After my mother died, my father spoke it seldom. Videssian goes better in my mouth."

Bagdasares shrugged. He returned to the language of the Empire. "My children, they will be the same, your Majesty. We are a small drop of ink, and Videssos a big pail of water. But now, Phos who made the princes first willing, you want to give all the Empire the coloring of that ink?"

The grandees from the capital muttered back and forth behind their hands. Samosates drummed his fingers on the polished oak of the tabletop. Seldom was heresy spoken so openly in a hypasteos' hall. Heads swung toward Maniakes, to hear how he would respond. If he espoused heresy, too, he would cost himself support—not among the grandees, who were too committed to abandon him for Genesios, but from simpler, more pious folk to whom word of what he said would surely spread, perhaps with exaggerations for effect.

To Bagdasares, he replied, "I fear most of the coloring has already bleached out of me. What the Videssians call orthodoxy suits me well enough."

He wondered if the wizard would rail at him for abandoning the doctrines of his forefathers. But Bagdasares shrugged again. "I know many others from among our folk who share your views. Some of them are good men, some bad, as is true of any other group. I do not condemn them out of hand."

"Good," Maniakes said with genuine relief. Only later would he wonder why a wizard's view should matter to an Avtokrator. He wasn't used to being Avtokrator, not yet. "To business," he declared. "Can you protect me against whatever spells Genesios' mages may hurl from Videssos the city?"

"I think I can, your Majesty," Bagdasares answered. "They'll be stronger sorcerers than I, you understand, but I'll be far closer to you, which also matters in struggles thaumaturgic."

"In these matters, you are the expert," Maniakes said. "Soldiers, as you know, have little to do with magic."

"And for good reason, too," the wizard said. "The stress and passion of the battlefield make sorcery too unreliable to be worth using. Unfortunately, however, it remains a very useful tool for assassins." He preened, just a little; few young men are without vanity, and even fewer can resist the temptation to show off. "As a result of which consideration, you have engaged my services."

"Exactly so," Maniakes said. "I am now going to seek my bedchamber for the night. Will you come with me and do what you can to make it safe against whatever sorceries Genesios can send against me?"

"Your Majesty, I will, if you will excuse me for one small moment." Bagdasares ducked out into the hall. He returned with a stout wooden case with brass fittings. Dipping his head to Maniakes, he said, "Now I am ready to rally to your cause, your Majesty. As well expect a swordsmith to beat out blades with no hammer or anvil as a wizard to work magic without his tools."

"Again, I yield to your expertise." Maniakes nodded to Samosates. "If a servant will be so kind as to show me to my chamber?"

In Videssos the city, the room would have been reckoned spare; it had bed, table, stools, a chamber pot, and a chest of drawers, but no ornamentation save an icon of Phos. For Opsikion, it was surely good enough.

Bagdasares beamed when he saw the icon. "The good god's protection will make mine more effective," he said, "even if the image is undoubtedly the work of a Videssian heretic."

Half grinning, he glanced over at Maniakes for his reaction. Maniakes was convinced the wizard was trying to get a rise out of him, and held his peace. Bagdasares chuckled, then stalked about the bedchamber muttering to himself, sometimes in Videssian, more often in the Vaspurakaners' native tongue.

At last he seemed to remember his client, and that said client claimed the throne of the Empire of Videssos and deserved to know what was going on. He said, "Your Majesty, this will not be a difficult room to seal. You have but one door, one window, two mouseholes that I found, and one small hole in the roof, probably under a broken tile. Seal those sorcerously and nothing can get in to trouble you. Oh, perhaps the mages in Videssos the city may try to shake down this whole building on your head, but at this distance I do not think they would succeed, though I may be wrong."

Maniakes wished the wizard hadn't added that qualifying phrase. Bagdasares walked up and down the bedchamber, whistling tunelessly between his teeth as he contemplated what needed doing. He began at the window. From his box he took what seemed to Maniakes an ordinary ball of twine. He used a knife to cut off two lengths of it, one of which he stretched across the window frame from side to side, the other from top to bottom. When he pointed a finger at them and spoke imperiously in Vaspurakaner, the two pieces of twine stayed where they were without pins or tacks to hold them in place.

Bagdasares muttered a spell in Videssian. The vertical string burst into gold flame, the horizontal into blue, both so bright that for a moment Maniakes, dazzled, turned his head to one side. When he looked back to the window, the strings had vanished.

"Excellent!" Bagdasares said in self-satisfied tones. "That window is well and truly sealed against unwelcome intrusion from without, whether physical or sorcerous. The morning breeze will get in, but nothing more."

"That's what I want," Maniakes said.

Bagdasares proceeded to treat both mouseholes in the same fashion. He grinned at Maniakes, showing white, white teeth in the midst of his tangled black beard. "The chamber should be clear of vermin for some time to come, your Majesty—it would take sorcery to get them inside now. This is a strenuous way to keep a room free from mice and rats, but no less effective on account of that."

He wiped sweat from his forehead with the sleeve of his robe. Any sorcery was strenuous; had it been easier, the arts of the Empire of Videssos would have been altogether different, with magecraft supplanting mechanic skills in areas as diverse as farming and forgery. But sorcerous talent was rare, and its application limited by the mental and physical strength of the operator.

Bagdasares clambered up onto a stool and sealed the hole in the roof. "If it rains, your Majesty, I think this chamber will not leak there, but I should be reluctant to take oath on it," he said. "I will swear, however, that nothing worse than rain can enter by this path."

"Very good," Maniakes said. "I always enjoy watching a fine craftsman at work, whatever his craft may be. Competence is not so common that we can take it for granted."

"You have spoken truth, your Majesty, and I thank you for the compliment." Bagdasares descended from his perch and turned toward the door. He rubbed his chin. "Here the problem is not so simple as it is with windows and incidental openings. You must be free to go in and out of the chamber, and so must not only your proper comrades but also—I assume—the servants of this establishment." He waited for Maniakes to nod, then went on, "At the same time, we must prevent evil influences from gaining entry. A complex problem, would you not agree?"

He did not wait to learn whether Maniakes agreed or disagreed. He walked over to the doorway. This time, he set two lengths of twine across it and three that reached up from floor to lintel. His first incantation seemed to Maniakes identical to that which he had used before. The upper piece of horizontal twine flared blue, the central vertical piece gold.

"Thus, the sealing spell," Bagdasares said. "Now to modify it: a cantrip of my own invention, I am proud to say."

The cantrip was in the guttural Vaspurakaner language. Every so often, Maniakes would hear a word or phrase he knew, but, while he seized it, the rest of the spell would flow on past him. Then Bagdasares shouted an invocation his father often used: "In the name of Vaspur, firstborn among mankind!" He smiled to recognize that, but failed to follow what Bagdasares wanted the eponymous founder of the Vaspurakaner folk to do.

Till that invocation, the extra pieces of twine had remained in their former condition. After it, though, they, too, began to glow, not so brightly as the other two had, but with soft lights of their own. The additional horizontal piece shone a darker, more nearly purple blue than that of the Videssian colors. To either side of the vertical that had flared golden, the others gleamed, one red, the other orange.

"Ah." Bagdasares rubbed his hands. "All is as it should be, your Majesty. You and your comrades and the servitors of this house may enter and leave as you see fit, but no one else—and no evil influence shall enter with anyone, so far as my skill can prevent."

"I thank you very much," Maniakes said; though he could not know for certain, he had formed the opinion that Bagdasares' skill was considerable. "Have you also protection for me when I am not in my chamber?"

"Aye, I can give you some, your Majesty, though my guess is that Genesios' mage, if any there be, would strike in dead of night, when he was most nearly certain of your location. Still, in your boots I'd not trust a wizard's guess, that I wouldn't." Bagdasares chuckled. He rummaged in his box and pulled out an amulet—a rayed golden sun-disk on a cord of braided blue and gold string. He turned the disk over to show Maniakes a red-brown stone set into the back. "Hematite, your Majesty, or bloodstone, as it's sometimes called. Having an affinity to blood, it will draw the magic that would otherwise spill yours. If you feel the disk grow hot against your skin, you are under assault. It will not long withstand the stronger sorceries, so seek a mage's aid as fast as you can."

Maniakes bent his head and let Bagdasares slip the cord around his neck. "Pure gold," he said, judging by the weight of it. The wizard nodded. "I shall repay it weight for weight in coin, over and above your fee," Maniakes told him.

"Have no fear about that," Bagdasares said. "The fee includes the gold in the amulet." He clapped a hand to his mouth, looking comically aggrieved with himself. "I shouldn't have told you that, should I? I just cost myself some money."

"That's what you get for being an honest man." Maniakes laughed. "If you're a true son of Vaspur, a true prince, I suspect you'll show a profit anyhow."

"I suspect you're right, your Majesty," Bagdasares replied, unabashed. "Going up against these grasping, ready-for-aught Videssians, an honest Vaspurakaner needs all the cunning he can come up with." By every indication, the wizard had enough and to spare. He closed his wooden chest, bowed to Maniakes, and left the chamber.

A few minutes later, Samosates' voice floated down the hall. "Are you there, your Majesty?"

"Aye, I'm here," Maniakes called to the hypasteos. "What's toward?"

"I was just wondering if, while you were in Opsikion, you would—" Samosates got up to the door and started to come through it. The way seemed open—and Bagdasares had gone out—but the hypasteos might have run headlong into a fence. A flash of light came from the open air. "What's this?" he cried, and tried again, with no better luck.

Suspicion flared in Maniakes: Bagdasares had vowed his spell would keep evil influences from entering the chamber, and now Samosates could not come in. Then Maniakes remembered who was allowed into the room—in the mage's own words, himself, his comrades, and the servitors in the hypasteos' residence. Samosates did not fall into any of those groups.

Chuckling, Maniakes said, "Send one of your men after Bagdasares, eminent sir. He can't have gone far yet, and his magic turned out to be a bit too literal." He explained what he thought the mage had done. Samosates did not see the humor in it. Samosates, Maniakes guessed, did not see the humor in a lot of things.

When Bagdasares returned, he was laughing. He chanted in front of the door for a few heartbeats, then bent his stocky frame in a bow to the hypasteos. "Try now, eminent sir, I beg of you," he said. Cautiously, Samosates stepped forward and into Maniakes' room. Bagdasares waved and left again.

"What were you wondering before Bagdasares' protective magic so rudely interrupted you, eminent sir?" Maniakes asked in tones as sympathetic as he could manage.

"I haven't the foggiest notion." Samosates still sounded flustered. He snapped his fingers, either in annoyance or to jar the vagrant memory loose. "Ah! I have it: I was about to ask if you intended to review the garrison here in Opsikion before incorporating it into your own forces."

"I don't think that will be necessary, though I thank you for the notion," Maniakes answered, diligently keeping his face straight. People who weren't in the habit of using troops to fight put great stock in reviews and other ceremonial. Maniakes was of the opinion that putting men into action did a better job of testing them.

Samosates looked disappointed. Maybe he had wanted to see troops all gathered together and glittering in armor. If so, he had no business being in a post as important as that of Opsikion's hypasteos. Maniakes shrugged. He would worry about such administrative changes later, after—and if—he effected a considerably greater one himself.

Doleful still, Samosates left. When Rhegorios knocked on the door, he had no trouble passing through it; as Bagdasares had promised, he had given Maniakes' companions full access to his chamber. "How soon will you be able to go on the march, cousin?" Maniakes demanded. "And how many men from Opsikion's garrison will you take west with you?"

"Whew!" Rhegorios leaned forward, as if into a headwind. "You *are* in a hurry, aren't you?"

"I begrudge every minute here," Maniakes said. "The longer we stay in any one place, the longer Genesios has to plan deviltry against me, whether by magic or simply by assassin's knife. A moving target is harder to hit. How fast will be we be able to get moving again?"

"Our men and horses are all unloaded," Rhegorios said. "That's taken care of. I think we can add a couple of thousand warriors from the local forces without leaving Opsikion in any great danger from a raid out of Khatrish. All that is as it should be: couldn't be better, in fact."

"But?" Maniakes asked. "There must be a 'but,' or you would have answered all my question, not just part of it."

Rhegorios sighed. "Phos grant mercy to the first fellow who tries to sneak anything past you once you take the throne—you'll give the wretch a thin time of it. We have men and horses aplenty, but a shortage of supply wagons. We can't very well sail our merchantmen along the southern slopes of the Paristrian Mountains. The Opsikianoi have wains enough for their own purposes, but not to keep our whole host fed as we fare west toward Videssos the city."

"A pestilence," Maniakes muttered under his breath. No one who wasn't a soldier, save perhaps a farmer whose fields had just been ravaged, ever thought about all it took to keep an army— essentially a city on the move—supplied with food, equipment, and weapons. But if you didn't take care of those essentials, the army would be in no condition to fight once it got where it was going, or else wouldn't get there at all.

"I haven't surveyed the town as a whole, to see what we can requisition from merchants and such," Rhegorios said. "I wanted to get your approval before I started anything like that, for I know it'll breed ill will."

"Do it anyhow," Maniakes said. "We'll make their losses good as we may. If we lose the war, goodwill won't matter. If we win, those who grumble can be brought round."

"Aye. When you put it like that, it makes perfect sense." Rhegorios scratched his head. "I wonder if I'm ruthless enough to make a proper captain."

Maniakes slapped him on the shoulder. "You'll do fine," he said. "You have the straight-ahead drive the job needs. You know how to do things that need doing. Before long, you'll see what those things are, too." He was only a handful of years older than his cousin but had vastly more experience as a commander. He felt like some old soldier of his father's generation heartening a recruit whose beard hadn't fully sprouted.

"I'll attend to it, then," Rhegorios said, and hurried away. The odd illusion Maniakes had known went with him, rather to his own relief.

He walked down to the harbor to talk with Domentziolos. He found the leader of Opsikion's flotilla closeted with Thrax, his own naval leader. As he walked in on them, Domentziolos was saying "Word of your rising must have reached Videssos the city by now—Genesios may not be good for much, but by Phos he can spy with the best of them. So—" His finger stabbed out at a map. "—We should expect to have to fight the fleet from the Key not long after we round the cape and head north and west toward the capital."

"Aye, likely you're right," Thrax replied, and then looked up and saw Maniakes. He jumped to his feet, as did Domentziolos. "Good day, your Majesty."

"Good day," Maniakes answered. "So the two of you think it'll come to a sea fight early, do you?" The prospect worried him. If the fleets of the Key and Videssos the city stayed loyal to Genesios, he could gather together every other ship in the Empire and still lose the war.

"Wouldn't be surprised," Domentziolos said. Thrax nodded. Domentziolos went on, "Of course, just because the drungarios of a fleet is loyal doesn't mean his captains will be, and a captain who flouts his crew's wishes will feed fishes if he doesn't know when to ease off."

"You do so much to ease my mind," Maniakes said dryly, which wrung a chuckle from Thrax. "I was hoping to reach the Key without having to fight my way there. That way, the lord with the great and good mind willing, we can get some use out of the grandees: let them soften up the officers, so to speak."

"Aye, well, that would be fine," Domentziolos allowed. "No guarantee it'll happen, though, and fair odds it won't."

"All right," Maniakes said. "How do we ready ourselves to defeat the Key's ships in sea battle?"

Domentziolos and Thrax looked at each other. Perhaps because he had been with Maniakes since Kalavria, Thrax answered the question: "Your Majesty, if the fleet is there in full force and loyal to Genesios, we won't defeat it."

Maniakes winced, then gave Thrax a formal military salute, setting his right fist over his heart. "I am grateful for your frankness. I shall remember and reward you for it. Too many Avtokrators have gone down to ruin, I think, because no one had the courage to tell them a simple but painful truth. Likinios would still be Avtokrator today, and we would have no need of rebellion, had someone only warned him he was mad to order troops to winter north of the Astris."

Domentziolos glanced over at Thrax again and then, with dawning wonder, at Maniakes. "Your Majesty," he said, "may I also speak plainly?"

"You had better," Maniakes answered.

"All right, then," Domentziolos said. But, even after Maniakes' urging, he hesitated before going on. "Truth of it is, your Majesty, I was bound and determined to back any man with the stomach to rise against Genesios, for I think it's as plain as his ugly face on our goldpieces these days that he's dragging the Empire straight down to Skotos' ice. But hearing you talk now, I begin to hope you're not just someone who's better than Genesios—there are as many men answering to that as grains of sand by the sea—but someone who may turn out to be good in his own right, if you take my meaning."

"Phos grant it be so," Maniakes said, and sketched the good god's sun-sign over his heart.

"You had better be good in your own right," Thrax said, "for if you're not, Sharbaraz King of Kings won't leave much of Videssos for you to rule."

"I know," Maniakes answered. "I know that all too well. He was vigorous half a dozen years ago, when my father and I helped restore him to his throne. He's grown since then. I hope I have, too."

Now Domentziolos murmured, "Phos grant it be so."

"What's worst is that I can't yet worry about Sharbaraz," Maniakes said. "Till Genesios is out of the way, the King of Kings and I don't impinge on each other, not directly." He shook his head "Funny to think of Genesios as Sharbaraz's buffer against me, but that's what he is . . . among other things."

He unlaced the mouth of a leather pouch he wore on his belt and fumbled in it till he found a goldpiece of Genesios'. The current ruler in Videssos the city had a triangular face, wide at the forehead and narrow at the chin, with a long nose and a thin fringe of beard. So the coin proclaimed, at any rate; Maniakes had never met the man it pictured. But he was willing to believe it gave an accurate portrayal of Genesios; it certainly looked nothing like the images on the goldpieces minted during the reign of Likinios.

"He's not that ugly," Maniakes said, sliding the coin back into the pouch. "Not on the outside, anyhow. If only he had some wit inside that head of his." He sighed. "But he doesn't. He rules by spies and murder, nothing else, and it's not enough. People fear him, but they hate him, too, and won't always do his bidding even when a particular order isn't bad in and of itself."

"Someone should have cast him down long ago," Thrax growled.

"No doubt," Maniakes answered. "But the soldiers weren't the only ones who rejoiced to see Likinios' head go up on a pike. He'd taxed the peasants and merchants and artisans to pay for his wars, so Genesios got goodwill he wouldn't have had otherwise. And then, when people began to see what he was, he put down the first few revolts so savagely that everyone had second thoughts about rebelling."

"And they knew that if Videssian fought Videssian, the only one who gained would be Sharbaraz," Domentziolos suggested.

Maniakes pursed his lips. "I'd like to believe that, and I hope it does hold true every now and again. But you know I have Vaspurakaner blood and heritage, and I sometimes see Videssos from outside, as it were. I speak without intending offense, but, to my way of looking at things, a whole great host of Videssians care for themselves first, their faction next, and after that, if they have any caring left over, they think about the Empire."

"The lord with the great and good mind knows I'd like to say you're wrong, your Majesty, but I fear you're right," Thrax said. "The civil war of a century and a half ago proves that: twin boys born to the Empress, with neither one willing to admit he was the younger. And so, because neither would set aside the wearing of the red boots, they tore the Empire apart."

"They almost put it in its grave, too," Maniakes said savagely. "They were so busy fighting each other, they emptied the frontier fortresses, and the Khamorth swarmed into our lands. And even then, I've heard it said, both greedy fools hired the nomads as mercenaries to bolster their own forces."

Domentziolos gave him a sly look. "Are you saying, your Majesty, that Vaspurakaners don't have faction fights? If that be so, why is the princes' land divided between Videssos and Makuran?"

"It's not," Thrax said. "Thanks to Genesios' blundering, Sharbaraz holds the whole of it these days."

"We have faction fights aplenty, clan against clan," Maniakes said. "That's often how warriors from Vaspurakan come to Videssos: they lose to their rivals in the next valley and have to flee their homes. But war inside a single clan, no, we see that but seldom."

Thrax ran a hand through his silvery hair. "To bring things back to where they were: if, when we round the cape, we find the fleet of the Key awaiting us, and if it still cleaves to Genesios, what then? Do we fight till we're slaughtered, or do we try to flee back to Kalavria? I see no other choices for us."

Maniakes gnawed at his underlip but was again grateful to his admiral for framing things so starkly. "We fight," he said at last. "If we flee, they'd follow and lay Kalavria waste. And we'd get cleaner ends dying in battle than we would were Genesios to take us prisoner."

"Aye, well, you're not wrong about that," Domentziolos said. "I hear he's imported a torturer from Mashiz. There if nowhere else, Sharbaraz is willing to lend him aid."

"That news hadn't got to Kalavria," Maniakes said heavily. "I wish it hadn't got here, either."

Maniakes worked like a mule, readying both the combined fleets of Kalavria and Opsikion and the cavalry Rhegorios would command for their separate pushes on Videssos the city. That the fleet had no certainty of success—and, indeed, was sure to fail if opposed by the full might of Genesios' navy—only made him work harder, as if his efforts could of themselves magically transmute defeat into triumph.

In the few hours he grudged to his bed, he slept like a corpse. Several of Samosates' serving women were young and pretty; more than one intimated she might be persuaded to do more on that bed than change its linen. He ignored all such offers, partly out of respect for Kourikos' feelings but even more because he was simply too tired to take advantage of them.

After a while, the serving women stopped dropping hints. He caught them talking about him behind their hands: evidently their regard for his masculinity had taken a beating. That would have infuriated some men. He found it laughable; the women's mockery would not make his prowess suffer.

Not long before the fleet was to sail south toward the cape, he awoke in darkness. He stared around, certain someone had rapped at the door. "Who's there?" he called, reaching for his sword. Midnight visitors seldom brought good news.

No one answered. Maniakes frowned. Had one of his officers needed to report some catastrophe, the man would have kept knocking. A skulking assassin, on the other hand . . . He shook his head. An assassin would not have knocked. Whom did that leave? A serving woman, perhaps, bent on revenge for being spurned? It came as close to making sense as anything he could think of.

Then the rapping came again. Maniakes' head whipped around, for the sound was not at the door this time but at the window. The shutters were open to let in cool night air. If anyone or anything stood at that window, he should have been able to see it. He saw nothing and no one.

The hair prickled up at the back of his neck. He sketched Phos' sun-circle over his heart, then clutched at the amulet Bagdasares had given him. He could guess what that rapping was likely to be: magic from the capital, probing at the defenses the Vaspurakaner mage had set up around him. And if it found a weak spot—

He wanted to rise from his bed and flee the chamber. Reason, though, told him that was the worst thing he could do. Here he lay in the center of all of Bagdasares' wards. If he ran from the sorcery prying at those wards, he would but leave himself more vulnerable to it. But holding still while being hunted came no easier for him than it did for a hare crouching in a thicket as hounds howled outside.

Another round of rapping began, this time on the ceiling. Maniakes remembered the hole Bagdasares had found and hoped he hadn't missed any. When nothing dreadful happened, he decided Bagdasares hadn't.

Before he could begin to relax, though, a mouse burst out of its hole and ran squeaking across the floor, its little nails ticking over boards. Maniakes had forgotten about the mouseholes. Bagdasares, he remembered, had not. His respect for the wizard grew. So did his fear: some stronger magic had forced the mouse through the wards and into his room.

The rapping sound came from each mousehole in turn. Like the rest of the openings into Maniakes' chamber, the mouseholes proved well and truly sealed. Maniakes pulled up the blankets and got ready to go back to sleep, certain now that Genesios' mage had been thwarted.

Reflecting later on what was liable to happen to a mage of Genesios' who failed in his task, he realized he had been naive. A shape appeared in the window. How much of that shape sprung from his own imagination and how much from the sending out of Videssos the city, he never knew. Any which way, it was quite frightening enough.

He could see the night sky through it. Most of it, in fact, seemed thin as gossamer: all but the mouth and the eyes. They were plenty to make up for the rest.

Every so often, fishermen brought sharks into Kastavala along with mackerel and tunny and squid and anchovies. Their jaws fascinated Maniakes: two curved saws of perfectly meshing, sharp-edged teeth. Any shark that swam in the sea would have envied this creature floating weightlessly outside his window now. The thing's mouth was not very large, or rather, not open very far. For some reason, he got the idea it could stretch quite a ways—and be lined with teeth from end to end no matter how far it stretched.

He was glad to take his eyes off that mouth, but doing so almost cost him his life. When his eyes met those of the creature, they were held fast. Try as he would, he could not pull them away. In the westlands and in Makuran, they had lions and even tigers. He had hunted lions a time or two and noted their lordly golden stare. But a lion with such powers of fascination in its gaze would have drawn in so much prey as to make it too fat even to waddle about.

Caught by a will not his own, Maniakes rose from his bed and walked toward the window. He understood the creature floating out in the darkness had not the power to enter while Bagdasares' charm remained in place. But if he were to sweep that charm aside, nothing would keep the creature from coming in . . . and showing him just how wide its jaws could open.

Each step closer to the window came more slowly than the one before as he struggled against the will that fought to turn him to its purpose. But each step was made. When he reached the windowsill, he knew he would brush away the protection Bagdasares had set there: the lengths of twine, or their sorcerous residuum. He knew what would happen afterward, too, but could not bring himself to care.

A mouse, undoubtedly the one disturbed by the prior sorcery of Genesios' mage, ran over his bare foot. That broke the spell and startled him, just enough for him to tear his eyes away from the creature. He staggered back from the window, throwing up an arm to shield himself against the deadly gaze outside.

He heard, or thought he heard, a bestial shriek of rage. It should have brought men running, swords and bows in their hands. But Samosates' residence remained quiet and still. Maybe he hadn't truly heard the rapping that tested his sorcerous defenses, either. Maybe all that, like the creature, existed only in his mind.

If so, he was convinced his mind had just done its level best to kill him. Ever so cautiously, he glanced toward the window. The creature was still out there. Its eyes probed at him again. Now, though, he had its measure. He felt the urge to let it into the chamber, but the compulsion that had tried to force him to action was gone.

If naming the mouse a noble would have helped the little creature in any way, he would have done it on the spot. Had Genesios' wizard not probed at his sorcerous protections before attacking, the attack surely would have succeeded. Maniakes savored the irony of that.

But he was not safe yet. When the creature hanging outside the window realized it could no longer force him to go tamely to destruction, it cried out again, even louder and more savagely than before. It drew back. For a moment, he thought that meant it was returning to the mage who had sent it forth. Then it darted toward the window, swift as a falcon, intent on battering its way through Bagdasares' wards if it could go no other way.

When it reached the pane of the window, where the Vaspurakaner wizard had crossed his pieces of twine, blue and gold lightning flared. Maniakes' eyes were briefly blinded; a clap of thunder smote his ears. He thought the light and noise, if not the anguished wail that came from the creature, plenty to rouse not just the folk of Samosates' residence but half the people of Opsikion with them.

But the night remained still and serene. Maniakes' vision cleared without the blinks he would have needed to recover from a veritable lightning bolt. As cautious as he had been before, he looked toward the window, ready to avert his gaze if the creature tried to lure him forward once more.

He saw no sign of it. Now of his own volition he advanced to the window. He peered out over Opsikion. In the sky to the west he thought he sensed a fading trail of light that might have led back toward Videssos the city, although it faded before he was sure he'd seen it. A dog or two began to bark, off in the distance. They might have sensed the magic that had sizzled around Samosates' residence. On the other hand, they might have smelled or seen a cat. Maniakes had no way to know.

All at once, he stopped worrying about the dogs. A new and urgent question filled his mind: was that the end of Genesios' sorcerous attacks, or only the beginning? His breath came quick and short as fear filled him. From many miles, that first assault had nearly breached Bagdasares' defenses. What could another, more heartily prepared stroke do?

He clutched the amulet Alvinos Bagdasares had given him. It did not seem unduly warm, which meant the wards had not been penetrated. If the wards did fail, it was his last line of defense. He did not like operating from his last line of defense in war, and cared for the idea no more in magecraft.

Nothing happened. A gentle night breeze blew into the room, carrying the sweet, heavy scent of jasmine along with the seaside city stinks of ordure and old fish. The ground did not open and swallow Samosates' residence. The sky did not crack and release a horde of winged demons, each one fiercer and uglier than the thing that had almost seized him.

"Thanks to a mouse—that's the only reason I'm here," he said wonderingly. "A mouse." He wondered how many great events turned on similar small, unrecorded circumstances. More than anyone guessed, he suspected.

He gradually began to believe that there would be only one attack in the night. Of course, that might have been a ploy to lull him into a false sense of ease before the next sorcerous storm struck, but somehow he did not think so—and, in any case, he was too sleepy to stay on his feet much longer. He got back into bed.

"If something comes in and eats me, I hope it doesn't wake me first this time," he muttered, pulling the covers up over his head.

Next thing he knew, the cool light of dawn came sliding through the window. He yawned, stretched, and got to his feet. At first he saw nothing at all out of the ordinary. Then he noticed four small charred patches on the window frame, at just about the spots where Bagdasares had sorcerously attached his vertical and horizontal lengths of twine. He hadn't seen those places there before. If the wards had indeed flared to protect him against magical attack, something of the sort might have resulted.

"Lucky the building didn't catch fire," he said, and decided he hadn't imagined the ghostly, fanged visitor after all.

He splashed water from the pitcher over his hands and face and, spluttering a little, went downstairs to his breakfast. After he had eaten his fill, he cut a large chunk off the round of cheese Samosates had set out and headed upstairs with it.

"You've made friends with your mice?" the hypasteos asked, chuckling at his own wit.

"With one of them, anyhow," Maniakes said from the foot of the steps. Samosates stared after him as he climbed them.

✦ III

The hills above Opsikion dropped away to the north. Rhegorios had led horsemen and rattling, squeaking supply wagons west toward Videssos the city two days earlier. With luck, his forces would reach the capital at about the same time as the fleet. Without luck, Maniakes would never see his cousin again.

Summer laid a heavier hand on the mainland than it ever did on Kalavria. The offshore wind blew the pungent fragrance of citrus orchards out to the ships that sailed south along the coast. No great mariner himself, Maniakes was just as glad when his captains stayed well within sight of land and beached their ships each night. He hadn't cared for the passage across the open sea that had brought him from Kastavala to Opsikion.

Every so often, the fleet would pass fishing boats bobbing in the light chop, each with a fisherman and perhaps a couple of sons or nephews working the nets. Sometimes the *Renewal* approached so close that Maniakes could see tanned, staring faces turned his way. He wondered what went through the fishermen's minds. *Probably the same thing that goes through an anchovy's mind when a shark swims by after bigger prey,* he thought.

The weather grew ever warmer as they sailed farther south. Maniakes came to understand why so many sailors often went about in nothing more than a loincloth. Had he not been mindful of his dignity, he might have done the same. As it was, he sweated in his robes, feeling rather like a loaf of bread trapped inside its oven.

Then one day the lookout in the crow's nest shouted and

pointed southwest. Maniakes' heart sprang into his mouth. Had the fellow spied Genesios' fleet? If he had, the chroniclers would write briefly of yet another failed rebellion during the reign of Genesios.

But the lookout's shout had words in it: "The cape! There's the cape ahead!"

Sure enough, before long Maniakes, too, could see how the land dwindled away to a single point washed by endless creamy waves. To the south, the sea stretched on forever, or at least to the distant, seldom-visited Hot Lands, home of elephants and other strange, half-legendary beasts.

As the fleet sailed past the point of the cape, Thrax and the other captains bawled orders. Sailors capered this way and that. Water muttered against steering oars that guided ships on a new course. Ropes creaked as the men swung the sails to catch the wind at a different angle. The masts themselves made small groaning noises; bent so long one way, they now were pushed another. The fleet swung northwest, sailing directly toward the imperial city.

"The Key," Maniakes muttered.

He didn't know he had spoken aloud till Kourikos, who stood close by, nodded. The logothete of the treasury said, "Indeed, your Majesty, that island and the fleets based thereon shall be the key to whether we stand or fall."

"I prefer to think of it as the key to Videssos the city and to hope it will turn smoothly in my hand," Maniakes said.

"Phos grant it be so, your Majesty," Kourikos answered. He hesitated slightly each time he spoke Maniakes' title. He had had no trouble bringing it out when he addressed the elder Maniakes, but to acknowledge someone years younger than he as a superior had to rankle. In Kourikos' sandals, Maniakes would have been thinking about having experience earn its proper reward. He wouldn't have been a bit surprised to learn that the same thoughts ran through Kourikos' head. *One more thing to worry about.* That had occurred to him a great many times lately.

Thrax visibly relaxed when the fleet rounded the cape without being assailed. "Now we have a chance," he declared. "If they meet us anywhere else on our way to Videssos the city, there'll be doubt in some of their hearts, and we'll be able to put it to good use. But they could have smashed us like a man setting his boot on a cockroach, and they didn't do it. I begin to think I'm not throwing my life away to no purpose."

"If you thought that, why did you sail with me?" Maniakes asked.

"Because there was always the chance I'd be wrong," his captain answered. "And because, if I do live, I'll do well for myself and I'll do well by Videssos, and both those things matter to me."

Maniakes wondered which mattered more. Thrax had put his own ambition ahead of his concern for the Empire. Maniakes judged that probably honest. He shrugged. As well ask men to give up food and wine as ask them to set anything ahead of their interests.

Every time the fleet put into shore, he had Alvinos Bagdasares renew the protective spells around him. Since that first attack in Opsikion, Genesios had not assailed him with magic. He wondered if that meant Genesios thought him dead, or if the mages at the capital concluded his shielding was too strong for them to penetrate. Neither supposition left him permanently secure. If Genesios thought him dead, sooner or later he would learn he was wrong. And Maniakes was closer to Videssos the city now than he had been in Opsikion. Wards that had sufficed then might fail now.

Every morning he woke relieved to have got through another night unmolested. Maybe, he thought, every wizard Genesios controlled had fled away from the detested sovereign, leaving the man who called himself Avtokrator no way to strike across the long leagues of ocean. Maybe that was so—but Maniakes did not count on it.

When he said as much to Bagdasares, the sorcerer nodded. "You are wise, your Majesty. Never rely on what a wizard may or may not do. We are tricksy, the lot of us." He tugged at his beard. "I wonder if I was wise to include myself in that. Ah, well, had I not, doubtless you would have attended to the matter for me."

"Doubtless," Maniakes said dryly. He had the fleet of the Key to worry about, too. It should have occupied all his thoughts. Instead, he had to spend time wondering whether he would wake up himself or as an earwig. He liked being himself. Gaining a couple of extra legs and a pincer on his backside did not strike him as a worthwhile exchange.

The fleet kept sailing north and west. The only sails the lookouts saw belonged to fishing boats like those that had bobbed in the chop outside Kastavala and Opsikion. Maniakes began to wonder where the fleet from the Key was. He certainly had not wanted to make its acquaintance as his own vessels were rounding the cape. Not seeing it then had been nothing but a relief. Not seeing it now made him fret. What in Skotos' cursed name were the captains based at the Key plotting?

Whatever it was, they didn't have long to put their plot into effect. In another couple of days, his fleet would sail between the Key and the mainland and make for Videssos the city. Was Genesios' plan to have the ships on the Key fall in behind his vessels and cut off their escape? That had risks, even if they did their job perfectly—if his fleet and land forces took the capital, they wouldn't need to escape.

The next morning, a fine bright day with the sun quickly burning off the light sea mist, the watchman in the crow's nest of the *Renewal* cried out, "Sail ho to northward!" A moment later, he corrected himself: "*Sails* ho to northward!" After another few minutes, he declared, "Those aren't fishing boats—sails are the wrong shape, and too big to boot. They're coming on fast."

Thrax cupped his hands into a trumpet: "Ready all for battle!" Horns blared the word to ships behind the leaders. Through their brazen cries, Maniakes heard other captains relay orders and other lookouts report sighting the oncoming vessels.

Then he saw them for himself. No, they were not fishing boats. They were warships like his own, spread across a good stretch of sea ahead. He looked from them to Thrax to his own fleet, trying to gauge numbers. He couldn't, not with any confidence. He keenly felt how much he was a landlubber afloat. At last, he turned and asked Thrax how the opposing forces matched up.

The captain ran a hand through his silvery hair. "Unless there's a whole lot of sail still under the horizon, that's not the whole of the fleet from the Key, nor even any great part of it. We can take 'em, your Majesty, likely without hurting ourselves too bad in the doing." He yelled orders to his trumpeter. "Pass word to widen the line! We'll sweep out beyond 'em to right and left."

Maniakes watched the ships obey the order. He could see they were not as smooth as they might have been. That did not much matter now. In some close-fought engagement, though, it might make the difference between victory and defeat.

"Their lead ship is showing shield of truce!" the lookout bawled.

Thrax peered ahead. So did Maniakes. They both wanted to make sure the lookout was right before doing anything else. When they had satisfied themselves of that, Thrax turned to Maniakes, a question in his eyes. Maniakes said, "We'll show shield of truce ourselves but have our ships go on with their maneuver."

"Aye, your Majesty." Thrax's voice throbbed with approval and relief. At his command, a sailor ran forward with a white-painted shield hung on a spearshaft.

Maniakes looked east and west. On both wings now, his fleet overlapped that from the Key. "We won't start a fight," he said, "but if they start one, we'll finish it, by Phos."

"Well said, your Majesty." Again, Thrax appeared imperfectly trusting of any captains who chose to serve under Genesios.

The fleets continued to approach each other. That from the Key did nothing to keep itself from being flanked, which worried Maniakes. In land combat, passions among soldiers ran so high as to make battle magic chancy at best and more often than not futile. He wasn't sure the same obtained in naval warfare: It seemed a more precise, more artisanly way of fighting than the melees into which land battles generally developed. Ships reminded him more of pieces in the Videssian board game.

He smiled when that thought crossed his mind. With luck, he would capture these ships and put them back on the board as part of his own force.

But would he have luck? No way to tell, not yet. As the fleets drew within hailing distance of each other, a leather-lunged sailor aboard the nearest ship from the Key bellowed across the green-blue water: "Why do you continue to move against us while still showing sign of truce?"

"Because we don't trust you," Maniakes answered bluntly, and his own herald shouted back at the oncoming dromon. He went on, "Genesios the usurper has tried to slay me once, so I have no good reason to trust him or his. But so long as you do not strike at us, we shall not strike at you."

The next question amused him. "Which Maniakes are you?"

"The younger, as I hope you'd see," he answered. Genesios hadn't even known at whom he was striking, then: *opponent* was label enough. Maniakes asked a question of his own. "Who seeks to know?"

After a moment, the reply came back. "You speak with Tiverhios, ypodrungarios of the fleet of the Key. Permission to come alongside to parley?"

"Wait," Maniakes told him. He turned to Kourikos and Triphylles. "Does either of you know this man?"

Triphylles was practically hopping up and down on the deck in excitement. "His brother is married to a cousin of mine, your Majesty. I was a groomsman at the wedding."

Kourikos also had a connection with Tiverhios, in a way perhaps even more intimate than that of Triphylles: "Your Majesty, he owes me seven hundred goldpieces, as well as a year's interest on them."

"Mm." Maniakes was not sure what to make of that. "Would he be more interested—forgive me, I did that by accident—in repaying you, in having you forgive his debt, or in slaughtering you so the matter becomes moot?"

"Oh, the indebtedness would not become moot were I to die suddenly," Kourikos assured him. "It is quite well documented, let me tell you, and would pass down to my heirs and assigns, Niphone receiving her fair portion from any eventual collection."

"You really mean that," Maniakes said in tones of wonder. Even after the six bloody, anarchic years of Genesios' reign, Kourikos remained confident the law would in the end exact payment from a recalcitrant debtor. Indeed, *remained confident* was an understatement; to the logothete of the treasury, no other result seemed conceivable. Maniakes wondered if he should enlighten his prospective father-in-law about the persuasive power of sharpened iron. A moment later, he wondered if Kourikos wasn't trying to enlighten him. He tried a different course. "For the sake of bringing him to our side, would you be willing to forgive his debt?"

"I suppose so," Kourikos said, sounding vaguely surprised. "It is one way of conveying advantage, after all."

"Well enough, then." To his own herald, Maniakes said, "Tell him he may come alongside." His calculation was not based solely upon the likelihood of Tiverhios' switching sides: he had taken the measure of the dromon in which the ypodrungarios of the fleet from the Key sailed and concluded the *Renewal* should have no trouble sinking it or winning any sort of boarding battle. That was reckoning as cold-blooded as any Kourikos made over whether to grant a loan, but made with lives rather than goldpieces.

Tiverhios' ship drew near. It had eyes painted on either side of the bow, to help it see over the waves. Some fishing boats followed that custom, as did some of the dromons in Maniakes' fleet. He wondered if it was magic or merely superstition—then he wondered if those two differed in any meaningful way. If he ever found some leisure, which looked unlikely, he would have to put both questions to Bagdasares.

Like every longtime seaman whose acquaintance Maniakes had made, Tiverhios was baked brown as an overdone loaf by the sun. His fancy robe and his arrogant stance made him easy to spy. As if they were not enough, he also shaved his cheeks and chin bare but wore a bushy mustache to prove his masculinity, an eccentric style by Videssian standards.

"Greetings, Maniakes, in the name of the lord with the great and good mind," he said, his voice all at once oddly formal.

Maniakes started to ask him about greetings in Genesios' name, but hesitated with the sardonic question still unspoken. A great many Videssian officers, probably most, were pious and prayerful men, but few put their piety into that kind of salutation. Tiverhios must have meant something special by it, even if Maniakes could not tell precisely what

His voice cautious, he replied, "Excellent sir, I return your greeting, also in the name of the lord with the great and good mind. May Phos' sun long shine upon you."

Tiverhios' nearly naked face split into a wide grin. "The good god bless you, sir, you're not the misbeliever they said you were."

Sir was not *your Majesty*; it wasn't even as much courtesy as Maniakes had tendered the ypodrungarios. But, coupled with the grin, it struck Maniakes as a good sign. He asked, "Who are 'they,' and what lies have they been spreading about me?"

"Genesios' men, sir," Tiverhios answered. "They came to the Key, excellent sir, and said you were a rebel, eminent sir, which I see is true, begging your pardon, your Highness, but they also said of you that you were a heretic and a misbeliever and a disbeliever, which I see isn't true at all, your Majesty."

Maniakes stared at him. He felt like some pious layman chosen by an Emperor as ecumenical patriarch and rushed through the grades of the ecclesiastical hierarchy so he would be juridically

fit to hold the office to which he had been named. In such pro-
motions, though, a man spent a day at each rung of the ladder.
Tiverhios had rushed him to his highest possible title in the space
of a sentence. It was dizzying.

"Unless I'm altogether mistaken, they will also have said of me
that I'm a cursed rug-peddler of a Vaspurakaner, doomed to Skotos' ice on account of my blood if for no other reason," Maniakes
said. "They will have said something about Vaspurakaners always
being heretics, too, won't they?"

Tiverhios' head bobbed up and down. It hardly seemed a
voluntary motion on his part: more as if the waves that slapped
against his ship were making him nod. "They did say something
like that, I think, but I didn't pay it any mind. Not me."

That would do for a round, thumping lie until a bigger one
came along. Had it been truth, Tiverhios wouldn't have readied
his loaded greeting and sprung it like a trap. But Maniakes was
willing to overlook it to win the ypodrungarios firmly to his
side. Sketching the sun-circle over his heart, he said, "True, my
ancestors came out of Vaspurakan, but I am of orthodox faith."
He hadn't been, not altogether, but the Videssians would pull
him down from the throne and burn him alive if he were mad
enough to try to impose his ancestral dogmas on them. Somehow that didn't always stop them from trying to impose theirs
on Vaspurakan when they had the chance, but they saw nothing
unusual in that disparity.

Tiverhios didn't go down on his belly in a full proskynesis, but
he did bow himself almost double. "Your Majesty, I had hoped—I
had prayed—that would be what you said. When it is seen to
be true all through the Empire, the crown and red boots will be
yours. So long as he be orthodox, any man alive is better on the
throne than Genesios."

Maniakes had to work to keep his face straight at such back-
handed praise. He worried only slightly about what the Empire
as a whole thought of his religious views. At the moment, what
the fleet thought of them was of paramount importance. Later,
if he won his way so far, what the ecumenical patriarch and the
people of Videssos the city thought would also matter. So would
the opinion of the army, though it was leavened with a good
many unconverted Vaspurakaners.

"What do you intend to do now, excellent sir?" he asked

Tiverhios. "Will all your ships join me? Will all the Key's ships join me?" He turned his head and in a lowered voice asked Thrax, "What part of the Key's fleet has he here?"

"Perhaps a third," Thrax answered. "A cautious strategy, coming out to meet us with so few." He sniffed. "In a civil war, caution is mostly wasted."

Tiverhios was also speaking: "Since I did not fully know your views, your Majesty, before setting out I promised—indeed, I swore—no harm would come to captains and crews either willing or unwilling to follow you, that depending on what you turned out to be." He looked anxious. "You will not make me violate my oath, I hope?"

Maniakes wondered how he had expected to be able to fight after giving an oath like that. He shrugged. The scent of heresy might have united the captains behind Genesios as nothing else could. He said, "No, those who prefer a bloodstained bungling butcher who aims to feed Videssos to Sharbaraz King of Kings piece by piece are welcome to go to him. Having such fools as his commanders will but weaken him."

Tiverhios thought that over and then, rather more slowly than Maniakes would have hoped for, got the point and laughed. "Well said! Now that you are shown to be orthodox, few from among my captains here will seek to desert your cause."

"From among your captains here?" Maniakes echoed. "What of the men still back at the Key?"

"More of them, I fear, will incline toward your enemy," Tiverhios said. "I took with me mostly ships whose captains, I thought, leaned your way."

Kourikos stepped up beside Maniakes at the starboard rail. Tiverhios' eyes widened when he recognized the logothete of the treasury. "Aye, I favor Maniakes," Kourikos said. "So do many from among the powerful at Videssos the city. That you do, too, in this hour of Videssos' need makes me set aside your debt to me in recognition of the debt the Empire owes to you."

"You're—very kind, eminent sir, and very generous." Tiverhios bowed almost as low to Kourikos as he had to Maniakes.

The logothete asked, "Is Erinakios still drungarios of the fleet at the Key?"

"Aye, eminent sir, he is," Tiverhios answered. "Genesios, he's slaughtered the generals till there's hardly a one that can tell north from sausage, if you know what I mean. But he hasn't much messed with us sailors. He doesn't trust himself to find better to take our place, unless I'm wrong."

"He hasn't found better to take the place of the generals he's murdered, either," Maniakes said. Lowering his voice, he said to Kourikos, "Tell me about this Erinakios. We Vaspurakaners don't know much about this business of fighting on the sea, either."

"He's a sharp-tempered man—all over prickles, you might say," Kourikos replied. "He's not broken with Genesios this past six years, not formally, but he didn't molest our merchantmen when we sailed by the Key, nor pursue us once we were past, though he might easily have done either. Where he'll stand now, I do not know."

Maniakes plucked at his beard. "What connections do our assembled nobles here have with him?"

"He borrowed money from me three years ago, about the same time Tiverhios did," the logothete answered. "He paid me back ahead of schedule." Kourikos sounded as if that were an affront, not something to be proud of. From his point of view, maybe it was: Erinakios had deprived him of some accrued interest. He went on, "I shall have to inquire. Offhand, I know of no close connections between any of my party and the drungarios."

"Well, we'll see what we can do." Maniakes did his best to keep his voice easy. In fact, he felt like pitching Kourikos and all his prominent companions into the sea. Here they had been boasting of all the important people they knew, but, the first time he really needed them, they let him down. He called across the water to Tiverhios: "Does Erinakios know why you chose the captains for the part of the fleet you led out to seek me?"

"Can't be sure," the ypodrungarios answered. "We didn't talk about it—nothing like that. But if he thinks about who's there and who's gone, he's going to figure it out. Erinakios, he may be spiny, but he's sharp the other way, too, that he is."

It was, Maniakes suspected with a hint of sadness, more than could be said for Tiverhios. Maniakes asked Thrax, "With these ships here added to ours, can we beat what's left of the force the Key has?"

Obviously unaware of what he was doing, the captain of the *Renewal* made several strange, thought-filled faces before answering "Your Majesty, I think we can, provided the fleet from Videssos the city doesn't come down to aid Erinakios. But if he fights with all he has, we'll not get away from the Key with enough to challenge the fleet that anchors at the capital."

Thrax had a way of sounding discouraged whether the situation truly warranted it or not. Maniakes was getting used to that, and included it in his calculations. He asked, "How likely is Erinakios to fight with everything he has?"

"If you're asking me, your Majesty, my guess is that he's not likely to do that," Thrax said. "If he'd intended fighting with everything he had, he'd have met us with his whole fleet a long way south of here. But I'm only guessing. If you really want to know, ask Tiverhios there."

"You're right." Maniakes called the question across the gap of ocean.

Tiverhios tugged at one end of his mustache as he considered. "Your Majesty, I just don't know. Some days, he'd be cursing Genesios up one side and down the other, the sort of curses that, were he a wizard, would slay a man in short order and leave him glad he was dead on account of the pain of his dying. But other times, he'd curse rebels every bit as hard. I don't think he knows himself what he'll do till the time comes to do it."

"That time is coming soon," Maniakes said.

The Key had two central mountain peaks. They loomed up from the sea, green on their lower slopes, the gray-brown of bare rock interspersed above. Neither was tall enough to hold snow in summer.

Maniakes cared nothing for the peaks, save that they marked where in the sea the island lay. His interest centered on the ports, particularly the southern one, Gavdos. The fleet still under Erinakios' command had put to sea and awaited him well out from the port. He would not catch the dromons tied up at the docks or beached nearby. Erinakios gave every appearance of being ready to fight.

Tiverhios' galley lay alongside the *Renewal*, so the ypodrungarios could tell Maniakes what he needed to know about captains and vessels of the opposing fleet. Maniakes called to him, "Which ship does Erinakios command?"

Tiverhios scanned the oncoming dromons. "It'd be easier to pick out under sail," he said a little peevishly, "but he's brailed up his canvas and stowed the mast for battle, same as everybody else. I think—there! Off to port a bit, the one with the red eyes painted by the ram."

"I see the one you mean," Maniakes said. The rowers on Erinakios' ship powered it through the water with swift, steady strokes. Maniakes couldn't remember seeing such polished efficiency before; it was as if a single hand worked all the oars. As the ship came up and over the waves, he got glimpses of its ram, the bronze turned green by the sea but the point cruelly sharp. That crew would make sure it did all the harm it could.

"Steer toward him," Maniakes said. "We'll show the shield of truce, but if he sprints at us, I want to be ready to fight on the instant."

"We'd better be," Thrax said. "Otherwise we'll be dead." He had also noted what Erinakios' rowers could do—and that the ship in which the drungarios sailed was larger and more formidable than the *Renewal.*

Erinakios' dromon drew closer appallingly fast. Maniakes saw no sign of a shield of truce—only the point of the ram, aimed always at a point just to port of his own bow. The enemy's oars rose and fell, rose and fell.

"A touch to port," Thrax called to the steersmen at the stern. "By Phos, he won't take the angle on us!" The *Renewal* made the slight course adjustment, but Erinakios and his rowers countered. Within moments, the green bronze ram aimed for the same point as before. Thrax bit his lip. "They're good. They're very good."

The two dromons were hardly a bowshot apart when a sailor in Erinakios' ship held up a white-painted shield. "Sheer off!" Maniakes shouted.

"What? Are you mad?" Thrax stared wildly. "It's a trick, your Majesty. Give him your flank and we'll be on the bottom in nothing flat."

"Sheer off," Maniakes repeated. "*Now!*" If he was right, Erinakios was seeing what kind of stomach he had for a tight place. If he was wrong . . . if he was wrong, the little fish and the urchins and the whelks that crawled across the bottom of the sea would feed well.

"Hard to starboard!" Thrax cried, raw pain coming from his throat with the words. They were so close to Erinakios' galley now that even sheering off was risky; if both ships dodged in the same direction, they might still collide.

Just for an instant, the flagship from the Key started to follow the *Renewal's* movement. Fear turned Maniakes' bowels to water. If Erinakios truly was committed to Genesios, he had the chance to do his sovereign a great service. But then the drungarios' dromon spun to starboard itself and slid past the *Renewal* on a parallel track, the tips of its oars almost brushing against those of the ship in which Maniakes sailed.

Across the narrow stretch of water, a hoarse voice bawled, "You want to see how close you can cut it, don't you?"

If that was Erinakios by the port rail, he looked as prickly as Kourikos had described him: a hawk-featured man with a red, angry face and a wolf-gray beard. To him, Maniakes called back, "Isn't that what you had in mind to find out, eminent sir?"

Erinakios' laugh sounded like the sharp, coughing bark of a wolf, too. "Aye, that's what I had in mind. What's it to you?"

Maniakes remembered the sudden, liquid terror he had known. A rush of anger all but burned it away. The first thing he thought of was revenge against Erinakios for reminding him of his mortality. Shame followed, extinguishing rage. Erinakios had a right to be concerned about what sort of sovereign he might get if he abandoned Genesios.

"Do I pass your test, eminent sir?" Maniakes asked.

The distance between the two dromons had lengthened. Erinakios had to raise his voice to answer: "You'll do." After a moment, almost as an afterthought, he added, "Your Majesty."

Maniakes nearly missed the offhand recognition of his sovereignty. He was looking out toward the wings of the two fleets. In the center, where captains on both sides saw their commanders parleying, they, too, had held back from fighting. Out on the wings, they had gone for each other. A couple of dromons had been rammed and were sinking; men splashed in the water, grabbing for oars and planks and other floating wreckage. More than one fire blazed upon the water, which could not extinguish the liquid incendiary the Videssian navy used.

"Will your trumpeter blow truce?" Maniakes asked. "In civil war, hurts cost the Empire double, for it bleeds when a man from either side dies."

"For that all on its lonesome I'd blow truce," Erinakios said.

"Genesios hasn't figured it out to this day, and won't if he lives to be a thousand." He turned to his trumpeter. The sweet notes of the truce call rang across the water. Maniakes nudged Thrax, who called to his own hornplayer. In a moment, the call to leave off fighting blared from both flagships.

Not all the captains obeyed the call, not at once. Some of the leaders of the fleet from the Key genuinely favored Genesios, no matter what their drungarios had to say. And some of Maniakes' captains, already engaged in battle when they heard the truce call, did not care to leave off fights they were winning.

Erinakios and Maniakes sorted things out together. Maniakes' dromons disengaged from battle as they could. Where they still fought Genesios' loyalists, they suddenly discovered allies among Erinakios' ships. Most of the dromons whose leaders backed Genesios soon sank or surrendered. On a couple, mutinies from the crew impelled such surrender.

But a few warships broke free and sprinted northwest toward Videssos the city, oars churning water white as they fled. Desperation lent them speed their foes could not match. "Genesios will be muttering into his mustache tomorrow, when word reaches him of rout and defection," Erinakios said. He bared his teeth. "I like the idea."

"And I," Maniakes said. "But that also means we'll have to look more to our safety from tomorrow on. Have you a wizard whose work you trust? The tyrant has already tried once to slay me by sorcery."

Erinakios made an impatient, disparaging gesture; every line of his body shouted contempt. "I'm a fighting man," he said. "I don't clutter my head worrying about magecraft."

"Have it as you will," Maniakes said, though he did not share the drungarios' scorn of sorcery: After the night in Opsikion, he hardly could. Aye, magic was hard to come by, difficult to execute properly, and of little use in time of battle. All that granted, it remained real, and could be deadly dangerous.

"D'you trust him, your Majesty?" Thrax whispered urgently. "Even without Tiverhios' ships, that fleet is a match for ours. If you add them into the bargain, we could be swamped."

"If Erinakios wanted to swamp us, he could have done it without this mime-show," Maniakes answered. "Having his ships waiting just past the cape would have taken care of the job nicely.

We *want* people to rally to our banner, Thrax; we've wanted that from the start. If it hadn't happened, we never could have come this far."

"I understand all that." Thrax stuck out his chin and looked stubborn. "But the thing of it is, we've come this far with people we know are loyal—most of 'em, anyhow. But if we take up this fleet and sail with it alongside ours or mixed together with ours against Videssos the city, and Erinakios turns on us then, why, it'd be like a man walking along on two legs and having one of 'em fall off."

"There's a pretty picture," Maniakes said. "But if we go against the city without the fleet from the Key, we're like a one-legged man setting out."

Thrax winced, but then nodded. "Something to that, too, I suppose. But watch yourself, your Majesty."

"I shall," Maniakes promised. He raised his voice and called to Erinakios: "Have you space at your docks for our ships?"

"Aye, we can take 'em all, in Gavdos or Sykeota around on the north coast," the drungarios of the Key answered. "I suppose you'll want more of my ships to go to one harbor and more of yours to the other, so you can surround yourself with armed men you trust."

He couldn't possibly have heard Maniakes and Thrax talking together. A glance at the distance between the *Renewal* and Erinakios' ship told Maniakes as much. He hadn't thought to give Erinakios any tests for wits, but the drungarios seemed to be setting his own—and passing them handily. Maniakes said, "If you think I won't take you up on that, eminent sir, you may think again."

Erinakios let out a couple of barking grunts of laughter. "You'd be a fool to say no till I prove my worth. Will you take Gavdos or Sykeota? The northern harbor's a trifle larger, but the southern's easier to get in and out of. Either which way, I suppose you'll want me for hostage?" He phrased it as a question, but his voice held certainty.

"Now that you mention it—yes," Maniakes answered, which drew another of those wolfish chuckles from Erinakios. Turning to Thrax, Maniakes asked, "Which harbor do you prefer?"

"Gavdos," Thrax answered without hesitation. "The drungarios is right—it's the easier of the two, and not all our captains and crews have been here before."

Kastavala had a good harbor, Opsikion had a good harbor. Videssos the city had three splendid harbors: north, south, and west. Only those last could stand comparison to the anchorage on the southern shore of the Key: it was as if Phos had scooped out three-fourths of a circle from an otherwise smooth coastline, giving a relatively small entrance to a wide, secure anchorage. Even storms would have their force muted before they smote with wind and wave the ships tied up there.

Had Videssos the city not stood at a crossroads of both land and sea routes, and had the imperial capital not kept itself rich by making potential rivals poor, the Empire might have been ruled from the Key. Maniakes wondered how the world might have looked had the islanders spread out and begun to rule the mainland instead of being ruled from it.

As it was, the town of Gavdos was far smaller than Kastavala, let alone Opsikion, let alone Videssos the city. Most of it seemed to be barracks and storehouses and taverns and brothels: but for the fleet, the place had no life.

"Is it the same at Sykeota in the north?" Maniakes asked.

Thrax did not need to have him explain himself. "Just the same, your Majesty. From time out of mind, this island's been given over to the navy and not much else. They don't grow enough grain here to feed all the sailors, and a city can't live on fish alone."

"So that's the way of it," Maniakes said thoughtfully. "If ever a drungarios of the fleet here decided to rebel, his men would get hungry by and by—provided they didn't win first, that is."

Triphylles came up and examined Gavdos with a jaundiced eye. "What a dreadful hole," he said, adding a shudder redolent of distaste. "I shall be ever so glad when this campaign is over and done and I can return to my villa in the city. Life anywhere else has proved altogether dreary, I fear."

"It would have been dreary to stay in Videssos the city after your head went up on the Milestone, I suppose," Maniakes remarked, deadpan.

"Well, yes, but even so—" Triphylles began. Then he realized he was being made sport of. With a sniff, he took himself elsewhere. Thrax suffered a coughing fit of epic proportions, but valiantly managed to hold back from laughing out loud.

Erinakios' flagship tied up just behind the *Renewal*. Maniakes walked up the gangplank to the dock. After so many days spent mostly at sea, dry land felt wobbly. Sailors with swords and shields came up onto the dock with him, in case Erinakios intended treachery even now.

But the drungarios, though he also got up on the dock as fast as he could—and though he swayed to and fro more than Maniakes—prostrated himself on the rough timbers before the man he had named his sovereign. "Get up, get up," Maniakes said impatiently. "We have a lot of planning to do, and not much time in which to do it."

Erinakios rose. Seen close up, he looked even tougher and grimmer than Kourikos had made him out to be and than he had seemed while aboard his dromon. Maniakes had twenty years fewer than he, but would not have cared to encounter him sword to sword or hand to hand.

But his fierce visage suddenly lightened into a smile, as if the sun had come out from behind thick clouds. "I am already seeing I made the right choice," he said. "Genesios knows nothing of planning. Something happens to him, happens to the Empire, and he goes and does the first thing that pops into his vicious head. Is it any wonder we're in our present state?"

"That we're in it is no wonder, but getting out won't be easy," Maniakes answered. "Falling down a hill is easier than slogging back up it once you've fallen, and straightforward viciousness has one thing in its favor: whoever gets in his way once isn't apt to be around to do it twice."

"Which is the only reason Genesios is still on the throne," Erinakios said. "But if he doesn't manage to murder you, I think you'll beat him. You can think—I can see that already. Most of the others who rose against him were just reacting. He could deal with them; his mind works the same way, and he had the advantages of already wearing the red boots and sitting in Videssos the city like a spider in the center of its web. You'll be tougher."

"May I ask you something?" Maniakes waited for Erinakios' gruff nod, then put his question: "Why didn't you go after the crown yourself?"

"I thought about it," Erinakios said, a dangerously honest answer—a man with imperial ambitions might be reckoned untrustworthy for that very reason. "Aye, I thought about it. But with only the fleet from the Key, I was too likely to lose. And I couldn't count on help from anyone else. I've made too many enemies over the years for that. Why do you suppose Genesios kept me on here? He's shortsighted, but he's not blind."

Maniakes pursed his lips. The drungarios' comment made considerable sense. Genesios had left the elder Maniakes alone on Kalavria, knowing that replacing him would cause more trouble. And he had retained an able but unpopular officer here lest his replacement prove able to forge alliances with other soldiers and sailors. No, that wasn't stupid. If only he had used more of his wits for the Empire's good.

"Going to have to put you up in the barracks," Erinakios said, pointing to a weathered wooden building. "Hope you don't mind—it's where *I* sleep."

"It's all right with me," Maniakes answered cheerfully. "Next to some of the places I've slept on campaign, it looks like the imperial palace." He glanced back toward the *Renewal.* "How the excellent Triphylles and the eminent Kourikos will take it is another matter, though. And I've another double handful of nobles from Videssos the city scattered through the rest of my ships."

"Well, if they want to get rid of Genesios, they'll have to take a bit of the rough so as they can have the smooth back," Erinakios said. "And if they don't fancy a couple of nights of hard beds and salt fish, to the ice with 'em."

Maniakes wouldn't have put it so bluntly, but the drungarios' assessment marched with his own. Some of the grandees seemed ready to make the best of their unprepossessing quarters, while others grumbled and fussed.

Erinakios spat scornfully when he saw that. "Pack of half-weaned brats, whining on account of Mama won't give 'em the tit."

"Let them be," Maniakes said, which got him a dirty look from the drungarios. He didn't care. The nobles from the capital might have been discontented with their lodgings, but they were finally doing what he had hoped they would. He watched them going around, mugs of rough wine in hand, to one of Erinakios' ship captains after another; whether through kinship or marriage or acquaintance or gold, they seemed to know most of the fleet's leading officers. The more they talked with those men, the stronger the bond they wove that bound the fleet of the Key to Maniakes.

"By tomorrow," Erinakios said in an appraising tone of voice, "Genesios will know you're here, and he'll know I've gone over to you. I don't think he'll be what you'd call happy about that."

"Then we should sail for the city tomorrow," Maniakes answered. "The faster we move, the less chance he'll have to figure out where we are and what we're up to."

Erinakios raised his cup of wine in salute. "Spoken like a soldier, your Majesty!" He drank again, then studied Maniakes. "The more I hear you talking, your Majesty, the more I like what I hear. Videssos won't prosper—by the good god, Videssos won't survive, the way things are these days—with a slugabed in the red boots."

"If I don't keep moving, I'm liable to be the one who doesn't survive," Maniakes said. "Genesios has already tried once to slay me by sorcery, as I've said. That's why I asked if you had a wizard warding you."

"And I told you, I have no truck with wizards. If sorcery hasn't slain me in all these years, I don't think it will bite on me now."

The logic behind that escaped Maniakes, but he held his tongue. If Erinakios wanted to substitute bravado for brains, that was his affair. And Genesios was in any case more likely to attack his rival Emperor than an underling, however high his rank.

"Do you mind if I send a boat around to Sykeota?" Maniakes asked Erinakios. "I want to make sure my men and ships there are getting on well and also to make sure fleets from both ports will sail against Videssos the city on the same day."

"Yes, that would be a good thing, wouldn't it?" Erinakios gave one of his barking chuckles. He waved a hand in Maniakes' direction, perhaps mocking the delicate gestures of the grandees from the city. "Go right ahead, your Majesty. In your boots, I'd do all the checking I could, too."

Maniakes went over to one of his officers and gave the necessary orders. The captain saluted with clenched fist over heart and went off to do his bidding. Maniakes was confident the fellow would find everything all right; the question had been more intended to find out how Erinakios would react. Had the drungarios tried to talk him out of seeing how things were going at the harbor where his ships were in the minority, he would have had something to worry about. Since Erinakios didn't mind, odds were he wasn't intending to try anything hostile over there.

"I hope all's going well with Rhegorios," Maniakes murmured, half to himself.

Erinakios overheard him. "That's your cousin with the horsemen? I hope it's well with him, too, your Majesty. The thinner Genesios has to spread his men—and his fears, and his hatred—the less he can concentrate on any one thing."

"Just what I was thinking," Maniakes said, and so it was, but only in part. The chief idea in his mind was that in Rhegorios he had a comrade he could trust without reservation. With all the new chieftains, with all the nobles from Videssos the city, he was constantly looking over his shoulder to make sure the hand patting him on the back hadn't first palmed a dagger.

Erinakios said, "Do I rightly remember hearing you also have a couple of brothers?"

"Aye—Tatoules and Parsmanios, both younger than I. They're officers in the westlands, of no great rank. I pray to the lord with the great and good mind that they're well; no word of them has come to Kastavala for a long time. With Sharbaraz rampaging through our lands there, anything might have happened to them."

"Too true—and you say nothing of all the revolts spawned in the westlands. But they won't have heard of your own rising?"

"I don't think so, no," Maniakes answered. "Not unless Genesios has sent for them to take vengeance for my move against him. But I don't think he can do that, either, not with the chaos there. From what I've heard, these days the Videssian armies in the westlands are fighting for themselves and for survival, nothing more. They don't much worry about orders from the capital."

"There you've heard true, your Majesty." Erinakios rolled his eyes to show how true it was. "But they don't work with one another, either, and so come off worse over and over against the Makuraners."

"Videssians do love faction-fighting," Maniakes observed. He couldn't have stated anything more obvious, save perhaps that air was needed for breathing, but several ship captains and three or four of the grandees from the capital looked askance at him nonetheless. He needed a moment to figure out why: he had publicly reminded them of his own Vaspurakaner blood. Many of them had been doing their best to forget about it so they could back him in good conscience.

Erinakios said, "You're sure you'll be able to sleep here in safety tonight, your Majesty?" It might have been real concern about

Maniakes' safety; then again, it might have been a taunt. With the drungarios, every sentence came out so drenched in vinegar that it was hard to tell.

Maniakes chose to think of it as real concern. "It should be all right. Genesios won't know tonight where I am, and in any case my wizard Alvinos is with me. His spells warded me in Opsikion and should protect me here, as well."

"Alvinos, eh?" Erinakios glanced over to the mage, who certainly looked more as if the Vaspurakaner appellation Bagdasares belonged to him than the bland, acceptable Videssian moniker he sometimes wore. Maniakes usually called him Bagdasares, too. This time he hadn't, precisely so he wouldn't bring up Vaspurakan in the minds of those who heard him.

Sensing that people were watching him, Bagdasares turned away from the captain with whom he had been talking, bowed, raised his wine cup in salute, and went back to the interrupted conversation. Maniakes smiled. The mage had a certain style of his own.

Servants lit torches to keep the gathering going after sunset. Maniakes stayed on his feet chatting until the man he had sent out to Sykeota returned with assurances all was well. Then Maniakes let out a couple of yawns so perfect, a mime at a Midwinter's Day festival would not have been ashamed to claim them for his own.

When you were Avtokrator of the Videssians, or even a claimant to the throne, such theatrics got results. Within minutes, dozens of captains, yawning themselves, set aside wine cups, went outside to use the slit trenches in back of the barracks, and flopped down on cots. Maniakes didn't expect his cot to be comfortable, and it wasn't. He slept like a log even so.

Breakfast was a rock-hard roll, a couple of little fried squid hot enough to scorch the fingers, and a mug of sour wine. To Maniakes' thinking, it was a naval variation on campaign food. To the grandees from Videssos the city, it might have been just this side of poisonous. Even Kourikos, who usually seemed the most reasonable of the bunch, didn't eat much.

"What are we to do?" Triphylles asked mournfully. He had nibbled a tiny piece off the roll, sipped the wine and set it down with a grimace of distaste, and turned up his sizable nose at the squid, although street vendors sold them in every quarter of Videssos the city.

To Maniakes, Erinakios remarked, "You know, your Majesty, I'm a grandfather now, but I remember when my oldest son was a little boy. He was what they call a fussy eater, I guess. When he didn't fancy something that was set before him, I'd say, 'Well, son, it's up to you. You can eat that or you can starve.' Like I say, I'm a grandfather now, so I guess he didn't starve."

Triphylles let out a loud, indignant sniff. A couple of the other nobles attacked their breakfasts with fresh vigor. Maniakes even saw one of them take a second helping of fried squid. So did Erinakios. His shoulders shook with suppressed mirth.

Kourikos came up to Maniakes and said, "Your Majesty, I don't think it proper that we should be made sport of for no better reason than our being unaccustomed to the rough fare of the military diet."

"Give me a chance, eminent sir, and I expect I could come up with some better reasons than that to make sport of you," Erinakios said with a maliciously gleeful grin.

Kourikos spluttered indignantly. He was used to twisting other people's words, not to having his own twisted. Maniakes held up a hand. He said, "Eminent sir, so far as I can tell, no one was making sport of anyone; the eminent drungarios happened to choose that moment to explain to me how he raised his son. That may prove useful when Niphone and I have children."

Now Kourikos sounded exasperated. "Really, your Majesty, you know perfectly well that—"

"What I know perfectly well, eminent sir," Maniakes interrupted, "is that on the Key there seems to be no food suitable for your delicate palate and those of your companions. Either you will have to take what the cooks dish out for you or you'll go hungry. When we win the war and the lot of you go back to your villas and manors, you can stuff yourselves with dainties to your hearts' content. Till then, you ought to remember the circumstances in which you find yourselves—and remember that, had you stayed in the city, you might be trying to eat through slit throats."

Angrily, Kourikos stomped away. Sulkily, he took a fried squid from a tray. Defiantly, he bit into it—the squid weren't hot any more. His eyebrows shot up in surprise. Maniakes wondered why he was surprised. Squid, bread crumbs, olive oil, minced garlic—nothing wrong with any of that.

Neither Maniakes nor Erinakios wanted to waste time. The sooner they were sailing for Videssos the city, the happier each would be. But sailing into battle without a plan was asking for trouble.

Erinakios led Maniakes to a chart of the capital with the harbors prominently displayed. Maniakes hadn't much worried about them when he had lived in Videssos the city. Even when he had taken ship, they had been just places from which to enter or leave. He hadn't thought about them in the military sense.

"You'll know the Neorhesian harbor on the north coast of the city is the one the navy mostly uses," Erinakios said, pointing to the chart. Maniakes nodded; he did know that much. Erinakios went on, "Now, the harbor of Kontoskalion in the south is every bit as good, mind you, if not as large. Law and custom say trading ships go there and the dromons to the Neorhesian harbor, but in a civil war nobody listens to what law and customs say, anyhow. Are you with me so far?"

"Aye. You've been very clear. When does it start getting complicated?"

Erinakios snorted. "Have no fear, your Majesty. We're getting there." He jabbed a thumb at the third harbor, this one at the blunt westernmost extremity of Videssos the city. "This anchorage is in the palace district, of course. Most of the time, there's not much tied up here: customs boats, a yacht if the Avtokrator happens to like sailing, a few fishing boats to help keep the palaces supplied, things like that. But the place will hold almost as much as the harbor of Kontoskalion. When an army goes over the Cattle Crossing to the westlands, for instance, some of it will go from there, because it's closest and most convenient. Still, because it's not used much, there's a chance the defenders will leave it out of their calculations. And if we can force a landing there—"

"We can seize the palaces and flush Genesios like a partridge from the gorse," Maniakes finished for him.

"That's how it'd work if everything goes the way it should," Erinakios agreed. "Of course, we'll never see the day when everything goes as it should, but the least making a move on the palaces will do is to force Genesios to shuffle his men all around, and that's part of the idea."

"If he spreads himself thin enough, we may be able to get men up and over the sea wall and move into the city that way," Maniakes said. "It's lower than the land wall, after all, and single, not double."

"It could happen," Erinakios said judiciously, "but I wouldn't count on it. If we do pull it off, it'll show that nobody in Genesios' force is standing by him, not his sailors or his soldiers, either. If that's so, we have him."

"If I understand the hints you've thrown around, you want us to make for the harbor of Kontoskalion and the one by the palaces, in the hope that they'll be less heavily defended than the Neorhesian," Maniakes said.

"That's what I'm thinking, all right," Erinakios said. "We may have a big sea fight before we can get up to the city. Then again, we may not. Depends on how confident Genesios and his captains are feeling when they find out we're on our way. If they hang back, they're afraid of us."

"What would you do in Genesios' sandals?" Maniakes asked.

"If I knew Erinakios was coming after me, you mean?" The drungarios puffed out his chest. "Your Majesty, I'd be afraid."

Maniakes was getting used to priests' giving him sour looks as they blessed his cause. They mistrusted his orthodoxy, but six years of Genesios had been enough to prove to almost everyone that orthodoxy alone did not guarantee a decent ruler.

"May the lord with the great and good mind watch over and protect you and your cause and our sacred orthodox faith," the priest said to Maniakes, making it clear that in his mind, at least, you could not be a decent ruler without orthodoxy, either. "May he grant peace, tranquility, and victory to Videssos. So may it be."

"So may it be," Maniakes echoed. "Thank you, holy sir." As far as he was concerned, the blue-robe had got the order backward: without victory, Videssos would know neither tranquility nor peace. This was, however, neither time nor place nor occasion for quarreling with a cleric.

"Thank you, your Majesty," the priest replied. "After your triumph, I pray you shall worship at the High Temple in Videssos the city. With its beauty and holiness, truly it seems the veritable home of Phos on earth." He sighed. "Ah, were it granted me to serve the good god in such a place—"

Maniakes had all he could do to keep his face straight. The priest might mislike his doctrine but was still angling to be translated from the Key to the capital. Videssians looked out for themselves, first, last, and always. He said, "When I win my way to Videssos the city, I shall indeed reward those who helped me get there."

Beaming, the priest blessed the ships so fulsomely that Maniakes marveled when they didn't close their painted eyes in embarrassment at the praise.

"Well, about time that's over and done with," Erinakios said when the cleric finally fell silent. The drungarios, while undoubtedly a believer, had a distinctly pragmatic attitude toward matters religious. "Now let's get on with the business of putting Genesios' head up on the Milestone and flinging his body onto a dung heap—not that I have anything personal against dung heaps, you understand."

"Everyone in Videssos has something personal against Genesios, I think," Maniakes said. "In fact, the only man I know of who doesn't is Sharbaraz King of Kings: Genesios has given away so much of the Empire to him that he's been an even greater benefactor than Likinios was—and all Likinios did, through my father and me, was to set Sharbaraz back on his throne."

"Your Majesty, you're wrong," Erinakios said. "Genesios has also made a whole host of executioners all through the Empire very happy men."

"There you have me," Maniakes said. "Now we need to—" He broke off. His right hand went to his chest. The amulet that rested against his skin there was suddenly burning hot. "Magic!"

The priest who had just blessed the fleet turned and fled, blue robe flapping around his ankles, shaved skull gleaming in the sun. Maniakes wished him dead and spending an eternity in Skotos' ice. In spite of the wish, the priest kept running. Maybe he wouldn't go to the ice, at least not for this. But one thing was certain: he would never, ever come to Videssos the city.

Bagdasares, on the other hand, ran toward trouble, not away from it. He shouted something in the Vaspurakaner tongue that Maniakes didn't quite catch; his hands twisted in quick passes. All at once, faster than metal and stone had any business doing, the amulet cooled again.

"Never mind me," Maniakes said. "I'm all right. Look to Erinakios."

"You're all right *now*, your Majesty," Bagdasares answered, panting. "How you would have been in another moment—"

But with that offhand remark, he turned his attention and his sorcerous skill to the drungarios. Erinakios stood swaying, his eyes wide and staring, lips pulled back from his teeth in a fearsome grimace, hands clenched into fists. As Maniakes watched in dismay, the naval officer's back began to arch so that he resembled nothing so much as a drawn bow.

Do something! Maniakes wanted to scream to Bagdasares. But if anyone had screamed at him in the middle of a battle, he might well have let the air out of the meddler with a well-placed sword thrust. And so, not feeling himself in any immediate danger, he simply stood and watched Bagdasares struggle against the onslaught of Genesios' mage.

"Why wouldn't you ward yourself against wizardry?" he demanded of Erinakios. The drungarios did not, could not, answer. Every muscle, every tendon in his face and neck, hands, and forearms—all Maniakes could see of his flesh—stood out, sharply defined. His back bent more and more. If it bent much further, it would snap.

Bagdasares incanted like a man possessed. He chanted charms in both Vaspurakaner and Videssian, sometimes in what sounded like the two languages commingled. His hands moved faster and more cleverly than those of a man playing a clavier. Greasy sweat ran down his face and dripped to the wood of the dock.

Still Erinakios' back bent.

When it came, the *snap!* reminded Maniakes of nothing so much as a good-sized stick being broken across a man's knee. Erinakios fell, as limp as he had been rigid. The latrine smell of death filled the air. With a groan, Bagdasares collapsed beside the drungarios.

Suddenly, instead of being helped by the mage, Maniakes was helping him. He rolled Bagdasares onto his back, made sure he was breathing, felt for a pulse. To his vast relief, he found one, firm and strong. "Phos be praised," he said shakily. "He's just fainted, I think. Someone flip water in his face."

For all the water that surrounded the Key, getting some in a bucket and splashing Bagdasares with it seemed to Maniakes to take an unconscionably long time. When the mage was finally splashed, he choked and spluttered. His eyes flew open. At first, only horror filled them. Reason slowly returned. "Phos be praised!" he said, sitting up. "Your Majesty yet lives."

"So I do, and glad of it," Maniakes said. "Poor Erinakios, though, wasn't so lucky."

Bagdasares' fleshy nostrils twitched, as if to pick up the death stench and confirm Maniakes' words. The wizard turned around and peered at the drungarios' corpse. "I'm sorry, your Majesty," he said, bowing his head. "I fought with all I had in me, but I could not save him."

Maniakes reached out a hand, pulled the mage to his feet. "Partly Erinakios' own fault, for disregarding sorcery of all sorts," he said.

"Partly, too, that Genesios' mage had time to prepare his attack, while I had to improvise the defense," Bagdasares said. "I understand that, but failure is never pleasant to contemplate. And Genesios' mage is very strong, to reach so far and to kill in my despite."

"How strong will he seem when we get closer?" Maniakes asked worriedly.

"Stronger than this, unless I miss my guess." Bagdasares' face glistened with sweat, as if he'd been running for miles. Magecraft was not easy, especially magecraft of the desperate sort he'd just been using. In a shaken voice, he went on, "The capital, by the nature of things, draws the best from every art. How good that best can be—" He shook his head. "Better than I had imagined, I can tell you so much."

"And we are now without the man who was plainly the best choice to lead our ships against the fleet from the city," Maniakes said.

The captains who had been staring at Erinakios' body returned with that to the world of the living, the world of rank and preferment. Tiverhios the ypodrungarios took half a step forward, as if to say that someone with appropriate qualifications might not be overhard to find. But, even though Tiverhios had declared for him right away, Maniakes was not keen to name the ypodrungarios his supreme commander on the sea. He strongly suspected an admixture of expedience in Tiverhios' choice. Besides, choosing Tiverhios would make the rest of the captains from the Key jealous.

And so Maniakes said, "Thrax, you'll command against Genesios' fleet. Tiverhios, you'll stay on as ypodrungarios, but ypodrungarios now of my whole fleet, not just the ships from the Key. To help show that's so, I'll raise your pay half a goldpiece a day, effective right now."

"Your Majesty is gracious," Tiverhios said enthusiastically, bowing almost double. If he resented being passed over for command of the whole fleet, he hid it very well. On brief acquaintance, Maniakes doubted he was a good enough actor to dissemble so well. And, if he had got in debt to Kourikos, the extra money had to look good to him. *One problem solved,* Maniakes thought; had Tiverhios proved difficult, everything might have unraveled right there.

"We have to go on," Maniakes said. "Only by casting down Genesios can we be sure outrages like this won't happen all across the Empire at a vicious brute's whim. By the good god, excellent sirs, my brave captains, I am a man, and I own to faults aplenty; only Phos and his sun are perfect things. But you will not need to fear—this—" He pointed to Erinakios' body. "—while I am on the throne."

They cheered him, louder than he had expected: perhaps they were venting the fear they had felt when Erinakios fell before their eyes. At Maniakes' wave, captains and sailors filed aboard their ships.

After Maniakes stood once more on the deck of the *Renewal,* he asked Bagdasares, "How do we protect ourselves if Genesios looses this murderous mage upon us once more?"

"I think we have a few days' grace before we need worry about that, your Majesty," Bagdasares said. "I stumble with weariness merely from having tried to withstand his sorcery. Having instigated it, he will be the next thing to dead this moment, and will need some days to recover before he next thinks about casting a spell."

Maniakes pondered that. It explained the long interval between the attack on him in Opsikion and this one now. He said, "Does that not suggest Genesios is down to a single wizard? If he had more, he would have been continually harassing us."

"It may well be so," Bagdasares answered. "If it is, though, the one he has is very powerful."

"I wonder what became of the others," Maniakes mused. "Would their heads have gone up on the Milestone when they failed to satisfy him?"

"With Genesios, I find that very likely," Bagdasares said.

"So do I," Maniakes said. "Tell me, how it is that an Avtokrator who is no magician himself, save perhaps in the sense of magically creating disaster for Videssos, can dominate sorcerers with great power?"

"The main reason, your Majesty, is that most magic requires slow preparation. If a man has a knife to his throat, or if his family is threatened, he is likely to obey a man who commands such immediate power." Bagdasares' chuckle sounded nervous. "Wizards do not widely broadcast this unfortunate fact."

"Yes, and I can see why," Maniakes said. "Well, Genesios' sorcerer, even if he succeeded against Erinakios, has twice failed to slay me now. Phos willing, Genesios will see that and act on it and solve our problem for us."

"May it be so." Bagdasares sketched the sun-circle over his heart.

Thrax came up to Maniakes and said, "Your pardon, your Majesty, but shall we sail?" Maniakes nodded. Thrax's trumpeter relayed the call to the fleet. Lines were cast off; oars churned the sea. The ships left the harbor of Gavdos and swung north against Videssos the city.

✦ IV

"The city! The city!" The lookout in the crow's nest cried. He was a Kalavrian lad and, so far as Maniakes knew, had never before set eyes on the imperial capital. But when any Videssian spoke of *the* city, no one could doubt what he meant.

Within a few minutes, Maniakes, too, made out the sparkle of the sun off the gilded globes topping the hundreds of temples dedicated to Phos in Videssos the city. Kourikos and Triphylles sighed like lovers returning to their beloved. "Home at last," Triphylles said, as if he had spent the time since he left the capital among the wild Khamorth of the Pardrayan plain rather than merely in the Empire's outlying provinces.

Then the lookout shouted, "Ship ho!" Fast as lightning, the cry ran through Maniakes' fleet. Thrax's trumpeter began blowing like a man possessed, relaying the drungarios' commands to the rest of the captains. Most of the dromons from the Key moved out to the flanks; a few of the larger, stouter vessels stayed in the center with the ships that had come from Kalavria, stiffening that force against the onslaught fast approaching.

Maniakes had picked the captains whose galleys would go into battle close by his. He had done his best to make sure they were loyal to him. But he did not know the men from the Key as he did those who had been in the rebellion from the beginning. If any of those captains turned on him, the sea fight could be lost all at once.

Or, of course, it could be lost in more conventional fashion.

The dromons ahead had already stowed their masts. They were ready to fight. Maniakes' captains did not wait for orders from Thrax to prepare their own vessels.

"Erinakios was ready for war, too, or so he seemed, at any rate, but he and his fleet went over to me," Maniakes said hopefully.

Thrax answered, "True, your Majesty, but if those bearing down on us are about to abandon Genesios, they're running a bluff that puts Erinakios' to shame."

"We'll go straight through them and make for the harbor of Kontoskalion," Maniakes said. "Once we get armed men inside the city, Genesios will have to flee or fall into our hands." He peered east, out past the capital's great double land wall, and clapped his hands with delight at the tents and pavilions that sprouted on the grass there like mushrooms. "Rhegorios has come, by the good god! He'll keep Genesios' soldiers at play while we overwhelm the tyrant's fleet."

"If we overwhelm the tyrant's fleet," Thrax said, imperfectly optimistic. His eyes scanned the sea from horizon to horizon. "They have a lot of ships, and I see no sign of—"

Before he could finish his sentence, a dromon bearing down on the *Renewal* let fly with its catapult. The dart, half as long as a man, hissed between Thrax and Maniakes and fell with a splash into the sea. The crew that served the dart-thrower loaded another missile into it and began winching back its flexion arms to shoot again.

"So much for the notion of their giving up without a fight," Maniakes said.

Thrax did not dignify that with a reply. He said, "Your pardon, your Majesty, but I have to fight this ship now," and ran back to the stern. There the men at the steering oars and the oarmaster could most clearly hear him as he shouted the commands that would keep the *Renewal* fighting—or send her to the bottom or see her smashed to kindling.

Maniakes had never given much thought to sea battles. When he had campaigned in the westlands, ships had sometimes brought supplies and reinforcements to Videssian ports, whence they had come to his army far faster than if they had made the whole journey by land. Kalavria kept up its fleet against pirates from out of the north, but that fleet hadn't been severely tested since he came to the island—and, in any case, he hadn't been aboard any of its vessels when they did see action.

The fight was, in its own way, an awe-inspiring spectacle. At first, it struck him as cleaner than a land battle. Catapults aboard the larger dromons hurled their great darts. Archers shot again and again whenever opposing vessels drew within range. All the same, the endless chorus of screams and groans that went with a battle of cavalry and infantry was missing here. Men shouted, aye, but in excitement and fear, not torment.

After a while, Maniakes realized that a sea battle was not man against man, as it was on land: here ship against ship was what counted most. He cried out in exultation as one of his galleys rammed a vessel whose crew was shouting for Genesios, then backed oars to let foaming water pour into the hole the dromon's bronze-shod beak had torn.

Men screamed then. Some were thrown into the sea, where they bobbed and began to sink—not all of them, nor even most, could swim. Some of the rowers seized oars and leapt off the stricken galley. Others fought sailors and officers for space aboard the ship's boat. That struck Maniakes as a more savage struggle than the larger battle of which it was a part.

One of Genesios' ships flung from its catapult not a dart but a large pot from which smoke trailed as it flew through the air. It crashed down onto the deck of a galley. Burning oil and pitch and sulfur started a fire on the planking that could not be put out. With cries of despair, men leapt into the sea: drowning was better than burning. Thick black smoke rose from the crackling flames that consumed the dromon.

A firepot from another of Genesios' ships flew wide of a vessel loyal to Maniakes. He cheered out loud when he saw the miss. But the firepot broke as it smacked into the sea and spread a coating of flame over the water. It clung to men floundering in the ocean, so they burned and drowned at the same time.

Few of Maniakes' ships from Kalavria could throw fire in that terrifying fashion: provincial fleets were seldom entrusted with the burning mixture, lest it fall into the hands of foreign foes. But the galleys from the Key answered Genesios' ships firepot for firepot, horror for horror.

"Every ship that burns is one more we won't have when we need them against Makuran or even Kubrat," Maniakes groaned.

Beside him, Kourikos said, "If too many of *our* ships burn, we shall not be the ones who worry about Makuran—or even

Kubrat." The logothete of the treasury looked as if he would rather have been anywhere else than on the deck of a galley in the middle of a sea fight, but, having no choice in the matter, he was doing his best to keep up a bold front despite qualms. Maniakes admired him for that.

The pitching deck of a dromon was not Maniakes' familiar haunt, either. He peered this way and that, trying to figure out which side was winning. In a land battle, but for blowing dust, it would have been relatively easy, even for a blind man: the changing cries of friend and foe told who advanced, who gave ground.

Here no dust intervened, but the line of battle extended much farther to either side than it would have on land, and the warships became so intermingled that Maniakes could not tell who was crying out in triumph, who shrieking in terror as his vessel was holed.

Instead of up and down the battle line, then, Maniakes looked ahead toward Videssos the city. The temples and hills and mansions seemed closer than they had when he'd looked before. With that in mind, he did glance at the line once more. As best he could tell, his fleet was moving forward with the *Renewal*.

He went back to the stern with Thrax. "We drive them," he said. "Does that mean we're winning?"

"We're not losing, at any rate," Thrax answered abstractedly. His eyes swung every which way. "Two points to port!" he called to the steersmen, and the dromon swung leftward, toward one of Genesios' galleys. The archers aboard it sent a volley that hit a couple of the *Renewal*'s oarsmen. That fouled the rowers' stroke, slowed the *Renewal*, and let the smaller enemy vessel escape ramming.

Not far away, a dromon crewed by men shouting for Genesios rammed one of Maniakes' ships. When it tried to pull free, though, it stuck fast. Sailors and rowers from Maniakes' galley, armed with knives, belaying pins, and every other sort of makeshift weapon, scrambled onto Genesios' ship and began battling the crew for a platform that would stay afloat. Before Maniakes could see how the fight turned out, other warships surged between it and the *Renewal*.

"There!" Thrax yelled, right in Maniakes' ear, loud and unexpectedly enough to make him jump. The captain pointed to port. "Those are our ships, your Majesty, a whole good-sized flotilla of them. They've broken free, and it looks like they're making for the harbor in the palace quarter."

Maniakes' gaze followed Thrax's outthrust finger. Sure enough, a score of dromons had outflanked their foes and were streaking toward the city, their oars churning the ocean to creamy foam as the oarmasters demanded—and got—the best from their rowers. Faint across the wide stretch of water, the crews' cheers floated back to the *Renewal.*

"Attack!" Thrax shouted. "All along the line, everything we have." The trumpeter blared the command to those ships near enough to hear it. Maniakes clapped his hands in excitement as other dromons' hornplayers relayed the order to more of his vessels.

And then, very suddenly, what had been a hard-fought struggle became a rout. Maybe that was because Genesios' captains saw their position turned and realized they could not keep Maniakes' fleet from reaching the harbors. Maybe, too, those captains saw in the determination of Maniakes' attack a warning of what might happen to them if they kept resisting and lost anyhow. And maybe, as some of them loudly proclaimed once the fight was through, they found themselves unable to stomach serving Genesios any longer. That impressed Maniakes until he remembered how long those captains *had* served his rival.

Explanations came later. Out there on the ocean south of Videssos the city, what he knew was that some enemy galleys were raising all their oars high out of the water in token of surrender. Others turned their sterns to his fleet and fled, some back toward the city, others toward more distant coastal towns or out to the open sea. Still others, stubborn or loyal, fought on, but more and more of them were overwhelmed as Maniakes' captains concentrated several dromons against each one.

"Phos be praised," Triphylles exclaimed. "Soon I'll be able to enjoy octopus in hot vinegar as it should be prepared." Maniakes had other reasons to be pleased at the victory, but he was willing to let the noble find his own.

"On to the harbor of Kontoskalion," he cried. "We'll enter the city and rout Genesios from whatever hole he hides in."

Beside him, Alvinos Bagdasares murmured what might have been a prayer or a spell or a little of both. The Vaspurakaner mage who sometimes used a Videssian name sketched the sun-circle over his heart. A prayer, then. Maniakes whispered Phos' creed, too. He knew Bagdasares was also worrying about Genesios' ferocious mage. They weren't in Opsikion any more, or on the Key. They were coming to Videssos the city, where Genesios' wizard would be almost as close to Maniakes as the mage who protected him.

The harbor swiftly drew nearer. People stared out toward the approaching dromons, pointing and exclaiming. Maniakes wished he knew what they were saying. If they were cursing him as a usurper surely bound for Skotos' ice, he was going to have trouble. Fighting his way through the streets of the capital against an angry city mob was the last thing he wanted.

Closer and closer the *Renewal* came. Maniakes hurried to the bow of the galley and craned his neck toward the docks and the people on them. He scowled in frustration; all he could hear at first was a confused babbling with no distinct words. Then someone unmistakably yelled, "Maniakes Avtokrator!"

Maniakes waved to the crowd to show them who he was. Some of the men and women waved back, as they might have for any incoming sailor. But others got the idea. A great cheer with his name in it rose from the people. He felt he had gulped half a jar of wine all at once.

Along with his name, though, people were also shouting that of Genesios. He wondered why that didn't touch off curses and fights and stabbings between the backers of the Avtokrator in the city and those who favored the man just entering it. All at once, though, a clear shouted sentence pierced the unintelligible racket: "Genesios Avtokrator is trying to flee the city!"

"Phos," Maniakes whispered. Now triumph was a brew more heady than any squeezed from the grape. He had known a moment even close to this only once before, when his forces and his father's had helped Sharbaraz beat Smerdis and take back the throne of the King of Kings of Makuran. But even that did not compare, not truly. Then he had been fighting for someone else's benefit. Now the gain, could he but seize that which so nearly lay in his hands, would belong to him alone.

"Don't let him get away," he called to the shore. "Five hundred goldpieces to the man who brings him to me, alive or dead."

That stirred up the crowd round the docks. Some of them cheered what looked like the fall of a hated ruler. Others, more pragmatic or perhaps just greedier, pushed away to start

Emperor-hunting. Maniakes nodded in satisfaction. The thinner the press of people at the shore, the more easily he could disembark his men and take control of the city.

"Back oars!" the oarmaster cried. The *Renewal* slowed, sliding to a stop alongside an outthrust dock. Sailors sprang up and roped the dromon fast. When the gangplank went out from ship to land, Maniakes rushed toward it, wanting to be first ashore but for those sailors. Other men, however, held him back. One of them said, "You wait, your Majesty. Let us make sure it's safe up there."

Brandishing knives and bludgeons, a dozen sailors swarmed up the gangplank. "Make way for Maniakes Avtokrator, curse you!" they shouted. The crowd of gawkers fell back before them, though some in that crowd were as well armed as they.

Only after the sailors had cleared some open space on the tar-smeared timbers of the pier did they wave for Maniakes to follow them. When he stepped off the gangplank, he drew his sword and said, "I shall not sheath this blade until Genesios the tyrant is captured!"

As he had hoped, that drew loud cheers from the crowd. Several men waved weapons of their own. That took a certain amount of courage, or at least bravado: the penalty for using a sword in a street brawl in Videssos the city was amputation of the thumbs.

Kourikos and Triphylles came across the gangplank after Maniakes. Triphylles got down on his knees, not to prostrate himself before the Avtokrator but fervently to kiss the timbers on which he stood, tar and white streaks of sea gull droppings deterring him not a bit. "Phos be praised, I'm home at last!" he cried, which in its manifest sincerity drew a cheer almost as loud as the one Maniakes had got.

Maniakes pointed to a nearby man who looked reasonably bright and asked, "How long have the soldiers under my cousin Rhegorios been outside the city?"

"Since day before yesterday, lord, uh, your Majesty," the fellow answered, adding, "The guards at the wall haven't attacked 'em, but they've held 'em off and not let 'em in."

"They will now," Maniakes declared. *They'd better,* he thought, *or I'm still in trouble here.* "Please stand aside, my friends, and let me come take my rightful place in the city."

The throne wasn't exactly his rightful place. He had no blood claim to it. He did have, though, a great many armed men who were of the opinion he belonged on it. He also had as his foe Genesios, which in and of itself went a long way toward cementing his claim.

More ships were tying up behind the *Renewal* and at the quays nearby. Sailors swarmed ashore. A cry went up: "Where now, lord?"

"To the palaces," Maniakes answered. "Once we take them, to the High Temple, to give thanks to Phos for letting this day come to pass." Getting the ecumenical patriarch's blessing would start him off on the right foot. If he didn't get the patriarch's blessing, he told himself, he would soon get a new ecumenical patriarch.

Some of the sailors now on the docks bore the shields and swords dromons carried so their men could repel boarders. They pushed the civilians back, shouting "Way! Make way for the Avtokrator!"

"I wish I had a horse," Maniakes said as they made their way up into the twisting maze of little streets north of the harbor of Kontoskalion. A cavalry officer, he didn't feel as if he could see enough from ground level.

"We'll get you one, by Phos," his escorts said. The first mounted man they came upon, they unceremoniously dragged from the saddle. Had the fellow said a word of protest, had he raised a hand to defend himself, they would have done worse than that.

Maniakes hadn't wanted to acquire a mount in such fashion, but didn't see how he could check his men, either—he wanted them enthusiastic on his behalf. To the unhorsed rider, he said, "Come to the palaces after I've driven Genesios from the throne for good. You'll have your beast back, and gold for my use of him."

"Phos bless you then, your Majesty!" the man cried, and people in the street took up the call. That eased Maniakes' mind, too; having the fickle city populace on his side while he seized power could only help him.

From his seat atop the newly acquired horse—a sedate and elderly mare with a very comfortable gait, provided you weren't in any hurry to get where you were going—he could see over the heads of his men and the swarms of locals in the streets. That helped him less than it would have on the battlefield, for the streets themselves twisted too much to let him see far.

He worried about that. His sailors could easily overpower any civilians who might try to stand against them, but if the Imperial Guards or any other troops in the city decided Genesios was worth fighting for, his men would be up against more than they could handle. They wore no armor, they carried only a few spears and bows, and they had no idea how to fight save as individuals. Disciplined soldiers would have massacred them.

But no soldiers appeared to try to bar his way. "We'll go north, toward Middle Street," he called to his men. The main east-west highway of Videssos the city would give him a long straight stretch, on which he could take his bearings.

Finding and then keeping to north in that warren wasn't as easy as when sailing by sun and stars. Many buildings were tall enough to hide the sun from sight. Sometimes balconies almost met overhead above the streets. That was supposed to be against the law, but Genesios had ignored laws far more important, so Maniakes had no reason to think he would have paid any attention to this one.

He had just reached Middle Street and was started down it toward the plaza of Palamas and the palace quarter beyond when a rumor coming from farther east overtook him from behind. "The gates are opening," people said. "No—the gates are open."

"We have him," Maniakes said to nobody in particular. If his own soldiers were in the city, nothing Genesios could do would stop it from falling. And Genesios did not seem able to do much in any case. His supporters had abandoned him outside the capital, and now the same looked to be happening within.

The only ways Maniakes could see losing now were a lone assassin . . . and Genesios' wizard. Against an assassin, he could take precautions. Against the wizard—Bagdasares was tramping along beside him. He didn't know if Bagdasares would be good enough, but he was the best available.

He rode past the red granite pile of the government offices. He had always thought the building squat and ugly when he had been in the capital before. Then his opinions on architecture had mattered to no one but himself. Now, if he wanted, he could change the way Videssos the city would look for generations yet to come.

He laughed at himself. He had more urgent things to worry about.

People stood under the covered colonnades that ran along both sides of Middle Street. Some cheered, some stared, some went about their business. A few people gaped from atop the colonnade, too. He thought that merely a curiosity until he realized it also made an ideal hiding place for a killer. Past clearing everyone off, which would have made him look foolish, he didn't know what he could do about it

He reached the plaza of Palamas unassassinated and stared across the broad stretch of cobbles to the lawns and splendid buildings of the palace quarter beyond. The plaza was crowded with people chaffering with merchants at stalls or booths or wagons or hand-held trays, buying everything from cloth to jewels to octopus tentacles; Maniakes glanced over at Triphylles. Other folk, even on a day when the crown of the Empire of Videssos changed hands, were out for a stroll, either to take the air or simply to see and be seen.

The vast bulk of the Amphitheater marked the southern boundary of the plaza of Palamas. To the west, just at the edge of the palace quarter, stood the Milestone, the granite obelisk from which all distances in the Empire were measured. Heads in great number were affixed to it, not just at the base as was usual, but for some distance up toward its pointed top. Placards, too distant to read across the square, set forth the alleged crimes of each victim. Unless Maniakes missed his guess, most of those boiled down to nothing more than falling foul of Genesios.

Beside the Milestone waited a small, bald, gray-bearded man in a robe of shimmering blue samite. Even with that fancy robe, Maniakes would have paid him no special attention had he not been surrounded by several soldiers in chainmail. They were very nearly the first soldiers not his own he had seen in the imperial capital.

He turned to Kourikos. "Who is that fellow there?" he asked, pointing.

The logothete of the treasury squinted. "That is the honor guard of the eparch of the city, your Majesty, unless I am mistaken, but I do not recognize the man whose honor they find themselves guarding."

"Whoever he is, he thinks he's important," Maniakes said. "Let's go over there and find out if he's right."

Getting across the plaza of Palamas wasn't easy, not even with the sailors from the fleet doing their best to clear the crowds out of the way. Some Videssians were intent on getting a close look at the man who was in the process of becoming their new Avtokrator, others on finishing the business for which they had come to the plaza in the first place. No one wanted to get out of the way. At last, the sailors went from shoving and shouting to hitting people with belaying pins. That touched off a few fights, but did eventually persuade the crowd to move back and make way.

The little bald man stared anxiously as Maniakes approached. "Are y-you the man I believe you to be?" he asked, stammering a little.

"That depends," Maniakes said. "But if you believe I'm Maniakes son of Maniakes, then you're right. And who, may I ask, are *you*, eminent sir?" The fancy robe and the armed retinue made the title a sure bet.

He had to wait for his answer, the little man promptly prostrated himself on the cobbles of the square. The delay made Maniakes notice the stench from the grisly collection of heads Genesios had on display at the Milestone. Some had been packed in salt like poor Hosios to keep them recognizable longer, but they still smelled like a butcher's shop much too long forgotten by its proprietor.

At last, the little man arose and said, "Your Majesty, I am Doulikhios. I have the honor to be eparch of the city, at least until you make a different appointment to that position, as is of course your privilege."

"Your Majesty, when my comrades and I left the city, the eparch was a certain Goulaion," Kourikos said.

Doulikhios pointed to the Milestone. "There is Goulaion's head. He was accused of conspiring against the Avtokrator, uh, the tyrant Genesios. And there below it is the head of Goulaion's successor Evdokimos. And there, right at the base of the column, is the head of Evdokimos' successor Levkates. Evdokimos was put to the sword for the same reason as Goulaion; I do not know how Levkates ended up displeasing Genesios, but he did."

No wonder the poor sod is nervous, Maniakes thought. The job he was holding did not seem one where the incumbent got much chance to learn from experience. "Well, eminent Doulikhios, in your place I do believe I'd have fled to a monastery," he said.

"I tried that," the eparch of the city answered bleakly. "Genesios dragged me out and forced me into this blue robe rather than the other."

Maniakes did not care to hear that; if Genesios had gone into a monastery after Doulikhios, he might have gone into a convent after Niphone. He forced himself not to think about that. "Am I to assume, eminent Doulikhios, that even though you are Genesios' appointee, you do not favor him as Avtokrator?"

At the question, Doulikhios drew himself up with the first pride he had shown. "Your Majesty, the mistake Goulaion made, and Evdokimos, and maybe Levkates, too, for all I know, was in plotting against Genesios *and getting caught*. Me, I plotted with Abasgios, the second-in-command of the Imperial Guards—and instead of reinforcing the troops on the land wall against your men out there, they moved on the tyrant this morning."

"You may just stay on as eparch of the city after all," Maniakes exclaimed.

"We botched it," Doulikhios said "Genesios was to have been slain, but he killed one of our men, wounded the other, and fled to the imperial harbor. I fear he got away in some small boat or another."

"We'll catch him, or at least I hope we will," Maniakes said. "We've had ships heading that way since they broke free of the sea battle."

"May it be so," Doulikhios said fervently.

Kourikos held up a hand. "A moment, if I may. Eminent Doulikhios—" He sounded so dubious about the title, it might have been an insult. "—I have spent my entire adult life among the nobility here at the capital, and I must confess I do not recall your being numbered among us. May I ask from what station Genesios elevated you to the eparchate?"

"Well, if you must know, eminent sir, I ran a fish market and pleased his I hope former Majesty with my wares," Doulikhios answered.

"Your Majesty!" Kourikos cried to Maniakes. "Surely you will not allow such a high office to be filled, surely you will not allow the ranks of the nobility to be polluted, by this, this *fishseller*." Spittle flew from his lips with the last word.

"If he can do the job, I don't see why not," Maniakes said. Kourikos goggled. Maniakes went on, "He's done me one great service already and deserves a reward for that. Anyhow, I have no time to worry about niceties of rank right now." He turned back to Doulikhios, leaving his prospective father-in-law gaping in dismay. "Tell me at once, eminent sir: do you know what's become of Genesios' chief mage? Can we find him at the Sorcerers' Collegium?" He heard the hot eagerness in his own voice. Genesios had put far too many heads up on the Milestone, but the wizard's was one that deserved to be there.

"I know the man you mean, your Majesty, but no, he's never had anything to do with the Sorcerers' Collegium," Doulikhios answered. "He's never had much to do with me, either, for which I give thanks to the lord with the great and good mind." He sketched the sun-circle above his heart, then shuddered. "He frightens me, and I'll not deny it. He's a tall man, and thin as a lath, and by the look of him he was born before your great-grandfather, but they say he's strong as a soldier in first flush of youth."

"Sounds like a hard man to miss, at any rate," Maniakes said. "We'll know him when we catch him, that's certain."

"Eminent sir—" When Kourikos spoke to Doulikhios now, he had scrubbed the scorn from his voice. That surprised Maniakes until the logothete of the treasury went on, "Have you any news of the fate of my wife and daughter, who took refuge in the convent of the holy Phostina? This affects more than me alone, for Niphone is affianced to his Majesty here."

"I don't know what to tell you, eminent sir," Doulikhios said slowly. "I never heard Genesios mention that name, or any like it, but that doesn't necessarily signify. And who knows what crazy orders he might have given since we tried to kill him but didn't do it, or who might have listened to them?"

"Where is this convent?" Maniakes demanded of Kourikos.

"In the northwestern corner of the city, north of the Makuraner district."

"We'll send men there," Maniakes said. He told off a couple of dozen sailors and, to guide them, found a local who knew where the convent was. That done, he went on, "As for the rest of us, we'll secure the palace quarter. Eminent Doulikhios, you come with us. If any of the soldiers there decide they're still on

Genesios' side, maybe you can explain he's fled. The fewer we have to fight, the better."

"As you say, your Majesty." Doulikhios did not prostrate himself again, but he bowed almost double.

As Maniakes was about to enter the palace quarter, unrest broke out on the eastern side of the plaza of Palamas, the side that fronted on the rest of Videssos the city. He looked back over his shoulder. Horsemen in bright chainmail were trying to force their way through the crowd that had re-formed after Maniakes made his way to Doulikhios.

At the head of those horsemen rode someone he recognized, even across the broad stretch of the plaza. From atop his own horse, he waved vigorously. "Rhegorios!" he shouted. "Cousin! To me!"

He didn't know whether Rhegorios heard him through the rack or spied him waving, but his cousin waved in return and booted his horse ahead. Cheering, the men he led followed. The folk of the capital did make way for them: It was that or be trampled.

Maniakes rode back into the crowd. Both men were grinning from ear to ear when they finally met. Rhegorios sheathed the sword he carried. "Cousin!" he cried, and then, "Your Majesty!" He thrust out the hand that had held the blade. Maniakes clasped it.

"Genesios' men are giving up and coming over to us wherever we find them," he said. "The only true fight they showed for him was on the sea south of the city. But even there, once we began to turn their position, they folded up. Videssos the city is ours."

"That it is, by the good god," Rhegorios said. "The men on the walls held us out till you came up with your fleet, though they didn't fight much doing it." He looked awed. "You don't have to do much fighting when you hold those walls and towers and gates. They'd stand off the whole world, so long as the soldiers atop them keep breathing. The soldiers needn't do much more than that, let me tell you."

"I'm glad you and your riders are here," Maniakes said. "If we find holdouts anywhere, they'll be in the palace quarter, and you can do a better job of overawing them than a ragtag and bobtail of sailors."

Rhegorios' grin stretched wider yet. "Do you know what, cousin of mine? When your brothers finally find out what we've been doing, they'll want to piss themselves out of sheer jealousy."

"I just hope they're alive and well," Maniakes answered. "That's first. Second is finding them enough important things to do—and rank to give them the power to do those things—to take away the sting. The state the Empire is in these days, that should be easy."

"Too true." By the way Rhegorios sat slightly straighter in the saddle and did his best to look capable and impressive, he was also looking for both rank and duties. That pleased Maniakes rather than alarming him. As he had said, the Empire had more than enough troubles to share out among all those who were trying to set them right.

"Come on," Maniakes said. "Let's take the palaces. I was about to do that when you rode up here. The company is better now." He turned back to his sailors. "Onward!" The men cheered. Some of them bayed like hungry wolves. Maniakes went on, "I don't mind you coming away with a trinket or three. The good god knows you've earned that. But I will not stand still for murder. You try killing to get your loot and your head goes up on the Milestone beside Genesios.'"

He did not add, *I mean what I say.* The men already knew as much—or if they didn't, they would soon find out.

The palace quarter was a world altogether different from the hustle and bustle of the plaza of Palamas. The generality of city folk were not allowed to disturb the calm quiet of those lanes set amid lawns and gardens and magnificent buildings. Only a few bureaucrats and beardless eunuchs strolled on them when Maniakes' forces brought the outside world crashing in. The bureaucrats fled with cries of horror. So did most of the eunuchs.

One of them, though, came up to the party of horsemen who led the advance. In a grave voice somewhere halfway between contralto and tenor, he asked, "Who among you is Maniakes son of Maniakes?" When Maniakes walked his mare up a couple of paces, the eunuch prostrated himself before him. Forehead still pressed to the cobbles, he said, "On behalf of all the palace servitors, your Majesty, I welcome you to this your new home. May your years be many and your line never fail."

He had probably said the same thing, maybe in the same words, to Genesios after Likinios and his sons met the headsman.

Maniakes did not hold that against him; the weak were well advised to keep clear of the quarrels of those more powerful than they. He said, "Thank you, esteemed sir." Eunuchs had their own honorifics, from which he chose the highest. "Rise, please, and give me your name."

"I am called Kameas, your Majesty, and have the honor to be vestiarios at the imperial residence." Kameas deserved that high honorific, then; he headed all the Avtokrator's servants. If the Avtokrator was weak, the vestiarios might become the most important man in the Empire. Maniakes did not intend to let that happen.

He said, "When Genesios fled the palaces, did he take with him whatever family he has?"

"No, your Majesty," Kameas answered gravely. "His wife and his young son and daughter remain in the imperial residence, awaiting your pleasure." He licked his lips. If Maniakes had a taste for blood, he would learn of it right now.

"I don't want to see them," Maniakes said. "If the woman and girl go into a convent and the boy to a monastery, that will satisfy me. Take them that message from me. But tell them also that if they ever try to come out or meddle in politics, their heads will answer for it. I do not want them to confuse mercy for weakness—tell them that, too."

"I shall carry your words exactly as you have spoken them." After a moment, Kameas added, "It will be good to have in the palaces once more an Avtokrator who understands the meaning of the word mercy." With a bow, he set off for the imperial residence.

Maniakes went on more slowly. He rode past the Hall of the Nineteen Couches, where fancy banquets were held. The building's great bronze doors stood open, as if inviting him in. He was hardly more eager to dine there than to see Genesios' family: the couches were for reclining while one ate, an antique style of feasting that had passed away everywhere save the palace quarter. He felt sure he would make a hash of it the first time he tried it.

He turned aside from the straight road to the imperial residence so he could examine the Grand Courtroom. It, too, had portals of bronze, these ones worked with reliefs so perfectly realistic they almost seemed to move. Large wings swept out to either side from the courtroom itself. Bureaucrats peered out from windows in those wings. As long as Maniakes' men did not harm them in this moment of transition, the change of rulers would affect them but little: if they were massacred, who would administer the Empire in their stead?

To one of them, Maniakes called, "What's behind that grove of trees there, off to the southwest?"

"That's a chapel to Phos, sir," the man answered, not realizing he was speaking to his sovereign. "It's been there many years, but seldom used of late: most Emperors have preferred to worship at the High Temple instead."

"I can understand that," Maniakes answered. He had trouble seeing how any man, given a choice, would worship anywhere save at the High Temple.

He stayed there a while chatting with the functionary, both to learn more about the buildings of the palace quarter and to give Kameas a chance to get Genesios' family out of the imperial residence without his officially having to notice them. When shouts and cries came from the west, he feared Genesios' wife and children were raising such a fuss that he would have to let them come to his attention.

But these were yells of joy and excitement, all in men's deep voices. Before long, he caught one rising above the rest: "We've got him!"

He dug his knees into the sides of the mare he was riding. The horse snorted indignantly at such treatment: how dare a rider try to rouse her to speed? Maniakes dared, and forced her into a reluctant trot. "You've got whom?" he called as his men streamed after him. "Have you laid hold of Genesios?"

When someone answered, "Aye, by Phos," his heart leapt within him; Genesios would not get away to stir up yet another round of civil war. His men loosed a torrent of cheers that soon formed words of their own: "Thou conquerest, Maniakes Avtokrator!"

Sailors came capering toward him from the direction of the harbor for the palace quarter. The imperial residence also lay in that direction; again he hoped Kameas had got Genesios' wife and children away; he wanted to spare them this. But whether they were off to convent and monastery or not, he gave the order he had to give: "Fetch Genesios here before me at once."

The sailors peeled back toward the anchorage, shouting his words ahead of them. He rode on after the men. Before long, they came in his direction again, shoving along a man whose hands were tied behind his back.

Maniakes recognized Genesios at once. The engraver at the imperial mint had accurately portrayed the man's features: wide forehead, narrow chin, a short thin fringe of beard, long straight nose. Now, though, Genesios did not wear the crown and rich robes that marked an Avtokrator of the Videssians. He was bare-headed—and, Maniakes noted with a touch of malice, going bald—and wore a plain linen tunic that came down to his knees, garb a fisherman might don before going out to work his nets.

Blood soaked the tunic now; Genesios must have fought before he was captured. He had a deep gash in his left arm and a cut across his forehead. More blood dripped from the slate on which he stood. A trail of it led back toward the harbor. Genesios, Maniakes thought, had left a trail of blood through the Empire ever since he murdered his way into the red boots.

He looked up at Maniakes. His face showed pain but not much fear; Maniakes remembered he had been a combat soldier. "All right, you have me," he said. His voice was deep, with the accent of a peasant from the westlands. He didn't ask what Maniakes was going to do with him—he had to have figured that out for himself.

"Aye, I have you," Maniakes said. "How could you have let Videssos come to such a pass?" He hadn't intended to ask that; it came out almost as a cry of pain.

Murky defiance lit in Genesios' eyes. "You're on top now, and you think you're such a great lord," he said, "but will you do any better?"

"By Phos, I hope so," Maniakes exclaimed. He looked around to the men who crowded close to see Genesios. He raised the sword he had carried ever since he set foot in Videssos the city. Now that the moment was come, though, he gulped. He had done plenty of fighting, but he had never been an executioner before. "Kneel," he told Genesios. When Genesios wouldn't, he spoke to the men who had frogmarched the defeated Avtokrator through the palace quarter: "Make him kneel."

They forced Genesios to his knees. He cursed them and Maniakes and Videssos all together, a torrent of vileness that had men making the sun-sign to turn aside words of evil omen. Maniakes clasped his blade two-handed, brought it up, and swung it with all his strength.

It bit into Genesios' neck with a meaty *chunnk!* His curses cut off in midword. Blood spurted, impossibly red in the bright sun. His body convulsed; his bowels and bladder let go. Maniakes swung the sword again, to sever his head completely.

"Take it through the city," he told his cheering followers. "Let everyone see Genesios is dead. Then it will go up on the Milestone." The cheers grew louder, fiercer. He held up a hand. "But that will be the end of it. We won't stop his slaughter to start our own."

"What shall we do with the body, your Majesty?" someone asked. It was still twitching feebly.

"Burn it," Maniakes answered, which prompted fresh cheers. He hadn't intended that; he had only wanted to get rid of a piece of carrion. But, now that it was done, he wouldn't turn aside the acclaim, either.

He rode on toward the imperial residence. Like the chapel, it was screened by trees: cherries here. They would be beautiful in springtime when they blossomed; the rest of the year, they were just there. The residence itself was as unprepossessing a structure as any in the palace quarter. Unlike most of the other buildings, it looked like a place where a man might actually live rather than be put on display.

Some of the soldiers who guarded the imperial residence were Videssians, others big blond Halogai who made Maniakes think of Rotrude. Kameas must have already come and gone, for as soon as Maniakes finished winding his way down the path through the cherry grove, all the guardsmen shouted, "Thou conquerest, Maniakes Avtokrator!" They went to their knees and then their bellies, honoring him with a full proskynesis.

"Get up, get up," he said, not wanting to make them resent him—after all, they would be protecting him now. "You served Genesios better than he deserved. I hope you'll serve me bravely, too."

"Thou conquerest!" the guards cried again, which he took for assent.

He swung down off his horse. He wanted to see what the imperial residence looked like on the inside. *I'll be living here the rest of my days,* he thought, *whether those be long or short.* From the shade of the doorway, pale smooth eunuch faces stared out at him. Like the guards, the servitors had to be wondering what sort of new master they would have.

Maniakes had just set his foot on the low, broad marble stairs that led up to the entrance when a breathless voice from behind him called, "Your Majesty, come quick! There's fighting in the northwest!"

He spun round to face the panting messengers. "Can't my officers handle it?" he snapped. "If they can't, what do I have them for?" Then a possible answer occurred to him, and urgency replaced anger in his voice: "Is it at the convent dedicated to the holy Phostina?"

"Aye, your Majesty," the messenger said. "A company of soldiers loyal to Genesios was trying to force their way in. The nuns had shut up the convent against them. They were doing their best to smash down the door when your men came up, but you didn't send enough to check them. They may be inside by now, and the good god only knows what outrages they'll work!"

Kourikos groaned. Maybe only Phos knew what outrages Genesios' men might commit, but he could imagine. "My daughter!" he cried piteously, and then, a moment slower than he should have, "My wife!"

Maniakes sprang back onto the mare. "I'm on my way!" he said. "Rhegorios, you and all your horses with me." That would leave the palace quarter to the doubtful mercy of the sailors, but it couldn't be helped. Horsemen would reach the convent in half the time folk on foot required.

The mare didn't want to trot, let alone gallop. Maniakes was in no mood to heed an animal's whims. Lacking spurs, he whacked it with the flat of the blade he had used to take Genesios' head. Once her attention was gained, the mare proved to have a fair turn of speed after all.

From behind, Kourikos called, "Wait!"

But Maniakes would not wait. "Gangway!" he shouted as he and his men neared the plaza of Palamas. For a moment after that, he glimpsed a sea of startled faces, all staring toward him. Then, with cries of alarm, people scattered every which way, some of them trampling others to keep the onrushing horses from trampling them.

He didn't think his mount ran over anyone. Horses didn't care to step on the soft, wiggling things people became when they fell to the ground. But from the screams that rose in back of him, some of the animals of his riders had been imperfectly careful about where they set their feet.

He had thundered out onto Middle Street before he realized he didn't know exactly where in the northwestern quadrant of the city the convent dedicated to the holy Phostina lay. He shouted the question back over his shoulder. "I can find it, your Majesty," one of his men said. "I grew up not far from there."

"Come forward, then," Maniakes said, and slowed his mare to let the city man take the lead. The mare snorted indignantly, as if asking him to make up his mind: first he'd called for more speed, so how dared he check her now? The animal complained again when he booted it in the ribs to make it keep up with the horse his guide was riding.

Once they swung north off Middle Street, the journey through the city became a nightmare for Maniakes. The streets were narrow and winding; he couldn't gallop full tilt no matter how much he wanted to. And if a mule-drawn wagon or donkey cart blocked the way, not all his curses or threats would clear the road for him until the driver could find a corner and turn.

At last he heard shouts of alarm and fury ahead that seemed to have nothing to do with the panic his own passage was causing. He muttered a quick prayer to Phos that they meant he was coming to the convent. A moment later, he burst out into the open space of a small square and found his prayer had been granted.

Blood splashed the cobbles of the square. A lot of the sailors he had sent were down, some dead, others thrashing with wounds. Others were down with them, men whose chainmail proclaimed them genuine soldiers. A good many more of them were trying to break into the convent dedicated to the holy Phostina.

They weren't having an easy time of it. Beneath the whitewash, the walls of the convent were solid stone, the windows mere slits too narrow to let a man through. The door was the only vulnerable point—and it didn't seem any too vulnerable, either.

Genesios' men here were all Videssians—they had no axe-wielding Halogai to make short work of the stout timbers. They had found a long, thick board to use as a ram, but, just as Maniakes rode into the square, the nuns poured a large tub of hot water down onto their attackers. The soldiers staggered back from the door, howling with pain.

"Yield or die!" Maniakes shouted at them and at the rest of the guardsmen trying to find other ways into the convent. The soldiers who had followed Genesios to—and past—the end stared in horrified dismay as cavalrymen, some with swords, some with light lances, but most with bows, filled the open space in front of the building.

A couple of Genesios' men stepped away from the convent and toward Maniakes and his followers with weapons still in hand. Bowstrings twanged. The guardsmen fell, screaming and twisting on the cobblestones. That was plenty to give their comrades the idea. Swords clattered as men threw them down. Maniakes waved some of his soldiers forward to take charge of the prisoners. Glumly, they let their hands be tied behind their backs and filed off into captivity.

Maniakes rode closer to the convent wall—but not too close. To the nuns at the second-story window, he called, "I am Maniakes son of Maniakes, now Avtokrator of the Videssians. Genesios the tyrant is dead. May I approach and confer with your abbess without fear of being boiled like a capon in a holiday stew?"

The nuns disappeared from the window without answering. After a couple of minutes, another, older, woman appeared there. "I am Nikaia, abbess of the convent dedicated to the memory of the holy Phostina," she said, and Maniakes believed her at once: her voice held authority any general would have been glad to own. She looked him over from beneath the blue head-scarf that concealed her hair, then went on, "How may I serve you . . . your Majesty?" By the hesitation, she remained imperfectly convinced he was who he claimed to be.

He said, "I am told by the eminent Kourikos, logothete of the treasury, that you have taking refuge within your walls his wife and daughter. As you will probably know, I am betrothed to Niphone. Now that I am returned to Videssos the city, now that the eminent Kourikos has accompanied me here, I would have you tell the noble ladies they are free and safe to come forth into the world once more, should they so desire."

"We have no 'noble ladies' here, only those who serve the lord with the great and good mind," Nikaia answered sternly. "Wait there, if you will." As the nuns had before her, the abbess left the window. She returned in a little while with another nun and pointed out at Maniakes. He heard her ask, "Is that the man?"

Was that Niphone there? Maniakes stared up at the window as the nun stared down at him. She was young; he could see that much. But her head scarf robbed her of much of her individuality, and, he discovered, the picture of his fiancée he had carried in his mind these past six years of exile had faded over time. He remembered Niphone as having a long, rather thin face, with delicate features and large eyes. That could have been she at the window, but he would not have dared take oath on it.

Whoever the woman was, she seemed similarly troubled. She said, "Mistress, I believe that is the younger Maniakes, but—I have trouble being certain."

Her voice was not far from what Maniakes remembered Niphone's sounding like, yet again he could not be sure. He called her name. She waved and nodded. He waited for a great surge of love and affection to pour from his heart and warm him from head to toe. He had been waiting to see her again for six years, after all. The surge didn't quite come, or rather did come but wasn't nearly so large as he had expected. He carried on as if it had been, saying to Nikaia, "Holy abbess, I ask you again: will you release this woman and her mother from the vows they took more to protect themselves from Genesios' evil designs than to resign from the world forever? Not that they are not pious, of course," he added hastily.

Niphone retreated; Nikaia came forward. "I have seen their piety these past months, your Majesty," the abbess said, "and it is far from inconsiderable. But, in any case, I have not the power to release them from vows they took of their own free will. Here in Videssos the city, that power rests only in the hands of the most holy ecumenical patriarch Agathios. If he so orders, and if the women be willing, I shall in obedience let them come forth from my convent. Until that time, I reckon them nuns no different from any others."

Maniakes admired her courage and rectitude, however much of a nuisance he found them. If he tried to disregard the abbess' wishes and take Niphone from the convent dedicated to the holy Phostina without patriarchal leave, he had no doubt boiling water would come rain down on him. He told Nikaia, "I'll see the most holy Agathios, then." To Rhegorios, he said, "Leave a third of your men here, to make sure we have no more problems with diehards—oh, and send a rider back to the eminent Kourikos, so he knows his wife and daughter are safe and well. You and the rest of your men will come with me to the High Temple."

Though both the convent and the High Temple lay in the northern part of Videssos the city, the fastest way to go from one to the other was to drop back down to Middle Street, ride west along it to the avenue that led up to the chief shrine of the Videssian faith, and then travel north along that avenue.

From the outside, the High Temple was massive rather than magnificent; the stout walls of golden stone needed to support the great central dome bore no special ornament. As with most Videssian homes, the treasures were on the inside, hidden from external view. Maniakes called to a priest ascending the low, broad stairs that led up to the entrance: "Holy sir, is the most holy patriarch at his devotions within?"

The priest needed no more than a heartbeat to realize who would approach the High Temple with hundreds of armed men at his back. Bowing, he replied, "No, your Majesty, I believe he is at present in the patriarchal residence nearby." He pointed. The High Temple dwarfed the residence, though anywhere else in the city it would have been reckoned a house of respectable size. A number of cypresses, gnarled and hoary with age, grew around it.

With a word of thanks, Maniakes led his troopers to the patriarchal residence. He dismounted and, Rhegorios at his side, walked up to the entrance and rapped on the door. The priest who answered was not an old man, as he knew Agathios to be, nor decked in the magnificent patriarchal vestments and the sky-blue boots that were as much a prerogative of Videssos' chief prelates as red ones were for the Avtokrator.

As a lot of people had done over the past few hours, the priest asked, "You are his Majesty, the Avtokrator Maniakes?"

Maniakes wondered if he should make a sign and hang it around his neck. He contented himself with saying, "Yes. Here with me is my cousin Rhegorios. And you, holy sir?"

"My name is Skombros, your Majesty," the priest replied. "I have the honor to be synkellos to the most holy Agathios." That meant he was Agathios' secretary, assistant, and, at need, keeper and watchdog for the Avtokrator.

"I am pleased to meet you, holy sir. Take me to the ecumenical patriarch at once."

Bowing, Skombros turned and obeyed. Maniakes followed him, with Rhegorios another pace behind. The patriarchal residence struck Maniakes as pleasant without being splendid; prelates were sworn to poverty, though not all of them took their vows seriously. Oaths aside, a greater display of luxury would not have surprised Maniakes.

Skombros rapped on a closed door. A soft voice answered. The synkellos worked the latch. "The most holy Agathios, ecumenical patriarch of the Videssians, awaits you, your Majesty—and you, eminent sir." He tacked on the last four words for Rhegorios' benefit.

Maniakes went into the chamber, only to be met by Agathios' pointing finger, which the patriarch wielded as if it were a spear. "Will you presume to make alterations in Videssos' pure and holy and orthodox faith?" he thundered, his voice soft no more. His eyes flashed. His long white beard seemed to crackle and stand away from his face, as if lightning had struck nearby. His beaky nose had the curve of a Kubrati scimitar. He was, in short, a most alarmingly holy old man.

He had, however, chosen a question Maniakes could answer without qualm of conscience. "No, most holy sir," he said, and watched Agathios deflate like a punctured pig's bladder.

"Oh, that's very good," the ecumenical patriarch said. His eyes stopped blazing; even his beard seemed to relax. Sounding much more like a grandfather than a righteous, wrathful cleric, he said, "I was concerned because of your Vaspurakaner blood, your Majesty. Heresy on the throne is a dreadful thing."

"You need have no fears on that account," Maniakes answered. He wondered what his father would say upon learning he had opted for unabashed orthodoxy. Something interesting and memorable, he had no doubt. But he was also sure the elder Maniakes would recognize the need.

"That's excellent, excellent." Now Agathios was beaming. His sudden swings put Maniakes in mind of a weathervane—he seemed liable to blow in any direction and to swing from one to another without warning. The patriarch said, "Would you have me crown you now, then, your Majesty?"

"Later today will do nicely. I would ask something else of you first," Maniakes said. Agathios' bushy white eyebrows rose: what could be more important than an imperial coronation? Maniakes explained what the abbess Nikaia had demanded of him.

"This is truly the wish of these women?" the patriarch demanded.

"Most holy sir, would I lie about such a matter, causing a rift with my own prelate before he has even set the crown on my head?"

"If you are wise, you would not," Agathios said, "but who can tell yet whether you are wise? Meaning no disrespect to you, your Majesty—Phos forbid!—we have seen our share and more of stupidity these past half-dozen years."

"And more," Maniakes agreed.

Before he could again ask the ecumenical patriarch to relieve his fiancée and her mother from the vows they had taken at the convent, Agathios called, "Skombros! Fetch me pen, parchment, and sealing wax—at once!"

"Certainly, most holy sir," the synkellos replied from the hall. Hovering near Agathios was part of his job. He soon returned with the articles the patriarch had asked of him.

Agathios inked the pen and wrote rapidly. When he was done, he showed the note to Maniakes. It was the release he had requested, couched in florid ecclesiastical style. Nodding, he returned it to the patriarch. Agathios rolled up the parchment, tied a ribbon around it, and then picked up a lamp. He used the flame from the wick to melt several drops of his special sky-blue sealing wax so they fell onto the parchment and the ribbon. While the wax was still soft, he pressed his signet ring into it. When he lifted the ring, the mark of his monogram remained in the wax. With a flourish, he handed Maniakes the completed document.

"Thank you, most holy sir," Maniakes said. He turned to Rhegorios. "Take this back to the convent dedicated to the holy Phostina, fast as you can ride. Then, if she will, bring Niphone here to me. The most holy Agathios will wed us and then proclaim us Avtokrator and Empress."

"I like that, by the good god," Rhegorios exclaimed, his eyes sparkling. "You'll put on two different crowns the same day."

Maniakes laughed. "True enough." Videssian custom was for a man and woman who joined together to don wreaths called crowns of marriage.

"It must be Phos' will, your Majesty," Agathios said, "to see you revealed as bridegroom and Avtokrator on the same day."

"I pray it proves a good omen," Maniakes said soberly. He slapped Rhegorios on the back. "While you're at it, bring Niphone's mother, the lady Phevronia, as well. And send riders to the palaces, too. Kameas will know where the true imperial crown is; I'd sooner have the most holy patriarch set it on my head than have him use some substitute. The same goes for the Empress' crown. And we'll need to bring the eminent Kourikos here, as well, to watch his daughter wed."

Rhegorios frowned in concentration. "Let me make sure I have all that," he said, and repeated it back. Maniakes listened, then nodded, pleased with his cousin. Independent command seemed to have made Rhegorios more responsible than he had been. He saluted with a clenched fist over his heart, then left the patriarch's chamber at a run. He almost ran over Skombros in the hallway; Maniakes listened to them exchanging apologies. Then Rhegorios' footsteps receded rapidly.

That made Agathios snap his fingers in annoyance at himself. "Here I sit, forgetting my manners! I crave pardon, your Majesty." He raised his voice. "Skombros! Fetch cakes and wine for the Avtokrator." He shook his head. "These should have come before business, not after."

"Most holy sir, ceremony is all very well in its place, but sometimes business has such urgency that it must lead," Maniakes replied. The ecumenical patriarch looked doubtful; Maniakes wondered if here, unwittingly, he had spoken heresy for the first time.

Skombros returned with food and drink on a silver tray. The cakes left Maniakes' fingers so sticky, he had to lick them clean: honey and chopped nuts between layers of thin, flaky pastry. The wine came golden from the jar into the silver cups that stood on the tray. Maniakes was no great connoisseur of such things, but he knew a noble vintage when he tasted one.

When Agathios emptied his cup, Skombros poured it full again—and, a little while later, again, then yet again and once more. The ecumenical patriarch seemed little affected by all he drank, but Maniakes noted how much that was. He wondered if Skombros had wanted him to note it. A synkellos' loyalty was liable to lie as much with the Avtokrator as with the patriarch.

"I shall pray for your success against the troubles besetting us from every side, your Majesty," Agathios said, only slightly slow speech showing the wine he had taken on. "How shall you drive the Makuraners forth from the westlands while the heathen Kubratoi oppress us from the north?"

That was a good question. It was, in fact, the very question Maniakes had been pondering since he'd rebelled against Genesios. "Most holy sir, the one thing I know for certain is that we can't fight them both at once." Given the parlous state to which the Empire had descended, he wasn't altogether sure Videssos could fight either one of its principal foes, but he did not tell that to Agathios. It was not the sort of thought he wanted noised about, and he was not sure how far he could trust either patriarch or synkellos.

"Will you make peace with one so that you may pursue war against the other?" Agathios persisted.

"It could be so." Maniakes held up a hand. "Till now, I've worried more about casting Genesios down from the throne he stole than what I would do once I held the throne myself." That wasn't strictly true, but it gave him an excuse not to go into details about his plans.

Skombros said, "Since you were benefactor to Sharbaraz King of Kings, perhaps he will give over his war against Videssos when he hears you have become Avtokrator. Phos grant it be so, anyhow."

"Perhaps," Maniakes said, though he didn't believe it. "As custom requires, I shall send him an embassy announcing my accession as soon as I can. Then we'll see."

"And against the Kubratoi?" Skombros asked. He was so long used to keeping track of what the patriarch said and did and planned, he automatically assumed he had the same right with the Avtokrator.

"Right now, holy sir, I don't know what I'll do," Maniakes replied, and in that he was completely truthful. "When I have an answer, be sure you will know along with the rest of the Videssos." Skombros bowed his head, recognizing he had just been reminded of his place in the world.

Heard dimly down the hall, the racket outside the patriarchal residence suddenly swelled. Agathios said to Skombros, "Go see if that betokens the arrival of his Majesty's bride or that of her father."

The synkellos returned with Kourikos, and with Kameas as well. The vestiarios was bearing not only the bejeweled dome of the imperial crown but also a pair of red boots and a stout shield on which the soldiers would raise Maniakes, symbolizing their acceptance of him as commander. He could no more rule without their blessing than without the patriarch's.

"We would not want the ceremony celebrated imperfectly," Kameas said with great seriousness. Maniakes nodded. Stories said eunuchs were often fussily precise. Stories said a good many things, though. Here, for once, they did not seem far wrong. Maniakes resolved to find ways in which Kameas' character could best serve him.

Kourikos said, "Thank you, your Majesty, for sending me word my daughter and wife are safe."

"It was something you needed to know." Maniakes cocked his head. The noise outside was rising again. He smiled. "And, unless I'm much mistaken, here they are now." He turned to Agathios. "Most holy sir, we're ready for you."

✦ V

Morning sun sneaking in through the shutters stabbed Maniakes in the eye and woke him. He yawned, stretched, sat up in bed. The motion disturbed Niphone, who also opened her eyes. He didn't know whether she was a naturally light sleeper or simply unused to sharing her bed with a man.

She smiled at him and made no effort to pull up the sheets to cover herself, as she had on the morning after they were wed. He'd laughed then, perhaps too loudly; he hadn't wanted to embarrass her. He had wanted a modest bride, and by all indications had got one. Modesty should have limits, though, or so he thought. He wasn't sure she agreed.

"I hope you slept well, your Majesty?" she said: formal as well as modest. He had thought well of that, too, till he found himself faced with the prospect of being yoked to it for as long as they both should live.

Truth was, he missed Rotrude, missed her openness, her easygoing acceptance, and the mind of her own that she most definitely had. The next opinion Niphone expressed about anything more profound than the state of the weather would be her first.

Very softly, Maniakes sighed to himself. He missed Rotrude for other reasons, too. Niphone's approach to the marriage bed was dutiful, little more; he had grown used to a partner who enjoyed what she was doing. He didn't think that was just because Niphone was only now passing from maidenhood, either. It sprang from a basic bit of who she was. He sighed again. Sometimes you had to make do with what you found in life.

Niphone tugged on a bell pull. Down the hall, a chime sounded in a maidservant's room. The serving woman came in to help the Empress dress. When she was done, Maniakes rang for Kameas with a different bell pull. The vestiarios slept in the room next to the imperial bedchamber.

"Good morning, your Majesty," the eunuch said. "Which robe shall it be today? The red, perhaps? Or the light blue with the golden embroidery?"

"The plain dark blue will do fine," Maniakes answered.

"As you wish, of course, although the light blue would go better with the gown your lovely Empress has chosen," Kameas said, gently inflexible. He nodded politely to Niphone. She returned the gesture. She was modest around Kameas, and Maniakes approved of that. He had watched the way the eunuch eyed women: all longing, with no possibility of satisfying it. Having Kameas in the bedchamber while Niphone robed herself would just have reminded the vestiarios the more strongly of his condition.

"And how will you break your fast, your Majesty?" Kameas asked once Maniakes' robe—the dark blue one; he had got his own way—was draped in a fashion of which he approved. "The cook has some fine young squab, if I may offer a suggestion."

"Yes, they'd do nicely, I think," Maniakes said. "Tell him to broil me a couple, and to bring them to me with bread and honey and a cup of wine." He glanced over at Niphone. "What about you, my dear?"

"Just bread and honey, I think," she answered. "These past few days, I've not had much of an appetite."

By Maniakes' standards, she had never had much of an appetite. "Maybe you got used to short commons in the convent of the holy Phostina," he said.

"It could be so," Niphone said indifferently. "The food here is far better, though."

Kameas bowed to her. "I shall tell the cook as much, and tell him of your requirements—and yours, your Majesty," he added for Maniakes' benefit before he went out the door.

After breakfast, Maniakes and Rhegorios put their heads together. His cousin was serving as his Sevastos—his chief minister—for the time being. He had sent a letter summoning the elder Maniakes and Symvatios to the capital, but it was still on the way to Kalavria.

He had also sent letters to the westlands after his brothers, but only the lord with the great and good mind knew when—or if—those letters would get to them. For now, Maniakes used the man upon whom he could most rely.

He flapped a parchment in front of Rhegorios' face, "Look at this!" he exclaimed—rhetorically, for Rhegorios had already seen the despatch. "Imbros sacked by the Kubratoi, half the wall pulled down, half the town burned, more than half the people run off to Kubrat so they can grow crops for the nomads. How am I supposed to fight off the Makuraners if the Kubratoi send everything to the ice up in the north?"

Rhegorios sighed. "Your Majesty, you can't."

Maniakes nodded. "I'd pretty much decided the same thing for myself, but I wanted to hear someone else say it, too." He also sighed. "That means I'll have to buy off the khagan of the Kubratoi. I hate it, but I don't see any other choice. I just pray old Etzilios won't want too much."

"How much is in the treasury?" Rhegorios asked. He managed a wry grin. "If you don't know, I'll ask your father-in-law. He'd tell me, right down to the last copper."

"The last copper is about what's there." Maniakes laughed bitterly. "No, I take that back: there are rats' nests and spiderwebs, too. Not much in the way of gold, though, nor even silver. I hope Skotos makes Genesios eat gold and silver down there in the ice." He paused to spit on the floor in rejection of the dark god, then went on, "For all I know, Genesios was eating them up here, too, for he certainly pissed them away. Maybe Phos knows what he spent his gold on, but I don't. Whatever it was, he got no good from it."

"And, of course, with the Makuraners raging through the westlands and the Kubratoi raiding down almost to the walls of the city here, a lot of taxes have gone uncollected," Rhegorios said. "That doesn't help the treasury, either."

"Too right it doesn't," Maniakes said. "I'm worried Etzilios will decide he can steal more than I'm able to give him."

"Or he might decide to take what you've given him and then go on stealing," Rhegorios put in.

"You're a cheerful soul, aren't you?" Maniakes said. "So he might. I'll offer him forty thousand goldpieces the first year of a truce, fifty thousand the second year, and sixty the third. That'll give him good reason to keep an agreement all the way through to the end."

"So it will," Rhegorios said. "It will also give you more time to scrape together the bigger sums."

"You're reading my mind," Maniakes said. "I even went over to the Sorcerers' Collegium to see if they could conjure up gold for me. If I hadn't been Avtokrator, they'd have laughed in my face. Now that I think on it, that makes sense: if they could conjure up gold whenever they wanted it, they'd be rich. No, they'd be richer than rich."

"So they would," Rhegorios said. "But tell me you didn't go there for another reason, too: to see if they'd had any luck tracking down Genesios' pet wizard for you."

"Can't do it," Maniakes admitted. "I wish I'd had some luck, but they've seen no sign of him, and their sorcery can't find him, either. They don't want to say it out loud, but I get the feeling they're scared of him. 'That terrible old man,' one of their wizards called him, and no one knows what his name was."

"If he's so old, maybe he dropped dead while you were taking the city, or maybe Genesios took his head for not finishing you but never got the chance to hang it up on the Milestone," Rhegorios said.

"Maybe," Maniakes said, though he remained unconvinced—such endings for villains were more the stuff of romance than real life. "I just hope Videssos never sees him again." In earnest of that hope, he sketched the sun-circle above his heart.

Triphylles rose from the proskynesis he had gone into after Kameas led him to the chamber in the imperial residence Maniakes used for private audiences. "How may I serve you, your Majesty?" he murmured as he took a chair.

Normally that was but a polite formality. Now Maniakes intended to ask important service of Triphylles. "I have a mission in mind for you, excellent sir," he answered. "Complete it satisfactorily and I shall enroll you among those reckoned eminent in the Empire."

"Command me, your Majesty!" Triphylles cried. Striking a dramatic pose while seated wasn't easy, but he managed. "To serve the Empire is my only purpose in existing." Being promoted to the highest level of Videssian nobility might never have entered his mind.

"All Videssos is indebted to your intrepid spirit," Maniakes said, which made Triphylles preen even more. The Avtokrator went on, "I knew I could not have chosen a better, bolder man to take my words to Etzilios, the khagan of Kubrat. With you as my envoy, I am confident my embassy to him will succeed."

Triphylles opened his mouth, but whatever he had started to say seemed stuck in his throat. His florid, fleshy face turned even redder than usual, then pale. At last, he managed to reply "You do me too much honor, your Majesty. I am unworthy to bring your word to the fearsome barbarian."

Maniakes got the idea that Triphylles was more worried by Etzilios' fearsomeness than his own unworthiness. He said, "I am sure you will do splendidly, excellent sir. After all, you so bravely endured the privations at Kastavala and on our return journey to the capital that I am sure you'll have no trouble withstanding a few more as you journey up into Kubrat." No sooner had he said that than he realized Triphylles might not have to travel to Kubrat; for all he knew, Etzilios might still be on Videssian soil after sacking Imbros.

Triphylles said, "I endured these hardships in the expectation of returning here to the capital. If I beard the vicious nomad in his den, what hope have I of faring home again?"

"It's not so bad as that, excellent sir," Maniakes said soothingly. "The Kubratoi haven't murdered an envoy of ours in close to thirty years." For some reason, that left Triphylles inadequately heartened. Maniakes went on, "Besides, you'll be going up there to offer Etzilios gold. He's not likely to kill you, because then he wouldn't get paid."

"Ah, your Majesty, you don't know how that relieves my mind," Triphylles said. Maniakes stared at the noble; he had not suspected Triphylles had such sarcasm in him. When the grandee didn't say anything more, Maniakes kept looking at him. At last Triphylles wilted under that steadfast gaze. "Very well, your Majesty, I shall do as you request," he muttered sullenly.

"Thank you, and may the lord with the great and good mind watch over you and decide the test in your favor," Maniakes said. When Triphylles still looked glum, he went on, "I'm not asking you to do anything I won't do myself. When the agreement is made, Etzilios and I will have to meet face to face to ratify it."

"Aye, your Majesty, *if* the agreement is made," Triphylles said. "If he chooses to slice me in strips and roast me over a horse-dung fire, though, you won't be coming after me to share my fate."

"I will come after you if that happens," Maniakes said. "I'll come after you with the whole weight of the army of Videssos behind me, to avenge the outrage." *Or as much of the Videssian army as I can afford to commit, what with the Makuraners rampaging through the westlands,* he thought. He did not share the qualification with Triphylles.

Having yielded, Triphylles got up to go. As he headed for the door, he muttered again, this time to himself. Maniakes did not catch all of it, but what he did hear angered him. Triphylles was complaining about having to go off to discomfort again after enduring so much of it in putting Maniakes on the throne.

"Halt," Maniakes snapped, as if to an insubordinate cavalry trooper. Triphylles peered back over his shoulder in alarm. Maniakes said, "If you worked to set me on the throne for no better reason than to let yourself come back to the fleshpots of the capital, you made a mistake. I thought you wanted me to rule to set Videssos' problems to rights. That is what I propose doing, and to do it I will seize any tool that comes to hand—including you."

Triphylles bit his lip, nodded, and took his leave before Maniakes could find any other reason to give him assignments he did not want. Maniakes plucked at his beard, wondering if he should have pretended to turn a deaf ear toward the grandee's grumbles. On reflection, he decided he probably should have, but it was too late to change his mind now. He could only go forward from what he had already done.

When you got down to it, that was all Videssos could do, too. But he was trying to take the Empire forward from what Genesios had done, and, so far as he could tell, Genesios had done everything wrong.

Meeting a returning envoy in the Grand Courtroom meant donning red boots, heavy ceremonial robe, and the even heavier imperial crown. In the hot, muggy weather of Videssos the city in summer, that was a torment Maniakes would just as soon have evaded. But Kameas politely insisted an emissary returning from the court of the King of Kings could not with propriety be met in the imperial residence. Maniakes was discovering that, while he ruled the Empire, his vestiarios was in charge of the palaces.

Fuming and sweating, Maniakes perched himself on the imperial throne and waited for his ambassador to make the long, slow advance between rows of marble columns. Sphrantzes was a man of an old noble family, one of the bureaucrats who did their best to keep the Empire on course even with a Genesios on the throne. Maniakes had sent him to Sharbaraz because he was both persuasive and honest, no more common a combination in Videssos the city than anywhere else.

He prostrated himself before Maniakes, turning what was for most people an awkward gesture of respect into one as flowing and graceful as part of a dance, then rose with the same fluid ease. He was about fifty, with a gray beard and a long, handsome, thoughtful face, one capable of expressing every shade of emotion he felt.

"How did you fare, eminent sir?" Maniakes asked. The logothetes and courtiers and functionaries who lined the way from the entrance to the throne leaned forward to hear better.

Sphrantzes' face grew longer yet. "Your Majesty, I regret I must tell you I failed in every particular," he said. His voice was deep and vibrant, a fit vehicle for the energy that filled him.

"Say on," Maniakes answered. Confessing failure before the Avtokrator and his court took courage. Most men would have claimed at least partial success before admitting such failures as they could not possibly deny.

The ambassador ticked off points on his fingers as he spoke. "Item: Sharbaraz does not recognize you as Avtokrator of the Videssians. He continues the mime-show of believing and claiming that the Videssian in fancy robes he keeps by himself is Hosios son of Likinios. I knew Hosios, your Majesty, and this lout is no Hosios."

"I knew him myself, and recognized his head when it came to Kastavala," Maniakes said, "so I know you are right about that. Go on."

"Item: he will not give over the war he is waging against Videssos, he says, until he sets the false Hosios on the throne you now occupy, your Majesty. This he terms obtaining vengeance for Likinios his benefactor."

"He conveniently forgets the Maniakai his benefactors," Maniakes said. "My father and I led the men who fought and bled to set him back on his own throne, and by the good god I wish we'd never done it."

"Item: he claims all Videssian territory his armies have overrun to be annexed to Makuran; his claim is that he shall hold it in trust for Hosios until the pretender's accession to the imperial throne." Sphrantzes raised an eyebrow in an elegant display of well-bred skepticism.

Maniakes translated without effort. "He'll keep it forever, he means. He wasn't arrogant when he knew he needed our help. Amazing what half a dozen years with nobody to tell him *no* have done." Every word Maniakes said was true. He also felt those words as a warning to himself. Who here in Videssos the city would tell him when he was being cruel or arrogant or foolish? Rhegorios might. The elder Maniakes would, when he got to the city. Past them, though, everyone knew currying favor with the Avtokrator was the way to rise. Nobody had told Genesios *no*, that was certain.

Like a sad bell, Sphrantzes tolled on. "Item: he proclaims all Vaspurakan annexed to Makuran in perpetuity."

Under other circumstances, that would have infuriated Maniakes. As it was, it seemed only to add insult to injury. Laughing, he said, "Let him proclaim, or simply claim, whatever he likes. Videssos and the princes of Vaspurakan will have more to say about that than he does."

"As you say, your Majesty," Sphrantzes replied. Maniakes thought he heard approval in the diplomat's voice. No less than Sharbaraz, Maniakes' own officials were taking his measure in the early days of his reign.

He said, "Did the King of Kings show any interest in my offer of tribute?" Videssos could not really afford to pay tribute to Makuran and Kubrat at the same time, but could afford war with either, let alone both, even less. If he could get a breathing spell no other way, Maniakes was willing to buy one.

But Sphrantzes mournfully shook his head. "Your Majesty, he says that since you are not the legitimate ruler of the Empire of Videssos—I hasten to add that these are his words, not mine—you have no right even to propose tribute to him. He adds that, once his Hosios is installed on your throne, he will regulate such matters to suit his own convenience. And he adds further that you need not pay him tribute, since he takes whatever he wants from Videssos as things stand now."

That made the assembled courtiers mutter angrily among

themselves. It angered Maniakes, too. Sighing, he said, "The wretch is revealed to be a man without gratitude. My father and I set him on his throne; now he begrudges me my place on this one. By the good god, eminent sir, if he wants war so badly, war he shall have."

The courtiers cried, "Thou conquerest, Maniakes!" Their acclamations came echoing back from the domed ceiling of the Grand Courtroom. Maniakes, though, knew he had only echoes of the Videssian army that had preserved the balance against Makuran for so long. As far as he could tell, only two reliable regiments remained in the westlands. When he finally did go forth to confront Sharbaraz, he would have to build up his forces from scratch.

To Sphrantzes he added, "Eminent sir, I am grateful for your courage and tact. You have served the Empire well."

"Not so well as I should have liked, your Majesty," Sphrantzes answered.

"Well spoken—a model we can all look up to," Maniakes said. "In these times, though, the Empire is in such a state that no one can do as much as he would like. If everyone does his best, that will have to be enough—and, if everyone does his best, I do not see how we shall fail of victory."

The courtiers cheered again, with apparently sincere enthusiasm. Maniakes had already learned to be wary of that. But trying truly to fire them was part of doing his best. He hoped he could be good enough.

"Delicious!" Maniakes said. The chef had done something interesting with mullet, sauteeing it in white wine and serving it up with a sauce of liquamen and garlic cloves baked in goose fat till they were soft and brown and tender. The garlic and fermented tunny were a perfect complement to the mullet's firm, tender flesh.

Or so Maniakes thought, at any rate. But while he was devouring his portion and soaking a heel of bread in the sauce left on his plate, Niphone picked at her supper and pushed it aside after two or three bites.

"Are you feeling well?" he asked. It was hard to be sure in ruddy lamplight, but he thought she looked pale. She hadn't eaten much at supper for several days, now that he thought back on it, or at breakfast, either.

"I think so," she said listlessly, fanning the air with her hand. "It's close in here, isn't it?"

Maniakes stared at her. The window to the small dining room was open, and admitted a cool breeze from off the Cattle Crossing. "*Are* you feeling well?" he repeated, his voice sharper this time. Like army camps, cities were breeding grounds for illnesses of all sorts. Videssos the city had the finest sorcerous healers in the world—and needed them.

Instead of answering him in words, Niphone yawned, covering her mouth with her hand. "I don't know what's come over me," she said. "Lately I want to go to bed as soon as the sun goes down and then sleep till noon. There's more to life than a mattress—or so I would have thought till now."

She certainly hadn't had much interest in matters of the mattress other than sleeping; Maniakes had to clamp his jaw shut to keep from saying something sardonic. The last time he had made love to her, she had complained his caresses made her breasts sore, though he didn't think he was doing anything different from the way he had stroked her since the day they became both man and wife and Emperor and Empress.

With that sarcastic retort still sizzling inside him, he wondered if he could find a discreet way to bring Rotrude to the imperial capital. She had never grumbled about his technique, except for a couple of months when . . .

"By the good god!" Maniakes said softly. He pointed a forefinger at Niphone, as if she were the key bit of evidence in a case he had to decide. And so, in a way, she was. Still quietly, he asked, "Could it be you're carrying a child?"

The way she gaped at him said the idea hadn't crossed her mind till now. "I don't know," she said, which annoyed him a little; a precise man himself, he preferred precise people around him. But, even if she didn't keep mental track of things as well as she might, she was not a fool. She started counting on her fingers. By the time she was done, an internal glow lit her face more brightly than the lamps could. "Why, I think I am!" she exclaimed. "My courses should have come ten days ago."

Maniakes hadn't noticed their failure, either, for which he reproached himself. He got up from the table and wrapped his arms around Niphone. "I won't pester you about eating any more," he said, "not for a while. I know you'll be doing the best you can."

A shadow crossed his wife's face, so fast he could hardly be sure he saw it. But he was. Niphone knew how he knew; she knew about Rotrude, and about Atalarikhos. He hadn't spoken of them himself, on the assumption that what he had done before he married her was his business. But she had mentioned them a couple of times, casually, in passing. He didn't know whether Kourikos had told her himself or mentioned them to his wife, who passed the news to Niphone. However it had happened, he was less than overjoyed about it.

By what seemed a distinct effort of will, Niphone made her features smooth and serene. She said, "I shall pray to the lord with the great and good mind that I give you a son and heir."

"May it be so," Maniakes said, and then, musingly, "In Makuran, I think; the wizards have ways to tell whether a child yet unborn will be a boy or a girl. If our Videssian mages can't do as well, I'll be surprised and disappointed." He chuckled. "The wizards won't want to disappoint the Avtokrator."

"Not after living through Genesios' reign, they won't," Niphone said, more spiritedly than she usually spoke. "Anyone who got on his wrong side went up on the Milestone without ever getting the chance to make amends." She shuddered; everyone in Videssos the city had memories of horror from the half-dozen years just past.

"I am not the sort of man, nor that sort of Avtokrator," Maniakes replied with a touch of injured pride. Then he laughed again. "Of course, if they don't fully realize that, and strive especially hard to please, me, I won't be altogether unhappy."

Niphone smiled. After a moment, the smile reached her eyes as well as her lips. That gladdened Maniakes. He didn't want her thinking about Rotrude . . . even if he had been doing the same thing himself.

He raised his wine cup in salute. "To our child!" he said loudly, and drank.

After that toast, Niphone's smile showed more than polite happiness. She lifted her own cup, murmured Phos' creed, and spat on the floor in rejection of Skotos. "To our child," she echoed, and drank with Maniakes.

He didn't recall her having been so pious before he had to sail for Kalavria. He wondered if he had failed to notice before—something an assotted young man might well do—or if her stay in the convent dedicated to the holy Phostina had brought out that side of her character. As far as he was concerned, the way you lived made a better proof of piety than ostentatious displays, but he knew not everyone in the Empire agreed. Videssians, he sometimes thought, got drunk on theology as easily as on wine.

So what? he thought. Trying to change the nature of the Empire was the fastest way he could imagine to make a whole host of rebels spring up against him. And if Niphone had found happiness in a close embrace of Phos, that was her concern. She had certainly embraced him, too—even if he had found more joy in the arms of another—or she would not be pregnant now.

"To our child!" he said again. If it proved a son, he would be overjoyed; if a daughter, he would give her all the affection he could . . . and try again as soon as the midwife gave him leave.

"Octopus in hot vinegar!" Triphylles exclaimed when a eunuch servitor brought in the supper Maniakes had ordered to celebrate his ambassador's return from Kubrat. "How kind of you to remember, your Majesty."

"After your weeks in the hinterlands and then in the plainsmen's country, eminent sir, I thought you would like something to remind you that you'd returned to civilization," Maniakes answered. He nodded to himself, pleased he had remembered to address Triphylles by the higher honorific he had promised him for going to Kubrat. Amazing what men would do for a change of title.

"Your Majesty, you know not what truth you speak." Triphylles ate octopus with every appearance of rapture. "Remind me to kidnap your cook—although, after some little while of elderly mutton without garlic, I doubt my palate is at its most discriminating right now."

Since his own mouth was full, Maniakes did not have to reply. He ate his octopus, too, though without feeling the ecstasies it inspired in Triphylles. He found the delicacy overrated: not only was the octopus a queer-looking beast, a man could die of old age trying to chew up each resilient, not particularly flavorful bite.

When supper was done and he and Triphylles were sipping on white wine from the north coast of the westlands, Maniakes said, "I gather from the despatch the couriers brought to me day before yesterday that your dicker with Etzilios went well."

"Fairly well, I'd say," Triphylles answered judiciously. "He is eager to receive tribute—"

"A great deal more eager than I am to pay it, I have no doubt," Maniakes said.

"As to that, I should not be surprised in the least," Triphylles said, nodding. "But the mighty khagan—and if you wonder about that, just ask Etzilios' opinion of himself—is, mm, imperfectly trustful of promises from an Avtokrator of the Videssians who overthrew his great friend Genesios."

"Of course he reckons Genesios his friend—Genesios was his lifesaver," Maniakes said. "Likinios was on the point of putting paid to the Kubratoi once and for all when Genesios overthrew him. And Genesios wasn't any good at fighting people who knew how to fight back, so he left Kubrat alone. Etzilios must feel he's lost the best friend he ever had."

"That was the impression he left with me, your Majesty," Triphylles agreed. "Accordingly, he set conditions on his agreement with you."

"What sort of conditions?" Maniakes asked. If Triphylles had taken revenge for being sent off to a barbarous land by acquiescing to onerous terms, Maniakes would think about feeding him to the octopi instead of the other way round, perhaps after first dunking him in hot vinegar.

But his envoy replied, "To assure himself of your goodwill toward him, your Majesty, he insists that you personally bring the first year's tribute to him, at a spot to be agreed upon by future negotiation. I gather he has in mind somewhere not far from the border between Videssos and Kubrat."

"On our side of it, I assume," Maniakes said sourly. He felt no goodwill toward Etzilios; he wished Likinios had succeeded in crushing Kubrat and pushing the Videssian frontier back up to the Astris River, where, to his mind, it belonged. But he had thought the khagan might demand something like that; Etzilios was a smaller menace than Sharbaraz, and so had to be accommodated until the threat from Makuran was gone. He sighed. "Very well. Let that be as pleases the khagan. What else?"

"That was the chiefest point," Triphylles said. "He also requires that your retinue include no more than five hundred soldiers, and swore by his sword to bring no more than that number with him. Among the Kubratoi, no stronger oath holds."

"Which means we either believe him or take precautions," Maniakes said. "I aim to take precautions. I shall swear to bring no more than five hundred men with me to the meeting with Etzilios, but I'll have others standing by not far away in case his strongest oath proves not strong enough."

For a moment, he thought about treachery of his own. If he managed to slay Etzilios, the benefits now might well repay any damage to his soul later: he would have plenty of time to do good works and found monasteries in expiation of the sin. But if he tried to kill the khagan and failed, the Kubratoi would have plenty of reason to ravage his land and sack his towns. From all he had seen, Etzilios was wily enough to have a good chance of escaping any plot. With pragmatism and moral scruples pulling him in the same direction, Maniakes decided against breaking a pledge once made.

Triphylles said, "May it please your Majesty, here you shall have a fine opportunity to overawe the barbarian with the splendor of Videssian court life. When he sees such a magnificent display, he will desire nothing more than to continue gaining the bounty you condescend to grant him."

"That would be good," Maniakes agreed. He found court life more nearly stupefying than awe-inspiring, but then he was stuck in the middle of it—like a fly stuck in honey, he sometimes thought. But indeed, to a sheep-raising nomad, the gold-encrusted robes, censer-swinging priests, and slow, stately eunuchs might be impressive. Unquestionably, Etzilios would never have seen anything like them.

"The last item the khagan demands, your Majesty, is twenty pounds of peppercorns a year in addition to the tribute of gold." Triphylles made a face. "The lord with the great and good mind alone knows what he purposes doing with the pepper, for he seemed utterly ignorant of its use in cookery."

"We shall survive that," Maniakes said. "We can give him his spice."

"Excellent, your Majesty." Triphylles beamed for a moment, then suddenly looked anxious. "Uh, your Majesty—I trust you won't need me to hammer out the details of your forthcoming visit to the borders of Kubrat?"

"I think the services you have already rendered the Empire will suffice for the time being, eminent sir," Maniakes said, and

Triphylles' fleshy face filled with relief. "High time now for you
to enjoy the comforts of Videssos the city, as you have indeed
labored so long and hard to keep them safe."

"Phos bless you, your Majesty," Triphylles said. His mobile
features bore a different message: *it's about time.*

Not every day did an ordinary, rather battered galley pull up
to the quays of the little harbor in the palace quarter. But then,
not every day did the father and uncle of the Avtokrator return
to Videssos the city after years of exile. When word the ship was
approaching came to the palaces, Maniakes set aside the tax register he had been studying and hurried down to the water's edge.
Had anyone asked him, he would have admitted he was glad for
an excuse to set aside the cadaster. No one presumed to ask. That
was one of the nice things about being Avtokrator.

Waves sloshed through one another and slapped against the
sea wall. The sound of the ocean pervaded Videssos the city, surrounded by water on three sides as it was. These days, Maniakes
often had to make a conscious effort to hear it. Time in the capital,
and before that in seaside Kastavala, had dulled his awareness.

Rhegorios came hurrying down to the docks. "Are they here
yet?" he said. "Oh, no, I see them. Another few minutes. Look,
there's Father in the bow—and your father, too." He waved. After
a moment, so did Maniakes. As often happened, his more spon-
taneous cousin got him moving.

The elder Maniakes waved back. Symvatios did, too. Rhegorios
had sharp eyes, to tell them apart so readily at such a distance.
Maniakes had to squint to be sure who was who.

Standing beside Symvatios was his daughter Lysia. She also
waved toward Maniakes and Rhegorios. That made Maniakes
wave harder. Rhegorios, though, put his hands down by his sides.
Maniakes poked him in the ribs with an elbow. "Aren't you going
to welcome your sister?" he demanded.

"What, and give her the chance to put on airs?" Rhegorios said
in mock horror. "She'd never let me forget it."

Maniakes snorted. He listened to the oarmaster calling the stroke
and then ordering back oars as the galley came alongside a quay.
Lines snaked out from the ship. Servitors ashore tied them fast.
Sailors and servitors wrestled the gangplank into place.

The elder Maniakes crossed to the wharf before anyone else.

Had anybody tried to precede him, his son thought he would have drawn the sword he wore on his belt and sent the presumptuous soul along the bridge it would either cross to reach Phos' heaven or fall from to descend to Skotos' ice.

With great dignity, the elder Maniakes bowed before the younger. "Your Majesty," he said, and then, with even greater pride, prostrated himself before the Avtokrator who happened to be his son.

"Get up, sir, please!" Maniakes said. This business of being Avtokrator kept having implications he didn't see till they upped and bit him. He stared around in no small alarm: what were people thinking of a father who had to perform a proskynesis before his son?

To his amazement, the servants and courtiers watching the elder Maniakes looked pleased and proud themselves. A couple softly clapped their hands at the spectacle. Whatever Maniakes had expected, that wasn't it.

Still bent on the dock, the elder Maniakes said, "Just let me finish my business here, son, if you please," and touched his forehead to the timbers. Then he did rise, grunting a little at the effort it cost him. Once he was back on his feet, he added, "Now that that's over and done, I can go back to clouting you when you do something stupid."

Where abject servility had brought nothing but approval from servitors and men of the court, that threat, obvious joke though it was, drew gasps. Maniakes rolled his eyes in wonder. Did they suppose he was going to punish his father for lese majesty?

By the way they kept staring from one of the Maniakai to the other, maybe they did. Maniakes walked over to his father, embraced him, and kissed him on both cheeks. That seemed to ease the minds of some of the spectators, but only made others more nervous.

Symvatios performed the proskynesis next. After he rose, he went on one knee before Rhegorios. "Your Highness," he said, as was proper in greeting the Sevastos of the Videssian Empire.

"Oh, Father, get up, for Phos' sake," Rhegorios said impatiently. Seeing the Sevastos imitate the Avtokrator's informality, the spectators sighed—things weren't going to be as they had been in the reign of the traditionalist Likinios. How things had been during Genesios' reign, they carefully chose not to remember.

After Symvatios had presented himself to his nephew and son, it was Lysia's turn. As before, Maniakes felt more embarrassed than exalted at having her prostrate herself. He got the strong feeling, though, that ordering her not to would have insulted her instead of making her happy. He shrugged. As he had seen with the way Triphylles lusted after an otherwise altogether unimportant title, ceremony was a strange business, almost a magic of its own.

"I'm glad you're here, cousin of mine," he said, giving Lysia a hug after she had greeted her brother. "When we left each other in Kastavala, we didn't know whether we'd ever see each other again."

"*I* knew," Lysia said, showing more confidence now than she had that day on the distant island. She said nothing about the embrace they had given each other then, though he would have bet it was in her mind as it was in his. The one they had just exchanged was decorously chaste.

The elder Maniakes said, "Son—your Majesty—have you had any word of your brothers?"

"No," Maniakes said. "It worries me. The westlands have been anything but safe for soldiers these past few years." That was an understatement. Not only had the armies of the westlands had to withstand a great onslaught from out of Makuran, they had also battered one another in endless, fruitless rounds of civil war.

"I pray the good god has not let my boys fall for nothing," the elder Maniakes said, his voice heavy with worry. "The good god grant that my line shall not fail now, at its greatest moment of triumph."

"The good god has already taken care of that, or so I hope," Maniakes replied with a grin. "We'll know for certain come spring."

"So you'll make me a grandfather, eh?" the elder Maniakes said. His chuckle was too bawdy to seem quite fitting at a ceremonial occasion. "You didn't waste much time, did you, eh? Good for you."

"Will you dine with me tonight, Father?" Maniakes said. "I shall be holding a feast in the Hall of the Nineteen Couches. Uncle, I bid you join us, too, and you, Lysia."

"The Hall of the Nineteen Couches?" The elder Maniakes rolled his eyes up toward the heavens. "We're going to have to eat reclining, aren't we? To think my own son would do such a thing to me, and at the same time make it impossible to say no."

Maniakes refused to let that half-piteous, half-sardonic appeal sway him. "If I can do it, you can do it. And if I spill fish sauce and wine down the front of my robe, with you there I'll have some reason to hope I shan't be the only one."

"See what an ungrateful child it is!" the elder Maniakes shouted out to whomever would hear him. But he spoiled the effect of his indignation by throwing back his head and laughing till he had to hold his sides.

The nineteen couches sat in a large horseshoe in the hall to which they had given their name. "Yours, of course, shall be at the center, in the keystone position, your Majesty," Kameas said, pointing to the one in question. "You shall have three times three on either side of you."

"We could invite many more than that if you'd only set out tables and chairs, the way they do it in every other dining hall in the Empire," Maniakes said testily.

"If elsewhere they forget the past, we should pity rather than emulate them," the vestiarios replied. "Here we recline, the last bastion of true elegance in a world gone shoddy and uncaring."

"I ought to start a new custom," Maniakes grumbled.

Kameas stared at him in horror that was, Maniakes realized, perfectly genuine. "No, your Majesty, I beg you!" the vestiarios cried. "In this hall, Stavrakios reclined after his great victories against Makuran, as did Yermanos before civil war tore the Empire to bits upon his death. Would you have your practices differ from theirs?"

Maniakes had his doubts about Stavrakios' reclining after his victories. From all he had ever read, the great soldier-Avtokrator had been more comfortable in the field than in the palaces. But that was not the point Kameas was trying to make. "Precedent is meant to guide, not to strangle," Maniakes said.

Kameas did not reply, not in words. He just stared at Maniakes with large, sorrowful eyes. "Your commands shall of course be obeyed, your Majesty," he said, sounding as if one of those commands were that he take poison.

Maniakes ended up eating on that central couch. He reclined on his left side, freeing his right hand for feeding himself. Not only did he find it a most awkward way to go about the business of supper, but before long his left arm, on which he leaned, seemed dead from elbow to fingertip.

Kameas beamed. So did the other servants who carried food and wine into the Hall of the Nineteen Couches and empty platters and goblets away from it. Maniakes wondered if keeping his servitors happy was worth this discomfort.

His sole consolation was that he wasn't alone in having trouble at the feast. Of all the guests there, only Kourikos, his wife Phevronia, and Triphylles seemed at ease. They had eaten this way in Likinios' day. Niphone might have been familiar with the arrangements, too, but at the moment she found facing food far more unpleasant a prospect than leaning on one elbow. If anything, for her the awkward position was an advantage: it meant she couldn't be expected to eat much.

Thrax the drungarios was the first person to dribble garum down his chin and onto his robe. He expressed his opinion of having to eat on couches so forcefully that several women turned their heads aside in embarrassment.

"Disgraceful," Niphone murmured.

A few couches down from Maniakes, Lysia giggled, then tried to pretend she hadn't. Maniakes caught her eye. She looked apprehensive till she saw him smile, but relieved after that. Moments later, Symvatios spilled sauce on himself. Lysia laughed out loud.

"Go ahead, mock your own father," Symvatios said, but his severity was as insincere as the elder Maniakes' had been earlier in the day at the harbor in the palace quarter.

After the blueberries candied in honey had been taken away, after the last toasts to the new Avtokrator and his family were drunk—mostly by the new Avtokrator and his family—the feasters began rising one by one and leaving the Hall of the Nineteen Couches. Kameas came hurrying up to Maniakes, worry on his smooth eunuch's face.

"I trust you enjoyed yourself, your Majesty?" He sounded anxious.

"More than I expected, yes," Maniakes admitted.

Kameas sketched Phos' sun-circle over his breast. "The good god be praised," he murmured to the heavens above before returning his attention to Maniakes. "Then you will not mind my scheduling further such entertainments?"

"Let's not get carried away," Maniakes said hastily. Kameas' face, which had begun to shine, crumpled again. Maniakes knew he would have to deal with a grumpy, disappointed vestiarios in the days ahead. He preferred that to the prospect of dealing with any of the nineteen couches any time soon.

One thing Maniakes hadn't anticipated before he donned the crown and the red boots: how much parchment an Avtokrator had to cope with every day. Letting clerks and logothetes take the burden could go only so far. If you didn't know what was going on inside Videssos, how could you be said to rule the Empire? To Maniakes' mind, you couldn't.

Genesios had let everything slip except matters that touched on his own hold on the throne—there he had been both wary and ruthless. But he hadn't delegated responsibility to anyone else. Things he didn't personally decide just got ignored.

"That's how Videssos got into the state it's in," Maniakes declared to anyone who would listen. Since he was Avtokrator, people had an incentive to listen to him. The flood of parchment that came to the imperial residence all but inundated him.

Most of the missives were in one way or another cries for help: towns wanting gold and artisans to rebuild walls, provinces wanting relief from taxes because their farmlands had been ravaged—he had no idea how to meet both those requests at the same time—generals wanting men and horses and weapons. He wished he had some to send them. He had managed to scrape together a couple of regiments of veteran troops, but didn't know where he could find more.

Here was a letter from another general:

> Tzikas commanding west of Amorion to Maniakes Avtokrator: Greetings. I have the honor to report, your Majesty, that your brother Tatoules formerly served with my command. This past spring, the Makuraners sent a column eastward past the southern edge of the territory within my assigned area of responsibility. I dispatched a force of my own southward to attempt to check the enemy column. My move was successful but, because my colleague, the excellent Provatos, showed the spirit of a sheep and did not similarly commit a detachment

of his own after promising to do so, the Makuraners were able to fall back rather than being destroyed. Our casualties were moderate, but I regret to inform you that your brother Tatoules did not return with the rest of the force. He is not certainly known to be slain. I regret I cannot convey more definite news as to his fate.

Maniakes regretted it, too; he had no way of knowing whether Tatoules was dead or alive and, if alive, whether he was wounded or in Makuraner captivity. He didn't think Sharbaraz would harm his brother if he knew he had him. They were enemies, yes, but because Makuran and Videssos were enemies. It wasn't personal, at least not as far as Maniakes was concerned. But the men of Makuran might have captured Tatoules without knowing he was brother to the Avtokrator—by all indications, he didn't know it himself. The lot of ordinary prisoners could be—too often was—harsh.

And yet that ambiguous letter from Tzikas gave him far more knowledge of Tatoules' actions and whereabouts than he had for Parsmanios. His other brother might have been swallowed by the earth, for all the report of him that came back from the westlands.

He noted that Tzikas had done his best to raise imperial wrath against Provatos, his fellow general in the westlands. Since he didn't know the circumstances under which the two men were supposed to have cooperated, he couldn't decide which of them was in the right here. That troubled him; he knew he needed to take firmer control over his officers if the army was ever to become effective against either Makuran or Kubrat.

But he could not simply leap atop the army and ride it as if it were a placid mare. The generals, especially in the westlands, had got used to taking matters into their own hands, for the good and simple reason that Genesios had given them no choice—he led not at all. Having gained power—even if not enough to hold back Sharbaraz—they were reluctant to surrender it to Videssos the city.

"To the ice with them all," Maniakes raged to Rhegorios. "They act like a herd of virgins fit for nothing but the convent and want me to waste my time seducing them one by one."

"The truth is, they're just a pack of whores," Rhegorios said.

While Maniakes agreed with that, it didn't help him find a way to deal with his independence-minded generals. He took the question to his father. The elder Maniakes plucked at his beard and said, "Having a good-sized army under your command in the westlands will bring them to heel soon enough."

"*Would* bring them to heel, you mean," the younger Maniakes said. "As things are now, the only way I'll be able to put troops in the westlands is buying off the Kubratoi so I can free up some of the men who are trying to hold them back. I hate that, but what choice have I?"

"None I can see," his father answered. "What you have to do, though, is make sure Etzilios can't find any way to cheat you."

"I've been doing my best there. My commissioners and the khagan's cronies have been dickering for weeks about where we'll meet, who we can bring with us, and other small details." Maniakes' smile showed his sardonic streak. He went on, "The only trouble is, while we're dickering, Etzilios' men keep raiding us. As best I can tell, he thinks that's part of the way negotiating gets done."

The elder Maniakes sighed. "He has gained our attention, hasn't he? The only way I can think of to make him stop is to threaten to go to war without limit against him if he doesn't give over, and that—"

"That will just make him laugh," the younger Maniakes finished. His father nodded. He went on, "He may be a barbarian, but he's no fool, worse luck. He knows the only way we can fight a big war with him is to quit fighting Makuran, and we can't afford to do that. Even if we did, we might get another mutiny out of it—the troops remember how Likinios tried to make them winter north of the Astris and what happened afterward."

"Ah, but would they mutiny for fear of having to spend the winter on the frozen steppe, or in hope of casting you down and setting another in your place?" The elder Maniakes spread his hands. "That wasn't a question I intended you to answer, son."

"The why doesn't much matter, anyway," the younger Maniakes said. "One more civil war and we pretty much hand Videssos over to Sharbaraz, anyhow. Then he'd have to try and rule it. Seeing him struggle with that is the one reason I can think of for losing." Before his father could speak, he added quickly, "I'm joking, by the good god."

"I know you are. I wasn't going to twit you about that. But I can make a pretty good guess, I think, about when Etzilios will rein in his raiders and graciously consent to accept the gold you want to give him."

"If I have enough gold to pay the tribute," the younger Maniakes said gloomily. "All right, Father, if you feel like foretelling, tell me when Etzilios will leave us in peace."

"Right about the time the harvest is done," the elder Maniakes answered. "He'll steal all he can up till then and take away as much grain as his horses can carry. Nomads often live right on the edge of starving and make up for what they can't raise themselves by robbing their neighbors. This way, Etzilios will have our farmers working for him."

"The ones he leaves alive, anyway," the younger Maniakes said. He considered. "You may well be right. That means another couple of months of attacks, though, and not much time after the harvest season to meet with Etzilios and pay him off before the fall rains turn the roads to muck."

"Maybe we should hope they start early," his father said. "The Kubratoi won't be able to do much in fall or winter, either. Come spring, you'd be able to pay the khagan and buy peace through the campaigning season."

"I'd like that," the younger Maniakes replied. "I see only one thing wrong with it." His father waited expectantly. He explained: "It would be convenient for us, and Etzilios won't let that happen."

The elder Maniakes barked a few syllables of wheezy laughter and clapped him on the shoulder. "I wish I could say you were wrong, but I don't think you are."

Bagdasares rose from his prostration with a quizzical look on his face. "You do me great honor, your Majesty," the wizard said, speaking Videssian with the throaty Vaspurakaner accent that put Maniakes in mind of his grandparents, "but truly, the mages of the Sorcerers' Collegium can do this as well as I. Better," he added in a burst of candor that made Maniakes like him very much.

"That may be so, but you can do it well enough," Maniakes answered, "and I trust you, which is more than I can say for the sorcerers of the Collegium. They were here through Genesios' reign. Who knows what some of them may have done?"

"He used that skinny old man for the worst of his conjurations," Bagdasares said.

"So everyone tells me—and that skinny old man is now conveniently vanished," Maniakes said. "As I say, I don't know what those others did and it's too late now for me to worry about it without evidence, but if I want to find out what's likely to come of my meeting with Etzilios, I'll ask you, not them."

"Very well, your Majesty," Bagdasares said. "I shall do my best not to disappoint you, although I must say, as with any effort to look ahead to what will be, I can give you no guarantee that all will transpire as now appears most likely."

"Yes, yes, I understand that," Maniakes said impatiently. "Just get on with it, if you'd be so kind. Unless the barbarian should yet again change what passes for his mind, I'll be departing to meet him before long."

"I shall attempt to learn what may be learned," Bagdasares replied, bowing. "I should also warn you that the Kubrati shamans may cloud what I see, either because they are also peering at what may be or because they are deliberately trying to keep me from seeing ahead."

Maniakes' gesture was so peremptory, he regretted it a moment later. However rude it was, though, it got Bagdasares moving, which was what Maniakes had intended. The Vaspurakaner mage emptied out his carpetbag on the polished top of a marble table. Rummaging in the pile of oddments, he selected a small jar of wine, a mirror of polished bronze, and a tiny, intricately carved cinnabar jar that held a glob of quicksilver.

"In the mirror, we shall see what we shall see," he explained. "We can touch the future only through the law of contagion, for it is, metaphorically speaking, in contact with the present. The spirits of the wine will give us the link between present and future, while the quicksilver—" He flicked it with his finger, to break it into several shining drops. "—symbolizes the mutability of all that lies ahead and has not yet been accomplished."

"Carry on," Maniakes said. Wizardry and its techniques often fascinated him, but not today. All he cared for were results.

"As you say, your Majesty." Bagdasares spent the next couple of minutes fussily gathering back into a single globule the quicksilver he had scattered, then slid a scrap of parchment under it so he could pick it up later.

Whistling tunelessly between his teeth, he poured some of the wine into a small cup with a white, shiny glaze. He left a finger's breadth of rim showing when he set aside the wine jar. Some of that margin disappeared when he let the quicksilver fall down into the wine. A couple of wine drops splashed out of the cup and onto the table. He wiped them up with a rag.

"No one should drink of this wine," he remarked. "It's been used in these rituals before and had quicksilver in it many times. Quicksilver's not the strongest poison I know, but it's not the weakest, either. Well—"

He spread his hands over the wine cup and began a slow, sonorous chant, some of it in the Vaspurakaner tongue, the rest in Videssian so archaic that Maniakes had trouble following it. He thought he understood that Bagdasares was using the spirits in the wine to harness the quicksilver's constant changes and turn them toward what would pass from the meeting with Etzilios.

Sweat rolled down Bagdasares' forehead and across his fleshy cheeks. "This is hard," he said. "I can feel resistance between me and my goal. I shall be the stronger, though; I shall prevail—Phos surely favors a man from among his firstborn." Maniakes wondered what Agathios would have to say about that. He himself, however, was more interested in what Bagdasares could tell him than in rooting out heresy wherever he found it.

When his incantation was complete, Bagdasares picked up a brightly polished silver spoon and filled it from the cup. Slowly and carefully, he brought it over to the mirror, which lay flat on the table. He poured the quicksilver-laden wine onto the smooth bronze surface. "Now you shall see what you shall see," he whispered to Maniakes.

At first, Maniakes saw only red wine spread over the surface of the mirror. Then the smeared wine became a filmy curtain and blew aside; it was as if he were peering through the mirror into infinite space filled neither with Phos' light nor Skotos' darkness. He wanted to blink—it was not something he thought man was meant to perceive—but found he could not.

After what might have been a heartbeat or some endlessly longer time, the mirror once more began to show an image. No longer did it reflect the ceiling or Maniakes' face, though. Instead, he saw the neck and head of a horse, as if he were riding on it; he thought the hands holding its reins his own. In the near distance were the walls of Videssos the city. The sun glinted from the globes of Phos' temples inside, just as it had when he approached by sea.

He wondered what lay behind him, but the image faded from his sight before he could find out. The mirror once more became its normal self. He looked away from it, scratching his head.

"Did you learn what you sought, your Majesty?" Bagdasares asked.

Maniakes glanced over to him in surprise. "Why do you ask? Didn't you see what I saw in the mirror?"

"No, your Majesty." The wizard shook his head. "The spell was created to enlighten you, not me. I know the sort of thing you experienced, as I've sometimes used that magic for my own purposes, but I did not share this particular vision with you."

"So that's the way of it, eh?" Maniakes was still bemused. "I don't know whether I saw what I needed to see or not. Your mirror showed that I will come back from my meeting with Etzilios, which is indeed a piece of news worth having, but it did not show anything of the meeting itself."

"As I said, your Majesty, I fear I was being impeded in my efforts by the Kubrati shamans," Bagdasares answered. "Whether they were trying to hinder me or simply creating uncertainty because of their own foreseeing attempts, I cannot tell you. I will say it is not impossible, or even improbable, that I have interfered with their magic, as well."

"Good." Maniakes thought of two stones being tossed into a calm pond at the same time and of ripples spreading out from each until those ripples met each other and either flattened out or pushed each other higher. In neither case would the water be as it had been before the waves ran through it. He went on, "So Etzilios will be as much in the dark as I will over what the meeting may bring?"

"From a sorcerous point of view, yes, I think so," Bagdasares said. "Sorcery, of course, may not be a decisive factor on whatever plans he has."

"Yes, there is that." Maniakes plucked at his beard, as he often did while thinking. When he got down to it, he had very little choice. "I'll treat with the barbarian. If he and I do not come to terms, how can we wage war against Makuran?" Bagdasares did not answer. He did not have to answer. Without a truce with Kubrat, Maniakes would fight in the westlands like a man with one arm tied behind his back.

Bagdasares fished the glob of quicksilver out of the cup into which he had dropped it, then put it back in the cinnabar jar. He poured the wine back into its jar, too, and tightly stoppered it. He dried and polished the bronze mirror before returning it and the rest of his sorcerous paraphernalia to the carpetbag in which he had carried them.

"I thank you for your help," Maniakes told him. The help hadn't been as complete as he might have hoped, but the more he had to do with magic, the more he realized it was a highly ambiguous business. Attempts to foresee the future might also influence it. If that was so, would it mean that what you had seen could no longer come to pass? But if what you had seen was false, how could it influence the true future? With a deliberate effort of will, he set aside that train of thought before it made him dizzy.

After Bagdasares left the imperial residence, Maniakes wanted to talk with someone about what he had seen. He discovered his father, cousin, and uncle had gone riding into the city while he was closeted with the mage. Since he hadn't gotten into the habit of confiding in Kameas—and since he wasn't sure getting into that habit was a good idea—he went looking for Niphone.

He found her in the imperial bedchamber. She was down on all fours on the floor, throwing up into a basin. Since she was an Empress of the Videssians, the basin was of solid silver, with low-relief images of holy men and their miracles ornamenting the outside. That didn't make being sick into it any more pleasant.

Maniakes stooped beside Niphone and held her hair back from her face till she was done. "Thank you," she said in a muffled voice. "There's a jar of wine on that chest there. Could you bring me a cup and let me rinse my mouth?"

"Of course," Maniakes said. While he was pouring it, Niphone rang for a maidservant. The woman came in and carried the basin away.

After Niphone had drunk some of the wine, she said, "That's a little better. I'm so tired of throwing up every day, I don't know how to begin to tell you."

"I believe that," Maniakes said as sympathetically as he could. "I just had Alvinos here—" When talking with Niphone, he used the Videssian name the wizard had given himself; Niphone didn't care to be reminded of the Vaspurakaners as a separate people. He explained what he had seen in the mirror, and what he hadn't as well.

"So long as you come back to the city safe," Niphone said, and that was the end of her interest in Bagdasares' magic. Maniakes told himself he wouldn't have been at his best just after being violently ill. That was true, but he had the feeling she would have been as indifferent were she perfectly well. She didn't care much—no, the truth, she didn't care at all—about how the Videssian Empire was run, though she was annoyed that the running of it kept him away from her more than she would have wanted.

Seeing he might as well have been talking to the wall, he left and wandered aimlessly through the halls of the imperial residence. Had he run into Kameas, he probably would have unburdened himself to him; not only did the vestiarios' position oblige him to listen, he had a good head for detail and might have had something useful to say.

But instead of Kameas, Maniakes found Lysia. His cousin was looking at some of the treasures stored up here. Not all of them were worth great piles of goldpieces. The battered iron helmet by which she stood, for instance, was nothing out of the ordinary to the eye. But it had once covered the head of a Makuraner King of Kings who had fallen to Videssian arms in Mashiz.

Lysia looked up at the sound of Maniakes' footsteps in the hallway and smiled to recognize him. The ceiling of the hall was set with thin alabaster panels that let in a pale, shimmering light. Lysia happened to be standing under one of them. She seemed ethereal, not quite of this world.

But there was nothing ethereal about what she said. "May you add Sharbaraz's helmet to go with the one we already have here."

"That would be fine," he said, nodding as he came up to her. "I can't even think about driving the Makuraners from our soil yet, though, let alone moving on Mashiz, not when I still have Kubrat to worry about." As he had with Niphone, he told of what Bagdasares' magic had shown him.

"You don't know what will happen before you come riding back to Videssos the city?" Lysia asked.

"No, and that's what worries me," Maniakes said. "It could be anything from the agreement I hope for to . . . just this side of being killed, I suppose."

"I don't blame you for worrying," she answered. "You ought to post troops close by, over and above the five hundred to which you've agreed, so they can come to your aid if Etzilios does prove to have treachery in mind.

"The trick of it," Lysia went on seriously, "will be finding places where they're near enough to do you some good but not so near as to make the Kubrati khagan think they endanger him—especially since he'll have his own men hanging about for the same reason."

Maniakes stared at her. "My dear cousin!" he exclaimed. "You're as clever as you are pretty, which says a good deal. Just what I aim to do, I don't think any of my generals or courtiers could have summed that up so neatly."

Under his intent gaze, Lysia looked down at the mosaicwork floor. "Your Majesty is too kind to me," she murmured.

He frowned. Along with everyone else in the Empire of Videssos, she was his subject, and protocol required that she remember it. But, as far as ceremony went, the crown still sat lightly on him, and he was used to her as a frank-spoken cousin, as near an equal as a woman was likely to become in Videssos' male-dominated society—although, from what he had seen, the Makuraners granted their women far fewer privileges than Videssians did.

He took a cousinly privilege and poked her in the ribs. She squeaked, started to poke him right back, and then checked herself. "No, you'd say I was guilty of lese majesty or some such, and cast me in a dungeon," she said, her eyes sparkling to show she was teasing him.

"Aye, no doubt, and you'd deserve it, but I need to keep you free so you can give me good advice," he answered. That could have been teasing, too, but it had enough of an earnest undercurrent to make her pause before she snapped back at him again. For that moment, at least, they liked each other very much.

✦ VI

Maniakes rode at the head of the procession that left Videssos the city through the Silver Gate, bound for the northern frontier and a meeting with Etzilios the khagan. After he had gone a couple of hundred yards, he reined in and turned to look back at everyone who was joining him in this effort to overawe the Kubrati ruler.

"We have a bit of everything here, don't we?" he said to Bagdasares, who had stopped his own horse at the same time.

"That we do, your Majesty," the wizard agreed soberly. He patted the side of his mount's neck. The mare let out a quiet, pleased snort.

Behind the Avtokrator and the mage rode the five hundred men who would serve as Maniakes' honor guard when he confronted Etzilios. Half of them wore blue surcoats over their chainmail, the other half gold. Blue and gold streamers fluttered from their lances. They gave the impression of being only for show, but every one was a first-rate fighting man.

Next after them came the baggage train: horses and mules and oxen and wagons with canvas tops that could be stretched over them in case of rain. The baggage for the Avtokrator's pavilion was separate from the rest, marked off by blue banners with gold sunbursts on them. Kameas and other imperial servitors accompanied it, ready to do their best to make the Avtokrator feel as if he had never left the palaces. The treasure Maniakes would give to Etzilios was also in that part of the baggage train, guarded by half a hundred hard-faced men who made no effort to seem anything but deadly dangerous.

After the baggage train rolled wagons of a different sort: these carried the members of a couple of the leading mime troupes in Videssos the city. The performers were veterans of many a Midwinter's Day skit in the Amphitheater, but they had never gone up before a more demanding audience. If the khagan didn't care for the shows they put on, he had blunter—or rather, sharper—ways to express his disapproval than flinging a rotten pumpkin.

"I wish we had a giant serpent to give Etzilios," Maniakes said suddenly. "I'd like to see what he'd do with one, by Phos. Give it back, unless I miss my guess—either that or feed his enemies to it."

"Such serpents seldom enough come from the Hot Lands to Videssos the city," Kameas said. "I daresay no plainsman has ever had to deal with one."

Since there were no serpents, a couple of dozen of the swiftest horses in the city followed the mime troupe's wagons. Maniakes aimed to put on horse races for the khagan. If Etzilios wanted to run his steppe ponies against these beasts, the Avtokrator wouldn't complain. And if Etzilios wanted to bet on the outcome, Maniakes figured he would win back some of the gold he was paying.

Last of all rode another fifteen hundred cavalrymen. Unlike the formal guard regiment, they lacked matching gear. If all went well, Etzilios would never see them. They accompanied the Avtokrator in case all failed to go well.

When the party—with so many noncombatants along, Maniakes had trouble thinking of it as a *force*—reached the Long Walls, the fortifications that protected the area surrounding Videssos the city from barbarian raids, he sent out his troops to check the nearby woods and copses to make sure no Kubratoi were lurking there. They found none of the nomads. That helped set Maniakes' mind at ease; Etzilios seemed to be living up to the agreements he had made.

On the road up to Imbros, Maniakes had no trouble sleeping in the elaborate pavilion of scarlet silk his servitors erected for him each night. He had had far worse beds on campaign. The servitors themselves, though, were used to life in the palaces and had trouble adjusting to being away from Videssos the city. They complained about the travel, about the food, about the noise at night, and about how drafty their tents were.

Kameas' shelter stood beside that of the Avtokrator and was the next most elaborate after it alone. Yet the vestiarios kept saying, over and over again, "Most unsatisfactory."

"What's wrong, esteemed sir?" Maniakes asked in honest bewilderment. "Seeing that we're traveling, I can't imagine doing it with any more luxury."

"It is inadequate," Kameas insisted. "The Avtokrator of the Videssians should not dine on rabbit stew, and if by chance he should, the dish should not be lacking in mushrooms to give it at least a hint of piquancy."

Maniakes ticked off points on his fingers. "First of all, I like rabbit stew. Second, I didn't so much as notice it came without mushrooms. Third, if this were a real campaign, I'd be eating out of the same pots as my men. That's the best way I know for a general to be sure their food is as good as it can be."

Kameas turned a delicate shade of green—or perhaps it was only a trick of the torchlight. "It strikes me as the best way for an Avtokrator to be sure his own food is as bad as it can be."

Barley porridge, hard rolls, onions, crumbly cheese, salted olives, garlicky smoked sausage of pork or mutton, wine sometimes halfway to vinegar . . . Maniakes decided he would be wiser not to admit a fondness for the food armies ate on the march, lest he bring a fit of apoplexy down on his vestiarios. But fond of such fare he was, no doubt because he had eaten it so often when he was young.

"How long shall we be away from the palaces, your Majesty?" Kameas asked.

"Two weeks; three at the most," Maniakes answered.

Kameas rolled his eyes, as if the Avtokrator had announced a separation of as many years. His sigh made his jowls wobble. "Perhaps we shall survive it," he said, though his tone implied he had his doubts.

Imbros was the nearest town of any size to the frontier with Kubrat, which also meant it was the town most exposed to Kubrati raiders. The farmland around it had brought in a lean harvest this year, *if* any.

Company by company, regiment by regiment, the extra cavalrymen

Maniakes had brought with him peeled off from the main body moving toward Imbros and took up concealed positions in the woods south of the city. Riders could easily summon them to come to the Avtokrator's aid or, at need, to avenge him. Given the vision Bagdasares had shown him, Maniakes did not think it would reach that point. As the walls of Imbros came into sight, he realized he was betting his life on that vision.

Those walls had known better days. He had heard as much, but seeing it with his own eyes was a shock. The Kubratoi had torn great gaps in the stonework, not during a siege but after they got into the town. Till the fortifications were repaired, the barbarians could force their way into Imbros any time they chose. Maniakes resolved to rebuild the walls as soon as he could. How soon that would be, he couldn't guess.

A horseman on a shaggy brown plains pony approached the Avtokrator's party from the north. He carried a white-painted shield hung from the end of a lance. As he drew near, Maniakes saw he was wearing trousers of stained and faded leather, a wolfskin cap, and a jacket of marten fur unfastened to show off the cloth-of-gold beneath it: the last a sure bit of loot from Videssian soil.

Maniakes ordered his own shield of truce displayed. At that, the rider, who had reined in, came forward once more. "I, Moundioukh, greets you, your Majesty, in the names of the great and fearsome khagans of the Kubratoi, Etzilios the magnifolent," he called in understandable but mangled Videssian.

"I greet you and your khagan in return; Etzilios your ruler is indeed most magnifolent," Maniakes said gravely, holding in a smile by main force. A couple of men behind him snickered, but Moundioukh, luckily, did not notice. He sat straight in the saddle, beaming with pride to hear the Avtokrator, as he thought, honor the khagan.

"Etzilios bewails for youse," Moundioukh said. "Where does youse wants to meets with him?"

"We need a stretch of flat, open ground," Maniakes answered, "the better to show off our mimes from the Amphitheater and the speed of our horses." He waved a hand. "Here where I am now would do well enough, if it pleases the magnifolent Etzilios." He warned himself to be careful with that, but liked it so well he had trouble heeding his own good sense.

"This should pleases him, yesly. I will takes your words his way." Moundioukh wheeled his horse and rode back toward and then past Imbros at a ground-eating trot the animal looked able to keep up all day.

Off in the distance, horns brayed like donkeys with throats of bronze, a cry more like a challenge than a fanfare. Maniakes tried making a joke of it. "Either that's Etzilios coming, or we're about to be attacked." Then he listened to himself. Just on the off chance, he made sure his sword was loose in its scabbard.

But Etzilios and his guardsmen advanced peaceably enough. Maniakes had no trouble picking out the khagan of the Kubratoi: his horse had trappings ornamented with gold, and he wore a gold circlet on his fur cap. As he got closer, Maniakes saw his sword also had a hilt covered with gold leaf.

The khagan was older than Maniakes had expected, his long, unkempt beard well on the way toward going white. He was stocky and wide-shouldered; even with those years on him, Maniakes would not have cared to meet him in a wrestling match. He had only a stump for the little finger of his left hand. His face was weathered and leathery; his nose had a list to the left.

His eyes . . . When Maniakes saw those eyes under gray, shaggy brows, he understood how Etzilios ruled his unruly people. He lacked the schooling, the formal training a man could acquire in the Empire of Videssos, but if he didn't prove one of the two or three shrewdest men Maniakes had ever seen, the Avtokrator would own himself mightily surprised. After a moment, Maniakes realized why Etzilios struck him so: the khagan put him in mind of a barbarous version of his own father.

Etzilios spoke a gruff word in his own language, then held up his right hand. The horsemen who had accompanied him halted at that word of command. He rode out alone into the open space between his party and Maniakes'. Halfway across it, he reined in and waited.

Maniakes knew a challenge when he saw one. He booted his horse in the ribs and advanced to meet the khagan. "Do you speak Videssian?" he called as he approached. "Or shall we need an interpreter?"

"I speak Videssian, so I can understand you people," Etzilios answered, using the imperial tongue far more accurately than Moundioukh had. "When I want you to understand me, I most often speak with this." His right hand covered the swordhilt.

"I know that speech, too," Maniakes said at once. He saw clearly that he dared not let Etzilios intimidate him or take advantage of him in any way, for, if the khagan ever gained an edge, he would never let it go. "You have but to begin it here and we shall go back to war. You will not find me or my men easy meat for your taking."

"I did not come here to fight," Etzilios said with the air of a man making a great concession. "You have said you will pay me gold to keep from fighting."

"That is so," Maniakes agreed. "Fear of the Kubratoi, I should tell you, is not the only reason I am taking this course. We can thrash you if we must—you did not beat Likinios' army, after all."

"And what does that have to do with the price of a good horse?" the khagan asked. "We still hold our land, and look what became of Likinios—yes, and of Genesios, too, who threw him down. The battles do not matter, Videssian Avtokrator. We won the war—otherwise, we would be paying you."

Almost, Maniakes pulled out his sword then and there and attacked Etzilios. Robbing the Kubratoi of a man of such long sight would be a great good for Videssos. But if an assassination failed, the barbarians would renew their assaults, fueled by righteous fury. Not for the first time, Maniakes regretfully set aside the thought of murder.

He said, "I have brought the forty thousand gold pieces of the first year's tribute to which you agreed with my envoy, the excellent Triphylles."

"That man talks too much and thinks too well of himself," Etzilios said.

Since Maniakes had noted both those flaws in Triphylles, he found silence on them the better part of prudence. Instead, he made a manful effort at returning to the subject at hand: "As I say, I have with me the gold I will pay you in exchange for a year's peace. I will give it to you after the entertainments I have planned in your honor."

"I'd just as soon have it now," Etzilios said. "What are these entertainments, anyhow?"

"For your enjoyment, I have brought from Videssos the city two of our leading mime troupes, whose antics will make you laugh," Maniakes said.

"People hopping around without saying anything and pretending they're funny?" Etzilios spat on the ground. "I've seen the like in towns of yours I've taken. I could live a long time without seeing it again. Why don't you just give me the gold and toss out the folderol? Then you can go home and worry about Makuran. That's what you have in mind, isn't it?"

Maniakes opened his mouth, then closed it again without saying anything. He had never heard Videssian civilization so cavalierly dismissed. And Etzilios couldn't have divined his purposes better had he been in the room when Maniakes hammered them out with Rhegorios, Triphylles, and his own father. At last, after a deep breath and a pause for thought, the Avtokrator said, "We've also brought fine horses for racing."

"You should have said that first," Etzilios told him. "I'll put up with anything to see good horses run. I'll even watch your stupid mimes, and I won't pick my nose to distract them while I'm doing it." He chuckled. Maniakes wondered if he had really done such a thing. If he had, it probably would have served its purpose.

"Let us feast together and rest this evening, your men and mine," Maniakes said, "and in the morning you can enjoy the mimes—or not—and we will hold horse races, and then, after we pray to the lord with the great and good mind to preserve the arrangement as we have made it, I will convey to you the gold and we shall be at peace."

"You pray to Phos," Etzilios answered. "Me, I worship my sword alone. It's served me better than your god ever did."

Maniakes stared at him. He had never heard the lord with the great and good mind not just rejected—the Makuraners worshiped their deity, the God, instead of Phos—but dismissed as unimportant. Etzilios was a resolute heathen, and his people with him. Most in Khatrish and Thatagush followed Phos these days, but the Kubratoi clung to the ways they had brought off the Pardrayan steppe.

"Other than on the prayers, are we agreed?" Maniakes asked.

"Oh, aye, we're agreed," Etzilios said. "If you'll hold on a bit, I'll even have my men bring your cooks some sheep they can use for the feast."

"Generous of you," Maniakes said tonelessly. He would have been more appreciative had he not been certain the sheep the Kubratoi were contributing came from Videssian flocks.

If Etzilios noticed the irony, he didn't show it. With a vague wave to Maniakes, he turned his horse and rode back toward his waiting men. Maniakes did the same. The cooks set some of his soldiers to work digging trenches and others cutting wood to fill those trenches and build racks above them for roasting meat. The cooks also broke out great tuns of fermented fish sauce and jars of peeled garlic cloves kept fresh and flavorful in olive oil. Maniakes wondered what the Kubratoi would make of the condiments. If they didn't fancy them, his own men would have more to eat. He hoped just that would happen.

As promised, the Kubratoi drove a flock of sheep to the Videssian cooks. They did indeed look like Videssian animals, but, for the sake of peace, Maniakes asked no questions. The sheep bleated in desperation as they were butchered; cattle lowed out a last futile protest. Before long, the savory smoke that rose from the cooking trenches had Maniakes' mouth watering.

He picked some of his most trusted soldiers, men who would not resent missing a chance to stuff themselves, and sent them out to form a perimeter around the camp. He also warned the goldpieces' guards to be especially wary. Then, satisfied he had done all he could to keep himself and the gold safe during the celebration, he began to hope he would enjoy himself.

He went over to the chief cook, an enormously fat man named Ostrys, and said, "Be generous with the wine you give the barbarians. The happier we make them, the more they're liable to reveal of what their master truly intends for tomorrow."

"It shall be just as you say, your Majesty," Ostrys replied, setting a pudgy finger by the side of his nose. But for his dark, heavy beard, his looks would have inclined Maniakes to guess him a eunuch: He was round enough for any two of the palace servitors. He knew, though, that Ostrys had not only a wife but several sons who looked like him and shared his nearly spherical contours.

The smell of cooking meat drew the Kubratoi in the same way it would have drawn hungry wolves from the forest. They fraternized amiably enough with their Videssian counterparts; some of them had fought one another before. Most of the nomads spoke some Videssian. Maniakes wondered how they had learned it—maybe from women they had stolen.

Priests paraded with thuribles, sending up clouds of sweet-scented incense that mingled with the odors of firewood and roasting mutton and beef to make the feast flavorful to the nose. The blue-robed clerics also sent up sonorous prayers for peace between Videssos and Kubrat, beseeching Phos to make both sides honest and righteous and to hold deceit away from them.

Maniakes glanced over to see how Etzilios would take that. The khagan's left hand twisted in a sign that looked like one of the gestures of aversion Videssian peasants used. "By the good god, they're not trying to ensorcel you," Maniakes said.

Etzilios looked down at his hand as if it had turned traitor. "I trust no magics but those of my shamans," he said, and smiled a carnivorous smile. "If they blunder, I can punish them."

Barbarian, Maniakes thought. *A clever barbarian, but a barbarian all the same. He sees what he wants now and he takes it now, without worrying about what will happen later. Later is a different world.*

What Etzilios seemed to want now was meat. He sat crosslegged on the grass, a growing pile of bones around him. He drank, too, though more moderately than Maniakes had expected; he nursed his wine well enough to wave on Videssian servitors about every other time they came by with fresh jars. That moderation did not keep him from belching cavernously. Maniakes was not offended; among the nomads, such rumblings signified approval of the fare offered.

"You Videssians should have done this years ago," Etzilios said, beaming at the feast. "But no—instead you thought to chase me, like dog after fox. But no fox am I—I am a wolf, as you have seen." He bared his teeth. They were yellow as a wolf's; in so much, if no further, he spoke the truth.

"We're making peace now. We shouldn't worry about past quarrels," Maniakes said. He wished his men were chasing the Kubratoi right now. Had he not faced war on two fronts, his men would have been doing just that. Saying as much to Etzilios struck him as unwise.

The khagan frowned, rubbed at his considerable belly. "You make this mutton too spicy, I think," he said, climbing to his feet. "My guts gripe me."

Maniakes remembered Triphylles' complaint about eating endless meals of mutton without garlic. What seemed mildly seasoned meat to a Videssian was liable to be too much for a Kubrati to appreciate. He was just glad Etzilios hadn't accused him of putting poison in the sauce.

"I will be back later," Etzilios said, and lumbered off toward a stand of elms not far away. Maniakes hadn't been sure the nomads bothered to seek privacy for performing their basic bodily functions. He hoped Etzilios had nothing worse than a bellyache. If he suddenly dropped dead now, the Kubratoi would think Maniakes had slain him—when in fact he had decided not to try.

Maniakes sipped his own wine. When he looked around at the feast, he felt reasonably pleased with himself. His men and the Kubratoi seemed to be getting along well, in spite of old enmity. Not far away, a Kubrati who didn't speak Videssian was using vivid hand gestures to show how one of his people's horses would leave all the Videssian nags in the dust. The imperials sitting by the nomad quite plainly disagreed, but nobody hauled out a sword to back up his opinion.

If Etzilios saw that, Maniakes hoped he would be pleased, too. The Avtokrator frowned. Etzilios still hadn't come back from that stand of trees. Whatever call of nature he had had to answer, he should have been done long since. Either he truly had been taken deathly ill in there, or—

A couple of couriers sat nearby. Turning to them, Maniakes said, "Mount and ride to our waiting horsemen. Tell them to be ready." The couriers got to their feet. Above the friendly din of the feast, Maniakes heard a drumroll of hoofbeats. "No, tell them to come. Run to your horses, before the Kubratoi here try to stop you."

"Is something amiss, your Majesty?" Kameas asked as the couriers dashed away. Then he heard the approaching horses, too. His face went from sallow to white. He sketched the sun-circle over his heart.

"Hide!" Maniakes told him urgently. "If you can, pick someplace where they won't ever find you. Good luck, esteemed sir."

That done, Maniakes had no more time to worry about the vestiarios. He scrambled to his own feet, cursing the insistence on ceremony that had made him deck himself out in the gold-encrusted imperial robe rather than chain mail. Even his sword was a ceremonial blade, not meant for real fighting.

Here came a sentry, riding as if Skotos were at his horse's heels. It wasn't the dark god, but it was the next worst thing: a whole great swarm of Kubratoi, thundering forward with gleaming scimitars upraised.

Seeing the blades gave Maniakes an instant of relief. The nomads would not loose a shower of arrows from their deadly bows, not with their own men so intermingled with his. He cherished that relief, suspecting it was all he would be able to enjoy for a long time to come.

"To arms, men of Videssos!" he shouted, as loud as he could. "We are betrayed!" He drew his ridiculous toy of a sword and slashed at a Kubrati noble sitting a few feet away. The leather of the nomad's sleeve was enough to armor his flesh against the dull edge's bite.

In an instant, peace exploded into pandemonium. Videssians and Kubratoi who had been chatting snatched out blades and went at one another. Some of the Videssians ran for their horses, the better to resist the barbarians bearing down on them. Someone also had the presence of mind to run down the rows of the nomads' mounts, shouting, slashing tethers, and whacking the animals with his blade. Not many of the Kubratoi from among the feasters got mounted themselves.

Maniakes saw only disjointed fragments of the action. The barbarian he had tried to cut down surged to his feet and drew his own curved blade, which was no toy. Maniakes didn't want to try turning it with his gilded toothpick. He snatched up a heavy silver wine cup and dashed its contents full in the Kubrati's face. The fellow roared like a branded bull and clapped his hands to his eyes. Maniakes hit him over the head with the cup. He crumpled. Maniakes threw away his ceremonial sword and grabbed the Kubrati scimitar. Now he had a blade with which he could fight.

And none too soon. The Kubratoi were upon him and his men. He slashed at a nomad horseman, then sprang aside to keep from being trampled. Instead of going after the Kubratoi themselves, he cut at their horses all around him. His blade bit again and again. Ponies squealed in pain. That kept their riders too busy trying to keep control to have too much time to devote to murdering him.

As he fought for his life, he wondered what sort of nonsense Bagdasares had shown him in the magic mirror. How was he supposed to break free of this murderous press and get back to

Videssos the city? As he dodged and ducked and cut, he knew he was lucky to be surviving from moment to moment.

A Kubrati close by snatched at an arrow that suddenly sprouted above one eye. A moment later, the nomad's hands relaxed and he slid, dead, from the saddle. Maniakes scrambled onto the little plains horse the Kubrati had been riding. Like a lot of his fellows, the Kubrati had kept his stirrup leathers very short so he could rise in the saddle to shoot. Maniakes felt as if he were trying to touch his ears with his knees.

He didn't care. On a horse, the barbarians still might slaughter him like a sheep. They couldn't mash him like a bug underfoot, though. He fought his way toward a knot of his own men who were still fighting with some kind of order. He wondered how long till his own reinforcements arrived.

Pressure on that knot of determined fighting men eased. It wasn't Videssians coming to the rescue, not yet. Some of the Kubratoi, instead of finishing their foes, were busy plundering the imperial pavilion and the rest of the camp. A separate fight broke out when they overran the guards protecting the horses that carried the tribute and started quarreling over the goldpieces like a pack of dogs over a juicy bone.

"Videssos!" he shouted, lest anyone see the pony and take him for a Kubrati. Since he was wearing the gaudy imperial robe and the red boots, that was highly unlikely, but no one can think of everything in the midst of battle.

"Your Majesty!" The soldiers toward whom he was fighting had no trouble recognizing him. When at last he joined them, he felt like a man who had managed to seize a spar after his ship sank in a sea fight.

The analogy had but one flaw: the spar he had seized was in itself in danger of sinking. The Kubratoi, both afoot and mounted, raged against their outnumbered Videssian foes. They shouted to one another in their own guttural language, captains urging their men away from the loot of the imperial tent, away from the spilled goldpieces, and into the fight. The captains were wise enough to know the time for looting was after a triumph, not before. The men were harder to convince.

Because of that, Maniakes and his guards, though beleaguered, had not been overwhelmed when horns rang out from the south. "Videssos!" This time the cry rang from hundreds of throats.

"Videssos!" Maniakes shouted again. He waved the scimitar to show he still lived. Had he been on his own horse, he would have urged it to rear. On a beast he had acquired so irregularly, though, he took no chances. As long as he was able to stay in the saddle, that sufficed.

One thing the arrival of Videssian reinforcements did: it reminded the Kubratoi they were in a fight, not just a plundering expedition. They had ignored their officers in the search for booty. Ignoring the prospect of being killed was something else again. They snatched bows from their cases and plied the oncoming imperials with arrows. The Videssians shot back. Even more than he had before, Maniakes wished he had a shield.

He waved again. "To me! To me!" he cried. If the reinforcements could reach him, what had been a chaotic struggle to keep from being ridden down and crushed could suddenly become a fight the Videssians might win . . . or might still lose. Maniakes looked about worriedly. More Kubratoi were still coming down from the north. He had brought fifteen hundred men, over and above those about whom he had agreed with Etzilios. He had the bad feeling the khagan had brought more.

No help for that. He spurred southward, fighting toward the imperials as they neared him. Squeezed between two forces, the Kubratoi who tried to bar his path gave way—and, suddenly, the spar Maniakes had seized seemed a boat instead.

"Your Majesty!" the men bawled. "Here, take this!" "And this!" Someone set a helmet on his head, someone else thrust a shield at him. Since the trooper who offered it had a mail-shirt while he wore no armor beneath his robes, he gladly took it. Sometimes, he thought, Phos did answer prayers.

He hadn't fought like a common trooper for years, thinking of nothing past himself and staying alive from minute to minute. He had led charges after he attained high rank, but then, even as he battled, he had had the shape of the whole fight in his mind. The struggle for survival brought him fresh awareness of what his soldiers went through. But now he had a proper battle to run. He waved men to left and right, widening his line and trying to keep the Kubratoi from outflanking the reinforcements as they had effortlessly done with his accepted force of guards.

He didn't care for the shape of this fight. Etzilios had too many men, and they were pressing too hard. Presumably Etzilios also had the priests and the mimes and the racehorses Maniakes had brought up from Videssos the city. The racehorses he would undoubtedly treat well. The Kubratoi, though, had resisted all efforts to get them to accept Phos' faith. The priests might become martyrs for the greater glory of the good god. And Phos would have to be the one who helped the mimes, too.

A rider came hurrying up to Maniakes and cried, "Your Majesty, try as we will, we can't hold them on the left. They keep overlapping us and forcing us to fall back. If we don't, they get round us, and then we are undone."

Maniakes looked that way. Sure enough, the line was sagging badly. He looked eastward, to the right. The line sagged there, too, though no one had come to tell him about it. "Blow 'retreat,'" he called to the trumpeters. "They'll surround us if we don't give ground."

The melancholy horn calls rang out. Videssian military doctrine didn't represent retreat as anything to cause shame. Realistically, no army could expect to win every fight. If you didn't win, staying to be slaughtered was stupider than drawing back, because it lowered your chances of winning the next fight.

But regardless of whether retreat was shameful, it was fraught with danger. If soldiers gave way to panic, they were just a mob, and they would be massacred as surely as if they had let the enemy surround them. "Hold together!" Maniakes shouted, over and over till his throat was raw. "If we hang together, they can't drive us like wolves after deer."

Sticking together as they drew back, as the Kubratoi poured arrows into them from both flanks and from ahead, took almost superhuman discipline. Maniakes looked around for Etzilios. If he could kill the khagan, the Kubratoi might collapse. He had had his chances earlier and passed them by. Now it was too late; Etzilios, like any sensible general, led his troops from behind. With a manifest victory developing before their eyes, they didn't need to see their ruler in action to be inspired.

More horns rang out, the braying horns of the barbarians. A quick charge at the right of Maniakes' crumbling line made him send men there to hold it. But the charge proved a feint. Screaming like fiends, the Kubratoi staged another charge into the Videssian center—and broke it.

The rout Maniakes had dreaded was on. With Kubratoi in among them as well as on their flanks, the imperials no longer even tried to hold firm. Giving up any thought of staying together, they fled southward singly and in small bands, no thought but escape in their minds. The Kubratoi pursued, baying on the chase.

Maniakes was swept along with the rest. A group of about fifty men clung together—too large for the Kubratoi to assail when so many smaller, easier targets were there for the taking. But then one of the nomads spotted the imperial raiment in among that band of Videssians, and after that they were never free of the foe again.

Had Etzilios been anywhere close by, he no doubt would have urged his men to go after the Avtokrator regardless of the casualties it cost them. But the khagan was elsewhere on the field, and none of the men dogging Maniakes thought to ride off again and ask what to do next: being barbarously self-sufficient, they believed themselves able to make their own choices.

Maniakes spied a stand of oaks ahead. "Let's ride in among them," he said.

"Aye, why not?" one of the soldiers said. "The trees will keep them from raining arrows on us the way they have been."

"We'd go faster through open country," another man said. "The closer we stick to the road, the better the time we'll make."

"How fast isn't everything," Maniakes answered. "How you go counts, too. Come on." He guided his horse toward the trees. Most of the men in the band went with him. Six or eight, though, struck off on their own in the hopes the road would give them a better chance to escape the nomads.

Once in among the trees, Maniakes brought his blowing horse to a halt and dismounted. "Here, your Majesty, you can piss later," a trooper said gruffly. Maniakes ignored him. He undid the golden belt that held his robe closed, and threw it on the ground. Then he pulled off the heavy robe with its precious metallic threads and draped it over a branch. Wearing only his thin linen undertunic and drawers, he climbed back onto the Kubrati pony. "Now they won't hound us so much," he said. "I don't look like the Avtokrator any more."

His troopers nodded approvingly. He himself felt low enough to walk under a mouse without ruffling its belly fur. What could be more dishonorable and disgraceful than abandoning the imperial raiment to escape with your hide unpunctured? Only one thing occurred to him: dying when you had a means of survival at hand. Even so, he knew he would replay this scene in his nightmares as long as he lived. Whether he would live long enough to have more nightmares remained an open question.

More than forty men emerged from the south side of the stand of oaks. Maniakes was suddenly much less conspicuous than he had been. Now the Kubratoi harassed his band no more than any other of like size. He wondered if he should also have thrown away the red boots. That would have made riding harder. Besides, keeping them on let him cling to the notion that he had salvaged something of the imperial regalia.

"Where now, your Majesty?" a trooper asked.

"Back to Videssos the city, as best we can," Maniakes answered. Bagdasares' magic—and how was Bagdasares now? and Kameas? and the servitors? and the mimes? and everyone else Maniakes had led on this disastrous jaunt?—had shown he would come back to the city. But it hadn't shown him safe inside the walls. Now more than ever, he wished he could have looked back over his shoulder and seen if anyone was gaining on him.

As the routed Videssians fled south, the pursuit grew more distant. Maniakes wanted to draw more consolation from that than he actually could. It wasn't so much that he and his comrades had outrun the nomads, though that was part of it. But more, Maniakes knew all too well, was that the Kubratoi were busy plundering not only his camp with all its riches but also the surrounding countryside. How many Videssian peasants would they round up and herd north to labor for them? Where would he find other peasants to replace the ones the barbarians were kidnapping? With the Kubratoi in the north and the Makuraners ranging as they pleased in the westlands, Videssos might have no people left in a few years' time.

"We have to be careful not to founder our horses," Maniakes warned his comrades in misfortune. "If they break down before we get home, I expect we're done for."

His own pony, the one he had taken from the dead Kubrati, was still working magnificently. It was an ugly little beast, short and rough-coated, but it could run. Every so often, he paused to let it rest and pull up some grass and weeds from the ground. It seemed happy enough with that.

After a while, his own stomach started growling. The eruption of the Kubratoi had come before he got a chance to eat much at the feast. He rummaged in the beast's saddlebags to see what its former owner had been carrying. The first thing he found was a skin that, when he untied it, gave off the odor of sour milk. He threw it away. The Kubratoi might live on such fare, but Videssians? A moment after he had rejected the stuff, he cursed himself for a fool. No matter how nasty it smelled, it was food of a sort, and he was liable to be hungry by the time he got to Videssos the city.

The nomad had also been carrying strips of sun-dried mutton and flat griddlecakes of barley. The mutton was so hard, he could hardly bite it. As for the griddlecakes, they came as close to having no flavor whatsoever as anything he had ever eaten. He wolfed them down regardless. They had kept the nomad going, and they would do the same for him.

Camp that night was a cold, miserable affair. No one dared light a fire, for fear it would draw the Kubratoi. A raw wind blew out of the northwest. It smelled of rain, though none fell that night. Maniakes and his companions counted themselves lucky there. They had only a few blankets among them, and huddled together for warmth like the luckless sheep Maniakes' cooks had butchered for what should have been a celebration of peace with the Kubratoi.

Trying to find someplace comfortable on the ground, trying to keep the rest of the Videssians from kicking or elbowing him, Maniakes dreamed up a whole flock of grandiose vengeances to visit upon Etzilios' head. The one he liked best involved loosing Genesios' wizard, the old man who had almost killed him, against the khagan. Setting that mage, whoever and wherever he was, on the foes of Videssos for a change struck him as only fitting and proper. He fell asleep still imagining revenge.

He woke several times in the night, from people poking him or just because he was cold. At last, though the trees, he saw the gray light of false dawn. Yawning, he got to his feet. A good many other men were already awake; the morning looked as wretched as the night had been.

The soldiers shared what food they had. By the time evening came again, their supplies would be gone. The horses let out snorts of complaint as the men clambered onto them. Maniakes' steppe pony seemed fresher than most of the larger, more elegant beasts around it.

They had just left the woods when a cold rain started falling. Though it soaked him to the skin, Maniakes was not altogether unhappy to see it. "Let's see the Kubratoi try to track us when everything turns to muck," he said, and punctuated the remark with a sneeze.

The sneeze notwithstanding, that was the first even slightly optimistic thing he had said since Etzilios proved more adept at treachery than he was at preparing for it. One of the troopers promptly ruined his comment by saying, "They don't hardly need to track us. Long as they keep coming south, they're liable to run into us, and they ain't got nowheres to go but south."

Sure enough, not half an hour later they came upon a band of nomads riding on a track paralleling theirs. The Kubratoi were there in numbers about equal to those of the imperials, but did not attack them. That puzzled Maniakes, till he burst out, "They don't want to go at us sword to sword, and the rain would get their bowstrings wet." He sneezed again, this time almost cheerfully.

As gloomy day darkened toward black night, they came upon a peasant village. The farmers there gave Maniakes some baggy wool trousers and a tunic to put on instead of his soaked drawers while those dried in front of a fire, and later over them. They fed the soldiers bread and cheese and eggs, and killed a few of the chickens that pecked on the dirt floors of their homes.

When Maniakes tried to tell them who he was and to promise he would be grateful once he got back to Videssos the city, he found they didn't believe he was the Avtokrator, not even after he showed them the red boots. That touched him to the heart, at least until an old man said, "Don't matter who y'be, so long as y'got soldiers at your back. Farmers what's smart, they don't say no to soldiers."

Maniakes had enough soldiers to overawe them, but not enough to protect them if the Kubratoi attacked in any numbers. And after his band left the village on the southbound road, no one would be left to protect it at all.

As he was preparing to ride out the next morning, the old man took him aside and said, "Young feller, all that talk about bein' Avtokrator's fine and funny when you spin it afore the likes of us. But if Genesios Avtokrator ever gets wind of it, he'll have your guts for garters, likely tell. He's one hard man, Genesios is, by all they say, and not much for joking."

"I'll remember that," Maniakes said, and left it there. He wondered if any isolated villages off in the hinterlands thought Likinios was still Avtokrator. If you didn't go to town and traders didn't come to you, how would you find out what the truth was?

He and his men worked their way southward, adding other bands of fugitives as they went until, by the time they reached the Long Walls, they numbered two or three hundred. They scared off a troop of Kubratoi not far from their own size and were beginning to feel like soldiers again.

"Two more days and we're back in the city," Maniakes said, trying to hearten them further. "We'll get reinforcements and we'll have our revenge." A few of the men raised a cheer. That made Maniakes feel worse, not better. Where would he come up with reinforcements, with so much of Videssos in turmoil? If he did come up with them, where would he get the goldpieces to pay them? Those were conjurations he would gladly have assigned to the mages of the Sorcerers' Collegium, if only he had thought they had some hope of success.

Then all thoughts of what might happen and what probably wouldn't happen were swept away by a cry of despair from the rearguard: "The Kubratoi! The Kubratoi are on our heels!"

Maniakes looked back over his shoulder. He had some hope of driving the barbarians off—till he saw their numbers. Those offered but one remedy. "Fly!" he shouted. "They'll ride us into the mud if we don't." He no longer thought Etzilios was following him in particular. It seemed far more likely the Kubratoi were just taking advantage of Videssian weakness to plunder as far south, as close to the imperial city, as they could. The cause didn't matter. The result did—and it was quite as bad as deliberate pursuit.

The horses were worn to shadows of themselves. What should have been gallops were exhausted trots. Had the Kubratoi pursued harder, they might have overhauled and overwhelmed the Videssian stragglers. But their horses were frazzled, too.

It made for a strange sort of chase. Maniakes was reminded of a mime troupe he had once seen at a Midwinter's Day celebration, where everyone moved as if half frozen, drawing out each action to preposterous lengths for the sake of a laugh from the crowd. Even the memory might have been funny had he not been fleeing for his life and had he not also remembered the Kubratoi

sweeping down on the two mime troupes he had brought from
the capital in hopes of amusing them.

Rain started coming down again, hard and cold. Road and
fields alike turned to mire, which made both pursued and pursuers slower still. Normally, the downpour would have helped
Maniakes shake the Kubratoi off his trail. Now, though, they
knew he was heading for Videssos the city. They didn't need to
see him to follow him.

He thought about breaking off and making for some provincial
town instead. But the Kubratoi had already sacked Imbros, one
of the more strongly fortified cities in their path. That meant no
provincial town was safe from them. If he could get behind the
indomitable walls of Videssos the city, the barbarians would storm
against them in vain. If—

Bagdasares' mirror had shown him approaching the imperial
city. Had he not known—or at least strongly believed—he would
get that far, he might have given way to despair. As it was, he kept
riding, hoping to meet a rescuing force coming out of the capital
and turning the tables on the nomads who pursued him.

No rescuers came forth. He was forced to conclude that he,
his comrades, and, worse luck, the Kubratoi had outridden news
of their coming. As far as anyone in Videssos the city knew, he
had paid Etzilios his tribute and bought three years' peace in
return.

"I wish I only knew as far as they did," he said when that
thought crossed his mind.

At last, he and those of his fellows whom the Kubratoi had
not taken came into sight of the imperial capital. The sun had
come out and was shining in a watery sort of way, as if to warn
that this stab at decent weather would not last long. Even watery
sunlight, though, was enough to make the gilded globes that
marked Phos' temples glitter and sparkle.

Here was the view the magic mirror had given him. From now
on, he realized, he was on his own. Past this point, he had no
guarantee of his own safety. He dug his heels into the barrel of
the poor worn steppe pony. The beast snorted in exhausted protest
but somehow managed to shamble on a little faster.

Maniakes and the riders with him began shouting toward the
walls. "A rescue! By the good god, come to our aid!"

An arrow whined past Maniakes' head. Some of the Kubratoi

still had shafts to shoot, then. Perhaps twenty feet away, a man cried out, slumped in the saddle, and slid from his horse: how cruel, to have escaped so much and yet to fall within sight of safety. Maniakes urged on his mount yet again. He was not safe himself, either.

And then, at last, a sound sweeter to him than the chorus of monks who hymned Phos' praises in the High Temple, catapults up on the wall and in the siege towers began to buck and thump, throwing darts and great stones at the Kubratoi. Chains rumbling, an iron-faced portcullis lifted. A regiment of mounted archers and javelin men rode out against the barbarians.

Resentfully, the Kubratoi withdrew, shooting over their shoulders at the Videssians who had driven them back from the walls of the capital. The imperials did not chase them far; they had a way of turning and mauling pursuers who broke ranks thinking the foe was done for.

The Videssians' commander, a handsome fellow on a handsome horse, looked down his nose at the draggled men he had rescued. "Who," he asked scornfully, "is in charge of this ragtag and bobtail?"

"I am," Maniakes answered, weary in every pore and hardly daring to believe he had won free to the capital at last.

He had forgotten what sort of spectacle he must have seemed, filthy, dressed in ill-fitting peasant clothes, and riding a Kubrati pony on its last legs. The impressive officer set hands on hips and demanded, "And who, sirrah, are *you*?"

Worn as they were, some of the men who had come down from Imbros muttered back and forth and smiled a little, waiting to see how he would respond to that.

"I am Maniakes son of Maniakes," he said. "Who are you, excellent sir?"

The handsome officer started to laugh, but was not quite altogether a fool. He looked at Maniakes' face, then at his boots, which, however mud-spattered they had become, were undeniably red beneath the grime. "Forgive your servant Ipokasios!" he cried, suddenly solicitous rather than scornful. "I failed to recognize you, your Majesty. A thousand pardons!"

In his alarm, he grew almost as flowery as a Makuraner. Maniakes held up a hand to stem the tide of self-reproach. "Excellent Ipokasios, for driving the Kubratoi from my trail I would forgive you a great deal more than not knowing who I am, though I hope you'll greet the next ragged traveler with a touch more forbearance than you showed me."

Ipokasios hung his handsome head. "It shall be just as you say, your Majesty." Maniakes wouldn't have risked a copper to win a pile of goldpieces that it would be as he had said—he knew well-bred arrogance when he saw it—but perhaps the officer believed he was telling the truth, and was properly apologetic any which way.

From behind Ipokasios, one of his men cried, "But, your Majesty, what *happened*?"

That was the question Ipokasios should have come up with himself. Maniakes and his comrades explained: variations on the theme of treachery. The men from Videssos the city cursed to hear what had happened to the imperial camp, the priests, the mimes, and the gold.

"To say nothing of all the peasants the Kubratoi raped away from the northern marches after they routed us," Maniakes added glumly. Without enough peasants, the rest of the Empire would soon grind to a halt, though city folk had trouble remembering it.

"Peasants." Ipokasios dismissed them with a short, contemptuous wave, which proved only that he had never paused to think about where the bread he ate every day came from.

"Enough chatter," Maniakes said; making Ipokasios understand that his view of the way the Empire worked was too simple would have taken more time than Maniakes had to spare and might have taken longer than winning the war would have done. "I need to get back to the palaces as fast as I can go. I blundered into disaster; now I have to start setting it to rights."

Few people on the streets of Videssos the city recognized him as he made his way across town toward the palace quarter. That he found refreshing; being the focus of everyone's gaze had quickly come to seem a trial. Next time he achieved the present effect, though, he vowed not to use such drastic means.

Few people recognized him in the palace quarter, either. The bureaucrats who deigned to notice him did so for his ragged clothes and scruffy horse. What they were wondering, very plainly, was how such a ragged fellow had become part of a body of imperial soldiers.

At the imperial residence, guards and eunuchs likewise failed to realize what he was—until one of the latter exclaimed in high-pitched tones of horror, "Phos preserve us! It is the Avtokrator, returned in this rough guise."

The servitors fell on him like an army, crying out the virtues of soaking and steaming and hot scented oil and clean linens and silk and squab stuffed with mushrooms and fine fragrant wine. He held up a hand. "Those all sound wonderful," he said, and, as if to prove it, his belly rumbled. "First, though, I'll see my wife and my father and let them know I'm alive and what's happened to me."

"Your Majesty," one of the eunuchs quavered, "where is the esteemed Kameas?"

Maniakes grimaced, but that question, like so many others, had to be faced. "If he's lucky, prominent sir, the Kubratoi have captured him. If he's not lucky—" He didn't think he had to elaborate on that.

The eunuch looked down at the stairs of the imperial residence. "If being captured by the barbarians is good fortune, Phos ward us from the bad," he said.

After dismissing the troops who had escorted him through the city—and praising those who had fought and fled with him from just outside Imbros—Maniakes went into the imperial residence. Drawn by the commotion, Niphone waited just inside the entrance. By the expression on her face, Maniakes gauged the state of his own decrepitude.

"I'll be all right," he said. "I'm just hungry and tired and dirty and worn to a nub. I wish the rest of my news were as good as what I can say about myself." In a few gloomy sentences, he told once more of Etzilios' assault.

Niphone's finger traced the sun-circle above her heart. "So long as you are safe," she whispered.

"I'm safe," Maniakes said, and, for the first time, began to believe it himself. Every moment of every day since the Kubrati surprise had passed for him as if he were a hunted animal, with the huntsman always about to fall on him. Only luck and watchfulness had saved him, and that watchfulness had grown so ingrained in a few short days that lifting it took strong, conscious effort. After a moment, he went on, "But so much and so many have been lost: Bagdasares, Kameas, the treasure I was to give the khagan in exchange for peace, the priests who would have blessed that peace, the mimes and horses Etzilios would have marveled to see. All gone."

Niphone sketched the sun-circle again. "May the men safely walk the bridge of the separator and reach Phos' light. As for the beasts and treasure, you are the Avtokrator. Of these things you can always get more."

"Would it were so easy!" Maniakes said with a bitter laugh. "If only I could order them from a storeroom or conjure them up and have them appear when I commanded. But I cannot do those things, and I do not know where to lay my hands on more gold."

"My father is logothete of the treasury," Niphone said, as if reminding him of something he had forgotten. "Speak to him. He will get gold for you."

Maniakes had spoken with Kourikos, more than once. The main thing his father-in-law had told him was that not only the coffers but also the yearly tax revenues were disastrously low. That was hardly surprising, after years of invasion and civil war, and with the Makuraners in the westlands and the Kubratoi not only working great destruction but also keeping tax collectors from even reaching huge tracts of land. Till some of the invaders were driven out, the imperial government would have to run on shoestrings and cheese parings.

No point in burdening Niphone with any of that, though. Maniakes said, "We'll do what we can, that's all. That's all I want to do for myself right now: bathe, eat, and sleep for a week."

Rotrude would have looked at him out of the corner of her eye and said, "And then?" He could all but hear the words, and the saucy flavor her Haloga drawl would lend them. Niphone just nodded earnestly. Maniakes sighed a silent sigh. *We'll do all we can, that's all*, he thought.

Stragglers from Maniakes' journey up to Imbros kept reaching Videssos the city, sometimes by ones and twos, sometimes in larger groups. A lot of them told terrible tales about what they had seen the Kubratoi doing to the countryside as they made their way south. None of what they said surprised Maniakes, who had seen some of that for himself and owned imagination enough to guess the rest.

Five days after he returned to the capital, Bagdasares arrived aboard a horse that looked fit only for slaughter. Like Maniakes, he had trouble getting the guards to believe he was who he said he was.

"You should have turned them into toads and let them sleep stupidly in the mud at the bottom of a pond till spring," Maniakes declared when the wizard finally gained admission to his presence.

"Speak to me not of spells of changing," Bagdasares answered with a shudder. "When I saw the nomads bearing down on the feast and the encampment, I gave myself the seeming of a Kubrati. The spell was, if anything, too thorough, for not only did I look like a barbarian, I even thought like one—or rather, I thought the way I thought a Kubrati would think, which proved quite sufficiently unpleasant, I assure you."

"In that case, I expect I'm lucky you decided to make your way south instead of heading back toward the Astris with the folk you imagined to be your tribesmates," Maniakes said.

"It is no laughing matter, I assure you," Bagdasares said, though Maniakes had not laughed. "In the confusion, I got to the woods and hid there, and for the life of me I could not be sure whether I was hiding from Videssians or Kubratoi. Fear for the most part makes magic fail. My fear powered the spell to greater heights than it had any business reaching."

"How did you decide who you truly were?" Maniakes asked.

"I had to skulk among the trees for a couple of days, till I could get free and start moving south," Bagdasares answered. "During that time, as the magic slowly waned, I began to be afraid of the nomads once more."

"I'm just glad you didn't ride off with them before your magic faded," Maniakes said.

"Not half so glad as I am," Bagdasares answered with great sincerity. "I wouldn't have cared to try to explain myself when the Kubratoi suddenly saw my true appearance rather than the seeming I had placed on myself. Mind you, I'm a much handsomer fellow than the barbarian I made myself appear to be, but there is a time and a place for everything."

The wizard's invincible self-importance made Maniakes smile, but he quickly sobered. "Magic is seldom as definite as it ought to be," he said. "I saw myself coming back to Videssos the city in your magic mirror, but I didn't see the Kubratoi riding after me, and so thought I'd concluded the treaty with them. And you wanted to seem a nomad, not to be one."

"'Be what you wish to seem' is a good rule for life, but not for magic," Bagdasares said. "Magic confuses being and seeming too much as is."

Maniakes clapped him on the shoulder. "Well, however you got here, I'm glad you did," he said. "I'll need your help in the future, and I'd have hated to break in a new wizard."

"You're kind, your Majesty, but there are swarms of sorcerers stronger than I am." Bagdasares hung his head. "Had I been better at what I do, you might have been properly warned that Etzilios planned treachery, for instance."

"You've given me good service, and my foibles don't seem to bother you," Maniakes said. "In my ledger, those count for more than raw strength."

"Don't be absurd, your Majesty." Bagdasares raised an admonitory index finger. "Avtokrators have no foibles."

His face was perfectly straight. Maniakes stared at him, then burst out laughing. "I haven't heard anything so funny in years. Likinios was a skinflint, Genesios murdered people for the sport of it, and I—"

"Yes, your Majesty?" Bagdasares asked innocently.

"I'm trying to save the Empire. Considering the state it's in right now, if that's not a foible, to the ice with me if I know what is."

Without Kameas, the imperial household ran less smoothly than it had before. The other eunuchs were willing and gracious, but the vestiarios had known how everything worked and where everything was. No one else attained to such omniscience. Maniakes caught a couple of servitors on the point of coming to blows over a crimson sash each of them claimed the other had mislaid. Such squabbles would not have happened with Kameas supervising the staff, or, if they had, Maniakes would never have known of them.

That the eunuchs were jockeying to be named vestiarios did nothing to improve matters. They all tried so hard to impress Maniakes that they ended up irking him as often as not. He kept putting off the decision; none of them completely satisfied him.

A couple of weeks after he returned from the north, the first snow fell. Maniakes watched the flakes swirl in the wind with something less than enthusiasm. When the cold froze the ground, the Kubratoi would be able to sweep over the roads and fields and steal whatever they had missed on earlier raids.

Sure enough, a couple of days later a band of nomads rode down into sight of the walls of Videssos the city. Maniakes went over to the wall to glare at them. They weren't doing much, just sitting their horses and staring at the capital's fortifications. Maniakes understood that; the great works were plenty to inspire awe even in a Videssian.

"Shall we drive them off, your Majesty?" Ipokasios asked. "We have force aplenty to do it."

Maniakes was sure he wanted to perform well in front of the Avtokrator's eye after his earlier embarrassment. But he answered, "No, let them look all they like. The more they see about Videssos that impresses them, the more they'll come to understand that, once our present troubles are over, we are not to be trifled with." He almost made the sun-circle as he replied; he seemed even to himself to be speaking more in pious hope than from any knowledge of when, if ever, Videssos' troubles would end.

But the Kubratoi, after spending some time looking at the wall from beyond the range of its stone- and dart-throwing engines, rode away to the north—all but one of them, who was left behind on foot. That one started slowly walking toward the wall. As he drew nearer, Maniakes saw he wore no beard. He plucked at his own whiskers; he had never seen nor heard of a clean-shaven Kubrati.

The fellow called up to the soldiers atop the wall. "Open the gate, I pray you, that I may enter." He spoke Videssian like a cultured man of the city. But was he a man? The voice could as easily have been contralto as tenor.

"Kameas!" Maniakes shouted. "Is it you?'

"More or less, your Majesty," the vestiarios answered. "I would be surer inside the city than I am out here. I have seen more of the wide, wild world than I ever expected to know."

"Let him in," Maniakes told the men on the wall. He hurried down a stairway at the rear of the wall and embraced Kameas when he came through the gateway they opened for him.

"Please, your Majesty, such familiarity is improper," Kameas said.

"You're not in the palaces, esteemed sir, not yet, nor in my pavilion. That means you don't tell me what to do. I tell you. And if I want to hug you, I bloody well will."

"Very well. Under these circumstances, I shall not be argumentative," Kameas said with the air of one making a great concession. Had he been his normal sprightly self, he might have given the Avtokrator more backtalk. But he was thin and worn and pale even for a eunuch, and, though the Kubratoi had dressed him in wool trousers and sheepskin jacket in place of his robes, he looked half frozen.

Concerned, Maniakes said, "Come on, esteemed sir. We'll get you back to the palaces, soak you in a warm pool, and feed you hot spiced wine and candied figs and apricots. Can you ride a horse across the city, or shall I have a litter brought for you?"

"I can ride a horse." Kameas rolled his eyes. "That is not a skill I ever thought I should acquire, but acquire it I have. From all I have seen, among the Kubratoi one either rides or is left behind for the delectation of the wolves." He shuddered. "After the journeys I have made, the trip to the palaces will be like a spring stroll through the cherry trees around the imperial residence when their blossoms fill the air with sweetness."

"I couldn't muster up that much poetry when I'm perfectly well, let alone after what you've been through," Maniakes told him. "Here, we'll get you a nice, gentle animal, not one of those steppe ponies with a mouth like iron and a will that comes straight from Skotos." He spat on the cobblestones.

"You're familiar with the breed, then," Kameas said. When Maniakes nodded, the vestiarios went on, "I did wonder if the problems I was having were entirely due to my own ineptitude. But the Kubratoi had no trouble with their horses. I suppose they're as harsh as the beasts they ride."

He swung up onto the mare that was fetched for him—the prospect of getting him a gelding had struck the Avtokrator as being in poor taste—and seemed capable enough in the saddle, if not what Maniakes would have called comfortable there. "How did they catch you?" he asked. "What happened to you then?"

"How did they catch me?" Kameas echoed. "Your Majesty, I shall always be grateful to you for your advice to hide; had the nomads spotted me out in the open, most likely they would have ridden me down and slaughtered me. But the places for proper concealment were few. I ran into a tent, covered myself over with bedding, and hoped for the best.

"Unfortunately for me, the Kubratoi soon proceeded to loot the tents. One of the blankets under which I lay was a quilted one with a fine cover of crimson silk. A barbarian pulled it away—and discovered me."

"Did he already know you were there?" Maniakes asked delicately; the vestiarios had been considerably bulkier on the day of the Kubrati surprise.

"Well, yes, your Majesty, you might say so. He had his breeches down around his ankles when he pulled the blanket off me. I spoke none of the Kubrati language then, and have learned but few words, most of them vile, since. Still, I had no trouble figuring out his disappointment that I was not a woman. Had I been a man of the ordinary sort, I think he would have slain me out of sheer pique.

"But he did not know what to make of me, and in his curiosity decided I might be more interesting alive than dead. He fetched me out and showed me to someone of higher rank than himself, who in turn took me to a barbarian of still more exalted rank—from excellent to eminent, you might say—and, shortly thereafter, I was fetched before Etzilios.

"He had seen me attending you, your Majesty, and knew I had to be one of your eunuchs, but he did not know what a eunuch was, at least not in detail. He kept insisting they must have made me into a woman. I denied this, but refused to, ah, let him examine the evidence for himself."

"Clever," Maniakes said. "The more curious he was about you, the less likely he'd hurt you."

"I thought of that only later," Kameas said. "Your Majesty, you are a gentleman of finest quality; you have never shown any unseemly interest in the nature of my mutilation. This has not always been the case among the powerful, in my experience." The vestiarios' voice was bleak. Maniakes wondered what indignities he had suffered during Genesios' reign.

Kameas went on, "Etzilios could have forced me to expose my nakedness, of course, but having me serve him amused him more: he boasted how he'd taken everything of yours, from the imperial robe—which he wore over his furs and leathers—to the imperial eunuch. Perhaps he thought I would poison him if I was sufficiently humiliated. I wish I had indeed had the wherewithal to prove him right."

"If he wanted you to serve him, why didn't he take you back to Kubrat with him?" Maniakes asked.

"Eventually, while attending to a call of nature, I was discovered by some of the ruffians in what passes for Etzilios' court," Kameas answered. "What they saw so bemused them that they burst out of the bushes where they were hiding and dragged me forthwith before the khagan, to exhibit me to him as if I were a two-headed snake or some other freak of nature." His sallow cheeks reddened with remembered indignation.

When he did not continue, Maniakes said, "And?"

"And Etzilios, having looked his fill, immediately sent me back to you, saying you were welcome to me." Kameas sniffed. "*I* consider his judgment a vindication."

"So do I," Maniakes said, reaching out to set a hand on his shoulder. "His loss is my great gain."

"Your Majesty is gracious."

✦ VII

About a week after the Midwinter's Day festivities had come and gone, Kameas interrupted Maniakes as the Avtokrator went over the accounts of revenue received from each province. Maniakes was glad to be interrupted; the numbers added up to *not enough*. To avoid that bleak contemplation, he slammed shut the register in front of him and said, "How now, esteemed sir?"

"Your Majesty, a man awaits you at the entrance to the residence here. He claims to be your brother Parsmanios," the vestiarios answered. "You of all people are best suited to judge the truth of this claim."

Maniakes' heart leapt within him. He sprang to his feet, exclaiming "At last something goes my way! I'll see him at once. And fetch my father there, too—he'll want this news no less than I."

"It shall be as you say, your Majesty."

Heedless of his imperial dignity, Maniakes ran down the hall toward the entrance. The closer he got, the colder the air grew. Hypocausts—brick-lined ducts under the floor—brought warmth from a central furnace to the rooms of the residence, but that warmth could not compete with the winter wind whistling outside.

He didn't care. The guardsmen out there—shivering Videssians and Halogai who looked far more comfortable now than they did in the muggy heat of midsummer at the capital—were keeping a wary eye on a tall dark fellow in a cavalryman's cloak and boots. One of the soldiers turned to Maniakes and said, "Well, your Majesty, is he your brother or do we fill him full of holes?"

554

The last time he had seen Parsmanios, not long before he went into exile and his brother off to fight in the westlands, Parsmanios' beard had still been on the downy side, with patches where the hair grew sparsely. Now it was full and thick, with a gray streak in it that looked to follow a scar whose upper portion seamed his left cheek.

"By the good god, brother of mine, you're a man," Maniakes said.

"By the good god, brother of mine, you're Avtokrator," Parsmanios replied. "How did that happen? I heard of it by chance in a tavern out toward the border with Vaspurakan—a merchant had managed to bring in a few donkeyloads of wine. I almost fell off my chair. Many good-byes to Genesios and all, but how did you end up wearing the red boots? I suppose I should prostrate myself to you, shouldn't I?"

"If you do, I'll kick you in the ribs," Maniakes promised. He briefly told how he had come to the throne, then went on, "So what of you? You were near the border with Vaspurakan, you say? Why didn't news get there sooner? I've sent letters out after you and Tatoules, but it was like shouting into a bottomless cavern: no echo came back."

Parsmanios spread his hands. "Who brings news? Traders, soldiers—travelers, anyhow. Haven't seen many of those lately, not in the little pisspot village where I've been stuck—place called Vryetion. The princes' land is under the thumb of the King of Kings these days, and his general Abivard led an army that sliced up and cut us off from getting any word out to the east. If he'd wanted to, he could have smashed us up, but he must have figured he had bigger fish to fry. For all I know, he may have been right."

"It wouldn't surprise me," Maniakes agreed. "I got to know Abivard when we were fighting to put Sharbaraz back on his throne. He knows his business, no way around that. He'd strike toward the heart of Videssos and leave detachments behind him to wither on the vine."

Before his younger brother could answer, the elder Maniakes came out and folded Parsmanios into a bearhug. "The more of this clan we have gathered in one place," he said, "the more cause our foes have to fear."

"Any word at all of Tatoules?" Parsmanios asked.

Maniakes told him of the short, unsatisfying report he had had from Tzikas. "I sent him a letter straightaway," he added, "but I've heard nothing further. He's been busy trying to hold Amorion against the Makuraners. If they take it, they can swarm straight down the valley of the Arandos to the sea and cut the westlands in half from west to east."

"When I got word of what had happened to you, I thought of coming here by way of Amorion and the river," Parsmanios said. "I figured I'd run into the boiler boys if I tried it, though, so I took the coast route instead. That worked well enough—I'm talking with you, anyway."

"To the ice with the boiler boys," Maniakes said, echoing his brother's use of the slangy Videssian nickname for heavy-armored Makuraner cavalry. He pointed to the doorway. "Here, come inside. We'll get some hot spiced wine inside you, make you feel like a new man."

"Hot spiced wine is good even if you feel like an old man," the elder Maniakes said.

Parsmanios laughed. "By Phos, Father, it's good to see you, and better still to hear you. If you have hot wine anywhere handy, I'll gladly drink some."

Over the wine, which was steaming and fragrant with cloves and cinnamon, the younger Maniakes said, "We'll put you up in one of the apartments in the wings off to the side of the Grand Courtroom. And—" He preened. "—you're going to be an uncle again."

"Good news," Parsmanios said, thumping him on the back. "Little by little, you're gathering in our whole clan." His face clouded. "Except Tatoules."

"We can but pray to the good god there," Maniakes said, and his brother nodded.

"If you'll recall," the elder Maniakes said to Parsmanios, "you were betrothed before you went off to the westlands. Evagria, that was the girl's name; I'm not too far into my dotage to remember it. I think Genesios took her father's head for something or other, but that's old news now, and I've forgotten what. She's still here in the city; odds are she'll be glad to see you."

Parsmanios coughed, more from discretion than catarrh. "Father, we've been based in Vryetion four or five years now. Summer before last, I wed a local girl named Zenonis. I have a baby boy myself; his name is Maniakes."

The elder Maniakes beamed. "You flatter me outrageously," he said. "As for the other, well, if you wed her, you wed her. A settlement of gold on Evagria's family will probably make them happy enough; they've been, oh, not poor, but poorish since her father got put to the sword." He turned to the younger Maniakes. "You'll take care of that?"

"I'll take care of it some way or other," Maniakes said. "We don't have the gold for what really needs doing, let alone for smaller things like this." He frowned, first in annoyance, then in thought. At last he beamed. "*I* have it! I'll promote them in the nobility. Not only won't that cost me anything, I may even be able to make them pay for the privilege."

Parsmanios stared at him. The elder Maniakes laughed uproariously. "Damn me to the ice if I think you're wrong, son." He snorted, drank, and snorted again. "The good god save the poor Makuraners when we're finally able to face them. Not only will we beat 'em in the field, we'll cheat 'em out of their armor and their boots and, if they're not careful, their drawers, too."

Kameas poked his head into the study where Maniakes was trying to figure out how to stretch his gold as far as it would go or, with luck, three steps farther. "Your Majesty, the Empress has pangs she believes to be labor pains. She just asked me to send for the midwife and arrange the Red Room for the birth of, Phos willing, the heir."

"Esteemed sir, you don't need my permission to attend to such matters," Maniakes answered. "As far as birth is concerned, Niphone's serving women have made it quite clear that I am, in their words, a large, stupid man, and not to be trusted with anything of greater weight than staying out of the way and not getting underfoot."

"I was not seeking permission, your Majesty, merely informing you of what I was about to do," the vestiarios said. "This notification, I trust, will enable you to succeed at the tasks the maidservants set you."

Maniakes considered that, then said, "Have a care with that wit of yours, lest you pierce someone with it by accident."

"As always, I obey your Majesty," Kameas said. Maniakes had the satisfaction of winning a rare smile from the eunuch before Kameas hurried off to do as Niphone had asked.

The midwife was a plump, middle-aged woman named Zoïle. By the way she strode confidently through the halls of the imperial residence, she had come here before: perhaps she had helped Genesios' wife give birth, or perhaps she had aided servants at their confinements. Maniakes didn't have the nerve to ask. She was the ruler of a province where he could not go and carried herself with a ruler's pride.

"Now you just sit yourself down, your Majesty—find someplace comfortable, let them fetch you some wine, and settle yourself down to wait," she said, echoing, consciously or unconsciously, the maidservants' advice. "It may take a while, but I'll make sure you get yourself a fine baby and a healthy lady, too."

"Thank you," Maniakes said. Large, stupid man though he was, he knew Zoïle could not make the guarantee she claimed. Women died in childbirth, and afterward from fever, in spite of everything midwives could do. If fever took Niphone, he had a healer-priest ready to summon. But even healers could do only so much, and their art told cruelly on them. He prayed he would not have to make the call for which he was prepared.

After a while, Kameas came into the chamber where he sat worrying. The vestiarios said, "Under Zoïle's direction, we have transferred her majesty to the Red Room. The heir, if such the birth should produce, shall come into the world in the chamber set aside for the confinements of Empresses."

Maniakes had been born by the side of the road. So had his father; he remembered his grandmother talking about it. However steeped in ceremony Videssos was, being born in the Red Room wasn't required for imperial rank. Kameas surely knew as much. Bluntly pointing it out, however, struck Maniakes as impolitic.

The vestiarios asked, "Does your Majesty require anything?"

"Nothing I can think of, esteemed sir; thank you," Maniakes answered. "Just come in and dust me off occasionally, as you need to."

"The process should not take so long as that," Kameas said with a hint of reproof in his voice. "In my admittedly limited experience—" He left it there, undoubtedly because part of his limited experience did involve Genesios' wife, and he was too polite to make much of that in Maniakes' presence.

Periodically reports came to Maniakes of what Genesios' survivors were doing in the monastery and convents where they lived out their days. The reports always boiled down to *nothing much*. So long as they kept boiling down to that, Maniakes was content, at least there.

Kameas went off to put the finishing touches on the feast that would celebrate the birth of Maniakes' first child. So it was described, anyhow, though the vestiarios knew he had a bastard son. He wondered how Atalarikhos was doing these days. If Niphone gave him legitimate children as fine as the son Rotrude had borne, he would be a lucky man.

With nothing to do but wait, he did that as well as he could. Every so often, his kinsfolk would come in to pat him on the shoulder and wish him and Niphone luck. "I know what you're going through, son," the elder Maniakes said. "It's never easy, though if you listen to the women, they'd gladly trade places with you."

A little while after his father left, Lysia peered into the chamber where Maniakes sat. "The good god grant everything goes well in the Red Room," she said.

He sketched the sun-circle over his heart. "May it be so," he said, and then, "She's been in there a long time, hasn't she?"

Lysia smiled at that. "It seems so to you, and no doubt it seems so to Niphone, but it's not really. These things do take a while, you know."

"I suppose so," he said vaguely. "I ought to be getting some work done, not just hiding myself away, but I've tried. I can't."

"I'd worry about you if you could," his cousin replied. "The Empire won't crumble to pieces because you're not watching it for a few hours. If you want to give the stack of parchments to Rhegorios, I'm sure he'd make short work of them." Her eyes twinkled.

"The work your brother would give them is too short to suit me," Maniakes answered with a snort. "He's a clever chap, and I'm glad to have him for my Sevastos even with Father here, but he sees the whole mosaic and doesn't pay enough attention to any one tessera in it."

"Of the two of us, I got that," Lysia's mouth twisted. "It does less good in me than it might in him, me being a woman."

"If I were to make you Sevastos, or rather Sevaste—"

"Don't mock me," Lysia said, more sharply than she was in the habit of speaking. "We both know that cannot be."

Maniakes looked at her as if he had never seen her before. "I'm sorry," he said slowly. "Till this moment, it never occurred to me that you might want the job."

"Why does that not surprise me?" she said, and then sighed. "I know why, of course. It could be worse. I know that, too. Even after I got done explaining myself, you still might not have had any idea what I was talking about. I'm glad you did figure it out, though."

"Cousin, much as I love you—" Maniakes began.

"If you loved me, you would take me seriously," Lysia broke in.

"Take you seriously? I do. I always have." Maniakes spread his hands. "If we ever find peace, maybe I'll get the chance to prove it to you. But if I'm fighting the Kubratoi and the Makuraners both, I can't set men and women in Videssos against each other, and if I appoint you to the rank you'd like—not that you wouldn't fill it well—that's what I'd do. We can't afford it. I have to find a better way."

"I know," she answered. "Realistically, I know. Sometimes, though, being kept for a brood mare and valued only for the marriage I might make and the sons I might bear is hard to stand."

"Whatever happens, you'll have a place with me," Maniakes said. "You always need to remember that."

Lysia sighed again. "You mean that well, and I thank you for it. It's far more than almost any woman in the Empire has. I hope you won't think me ungrateful if I say it's not enough." She turned and walked out before he could find an answer. He had the feeling she might have waited a long time before he came up with a good one.

But she did not have to wait now. He did. The waiting went on for what became by anyone's standards a long time. Kameas brought him supper—he ate without noticing what was on the plate in front of him—put him to bed, and then, when he woke, served him breakfast. No word came from the Red Room.

"They've been in there most of the day now," he said. "How much longer can it be?"

"I have spoken with Zoïle," the vestiarios answered. "From what she says, the lady your wife is doing as well as can be expected for a first birth, but proceeding more slowly than is often the case."

"A lot more slowly," Maniakes said. Would a midwife tell a chamberlain all she knew—or feared? Would Kameas shade whatever he did hear from the midwife? The answers that formed in Maniakes' mind were *not necessarily* and *very likely*, respectively.

When he tried to go to the door of the Red Room himself, all his servants reacted with such dismay that he never got the chance to ask any questions of Zoïle herself. "Her Majesty is very tired" was as much as anyone would tell him. Since she had been in there more than a day by then, it wasn't anything he hadn't been able to figure out for himself. He stalked down the hall, scowling at everybody he saw.

He had been worried since Niphone went into labor. It was more than worry now; it was alarm. What if he lost her? To his own embarrassment, he had never been able to call up more than a fraction of the feeling he had had for her before he was forced to sail off to Kalavria. That was a long way from saying he would have been happier without her.

He drank more wine than he should have, and felt hazy and stupid and belligerent all afternoon. He headed back to the Red Room, the wine fueling his determination to get answers one way or another.

But before he got to the door, though, a cry from within the chamber froze him in his tracks. Niphone's voice was high and thin and rather breathy; he had never imagined such a piercing sound passing her lips. He heard torment and exhaustion there, but something else, too, something he had a harder time naming. *Effort* wasn't the word he wanted, but it came closer than any other he could find.

The cry faded. Maniakes needed a moment before he could nerve himself to go on. He had just taken another step toward the closed door when Niphone cried out again. This—shriek? moan? wail?—lasted even longer than the one before it had, and sounded far more dire.

Zoïle's voice came through the door, too. He couldn't hear what the midwife said, only her tone of voice. After a moment, he recognized it: it was the same one he had used to urge on his failing Kubrati pony as it neared the walls of Videssos the city. Was Niphone failing, too? His nails bit into the palms of his hands.

Niphone let out yet another cry. It cut off in the middle.

Maniakes' heart leapt into his mouth. Rotrude had never made noises like these. She had been grimly silent through the whole business of childbirth till, six or eight hours after she began, she presented him with a baby boy. Was Niphone in greater pain? Was she just more sensitive to whatever pain she felt? Or was she truly at the point of . . . failing? For fear of evil omen, Maniakes did not let *dying* cross his mind.

Silence followed. He reached for the latch. As his hand fell on it, a new cry came through the door: new in the most literal sense of the word. The high, thin wail could only have sprung from the throat of a newborn. Maniakes sagged where he stood. He had a living child. That was something. Now he needed to find out about Niphone.

The door to the Red Room opened. Zoïle came out and almost ran headlong into Maniakes. "Your Majesty!" the midwife exclaimed. She looked exhausted herself, drawn and sweaty, with dark circles under her eyes. She drew back half a pace from the Avtokrator. "Your Majesty, you have a daughter."

Bagdasares had thought it more likely he would have a son. He would twit the mage about that another time. "How is Niphone?" he demanded.

"I won't lie to you, your Majesty," Zoïle answered. "It was touch and go there for a while. I thought I might have to summon a surgeon to cut her open and try to get the baby out, aye, and a healer-priest to see if he could fix the wounds afterward before she bled to death."

"Phos!" Maniakes drew a quick sun-circle over his heart. He knew a woman lay down with death in childbed, but he had never expected to be so brutally reminded of it. Not even the luxuries of the palaces could hold all dangers at bay.

Zoïle went on, "From somewhere, though, she found enough strength to bring forth the babe at last. She has courage, your lady; I've seen women give up and die who worked less hard than she did."

"May I see her?" Maniakes asked. He didn't really want to go into the Red Room now; it had a sickroom stink of stale sweat and slops and even blood that repelled him. But after what Niphone had been through, what he wanted and what he liked seemed small things.

Still, he was not altogether sorry when Zoïle shook her head.

"She wouldn't know you, your Majesty, not yet. As soon as she passed the afterbirth, she fell asleep—or passed out, whichever you'd rather. Either way, I'd sooner you let her rest." The midwife looked worried. "I hope she's not bleeding inside. I don't *think* she is—her pulse has been strong all through this—but it's hard to know for certain."

Maniakes' hands folded into fists. Even now, with the delivery done, Niphone still was not safe. He had to trust Zoïle that she would be all right—and Zoïle sounded none too sure. He found another question: "May I see my daughter?"

Now the midwife gave him a smile that pierced her worry like a sunbeam lancing through a break in dark clouds. "That you can, your Majesty. You wait here a moment, and I'll fetch her." She opened the door to the Red Room. More of the sick-room smell wafted out. Maniakes got a glimpse of his wife lying still and pale on the bed where she had given birth. He wished he could rush to her, but sensed Zoïle was right—for now, rest would do her the most good. But standing out here alone in the hall was hard.

The midwife came out again, carrying a small, swaddled bundle. Maniakes held out his hands to take his daughter. She seemed to weigh nothing at all. Her skin was astonishingly thin and fine; not a parchment-maker in the Empire could do work like that. Her eyes, a dark blue, were open. She looked up at him—or perhaps through him. He had no idea what she was seeing.

"She looks like you, your Majesty," the midwife said.

"Does she?" Maniakes couldn't see it. To his inexperienced eyes, she looked like a baby, nothing else.

"What will you name her?" Zoïle asked.

He and Niphone hadn't talked much about names for a girl. "We'll call her Evtropia, I think," he answered, "after Niphone's grandmother." That would make her side of the family happy, and he didn't mind the name.

"Evtropia." Zoïle tasted it in her mouth and nodded. "Not bad." The midwife paused, then went on, "When she found out the baby was a girl, your Majesty, the Empress asked me to apologize to you. This was just before exhaustion took her."

Maniakes shook his head. "Foolishness. A girl baby's a long way from the end of the world. When I learned she was pregnant this time, I told her as much. We'll try again after she gets her strength back, that's all." Zoïle didn't say anything, but he saw her frown and asked, "What's wrong?"

"Your Majesty, this was a hard birth. If the Empress has another one like it . . . even with a healer-priest standing by, she'd be taking a great risk, a risk of her life."

Maniakes stared, first at Zoïle and then down at his newborn daughter. Would she be the only fruit of his loins? What would happen to the throne then? Would he pass it to a son-in-law? To his brother? To a nephew? To Rhegorios or whatever heirs he might have? With a couple of sentences, the midwife had made his life more complicated.

She saw that and said, "I'm sorry, but you'd best know the truth."

"Yes." He shook his head again, this time to clear it. "Do you think her next birth would be as difficult as this one was?"

"No way to know that for certain, not till the day comes. But a woman who's had a hard time in childbed once, she's more likely to have one again. I don't think any midwife would tell you different."

"No, I suppose not." Maniakes sighed. "Thank you for your honesty. You've given me a great deal to think about." He looked down at Evtropia again. Would she be his only legitimate heir? She stared up at him, through him, past him. Her tiny features held no answers; she was trying to do nothing more than figure out the strange new world in which she found herself. At the moment, so was he.

Kourikos looked apprehensive. "Your Majesty," he said, "I am not a mage. I cannot make gold magically appear where there is none to be had."

"I understand that, eminent sir," Maniakes answered. "But without gold, the Empire is hamstrung. Soon I'll be at the point where I can't pay my soldiers—isn't that what the accountants say? If I can't pay them, either they'll mutiny, which will be a disaster—or they'll up and go home—which will be a disaster. How many more disasters do you think Videssos can stand?" He didn't expect the logothete of the treasury to give him an exact answer, but they both understood the number was not very large.

Licking his lips, Kourikos said, "Revenue enhancements from

the merchants in the city and other towns could bring in a certain amount of new gold."

"Aye, but not enough," Maniakes said. "For one thing, we don't have enough merchants to let what we gain from them offset what we lose from the peasants, who are nine parts in ten, maybe nineteen parts in twenty, of all our folk. For another, thanks to all the enemy onslaughts, trade has sunk like a ship in a storm, too. The merchants can afford to give but little."

"In all this you speak truth, your Majesty," Kourikos agreed mournfully. "You have set your finger on the reasons why the treasury is in its present state."

"Knowing why is easy. Doing something about it is another matter altogether." Maniakes' voice turned pleading: "Eminent Kourikos, father-in-law of mine, how can I lay my hands on more gold? You are the acknowledged expert here; if you know no way, what am I to do?"

The logothete of the treasury licked his lips again. "One way to stretch what gold we have comes to mind." He stared down at the cup of wine on the table in front of him and said no more.

"Speak!" Maniakes urged him. "Give forth. How can I judge what you say unless you say it?"

"Very well, then." Kourikos looked like a man about to repeat an obscenity. "If we put less gold in each coin, and make up the weight with silver or copper, we can mint more goldpieces for the same amount of metal."

Maniakes stared at him. "How long has it been since an Avtokrator tampered with the currency?"

"About three hundred years, your Majesty, maybe more," Kourikos answered unhappily. "The Avtokrator Gordianos cheapened his goldpieces to help restore the Amphitheater after an earthquake."

"And you want me to break that string, eh?"

"I never stated, nor do I feel, any such desire," Kourikos said. "You asked me how gold might go further. That is one way."

Maniakes gnawed on his underlip. Videssian gold coins passed current all over the world, precisely because of their long tradition of purity. Still . . . "How much can we debase our goldpieces without drawing much notice?"

"One part in ten should cause no problem of that sort, your Majesty," the logothete of the treasury answered. Maniakes wondered what sort of experiments he had run to come back with that quick and confident reply.

"One part it is, then." Maniakes aimed a stern forefinger at Kourikos. "But only during this emergency, mind you. As soon as the worst of the crisis is past, we go back to full value for the weight. Is that understood?" His father-in-law nodded. Maniakes felt as if he had just bathed in mud—but if he didn't get the gold he needed now, having it later might do him no good. Half to himself, he went on, "One part in ten isn't enough, not when we're short by so much more than that. We don't need only to stretch the gold we have; we need more, as well. I don't know where to get it."

Kourikos coughed. "Your Majesty, I know one place where there's gold and silver aplenty, waiting to be stamped into coins."

"Aye, no doubt, and roast pigs lie around in the streets waiting to be eaten, too," Maniakes said. "If gold and silver lay ready to hand, don't you think I would have seized them?"

"That would depend on whether you saw them." Kourikos shook his head, a quick, nervous gesture. "No, not whether you saw them, for you see them every day. Say rather, on whether you realized what you saw."

"Eminent sir, don't play at riddles with me; I haven't the time for it now. If you know where I can get gold, tell me. If you don't and you're trying to show how clever you are ... be thankful I'm married to your daughter. The state the Empire's in, even that may not save you. Speak up, if you have anything to say."

Kourikos looked as if he wished he had never raised the subject. He went to the doorway of the little chamber in the imperial residence and peered up and down the hall to make sure no servants were in earshot. When he came back, he dropped his voice to a hoarse whisper: "Your Majesty, if you need it badly enough, there is gold and silver aplenty in the temples." No sooner had the words passed his lips than he jumped up to reassure himself he hadn't been overheard.

Maniakes didn't blame him. "Rob the temples?" he exclaimed, also in a whisper. "Agathios would scream like a branded bullock, and so would every other priest and prelate in the Empire. By the good god, eminent sir, it might touch off another round of civil war on top of the Makuraners and the Kubratoi."

"I never said the gold would be easy to take," Kourikos reminded him. "I said it was there, and it is."

He was right about that. Aside from the vast sums that had gone into building the High Temple, the ornaments and the great altar at which the patriarch presided were massy lumps of precious metal. Other temples throughout Videssos, though less lavish than the chief shrine, also had riches stored away inside.

With more regret than he would have imagined a moment before, Maniakes shook his head. "Ah, eminent sir, you frustrate me worse than you know. For you're right: the gold is there, and that it's there never once crossed my mind. But I don't know if I can lay hold of it, not if I want to hold the throne, too."

"Your Majesty must be the judge of that," Kourikos said, bowing his head.

"It cannot be," Maniakes said, and then, "I don't think it can be." He could order the ecclesiastical hierarchy about as he wished, so long as he did not lapse into heresy. He could depose the ecumenical patriarch and have a synod choose a successor from among three candidates he had picked himself. But take gold from the temples? Maybe Avtokrators had dreamt of it, but no one, not even Genesios, had dared try. A man would have to be desperate even to contemplate it seriously.

Maniakes learned how desperate he was by one simple fact: The idea, once lodged in his mind, would not go away.

With a sort of cautious passion, Niphone wrapped her arms around Maniakes. It was the first time they had joined since Evtropia was born. Maniakes did his best to be gentle with her. And, remembering what Zoïle had said, when the moment came when he could hold back no more, he pulled out of her and spurted his seed onto her belly.

She stared up at him. Only one lamp was lit in the imperial bedchamber, but the dim light it threw was plenty to show her expression of rebuke. "Why did you do that?" she demanded. "How are we to get an heir if you don't make me pregnant again?"

He had never heard her speak so sharply; it was all the more surprising because her thighs still clasped him. "The midwife said you might die if you tried to bear another child," he said.

"To the ice with the midwife," Niphone said. "For one thing, how can she possibly know?"

"The time you had bearing Evtropia was warning enough for her," Maniakes said. "It ought to be warning enough for you, too."

She ignored him. From the moment Agathios wed them, she had been as modest and submissive a wife as he had ever imagined: to a fault, if anything. Now, all at once, she made a lie out of everything he had thought she was, continuing, "For another, come what may, my son will sit on the throne of the Empire of Videssos after you. Will you cheat my family of its place?"

He hadn't thought of it like that. He had plenty of relatives of one sort or another to succeed him; he would have preferred a son, certainly, but his family's line would not fail if he didn't produce one. But if a nephew or cousin or even brother of his donned the red boots, Niphone's kin would lose their place in the sun, with no way to get it back.

She went on, "My husband—your Majesty—we shall have an heir of your body, and of mine." She reached down to restore his wilted vigor, plainly intending to start trying to conceive that heir on the instant.

He took hold of her wrist. "Easy, there. I can't go again quite as fast as I could ten years ago. And even if I could, I told you already the price of a boy child is more than I care to risk."

"*You* care to risk?" Niphone said. "The risk is mine to make, not yours. Life is risk, for men and women. Men go off to war; women lie down in childbed. When men win, they bring themselves home alive, no more. But women, now, women lie down as one and get up as two. You have no right to say I may not do this."

Maniakes opened his mouth, then closed it again. If he held Parsmanios, say, out of a battle with the Makuraners for fear of what might happen to him, his brother would have reason to be furious with him. Women, though, were supposed to be protected from such risk. What if a woman didn't want to be protected? What then? Till this moment, he hadn't imagined such a thing.

He was trying to keep her alive. She should have been grateful. Since she seemed anything but, he took his most imperious and imperial tone and declared, "I am your husband. I have the right to tell you what we shall do—and what we shall not."

For a moment, he had hopes the ploy would work. Niphone was a girl conservatively reared even by the conservative standards of her family; her attitude toward her husband's decrees should have approached that of a Makuraner wife locked away in the women's quarters of her noble husband's stronghold.

Should have. Niphone looked at him. In the dim lamplight, he could not make out the expression on her face. Then she reached out and took hold of him again. She wasn't usually so bold. "One of the things that makes you my husband is *this*," she said, squeezing gently. "If you deny it to me, is that not grounds for making our marriage as if it had never been?"

The Videssian military knew retreat could be a virtue. Maniakes decided this was a time he would have to retreat—especially since, inside her hand, part of him was advancing. He took her in his arms, kissed her mouth and her neck and the hollow of her shoulder and her breasts. When the time came for them to join, he rolled onto his back—not only was that easier for his second round, but also for her not long out of childbed.

She carefully lowered herself onto him. "You win," he said in a voice that was all breath.

"No," she said, raising up and then filling herself with him again. "We do."

Maniakes stared at the messenger who had come hotfoot from the walls of Videssos the city. "There's a what out there?" he demanded, digging a finger into his ear. "I can't have heard you rightly."

"May it please your Majesty, you did," the messenger said. "There's a band of Kubratoi out there, just past dart-thrower range. The fellow who sounds like he's in charge—I misremember his name, but he speaks Videssian like it was an egg he's beating in a bowl—"

"Is he called Moundioukh, by any chance?" Maniakes asked.

"That's it, your Majesty," the messenger agreed. "You know of him?"

"I know of him," Maniakes said grimly. "Very well, admit him to the city. Surround his force, however large it may be, with armed men. Be particularly careful not to give him any promise of safe-conduct whatsoever. I will meet with him—and him alone—in the Grand Courtroom in two hours' time. Separate him from his men and make sure they are treated well unless you hear otherwise from me. Have you got all that?"

"Would your Majesty be kind enough to repeat it?" the man

said. Maniakes did. The messenger gave it back to his satisfaction. Nodding, he sent the fellow back to the wall, then shouted for Kameas.

Two hours later, he sat on the imperial throne in raiment almost as splendid as that which he had had to discard after the Kubrati surprise. Hastily assembled dignitaries took their places to either side of the colonnaded aisle down which Moundioukh would walk.

But for the sounds of Moundioukh's footfalls, the Grand Courtroom was altogether silent as the Kubrati advanced toward the throne. At the prescribed distance from it, he prostrated himself before Maniakes. With a *skreek* of gearing, servitors behind the far wall raised the imperial throne several feet in the air. When Moundioukh started to get up afterward, the Avtokrator snapped, "I did not give you leave to rise."

Moundioukh flattened himself against the marble once more. He turned his head to glance up at the Avtokrator. His eyes blazed; he did not seem impressed by the rising throne. "Youse gets smarts with me, your Majesties, and the magnifolent Etzilios, he will pull the Empires down around your heads," he said.

"What? Will he do worse than he has already?" Maniakes said.

"Much worser, your Majestive. There will be a slaughtering the likes of which the world has never seen the likes of," Moundioukh declared.

"Rise," Maniakes said. Moundioukh climbed to his feet, looking smug. Then he saw the expression on Maniakes' face, and his own confidence leaked away. Maniakes said, "Take this message back to Etzilios the cheat, Etzilios the robber, Etzilios the traitor: If his ravages go on, I will pull all my forces from the westlands, settle him once for all, and then go back to fighting Makuran."

"Youse is bluffing!" Moundioukh said.

"Why on earth do you think so?" Maniakes said. "The King of Kings can't hurt me worse in the west than Etzilios does in the north—and if I beat Etzilios once, he may stay beaten, while Makuran won't."

Moundioukh exclaimed, "Youse will be sorry for these!" but he sounded dismayed, not fierce and threatening. He went on, "I did not come here for insulteds. I earned to offer my magnifolent khagan's mercies to youse. Youse gives him golds, he will goes away and not bothers the towns of youse."

Maniakes laughed in his face, a long, bitter laugh. "He said that last year, and look what we got for it. Does he want me to come to Imbros again?"

"Uh, no, your Majesties." Barbarian though Moundioukh was, he did not seem immune to embarrassment.

"Well, then." Maniakes folded his arms across his chest and stared down at the Kubrati emissary. "Tell him the choice is his: he may have peace, or he may have war without limits. Videssos was here long before you Kubratoi came off the Pardrayan steppe; Videssos will be here long after you are forgotten. Look around you, Moundioukh. You are in a real city now."

Moundioukh looked, and looked uncomfortable. Phos' High Temple would have been the best place in Videssos the city for him to see the difference between what his people could do and what the Videssians had accomplished over the centuries, but the Grand Courtroom ran a strong second.

Yet the Kubratoi had their talents, too, as he reminded Maniakes: "Youse Videssians, youse makes pretties, but youse can'ts fight for nothings. Bring on soldiers. Us slaughters they." He paused. "Unless youse pays we not to."

Maniakes did not want to pay the Kubratoi tribute. He wanted it even less now than he had when he had agreed to the three-year truce the autumn before. But he knew he could not bring the entire Videssian army—such as it was—out of the westlands. Even if he beat the Kubratoi with those forces, Makuran would make sure he got no profit from it.

Freighting his voice with all the scorn he could muster, he said, "I might give you fifteen thousand goldpieces, simply to be rid of you." They would all be cheapened ones, too, he resolved to himself.

"We takes," Moundioukh answered at once. "A one years of pieces, youse gets."

Maniakes stared at him. "You mean that," he blurted in amazement. Moundioukh nodded. Still startled, Maniakes went on, "The magnifolent Etzilios is a fool. He could have had better than three times as much for this year if he hadn't attacked me up by Imbros."

"I tells him not to does it," Moundioukh answered. "But him

do not listens. Him are magnifolent, like youse says. Him listen only to himsownself. Him say, catch Avtokrators, not have tributes, have Videssos."

"He'll never get another chance," Maniakes ground out. The khagan had certainly had a point; if he had captured or killed Maniakes, all of Videssos down to the imperial city might have been his for the taking. He had done enough damage to the Empire without getting hold of the Avtokrator. Maniakes continued, "Why does Etzilios think I can trust him to keep the peace now when he broke it before? I have better things to do with my gold than throw it away for nothing."

Moundioukh let out a long, heartfelt sigh. "Him give hostages," he answered unwillingly. "Men of Kubrat, we breaks the pieces, youse does what youse wants to hostages."

"And what sort of hostages will he give?" Knowing Etzilios' wiles, Maniakes would not have been surprised to get either men of no account or outright rivals to the khagan, who would then have no trouble restraining his grief if they were executed in reprisal for his own treachery.

But, sounding unhappier still, Moundioukh answered, "Him gives I an all him send down with I. Him breaks bargains, youse breaks we."

Etzilios had used Moundioukh as an emissary before he had attacked Maniakes. That argued the khagan had a reasonably high opinion of him. "We shall see who these other men are," Maniakes said. "If they prove suitable, perhaps we have a bargain." *If I can scrape together fifteen thousand goldpieces, even cheapened ones.* He scowled down at Moundioukh. "For now, you are dismissed. This audience is ended. You will be housed as fits your station."

Moundioukh knew court etiquette; perhaps he had visited Videssos the city during Genesios' reign. He prostrated himself again, then rose and backed away from the throne till he had gone far enough to turn his back without committing lese majesty. The housing Maniakes would have liked to give him was a deep but narrow hole in the ground, but he didn't need more trouble with Etzilios than he already had.

Having Kubrati hostages went some way toward restoring his pride after the humiliation of the previous autumn. He frowned thoughtfully as the throne descended and he got down off it. His courtiers were shouting "Thou conquerest, Maniakes Avtokrator!"

but he wondered whether he had gained a victory or simply given Etzilios what he wanted once more.

He shrugged. The way things were, he had very little choice but to accept the khagan's offer. He still had a long road ahead of him before he could think about having many choices when it came to dealing with the Empire's foes.

Agathios performed a proskynesis before Maniakes. "Rise, most holy sir, by all means rise," Maniakes told the ecumenical patriarch as he finished the prostration. "Here, take this couch. My vestiarios will be fetching us refreshments directly—ah, here he is now."

Right on cue, Kameas brought in a silver tray that held a jar of wine, two cups of cut and faceted crystal, and a bowl full of boiled baby squid in a sauce of wine vinegar. Agathios beamed when he saw the squid. "My favorite delicacy!" he exclaimed. "What a lucky choice, your Majesty."

"I'm fond of them, too," Maniakes said, about a two-thirds truth. To bolster it, he ate one. The choice had not been luck; a few discreet questions from Kameas to Skombros yielded the secrets of the patriarch's taste. The synkellos knew them as well as Agathios did himself, and was not shy about telling them to the vestiarios. Had he been shy in that way, Agathios would soon have found himself with a new synkellos.

Maniakes made small talk with the ecumenical patriarch till Agathios' wine cup had been refilled once and the bowl of lightly pickled squid almost emptied. Then he said, "Most holy sir, I hope the temples have income adequate to all the tasks they undertake."

"Ah, your Majesty, we never have as much as we would like," Agathios answered solemnly. "Our charitable enterprises have stretched very thin because of the ravages of the barbarians in the north and the Makuraners in the westlands. Generous as imperial contributions have been in the past, we could always put more gold to good use."

Maniakes stifled a giggle. Agathios had come to the imperial residence ready to put the bite on him for more funds. Considering the purpose for which he had summoned the patriarch, the irony there was worth savoring.

"I'm sure you could, mostly holy sir," he said. "When the time comes that we may give you more gold from the fisc, be assured we shall gladly do so."

"Your Majesty is generous," Agathios said.

My Majesty is nothing of the sort, Maniakes thought. Aloud, he said, "The pity of it is, we can't do that now. The invaders' inroads have taken a deep bite out of the tax revenues that would normally come into the treasury."

"I sympathize with your plight," Agathios murmured.

That gave Maniakes the opening for which he had hoped. He took advantage of it, saying "I was sure you would, most holy sir. I know the temples will do everything they can to aid Videssos in our hour of need."

Had Agathios been a naively pious cleric, he would have said something like *Whatever the Empire requires, your Majesty!*—most likely in ringing tones full of self-sacrifice. He understood, though, that he was a political as well as a religious figure. Cautiously, he replied, "With our own funds strapped, as I noted, your Majesty, how could we do more?"

"I know the High Temple has vessels and censers and candelabra and other ornaments of gold and silver where bronze or glass or clay would serve as well," Maniakes said. "This is also true of other temples in Videssos the city and all around the Empire, though in lesser measure. The treasury is in desperate need of gold and silver, most holy sir. I should like to requisition some of this holy gear to aid us in our time of trouble, and pay it back weight for weight, measure for measure, when the crisis is past."

Agathios stared at him. "You would have us give up our holy vessels so the metal in them can be put to secular use? Your Majesty, forgive me, but I fear this cannot be."

"Why not?" Maniakes said; Agathios hadn't started screaming anathemas at him, as he had feared might happen. "If Videssos goes down in ruin, the temples fall with the rest. The Kubratoi are heathens; the Makuraners reverence the God, not the lord with the great and good mind."

The ecumenical patriarch *was* a political animal; his protest came out in terms of legalisms rather than theology: "But, your Majesty, such confiscations have never been heard of in all the history of the Empire. You would be setting a potentially disastrous precedent."

"Having the Empire collapse also sets a bad precedent," Maniakes pointed out, "and one much harder to mend." Emboldened by Agathios' cautious response, he went on, "Most holy sir, I regret the need that drives me to ask this of you. Without gold, without silver, we cannot pay our soldiers, and without soldiers we cannot fight either Kubrat or Makuran, let alone both. I will give you my pledge in writing to restore what we have taken as soon as we have gold from anywhere else."

"So you say now," Agathios answered suspiciously. "But what will you say come the day redemption is due?"

"I hope I'll say 'Most holy sir, here is the full weight of gold and silver the fisc borrowed from the temples. My thanks for helping Videssos get through its hour of danger,'" Maniakes told him. "If I don't say that, I expect you'll anathematize me from the pulpit of the High Temple." He had feared—he had expected—Agathios wouldn't wait so long.

The patriarch licked his lips. A bold prelate could indeed do such a thing. It was liable to touch off riots and could get a man kicked off the patriarchal throne, but it was an available weapon. Agathios had never struck Maniakes as a man overly concerned with the spiritual side of his job; administering the temples and enjoying the perquisites of office seemed to rank higher with him. The wealth the temples held, though, touched him there, and he might use the spiritual power if it was not repaid to the last silver coin.

"Let it be as you require, your Majesty," he said now, bowing his head. "I shall send the sakellarios of the High Temple to confer with the logothete of the treasury on the best way to make sure we have an exact record of how much gold and silver is borrowed from each shrine we control."

"I'm sure your treasurer and mine will quickly agree on those procedures," Maniakes said. "By giving up some of your wealth for a little while, you help preserve Phos' faith on earth."

"I hope what you say is true," Agathios answered heavily. "Should it prove otherwise, you will have a great deal for which to answer, not merely to me—I am, after all, but a man—but to the lord with the great and good mind. By your leave—" Robes swirling about him, he swept out of the imperial residence.

A couple of days later, a messenger brought Maniakes a note sealed with the treasury's signet. "Kourikos to Maniakes Avtokrator:

Greetings. May your boldness against foreign foes be rewarded with victories no less splendid—and no less startling."

Maniakes read the note twice, then folded the scrap of parchment on which it was written. "If Phos grants me that," he said, "I'll take it."

"Not long after Midwinter's Day, you say?" Maniakes stared at Niphone and shook his head. "I thought you'd have more time to recover from your last birth before you had to start thinking about"—a euphemism for *worrying about*—"another one."

"It is as the good god wills." Niphone sketched the sun-circle over her heart. "I am in Phos' hands now, as I have been all my life. He will do with me as he thinks best. I cannot believe he would deny you the heir Videssos needs."

"An heir is all very well," Maniakes said, "but—" He didn't go on. How were you supposed to tell your wife, *But I'm afraid this birth will be the death of you?* You couldn't. Besides, she knew the risks as well as he did. She had been the one who wanted to press ahead, where he would have protected her if she had let him.

Evtropia was almost two months old, but Niphone still looked worn from the struggle she had had bringing her daughter into the world. Could she gather enough strength to go through labor again so soon?

"We'll have a healer-priest standing by outside the Red Room," Maniakes declared. Niphone nodded obediently. *We'll have a surgeon there, too, in case we have to take the babe,* Maniakes thought. That he kept to himself.

"Everything will be all right," Niphone said, but then, as if she wasn't quite convinced of that herself, she added, "and if not, I'll dwell in Phos' eternal light forevermore."

"We'll have no more talk of that sort," Maniakes said firmly; he might have been dressing down a young soldier who wasn't shaping quite as well as he had hoped. Niphone nodded, accepting the rebuke. Maniakes hugged her to show he wasn't really angry, then walked into the hall.

He almost bumped into Rhegorios. "Have a care there, my cousin your Majesty," the Sevastos said with a grin. Then he got a look at Maniakes' face. "Oh, by the good god, what's gone wrong now?"

"Eh? Nothing. Very much the opposite, as a matter of fact."

Maniakes steered Rhegorios down the hall so he could talk without his wife's overhearing. "Niphone's going to have another baby."

"That's good news, for a change," Rhegorios agreed. "Why do you look as if the Makuraners just showed up at the Cattle Crossing?" Then his eyes widened. "You're that worried about her?"

"I am," Maniakes answered. "The midwife as much as told me that if she got pregnant again—" He stopped, not wanting to speak words of evil omen, and went on at a tangent, "But Niphone was the one who wanted to try again as soon as might be, and so—" He stopped again.

Rhegorios sketched the sun-circle over his heart. "May the lord with the great and good mind look after her and the babe both. Now I understand why your face was so long."

"We'll have to see how things go, that's all." Maniakes scowled. "I wish that, somewhere in the Empire, I could make things happen, not wait for what happens and have to react to it."

"Well, if the Kubratoi stay quiet, you'll be able to take the field against the Makuraners this summer," Rhegorios said. "That looks to be fifteen thousand goldpieces well spent."

"If the Kubratoi stay quiet," Maniakes said. "And if I can find any soldiers with whom to fight Abivard and the rest of Sharbaraz's generals. And if I can find officers who won't run away. And if I can find the money to pay them—no, robbing the temples will take care of that, I admit, but it gives me more troubles further down the line."

"Parsmanios won't run away from the Makuraners," Rhegorios said, "and he won't be sorry to get out of the city and take a command, either."

Maniakes started to answer, then paused: it was his turn to study Rhegorios' face. "You won't be sorry to see him go, will you?"

"Well, no," his cousin answered. "He's been—testy—because you didn't make him Sevastos in my place."

"I know," Maniakes said, "but I couldn't see the justice in taking you out of the post when you've done well in it. Maybe Father can make him see the sense of that. I own I haven't had much luck. But then, I haven't had much luck in anything since the crown landed on my head."

Rhegorios opened his mouth, probably to deny that, then stopped and thought about everything that had happened since Maniakes took the throne. What went through his mind was easy to read on his face; he hadn't fully learned the courtier's art of dissimulation. After a pause just short of awkward, he said, "The good god grant things get better."

"May it be so," Maniakes agreed. "When I meet Abivard again, I want to face him on something like even terms." He sighed. "We might be friends, he and I, did we not spring from different lands. We got on well when we worked together to put Sharbaraz back on his throne."

"Yes, and look at the gratitude he's shown since," Rhegorios said bitterly.

"He did claim to be avenging Likinios when he invaded us," Maniakes answered. "Maybe he even partway believed it at the time. Of course, he still makes the same claim now, but I don't know of anyone on either side of the border who takes it seriously these days."

"On the other hand, the border's not where it was when he started the invasions, either," Rhegorios said. "It's moved a lot farther east."

"That's one of the things I shall have to attend to—if I can." Maniakes sighed again. "The way things have gone wrong here at the Empire's heart, I sometimes wonder if I wouldn't be better off sailing away to Kastavala and carrying on the fight from a land I could really control."

Rhegorios looked alarmed. "If you're wise, my cousin your Majesty, you'll never say that where anyone but I can hear it. I can't think of a better way to start panic here, and if you don't keep a tight grip on Videssos the city, you won't hold your grip on Videssos the Empire, either."

Maniakes weighed that. "Mm, you're probably right. But I miss being able to operate from a place where I needn't fear treachery if I stir out of the imperial residence and defeat if I go beyond the city walls."

"It will get better, your Majesty," Rhegorios said loyally.

"I hope you're right," Maniakes said, "but damn me to the ice if I see how."

"Maniakes, how could you?" Lysia demanded. He could have been angry at her for forgetting protocol, but, when even his wife called him "your Majesty," he rather relished being treated like a mere human being.

"I don't know. How could I?" he asked, and then, "How could I what?"

Now his cousin hesitated: not out of deference to him, he judged, but from reluctance to mention matters out of the usual ken of unmarried Videssian women. At last, visibly gathering her nerve, she went on, "How could you get your wife with child, knowing what might happen at the end of the confinement?"

He gave her an ironic bow. "That is an excellent question, cousin of mine. As a matter of fact, I asked it of myself, and came up with no good answer."

Lysia set hands on hips. "Well, then? I thought I knew you better than to imagine you'd do such a thing."

"I wouldn't have, were it up to me alone," Maniakes answered. "As with a lot of things, though, more than one person had a say here. When Niphone insisted she wanted to take the risk, how was I to tell her no? You'd have to be wiser than I was to find a way that might work."

"She wanted to? Oh," Lysia said in a small voice. "Men being what they are, when I heard the news I assumed—" She looked down at the hunting mosaic on the floor. "I think I owe you an apology, cousin of mine."

"Maybe for that 'men being what they are,'" Maniakes said. "Have you seen me dragging serving maids off behind the cherry trees?"

Lysia looked down at the floor again; he had embarrassed her. But she managed a mischievous smile as she answered, "No, but then I wouldn't, would I, what with them being in full leaf and flower?"

He stared at her, then started to laugh. "A point, a distinct point. But I had all winter, too, and the grove was bare then."

"So it was." Lysia dipped her head to him. "I am sorry. I thought you were more worried about the dynasty than you were about your wife."

"Niphone's the one who's more worried about the dynasty than she is about herself," Maniakes replied. "Even if I have no children, the crown will stay in my family. But if she dies without bearing an heir, her clan is cut off from the throne forever. She doesn't want that; she's made it very plain. I can't say that I blame her, and—"

"And she is your wife," Lysia finished for him. "As things are,

I would have understood if you were taking up with serving maids now and again. But if Niphone is so dead set on having a boy child—" Her fingers writhed in a sign that turned aside words of evil omen.

"It will be all right," Maniakes said, as much to convince himself as to reassure her. After a moment, he went on, "I'm lucky in my family, too. You thought I was in the wrong, and you up and told me. Nice to know people still think they can tell me the truth even if I won't like it."

"But what I told you wasn't the truth," Lysia said. "I thought it was, but—"

"That's what I meant," Maniakes broke in. "Do you think anyone ever told Genesios he was making a mistake? Maybe one or two people did, right at the beginning of his reign. After their heads went up on the Milestone, do you suppose anyone had the nerve to try that again?"

"You're not Genesios," his cousin said.

"Phos be praised for that!" Maniakes exclaimed. "I'm just glad everyone understands it."

"If people didn't understand it, you would have lost the civil war," Lysia said. "Genesios had Videssos the city, he had most of the army, he had most of the fleet. But no one would fight for him, and so you won."

"And so I won." Maniakes' smile was crooked. "And so, instead of the army and the fleet against me, I have my cousin—a much more dangerous foe."

Lysia scowled at him. "I don't ever want to be your foe or a danger to you—and you ought to know that perfectly well." He started to assure her that he did, but she overrode him: "But that doesn't mean I can't worry about what you do and why you do it. And I worry about Niphone. After so hard a time with her first birth, and then to be expecting another so soon . . . Women don't have an easy time of it."

"I suppose not," Maniakes said—uneasily. Now he stared down at the shining glass tiles set into the floor. "But for all of me, you may ask Niphone if this wasn't her idea, and none of mine."

"How would I say such a thing?" Lysia put up her hands, as if to push away the very idea. "And why would I? I believe you, even if I think she's foolish. But *if*—Phos prevent it—all should not go as she hopes, what would you do? She links our clan to the bureaucratic families of the city. We need their support."

"We need them quiet, at any rate," Maniakes said. "One thing about having so many enemies outside the Empire: sometimes it keeps even Videssians from fighting among themselves."

"And sometimes it doesn't, if you'll remember what happened all through Genesios' reign," Lysia retorted.

"True." Maniakes sighed. "Too true. These Videssians—" He started to laugh. He was of pure Vaspurakaner blood, but his parents had been born in the Empire and he himself thought more like a Videssian than like a man newly come from the princes' land. He might say *these Videssians*, but he felt at home among them.

"What *would* you do?" Lysia said. "I mean, if—" She didn't go on, but she didn't need to, either.

She had a point. What with Zoïle's warnings, Niphone's health was something about which he did have to worry. Thinking aloud, he said, "I suppose I could bring Rotrude here from Kalavria—"

Lysia's lip curled. Again, she didn't say anything. Again, she didn't need to. He couldn't marry Rotrude, not as Avtokrator; she not only too obviously wasn't of Videssian blood, but she also didn't—and didn't want to—think like a Videssian. He would have a hard time legitimating Atalarikhos, too, for the same reasons. If he did make his bastard son legitimate, the boy would be a weak heir, open to challenge from ambitious generals and the men of his own clan both. Better Atalarikhos stayed far from the city.

Maniakes spread his hands. "What would you have me do, then?" he said. "Marry only for the sake of the girl's family, and not care whether I feel anything for her? I've done that once, by the good god, and once is plenty. Or maybe I should put on a blue robe with the red boots, and be Avtokrator and monk at the same time? I haven't the temper for that, I fear."

"Please," Lysia whispered.

"I'm sorry," he answered. "I shouldn't say those things. I shouldn't even think them. I know that. I should be thinking everything with Niphone will be fine: Phos grant it be so. That's what you get for being my dear cousin, you know. I'm used to talking things over with you, and when you ask me a question, I do my best to answer it."

"It's all right," Lysia said, and might halfway have meant it. "It's just that you startled me—I hadn't expected so much to come welling up. Even if you wear the red boots, you're still a man; you need someplace to go with your troubles. If I can help there, I'm glad to do it."

"You did," Maniakes said, and slipped an arm around her shoulder for a moment. In a musing voice, more to himself than to her, he went on, "You know, should the occasion arise—which Phos prevent, as we both said—I could do much worse for myself than to marry you."

"Our fathers are brothers," she said. He cocked his head to one side, trying to make sure of her tone of voice. He didn't think she sounded shocked, as she very well might have. It was, he thought, more as if she was reminding him of a certain practical difficulty that would have to be met.

He was shocked himself, but less than he might have been. He and Lysia had always got on well, and he thought the spark of something more might be there. He had felt it when they said farewell back at Kastavala, and he thought she had, too.

His laugh sounded nervous, even to himself. "I can't think of a better way to make the most holy ecumenical patriarch Agathios have kittens." Then he laughed again, this time with real humor. "No, I take that back. Borrowing gold from the temples probably outraged him more than anything two people, even two cousins, could do."

"Don't be too sure," Lysia answered. "If we weren't cousins—" She shook her head and didn't go on.

Just as well, Maniakes thought. "All this is moonshine and foolishness, anyhow. Zoïle is a good midwife, none better; she'll bring Niphone through without any trouble. And if there is trouble, she'll have a healer-priest standing by. She's said as much. With any luck at all, we'll have an heir. If Phos is kind, he'll live to grow up and come after me, and the two of us can forget what we've said here. No, not forget, but pretend it didn't happen."

"That may be the wisest thing to do." Lysia turned and walked down the hall. He watched her go, and wondered: was he relieved or disappointed or both at once? He sketched Phos' sun-circle above his heart. If the good god was kind, he would never have to find out.

✦ VIII

When an Avtokrator sailed over the narrow strait of the Cattle Crossing to campaign against the King of Kings of Makuran, it was often an occasion of great ceremony. The patriarch would bless the Emperor and the grand and glorious host he had with him. The people of Videssos the city would cheer the soldiers as they filed onto the troopships. In flush times, palace servitors would hand out largess to the crowd. Sometimes, as Kameas reminded Maniakes, a chorus would sing of the victories the great Stavrakios had won in the west, to inspire those who came after him to do likewise.

But for having Agathios the patriarch present when he sailed, Maniakes broke with most of those traditions. He was leading only a couple of regiments out from the capital: if he was to keep the walls garrisoned, he had no more to lead. He did not want the people of the city to gawp at his little force, lest the Makuraners learn how small it was. He couldn't afford to dole out largess; he could barely afford to pay his troops. As for the triumphal chorus, Videssian soldiers had gained so little glory against the armies of the King of Kings lately that he feared they would take Stavrakios' triumphs more as reproach than inspiration.

Agathios spat on the planks of the pier in rejection of Skotos, then raised his hands toward Phos' sun as he said, "May the lord with the great and good mind bless our armament here and instill in Maniakes Avtokrator, his viceregent on earth, the courage and steadfastness to persist even in the face of the many troubles that lie before us. May he keep our brave men safe from harm, and may they restore the Empire and its temples to the grandeur that once was theirs. So may it be."

"So may it be." The response went up from Maniakes, from his brother Parsmanios, and from the men who would accompany them into the west.

Maniakes tried to ignore the sour look Agathios sent him. When the ecumenical patriarch talked about restoring the temples to the grandeur that once was theirs, he meant not only liberating those in land under Makuraner occupation. He also had in mind getting back the gold and silver that had gone from the temples to the imperial mints.

"Thank you for the prayer wishing us success, most holy sir," Maniakes said. "You're wise to pray for our victory, for, if we fail, you assuredly shall not not be repaid."

"I promise you, your Majesty, such mundane considerations were far from my thoughts," Agathios murmured. He sounded most sincere, but sounding sincere was part of the patriarch's job.

Maniakes wondered how Agathios would have sounded had he mentioned that he and his first cousin were drawn to each other. No doubt his outraged indignation would have been . . . most sincere.

In lieu of that confrontation—one that he hoped never to have to bring up—Maniakes turned to his father and Rhegorios. "I'm going to trust the two of you not to give this half of the Empire to Etzilios while I'm busy in the westlands," he said. He intended it as a joke, but it came out sounding more like a plea.

"He seems quiet now," the elder Maniakes said. "Phos grant that he stay so."

Rhegorios added, "Have a care in the westlands, too, my cousin your Majesty. Remember, don't get too bold too fast. The Makuraners have been winning for a long time, and our side losing. Don't take on a lot of battles you haven't much chance of winning, or you'll give our men the notion they can't beat Makuran no matter what."

"I'll remember that," Maniakes answered. If headstrong Rhegorios was advising him to be careful, he had to think that was a good idea. And yet, if he did not go out and try to drive the armies of the King of Kings from the westlands, he might as well hand them over to Makuran.

"You'll have to remember it, son," the elder Maniakes said.

"You haven't any large army here, and the ones in the westlands have been battered to bits in the past six—no, seven now—years. If you want to do anything worthwhile, you'll have to train up some soldiers who aren't used to getting trounced."

"That's one of the things I intend to do," Maniakes said, nodding. Then he grimaced. "Of course, what I intend to do and what Abivard lets me do aren't likely to be one and the same thing."

On that imperfectly optimistic note, he embraced first the elder Maniakes and then his cousin. That done, he boarded the *Renewal* for the short trip over the Cattle Crossing.

The suburb on the western shore of the strait was simply called Across, in reference to its position in relation to that of Videssos the city. The *Renewal* beached there, the rowers driving it well up onto the sand. Sailors let down the gangplank so Maniakes could descend first. He had thought about making a speech pointing out his presence in the westlands; Genesios hadn't fared forth to fight the Makuraners in all his years on the throne, while Likinios, though far more able an Avtokrator than the man who had stolen his throne, had not been a soldier and seldom took the field at the head of his own troops.

In the end, though, Maniakes said, "Let's go," and let it go at that. Speeches a long way from the battlefield did nothing to win wars, and making great claims after suffering great defeats struck him as an easy way to get a name as either a brainless braggart or a desperate man.

He *was* a desperate man, but didn't care to advertise it.

The rest of the fleet beached itself. Videssian law banned the suburbs of the imperial capital from improving their harbors with docks, assuring that the greatest proportion of commerce went through Videssos the city.

Sailors, troopers, and grooms coaxed horses off bulky, beamy transports. The animals kicked up sand on the beach, obviously glad to be off the rolling, shifting sea. Maniakes had seen that with every sea journey a cavalry force had ever undertaken. Horses were marvelous beasts on dry land but hated travel by water.

Maniakes turned to Parsmanios, who had descended from the *Renewal* after him. "You'll head up our vanguard," he said. "You've been through this country more recently than anyone else here; I expect you'll know where we can safely go and where we'd best avoid."

"I hope so," his brother answered. "When I was making my way to the city, Tzikas still held Amorion, which meant the whole valley of the Arandos was under our sway. If Amorion falls—"

"We're in even more trouble than we thought we were," Maniakes finished for him. "By the good god, we're in so much already, how much harm could a little more do?" He laughed. Parsmanios gave him an odd look. If you were Avtokrator, though, not even your brother could get away with telling the world at large you had softening of the brain.

Forming up on the beach, helmets and javelin points glittering in the morning sun, baggy surcoats flapping in the breeze, the regiments Maniakes had brought with him from Videssos the city made a fine martial display. He had no doubt they could crush an equal number of Makuraners. The trouble was, far more Makuraners than two regiments could hope to handle were loose in the westlands.

Parsmanios went up to take his place at the van. Maniakes looked around for someone with whom he could talk. He waved to Bagdasares. "Joining up with whatever forces we already have here won't be enough. We'll have to form a whole new army if we expect to beat back the Makuraners."

"That won't be easy, your Majesty, not with the enemy roaming as he would through the countryside," the wizard answered. "We're liable to be too busy fighting to do much in the way of recruiting."

"The same thought's running through my mind, and I'm not what you'd call happy with it, either," Maniakes said gloomily. "But if we don't have enough veteran troops and we can't raise new ones, what does that leave us? Not much I can see—outside of losing the war, I mean."

"Your reasoning is so straightforward, only a lawyer or a theologian could be displeased with it," Bagdasares said, which drew a snort from his sovereign. "Still, if the Arandos valley remains in our hands, it should prove a fertile recruiting ground in more ways than one."

Maniakes snorted again. "I wish that were true, but it's not. It might be, if we'd won a few victories. As is, though, the only thing men of fighting age will have heard for the past seven years is how the Makuraner heavy cavalry has chewed to rags everything we've sent against it. Hardly anyone volunteers for the privilege of dying messily in a losing war."

Bagdasares dipped his head. "Your Majesty is wiser than I."

"Really? If I'm so clever, why did I want to be Avtokrator in the first place?" Maniakes rolled his eyes. "What wearing the red boots will do to you is make you distrust every noble-sounding scheme you've ever heard from anyone. You start wondering what the fellow thinks he stands to gain from it."

"If you keep looking at the world that way, you'll—" Bagdasares stopped talking. If the Avtokrator learned cynicism, those around him learned caution.

"Say it, whatever it is," Maniakes said; he knew that too well. "If I don't know what people are thinking, I'm going to make more mistakes than I would otherwise. Whatever you were going to tell me, I want to hear it."

"Of course I obey your Majesty," the mage said with a sigh that argued he was unhappy about said obedience. "I was going to say, if you look for the worst in people, you'll surely find it, and end up as sour as poor dead Likinios."

"Mm," Maniakes said judiciously. "I remember the way Likinios was toward the end of his reign—wouldn't trust his own shadow if it got behind his back where he couldn't watch it. No, I don't care to have that happen to me, but I don't care to ignore trouble ahead, either."

"You walk a fine line," Bagdasares said.

And so do all the people around me, Maniakes thought. *They've seen I'm not a brainless bloodthirsty beast like Genesios, which has to ease their minds, but they have to wonder if I'll turn cold and distant the way Likinios did. I wonder about that myself.*

To keep from having to think about it, Maniakes walked over to the nearest transport that was unloading horses. He climbed aboard the black gelding he had been riding since he returned from the disastrous meeting with Etzilios. Since he had got back to Videssos the city, he hadn't been on the steppe pony he had managed to seize in the fighting. He was thinking about breeding it to some of the mares in the imperial stables, in the hopes of adding its phenomenal endurance to the bloodlines of his beasts.

Looking at the ugly, rough-coated little animal, his grooms had been uniformly aghast at the idea. He hadn't had time to persuade them before he set out on campaign. After he got back, if he remembered . . .

✦   ✦   ✦

Despite the ruin that had overtaken so much of the westlands, the farmers of the coastal lowlands still lived contented, almost untroubled lives. The warm, moist air and rich soil let them bring in two crops a year, and left them enough after they paid their taxes that famine was no more to be imagined than, say, an invasion from the armies of the King of Kings.

Men dressed in no more than loincloths and women in calf-length shifts of thin linen, the farmers labored in green fields and black earth. The soldiers making their way down the paths through those fields might have come from another world, one that did not impinge on the peasants.

Maniakes sent riders ahead of his little army and off to either side of its route, crying out for men to join the struggle and help cast the invaders from the Empire of Videssos. Only a tiny trickle of would-be warriors presented themselves at each night's campsite, though. Maniakes had horses, weapons, and armor for all of them, and would have had mounts and gear for five times their number.

On the third night out from Videssos the city, he looked at the latest handful of new recruits and asked, "If I sent you men back to your villages to bring in your fellows, do you think you could do a better job of it than my troopers have managed?" As he spoke, he sent up a silent prayer to Phos that the answer would be yes.

But, to a man, the new soldiers shook their heads. One of them slapped his belly and said, "Begging your pardon, your Majesty, but we eat well in these parts. Most of your soldiers, now, they're hungry men."

That was true. Maniakes had seen it often enough: the men likeliest to take up fighting for their trade were those whose farms had failed or who hadn't managed to make a go of it for themselves in the city. He spoke to the fellow who had answered him. "If you have a full stomach, what are you doing here?"

"If I don't fight the Makuraners somewheres else, looks like I'd have to fight 'em on my own land," the farmer told him. "Trouble is, most people, they can't see far enough to worry that kind of way."

"You don't know how right you are," Maniakes said feelingly. "What I ought to do is, I ought to send you back to Videssos the city and make you into a logothete. I have the feeling you'd be wasted as a common soldier. What's your name?"

"I'm Himerios, your Majesty," the peasant said, his eyes wide. "D'you really mean that? Have to tell you, in case you do, I can't read nor write my name."

"That would help, I admit," Maniakes said. "You'd best stay in the army after all, Himerios. I will keep my eye on you, though. I just wish you—and all your comrades here—had brought your brothers and cousins with you when you decided to join us."

"My cousin said good riddance, is what he said," Himerios answered, spitting on the ground to show what he thought of that. "He's got an eye on my plot of ground, he does. His'd be better if he took more time tending it, the fat, lazy son of a donkey." He chuckled. "He's on my mother's side of the family, you gather."

One of the men who evidently knew Himerios dug an elbow into his ribs and said, "Hey, if you could fight as good as you talk, the Makuraners, they'd be running back to their own country already."

Amid general laughter, Himerios cursed his friend up and down, back and forth, inside and out. Maniakes laughed, too, but the mirth slipped from his face after he left the campfire around which the new recruits sat. Better than having Himerios fight like five men would have been his bringing five men with him. That hadn't happened. Because it hadn't, Maniakes would have an even harder time against the Makuraners than he had expected.

The Arandos flowed lazily through the coastal lowlands, its waters turbid with sediment and, downstream from villages, sometimes foul-smelling from the wastes dumped into it. Maniakes made it a point never to camp where the water did smell bad. He had seen armies melt away like snow in the early days of spring when a flux of the bowels ran through them. Some men died, some who didn't got too sick to be worth anything as fighters, and some who got only a touch of the disease took off for home anyhow.

To Parsmanios, he said, "If men start coming down with the flux, we're ruined, because it'll spread faster than the healer-priests can hope to stop it."

"You're not telling me anything I don't know, brother of mine—er, your Majesty," Parsmanios answered. "The one good thing I can say about Vryetion, where I was stuck for so long, is that the water was always pure there. Now that I think on it, it's likely one of the reasons we based ourselves there."

"The one good thing you can say about the town?" Maniakes asked slyly. "I'll have to remember that, come the day I meet your wife. I wonder what she'd have to say about it."

"Something interesting and memorable, I have no doubt," Parsmanios answered. "No one ever wonders where Zenonis stands about anything."

"She'd need to be headstrong, to stay with one of us," Maniakes said. "Anyone who thinks our clan shy and retiring hasn't met us yet." He spoke with more than a little pride; having a reputation for being cantankerous wasn't the worst thing in the world.

Parsmanios smiled and nodded, but then said, "What of Niphone? Not that I know her well, but she seems quiet enough, willing to stand in your shadow."

"You probably know better than I that what outsiders see of husband and wife isn't everything that's there," Maniakes answered. His brother nodded again. He didn't go on to explain that, had Niphone truly been as modest and self-effacing as she seemed, she wouldn't have had a new baby growing in her belly now.

Parsmanios said, "And what of our cousin, Rhegorios? When do you aim to marry him off?" He spoke carefully, doing his best to conceal his resentment at the place Rhegorios held at court.

"His own father will have a good deal to say about that," Maniakes answered. "Uncle Symvatios is hardly one to curl up and pretend he's not there, either, though he is better-natured about going after what he wants than some blood kin I could name."

If Parsmanios thought that applied to him, he didn't show it. "The final word will be yours, of course," he said, in his persistence unwittingly proving his brother's point. "You're the Avtokrator, after all. I suppose you'll settle on a girl from one of the high bureaucratic families, to bind it to us. You won't want to pick anyone from too prominent a clan, though, or with backing like that Rhegorios might decide to see how his feet look in the red boots."

"If you already know all the answers, brother of mine, why ask the questions?" Maniakes said. "Actually, I don't worry too much about Rhegorios' trying to steal the throne. This past year, he's seen how much the Avtokrator has to do. By all the signs, it's more than he cares for."

"Maybe so," Parsmanios said darkly, "but you never can tell." Since Videssos' recent history proved how true that was—who would have expected a no-account captain like Genesios to murder his way to the throne?—Maniakes had to nod. Parsmanios went on, "And you'll be thinking about the same sorts of things for Lysia, no doubt. Whoever marries her may get ideas because he's so close to the throne. You'll have to keep an eye on that."

"So I will." Thinking about a husband for Lysia made Maniakes uncomfortable. Recognizing that made him even more uncomfortable. He breathed a silent prayer that Niphone would be safely delivered of a son.

Parsmanios didn't notice the short reply. He was building a chain of logic, and as intent on his work as any shaven-skulled theologian. "She'd long since have been wed if the lot of you hadn't been sent to Kalavria," he said. "I don't suppose our uncle was able to find a suitable match for her there."

"Well, no, he couldn't," Maniakes said, and then changed the subject by main force: "We'll be getting into Kyzikos tomorrow, I expect. I'll want you to use some of the vanguard—men you can count on, mind you—to surround the mint there and make sure it's not plundered. I don't know how much gold we'll be able to draw from it, but the one thing we can't do is get in arrears on the soldiers' pay."

"I shall attend to it," Parsmanios promised. "I'll speak to my captains tonight, let them help me pick out a good, reliable company."

Maniakes frowned. His brother should already have had a good idea of which companies under his command were good ones, which not so good. Till he came to Videssos the city, he hadn't enjoyed high rank. If you were to deserve high rank, though, you couldn't just enjoy it; you also had to meet the demands it set on you. Maniakes hoped Parsmanios would learn that. He didn't have much time.

As Maniakes' little force headed west along the north bank of the Arandos, the land began to rise toward the central plateau, at first so slowly it was hard to notice, then more rapidly. The Arandos itself seemed to shake off age as the Avtokrator moved farther from its mouth. It flowed more rapidly and in a straighter course, giving up on looping back on itself as it bumped over a series of rapids as the plateau drew near.

Garsavra lay at the very edge of the westlands' central plateau, at the confluence of the Arandos and the Eriza, which came down from the north. Had it not been for the rapids that hindered trade coming up from the east, Garsavra might have grown into a great city. Even as things stood, it was the chief trading town for the eastern part of the plateau.

It also had stout fortifications in excellent repair. When the hypasteos, a plump, important-looking little fellow named Rhousas, came out of the city to prostrate himself before Maniakes, the Avtokrator complimented him on that.

"Oh, I thank you very much, your Majesty," Rhousas answered as he rose. "I do my best to keep this city ready to hold out as long as may be against the attacks of the fearsome Makuraners, who know not Phos." By the way he strutted in place, he might have been personally responsible for every stone that had gone into the wall.

Maniakes had heard that sort of self-aggrandizement too often in his nearly a year on the throne to let it impress him. "I suppose your garrison commander had nothing to do with getting your city ready to defend itself."

He had seen officials deflate like popped pigs' bladders when he made that sort of remark to them. He glanced over to the garrison commander, a gray-bearded, weatherbeaten man who seemed half asleep. Rhousas said, "Oh, yes, the excellent Byzakios did lend a hand. But the garrison numbers only a couple of hundred, and he was so busy seeking to form a city militia that he and his men played but a small role in the recent reconstruction."

"A couple of hundred? For a town this large and important, in a time when we're invaded?" Maniakes turned to Byzakios. "Surely you had more men once. What happened to the rest of them?"

"'Bout what you'd expect, your Majesty," Byzakios answered, his voice full of an upcountry twang. "Some of 'em got killed in this fight or that. And others, well, they were just stolen, you ask me. Every time a rebel came through, he'd pull away a few more. I sent Tzikas a draft of three hundred; I reckoned he'd need 'em worse'n I did."

"I think you're right," Maniakes answered. "I think you did

very well indeed to train up a militia to take the place of your departed soldiers, too. In a pinch, will they fight?"

"You never know till the day comes," Byzakios said. "Maybe so, maybe not. Best guess is, they'll do all right up on the wall, but Phos' light take their souls if the Makuraners break in despite 'em."

"Aye, that sounds likely," Maniakes agreed. "When amateurs like that get into hand-to-hand with professional soldiers, they'll come off second best every time." He sighed. "You're stripped down to a couple of hundred regulars? I can't take many away from you, then."

"May I talk frank, your Majesty?" Byzakios asked. When Maniakes nodded, the commandant studied him, then muttered, half to himself, "Well, he *was* a soldier his own self." To Maniakes, he said, "You better not take any, not if you want this town to have any chance of holding. You want my head because the mouth in it's too big, you've got your excuse to take it."

"It seems to be doing a good enough job up there on your shoulders, excellent sir," Maniakes said. "We'll leave it there for now."

A look passed between Byzakios and Rhousas. Maniakes had seen that look before when he dealt for the first time with officials who didn't know him personally. It said, *He's not Genesios,* and pleased and saddened him at the same time. True, it was a compliment, but one that should have been superfluous. Genesios had a great deal for which to answer; Maniakes suspected he would be answering to Skotos for all eternity.

Rhousas said, "I am sorry, your Majesty, but we have little revenue for the fisc. Commerce these past few years has been very bad. Goods come in down the Arandos and the Eriza, but not much goes out, especially to westward. In good years, we'd send caravan after caravan to the *panegyris,* the trade fair, at Amorion. This year—" He spread his hands in regret.

"Not much point going on to Amorion when you know you can't go further without likely getting robbed and murdered," Byzakios said.

"Too true," Maniakes said mournfully. "For that matter, there's the risk of getting robbed and murdered *inside* Amorion. What news have you from there? Are the Makuraners pressing against the city, and what force has Tzikas inside it to hold them at bay?"

"They are moving, there west of Amorion," Byzakios answered. "We don't know all we ought to from out there: Have to rely on spies and such in what by rights is our very own land." He shook his head indignantly. "Terrible thing. Anyways, Tzikas has several thousand soldiers, along with whatever he's done about getting the townsfolk ready to fight. They'll fight hard, I reckon. They know nothing good'll happen to 'em if they yield themselves up, that's sure: prisoners go to digging underground, it's said."

"Can Tzikas hold, if Abivard throws everything he has against the place?" Maniakes asked.

Byzakios and Rhousas looked at each other again. This time, the unspoken question was, *How much truth can we tell?* At last, Byzakios answered a question with another question: "Your Majesty, when the Makuraners throw everything these days, what holds?"

"Something had better start holding," Maniakes said, kicking at the dirt, "or the whole Empire will come crashing down. Curse it, we can beat the Makuraners in battle. My father and I did it at the end of Likinios' reign. By the good god, Stavrakios sacked Mashiz."

"Ah, your Majesty, but that was a long time ago," Rhousas answered sadly. Maniakes couldn't tell whether the city governor meant Stavrakios' exploits or his own.

Garsavra gave every sign of being a town with a prosperous history. The local shrine, like a lot of such centers all through the Empire, was modeled after the High Temple in Videssos the city. A lot of such imitations deserved the name more by intent than by its execution, but from Garsavra's shrine one could get at least a feeling for what the original was like.

The local temple fronted on the market square in the center of town. That expanse of cobbles was almost as big as the plaza of Palamas back in the capital. Everyone from Rhousas down to the apprentice grooms in the stables spoke of how that square had been packed with merchants from the capital, from Opsikion and even Kalavria in the east, from Amorion and Vaspurakan and Mashiz in the west.

It was not packed now. A couple of potters had set up forlorn booths in one corner, displaying earthenware made from the grayish-yellow local clay. A herder had half a dozen lambs to sell.

A couple of weavers displayed bolts of wool. At a portable desk, a scribe wrote a letter for a patron who could not. Over most of the square, though, pigeons strutted in search of crumbs, with scrawny cats prowling after them.

When Maniakes came out of the hypasteos' residence to walk across to the temple to pray, the merchants abandoned their stalls and ran up to him, crying, "Mercy, your Majesty!" "How can we pay the hearth tax and the head tax, let alone that on our profits?" "We have no profits, by the good god!" "Mercy, mercy!"

He wondered how many merchants in how many cities would have sung the same tune had he appeared before them. Too many; he knew that much. "I'll do what I can for you," he said, and felt how inadequate the words were. The best thing he could do to help the merchants—the best thing he could do to help the Empire—would be to drive the Makuraners out of Videssian territory once and for all. He had never had any trouble figuring out what wanted doing. How to do it was something else again.

After a couple of days' rest and resupply, Maniakes and his little army made for Amorion. Once they were up on the plateau, the weather got less muggy, though it continued blazing hot. Grain and fruit trees grew close by the Arandos and along the banks of its small tributaries. Away from water, the land was baked dusty, with only scrubby grass and brush growing on it. Cattle and sheep grazed on the scrub.

"We'll be able to keep the army fed and watered, even if the supply lines fail," Parsmanios observed at camp one evening. "My little force in Vryetion lived off the local herds a good deal of the time."

"I'd like to be able to pay for any animals I end up having to take," Maniakes said. "Of course, what I'd like to do and what I can do are liable to be two different beasts. Wearing the red boots has taught me that."

"Any command will," Parsmanios agreed. "The bigger the command, I suppose, the harder the lesson."

Maniakes listened carefully to his brother's tone. Another thing sitting on the imperial throne had taught him was that you couldn't trust anybody. He hated having to try to gauge how sour Parsmanios sounded at any given moment, but couldn't see what choice he had.

He said, "Another three or four days and we'll be in Amorion.

Then we can stop worrying about our supply lines for a while—and start worrying about whether Abivard is going to try storming the place with us inside it." His laugh was anything but jolly. "Another thing you learn is that you're always worrying about something. The day you think everything is fine is the day you haven't noticed the plot against you just starting to bubble."

"I expect you're right." Parsmanios rose and sketched a salute. "I'm going to see to my men and then turn in."

"Good enough, brother of mine." Maniakes liked the way Parsmanios assumed the responsibility that went with commanding the vanguard. It was a far bigger command than he had ever had before, but he was shaping well in it—Maniakes had not had any complaints about his diligence since that evening outside of Kyzikos. If he ever scraped together enough troops to operate with two armies at the same time, Parsmanios might well make a capable commander for one of them. The Avtokrator rubbed his chin. Tzikas was already commanding an army, and had been doing so as a virtually independent lord for several years now. Promoting Parsmanios over his head would not please him. Would it touch off a revolt? Maniakes would have to think about that, too.

"Wearing the red boots also teaches you life is much more complicated than you'd ever imagined," he told the silk walls of his tent. Unlike his livelier subjects, they did not argue with him.

The scout who came galloping back to Maniakes kicked up a plume of dust. Maniakes spied it long before the scout himself became visible. The fellow reined in; his horse was lathered and blowing. After saluting Maniakes with clenched right fist over his heart, he said, "We've spotted dust ahead, your Majesty—lots of it, and getting closer fast."

Maniakes frowned. "Any idea who's kicking it up?"

"No, your Majesty," the scout said.

"Could be reinforcements," Maniakes said hopefully. But even he didn't think that was likely. "Reinforcements hereabouts should be heading straight for Amorion, not for us."

"That's so, your Majesty," the rider agreed. "Whatever that is, it's heading dead away from Amorion, no two ways about it."

"No." Maniakes shaded his eyes with his left hand and peered westward. He clicked his tongue between his teeth. "I don't see anything—yet. But if a lot of men are coming from Amorion, odds are they're either our troopers fleeing the place—or Makuraners who've taken it. Ride back to your place; be ready if Parsmanios needs you to carry more messages."

"Aye." The horseman saluted again and set spurs to his mount, urging the animal up into a gallop as fast as he could.

Maniakes turned to the trumpeters who were never far from his person on campaign. "Order the army into battle array," he said. The musicians saluted, raised the long, straight brass horns to their lips, and blared out the signal that would take Maniakes' little force out of column and into line. "We'll anchor our left on the Arandos," he shouted.

Each regiment broke in two. Half of one regiment stayed back to protect the baggage train and form a reserve. The other half and the whole regiment deployed in three elements, the center one—the one Maniakes led—forward. It was a flexible formation, well prepared to deal with anything . . . except overwhelming numbers.

The force had practiced going from column into line of battle many times and moved now without undue fuss or wasted motion. Even so, by the time they were ready to fight, Maniakes could clearly see the dust the men of the vanguard had already spotted. He clamped his jaw down hard to help keep from showing his worry. As the scout had said, somebody out there was kicking up a *lot* of dust.

Then horsemen in mail shirts emerged from out of the dust. He recognized some of their surcoats and banners—his own vanguard was mixed in among them. A shout rose above the drumming of the horses' hooves: "Amorion is fallen!"

When he understood that cry, he grunted as if he had taken a blow to the belly. In truth, the Empire of Videssos had taken the blow. For years, the fortress at Amorion had kept the Makuraners from overrunning the Arandos valley and perhaps from reaching the Sailors' Sea. If Abivard had at last forced his way into Amorion—

"You, there!" Maniakes shouted, pointing to a fleeing horseman who did not belong to his own vanguard. "Tell me at once what happened off to the west."

For a moment, he thought the soldier would ride on by without stopping or answering. He hadn't been part of a rout till Etzilios ambushed him outside Imbros, but now he knew how to recognize one. At the last instant, though, the fellow reined in and shouted, "Amorion is fallen!"

It might have been a cry of lamentation like those in Phos' sacred scriptures, wherein the lord with the great and good mind nearly despaired over the wicked way of mankind. The fugitives took it up again and again: "Amorion is fallen!" "—is fallen!" "—is fallen!" "—is fallen!"

As the cry echoed and reechoed, Maniakes' men cried out, too, in anger and alarm. They knew—he had taken pains to impress upon them—how important the city at the west end of the Arandos was. And, unschooled in formal logic though they were, they could reason out the misfortune its fall implied.

"Does Tzikas still live?" Maniakes called to the man who had stopped.

"Aye, so he does," the cavalryman answered, and then, recognizing Maniakes' regalia, added, "your Majesty." He wiped sweat from his forehead with the sleeve of his surcoat before going on. "He commands the rear guards; Phos bless him and keep him safe, he's still trying to hold the boiler boys away from the rest of us."

"Get into line with us," Maniakes said, not just to him but to all the fugitives within earshot. "We'll ride forward to Tzikas' aid and, the good god willing, surprise the Makuraners and steal a victory from them."

His calm and the good order of the force he led persuaded some of the soldiers who had abandoned Amorion to try fighting again. Others, though, kept on going, thinking flight their only refuge. Maniakes did not have enough men to hold them in line by force. And their fear infected some of the warriors who had been with him since Videssos the city, so that they wheeled their horses and fled with the fugitives. Their companions tried to stop them, but too often in vain.

Another scout rode back to Maniakes from the vanguard. Saluting, the fellow said, "Your Majesty, the most eminent sir your brother bids me warn you his force is cracking to pieces like the ice on a stream at the start of springtime. His very words."

"Tell him he may fall back on the main body here, but—" Maniakes waved an arm to show the chaos all around him. "—we're in the same boat, and I fear the boat is sinking." The scout saluted and rode back toward the vanguard. The scores of men coming the other way stared at him and shouted out warnings. One or two took courage from his example and stayed to fight alongside the Avtokrator. Most, though, just shook their heads and kept on fleeing.

Along with the vanguard Parsmanios commanded, a new group of warriors approached Maniakes and his men. Among them was a standard bearer still holding the Videssian banner, gold sunburst on blue, on high. Next to him rode a gray-bearded fellow in gilded chain mail on a fine gray horse.

"Eminent Tzikas!" Maniakes shouted, loud as he could.

The gray-bearded man's head came up. Maniakes waved to him. He started to wave back, then seemed to recognize Maniakes and changed the gesture to a salute. "Your Majesty!" he called, and rode toward the Avtokrator.

Maniakes waved at the chaos all around them. "What happened?" he asked. "After holding so long—"

Tzikas shrugged, as if to deny that any of the sorry spectacle was his fault. "We lost, your Majesty," he answered. "That's what happens when every Makuraner in the world comes at you, when none of the other generals in the westlands will lend you a counterfeit copper's worth of aid, when all we hear from Videssos the city is that there's no help to be had there, either, or else that your head is forfeit if you ever take a pace away from the soldiers who protect you—" He made a disgusted gesture. "I could go on, but what's the use? To the ice with it. To the ice with everything."

"Amorion's gone to the ice, seems like," Maniakes said. He remembered that Tzikas had blamed the failings of one of his fellow generals for the defeat in which Tatoules disappeared, and wondered if the man knew how to take responsibility for his own actions.

"Do you think you'd have done better, your Majesty?" Tzikas growled—almost the same question Genesios had put to Maniakes when he was captured.

"Who can say?" Maniakes looked Tzikas up and down. "Splendid footgear you have there, eminent sir," he remarked. But for a couple of narrow black stripes, Tzikas' boots were of imperial crimson. At any distance, they would have looked like the red boots reserved for the Avtokrator alone.

The general shrugged again. "The way things have been, all

the Videssian authority around these parts has been invested in me—nothing much coming from the capital but trouble, as I said. I thought I ought to look the part, or come as close to it as I could in law and custom."

He was on this side of both law and custom—barely on this side, but inarguably so. Maniakes wondered if, one fine day, he might have pulled on boots without any black stripes. The Avtokrator wouldn't have been a bit surprised. Taking Tzikas to task, though, would have to wait. "Are you pursued?" he asked the ever-so-punctilious general.

"We're not riding east to settle our supper, your Majesty," Tzikas answered. "Aye, the boiler boys are on our trail, great droves of 'em." He peered north, then south, gauging the forces Maniakes had with him. "No point even standing in their way. They'll go through you like a knife through fat bacon."

"Mm, not necessarily," Maniakes answered after a moment's thought. "They're chasing what they think is a broken band of fugitives, after all. If we hit the ones out in front of the pursuit and hit them hard, we may be able to knock their whole army back on its heels. Phos willing, we'll save the Arandos valley for this year, or most of it, anyhow."

Tzikas' face was pinched and narrow, not one for showing joy under the best of circumstances. Now that circumstances were far from the best, he all but radiated gloom. "Your Majesty, if you press forward and see the numbers arrayed against us, you will know resistance is hopeless."

"Until I see them for myself, I don't know anything of the kind," Maniakes answered. "Eminent sir, if you and as many of your men as you can bring want to ride with us, you'll be welcome and you can give useful aid. If not, then kindly keep running east; don't stay around infecting us with the notion that everything is lost."

He waited to see how Tzikas would take that. The general scowled; he wasn't used to taking orders or to being dismissed so peremptorily. After a moment, he said, "You are the Avtokrator; it shall be as you command." His voice was flat, empty of any feeling whatsoever, for good or ill.

Maniakes could not fault him when he started shouting to his men to rally. He had a bigger voice than his slim frame suggested, and used it to good effect. Some of the horsemen fleeing the fall of Amorion kept right on fleeing, but others reined in and began adding themselves to Maniakes' regiments. Maniakes' troopers seemed to gain fresh heart, too, seeing that not everything was falling to pieces before their eyes.

"Forward!" Maniakes shouted. The trumpeters sent the command to the whole force, as if the men were ships spread across the sea. They advanced at a trot they could quickly kick up to a gallop at need.

Here and there, they passed Videssians leading lame horses and men on foot whose horses must have foundered altogether or been killed. Those soldiers stared in disbelief at the spectacle of a strong force from their own side heading toward the oncoming Makuraners rather than away from them.

They also passed dead horses and dead men—freshly dead, not yet bloated and stinking. Those would have been wounded when they fled Amorion and its environs, but they hadn't made it to safety. Maniakes' mouth was a thin, bitter line. So many men thrown away these past seven years. Genesios couldn't have done a better job of gutting the Empire if he had set out to accomplish exactly that.

Then Maniakes spied another body of soldiery riding east. At first, from a distance, he thought they were more imperials trying to break free from the Makuraners. After a moment, he realized they were the Makuraners from whom the garrison at Amorion had been trying to get free.

They rode big, strong horses. With their style of fighting, they needed such sturdy beasts, too. The riders wore full armor of chain and splints, with lamellae protecting their arms and legs. Chainmail veils of iron rings hung from their helmets to ward their faces. Only their eyes and hands showed, and iron half-gauntlets held weapons away from the backs of those hands.

Even their horses wore iron scales mounted on leather, an armor that reached back to the animals' flanks. The riders carried long, heavy spears, with swords slung in scabbards on their left sides so they could protect themselves if their spearshafts broke in battle.

"Ply them with arrows!" Maniakes shouted. "Stay at long range and scattered—don't come to close quarters with them." Those were standard tactics for Videssians fighting their western neighbors. Videssian cavalrymen wore mail shirt and helmet only, and never rode armored horses. The Makuraner horsemen and their mounts had to be sweltering in the heat, which was why the Videssians had given them the scornful "boiler boy" nickname.

The Makuraners' lances came down to point straight at their foes; the sun sparkled off sharp-edged iron. "Sharbaraz King of Kings!" the heavy-armored cavalrymen shouted in their own language. Maniakes spoke it, not with any great fluency but enough to make himself understood. The Makuraners had other cries, too: "Abivard!" and "Hosios Avtokrator!"

Maniakes looked around for Abivard but did not see him. The enemy who had been his friend must not have been with his foremost troops. His own men yelled "Videssos!" and "Maniakes Avtokrator!" back at the Makuraners. A few Videssians also yelled "Tzikas!" They all sounded fierce and spirited, which made Maniakes' heart leap. Videssians had lost so many fights lately that any show of courage had to come as a surprise to their foes.

His troopers reached back over their shoulders to pluck arrows from their quivers, then nocked them, drew bows back to their eyes, and let fly. A couple of hundred years before, such horse archery would have been much more difficult, but stirrups let a rider control his mount well enough that he could without hesitation use both hands to shoot. Stirrups also let the Makuraners charge with the lance without fear of being unseated: Videssos and Makuran had taken the same notion and gone in different directions with it

Not all of Maniakes' troops were archers. For closer-in work, javelin men nipped toward the enemy, flung their darts, and then tried to make off before the Makuraners could draw near enough to spear them out of the saddle. Not all of them escaped as they would have hoped. At close quarters, an armored Makuraner boiler boy was more than a match for any one Videssian horseman.

The trick, though, was not to let the Makuraners use their superior power to full advantage. Maniakes' men outnumbered their foes. No armor covered every part of a man's body; no armor kept every shaft from penetrating. After a short, sharp combat, the Makuraners broke off and tried to escape.

That wasn't easy. Their horses still had to carry the extra weight of iron they bore. And the horses wore no armor behind. The Videssians plied their vulnerable haunches with arrows. The horses screamed in pain and terror. Their harassed riders fought hard to master them.

Maniakes' troopers cheered like wild men at the startling sight of Makuraners showing their backs. They galloped after the boiler boys with more spirit and excitement than Videssian troops had shown in the westlands for years.

"How far will you let them go?" Tzikas asked, adding "your Majesty" half a beat late. "Before long, either the Makuraners will rally or they'll find more of their kind and punish us for our presumption."

He was very possibly right. Biting his lip, Maniakes acknowledged that with a grudged nod. But, with fussy caution such as Tzikas had shown, no wonder the Makuraners had run wild through the westlands. If you assumed taking the initiative against them was presumption, you wouldn't take the initiative. Tzikas might well be a genius of a defensive fighter; he probably was, to have held Amorion so long. Still, while lack of defense could make you lose a war, having it was no guarantee you would win.

Maniakes realized he hadn't answered the general's question, which, phrased differently, had also been in his own mind. "We'll go a little farther," he said. "Having the men know they can beat the boiler boys may be worth more to us than goldpieces."

"Having them think they can beat the Makuraners only to discover they're wrong may cost us more than goldpieces," Tzikas answered dolorously.

Again, Maniakes nodded. He waved on his horsemen nonetheless. It occurred to him that he might need to worry less than he had thought about Tzikas' trying to usurp the throne. By all signs, the man was too cautious to go squat behind a bush at night without shining a torch there to make sure he wouldn't meet a bear.

Maniakes drew his sword. So did Tzikas. His face stayed set in disapproving lines, but he did not lack animal courage. Together, they joined the Videssian cavalry in pursuit of the Makuraners.

The leaders from among Maniakes' men had got well ahead of the Avtokrator and the general. Maniakes urged his gelding after them. Just before he caught them up, fresh horn calls came up ahead, horn calls different from those Videssos used. "Straighten up, there!" Maniakes shouted to the horsemen in front of him.

"Form line of battle. Don't pelt after them like a herd of sheep gone mad on crazyweed."

"There are a lot of Makuraners up there," Tzikas remarked. It wasn't *I told you so*, but it might as well have been.

Along with the horn calls, shouts and screams rang out. All at once, Maniakes' horsemen were no longer pursuers but pursued. They came galloping back toward him, riding harder than they had after the fleeing Makuraner heavy cavalry. Horses' barrels ran with blood from frantic spurring; animals' flanks showed lines from the whip.

Close behind them, in no better order, coursed more Makuraner riders. These were not boiler boys, but the light cavalry the King of Kings used to bulk up his forces. They were armed with bows and swords, and armored for the most part with nothing more than iron pots for their heads and heavy leather jerkins. Maniakes knew their kind: wild and fierce when they had the advantage, and as quick to panic if things went wrong or they were checked.

But how to check them? "Stand fast!" Maniakes cried; individually, his men enjoyed the same advantage over the Makuraner light horsemen as the heavy cavalry did over the Videssians. But the imperials would not stand fast, not when they saw enemy horsemen sliding round their flanks.

In a fury, Maniakes spurred toward the Makuraners. They scattered before him; they had no taste for hand-to-hand combat with a man both well protected and bold. Tzikas stayed at his right hand, slashing with his sword. A few other imperials rode with them, doing their best to stem the building rout.

Maniakes traded sword strokes with a Makuraner too hemmed in to evade him. Whatever words the fellow shouted were lost in the general din of combat. Sweat carved canyons through the pale dust covering the soldier's swarthy skin. His face was long, rectangular, solemn, with large, dark, deep-set eyes that could show soulful seriousness but now blazed with blood lust.

With a cunning stroke, Maniakes knocked the sword from his hand. It flew spinning into the dirt. But, before the Avtokrator could finish him, another Makuraner made straight for him. He had to twist awkwardly to meet the new onslaught, and knew a moment's stark fear that he would not be able to twist in time.

Then Tzikas attacked the oncoming horseman, forcing him to sheer off before he could strike at the Avtokrator. "My thanks," Maniakes said. He turned back toward the Makuraner he had disarmed, but the fellow had taken advantage of his moment of distraction to get away.

"I am privileged to serve your Majesty," Tzikas said. Maniakes had trouble reading anything into his tone. Was that simple statement of fact, submissiveness, or irony? The Avtokrator could not tell.

He got no time to worry about it, either. More Makuraner horns were winded. He had a brief glimpse of more horsemen riding to the growing fight from out of the west. Grimacing, he nodded toward Tzikas. "Seems you were right, eminent sir," he said. "Now let's see how we can get ourselves out of this mess."

"Aye, your Majesty." Tzikas hesitated, then went on, "Do you know, neither Likinios nor Genesios, so far as I remember, ever admitted he was wrong."

"Maybe I'm just new on the throne," Maniakes said, his voice dry. Tzikas sent him a sharp look, then decided it was a joke and laughed. Maniakes continued, "Admitting I made the mistake doesn't much help me put it to rights now."

"No, not this time," Tzikas agreed. "But that may not be so on some other occasion—provided we live to see other occasions."

"Yes, provided," Maniakes said. Given the number of Makuraners who swarmed forward to shoot arrows at his men, that was by no means obvious. The tactical solution presenting itself—that was all too obvious, with headlong retreat the only possible choice to escape catastrophe.

Though Videssian doctrine dealt matter-of-factly with retreat, Maniakes bared his teeth in an anguished scowl. His own willingness to push forward to meet Etzilios had led to disaster outside of Imbros. Now he had been impetuous again, and was again paying the price for it.

"I wish I were a turtle," he said to no one in particular. "I'd go into my shell and never come out."

"This can have its advantages," Tzikas said with a grave nod. "Thus Amorion remained in our hands throughout Genesios' unhappy reign."

"And thus it was lost in mine," Maniakes answered. "A proud record, isn't it? But you may be right more often than not—you certainly are this time. I can't help thinking, though, that some-times the cure for too much boldness is more, not less."

Tzikas' dark, mournful eyes did all the contradicting he couldn't speak aloud. For now, though, boldness in attack was simply out of the question. Avtokrator and general rode side by side, right-ing when they had to and doing their best to hold the retreat in check.

"Rally! Rally!" someone cried in Videssian: Parsmanios. When he spied his brother, he said, "Here's a fine mixed-up day, where the leader of the main force gets ahead of the leader of the van."

"Here's a fine dreadful day," Maniakes said. Then he added his own voice to Parsmanios', trying to persuade his cavalrymen and those who had originally ridden with Tzikas to hold fast. Now and again, he thought he would succeed. But then either more Makuraners would come up or the Videssians would begin to melt away, and he would have to fall back and try again.

At last, not long before sunset, his forces succeeded not in halt-ing the Makuraners but in breaking free of them and being able to set up camp without getting attacked while they were going about it. A miserable camp it was, too. Wounded men groaned and cursed. Here and there, healer-priests labored to bring forth their curative magic and restore to health some warriors who had been grievously wounded.

As always, Maniakes watched the blue-robes with more than a little awe. When one of them laid hands on a man, even someone as blind to magic as the Avtokrator could sense the current of healing passing to the one who was hurt. And, when the priest took his hands away, the healed wound would look as if it had been suffered years before.

But the cost on the healer-priests was high. After each man they treated, they would emerge from their healing trance like men awakening from some killing labor after not enough rest. They would gulp food and swill down wine, then lurch on to the next desperate case. And, after they had healed two or perhaps three men each, they would fall asleep so deeply that even kicking at them did no more than make them stir and mutter.

Men whose hurts were not bad enough to require such dras-tic intervention made do with surgeons who drew arrows and sewed up gashes and poured wine over wounds to keep them from 'rotting. So the surgeons said, at any rate. Maniakes often wondered if they helped as many men as they hurt.

He strode through the camp, doing his best to keep up the soldiers' spirits. He found Bagdasares sitting on the ground with his head in his hands, as if afraid it would fall off if he didn't keep tight hold on it. "Magical sir, have you any skill in healing?" Maniakes asked.

Bagdasares looked up. "What's that?" he said blankly. "Oh, your Majesty. No, I'm sorry, I fear I have none whatever. Even among mages, healers are a special breed. Their gift can be trained if it is present, but it must be inborn; I know of no man without that innate talent who ever succeeded in relieving another's misery."

Maniakes sighed. "I thought you would say something of the sort, else you would have been laboring with the priests as best you could. By the good god, though, I wish it were otherwise. If you cannot heal, what can you accomplish for us in this joyless place?"

"Not even as much as a fighting man could," Bagdasares answered with a guilty frown. "All I'm good for is eating up food that might instead go to someone who has a chance of keeping both himself and me alive."

"How do we change that in the future?" Maniakes asked. "Wizards should not have so many limits on their sorcerous powers."

"We do better than we once did," Bagdasares said. "In the days of Stavrakios the Great, the healing art was but newly born, and as likely to kill a healer-priest as to cure the poor chap he was trying to save."

"We know more of other arts than they did in his day, too," Maniakes said. "I was thinking about that not so long ago—you read the accounts of his campaigns and you'll see he and his followers didn't know the use of stirrups. I wouldn't like to try riding without them, I tell you that."

He rubbed his chin, thinking how strange it was to be talking about changes from long-ago days after a lost battle. Even thinking about changes from long-ago days felt strange. He hadn't noted any changes in the way he lived through his whole lifetime, save those that went with his own change in age and station. He didn't ever remember his father talking about such changes, either; if they had gone on, they had done so at a pace too slow for any one man to notice.

But go on they had. A river would eventually shift its bed with the passing years. So, too, when you looked far enough, the course of human knowledge and endeavor shifted. He supposed that accumulation of slow, steady, but in the end significant changes had been growing since the day when Phos created Vaspur, first-born of all mankind.

He let out a snort. If he was to be properly orthodox by Videssian standards, he could not let himself believe in the tale of Vaspur and other doctrinal matters the most holy Agathios would no doubt term heretical. He shook his head. No—he could not let himself be seen to believe in the tale of Vaspur and the rest.

"Your Majesty?" Bagdasares asked, wondering what the snort and the headshake meant.

"Never mind," Maniakes said. "Fuzz on the brain, that's all. Amazing, the notions I can come up with to keep from thinking about the mess we're in."

"Ah, yes," Bagdasares answered. "The mess we're in. What do we do about it? What *can* we do about it?"

"Nothing I can see," Maniakes said, the words bitter as alum in his mouth. "Come morning, the Makuraners are going to attack us again. They'll have more men than we will, and they'll have their peckers up because they've beaten us once."

"They've beaten us more than once," Bagdasares said incautiously.

"Too true," Maniakes said. "So long as they keep it in mind—as we have to as well—it'll be worth extra men to their side . . . not that they'll need extra men tomorrow. They'll attack us, they'll beat us, and we'll have to retreat again. Pretty soon we'll be back in Garsavra, at the edge of the plateau." He scowled. "By the good god, pretty soon we'll be back in Videssos the city, with all the westlands lost."

"Surely it won't be so bad as that," Bagdasares said.

"You're right," Maniakes said glumly. "It's liable to be worse."

Scouts from the rear guard came galloping into Maniakes' miserable camp not long after dawn began painting the eastern sky with pink and gold. "The Makuraners are moving!" they shouted in tones that could have been no more horror-stricken were they announcing the end of the world.

As far as the Empire of Videssos went, they might as well have been announcing the end of the world.

Maniakes had hoped to mount a defense, maybe even a counterattack, against the men from Makuran. One look at his army's
reaction to the news that the enemy was on the way drove that
thought from his head. Men cried out in alarm. Some fled on
foot; others made as if to rush the guards who were keeping
watch on the long lines of tethered horses. No one showed the
slightest eagerness to fight

"What now, your Majesty?" Tzikas asked. He still wasn't saying *I told you so,* but by his expression he was thinking it very
loudly now.

"We fall back," Maniakes answered bleakly. "What else can we
do?" While Videssian military doctrine did not necessarily condemn retreat, after a while you got to the point where you had
no room left in which to retreat. His situation in the westlands
was rapidly approaching that point.

Tzikas sighed with more resignation than Maniakes could make
himself feel. "Ah, well, your Majesty," he said, evidently trying to
console, "had we not run into them yesterday, they would have
come upon us in short order."

"Which doesn't make our predicament here any better." Maniakes
raised his voice to a shout that carried through the camp: "Parsmanios!"

His brother hurried up to his tent a couple of minutes later.
"Aye, your Majesty?" he asked, as formally polite as if unrelated
to the Avtokrator.

"You'll go from vanguard commander to rear guard today,"
Maniakes said. "I don't expect miracles; just try to keep 'em off
us as best you can."

"I'll do whatever I'm able to," Parsmanios answered. He hurried away.

"Command me, your Majesty," Tzikas said.

Maniakes was reluctant to do that; he gauged Tzikas' obedience as springing more from policy than from conviction. But,
without any choice, he said, "Stay by me. We'll fight side by side,
as we did yesterday."

"Let it be as you say," Tzikas replied. Even as he spoke, the sound
of Makuraner horns blown in excitement and triumph came faintly
to Maniakes' ear across a rapidly shrinking stretch of ground.

"Fall back!" the Avtokrator ordered, and his own horn-players
relayed the dolorous call to everyone within earshot.

It wasn't a complete rout, not quite. Maniakes' soldiers hung together as a unit instead of wildly riding off every which way in search of safety. Maniakes hoped that was because of the discipline he had helped instill in them on their way to the encounter with the Makuraners. He was, however, realistic enough to suspect that the troopers stuck together only because they thought they were likelier to survive by doing so.

The running fight lasted from dawn till late afternoon. Then Maniakes set an ambush in a grove of almond trees not far from the Arandos. The only way he could get his men to stay there and await the Makuraners was to lead the ambush party himself. Even then, he had to growl at one nervous horseman: "You try and run off on me and I'll kill you myself."

Before long, the Makuraners came up, a few boiler boys mixed with a larger band of light horsemen. They rode in loose order, laughing and joking and plainly not looking for any trouble. *Why should they?* Maniakes thought bitterly. *We haven't given them any up till now.*

He drew his sword. "Videssos!" he shouted, and spurred his horse out of its hiding place.

For a hideous instant, he thought the men he had gathered would let him ride to his doom all alone. Then more shouts of "Videssos!" and some of "Maniakes!" split the air. The thunder of hoofbeats behind him was some of the sweetest music he had ever heard.

The Makuraners looked almost comically horrified as he and his men barreled toward them. The fight was over bare moments after it began. The Videssians rode through and over their foes, plying bow, javelin, and sword with a will. A few Makuraners managed to break out of the engagement, their cries of terror loud and lovely in Maniakes' ears. More, though, either died at once or were overtaken and slain from behind.

"A victory! A great victory!" yelled the man Maniakes had threatened to kill. He was bold now, even if he hadn't been then, and the Avtokrator did not begrudge him his sudden access of spirit. Seeing Maniakes, he asked, "What does our victory bring us, your Majesty?"

Maniakes wished he would have picked almost any other question. He didn't answer aloud, but all he had won by routing the Makuraners' advance party was the chance to camp for the night without being attacked and then, when morning came, to resume the retreat.

Tzikas undoubtedly would have thought he was lucky to get even that much. Maybe Tzikas was right; in his stand at Amorion, he had shown himself a master of defensive fighting. But Maniakes remained convinced he could not win by merely defending. As soon as he could, he aimed to take the offensive.

As soon as he could, though, wouldn't be any time soon. And, moreover—"Take the offensive where?" he said. Try as he would, he found no answer.

✦ IX

From the little harbor in the palace quarter, Maniakes glumly peered west over the Cattle Crossing at the smoke rising in great fat columns above the suburb called Across. Only that narrow stretch of water—and the dromons that unceasingly patrolled it—held the armies of the King of Kings away from Videssos the city.

"In all the wars we've ever fought with the Makuraners, they've never reached the Cattle Crossing before," he said morosely.

His father sighed and clapped him on the shoulder. "So long as they don't get across the strait, you still have the chance to go down in history as the great hero who drove them back from the very brink of victory," the elder Maniakes said.

"What brink?" Maniakes said. "They have their victory, right there. And how am I supposed to drive them back? They've cut me off from the westlands, and we draw most of our tax revenues from that part of the Empire. How will I pay my soldiers? Phos, Father, they aren't even ravaging Across and letting it go at that. From what the sailors say, they're settling in to winter there."

"I would, in their sandals," the elder Maniakes answered calmly. "Still, just because they're at Across doesn't mean they hold all the westlands."

"I know that," Maniakes said. "We're still strong in the hill country of the southeast, and not far from the border with Vaspurakan, and we still hold a good many towns. But with Abivard's army plugging the way against us, we can't do much to support the forces we still have there, and we can't do anything at all to get revenue out of the western provinces."

"I wish I could tell you you're wrong," his father said, "but you're not. One good thing I can see is that Abivard's men have done such a fine job burning out the croplands all around Across that they'll have a hard time keeping themselves fed through the winter, especially if our horsemen can nip in and pinch off their supply lines."

Maniakes grunted. When you had to look at the worst part of a disaster and figure out how it might—eventually—redound to your advantage, you were hard up indeed. As a matter of fact, the Empire of Videssos was hard up indeed.

The wind began to rise. It had a nip to it; before long, the fall rains would start, and then the winter snows. He couldn't do anything much about solving the Empire's problems now, no matter how much he wanted to. Come spring, if he was wise enough—and lucky enough—he might improve the situation.

"Niphone seems to be doing well," the elder Maniakes said, sketching the sun-sign to take his words straight up to Phos. "And your daughter has a squawk that would make her a fine herald if she were a man."

"All very well," Maniakes answered, "and the lord with the great and good mind knows I'm grateful for what he chooses to give me. But when set against *that*—" He waved toward the Makuraners on the far side of the Cattle Crossing. "—my personal affairs seem like coppers set against goldpieces."

His father shook his head. "Never belittle your personal affairs. If you're miserable at home, you'll go and do stupid things when you take the field. More stupid things than you would otherwise, I mean."

"Ha!" Maniakes clapped a hand to his forehead. "I was enough of an idiot out there for any eight miserable men you could name. Do you know what Genesios asked me just before I cut off his head? He asked if I'd rule the Empire any better than he had. From what happened my first year, I'd have to say the answer is no."

"Don't take it too much to heart," the elder Maniakes said. "You're still trying to muck out the stables he left you—and he left a lot of muck in them, too."

"Oh, by the good god, didn't he!" Maniakes sighed. "You make me feel better—a little better. But even if the muck isn't all my fault, I can still smell its stink. We'll have to move it farther from the castle." He gestured again toward the smoke rising from Across.

"They can't spend the winter there," his father said. "They can't. After a while, they'll see they can't cross the strait to menace the city, either, and they'll pull back."

But the Makuraners didn't.

Kameas came into the chamber where Maniakes was fighting a losing battle against the provincial tax registers. If no gold came in, how was he supposed to keep doling it out? Could he rob—or, to put it more politely, borrow from—the temples again? Did they have enough gold and silver left to make that worthwhile?

He looked up, in the hope the vestiarios would bear news interesting enough to distract him from his worries. Kameas did: "May it please your Majesty, a messenger has come from the palace harbor. He reports that the Makuraner general Abivard, over in Across, has sent word to one of your ship captains that he would have speech with you."

"Would he?" Maniakes' eyebrows shot up.

"Aye, your Majesty, he would," answered Kameas, who could be quite literal-minded. He went on, "Further, he pledges your safe return if you go over the Cattle Crossing to Across."

Maniakes laughed long and bitterly at that. "Does he indeed? Etzilios made me the same pledge, and see how well that turned out. I may be a fool, but I *can* learn. No matter how generous Abivard is with pledges, I shall not put my head inside the Makuraners' jaws and invite them to bite down."

"Then you will not meet with him?" The vestiarios sounded disappointed, which made Maniakes thoughtful. Kameas went on, "Any chance to compose our differences—"

"Is most unlikely," Maniakes interrupted. Kameas looked as if the Avtokrator had just kicked his puppy. Maniakes held out a hand. "You needn't pout, esteemed sir. I'll talk with him, if he wants to talk with me. But I don't expect miracles. And we're hardly in a position to demand concessions from Abivard, are we?"

"No, your Majesty, though I wish we were," Kameas said. "I shall convey your words to the messenger, who in turn can pass them on to the Makuraner general."

"Thank you, esteemed sir. Tell the messenger to tell Abivard that I will meet with him at the fourth hour of the day tomorrow." Videssos—and Makuran, too—divided day and night into twelve hours each, beginning at sunrise and sunset, respectively. "Let him put his standard on the shore, and I will come and speak to him from a boat. My war galleys will be close by, to prevent any treachery."

"It shall be as you say," Kameas answered, and waddled out to pass on the conditions to the messenger. Maniakes lowered his eyes to the cadaster he had been studying when the vestiarios came in. The numbers refused to mean anything to him. He shut the tax register and thought about seeing Abivard again. As he had told Kameas, it wasn't likely anything would come of talking with him. But hope, like any other hearty weed, was hard to root out altogether.

"There, your Majesty." The officer in command of the boat in which Maniakes rode pointed. "You see the red lion banner flapping on the beach."

"Aye, I see it," Maniakes answered. "By the good god, I hope it's never seen on a Videssian beach again." He glanced back over his shoulder. There on the eastern shore of the Cattle Crossing, he was still Avtokrator, his word obeyed—by those outside his immediate household—as if he were incarnate law. In the land he was approaching, though, Sharbaraz's word, not his, was law.

There beside the Makuraner banner stood a tall man in a fancy striped caftan of fine, soft wool; the fellow wore a sword on his belt and a conical helmet with a feathered crest and a bar nasal on his head. At first Maniakes did not think he could be Abivard, for he had streaks of gray in his beard. As the boat drew closer, though, Maniakes recognized the grandee who had stayed with Sharbaraz even when his cause looked blackest.

He waved. Abivard waved back. "Take us well inside arrow range," Maniakes told the boat captain. "I want to be able to talk without screaming my lungs out."

The fellow gave him a dubious look. "Very well, your Majesty," he said at last, but warned the rowers, "Be ready to get us out of here as fast as you can work the oars." Since Maniakes found that a sensible precaution, he nodded without comment.

In the Makuraner language, Abivard called, "I greet you, Maniakes." No respectful title went with the name; the men of

Makuran did not recognize Maniakes as legitimate Avtokrator of the Videssians.

"I greet you, Abivard," Maniakes replied in Videssian. Abivard had mastered some of the Empire's tongue when he and Maniakes campaigned together against Smerdis the Makuraner usurper. Since he had spent so much time in Videssian territory since those days, he probably had more now.

Maniakes expected him either to get on with what he had come to say or to launch into a florid Makuraner harangue about Videssian iniquity. He did neither. Instead, he said, "Have you or your guardsmen any silver shields?"

"Is he daft?" the captain of the small boat murmured.

"I don't know," Maniakes murmured back. By Abivard's intense tone, by the way he stared intently across the water at Maniakes, he meant the question to be taken seriously. Maniakes raised his voice. "No, Abivard. Silver shields are not part of my guards' ceremonial dress, nor of my own. Why do you ask?"

The *no* made Abivard's shoulder slump; Maniakes could see as much, even across the water that separated them. But the Makuraner general rallied and said, "Maniakes, the King of Kings and the Avtokrator should not be at odds with each other, but should govern their states like true brothers. For there is no other empire like these."

"Abivard, I would better like hearing that from you if we were not at war, and if you called me 'Majesty' instead of the fraud and pretender whom Sharbaraz King of Kings—you see, I recognize him; he would not be King of Kings if Videssos had not recognized him—raised up in my place. Sharbaraz wants to be Videssos' big brother, to watch over us and tell us what to do. If you speak of brotherhood, go back to your proper border and do it there, not here at the Cattle Crossing."

"If you will come to an understanding with Sharbaraz King of Kings, may his years be many and his realm increase, the states of Makuran and Videssos will not let their thoughts drift apart from each other. They should be eager to become friendly and to agree," Abivard answered.

Florid Makuraner harangue, indeed, Maniakes thought. Aloud, he replied, "When you say we should become friendly and agree, you mean I should become Sharbaraz's slave."

"If you acknowledge his supremacy, he will grant you a treaty admitting your place on the Videssian throne," Abivard said. "So he has told me, swearing by the God and the Four Prophets. The greatness of this treaty will endure, for when goodwill and friendship toward each other prevail by our using concern and good counsel, it would be unholy to raise arms against each other and unjustly distress and harass our subjects."

"Does that mean you'll be leaving Across this afternoon, or will you wait till tomorrow?" Maniakes asked sweetly.

Abivard ignored him. He had his speech set and he was going to finish it: "What will come of this? If you acknowledge the authority of Sharbaraz King of Kings, may his years be many and his realm increase, you will be more fortunate than other men, and throughout your life you will be admirable and deserve emulation. But if you let this chance go and decline to make a great and good peace—if you do not figure out what is to your advantage—you will see instead hostility and enmity. You will cause all-out, discordant, impossible warfare, and it is only too likely that you will be choosing great toil and exertion, and will spend many lives. You will spend your treasures but will create only the maximum of destruction. In general, the war's end will result only in great evil for you. You can see this from what has happened since I invaded Videssian territory, and from the terrible things it has seen and suffered. But with peace, the condition of your state will stop being so very pitiful and wretched."

"Frankly, Abivard, I don't believe a word of it," Maniakes said. "If you want peace, if Sharbaraz King of Kings wants peace, you may have it any time you like. All you need do is pack up your soldiers and go back to Makuran. Leave Videssian soil and we shall have peace."

Abivard shook his head. Maniakes would have been astonished had he done anything else. The Makuraner general said, "Peace can be yours, if you want it. Send envoys dealing with that matter to Sharbaraz King of Kings. He will be persuaded by me, I am sure, and will come around to your point of view. Make peace now, secure and pure for all time to come."

In and of itself, that was more of a concession than Maniakes had thought to get from Abivard. But he answered, "From all I have seen, Sharbaraz King of Kings is persuaded by no man these days. He does as he pleases, and if it pleases him to outrage my envoys, he will, with no one to let or hinder him."

"His principal wife is my sister," Abivard said, speaking with rather than at Maniakes for the first time since his odd question about silver shields. "If he heeds anyone, he heeds me."

Maniakes studied him. "How often does he heed anyone? But seldom, or I miss my guess."

"The King of Kings is his own judge, as a man who calls himself Avtokrator should know," Abivard said.

"That is true, but a man who listens only to himself will sooner or later hear the words of a fool, with no one to tell him so," Maniakes answered. "How can you weigh the proper course when you don't know all the choices?"

"Consider where we are talking, Maniakes," Abivard said, "and think whether this King of Kings or the Avtokrator has planned more wisely. If we were speaking outside Mashiz, I might think your point better taken."

"I said, 'sooner or later,' " Maniakes replied. "That something has not happened yet doesn't mean it can never happen. Do you play at dice?" He waited for Abivard's nod before going on, "Then you know that just because no one has rolled the double ones of Phos' little suns for a long time doesn't mean they can't come up on the next throw."

"With us, a double two is the winning throw—we call it 'the Prophets Four,' " Abivard said. "One and three ranks next; some of us call that 'Fraortish and the rest,' others 'the lady Shivini and the men.' " He kicked at the sand of the beach. "But I did not ask you here to talk about dice. I take it you will not yield even if reason calls on you to do so?"

"I will not. I cannot," Maniakes said. "Stavrakios took Mashiz, but you Makuraners went on, and now you have won a triumph. You will not take Videssos the city, and we, too, shall rise from the ruins."

"Videssos the city cries out to be sacked," Abivard said. "It may yet happen, Maniakes, and sooner than you think."

"Say what you will," Maniakes answered, "but if you so much as dip a toe into the waters of the Cattle Crossing, a dromon will row up and slice it off."

Abivard scowled. Maniakes knew he had angered him. That bothered the Avtokrator not at all. The Makuraners were fine horsemen and clever artificers; in close combat on land and in siege operations they were a match for their Videssian neighbors.

One thing they were not, though, was sailors. They could look over the Cattle Crossing at Videssos the city, but the imperial navy kept them from getting to the other side of that little strip of water.

"I have no more to say to you, Maniakes," Abivard said. "When we meet again, we shall be at war once more."

"Be it so, then." Maniakes turned to the captain of the light boat. "It is over. It accomplished nothing. Take me back to the docks in the palace quarter."

"As you say, your Majesty," the officer answered, and gave the oarsmen their orders. The light boat pulled away from the beach by Across. Maniakes looked back over his shoulder. Abivard stood on the sand, watching him go. The Makuraner general took a couple of steps toward the Cattle Crossing, but did not try to get his feet wet.

Alvinos Bagdasares plucked at his thick black beard. "Let me make sure I understand you correctly, your Majesty," he said. "You want me to learn why Abivard was so interested in finding out whether you or your retinue had along a silver shield when you spoke with him the other day?"

"That's right," Maniakes said. "It meant something important to him, and he was disappointed when I told him no. If I know why, it may tell me something I can use to help drive the Makuraners back where they belong. Can you learn for me what it is?"

"I don't know," Bagdasares answered. "If the answer is in some way connected with sorcery, other sorcery may be able to uncover it. But if it springs from something that happened to Abivard on campaign, say, odds are long against our ever knowing what was in his question."

"Do everything you can," Maniakes said. "If you don't find the answer, we're no worse off than we would have been had you not tried."

"This is not something I can accomplish overnight," the wizard warned him. "It will take research into the spell most likely to be effective, and more time, perhaps, to gather the materials to complement the symbolic portion of the enchantment."

"Take your time." Maniakes' mouth twisted. "Why not? By all the signs, Abivard is going to winter in Across after all. I don't know what he gains by it except humiliating us, but he certainly does that. Still, it's not as if we haven't been humiliated enough other ways lately."

"I'm sure it could be worse, your Majesty," Bagdasares said.

Maniakes fixed him with a baleful glare. "Really, sorcerous sir? How?"

He gave Bagdasares credit; instead of mumbling an apology, the mage quite visibly thought about how things might be worse. At last he said, "Well, the Makuraners and Kubratoi could make common cause against us."

"Phos forbid it!" Maniakes burst out, appalled. "You're right. That would be worse. The good god grant Sharbaraz never thinks of it. It wouldn't be easy to arrange, not with our war galleys holding Abivard off in the westlands. A good thing they are, too—otherwise I'd have something new and dreadful to worry about, alongside all the old dreadful things on my mind now."

Bagdasares bowed. "I did not mean to trouble you, your Majesty. I sought but to obey."

"You succeeded all too well," Maniakes said. "Go on, now; see how to go about finding what was in Abivard's mind. And I—" He sighed and reached for a cadaster from the westlands. He knew what revenues would be recorded inside: none. "I shall set about making bronze without tin—and without copper, too, come to that."

After a little while, Maniakes' interest in seeing how little the Empire would be able to spend in the year to come palled. He got up from the table where he had been depressing himself and went wandering through the halls of the imperial residence. Those halls were chilly; winter would soon be at hand. Maniakes glanced west; he could not see the Makuraners lording it over the suburbs of the imperial capital, but he felt their presence. The humiliation of which he had spoken to Bagdasares burned at him like vinegar poured onto a wound.

The hallways of the residence held mementos of Avtokrators past. Genesios, fortunately, had not tried to immortalize himself in that particular way. If he had, Maniakes would have thrown whatever he had left behind onto the rubbish heap. The best memorial Genesios could have had was the pretense that he had never existed.

Not wanting to think about Genesios, Maniakes paused awhile in front of a portrait of Stavrakios. The Avtokrator of old wore the red boots, the heavy crown, and the gilded chainmail that went with his office, but in spite of those trappings resembled a veteran underofficer much more than anyone's expectations of what an Emperor should look like. He was painted as squat and muscular, with blunt, battered features, dark pouches under his eyes, and an expression that warned the whole world to get out of his way. Not all of the world had listened, so Stavrakios spent most of his long reign forcibly moving it aside.

Maniakes, who now needed to salute no living man—no matter what Sharbaraz had demanded of him—gave Stavrakios a formal salute, clenched right fist over his heart. "If you could beat the Makuraners, no reason I can't," he said.

The old picture, of course, didn't answer. If it had, Maniakes would have suspected either that he was losing his wits or that Bagdasares was playing a sorcerous joke on him. All the same, he could almost hear what the great Avtokrator of days gone by was thinking: *Well, if you're going to, what are you waiting for?* In his mind's ear, Stavrakios sounded a lot like his own father.

He studied the portrait a while longer, wondering how Stavrakios would have got out of this predicament—or how he would have kept from getting into it in the first place. The best answer Maniakes could come up with was that Stavrakios wouldn't have gone into anything with an inadequate force. Maniakes had done that twice now, first against the Kubratoi—he had anticipated treachery there, but not on the scale Etzilios had planned—and then against the Makuraners. Again, that hadn't been altogether his fault—how could he have anticipated Amorion falling just before he got to it?—but the results had been disastrously similar.

He nodded to Stavrakios. "All right, sir, I was stupid twice, which is once more than I'm entitled to, but I promise you this: next time I put troops into battle, the numbers will be on my side."

"They'd better be."

For a moment, Maniakes thought he was again imagining Stavrakios' reply. Then he realized he really had heard the words, and whirled around in surprise. His father grinned at him. "Sorry to break in like that, son—your Majesty—but you'd just said something that makes a good deal of sense. I wanted to make sure you'd remember it."

"You managed that, by the good god," Maniakes said. Now he

set the palm of his hand over his heart, which was still pounding in his chest. "To say nothing of scaring me out of six months' growth."

His father's grin got wider, and rather unpleasant. "Fair enough—we'll say nothing of that. But what you said was wise: if you're going to hit the other fellow, make sure you hit him so hard he can't get back up. Try and do things by halves and you'll just end up throwing both halves away."

"Yes, I've seen that," Maniakes agreed. "But the goldpiece has two faces. If I charge ahead on one course with everything I have, it had better be the right one, or else I only make my mistake larger and juicier than it would have been."

"Juicier, eh? I like that." The elder Maniakes let out a wheezing chuckle. "Well, son, you're right—no two faces on the goldpiece there. You'd better be right for Videssos' sake, too. We're at the point now where being even a little wrong could sink us. Even bad luck might. Do you know that, when I was a boy, old men would talk about one year when they were children that was so cold, the Cattle Crossing froze from here all the way over to Across, and you could go to and from the westlands dryshod? If we get that kind of winter again—"

"Our dromons won't be able to patrol the strait, and the Makuraners will be able to cross from the westlands and lay siege to us," Maniakes finished for him. "You do so relieve my mind. Every time it snows this winter now, I'll be looking up and wondering how long it will last and how bad it will be. As if I didn't have enough things to worry about."

The elder Maniakes chuckled again. "Maybe now you understand why, when the eminent Kourikos tried to put the red boots on me, I turned him down flat."

Niphone got up out of bed to use the chamber pot. The cold air that got in when she lifted up the quilts and sheepskins that held winter at bay woke Maniakes. He grunted and stretched.

"I'm sorry," Niphone said. "I didn't mean to bother you."

"It's all right," Maniakes said as she slid back into bed. "There's already the beginning of light in the east, so it can't be too early. In fact, since today's Midwinter's Day, it's getting light as late as it does any time during the year."

"That's true." Niphone cocked her head, listening. "I think the snow's given way to rain." She shivered. "I'd rather have snow. The rain will turn to ice as soon as it touches the ground, and people and horses will be sliding everywhere."

"It won't freeze on the Cattle Crossing, which is all that matters to me . . . almost all," Maniakes amended, slipping a hand up under her wool nightdress so that his palm rested on her bulging belly. As if to oblige him, the baby she was carrying kicked. He laughed in delight

"This one kicks harder than Evtropia did, I think," Niphone said. "Maybe that means it will be a boy."

"Maybe it does," Maniakes said. "Bagdasares thinks it will be a boy—but then, he thought Evtropia would be a boy, too. He's not always as smart as he thinks he is."

That was one reason Maniakes had not asked his wizard to try to learn how Niphone would fare in her confinement. Another was that Bagdasares hadn't yet figured out why Abivard had been interested in a silver shield. He had warned that would take time, but Maniakes hadn't expected it to stretch into months. And if he couldn't manage the one, how could the Avtokrator rely on his answer to the other?

"When does the mime show at the Amphitheater begin today?" Niphone asked.

"We've spread word through the city that it will start in the third hour," Maniakes answered. "Any which way, though, it won't start till we're there."

"We don't want to make the people angry," Niphone said, "nor to anger the lord with the great and good mind, either." The covers shifted as she sketched Phos' sun-sign above her heart.

He nodded. "No, not this year." Midwinter's Day marked the time when the sun was at its lowest ebb in the sky, when Skotos snatched most strongly at it, trying to steal its light and leave the world in eternal frozen darkness. As the days went by, the sun would rise ever higher, escaping the evil god's clutches. But, after this year of disasters, did Phos still care about Videssos? Would the sun move higher in the sky once more? Priests and wizards would watch anxiously till they learned the answer.

Niphone rode to the Amphitheater in a litter borne by stalwart guardsmen. Maniakes walked alongside, with more guardsmen to protect him from assassins and to force a way through the crowds that packed the plaza of Palamas. A dozen parasol-bearers carrying bright silk canopies proclaimed his imperial status to the people.

Bonfires blazed here and there across the square. Men and women queued up to leap over them, shouting, "Burn, ill-luck!" as they jumped. Maniakes broke away from his guards to join one of the lines. People greeted him by name and slapped him on the back, as if he were a pig butcher popular with his neighbors. On any other day of the year, that would have been lese majesty. Today, almost anything went.

Maniakes reached the head of the line. He ran, jumped, and shouted. When he landed on the far side of the fire, he stumbled as his booted foot hit a slushy bit of ground. Somebody grabbed his elbow to keep him from falling. "Thanks," he gasped.

"Any time," his benefactor said. "Here, why don't you stay and see if you can't catch somebody, too? It'd make a man's day, or a lady's even more." The fellow winked at him. "And they do say anything can happen on Midwinter's Day."

Because they said that, if babies born about the time of the autumnal equinox didn't happen to look a great deal like their mothers' husbands, few people raised eyebrows. One day of license a year helped keep you to the straight and narrow the rest of the time.

The next few people in the queue sailed over the bonfires without difficulty. Then a woman leapt short and almost landed in the flames. Maniakes ran forward to drag her away. "Niphone!" he exclaimed. "What were you doing, jumping there?"

"The same thing you were," his wife answered, defiantly lifting her chin. "Making sure I start the new year without the bad luck piled up from the old one."

Maniakes exhaled through his nose, trying to hold on to patience. "I put you in the litter so you wouldn't tire yourself out walking or go into labor sooner than you should, and you go and run and jump?"

"Yes, I do, and what are you going to do about it?" Niphone said. "This is Midwinter's Day, when everyone does as he—or she—pleases."

Faced by open mutiny, Maniakes did the only thing he could: he cut his losses. "Now that you have jumped, will you please get back into the litter so we can go on to the Amphitheater?'

"Of course, your Majesty." Niphone demurely cast her eyes

down to the cobbles of the plaza of Palamas. "I obey you in all things." She walked back toward the bearers and other guardsmen, leaving him staring after her. *I obey you in all things,* his mind translated, *except when I don't feel like it.*

When the parasol-bearers emerged through the Avtokrator's private entrance, waves of cheers and clapping rolled down on Maniakes like surf from a stormy sea. He raised a hand to acknowledge them, knowing they weren't for him in particular but in anticipation of the mime show that now would soon begin.

He took his seat at the center of the long spine that ran down the middle of the Amphitheater's floor. Most days, the enormous structure was used for horse races; the spine defined the inner margin of the course. Today, though—

Today Maniakes said, "People of Videssos—" and the crowd quieted at once. A magic, not of sorcery but of architecture, let everyone in the Amphitheater hear his voice when he spoke from that one spot. "People of Videssos," he repeated, and then went on, "May Phos be with you—may Phos be with us—all through the coming year. As the sun rises higher in the sky from this day forward, so may the fortunes of the Empire of Videssos rise from the low estate in which they now find themselves."

"So may it be!" the multitude cried with one voice. Maniakes thought the top of his head would come off. Not only could everyone in the Amphitheater hear him when he spoke from that one spot, as long as he stayed there all the noise in the great tureen of a building poured right down on him.

He gestured to Agathios, who sat not far away. The ecumenical patriarch led the tens of thousands of spectators in Phos' creed. Again the noise of the response dinned in the Avtokrator's ears.

Maniakes said, "To sweeten the year to come, I give you the mime troupes of Videssos the city!"

Applause rocked him once more. He sat down, leaned back in the throne set on the spine for him, and prepared to enjoy the mimes as best he could—and to endure what he could not enjoy. Everything save Phos himself was fair game on Midwinter's Day; an Avtokrator who could not take what the mimes dished out lost favor with the fickle populace of the city.

Leaning over to Agathios, Maniakes asked, "Did Genesios let himself be lampooned here?"

"He did, your Majesty," the patriarch answered. "The one year he tried to check the mime troupes, the people rioted and his guardsmen looked likely to go over to them instead of keeping them in check. After that, he sat quiet and did his best to pretend nothing was happening."

"What a pity," Maniakes said. "I was hoping he would give me a precedent for massacring any troupe that didn't strike my fancy." Agathios stared at him, then decided he was joking and started to laugh.

Maniakes was joking—after a fashion. But worries about offending the Avtokrator went out the window on Midwinter's Day along with everything else. Mime troupes were supposed to mock the man who held the throne—and he was supposed to take it in good part, no matter how much he wanted to set his guardsmen on the impudent actors.

Out came the first troupe. Most of them were dressed up as extravagant caricatures of Makuraner boiler boys, though they weren't mounted. One fellow, though, wore an even more exaggerated likeness of the imperial regalia Maniakes had on. The troupe's act was of the utmost simplicity: the boiler boys chased the fellow playing Maniakes around and around the racetrack. The crowd thought that was very funny. Had he been sitting up near the top of the Amphitheater, with no concerns past his own belly and perhaps his family, Maniakes might have found it funny, too. As it was, he smiled and clapped his hands and did his best to hold his temper.

He had a long morning ahead of him. One troupe had him and Parsmanios out looking for Tatoules, and finding a horse apple instead. Another had made a huge parchment map of the Empire of Videssos—it must have cost them a good many goldpieces—and proceeded to tear it in half and burn up the part that held the westlands. Still another had him running from first the Kubratoi and then the Makuraners, and the two sets of Videssos' foes colliding with each other and getting into a brawl.

Maniakes really did clap over that one. Then he realized that, if the Kubratoi and Makuraners really did meet, they would of necessity do so over the corpse of the Empire. He wondered if the mimes—or the audience—fully understood that. He hoped not.

At last the show ended. Maniakes rose and led the audience in a cheer for the performers who had entertained them—and embarrassed him. He hadn't been the least bit sorry when rotten fruit greeted a couple of troupes that lacked the saving grace of being funny. Had he had a basket of rotten apples at his feet, he would have pelted most of the mimes. As it was, he took the mockery as best he could.

People filed out of the Amphitheater, off to revel through the rest of the short day and the long night. Maniakes walked back to the imperial residence beside Niphone's litter; this time, the Empress stayed inside. That relieved him as much as having the mime shows end.

No sooner had he returned to the residence, though, than Kameas came up to him and said, "Your Majesty, the wizard Alvinos waits at the southern entrance. He would have speech with you, if you care to receive him."

For a moment, Maniakes failed to recognize the Videssian-sounding name Bagdasares sometimes used. When he did, he said, "Thank you, esteemed sir. Yes, I'll see him. Perhaps he's had some success with his magic after all. That would be a pleasant change."

Bagdasares prostrated himself before Maniakes. The Avtokrator hadn't always made him bother with a full proskynesis, but did today: he was less than pleased with the mage, and wanted him to know it. Bagdasares did; when Maniakes finally gave him leave to rise, he said, "Your Majesty, I apologize for the long delay in learning what you required of me—"

"Quite all right, magical sir," Maniakes answered. "No doubt you had a more important client with more pressing business."

Bagdasares stared, then chuckled uneasily. "Your Majesty is pleased to jest with me."

"I do wish I'd heard more from you sooner, and that's a fact," Maniakes said. "Here it is Midwinter's Day, by the good god, and I set you the problem a few days after I met with Abivard. When I told you to take your time, I own I didn't expect you to take *all* of it."

"Your Majesty, sometimes seeing the problem is easier than seeing the answer to it," Bagdasares replied. "I'm still not sure I have that answer, only a way toward it. But this is Midwinter's Day, as you said. If you have it in mind to revel rather than worry about such things, tell me and I shall return tomorrow."

"No, no, never mind that," Maniakes said impatiently. He could see all the problems Genesios had left him, but, as Bagdasares had said, seeing how to surmount them was another matter. "It's possible I owe you an apology. Say on, sorcerous sir."

"Learning why someone does something is always tricky, your Majesty," the wizard said. "Sometimes even he does not know, and sometimes the reasons he thinks he has are not the ones truly in his heart. Finding those reasons is like listening to the howl of yesterday's wind."

"As you say," Maniakes answered. "And have you managed to capture the sound of yesterday's wind for today's ears?"

"I shall make the attempt to capture it, at any rate," Bagdasares said. "I have tried this before, with uniform lack of success, but in my previous conjurations I always assumed Abivard's question arose from some connection with Sharbaraz King of Kings or with some mage from Mashiz or both. Failure has forced me to abandon this belief, however."

Maniakes wondered if Bagdasares was wrong or merely lacked the strength and skill to prove himself right. He did not say that; making a mage question his own ability weakened him further. Instead he asked, "What assumption do you set in its place, then?"

"That Abivard acquired this concern independently of the King of Kings, perhaps in opposition to him—would it not be fine to see Mashiz rather than Videssos engulfed in civil strife?—or perhaps from before the time when he made Sharbaraz's acquaintance."

"Mm, it could be so," Maniakes admitted. "If it is, how do you go about demonstrating it?"

"You have indeed set your finger on the problem, your Majesty," Bagdasares said, bowing. "Recapturing ephemera, especially long-vanished ephemera, is difficult in the extreme, not least because the application of the laws of similarity and contagion often seems irrelevant."

"Seems irrelevant, you say?" Maniakes' ear had been sensitized to subtle shades of meaning by more than a year on the throne. "You want me to understand that you have found a way around this difficulty."

"I think I have, at any rate," Bagdasares said. "I've not yet tested it; I thought you might care to be present."

"So I can see how clever you've been, you mean," Maniakes said. Bagdasares looked injured, but the Avtokrator spoke without much malice. He went on, "By all means, sorcerous sir, dazzle me with your brilliance."

"If I can but give satisfaction, your Majesty, that will be enough and to spare," the mage answered. He was not usually so self-effacing, but he didn't usually keep the Avtokrator waiting a couple of months for a response, either. Now he was all briskness. "If I may proceed, your Majesty?"

Without waiting for Maniakes' consent, he drew from his carpetbag a lamp, a clay jar—at the moment tightly stoppered—and a silver disk about as wide as the palm of his hand. A rawhide cord ran from one side of the disk to the other, to symbolize the support by which a soldier carried a shield.

Bagdasares worked the stopper from the jar and poured water in a narrow stream on a tabletop. "This is seawater, taken from the Cattle Crossing," he said. He set the silver disk close by it, then made a few quick passes over the lamp. Not only did it light, but with a flame far more brilliant than the usual, so that Maniakes had to squint and shield his eyes against it.

"It's as if you brought the summer sun into the imperial residence," he said.

"The effect does not last long, but will be useful here," Bagdasares answered. He picked up the disk and used it to reflect the sorcerously enhanced light into Maniakes' face. The Avtokrator blinked and squinted again. Nodding in satisfaction, Bagdasares said, "Here we have a silver shield shining across a narrow sea, not so?"

"Exactly so," Maniakes agreed.

"Now to uncover the origins of the phrase," Bagdasares said, and began to chant not in Videssian but in the throaty Vaspurakaner language. After a moment, Maniakes recognized what he was chanting: the story of how Phos had created Vaspur, firstborn of all mankind Between verses, the mage murmured, "Thus do we approach the problem of origins." Then he was chanting again—verses Agathios would surely have condemned as heretical. Agathios, however, wasn't here. Maniakes had grown up with these verses. They didn't bother him.

Suddenly, out of the air, a deep, rich voice spoke. Maniakes habitually thought in Videssian. He had just been listening to a chant in the Vaspurakaner tongue. Now he quickly had to adjust to yet another language, for the words, wherever they came from—and he could see no source for them—were in Makuraner: "Son of the *dihqan*, I see a broad field that is not a field, a tower on a hill where honor shall be won and lost, and a silver shield shining across a narrow sea."

Maniakes cocked his head to one side, wondering if more would come, but found only silence. Bagdasares, his broad forehead glistening with sweat despite the chill of Midwinter's Day, staggered and almost fell. He looked worn to exhaustion, and sounded it, too, saying "Did you understand that, your Majesty? It was not in a tongue I know."

"I understood it, yes," Maniakes answered, and did his best to render it into Videssian for the mage. He went on, "It sounds to me as if you called back into being a prophecy from long ago."

"So it would seem, indeed." Shoulders bent, gait halting, Bagdasares hobbled over to a chair and sank into it. "Might I trouble you for some wine? I find myself fordone."

Maniakes called for a servitor. Response came slowly; like so many others throughout Videssos the city, most of his household staff were out reveling on the holiday. Presently, though, a serving woman brought in a jar of wine and two cups. Bagdasares spat on the floor in rejection of Skotos, then drank down what the servant had poured him.

After a couple of slower sips of his own, Maniakes said, "When I campaigned with Abivard and Sharbaraz against Smerdis the usurper, Abivard had with him a soothsayer named . . ." He hesitated, trying to dredge up the memory. "Tanshar, that's what he called himself."

"Was it his voice we heard, then?" Bagdasares asked.

"I'd not have thought so, though I had scant dealings with him myself," Maniakes answered. "His beard was white, not gray. I can hardly imagine him sounding as . . . as virile as did that voice you summoned from the deep."

"If he was the one who gave the prophecy I recalled here, who can say what power was speaking through him?" Bagdasares sketched the sun-sign. "Not all such powers conform to our usual notions of fitness, that much I can tell you."

"I'd like to be surer than 'Well, this is possible,'" Maniakes said. He ruefully shook his head. "What I'd like and what I get are apt to be two different things. You needn't remind me of that, magical sir, for I've already learned it for myself. Still and all, though, Abivard was responding to something in his past he reckoned important. 'A broad field that is not a field'—I wonder what that meant, other than that the soothsayer had a gift for obscurity."

"Abivard could tell us—provided the prophecy came true," Bagdasares said. "But then, if some of it hadn't come true, I don't suppose Abivard would have been worrying about the rest—and I don't suppose we could have reconstructed it so readily. My magic, I think, responded to magic already in the prophecy."

"That sounds reasonable, sorcerous sir," Maniakes agreed. "So now we have the answer to the question that's been troubling us since I met with Abivard. But, even knowing the answer, we still don't know why Abivard wanted to see, or would see, that shining silver shield. What conclusions do you draw from that?"

"Two possibilities occur to me," Bagdasares answered. "One is that we were simply asking the wrong question. The other is that the question was indeed the right one, but the fullness of time for the answer has not yet come round."

Maniakes nodded. "And there's no way to know which until the fullness of time does come round—if it ever does." He sighed. "Thank you, sorcerous sir—I think."

Triphylles puffed a little as he rose from his proskynesis. "Your Majesty, you honor me beyond my worth by summoning me before your august presence this day. How may I serve you? Command me." His rather doughy face took on an expression intended to convey stern devotion to duty.

The last time Maniakes had commanded him—to fare north as envoy to the Kubratoi—he had also had to cajole him with the promise of a boost in rank. He couldn't do that again; *eminent* was the highest rung on the ladder. He had to hope Triphylles really did own a living, breathing sense of duty. "Eminent sir, no doubt you will recall that last fall I met with the Makuraner warlord Abivard, whose forces, worse luck for us, still occupy Across."

"Of course, your Majesty." Triphylles looked westward, though all he saw in that direction was a wall of the chamber in which Maniakes had received him. "The smoke from their burnings is a stench in the nostrils of every right-thinking man of Videssian blood."

"So it is," Maniakes said hastily; Triphylles looked set to launch into an oration. The Avtokrator went on, "Abivard suggested that one way in which the Makuraners might possibly be persuaded to withdraw was through the good offices of an embassy sent to Sharbaraz King of Kings."

He got no further than that. In a baritone scream, Triphylles bellowed, "And you want me to be that embassy? Your Majesty, how have I offended you to the point where you keep sending me off to loathsome places in the confident expectation I shall be killed?"

"There, there," Maniakes said, as soothingly as he could. "Mashiz is not a loathsome place; I've been there myself. And Sharbaraz isn't the cheerful sort of murderer Etzilios is, either—or at least he wasn't back in the days when I knew him, at any rate."

"You will, I trust, forgive me for reminding you that in the years since then his disposition does not seem to have changed for the better?" Triphylles was not normally a man of inspired sarcasm; *amazing what being a little bit unhappy can do,* Maniakes thought.

Aloud, he said, "You will be an embassy, eminent sir, and the law of nations prohibits such from being assaulted in any way."

"Oh, indeed, your Majesty, just as the law of nations prevented Etzilios from assailing you at what was claimed to be a peace party." Triphylles still looked frightened and defiant, and was upset enough to be more imaginatively sardonic than Maniakes had thought possible for him.

The Avtokrator said, "I didn't have any reason to want to be rid of you, eminent sir, but you'll give me one if you keep on with your complaints."

"A paradox worthy of a theologian," Triphylles exclaimed. "If I am silent, you'll send me away, thinking I consent, whereas if I tell you I don't consent, that will give you what you reckon good cause to send me away."

Maniakes tried again: "I want to send you to speak to Sharbaraz because I think you are the man best suited to the task. You've shown yourself a gifted speaker again and again—not least here today."

"If I truly were gifted, I would have talked you out of sending me to Etzilios," Triphylles said darkly. "And now Mashiz? No seafood, date wine, women locked away as if they were prisoners—"

"Less so than they were before Sharbaraz took the throne," Maniakes interrupted. "The King of Kings and Abivard both have strong-willed wives—Sharbaraz is married to Abivard's sister, as a matter of fact."

"And to a good many others, by all accounts," Triphylles said. "But I was simply using that as an example of the reasons I shall be most distressed to travel to a far land yet again."

You had to listen carefully with Triphylles, as with most Videssian courtiers. He had said *shall*, not *should*. He didn't do such things by accident; he meant he had resigned himself to going. Maniakes said, "Thank you, eminent sir. I promise, you won't be sorry when you return from Mashiz."

"A good thing, too, for I shall certainly be sorry on the journey thither and while I'm there—very likely on the way back, too," Triphylles said. "But if I must leave the queen of cities, what am I to say to the King of Kings when I am ushered into his gloomy presence?"

"One of the reasons I send you forth is my confidence that you will know what to tell Sharbaraz and how to say it when the time comes," Maniakes answered. "You know what Videssos needs from him: that he recognize me as Avtokrator and pension off his false Hosios, and that his troops leave the westlands as soon as may be." He scowled. "I will pay him tribute for as long as five years, much as I hate doing it, to give us the chance to get back on our feet."

"How much per year will you give him?" Despite complaints, Triphylles turned businesslike.

Maniakes sighed. "Whatever he demands, more or less. We're in a worse position for hard bargaining than we were with Etzilios."

"Indeed, and look what I won for you with that negotiation," Triphylles said. "The chance to be captured and just as nearly killed."

"Ah, but now you've had practice," Maniakes said blandly. "I'm sure you'll do much better with Sharbaraz. I *am* sure you'll do better, eminent sir, else I'd not send you out."

"You flatter me beyond my worth," Triphylles said, and what was usually a polite disclaimer and nothing more now sounded sour in his mouth. He sighed, too, hard enough to make a lamp flicker. "Very well, your Majesty, I obey, but by the good god I wish you'd picked another man. When do you aim to send me off into the Makuraner's maw?"

"As soon as may be."

"I might have known."

Maniakes went on as if Triphylles had not spoken: "You make your preparations as quickly as you can. I'll arrange a safe-conduct for you with Abivard, and perhaps an escort of Makuraner horsemen, as well, to keep you safe on the road to Mashiz." He smacked a frustrated fist into his open palm. "Eminent sir, you have no notion how much it galls me to have to say that, but I will do it, for your sake and for the sake of your mission."

"Your Majesty is gracious," Triphylles said. Maniakes thought he would leave it at that, but he evidently took courage from having spoken freely before without anything dreadful happening to him, so he added, "You might as well be honest and put the mission ahead of me, as you surely do in your own mind."

If he hadn't been dead right, Maniakes would have felt insulted.

South and east of the wall of Videssos the city lay a broad meadow on which soldiers were in the habit of exercising. Maniakes drilled his troops there all through the winter, except on days when it was raining or snowing too hard for them to go out.

Some of the men grumbled at having to work so hard. When they did, the Avtokrator pointed west over the Cattle Crossing. "The smoke that goes up from Across comes from the Makuraners," he said. "How many of you have your homes in the westlands?" He waited for some of the troopers to nod, then told them, "If you ever want to see those homes again, we'll have to drive the Makuraners out of them. We can't do that by fighting the way we have the past few years. And so—we drill."

That didn't stop the grumbling—soldiers wouldn't have been soldiers if they didn't complain. But it did ease things, which was what Maniakes had intended.

Along with his father and Rhegorios, Parsmanios, and Tzikas, he worked hard to make the exercises as realistic as he could, to give the men the taste of battle without actual danger—or with as little as possible, at any rate. They fought with sticks instead of swords, with pointless javelins, with arrows that had round wooden balls at their heads instead of sharp iron.

Everyone went back to the barracks covered with bruises, but only a few men got hurt worse than that: one luckless fellow lost an eye when an arrow struck him just wrong. He was only a trooper, but Maniakes promised him a captain's pension. You had to know when to spend what gold you had.

Sometimes, when the exercises were done, Maniakes would ride up to the edge of the Cattle Crossing and peer west at Across. Every now and then, when the day was sunny, he saw moving glints he thought were Makuraners in their heavy armor. They, too, were readying themselves for the day when their army and his would come to grips with each other again.

"I wish it weren't so built up over there," he complained to Rhegorios one day. "We'd have a better idea of what they were up to."

"That's what we get for raising a city there," his cousin answered with an impudent grin. Then, growing thoughtful, Rhegorios waved back to the Videssians' practice field. "Not much cover here. If they have men with sharp eyes down by the shore, they shouldn't have much trouble figuring out what we do."

"True enough," Maniakes said. "But that shouldn't be any great surprise to them, anyhow. They must know we have to ready ourselves to fight them as best we can. Whether it will be good enough—" He set his jaw. "These past seven years, it hasn't been."

"The lord with the great and good mind bless our fleets," Rhegorios observed. "They can't fight our battles for us, but they keep the Makuraners from setting all the terms for the war."

"It's always a good idea to go on campaign with a shield," Maniakes agreed. "It will help keep you safe. But if you go with only a shield, you won't win your war. You need a sword to strike with as well as the shield for protection."

"The fleet could ascend a fair number of rivers in the westlands a good distance," Rhegorios said in the tones of a man thinking aloud.

"That doesn't do us as much good as we'd like, though," Maniakes said. "The dromons can't interdict rivers the way they can the Cattle Crossing. For one thing, we don't have enough of them for that. For another, the rivers in the westlands are too narrow to keep the Makuraners from bombarding them with catapults from the shore."

Approaching hoofbeats made him look up. The rider wasn't one of his troopers, but a messenger. "News from the north, your Majesty," he called, holding out a boiled-leather message tube to Maniakes.

The Avtokrator and Rhegorios looked at each other in alarm. Urgent news from the north was liable to be bad news: Etzilios on the move was the first thing that crossed Maniakes' mind. While he would have taken a certain grim pleasure in separating Moundioukh's head from his shoulders, that alone would not have compensated him for the damage a large-scale Kubrati raid would cause. Trapped between the steppe nomads and the Makuraners, the Empire of Videssos held little territory it could call its own these days.

Maniakes unsealed the message tube with more than a little trepidation. "Tarasios hypasteos of Varna to Maniakes Avtokrator. Greetings." Maniakes had to pause a moment to remember where Varna was: a coastal town, northwest of Imbros. His eyes swept down the parchment.

Tarasios continued, "I regret to have to inform your Majesty that the Kubratoi raided our harbor two days before my writing of this dispatch. They came by sea, in the *monoxyla* they habitually use for such incursions: boats made by hollowing out single large logs through fire, and then equipping them with rowers, low masts, and leather sails. Such vessels cannot challenge dromons, of course, but are more formidable than the description would suggest, not least because they are capable of accommodating a dismaying number of armed men.

"Varna, unfortunately, had no dromons present when the raiders descended upon us. They plundered a couple of merchantmen tied up at the quays, then threw fire onto those quays, the merchantmen, and the fishing boats nearby. But the fire did not spread from the harbor to the town, and the garrison repelled the barbarians upon their attempt to force entry into Varna by scaling the sea wall. That effort failing, they returned to their *monoxyla* and sailed away northward."

The hypasteos went on to request aid for his beleaguered city from the imperial fisc. The fisc was at least as beleaguered as Varna, but perhaps Tarasios didn't know that. Maniakes resolved to do something for him, although he knew that something wouldn't be much.

Rhegorios said, "Well, my cousin your Majesty, who's gone and pissed in the soup pot now?"

"How do you think Moundioukh's head would look hanging from the Milestone?' Maniakes asked dreamily. "The Kubratoi have violated the truce I bought, so I have the right to take it." He passed his cousin the message from Tarasios.

Rhegorios went through it, lips moving as he read. "Isn't that peculiar?" he said when he was through. "It doesn't sound like a big raid. I wonder if it wasn't some of the Kubratoi going off on their own to see what they could steal, maybe without Etzilios' even knowing about it."

"It could be so," Maniakes agreed. "My guess is that Etzilios will say it's so, whether it is or whether it isn't. I won't take Moundioukh's head right away, however much I think he'd be improved without it. What I will do is send a message straight to Etzilios, asking him what's going on here. If I don't get an answer I like, that will be time enough to settle with Moundioukh."

The messenger bearing Maniakes' query left Videssos the city the next day. Two weeks after that, he returned in the company of a small troop of Kubratoi who rode under shield of truce. The Avtokrator met their leader, a bearded barbarian named Ghizat, in the Grand Courtroom.

Ghizat approached the throne with a large leather sack under one arm. He set it down beside him while he performed a proskynesis. "Rise," Maniakes said in a voice colder than the chilly air outside. "Has your khagan forgotten the truce he made with us?"

"No, him not forgets, youse Majesty," said Ghizat, who seemed to have learned his Videssian from Moundioukh. "Him sended I down to these city with presents about you."

"What sort of present?" Maniakes asked. The size and shape of the leather sack made him hope he knew the answer, but Etzilios had taught him never to rely too much on hope.

Ghizat fumbled with the rawhide lashing that held the mouth of the sack closed. He turned it upside down and dumped a severed head out onto the polished marble floor of the courtroom. In violation of every canon of court etiquette, exclamations of shock and horror rose from the assembled bureaucrats and courtiers.

"This thing," Ghizat said, spurning the head with his foot, "this thing once upon a time it belongs to Paghan. This here Paghan, him leads *monoxyla* fleets what sails up along Varna. Etzilios the magnumperous, him not knows nothing about this fleets till too late."

The late Paghan stared up toward Maniakes with dull, dead eyes. The weather had remained wintry, so his mortal fragment was neither badly bloated nor stinking. Maniakes said, "How do I know he's not some no-account Kubrati sacrificed to let your khagan claim he's keeping the peace?"

"Couple kinds way," Ghizat answered. "First kind ways is, we Kubratoi never does nothing like these, no ways, nohow. Second kind ways is, Moundioukh and them other hostages personages, them knows Paghan, them tells youse what him are. Them knows other six headses us brings, too, know they when they still on bodies, yes sir."

Maniakes clicked his tongue between his teeth. He could indeed check that. He wouldn't know for certain whether these particular barbarians had in fact led the attack on Varna, but he could learn whether they were prominent among their people.

"Fair enough," he said. "Give me the names and stations of these men whose heads you've brought. If Moundioukh's account of them tallies with yours, I shall accept that Etzilios is not to blame for this raid."

"Youse Majesty, the bargains you have," Ghizat said, and told him the names of the other nomads now shorter by a head. "You does what you wants over they. Put headses up on big pointy stone prick—what you call it?"

"The Milestone," Maniakes answered dryly. A couple of court-iers tittered and then did their best to pretend they hadn't: it was a pretty good description. "I'll do that with some, I think, and send the rest to Varna so the people there know the raiders have been punished."

"Howsomever. They yourses now," Ghizat said. He prostrated himself again, to show he had said everything he intended to say.

"You will stay in the city until Moundioukh confirms what you and Etzilios have told me," Maniakes said; Ghizat knocked his head against the stone to show he understood. Maniakes turned to Kameas. He pointed to Paghan's head. "Take charge of that, eminent sir. Convey it first to Moundioukh with the others and then to the Milestone."

"Er—yes, your Majesty." Looking anything but delighted, the

vestiarios approached the head and picked it up by the very tip of its tangled beard with his thumb and forefinger. If his expression was any guide, he would sooner have handled it with a long pair of smith's tongs. He carried it away.

Ghizat rose, backed away from the throne till he had reached the distance protocol prescribed, and then turned and left the Grand Courtroom. From behind, his bowlegged swagger was amusing to watch.

After the audience ended, Maniakes returned to the imperial residence. Kameas, looking a bit green, presently reported to him: "Your Majesty, Moundioukh applies the same names to the Kubratoi—or rather, the abridged selection from the Kubratoi—as Ghizat gave them. The distinguished barbarous gentleman expressed forceful if ungrammatical surprise at discovering these individuals in their present state."

"Did he?" Maniakes said. "Well, by the good god, that's something. I take it to mean Etzilios will likely look for more tribute this year, and also to mean he'll keep his men quiet if we pay him enough."

"May it be so." Kameas hesitated, then decided to go on: "And, may it please your Majesty, I should be indebted to you if I were spared such, ah, grisly duties in the future. Most, ah, disturbing."

Maniakes reminded himself that the vestiarios' sole experience of war and battle had been Etzilios' assault on the imperial camp by Imbros. "I'll do what I can to oblige you, eminent sir. I must remind you, though, that life comes with no guarantee."

"I am aware of that, your Majesty, I assure you," Kameas answered tonelessly. Maniakes' cheeks heated. A eunuch was aware of it in ways no entire man ever could be.

Feeling foolish and flustered, Maniakes dismissed the vestiarios. He hoped Kameas would go have a mug of wine, or maybe several. If he ordered him to do something like that, though, Kameas was liable to be touchy enough to disobey because he had just been commanded to do something else he didn't care for. Sometimes you got better results with a loose rein.

Sometimes, of course, you didn't. The Makuraners were not going to leave the westlands unless Videssos drove them out, not unless Triphylles worked a miracle bigger than most of the ones accomplished through thaumaturgy. Keeping peace with

the Kubratoi would help with the fight against Makuran, but, as
he had told Kameas, life came with no guarantee. Pretty soon,
Niphone would bear their second child. If it was a boy, he would
become heir to the throne. Maniakes wanted to be sure he had
an Empire left to inherit.

The soup was rich with mussels, tunny, crab meat, mushrooms, and onions. Niphone paused with silver spoon halfway to her mouth, "I don't think I'd better eat any more," she said in a thoughtful voice.

Maniakes stared across the table at her. She sat some distance back from it; her bulging belly made sure she could come no closer. "Do you mean what I think you mean?" he asked.

He had spoken quietly. She didn't answer for a little while, so he wondered if she had heard him. Her gaze was searching, inward. But then she nodded with abrupt decision, as if she were a captain ordering troops forward into a breach in enemy lines. "Yes, there's another pang," she said. "Once you've known labor once, you don't confuse it with the tightenings you feel all through the last part of your confinement. This baby will be born tonight or tomorrow."

"We're ready," Maniakes said. "Everything will go exactly as it should, Phos willing." He sketched the sun-circle over his heart, a shorthand prayer to the lord with the great and good mind. Then, raising his voice, he called for Kameas. When the vestiarios came into the dining room, he spoke one word: "Now."

Kameas' eyes widened. As Maniakes had before him, he drew the sun-circle above his left breast. "I shall send for the lady Zoïle directly," he declared, "and make all other necessary preparations as well."

Those necessary preparations had nothing to do with the Red Room; the imperial birthing chamber had been ready for months. What Kameas meant was that he would summon, along with Zoïle, a healer-priest from the Sorcerers' Collegium and a surgeon. Coming out and saying that in front of Niphone would have reminded her of the risks she took; Maniakes was grateful for the vestiarios' tact.

Kameas bowed and hurried away. Maniakes got up from his seat, went around the table, and set his hands on Niphone's shoulders. "Everything will go perfectly," he repeated, as if saying it could make it so.

"Of course it will," his wife answered. "Why—" She paused as another labor pain came and went. "—shouldn't it?"

"No reason at all," Maniakes said heartily. "We'll have ourselves a fine boy by this time tomorrow." He hesitated. "Are the pains bad yet?"

"No, not yet," Niphone said, "but I know what lies ahead." She shrugged. "I endured it once. I can do it again."

Maniakes waited nervously for Zoïle to arrive. When Kameas escorted her into the dining room, she did not bother prostrating herself before the Avtokrator: She ruled the domain Niphone was reentering. She went over to the Empress, looked into her eyes, felt her pulse, and finally nodded.

"How does she seem?" Maniakes asked.

"Pregnant," Zoïle snapped, whereupon the Avtokrator shut up. The midwife gave her attention back to Niphone. Solicitude returned to her voice. "Can you walk, your Majesty?"

"Of course I can," Niphone said indignantly. To prove it, she got to her feet

Zoïle beamed at her. "In that case, your Majesty, why don't you take yourself to the Red Room, and get as comfortable as you can? I'll be along shortly; as you'll remember, much of the first part of labor can be boring."

"I remember what comes afterward, too," Niphone said, the first sign of apprehension she had shown in all her pregnancy. She turned back to Maniakes. "I will give you a son."

"Come through safe, that's all," he told her. He might as well not have spoken. Her head held high, she waddled out through the door and down the hall toward the chamber where legitimate Emperors who were the sons of Emperors came into the world: where dynasties, in other words, were born along with babies.

Zoïle looked out the door to see how far Niphone had gone.

Far enough, evidently, for Zoïle turned back to Maniakes and said, "Aye, she's pregnant again, your Majesty, and by the good god I wish she weren't."

Maniakes had no trouble interpreting the glare in the midwife's black eyes. *Men*, it said. In a hurt voice, he remarked, "Why does everyone think this is my fault?"

"Are you telling me you're *not* the father?" Zoïle asked sweetly, at which point the Avtokrator threw his hands in the air and gave up on convincing her he wasn't a stupid, lecherous brute. If she wanted to think that, she would, and he didn't seem able to do anything about it.

"Do the best you can for her," he said.

"I would anyhow, your Majesty, for my own sake," the midwife replied with quiet pride. Her mouth thinned into a bloodless line. "And if I can't, Phos willing the healer and the surgeon can. You've sent for them?"

"Yes," Maniakes said. "I don't want them to come into the residence, though, till Niphone goes inside the Red Room and you close the door. If she saw them, it would just make her worry more."

Zoïle considered that, tasting the words one by one. "Maybe there's hope for you yet," she said, and went down the hallway after the Empress before Maniakes could think of any fit reply.

A couple of minutes later, Kameas led two men into the dining room. "Your Majesty, I present to you the healer-priest Philetos and the surgeon Osrhoenes." Both men prostrated themselves before Maniakes. Philetos was tall and lean, with a lined face, dark freckles on his shaven crown, and a beard white as clean snow. He wore a plain blue robe, its only ornamentation the cloth-of-gold circle on his left breast that symbolized Phos' sun.

Osrhoenes was also tall, but heavyset He was some years younger than Philetos; gray rested lightly in his hair and beard. He wore a black robe; Maniakes peered closely at it, trying to see whether the somber color masked old bloodstains. He couldn't tell. Osrhoenes carried a small leather case, also black. Maniakes tried not to think about the sharp blades inside.

To Osrhoenes he said, "Sir," and to Philetos, "Holy sir," then went on to both of them together: "I trust you will forgive me when I say I hope your services won't be needed here today, though of course I shall pay you for your time regardless."

"Part of the gold you give me shall go to the sakellarios at the High Temple so as to swell the ecclesiastical treasure, the rest to the upkeep of the Sorcerers' Collegium," Philetos said; healers, like other priests, were constrained by vows of poverty.

Osrhoenes merely bowed to Maniakes. He was a secular man; the fee he got from Maniakes would go into his own belt pouch.

To Kameas the Avtokrator said, "If you would be so kind, escort these gentlemen to their place opposite the doorway to the Red Room. Perhaps you will find them chairs, so they may wait comfortably. If they want food or wine or anything else, see that they have it."

"Certainly, your Majesty," Kameas said. Maniakes was certain his instructions had been unnecessary; to the vestiarios, perfect service was a matter not only of pride but also of routine. Fortunately, that perfect service included not showing up the Avtokrator. If Maniakes was too nervous to let Kameas do what was required without nagging, Kameas would condescend not to notice.

The eunuch led Philetos and Osrhoenes away. That left Maniakes alone with his worries, which he would rather not have been. Zoïle's warnings after Niphone's last confinement, the midwife's worried look now, Niphone's insistence on bearing an heir or dying in the attempt, his own fear over his wife's safety . . . Mixed together, they made a corrosive brew that griped his belly and made his heart pound as it would have before combat.

He jumped and spun around when someone tapped on the doorframe. "I didn't mean to startle you," Lysia said. "I just wanted to tell you that I pray the lord with the great and good mind will grant you a son and heir—and that the Empress comes through safe."

"Thank you, cousin of mine," Maniakes said. "My prayers ride along the same path. May Phos heed them all." As he had so often lately, he sketched the sun-circle over his heart. So did Lysia.

He waited for her to reassure him that everything would surely be all right. Instead, she said, "I didn't think you'd want to be here by yourself, fretting because you can't do anything but fret."

"Thank you," he said. "That was kind." He made himself produce something that sounded a little like a laugh. "Now I can be here with you, fretting because I can't do anything but fret."

Lysia smiled. "Yes, I suppose you will be, but maybe not as

much. Shall I call one of the servants and have him bring you a jar of wine? That might take the edge off your worry."

"Another kind thought, but no," Maniakes answered. "If I started drinking wine now, I don't think I'd stop till I was sodden. And that wouldn't do when Niphone or the midwife hands me the baby, and it won't do now. Nothing wrong with being worried when you have something to worry about. Before too long, the reason will go away and everything will be fine."

"Phos grant it be so." Lysia took a breath, as if to add something else, then looked away and shook her head. "Phos grant it be so," she repeated softly. Maniakes thought about asking her what she had been on the point of saying, then decided he would probably be better off not knowing.

He made awkward small talk for a couple of minutes. Then his father came into the chamber. The elder Maniakes seemed not in the least surprised to find Lysia there before him. "I remember waiting and pacing while *you* were being born," he told the Avtokrator. "I thought it was taking forever, though I daresay your mother thought it was taking a good deal longer than that." He sighed. "Nobody can tell me that was more than two or three years ago, and look at you!"

Rhegorios joined them a little later, and Symvatios moments after his son. Parsmanios did not make his quarters in the imperial residence, so he took longer to arrive. Kourikos' home was outside the palace quarter altogether; close to two hours went by before he and Phevronia came to join the wait for their second grandchild from Niphone.

By then, Maniakes had long since called for the wine he had turned down when Lysia suggested it. He even sipped at a cup, nursing it, savoring the flavor, but not drinking enough to let it affect him much. Having family around him did make things easier to bear—but the burden remained on him . . . and on his wife.

Parsmanios thumped him on the shoulder. "It takes time, brother of mine. Nothing to be done but wait."

"I know," Maniakes replied abstractedly. It had taken a very long time when Evtropia was born. He had hoped it would go faster this time; women's second labors, from what he had heard, often did. The sooner Niphone gave birth and began to recover, the happier he would be.

But no word came from the Red Room. Leaving his relatives

behind, he walked down the hall to the birthing chamber. Philetos and Osrhoenes sat in their chairs, a board for the war game set on a little table between them. A quick glance showed Maniakes that the healer-priest had the surgeon on the run.

Inside the Red Room, Niphone groaned. The sound made Maniakes flinch. "Do you know how she fares?" he asked the two men. "Has Zoïle come out?"

Almost in unison, the two men shook their heads. "No, your Majesty," they said together. Philetos went on, "One lesson I have learned as a healer-priest, and that is never to joggle a midwife's elbow." The expression of most unclerical rue that passed over his face suggested he had learned the lesson the hard way. By the way Osrhoenes rolled his eyes, he had had the same lesson, and maybe the same teacher.

Niphone groaned again—or perhaps this cry was closer to a scream. It wasn't quite like any of the sounds of agony Maniakes had heard on the battlefield, so he had trouble assigning it a proper name. That didn't make it any less appalling, especially since it came not from a wounded soldier but from his wife.

But while he winced, Osrhoenes and Philetos went back to studying the game board—covertly, because he still stood by them, but unmistakably. He took that to mean they had heard such cries before, which meant—which he hoped meant—such cries were a normal part of giving birth. All the same, he could not bear to listen to them. He retreated back up the hall. When he looked over his shoulder, he saw that the physician and healer-priest had returned to their game.

His father clucked sympathetically on seeing his face. "Going to be a while yet, eh?" the elder Maniakes said.

"Looks that way," the Avtokrator said. He wore the red boots that marked him as ruler of all Videssos, but some things not even a ruler could command. Niphone's cries painfully reminded him of the limits to his power.

He waited . . . endlessly. He made small talk, and forgot what he had said the moment the words passed his lips. Kameas brought in a meal. Maniakes ate without tasting what was set before him. It got dark outside. Servitors lit lamps. Presently Kameas brought in more food, and Maniakes realized it was long enough since the last time for him to be hungry again.

By then, Parsmanios had fallen asleep in his chair and begun to snore. Symvatios' face, usually jolly, was full of shadow-filled lines and wrinkles. "Hard," he said to Maniakes, who nodded.

Kameas came into the chamber. "Can I bring you anything, your Majesty?" he asked, his voice low so as not to disturb Parsmanios—or Rhegorios, who was also dozing. The vestiarios' face, though smoother than Symvatios', showed no less concern.

"Esteemed sir, what I want now you can't bring me," Maniakes answered.

"That is so," Kameas said gravely. "May the good god grant that you receive it nonetheless." He dipped his head and slipped out of the room. His soft-soled shoes flapped against the marble and tile of the floor.

Lysia got up, walked over to Maniakes, and set a hand on his shoulder without saying anything. Gratefully he put his own hand on top of hers. Symvatios' head bobbed up and down like a fishing float in choppy water. The elder Maniakes' face was shadowed; the Avtokrator could not make out his father's expression.

Someone—not Kameas—came running up the corridor. "Your Majesty, your Majesty!" Zoïle was shouting.

Parsmanios awoke with a start. Rhegorios jerked out of his light sleep, too. "I don't fancy the sound of that," he said, rubbing at his eyes.

Maniakes didn't fancy it, either. He stepped out into the hallway—and recoiled in dismay at the sight of the midwife. Zoïle's arms were red to the elbows with blood; it soaked the front of her robe and dripped from her hands to the colored tiles of the floor mosaic.

"Come quick, your Majesty," she said, reaching out to grab at Maniakes' sleeve in spite of her gory fingers. "There's no hope to stop the bleeding—I've tried, Philetos has tried, and it's beyond what we can do. But we still may get the baby out of her alive, and with that done, the healer-priest may yet have another chance, a tiny one, to save your lady's life."

The hot-iron stink of blood filled the corridor. It made thinking straighter all the harder for Maniakes, arousing as it did the panic of the battlefield. At last, he managed, "Do as you must, of course, but why do you need me?"

Zoïle looked at him as if he were an idiot. "Why, to give the knife into Osrhoenes' hands and show your assent to his cutting. It would be for your lady, but she's too far gone to do it."

Seeing the state the midwife was in should have told Maniakes as much. Maybe he was an idiot. He also realized that, if Niphone was in such desperate straits, Philetos' chances of saving her after the surgeon had done his work were forlorn indeed. He moaned and shook his head, wishing he could have kept the illusion of hope.

No time for that now. No time for anything now. He trotted down the hall toward the Red Room, Zoïle at his elbow. Osrhoenes stood waiting outside the door. Seeing Maniakes, he reached into his bag and drew out a lancet. The keen blade glittered in the lamplight. Had any of the Avtokrator's guardsmen seen him, he might have died in the next instant for daring to draw a weapon in the presence of the Emperor.

Maniakes thought of that only later. When Osrhoenes held out the lancet to him, it was not a threat but a gesture as formal as a proskynesis. Maniakes took the knife, held it a moment, and returned it to the surgeon. "Do what you can," he said. "You shall not be blamed, come what may."

Osrhoenes bowed to him, then turned and went into the Red Room. Zoïle followed him. Maniakes had a brief glimpse of Niphone lying motionless on a bed in the center of the chamber, her face slack and pale as death. Philetos, his shoulders slumped, stood beside her. The midwife closed the door and he saw no more.

Nails biting into his palm, he waited for Niphone's shriek as the knife laid her belly open. No shriek came. For a moment, he was relieved, but then his heart sank further: if she was silent, it could only be because she was too nearly gone to feel anything.

He feared he would hear no sound from the Red Room but the frantic, muffled talk from Zoïle, Osrhoenes, and Philetos that leaked through the thick doors of the chamber. That would mean everything had been too late, that the baby was gone along with its mother.

He tried to figure out what that would mean for Videssos, what he would have to do next if it was so. He found his mind utterly stunned and blank. He tried to flog it into action, but had no luck. Past *my wife is dead, and my baby, too,* nothing meant anything.

Then, after what seemed an eternity but could not have been more than a handful of minutes, a newborn's angry, indignant wail pierced the portal of the Red Room. Maniakes needed a moment to recognize the sound for what it was. He had been so certain he would not hear it, he had trouble believing it when it came.

He stood rigid, leaning toward the Red Room. Of itself, his right hand sketched the sun-sign above his heart. If the baby lived, why not Niphone, too? "Please, Phos," he whispered.

When Zoïle came out, she carried a tiny bundle, tightly swaddled in a lambswool blanket. "You have a son, your Majesty," she said.

Instead of being joyful, her voice was numb with fatigue and grief. She had torn the neck opening of her robe, too, a sign of mourning. Maniakes asked the question anyhow. "Niphone?"

Tears ran down the midwife's cheeks. She bowed her head. "They—we—all of us—did everything we could to save her, your Majesty, but even to get the babe out alive and well . . . I think we thank the lord with the great and good mind for that much. I wouldn't have guessed Osrhoenes could do it, and I've never seen anyone faster with a knife than he is."

"Give me the boy," Maniakes said. He undid the blanket enough to make sure the baby had the proper number of fingers on each hand and toes on each foot and that it was indeed a boy child. No doubt there; its private parts were out of proportion to the rest of it. "Are they supposed to be like that?" Maniakes asked, pointing.

"That they are, your Majesty," Zoïle answered, seeming glad to talk about the baby rather than its mother. "Every boy comes into the world so." He would have guessed she followed that with a ribald joke after most births. Not tonight, not here.

He wrapped his son in the blanket once more. As he had when he had lost the fight east of Amorion, he made himself go on even in defeat. "Philetos couldn't save her after the cuts?" he asked, still trying to find out what had gone wrong.

"It's not like that, not Philetos' fault," Zoïle said. "A surgeon doesn't try to take a babe out of a mother unless she's on the point of dying anyhow. The ones the healers save after that are the special miracles, the ones priests talk of from before the altar to point out how we should never give up striving and hoping for the good. But most of the time, we lose the mother when the surgeon cuts."

"What do I do now?" Maniakes asked. He wasn't really talking to the midwife. Maybe he wasn't talking to anyone, maybe he spoke to Phos, maybe to himself. The good god did not swoop miraculously out of the sky with answers. If there were any, he would have to find them.

Zoïle said, "The baby is all he should be, your Majesty. He turned pink nice as you please when Osrhoenes drew him forth and cut the cord. Phos willing, he'll do well. Have you chosen a name for him?"

"We were going to call him Likarios," Maniakes answered. "We—" He stopped. *We* didn't mean anything, not any more. Tears rolled down his cheeks. He might not have loved Niphone with the passion he had felt for her after they were first betrothed, but he cared for her, admired her bravery, and mourned her loss. It left an empty place in his life, and a bigger one than he had imagined till this moment when the event made imagination real.

"We'll tend to things here, your Majesty, prepare the body for the funeral," Zoïle said gently. Maniakes' head bobbed up and down, as if on a spring; he hadn't even thought about the funeral yet. Having a son and suddenly not having a wife had been all he could take in. The midwife, no doubt, had seen that before. She reminded him of what needed doing next. "Why don't you take your son—take Likarios—and show him to your kinsfolk? They'll be worried; they'll need to know what's happened here."

"Yes, of course," Maniakes said; it all seemed very easy, once someone took charge of you.

He started up the hallway toward the chamber where his relatives waited. He thought he was doing fine till he walked past the corridor on which he was supposed to turn. Shaking his head, he went back and did it right.

No one had presumed to come after him. His father and Lysia waited outside the chamber from which he had been summoned. Rhegorios stood inside, but had his head out the door. Maniakes didn't see anyone else. *The rest of them must be inside,* he thought, pleased with his talent for logical deduction.

In his arms, Likarios twitched and began to cry. He rocked the baby back and forth. He had had some practice doing that with Evtropia before he had gone out on campaign the summer before. She was bigger when he had gotten back; holding her didn't feel the same any more. *They grow. You stay the same from one day to the next—or you think you do. With them, there's no room to think that.*

"Is it a boy you're holding there?" the elder Maniakes called.

At the same time, Lysia asked, "Niphone—how is she?"

"Aye, Father, a boy," Maniakes replied. When he didn't answer Lysia, she groaned and covered her face with her hands. She knew what that had to mean.

So did the elder Maniakes. He stepped forward to fold the Avtokrator into an embrace—an awkward one, because Maniakes still held his newborn son in the crook of his elbow. "Ah, lad," the elder Maniakes said, his voice heavy with grief, "I lost your mother in childbed. I never dreamed the same ill-luck would strike you and your lady, too."

"I feared it," Maniakes said dully. "After she bore Evtropia, the midwife warned her—warned me—she shouldn't have another. I would have been content to see the throne come down to a brother or a cousin or a nephew, but Niphone insisted that she try to bear a son to succeed me. And so she did, but the price—"

Kourikos and Phevronia came out into the hallway. The face of the logothete of the treasury was even more pinched and drawn than usual; Phevronia, her hair all unpinned, looked haggard and frightened. Kourikos stammered slightly as he spoke, as if the words did not want to pass his lips: "Your Majesty, I pray you, tell me I have misunderstood your words to your father."

Maniakes could hardly blame him. "Behold your grandson, father-in-law of mine," he said, and held Likarios out to Kourikos. The logothete took the baby with a sure touch that said he hadn't forgotten everything he had once known about children. Maniakes went on, "More than anything, I wish I could tell you—tell you and your lady—that you have misunderstood me. The truth is, I cannot; you have not. Niphone . . . your daughter . . . my wife—" He looked down at the floor. The hunting mosaic blurred as his eyes filled with tears.

Phevronia wailed. Kourikos put his free arm around her. She buried her face in his shoulder and wept like a soul damned to the eternal ice.

Gravely Kameas said, "I share your sorrow, your Majesty. I shall set in train arrangements for care of the young Majesty here and, with your permission, shall also begin preparations for the Empress' funeral obsequies. The weather remains cool, so the matter is not so urgent as it might otherwise be, but nevertheless—"

Phevronia wept harder yet. Kourikos started to bristle at the vestiarios' suggestion, then seemed to slump in on himself. He nodded jerkily. So did Maniakes. *You have to go on,* he told himself, and wondered how to make himself believe it.

As with anything else connected with the imperial household, the funeral carried a heavy weight of ceremonial, in this case melancholy ceremonial. The limestone sarcophagus in which Niphone was laid to rest bore carved scenes showing the bridge of the separator, the narrow passage souls walked after death. Demons snatched those who failed Phos' stern judgment and fell from the bridge, dragging them down to Skotos' ice. The last panel of the relief, though, showed one soul, intended to represent Niphone, winging upward toward Phos' eternal light.

Deceased Avtokrators and their kinsfolk were by ancient tradition interred beneath a temple in the western part of Videssos the city, not far from the Forum of the Ox, the capital's ancient cattle market. The temple, dedicated to the memory of the holy Phravitas, an ecumenical patriarch from before the days of Stavrakios, was ancient, too, though not so ancient as the Forum of the Ox.

Kameas produced for Maniakes a robe of black silk shot through with silver threads. The Avtokrator had no idea of where the robe came from; it certainly did not hang in the closet adjoining the imperial bedchamber. It smelled strongly of camphor, and its wrinkles and creases were as firmly set as if it were made of metal rather than fabric.

"Be gentle with it, your Majesty," Kameas said. "The cloth is fragile these days."

"As you say," Maniakes answered. "How old is it, anyhow?"

The vestiarios' shrug made his several chins wobble. "I apologize, your Majesty, but I cannot tell you. My predecessor at this post, the esteemed Isoes, was himself ignorant of that, and told me his predecessor did not know the answer, either. I also cannot tell you how long the answer has been lost. That might have happened in the days of Isoes' predecessor, or it might have been a hundred years before his time."

Maniakes fingered the silk. He doubted the mourning robe had been new in his grandfather's days, but had no way to prove that. Kameas also brought him polished black leather covers for his boots. Strips cut in them let a little of the imperial crimson shine through; even in mourning, the Avtokrator remained the

Avtokrator. But, looking down at himself, Maniakes saw that he made a somber spectacle indeed.

The other mourners in the funeral party—Kourikos and Phevronia, the elder Maniakes, Parsmanios, Rhegorios, Lysia, and Symvatios—wore unrelieved black. The horses drawing the wagon on which the sarcophagus lay were also black—though Maniakes knew a groom of the imperial stables had carefully painted over a white blaze on one of the animals.

Also in black surcoats, with black streamers hanging from their spears, were the guardsmen who marched with the mourners and the funeral wagon. For the day, the parasol-bearers who preceded the Avtokrator in all his public appearances carried black canopies rather than their usual colorful ones.

As the funeral party approached the plaza of Palamas, Maniakes saw it was packed with people; the folk of Videssos the city were eager for any spectacle, no matter how sorrowful. Some of the people wore black to show their sympathy for the Avtokrator. Others had dressed in their holiday best: for them, one show was as good as another.

At the edge of the plaza nearest the palace quarter waited the ecumenical patriarch Agathios. His regalia had not changed; he still wore the blue boots and a cloth-of-gold robe encrusted with pearls and gems, as he would have at a wedding or any joyous occasion. But his face was somber as he prostrated himself before Maniakes. "Your Majesty, I beg you to accept my condolences for your tragic loss."

"Thank you, most holy sir," Maniakes answered. "Let's get on with it, shall we?" As soon as the words were out of his mouth, he regretted them; Agathios looked scandalized. Maniakes had not meant anything more than wanting to have the funeral over so he could grieve in private, but anything an Avtokrator said that could be misinterpreted probably would be, and he knew too well he had left himself open to such misinterpretation.

Without a word to Maniakes, Agathios turned away and took his place at the head of the mournful procession. He called in a great voice to the crowds filling the plaza of Palamas. "Stand aside, people of Videssos! Make way for the last journey of Niphone, once Empress of the Videssians, now bathed in Phos' eternal light."

"May it be so," the people answered, their voices rising and falling like the surf that beat against the seawall. As best they could, they did clear a path through the plaza. Where their own efforts were not enough, the guards moved them aside with their spearshafts.

Even as the people moved back to make way for the funeral procession, they also pushed forward to speak a word of consolation to Maniakes or to his family. Some of them also pressed forward to get a glimpse of Niphone, who lay pale and still and forever unmoving inside the sarcophagus.

"I pray she knew she gave you a son," a man said to Maniakes. He nodded, though Niphone had known nothing of the sort.

A few of the folk in the plaza kept their hands at the hems of their tunics, ready to use the garments to help catch any largess the Avtokrator might choose to dispense. That thought had never entered his mind, not for today's occasion. He shook his head, bemused at the vagaries of human nature to which his position exposed him.

Though the plaza of Palamas was far wider than Middle Street, the procession had better going on the capital's main thoroughfare. The crowds there stayed off the street itself and under the covered colonnades to either side. When Maniakes glanced up, he saw a goodly number of people atop the colonnades as well, peering down at him and at the woman who had given him two children in just over a year and a half and now would give no more ever again.

Maniakes slowly walked past the government office buildings. Faces stared out at him from almost every window as clerks and bureaucrats escaped their scrolls and counting boards for a little while. The farther he went, the harder keeping up a dignified front before the people became.

In the Forum of the Ox, the crowds grew thick and hard to manage once more. The forum had once been the chief marketplace of Videssos the city for cattle and all other goods, a position long since usurped by the plaza of Palamas. Now most of what was bought and sold here was not fine enough to succeed in the newer square close by the palaces. The Forum of the Ox, even packed as it was now, seemed tired and sad and shabby and rundown.

Again the ecumenical patriarch appealed to the crowd to stand back and let the funeral procession pass. The people responded more slowly than they had in the plaza of Palamas. That was partly because the Forum of the Ox was even more crowded than the plaza had been, and partly because the people who crowded it looked to be less inclined to listen to requests from anyone than were the more prosperous Videssians who frequented the plaza of Palamas.

Little by little, the procession inched its way across the square and back onto Middle Street. After a couple of short blocks, the parasol-bearers followed Agathios south down a narrow, twisting lane that led toward the temple dedicated to the memory of the holy Phravitas.

As was true on a lot of such lanes, second- and third-story balconies grew close to each other above the street until they all but cut off light and air from it. Maniakes remembered thinking when he first came back to Videssos the city that the ordinance mandating balconies to keep a proper distance from one another had not been enforced during Genesios' reign. It didn't look as if building inspectors were doing much better now that he wore the red boots. He exhaled through his nose. He had had a few more immediately urgent things to worry about than whether balconies conformed to law in all particulars.

Legal or not, the balconies were jammed full of people. When Maniakes looked up to the narrow strip of sky between them, he saw dozens of faces staring down at him. One of those faces, a woman's, up on a third-floor balcony, was not only staring but deathly pale, pale as Niphone, pale enough to draw Maniakes' notice even in the midst of the crowd, even in the midst of his sorrow.

The woman leaned over the wooden rail of the balcony. Her mouth opened wide. Maniakes thought she meant to call something to him, although he would have had trouble hearing her through the noise of the crowd. Perhaps that was what she intended, but it was not what happened. She choked and gagged and vomited down onto the funeral procession.

The stinking stuff splashed the sarcophagus, the funeral wagon, and one of the guardsmen. He leapt aside with a cry of disgust. Maniakes pointed a furious finger up at the woman. Afterward, he regretted showing his anger so openly, but that was afterward.

The guard's was not the only disgusted cry to go up. Other cries rose, too, cries of "Shame!" and "Sacrilege!" and "Profanation!"

and, inevitably, "Blasphemy!" Those cries rang loudest from the balconies, and loudest of all from the balcony where the luckless woman stood. Other people standing there with her seized her, lifted her, and, while she screamed, flung her down to the cobbles below. The scream abruptly cut off.

Maniakes whirled and stared in horror at the body of the woman who sprawled only a few feet behind him. By the unnatural angle at which her head joined her body, her neck was broken. She would never rise from the street again. Maniakes' hand drew the sun-sign over his heart. "By the lord with the great and good mind," he cried, his voice full of anguish, "must even the funeral of my wife grow wrong?"

But other shouts went up from the crowd, shouts of fierce exhilaration: "Death to defilers!" "She got what she deserved!" "We avenge you, Niphone!" and even, "Thou conquerest, Empress Niphone!"

Far from being ashamed at what they had done, the men who had thrown the woman to her death raised their arms in triumph, clenched fists pumping the air. The cheers that echoed up and down the narrow street said not just they but also the city mob thought of them as heroes.

Maniakes looked helplessly toward his father. The elder Maniakes spread his hands, as if to ask *What can you do?* The Avtokrator knew the answer to that only too well: *not much.* If he sent his guardsmen into that building after the killers, they would have to fight through the crowd to get inside, fight their way upstairs, and then come down with their prisoners to face the wrath of the mob again. Having the capital erupt in riots was not something he could afford, not with all the other bitter troubles the Empire had these days.

"Forward!" he shouted, and then again: "Forward! Let us grant Niphone such dignity as we can, such dignity as she deserves."

That reached the crowd. Their baying, which had reminded him of nothing so much as a pack of wolves in full cry on a winter's night, eased. Still shaking his head in amazement and disbelief, he hurried on toward the temple dedicated to the memory of the holy Phravitas.

If that temple wasn't the oldest building in Videssos the city, it was among them. In the High Temple and shrines modeled after it, the altar stood under a dome at the center of the worship area, with pews approaching it from each of the cardinal directions. The temple of the holy Phravitas conformed to a more antique pattern. It was a rectangular building of red brick, the bricks themselves darkened and smoothed by age. Its entrance was at the west side; all seats faced the east, the direction from which Phos' sun rose each day.

Agathios strode to the altar, his gleaming robes swirling about him. The senior priest normally responsible for the temple bowed low to his ecclesiastical superior and kissed his outstretched hand in token of submission. Maniakes' guardsmen lifted Niphone's sarcophagus off the wagon that had borne it hither and carried it to a black-draped bier by the side of the altar.

Maniakes and his family took their places in the pews nearest the holy table. When other mourners, some nobles, some simply townsfolk, had filled the rest of the seats, Agathios raised his hands to the heavens, not in triumph but in supplication. That was the signal for those in the temple to rise once more.

"We bless thee, Phos, lord with the great and good mind," Agathios intoned, "by thy grace our protector, watchful beforehand that the great test of life may be decided in our favor."

By its very familiarity, repeating the creed helped steady Maniakes: Not that his grief diminished, but it was channeled into pathways where his mind regularly traveled. The ecumenical patriarch gestured. Maniakes and his companions sat back down. Being in a temple—even if not the one where he usually prayed—and listening to the patriarch also helped transmute anguish into routine, which was easier for the mind to grasp and deal with.

Agathios said, "We are gathered here today to commend to Phos and his eternal light the soul of our sister Niphone, who died in the most noble way given to a woman: that is to say, in bringing new life into our world."

Phevronia sobbed noisily. Kourikos patted his wife's shoulder, doing his best to comfort her. His best struck Maniakes as ineffectual, but then, Phevronia had a right to her sorrow. Losing parents was hard. Losing a spouse was harder. Losing a child, especially a child in what should have been the prime of life, turned the natural order of things on its head.

Maniakes wondered if he ought to be angry with Niphone's mother and father for making her feel she had to bear him a son so as to keep alive her family's influence over the imperial line. He had tried calling up that anger, it would have made his grief easier to bear. He hadn't managed it, though. Many would have taken the same risk Niphone had, and she had done it of her own free will.

"Surely the good god will demonstrate his bounteous compassion and will suffer our sister Niphone to cross the bridge of the separator unharried by the demons who mount up from the eternal ice," Agathios said. "Surely she shall have no part of Skotos and his devices." The ecumenical patriarch spat in rejection of the dark god. Maniakes and the other mourners imitated him.

Agathios went on for some time, describing Niphone's manifest virtues. He had spoken with Maniakes about those, and with Kourikos and Phevronia, and with Nikaia, the abbess of the convent dedicated to the memory of the holy Phostina. So far as Maniakes could tell, every word he said was true.

If Niphone had all those virtues, why did she have to die so young? That was a silent scream inside Maniakes, the way, no doubt, it had been a silent scream in every generation of mankind all the way back to Vaspur the Firstborn—of whom Agathios did not think in those terms. If the ecumenical patriarch had any new light to shed on the question, he did not show it to Maniakes.

After praising Niphone and reassuring everyone who heard him that Phos had indeed taken her soul into the realm of eternal light, after leading his listeners in Phos' creed once more, Agathios said, "And now let her discarded earthly remains be consigned to their final resting place."

That was the signal for Maniakes, Kourikos, and Phevronia to come forward and stand by the sarcophagus. Before the guardsmen lifted it from the bier, Maniakes looked into it one last time. Niphone seemed at peace. He had seen too many dead men on the battlefield to lie to himself by thinking she merely looked asleep, but he could hope she had indeed passed over the bridge of the separator.

The priest who normally presided at the temple dedicated to the memory of the holy Phravitas handed Agathios a lighted torch, murmuring, "The lamps in the memorial chamber below have been kindled, most holy sir."

"Thank you, holy sir," the patriarch answered. He gathered up

Niphone's closest survivors and the guardsmen by eye, then went down a stone staircase to the chamber below the temple.

When Genesios toppled Likinios, he had thrown the dead Avtokrator's body and those of his sons into the sea and sent their heads far and wide to prove they were dead. After Maniakes cast down Genesios in turn, the tyrant's head had gone up on the Milestone and his body was burned. The imperial tombs, then, had not had anyone inhumed in them for some years.

The chamber was very quiet. The thick, still air seemed to swallow the sound of footsteps. Lamplight played off marble and cast flickering shadows on inscriptions and reliefs of Avtokrators and Empresses who had been dead for decades, centuries, even a millennium. On some of the oldest inscriptions, the Videssian was of so antique a mode that Maniakes could hardly read it.

Amid all the whiteness of the marble, one space in the back of the chamber gaped black. Quietly grunting with the effort, the guardsmen slid Niphone's sarcophagus into it. Agathios said, "In a year's time, your Majesty, you or the Empress' sadly bereaved parents may set a memorial tablet here, one properly describing her courage and virtues. Please know that I share your sorrow and offer you my deepest and most sincere sympathy."

"Thank you, most holy sir," Maniakes answered. Kourikos and Phevronia echoed him. Even as he spoke, though, the Avtokrator wondered how sincere Agathios truly was. He had said all the proper things, but said them in a way that suggested duty more than piety. Maniakes sighed. The patriarch was at least as much a political creature as he was a holy man.

"It's over," Phevronia said in a dazed, wondering voice. "It's over, and there's nothing left of her, not any more, not ever again."

She was right. It was over. Nothing was left. Feeling altogether empty inside, Maniakes started back toward the stairs. Agathios hurried to get in front of him, to lead the upward-bound procession as he had the one going down. The guardsmen came next. More slowly, Kourikos and Phevronia followed, leaving the chamber under the temple dedicated to the memory of the holy Phravitas empty until the next time someone from the royal house died.

Kameas said, "May it please your Majesty, a messenger has just come bearing word from Abivard the Makuraner general."

"What can he want of us now?" Maniakes wondered. He had

trouble concentrating on the affairs of Videssos; he had laid Niphone to rest only a few days before. Gamely he tried to bring his mind to the business at hand. "Have him enter, esteemed sir."

The messenger prostrated himself, then handed Maniakes a rolled parchment sealed with ribbon and wax. As he broke the seal, he wondered if he would be able to make sense of the letter inside. He spoke Makuraner fairly well but didn't read it

Abivard, though, must have had a local translate his thoughts for him, for the missive was written in Videssian: "Abivard the general serving the mighty Sharbaraz King of Kings, may his years be many and his realm increase, to Maniakes styling himself Avtokrator: Greetings. I learn with sadness of the death of your wife. Accept, please, my condolences on this, your personal loss; may the Prophets Four guide her to union with the God."

Maniakes turned to Kameas. "Bring me sealing wax, please, esteemed sir." As the vestiarios hurried off to get it, Maniakes inked a reed pen and wrote rapidly on a sheet of parchment: "Maniakes Avtokrator to the Makuraner general Abivard: Greetings. My thanks for your kind personal wishes. My own wish is that you and your army would withdraw from lands to which you have no right. I speak there both as Avtokrator of the Videssians and in my own person. It was for that purpose that I sent the eminent Triphylles as ambassador to Sharbaraz King of Kings. Have you yet any word of the progress of his embassy?"

He rolled up the parchment and tied it with one of the ribbons he normally used for decrees. Kameas returned with a stick of the crimson sealing wax reserved for the Avtokrator alone. The eunuch handed the wax to him, then picked up a lamp. Maniakes held the lamp to the flame. Several drops fell onto the ribbon and parchment. While they were still soft, Maniakes pressed his sunburst signet into them. He withdrew the ring, waved the sealed letter in the air to make sure it hardened properly, and gave it to the messenger. "Be sure this reaches Abivard, by whatever means you have of arranging such things." He didn't need to know the details, and so did not inquire after them.

The messenger took the parchment, stuffed it into a waterproof tube of boiled, waxed leather, and, after prostrating himself to Maniakes once more, hurried out of the imperial residence. "May I see what the Makuraner general wrote, your Majesty?" Kameas asked.

"Yes, go ahead," Maniakes answered. Maybe Stavrakios had been bold enough to keep his vestiarios from knowing everything that happened to him. Few Avtokrators since had been. Maniakes certainly was not.

Kameas said, "He speaks you fair, no doubt of that. One thing the Makuraners have shown, though, is that their deeds don't commonly live up to the words they use to cloak them."

"Too true," Maniakes said. "The same holds true for the Kubratoi. The same held true for Videssos, too, during the reign of my late and unlamented predecessor. I, of course, am the very Milestone of truthfulness."

"Of course, your Majesty," Kameas said, so seriously that Maniakes doubted whether he had caught the intended irony. Then the vestiarios let out the smallest, most discreet snort imaginable.

"Go on, esteemed sir," Maniakes told him, starting to laugh. "Take yourself elsewhere."

"Yes, your Majesty," the vestiarios replied. "The good god grant that Abivard give you good news concerning the eminent Triphylles."

He turned and swept away, leaving Maniakes staring after him in astonishment. He hadn't seen what the Avtokrator had written; he hadn't been in the chamber then. "How did you know?" Maniakes asked. But by then Kameas was a long way down the hall. If he heard, he gave no sign.

Great pillars of smoke rose from Across, as they had when Abivard's forces entered the suburb the autumn before. Now they were leaving, giving Maniakes easy access to the westlands if he wanted to try conclusions with the Makuraners again this summer.

Wondering whether he did was only part of what worried him. He turned and put the other part to Rhegorios: "If he's leaving there, where in Phos' holy name is he going?"

"My cousin your Majesty, damn me to the ice if I know." Rhegorios spat on the ground in rejection of Skotos. "All I can say is, he's likely headed where he thinks he can do us the most harm."

"He could have done worse staying right where he was," Maniakes said, discontent in his voice. "Across was like the stopper in the jar; his holding it kept us out of the westlands. Now we can go back, if we dare. But what will happen to us if we do?"

"Can't tell that till we try it—if we try it," Rhegorios answered. "But I can tell you what happens if we don't: the Makuraners get to keep the countryside for another year and make it even harder for us to get it back when we do finally work up the nerve to try."

Maniakes grimaced. That his cousin was blunt did not mean he was wrong. Maniakes said, "I wish I thought our army was in better shape. We've worked hard this winter, but . . ." He let that hang.

"You could take Tzikas' advice," Rhegorios said with a curl of his lip. "If you stay right here in Videssos the city, you know, and only wait long enough, why, eventually every single fellow who opposes you now will die of old age, and then Videssos will be free to take back its own."

"Ha-ha," Maniakes said in a hollow voice. His cousin exaggerated Tzikas' cautious approach to war, but only slightly. "We have to fight the Makuraners, we have to do it in the westlands, and we have to do it on our own terms. We can't afford any more fiascoes like the one last summer. If we aren't in a position to go out there and win, we shouldn't fight."

"How do you propose to guarantee that?" Rhegorios asked. "Just about every time there's a battle, the bastards on the other side have a nasty habit of fighting back. You can't simply count on them to lie down and die, no matter how much you wish they would."

"To the ice with you," Maniakes said, laughing in spite of himself. "You know what I mean, no matter how clumsily I say it. I can't let myself get lured into situations where I don't have the advantage. The more of what's ours we take, the more men and resources we gather for the next step."

"If we can start by taking back Across, that will be something," Rhegorios said.

Take it back they did, after the dromons on endless patrol in the Cattle Crossing reported that Abivard and his horsemen had indeed abandoned the suburb. Soon after imperial soldiers reentered Across, Maniakes sailed over the strait to the westlands to see what the Makuraners had done to it.

His first impression was that what his men had taken was not worth having and that the Makuraners had abandoned it only because nothing was left to wreck. Most of what could burn had been burned; what hadn't been burned had been torn apart to get fuel for the fires made of the rest.

In ever-growing streams, people emerged from the ruins to spin him tales of woe and horror. He listened to them sympathetically but without much surprise; he knew how armies treated a countryside populated by enemies. The Makuraners had done nothing out of the ordinary. Robberies and rapes were part of the long, sad litany of man's inhumanity to man—and to woman.

"But, your Majesty," said an aggrieved merchant whose stock of fine boots now adorned Makuraner feet, "aren't you going to chase after those thieving heathens and make 'em pay for what they done?" By his tone, he expected Maniakes to set a properly itemized bill before Abivard the next time he saw him.

"I'll do everything I can," Maniakes said evasively; he didn't care to answer that just being in the westlands this year was as much as he had hoped for. "Consolidating my position here comes first, though. After all, we don't want the Makuraners back, do we?"

"What we want and what we get aren't always the same thing," the merchant answered, his voice sour. Only after the words were out of his mouth did he seem to realize they might be taken as criticism of Maniakes. A moment after that, he had made himself scarce. Maniakes ruefully shook his head. It wasn't as if the same thought hadn't crossed his mind a time or twelve.

Engineers surveyed the ground west of Across, seeking the best line on which to establish field fortifications. The suburbs on the far side of the Cattle Crossing from Videssos the city had been unwalled for hundreds upon hundreds of years. Who could have imagined an enemy dangerous enough to penetrate to the very heart of the Empire? Imagined or not, the Makuraners had been here; the evidence of that was only too obvious.

The chief engineer, a stocky, dour man named Stotzas, said, "I can lay you out the sites for some fine works, your Majesty. I see one trouble, though—no, two." He was the sort who saw more troubles the longer he looked at something.

Maniakes had no trouble seeing these for himself. He held up his thumb. "Where am I going to find the men to build the works you lay out?" He stuck up his index finger beside thumb.

"Where am I going to find soldiers to put in the works even if you do manage to build them?"

"You've just rolled Phos' little suns," Stotzas said. His big, blunt-featured head bobbed up and down as he nodded. "Mind you, your Majesty, I'll do everything I can for you, but . . ." His voice trailed away. He didn't flee, as the merchant had, but he didn't look delighted about speaking the whole truth, either.

"But there's liable not to be much you can do, what with man-power being the way it is," Maniakes suggested.

Stotzas nodded, glad for the respite. He said, "At that, I've got it easy. Brick and stone don't argue back. The lord with the great and good mind may know what to do about the mess with the temples, but I'm bound for the ice if I do."

"Nor I," Maniakes answered, feeling a good deal less than impudent. "Whoever came up with the idea of forcing priests in places the Makuraners hold to adopt Vaspurakaner usages was a fiendishly clever man. Some of the priests will have done it sincerely, others to curry favor with the invaders, others just to survive. Sorting out who did what for which reasons is liable to take years, especially when everybody's busy calling everybody else a liar."

"Like I said, bricks and stone, they keep quiet," Stotzas replied. "Shave a man's head and put a blue robe on him and it doesn't seem like he'll ever shut up."

That wasn't altogether fair. A great deal of the monastic life, for instance, was passed in prayerful silence. But the chief engineer had a point. In defending themselves and accusing their neigh-bors, the clerics who jostled for audience with Maniakes did the reputation of the temples no good.

After listening to one set of denunciations and counter-denunciations, all of them backed with documents—each side insisting the documents of the other were forgeries—Maniakes burst out, "A pox take the lot of you, holy sirs!" That wasn't the way a good and pious ruler was supposed to address his clerics, but he was too fed up to care. "You may send this whole great mound of tripe to the most holy Agathios, to let him deal with it as he will. Until such times as he decides the case, I command you to live at peace with one another and to respect one another as orthodox, regardless of who may have done what to whom while the Makuraners were here."

"But, your Majesty," one blue-robe cried, "these wretches reveled in their lapse into heresy, glorying in the chance to bring the temples into disrepute."

A priest of the other faction shouted, "You're the ones who dragged the good name of the temples through the wineshops and bathhouses with your shameless pandering to the invaders."

The two sides started calling each other liars and apostates again, just as they had when they first came before Maniakes. He slammed his open palm down on the table in front of him. The small thunderclap of noise made clerics from both sides momentarily fall silent in surprise.

"Perhaps you misunderstood me, holy sirs," Maniakes said into that brief silence. "You may respect one another as orthodox until the ecumenical patriarch renders his decision on your cases, or you may call one another heretics to your hearts' content—in gaol. Which will it be?"

The clerics weren't screaming at one another when they left his presence, which represented progress of a sort. When they were gone, he slumped back in his chair and covered his face with his hands. Rhegorios came over and thumped him on the shoulder. "Cheer up, my cousin your Majesty. You'll have cases like that in every town we reconquer from the Makuraners."

"No, I won't, by the good god," Maniakes burst out. "Agathios will, and we'll find out what—if anything—the most holy sir is made of and what he's good for." Given what he had seen of Agathios, that wasn't apt to be much. He screwed his face up, as if he had tasted wine gone into vinegar. "You've given me the first decent argument I've heard for letting the Makuraners keep the westlands."

Rhegorios laughed, as if he had made a joke.

From Across, Videssian forces cautiously pushed south and west. It was by no means a reconquest of the westlands but a slow, wary reoccupation of territory Abivard had, for the time being, abandoned. In somewhat bolder style, Maniakes ordered a few bands of horsemen deeper into the westlands to see if they could nip in behind big Makuraner forces and wreck the supply columns that kept them stocked with arrows and spear-points and iron splints for their cuirasses.

He ordered his men not to attack the Makuraner field armies. "Not this year," he said. "First we learn to hurt them in other ways. Once we know we can do that, we think about facing them in open battle again. Meanwhile, let's see how they like moving through a hostile countryside."

The short answer was, the Makuraners didn't like it. They started burning villages to show they didn't like it. Maniakes didn't know whether to mourn or cheer when he got that news. It would depend on whether the Makuraners cowed the westlands or infuriated them.

In response, he sent for more raiding parties, many of them aboard ship to go to the northern and southern coasts of the westlands and strike inland from there. "Maybe, just maybe," he told his father, "we'll be able to force the boiler boys off balance for a change. The one place where they can't match us is on the sea."

"That's so," the elder Maniakes agreed. He plucked a long white hair from his beard and held it out at arm's length so he could see it clearly. After he let it fall to the ground, he looked sidelong at his son and asked, "Have you got a naval captain whose head you wouldn't mind seeing up on the block?"

"I could probably come up with one," Maniakes allowed. "Why would I want to, though?"

His father's eyes twinkled. "The Kubratoi can't match us on the sea, either. Those *monoxyla* of theirs are all very well—until they run up against a dromon. After that, they're wreckage with butchered meat inside. I was just thinking you could send a captain up along the coast of Kubrat to raid and then, when Etzilios screamed blue murder, send him the fellow's head and say it was his idea all along."

Maniakes gaped, then laughed till the tears came. "By the good god, Father, now you've gone and tempted me. Every time I look north, I'm going to think of doing just what you said. It might not even make the khagan go back to war with us; he's clever enough, curse him, to see the joke."

"If you weren't at war with Makuran . . ." the elder Maniakes said.

"And if I had a ship's captain I really wanted to be rid of," the Avtokrator added. "It would hardly be fair to an up-and-coming officer."

"That's true," the elder Maniakes said. "He wouldn't be up-and-coming afterward; he'd be down-and-going, or rather gone."

They both laughed then, long and hard enough that Kameas stuck his head into the chamber to find out what was going on. After they had explained—each more sheepish than the other—the vestiarios said, "In times like these, any cause for mirth, no matter how foolish, is to be cherished."

"He's right," Maniakes said after Kameas left. "Between the way the war is going and losing Niphone, the imperial residence has been a gloomy place."

"A man who's happy without reason is likely either a fool or a drunk, or else both," his father answered. "We'll get back down to business soon enough. I'm sure of that."

His prophecy was fulfilled a couple of days later, when a messenger delivered a dispatch from Abivard, brought to Videssian-held territory behind a shield of truce. Maniakes drew it out of its boiled-leather tube. Like the one the Makuraner general had sent before, it was written in Videssian, though not in the same hand as the earlier missive had been:

> Abivard general to Sharbaraz King of Kings, may his years be many and his realm increase, to Maniakes styling himself Avtokrator of the Videssians: Greetings. In reply to your recent communication regarding the status of the man Triphylles whom you sent as embassy to the good, pacific, and benevolent Sharbaraz, favorite of the God, beloved of the Prophets Four, I am bidden by his puissant majesty to inform you that the aforesaid man Triphylles, in just punishment for his intolerable insolence, has been confined to prison outside Mashiz to ponder his folly.

The message stopped there. Maniakes' eyes kept going for a couple of lines' worth of blank parchment, as if to force more meaning from the sheet he held. "He can't do that," the Avtokrator exclaimed—to whom, he could not have said.

"Your Majesty?" The messenger hadn't the slightest idea what Maniakes was talking about.

"He can't do that," Maniakes repeated. "Sharbaraz can't just throw an ambassador into jail because he doesn't fancy the way he talks." If that were the only criterion, Moundioukh, for instance, would never see the outside of a cell again. Maniakes went on, "It violates every law of civilized conduct between empires."

"Why should Sharbaraz care a fig about anything like that?" the messenger said. "For one thing, he's a cursed Makuraner. For another, he's winning the war, so who's going to stop him from doing whatever he pleases?"

Maniakes stared at him without answering. The fellow was right, of course. Who would—who could—stop Sharbaraz King of Kings from doing whatever he pleased? Maniakes had proved singularly unable to pull off the trick.

"Is there a reply, your Majesty?" the messenger asked.

"Yes, by the good god." Maniakes dipped a pen in a pot of ink and began to write on a sheet of parchment he had been about to use to authorize more expenditures for repairing the walls of Imbros. This was more urgent—unless, of course, Etzilios decided to break the truce for whose extension Maniakes had just paid.

"Maniakes Avtokrator of the Videssians to Abivard general of Makuran: Greetings." The pen scratched gently as it raced over the writing surface. "I am shocked and dismayed to learn that Sharbaraz King of Kings would so forget the law of nations as to imprison my ambassador, the eminent Triphylles. I demand his immediate release." *How? On pain of war?* his mind jeered. *You're already at war—and losing.* "I further demand proper compensation for the outrage he has suffered, and his immediate return to Videssos the city, where he may recuperate from his travail. I do not judge you guilty in this matter. Pass my letter on to your sovereign, that he may act on it in all possible haste."

He called for sealing wax from Kameas and closed the letter in on itself before giving it to the messenger. "How much good this will do, Phos alone knows," the Avtokrator said, "but Phos also knows no good at all can come unless I do protest."

After the messenger departed, Maniakes spent a little while calling curses down on Abivard's head. Had the Makuraner general not urged the course upon him, he never would have sent Triphylles off to Sharbaraz. He had assumed the King of Kings would not mistreat an envoy, and also that Sharbaraz would be interested in extracting tribute money from Videssos.

But Sharbaraz was already extracting money from Videssos. With enough plunder coming in, he cared nothing for tribute.

Maniakes kicked at the floor. For an angry moment, he wished Kourikos and Triphylles had never come to Kastavala. Niphone would still be alive if they had stayed in Videssos the city, and it was hard to see how the empire could have been in worse shape under Genesios than it was now under his own rule. And he himself would still have been back on the island of Kalavria with his mistress and his bastard son, and none of the catastrophes befalling his homeland would have been his fault.

He sighed. "Some people are meant to start fires, some are meant to put them out," he said, though no one was there to hear him. "Genesios started this one, and somehow or other I have to figure out how to pour water on it."

He sat down and thought hard. Things were better now than they had been the year before. Then he had tried to match the Makuraners at their own game. It hadn't worked; Videssos had been—and remained—in too much chaos for that. Now he was trying something new. He didn't know how well his strategy of raids and pinpricks would work, but it could hardly fare worse than what had gone before it. With luck, it would rock Abivard back on his heels. The Makuraners in the westlands hadn't had even that much happen to them for a long time.

"Even if it works, it's not enough," he muttered. Harassing Abivard's forces wouldn't drive them off Videssian soil. He couldn't think of anything within the Empire's capacity that would.

✦ XI

Maniakes thrust a parchment at Tzikas. He wished he had the leather tube in which the message had reached Videssos the city; he would have hit his gloomy general over the head with it. "Here, eminent sir, read this," he said. "Do you see?"

Tzikas took his own sweet time unrolling the parchment and scanning its contents. "Any good news is always welcome, your Majesty," he said, politely—and infuriatingly—unimpressed, "but destroying a few Makuraner wagons west of Amorion doesn't strike me as reason enough for Agathios to declare a day of thanksgiving."

By his tone, he would not have been impressed had the message reported the capture of Mashiz. Nothing Maniakes could do would satisfy him, save possibly to hand him the red boots. Had he not been such a good general, Maniakes would have had no qualms about forcing him into retirement—but his being such a good general was precisely what made him a threat now.

Keeping a tight rein on his temper, Maniakes said, "Eminent sir, destroying the wagons is not the point. The point is that we have warriors raiding deep into territory the Makuraners have held since the early days of Genesios' reign—and coming out safe again to tell the tale."

More than your warriors in Amorion did, he thought, all the while knowing that was unfair. Tzikas had done well to hold out in the garrison town for as long as he had. Expecting him to have hit back, too, was asking too much.

The general handed the note back to him. "May we have many more such glorious successes, your Majesty." Was that sarcasm? Luckily for Tzikas, Maniakes couldn't quite be sure.

"May we indeed," he answered, taking the comment at face value. "If we can't win large fights, by all means let us win the small ones. If we win enough small ones, perhaps the Makuraners will have suffered too much damage to engage us in so many of the large ones."

"Did it come to pass, that would be very good," Tzikas agreed. "But, your Majesty—and I hope you will forgive me for speaking so plainly—I don't see it as likely. They have too strong a grip on the westlands for even a swarm of fleabites to drive them out."

"Eminent sir, if neither large fights nor small ones will get the Makuraners out of the westlands, isn't that the same as saying the westlands by rights belong to them these days?"

"I wouldn't go quite that far, your Majesty," Tzikas said, cautious as usual. Maniakes, by now, had the distinct impression Tzikas wouldn't go very far for anything—a more relentlessly moderate man would have been hard to imagine. In a way, that was a relief, for Maniakes could hope it meant Tzikas wouldn't go far in trying to overthrow him, either.

But it limited what he could do with the general. Send Tzikas to lead what should have been a dashing cavalry pursuit and you would find he had decorously ridden after the foe for a few miles before deciding he had done enough for the day and breaking off. No doubt he was a clever, resourceful defensive strategist, but a soldier who wouldn't go out and fight was worth less than he might have been otherwise.

Maniakes gave it up and went to see how his children were doing. Evtropia greeted him with a squeal of glee and came toddling over to wrap her arms around his leg. "Papapapa," she said. "Good!" She talked much more than he remembered Atalarikhos doing at the same age. All the serving women maintained she was astonishingly precocious. Since she seemed a clever child to him, too, he dared hope that wasn't the usual flattery an Avtokrator heard.

A wet nurse was feeding Likarios. Nodding to Maniakes, she said, "He is a hungry one, your Majesty. Odds are that means he'll be a big man when he comes into his full growth."

"We'll have to wait and see," Maniakes answered. That was flattery, nothing else but.

"He quite favors you, I think," the wet nurse said, trying again. Maniakes shrugged. Whenever he looked at his infant son, he saw Niphone's still, pale face in the sarcophagus. It wasn't as if the baby had done that deliberately, nor even that he felt anger at his son because of what had happened to Niphone. But the association would not go away.

Maniakes walked over to look down at the boy. Likarios recognized him and tried to smile with the wet nurse's nipple still in his mouth. Milk dribbled down his chin. The wet nurse laughed. So did Maniakes, in spite of everything—his son looked very foolish.

"He's a fine baby, your Majesty," the wet nurse said. "He eats and eats and eats and hardly ever fusses. He smiles almost all the time."

"That's good," Maniakes said. Hearing his voice, Likarios did smile again. Maniakes found himself smiling back. He remembered Evtropia from the fall before, when she had been a few months older than her little brother was now. She had thrown her whole body into a smile, wiggling and thrashing from sheer glee. She hadn't cared then—she still didn't care—that the Makuraners had conquered the westlands and were sitting in Across. As long as someone had been there to smile at her, she had stayed happy. He envied that.

The wet nurse stuck a cloth up on her shoulder and transferred Likarios from her breast. She patted him on the back till he produced a belch and a little sour milk. "That's a good boy!" she said, and then, to Maniakes, "He's a healthy baby, too." She quickly sketched the sun-circle over her still-bare left breast. "He hasn't had many fevers or fluxes or anything of the sort. He just goes on about his business, is what he does."

"That's what he's supposed to do," Maniakes answered, also sketching the sun-sign. "Nice to see someone doing what he's supposed to do and not fouling up the job."

"Your Majesty?" the wet nurse said. Politics wasn't her first worry, either. Whatever happened outside her immediate circle of attention could have been off beyond Makuran, as far as she was concerned. Maniakes wished he could view matters the same way. Unfortunately, he knew too well that what happened far away now could matter in Videssos the city later. If he and his father hadn't helped restore Sharbaraz to his throne, the westlands likely would have remained in Videssian hands to this day.

"Papapapa!" Evtropia wasn't going to let her brother keep all his attention. She came over to Maniakes and demanded, "Pick up me."

"How smart she is," the wet nurse said as Maniakes obeyed his daughter. "Hardly any children that little make real sentences."

Evtropia squealed with glee while Maniakes swung her through the air. Then she got bored and said, "Put down me," so he did that. She went off to play with a doll stuffed with feathers.

The wet nurse made no effort to put her dress to rights. Maniakes wondered whether that was because she thought Likarios would want more to eat or so she could display herself for him. Even if he slept with her only once, she could expect rich presents. If he made her pregnant, she would never want for anything. And if, as in a romance, she swept him off his feet and he married her . . .

But he didn't want to marry her, or even to take her to bed. After a while, she must have realized that, for she slipped her arm back into the left sleeve of the dress. The baby had fallen asleep. She got up and put him in his cradle.

Maniakes played with Evtropia for a while. Then she started to get cranky. One of the serving women said, "It will be time for her nap soon, your Majesty."

"No nap," Evtropia said. "*No nap!*" The second repetition was loud enough to make everyone in the room flinch—except her brother; he never stirred. Even as she screamed, though, Evtropia betrayed herself with a yawn. Maniakes and the serving woman exchanged knowing glances. It wouldn't be long.

The Avtokrator felt better after he left his children. Unlike most of the Empire, they were doing well. *Yes, and look at the price you paid.* But he hadn't paid the price. Poor Niphone had.

He missed her more than he had thought he would: not just waking up alone in the large bed in the imperial bedchamber but talking with her. She had never been afraid to tell him what she thought. For an Avtokrator, that was precious. Most people told him what they thought he wanted to hear, nothing more. Only among his own blood kin could he hope to find honesty now.

Slowly he walked down the hallway and out of the imperial residence. The guards on the low, broad stairs stiffened to attention. He nodded to them—letting your bodyguards think you took them for granted wasn't smart. His real attention, though, was on the westlands.

Rebuilding in Across went on by fits and starts. A few of the burned temples there had been restored; the gilded domes that topped their spires glinted in the sunlight. The Makuraner army that had held the suburb was now ravaging its way across the westlands. Despite Maniakes' pinpricks, he could not keep that army from going where it would, wrecking what it would.

And if, as they might, Abivard and his men chose to winter in Across yet again? Could he hope to hold them away from the nearest approach to the capital? He wondered whether he could get away with telling himself what he wanted to hear: that the reconstituted Videssian forces would surely drive the invaders far, far away.

"The only problem being, it's not true," he muttered. If Abivard decided to come back to Across, he could, and all the hopeful restorations would go up in flames like the buildings they were replacing.

He wondered if it was worthwhile to go out and fight the Makuraners west or south of Across. Regretfully, he concluded it wasn't, not till he could fight with some hope of winning. Videssos couldn't afford to throw men away in losing fights, not any more. Yes, the Makuraners would go on ravaging the countryside if he didn't fight them, but if he did, they would smash up his army and then go on ravaging the countryside.

"To the ice with choices between bad and worse," he said, but he had no means to consign those choices there.

Summer advanced, hot and muggy. Maniakes let Moundioukh and his fellow hostages ride north from Videssos the city toward Kubrat, not so much because he was convinced of Etzilios' goodwill as because holding hostages indefinitely was bad form and could create ill-will even if none had existed before.

"Youse not regrets thises, majesties," Moundioukh assured him. Maniakes already regretted it, but found it impolitic to say so.

Over in the westlands, Abivard took enough raids from the southeastern hill country that he finally hurled his mobile force against it, to try to end the annoyance once and for all. When word of that came to Videssos the city, Maniakes felt like celebrating.

So did his father. With an evil chuckle, the elder Maniakes said, "I don't think he knows what he's getting into. That country is almost as hard for a big force to operate in as Vaspurakan: it's all cut up into dales and valleys and badlands, and if you take one of them, that helps you not a bit with the next one just over the ridge."

"With a little luck, he may get stuck there like a fly in a spiderweb," Maniakes said. "That would be lovely, wouldn't it? We'd have a chance to get back real chunks of the westlands then."

"Don't count your flies till you've sucked them dry," his father warned. "Going into the southeast was a mistake; getting stuck there would be a worse one. From what I recall of Abivard, we're lucky he's made one mistake, but we'd be fools to count on two."

"Have to take all the advantage we can of the one," Maniakes said. "In a lot of places in the coastal lowlands, they bring in two crops a year. If Abivard stays busy in the southeast, we might even see a bit of revenue from them." He scowled. "I wish I could lay siege to some of the towns he's garrisoned, but I can't think of anything that would make him bring his main force back faster. I'd sooner let him play his own games down there for as long as he likes."

"Yes, that's wise." The elder Maniakes nodded. "We didn't get into this mess in one campaigning season, and we won't get out of it in one, either." He coughed, then wiped his mouth on his sleeve. "Anybody who thinks there are quick, easy answers to hard questions is a fool."

"I suppose so." Maniakes let out a wistful sigh. "What do you call somebody who *wishes* there were quick, easy answers to hard questions?"

His father rumbled laughter. "I don't know, boy. A human being, maybe?"

As the weeks passed, some revenue did reach Videssos the city from the nearer regions of the westlands. Maniakes had to fight the temptation to tax them till their eyes popped, just for the sake of immediate gold. If you flayed the hide off the sheep this year, what would you do for wool the next?

Kourikos said, "But, your Majesty, without significant revenue enhancements, how can we continue our necessary activities?"

"To the ice with me if I know," Maniakes answered with what he hoped wasn't deathbed cheeriness. "As I read the numbers, though, eminent sir, with this new gold coming in, why, we're almost back to bankrupt. We haven't been that well off since Likinios was still wearing his head."

The logothete of the treasury studied him. He watched Kourikos trying to decide whether he was serious—and not having the nerve to come right out and ask. He hadn't seen a funnier spectacle since Midwinter's Day.

"Joke, eminent sir," he said at last, to put the logothete out of his misery.

Kourikos tried a smile on for size. It didn't fit well; he hadn't smiled much since he had lost his daughter. "It might as easily have been simply a vivid metaphor for our present predicament."

Maniakes thought that was what a joke was, but knew he lacked the erudition to get into a literary discussion with Kourikos. "I haven't seen Makuraners or even Kubratoi swarming over the walls of the city, eminent sir. Until I do, I'm going to try to keep believing we have hope."

"Very well, your Majesty," Kourikos replied. "I have heard the patriarch say despair is the one sin that admits of no forgiveness."

"Have you?" Maniakes looked at him in no small surprise. "I wouldn't have thought the most holy sir had so much wisdom hidden in him."

Now Kourikos looked thoroughly scandalized, which was the very thing the Avtokrator had in mind.

Maniakes had hoped that, when Abivard decided he had had enough of grinding his army to bits in the hills and valleys and badlands of the southeastern part of the westlands, he would pull back into the central plateau and rest and recuperate there. He rejoiced when dispatch riders brought word that Abivard had apparently had enough of the southeast. Hard on the heels of those men, though, came other riders warning that the Makuraners, instead of drawing back to lick their wounds, were heading north with a large force.

"North through the lowlands?" Maniakes asked in dismay. He clung to disbelief as long as he could, which wasn't long: by the way Abivard was moving, he did intend to pass the winter just over the Cattle Crossing from Videssos the city, as he had the year before. Maniakes examined a parchment map of the westlands, hoping to find something different on it from what he had seen earlier in the year. "Any chance of holding them at the line of the Arandos?"

"There would be, if we had a real army to match his instead of a scant few regiments we can count on not to run screaming the first time they set eyes on a boiler boy," Rhegorios answered glumly.

The Avtokrator let out a long sigh. If Rhegorios, aggressive as he was, didn't think the Makuraners could be held at the river, then they couldn't be. "If we had forces south of the river to slow them down, we might get more men into place to stop them," he said, and then sighed again. The only forces Videssos had south of the Arandos were the hillmen of the southeast. They were fine, fighting where the terrain favored them. But they lacked both numbers and skill to confront the Makuraners on the flat ground of the lowlands, and they wouldn't just be pursuing Abivard's army, they would have to get in front of it. Thinking with his head rather than his heart, Maniakes knew the thing couldn't be done.

Rhegorios said, "At least we have forces down almost as far as the Arandos. Considering where we were last year after Amorion fell, that's progress of a sort. We haven't written off the whole of the westlands, as I'd feared we might."

"Haven't we?" Maniakes asked, his voice bitter. "If Abivard can travel through them as he pleases and the most we can do is bother him a bit now and then, do they belong to us or to him? It was generous of him to let us use some of them a bit this summer, but you can't say he's given them back."

"You can pray for miracles, your Majesty cousin of mine, but that doesn't always mean Phos will grant them," Rhegorios said. "If the good god did grant them all the time, they wouldn't be miracles any more, would they?"

One of Maniakes' eyebrows quirked upward. "Shall we send for Agathios to shave your head and give you a blue robe? You argue like a priest."

"I haven't it in me to be a priest," Rhegorios answered, his eyes twinkling. "I like pretty girls too well, and I'd sooner have it in them." When Maniakes made as if to throw a punch at him, he skipped back with a laugh, but persisted. "Was I right or wrong, eh?"

"What, about miracles or about pretty girls?" Just making the quip sobered Maniakes. He had bedded a couple of serving maids since Niphone died. He had been ashamed after each time but, like his cousin, found himself even more miserable as a celibate. Somberly, he went on, "Yes, you're right about miracles. Shall I go on and give the rest of your speech for you?"

"No, as long as I'm here, I may as well do it," Rhegorios said; try as you would, you couldn't keep him serious for long. "Given the mess Genesios left you, doing anything worth speaking of in the first couple of years of your reign would have taken a miracle. Phos didn't give you one. So what?"

"Now you sound like my father," Maniakes replied. "But if the Makuraners were shipbuilders, the Empire probably would go under: that's so what. The best we could hope for would be to stand siege here."

"Videssos the city will never fall to a siege," Rhegorios said confidently.

"You're right; it would probably take a miracle to make that happen—but suppose the God doled one out to the Makuraners?" Maniakes said, deadpan.

Rhegorios started to answer, stopped, stared at the Avtokrator, then tried again: "You almost caught me there, do you know that? For one thing, the God is only a figment of the Makuraners' imaginations. And for another, I don't think we've been quite sinful enough for Skotos to rise up and smite us that particular way. If the sun turned north again after last Midwinter's Day, we're good for a while longer, or I miss my guess."

Maniakes sketched the sun-circle over his heart. "May you prove right." He studied the map some more. "If we can't hold them at the Arandos, we certainly can't hold them anywhere between there and Across. Can we hold them with the new works we've built outside Across?"

He wasn't asking Rhegorios the question; he was asking himself. His cousin assumed the burden of answering it, though: "Doesn't seem likely, does it?"

"No," Maniakes said, and the word tasted like death in his mouth. "Why did we waste our time and substance rebuilding, then?" But it wasn't *we*. He had given the orders. He slammed his fist against the map. Pain shot up his arm. "I made the same mistake I've been making ever since I put on the red boots: I thought we were stronger than we are."

"It's done now," Rhegorios said, an epitaph for any number of unfortunate occurrences. "Are you going to send an army into the westlands to try to defend what we've rebuilt?"

"You're trying to find out if I'll make the same mistake one more time even now, aren't you?" Maniakes asked.

Rhegorios grinned at him, utterly unabashed. "Now that you mention it, yes."

"You're as bad as my father," Maniakes said. "He's had all those years land on him to make him so warped and devious; what's your excuse? . . . But I haven't answered your question, have I? No, I'm not going to send an army over to Across. If Abivard wants it so badly, he can have it."

Rhegorios nodded, gave the map a thoughtful tap, and left the chamber where it hung. Maniakes stared at the inked lines on the parchment: provinces and roads where his word did not run. All at once, he strode to the door, shouting for wine. He got very drunk.

The *Renewal* bounced in the chop of the Cattle Crossing. Makuraners stood on the western shore, jeering at the dromon and calling in bad Videssian for it to come beach itself on the golden, inviting sand. "We hello you, oh yes," one of them shouted. "You never forget you meet us, not never so long as you live." His teeth flashed white in the midst of his black beard.

Maniakes turned to Thrax. "Hurl a couple of darts at them," he said. "We'll see if they jeer out of the other side of their mouths."

"Aye, your Majesty," the drungarios of the fleet replied. He turned to his sailors. One of them set an iron-headed dart, its shaft as long as an arm and thicker than a stout man's middle finger, in the trough of the catapult. Others turned windlasses to draw back the engine's casting arms, which creaked and groaned under the strain. Thrax called orders to the oarsmen, who turned the *Renewal* so it bore on the knot of Makuraners. "Loose!" the drungarios shouted as a wave lifted the bow slightly.

The catapult snapped and bucked like a wild ass. The dart hurtled across the water. A scream went up from the shore—it had skewered someone. Yelling with glee, the catapult crew loaded another missile into the engine and began readying it to shoot again.

Maniakes had expected the Makuraners to disperse. Instead, all of them with bows shot back at the *Renewal*. Their arrows raised little splashes as they plinked into the water well short of their target. The sailors laughed at the foe.

"Loose!" Thrax cried again. Another dart leapt forth. This time the sailors—and Maniakes with them—cursed and groaned, for it hit no one. But the Makuraners scattered like frightened birds even so. That changed Maniakes' curses into cries of delight. Soldier against soldier, the boiler boys were still more than the Videssians could face with any hope of victory. But, when they came up against the imperial fleet, the Makuraners found foes they could not withstand.

"We rule the westlands!" Maniakes shouted, making the sailors stare at him before he added, "Or as much of them as isn't more than two bowshots from shore."

The sailors laughed, which was what he had had in mind. Thrax, earnest and serious as usual, said, "If it please your Majesty, I'll order the dromons in close to shore so they can shoot at clumps of the enemy who have come down too close to the sea."

"Yes, do that," Maniakes said. "It will remind them we don't tamely yield our land to Abivard and the King of Kings. It may even do the Makuraners a little real harm, too, which wouldn't be the worst thing in the world."

Maniakes hoped darts flying at them from beyond bow range would convince the Makuraners to stay away from the seaside, which might have let him land raiders with impunity. Instead, Abivard's men set up catapults of their own, close by the edge of the sea. Some of them threw stones big and heavy enough to sink a dromon if they hit it square. But they didn't—they couldn't— and in a few days the engines vanished from the beaches. The Makuraner engineers weren't used to turning their machines to aim at a target more mobile than a wall, and especially weren't used to shifting them to hit a target that was not only moving but doing its best not to get hit.

And the Videssian sailors, who compensated for wave action whenever they used their dart-throwers and who practiced hitting land targets, had a fine time shooting at catapults that had to stay in one place and take it. They damaged several and killed a fair number of the engineers who served them before Abivard figured out he was involved in a losing game and pulled back his machines.

A few days later, the first snow fell. Maniakes hoped Abivard's men would freeze inside Across, yet at the same time could not wish for too savage a winter. If the Cattle Crossing iced up, Abivard might have his revenge for the little wounds the catapult crews on the dromons had inflicted on his force. Maniakes wished his father hadn't told him the story of that dreadful winter.

He went back to drilling his soldiers on the practice field out by the southern end of the city wall. As they had the winter before, the Makuraners sometimes came out to see what they could see. Sometimes, now, a dromon would chase them away from the beach of Across. Maniakes took considerable satisfaction whenever he saw that happen.

No less an authority than Tzikas said, "Your Majesty, they look more like fighting men than they did a year ago—and you have more of them now, too." He tempered that by adding, "Whether you have enough men, whether they'll be good enough: those are different questions."

"So they are." Maniakes shaded his eyes with his hand and peered west over the Cattle Crossing. He saw no Makuraners today; a dromon slid smoothly through the channel, not pausing to harass any of Abivard's men. But Maniakes knew they were there, whether he could see them or not. Not all the smoke that rose above Across came from cookfires. The Makuraners were busy wrecking the suburb all over again.

"Come the spring, I expect you will put them to the test." By the way Tzikas sounded, that was more a judgment against Maniakes' character than an expression of hope for victory.

"Spring feels a million years, a million miles away." Maniakes kicked at the yellow-brown dead grass under his boots. Frustration gnawed at him like an ulcer that would not heal. "I want to go against them now, to drive them off Videssian soil with a great swift blow."

"You tried that once, your Majesty. The results were imperfectly salubrious, from our point of view." Tzikas might have been a litterateur criticizing a bad piece of poetry rather than a general commenting on a campaign.

Maniakes regarded him with reluctant respect. That he criticized his sovereign at all bespoke a certain courage and integrity—or perhaps such a perfect confidence in his own rightness as to blind him to any offense he might give.

Either way, he also seemed blind to how much Maniakes hated acknowledging himself unable to strike back at Abivard's army. He was glad to get back inside the walls of Videssos the city. In there, try as he would, he could not see the Cattle Crossing, let alone the land on the western shore. He could try to pretend all of it still yielded up taxes to the fisc, still recognized him as its ruler.

Before he had gone far into the city, he discovered—not for the first time—he was no good at fooling himself. When he got to the palace quarter, he could distinguish once more the smoke, rising from Across, from that coming off the myriad fires within Videssos the city. Even had his pretense survived so long, that would have killed it.

Oblivious to his worries, Rhegorios said, "To the ice with Tzikas; he's the sort who'd order up a lemon for his sweet." That was true, but did little to lift Maniakes' spirits. When he didn't answer, Rhegorios let out an indignant sniff. At the imperial residence, he went off in a huff.

"Wine, your Majesty?" Kameas asked. The only reply he got was a shake of the head. He was trained not to show annoyance, and very emphatically didn't show it. Maniakes wondered if the night's supper would suffer on account of that. No, he decided. Kameas also had great pride in service.

"Nice to know someone has pride in something," Maniakes muttered. Everything he had spent so much time and effort and gold rebuilding in the spring and summer had fallen to pieces in a few weeks as fall approached. Maybe things would get better when spring came once more . . . or maybe the good weather would just lead to yet another round of catastrophes.

He went into the chamber where he was in the habit of trying to match the dribbles of revenue that came into the fisc with the unending flood of gold that poured out of it. He had had a new, slender trickle of gold coming in from those parts of the westlands closest to Videssos the city, but he couldn't rob—or even borrow from—the temples nearly so much this year: they didn't have much, either. That meant he had to pay out less or cheapen the currency again, which amounted to the same thing.

If he stopped paying everyone but the soldiers . . . he wouldn't have any bureaucrats to collect next year's taxes. If he put more copper in the goldpieces, people would start hoarding good money, traders would stop doing business . . . and he wouldn't have much in the way of taxes to collect next year.

Someone rapped on the door. "Go away," he growled without looking up, assuming it was Kameas coming to try to make him feel better.

But the voice that said "Very well" didn't belong to Kameas: it was Lysia's. Maniakes' head came up with a jerk. There weren't many people in the city he didn't want to irk, but she was one of them.

"I'm sorry," he said. "I thought you were someone else. Please come in." She had already started to turn away. For a moment, he thought she would ignore the invitation; stubbornness ran all through his family. He said, "If you don't come in here this instant, cousin of mine, I'll call you up before the Avtokrator on a charge of lese majesty through wanton and willful disobedience."

He hoped that would amuse her instead of making her angry, and it did. "Not that!" she cried. "Anything but that! I abase myself before your Majesty."

She really did start a proskynesis. "Never mind that, by the good god," Maniakes exclaimed. They both started to laugh, then looked warily at each other. Since Niphone died, they had been cautious when they were together, and they hadn't been together much. Maniakes sighed, scowled, and shook his head. "I think back on how things were at Kastavala, and do you know what, cousin of mine? They don't look so bad. I didn't have to look over my shoulder whenever I wanted to talk to you, and I didn't have to worry about peering over the water and seeing the Makuraners wrecking everything in sight." He sighed again. "It might even be better back there now, come to think of it."

"Don't let your father hear you say that," Lysia warned. "He'd box your ears for you, whether you wear the red boots or no. I can't say I'd blame him, either. How could you fight the Makuraners in the westlands if you were back on Kalavria?"

"How can I fight them now?" he asked. "I was watching their smoke rise up from Across while I was out with the troops at the practice field. There they sit, right at the very heart of the

Empire, and I dare not do anything more against them than the little pinprick raids we tried this summer."

"They aren't at the heart of the Empire," Lysia said. "We are, here at Videssos the city. As long as we hold the heart, we can bring the rest back to life one day, no matter how bad things are in the westlands."

"So everyone says. So I've thought," Maniakes answered. "I really do wonder if it's true, though." Suddenly the notion of sailing back to Kalavria, leaving behind the hateful reminders of how weak the Empire of Videssos had grown, seemed sweeter than honey to him. Back at the old fortress above Kastavala, he could think of the Empire as it had always been, not in its present mutilated state, and could rule it without worrying so much about the day-to-day emergencies that made life here in the capital feel so difficult.

But, before he could make clear to Lysia his vision of the benefits abandoning Videssos the city might bring, she said, "Of course it's true. There's never been a fortress, never been a port, like this one in the history of the world. And if you give up on Videssos the city, why shouldn't the people here give up on you?"

He paused thoughtfully. She had a point. She had a couple of points, in fact. If the fickle city mob raised up a new Avtokrator, that man, whoever he was, would gain a tincture of legitimacy because he held Videssos the city. He would also gain its walls, its dromons . . . and even Genesios the unspeakable had reigned half a dozen years with those advantages.

And so, keeping his longing for Kalavria to himself, he said, "Maybe you're right. I told you once you had the wit to be Sevastos. I know you got angry at me then—"

"And if you tell me again, I'll get angry at you now," Lysia said. By the way her nostrils flared, she *was* angry. "The city mob wouldn't let me do that any more than they'd let you sail away. And," she added grudgingly, "my brother has shaped well in the job."

Maniakes got up from the table piled high with receipts and registers and requests for gold he did not have. Any excuse for escaping from those requests was a good one, as far as he was concerned. He walked over to Lysia and set his hands on her shoulders. "I am sorry, cousin of mine," he said. "It just seems as if everything has gone to the ice since we came to Videssos the city. I should never have named my flagship the *Renewal*. Every time I board it, that strikes me as a cruel joke—maybe on myself, maybe on the Empire."

"It'll come right in the end," she said, hugging him. In the sea fights before he took Videssos the city, he had watched floundering men find floating planks and cling to them as if they were life itself. That was how he clung to Lysia now. She still had faith in him, no matter how much trouble he had holding onto faith in himself.

He was also acutely aware of holding a woman in his arms. After a little while, she could hardly have failed to notice his body responding to hers. He never was sure whether she first raised her head or he lowered his. When their lips met, it was with as much desperation as passion—but the passion was there.

At last they drew back, just a little. "Are you sure?" Lysia said softly.

He didn't need to ask what she meant. His laugh rang harsh. "I'm not sure of anything any more," he said. "But—" He went to the door of the chamber and closed it. Before he let the bar fall, he said, "You can still go out if you like. We've talked about this before, after all. If we go on from here, it will complicate both our lives more than either of us can guess now, and I have no idea whether it will come right in the end, whether it will turn out to be worth it."

"Neither do I," Lysia said, still in a low voice. She didn't leave. She urged no course on him. He stood a moment, irresolute. Then, very carefully, he set the bar in its bracket. He took a step toward her. She met him halfway.

It was chilly and awkward and they had no comfortable place in the room—and none of that mattered. Their two robes and their drawers on the mosaic floor did well enough. Maniakes expected to find her a maiden, and he did. Past that, everything was a surprise.

He had thought to be slow and gentle, as he had been with Niphone their first night together, bare hours after Agathios set the imperial crown on his head. Lysia did grimace and stiffen for a moment when he entered her to the hilt, but she startled him by taking pleasure afterward. She had no practiced skill at what they did, but enthusiasm made up for a great deal.

She exclaimed in surprise and delight a moment before he could hold back no longer. Even as he spent, he thought of pulling free of her and spurting his seed onto her belly, as he had that once with Niphone. But he discovered that thinking of a thing and being able to do it were not one and the same: even as the idea skittered over the topmost part of his mind, his body drove ever deeper into hers and, for a little while, all thought went away.

It returned too quickly, as thought has a way of doing at such times. "Now what?" he murmured, his face scant inches from hers. He wasn't really talking to her, or to anyone.

She answered with a woman's practicality. "Now let me breathe, please."

"I'm sorry," Maniakes said, and got off her. She had a sunburst print between her breasts from the amulet Bagdasares had given him.

Sliding away from him, she started to dress. When she got a look at her drawers, she clucked to herself. "There won't be any hiding this from the serving women." Her mouth twisted in wry amusement. "Not that I'd bet anything above a worn copper that the servants don't already know."

Maniakes glanced toward the barred door that had given them privacy—or its illusion. "I wouldn't be surprised if you're right." He put on his clothes a little faster than he would have without her words. After running his fingers through his hair, he said "Now what?" again.

"Easiest, maybe, would be to pretend this never happened," Lysia answered. She paused, then shook her head. "No, not easiest. Most convenient, I should say."

"To the ice with convenience," Maniakes burst out. "Besides, you just said the servants will know, and you're right. And what the servants know today is gossip in the plaza of Palamas day after tomorrow."

"That's true." Lysia cocked her head to one side and studied him. "What then, my cousin your Majesty?"

"I know what I'd do if you weren't my cousin," Maniakes said. "If you weren't my cousin, I expect we'd have married years ago, out on Kalavria."

"You're probably right." Lysia hesitated, then went on, "I hope you won't be angry if I tell you there were times when I was very jealous of Rotrude."

"Angry?" Maniakes shook his head. "No, of course not. I—had

feelings for you that way. I didn't think you had them, too, not till I was about to sail off to see if I could overthrow Genesios."

"And you were sailing to Niphone," Lysia added. "What was I supposed to do then? I did what I thought I had to do. But now? Whatever we do now, we're going to make a scandal."

"I know," Maniakes said. They also took the chance of having the scandal become all too dreadfully obvious in nine months' time—although actually, if that befell, it would become obvious rather sooner. With that worry in mind, he went on, "The best way I can think of to deal with this is for me to marry you now, in spite of everything . . . if that's what you want to do, of course."

"It's what I'd like," she said, nodding. "But will a priest marry us? If he does, will Agathios anathematize him? And what will our families say?"

"I'm sure I can find a priest who will do as I tell him," Maniakes answered. "What Agathios will do . . . I don't know. He's a political beast, but this—We'll just have to find out." If Agathios thundered of sin, the city mob was liable to erupt. "We'll have to find out about our fathers, too, and our brothers." He had known this would complicate his life. Maybe he hadn't let himself think about how much.

And maybe the same thoughts were running through Lysia's mind. She said, "It really might be easiest to pretend this didn't—" She stopped and shook her head. Plainly, she didn't want to do that.

Neither did Maniakes. He said, "I've loved you as a cousin for as long as I can remember, and I've always thought a lot of your good sense. And now, with this—" Even after they had made love, he hesitated about openly saying so. "—I can't imagine wanting anyone else as my wife." He went over to her and took her in his arms. She clung to him, nodding against his chest.

"We'll just have to get through it, that's all," she said, her voice muffled.

"So we will," Maniakes said. "Maybe it won't be so hard."

After squeezing her once more, he went to the door and unbarred it. Then he opened it and looked up and down the corridor. He saw no one, heard no one. For a moment, he was relieved; *we got away with it* ran through his mind. Then he thought about how seldom the corridors of the imperial residence were so eerily quiet and deserted. Odds were that the servants were deliberately avoiding going anywhere near that door he had just unlocked.

He clicked his tongue between his teeth. A serving maid wouldn't have to see Lysia's drawers. The secret was already out.

The elder Maniakes took a long swallow of wine. He peered down into the depths of the silver cup, as if he were Bagdasares, using it as a scrying tool. "You aim to do what?" he rumbled.

"To marry my cousin," Maniakes answered. "We love each other, she has the best head on her shoulders of anyone in the family except maybe you, and . . . we love each other." His ears heated at the repetition, but it was done.

His father raised the cup again, draining it this time. He was careless when he set it down on the table, and it fell over, ringing sweetly as a goldpiece. He muttered to himself as he straightened it. To Maniakes' amazement, he started to laugh. "It does keep things in the family, doesn't it?"

"Is that all you have to say?" Maniakes demanded.

"No, not by a long shot," the elder Maniakes said. "Phos only knows what my brother will do—is Lysia telling him?" He waited for Maniakes to nod before continuing, "The patriarch will scream 'Incest!' at the top of his lungs, you know. Have you thought about that?"

Maniakes nodded again. "Oh, yes." Part of him was screaming the same thing. He was doing his best not to listen to it. The same probably held true for Lysia. That was one more complication he hadn't thoroughly thought through. And yet—"It didn't just . . . happen out of the blue, you know."

"Oh, yes, I do know that," his father answered. "One day back on Kalavria when Rotrude was pregnant with your boy—" He put one hand out in front of his own considerable belly. "—she told me she'd stick a knife in you if she ever caught you in bed with your cousin."

"Did she?" Maniakes said, amazed. He was, in fact, amazed for a couple of reasons. "I would have guessed she'd tell me that, not you."

"So would I," the elder Maniakes said. "I think being with child might have had something to do with her acting so weak and womanish." He rolled his eyes to show he did not intend that to be taken seriously. "But the point of it is, she'd noticed the two of you. I had, too, but I wasn't so sure. I'd known the both of you longer than she had, of course, and I knew you'd always been friendly. She was the one who saw it was something more than that."

"Rotrude always knew me pretty well," Maniakes said soberly. "Seems she knew me better than I knew myself there." He walked over to the pitcher of wine, which had on it a low relief of a fat old man drunkenly chasing a maiden who was neither fat nor old nor overburdened with clothing. After pouring his own cup full, he raised it to his lips and drank it down without drawing breath. Then he filled it again. "But, Father, what am I going to do?"

"Eh?" The elder Maniakes dug a finger in his ear. "You told me what you were going to do. You're going to marry her, aren't you? What do you expect me to do about it? Tell you I think you're a fool? I do think you're a fool—a couple of fools, I gather. But am I going to take a leather strap and turn your arse red? Send you to your room without supper? By the good god, son, you're a man now, and entitled to your choices, no matter how stupid I think they are. And you're the Avtokrator. I've read the chronicles, I have. Avtokrators' fathers who try giving them orders have a curious way of ending up shorter by a head."

Maniakes stared at him in genuine horror. "If you think I'd do such a thing, I'd better take off the red boots and shave my own head for a monk."

"No, son, the monastery is the other place for fathers who make their imperial sons unhappy," the elder Maniakes said. He studied the Avtokrator. "Are you sure this can't be settled somewhere short of marriage?"

"You mean, by keeping her as mistress?" Maniakes asked. His father nodded. He shook his head. "I wouldn't take honor away from her." His laugh held irony. "Some would say falling in love with her did that, wouldn't they? Well, let them. But that's not the only problem I see. Suppose we don't wed, but I do take another wife one day. What would she and her family think about the arrangement Lysia and I have?"

"Nothing good, I've no doubt," the elder Maniakes said. "Suppose instead that you put your cousin aside now? What then?"

"Then my life looks cold and empty and dark as Skotos' icy hell," Maniakes answered, spitting on the floor in rejection of the dark god. "When I look out at the Empire, gloom is all I see. Must I see the same when I look here at the imperial residence?"

"I told you, son, you're a man grown," his father answered. "If this is what you want and what my niece wants—" He coughed a little at that, but went on gamely enough. "—then it's what you will have. Where we go from there is any man's guess, but I expect we'll find out before long."

Kameas said, "Your Majesty, the most holy ecumenical patriarch Agathios has arrived at the residence in response to your summons."

"Good." Maniakes' stomach knotted within him at the prospect of the meeting that lay ahead, but he did not show it. "Bring him to me. Full formality throughout here, mind you; he is not summoned for a friendly chat."

"I shall observe your Majesty's requirements in all particulars," the vestiarios replied with dignity. He swept away. The tiny, mincing steps he took under his long robe made him seem to float as he moved, like a ship running before the wind.

"Your Majesty," Agathios said at the doorway after Kameas announced him. He went down to his knees and then to his belly in full proskynesis. When he started to get up before Maniakes had given him leave, the Avtokrator coughed sharply. Agathios bent his back once more, touching his forehead to the marble floor.

"Rise, most holy sir," Maniakes said after a wait he judged suitable. "You may take a seat."

"Er—thank you, your Majesty." Warily, the patriarch sat down. He suited his tone to the one Maniakes had taken: "In what way may I be of service to your Majesty this morning?"

"We have thought the time ripe to abandon the single life and choose for ourself another bride," Maniakes answered. He couldn't remember the last time he had bothered with the imperial *we*, but he would try anything to overawe Agathios today, which was why he had summoned the patriarch to the palace quarter rather than visiting him at his own residence next to the High Temple.

"I rejoice at the news and wish you joy, your Majesty," Agathios said, fulsomely if without any great warmth. He hesitated, then asked, "And to whom have you chosen to yoke yourself for what I pray will be many happy and fruitful years?"

Maniakes didn't miss that hesitation. He wondered what sort of rumors the ecumenical patriarch had heard. None had got back to him yet from the plaza of Palamas, which did not mean they were not there. Carefully, he said, "We have chosen to wed Lysia the daughter of the most noble Symvatios." He made no mention of Lysia's relationship to him; if anyone was going to raise that issue, it would have to be Agathios.

The patriarch did raise it, in a sidelong manner. "Has the most noble Symvatios given this union his approval?"

"Yes, most holy sir, he has," Maniakes answered. "You may ask this of him yourself if you doubt me." He had spoken the truth; his uncle hadn't said no. But if Symvatios had been enthusiastic at the prospect of his daughter's becoming Empress, he had concealed that enthusiasm very well.

"Of course I rely on your Majesty's assurance." Agathios hesitated again, coughed, and looked this way and that. Maniakes sat silent, willing him to keep quiet. Here in the imperial residence, Agathios, a malleable soul if ever there was one, would surely be too intimidated to argue from a doctrinal standpoint . . . wouldn't he? After that long, long pause, the ecumenical patriarch resumed: "Be that as it may, however, I must bring it to your Majesty's attention that the bride you propose to wed is, ah, within the prohibited degrees of relationship long established in canon law and also forbidden under all imperial law codes."

He hadn't screamed *incest* at the top of his lungs, but that was what his polite, nervous phrases amounted to. And what he would do back at the High Temple was anyone's guess. Maniakes said, "Most holy sir, what pleases the Avtokrator has the force of law in Videssos, as you know. In this particular case, it pleases us to exempt ourself from the secular laws you mention. That is within our power. Similarly, it is within your power to grant us a dispensation from the strictures of canon law. So we ask and so we instruct you to do."

Agathios looked unhappy. In his boots, Maniakes would have looked unhappy, too. Had the patriarch had a little less backbone, he would have yielded, and that would have been that. As it was, he said, "Let me remind your Majesty of the pledge he gave on entering Videssos the city to assume the imperial dignity, wherein he promised he would make no alterations in the faith we have received from our fathers."

"We do not seek to alter the faith, only to be dispensed from one small provision of it," Maniakes answered. "Surely there is precedent for such."

"A man who lives by precedent alone can, should he search, find justification for almost anything," Agathios said. "Whether the results of breaking justify one doing so is, you will forgive me, debatable."

Maniakes glared at him. "Most holy sir, do you tell me straight out that you will not do as I instruct you?" He kicked at the floor in annoyance—he had fallen out of the imperial *we*.

Agathios looked even unhappier. "May it please your Majesty—"

"It pleases me not at all," Maniakes snapped.

"May it please your Majesty," the patriarch repeated, "I must in this matter, however much I regret doing so, heed the dictates of my conscience and of anciently established canon law."

"However much you regret it now, you'll regret it more later," Maniakes said. "I daresay I can find another patriarch, one willing to listen to common sense."

"Avtokrators have indeed cast patriarchs down from their seats in the past," Agathios agreed gravely. "Should your Majesty undertake to do so in this instance, however, and for this cause, my opinion is that he will bring to birth a schism among the priests and prelates of the holy temples."

Maniakes bit into that one like a man stubbing his tooth on an unseen bone in his meat. "The Empire cannot afford such a schism, not now."

"Far be it from me to disagree with what is so self-evidently true," Agathios said.

"Then you will do my bidding and marry me to the woman I love," Maniakes said.

"She is your first cousin, your Majesty. She is within the degrees of relationship prohibited for marriage," the patriarch said, as he had before. "If I were to perform such a marriage in the High Temple, the temples throughout the Empire would likely see schism. If you oust me, rigorists would rebel against whatever pliant prelate you put in my place. If I acceded to your demands, those same rigorists would rebel against me."

Knowing the temper of Videssian priests, Maniakes judged that all too likely. "I do not wish to have to live with Lysia without the sanction of marriage," he said, "nor she with me. If you will not perform the ceremony in the High Temple, most holy sir, will you let it be done here at the small temple in the palace quarter by some priest who does not find the notion as abominable as you seem to?" He had yielded ground to Etzilios. He had yielded ground to Abivard. Now he found himself yielding ground to Agathios. He stood straighter. A private wedding was the only concession he would so much as consider.

With what looked like genuine regret, Agathios shook his head. "You ask me to designate someone else to commit what I still reckon to be a sin. I am sorry, your Majesty, but the matter admits of no such facile compromise."

Maniakes let out a long, unhappy breath. He didn't want to dismiss the ecumenical patriarch. Sure as sure, that would start a tempest in the temples, and Videssos might fall apart under such stress.

Agathios might have been reading his thoughts. "Since affairs of state have come to such a pass of hardship and difficulty," the patriarch said, "I urge you to incline toward putting your own affairs in good order. Do not contemplate this lawless action rejected by the statutes of Videssos, nor transgress decency with your cousin."

"You have said what you think good," Maniakes answered, "but you do not persuade me. I shall act as I think best, and the consequences of my action shall rest on me alone."

"So they shall, your Majesty," Agathios said sadly. "So they shall."

Some of Maniakes' bodyguards entered the High Temple with him. Others, the big fair men from Halogaland who did not follow Phos, waited outside. One of them yawned. "I hope your head priest will not talk long today," he said in slow Videssian. "Too nice the day for standing about."

Maniakes thought it was chilly and raw, but Halogaland routinely knew winters like the one of which his father had spoken in horror. "However long he speaks, I'll hear him out," he said. The tall, blond Haloga dipped his head in resigned acquiescence.

In the exonarthex, priests bowed low to Maniakes. They did not prostrate themselves, not here. In the High Temple, Phos' authority was highest, that of the Avtokrator lowest, of anywhere in the Empire.

A small opening in a side wall gave onto a stairway leading up to the small chamber reserved for the imperial family. Maniakes climbed those stairs. His Videssian guards mounted them with him. A couple of men stopped just out of sight of the bottom of the stairway; the rest accompanied him to the chamber and posted themselves outside the door.

As Maniakes peered out through the filigree grillwork that gave Avtokrators and their families privacy when they cared to have it, he saw one of the blue-robed priests who had greeted him hurry down the aisle and speak to Agathios, who was standing by the altar in the center of the temple.

Agathios heard him out, then nodded. His gaze went to the grill. From times when he had worshiped in the public area of the High Temple, Maniakes knew he was effectively invisible behind it. All the same, for a moment he and the patriarch seemed to lock eyes.

Then Agathios looked away from him and up toward the great dome that was the architectural centerpiece of the High Temple. Maniakes' eyes traveled up to the dome, too, and to the mosaic of Phos in stern judgment covering its inner surface. The good god's eyes seemed to look into his, as they would have had he been anywhere in the High Temple. The Phos in the dome there was the model for depictions of the good god in temples throughout the Empire. Some of the provincial imitations looked even fiercer than the original, but none could approach it for awe-inspiring majesty. You would have to think twice before contemplating sin under that gaze.

Try as he would, though, Maniakes had trouble seeing the desire to marry his cousin as something for which the lord with the great and good mind would condemn him to the eternal ice. In his time on the throne, he had seen the difference between rules in place because they made sense and those in place because they were in place. He reckoned the prohibition that so exercised Agathios one of the latter.

The patriarch kept looking up into the dome. His back was straighter when at last he gave his attention to the growing number of worshipers filing into the pews that led up to the altar. Presently Maniakes heard and felt priests shutting the doors down below him.

Agathios lifted up his hands. The congregants rose. Behind the filigree screen, Maniakes stood with everyone else, though no one except that Phos brooding in righteousness could have seen him had he stayed seated. Along with the rest of the worshipers, he followed the patriarch's lead in reciting Phos' creed, then sat once more as a chorus of priests sang the good god's praises.

Going through the infinitely familiar liturgy, rising and sitting, praying and chanting, cleansed Maniakes' spirit of some of the worry with which he had entered the High Temple. It served to unite him to the good god and also to unite the people of the Empire with one another. Wherever Videssos' dominions ran, men and women prayed in the same way and acknowledged the same clerical hierarchy. A schism would shatter that unity hardly less than the Makuraner occupation of the westlands had.

Following Agathios' lead, the worshipers stood for a last time, repeated Phos' creed, and then sat back down to hear the ecumenical patriarch's sermon. That, of course, varied from day to day, from week to week, and from temple to temple. Maniakes leaned forward and put his ear close to the grillwork so as to miss nothing. It was principally for the sermon he had come, not for the liturgy, comforting though that was.

"May the lord with the great and good mind look down kindly upon Videssos and ensure that we pass through the present crisis unharmed," Agathios said. Small murmurs of "So may it be" floated up to Maniakes from the pews; a good half the congregants sketched the sun-circle over their hearts. Maniakes traced a quick sun-circle himself.

The patriarch went on, "May the lord with the great and good mind also instill piety and wisdom into the heart of the Avtokrator. The course he presently contemplates would make it difficult for Phos to grant his blessings to him in particular and to the Empire as a whole. While I grieve with his Majesty and sympathize with the loneliness now engulfing him, I must respectfully remind you all that the laws of the temples are not a bill of fare at an eatery, wherefrom a man may choose those courses pleasing to him while paying no heed to the rest. They form a seamless garment, which will fall to rags if any one of them be torn from it."

He looked up toward the grillwork behind which Maniakes sat. "The Avtokrator is of course Phos' viceregent on earth, and heads the Empire consecrated to the good god's true and holy faith. He is at the same time a man, far from being the good god's son or any other such outlandish notion, and is subject to the same fleshly temptations as other men. Such temptations are lures of Skotos, to be resisted with all the power a man shall have."

Agathios went on in that vein for some time. He was polite, reasonable; he did not shout about incest or urge the people of Videssos either to rise against their Avtokrator or risk the imperilment of their souls. As Maniakes had seen, Agathios enjoyed being patriarch and wanted to hold the job. He was giving Maniakes as little excuse to oust him as he could—but he also was not retreating from the position he had set forth in the imperial residence.

It was, in its own way, a masterful performance. In the abstract, Maniakes admired it. He was, however, not much given to abstraction at the moment.

As Agathios dismissed the congregants from the liturgy, Maniakes rose from his seat and left the private imperial box. The guards nodded to him as he came out. One asked, "Did the sermon please you, your Majesty?"

He didn't mean anything by it: by his tone, it was just a question for the sake of casual conversation. But it was not the question Maniakes wanted to hear then. "No," he snapped.

"Will you sack him then, your Majesty?" the guard asked eagerly. The eyes of all his companions lit up. Doctrinal controversy was meat and drink to anyone who lived in Videssos the city.

"I hope not," Maniakes answered, visibly disappointing the soldiers. They were still trying to get more out of him when he left the temple and came out to where the Halogai waited.

The northerners found Videssian theological squabbles inordinately complex. "This stupid priest does not do what you want, your Majesty, you put his head up on the Milestone," one of them said. "The next chief priest you pick, he do what you tell him." He hefted his axe. By the look of him, he was ready to carry out the sentence he had passed on Agathios.

"It's not that simple," Maniakes said with a regretful sigh. The Halogai all laughed. In their bloodthirsty code, everything was simple.

Despite more prodding from the Videssian guards, Maniakes stayed quiet and thoughtful all the way back to the imperial residence. When he got there, he called for Kameas. "How may I serve you, your Majesty?" the vestiarios asked.

"Summon me the healer-priest Philetos," Maniakes answered.

"Of course, your Majesty." Kameas' smooth, beardless face twisted in concern. "Is your Majesty ill?"

"No," Maniakes said, but then amended that: "I'm sick to death of Agathios, I'll tell you so much."

"I . . . see," Kameas said slowly. In a speculative tone of voice, he went on, "The holy Philetos, being so much concerned with his healing researches, is apt to be of less certain obedience to the most holy ecumenical patriarch than a good many others from the ecclesiastical hierarchy whose names spring to mind."

"Really?" Maniakes said in mock surprise. "How on earth can you suppose such a consideration might matter to me?"

"It is my duty to serve your Majesty in every possible way," Kameas answered; it was not quite responsive, but informative enough in its way. The vestiarios went on, "I shall summon the holy sir directly."

"Good," Maniakes said.

After Philetos had prostrated himself before the Avtokrator, he asked, "How may I serve your Majesty?" He sounded genuinely curious, which Maniakes took as a sign that he was too busy with his research to care about what was going on in the wider world around him.

"I want you to perform the ceremony of marriage for me," the Avtokrator said, coming straight to the point. If Agathios wouldn't ask a cooperative priest to tend to that, he would do it himself.

Philetos' gray eyebrows rose, "Of course I shall obey, and I—I am honored that you should think of me," he stammered, "but I can't imagine why you have chosen me rather than the ecumenical patriarch. And—er, forgive me, but to whom would you have me join you in marriage?"

He *was* naive. Again, Maniakes answered directly. "To my cousin Lysia." He did not waste time skirting the relationship, as he had with Agathios.

If Philetos had been surprised before, he was astonished now. "She is your first cousin, is she not, your Majesty?" he asked, and then answered his own question: "Yes, of course she is. Have you a dispensation from the patriarch for this union?"

"No," Maniakes said. "I ask it of you even so."

Philetos stared at him. "Your Majesty, you put me in a difficult position. If I obey you, I suffer the wrath of my ecclesiastical superior, while if I disobey—" He spread his hands. He knew under whose wrath he fell if he disobeyed the Avtokrator.

"That is the choice you must make, and you must make it now," Maniakes said.

"Your Majesty, I have never performed the ceremony of marriage in all my days in the priesthood," Philetos said. "My interest has centered on applying Phos' goodness and mercy to broken and infirm bodies, and I took my priestly vows for that purpose alone. I—"

Maniakes cut him off. "You are not prevented from serving the part of a priest with less abstruse concerns, are you?"

"Well, no, but—" Philetos began.

"Very well, then," Maniakes broke in again. "Your answer, holy sir."

Philetos looked trapped. He was trapped, as Maniakes knew very well. The Avtokrator thought about pledging some large sum of gold to the Sorcerers' Collegium after the ceremony was done, but found a couple of reasons not to do so. Such promises were as likely to offend as to accomplish their purpose. Even more to the point, he couldn't lay his hands on any large sum of gold for the Collegium.

"Very well, your Majesty," Philetos said at last. "I shall do as you say, but I warn you that trouble is likelier than joy to spring from your decision."

"Oh, I know it will cause trouble." Maniakes' laugh held scant humor. "But I have so much trouble already, what's some more? And wedding Lysia will bring me joy. I know that, too. Aren't I entitled to a little now and then?"

"Joy is every man's portion from Phos," Philetos answered gravely. Maniakes suddenly wondered if he was yielding because he felt guilty over having failed to save Niphone and was seeking this way to make amends. He didn't ask. He didn't want to know, not for certain; finding out would make him feel guilty in turn. Philetos went on, "When would you like the ceremony celebrated?"

"At once," Maniakes said. *I don't want to give you the chance to change your mind.* He called for Kameas. When the vestiarios came in, he said, "Gather together Lysia, my father, her father, and Rhegorios. The wedding will go forward."

"Your Majesty, when you bade me summon the holy sir here,

I took the liberty of alerting the people whom you mention to that possibility," Kameas replied. "They are all in readiness."

"That's—most efficient of you," Maniakes said. "I suppose I shouldn't be surprised at such things anymore, but every once in a while I still am."

"I aim to be taken for granted, your Majesty," Kameas said.

While Maniakes was still trying to figure out how to reply to that, Philetos asked, "Where will the wedding take place, your Majesty? I gather you do not care to draw a great deal of attention to it—"

"You gather correctly, holy sir," Maniakes answered. "I had in mind the small temple here in the palace compound. It may be in something less than perfect repair, as it's not been used a great deal by the past few Avtokrators, but I did think it would serve."

Kameas coughed. "Again anticipating your Majesty, I have sent a crew of cleaners to that small temple, to make such efforts as they can toward improving its appearance and comfort."

Maniakes stared at him. "Esteemed sir, you *are* a marvel."

"Your Majesty," Kameas said with considerable dignity, "if something is to be done, it is to be done properly."

✦ XII

Parsmanios scowled at Maniakes. "Brother of mine, you didn't do that properly, not even close to it. The whole city's buzzing now that word's seeped out."

"Yes, the people are buzzing," Maniakes admitted. "They aren't screaming, though, the way I was afraid they would. With luck the buzz will die down and I'll be able to go on about my business."

His brother continued as if he hadn't spoken: "And I don't much fancy you going and tying yourself to Symvatios and Rhegorios, either, let me tell you that. You treat them better than you do your own flesh and blood, and there's a fact."

"There's your problem, brother of mine," Maniakes said. "You're not jealous of Lysia; you're jealous of Rhegorios."

"And why shouldn't I be?" Parsmanios retorted. "If you're Avtokrator, he has the place that should be mine by right. You had no business naming a cousin Sevastos when you had a brother ready to hand."

Maniakes exhaled through his nose. "First of all, you weren't 'ready to hand' when I needed a Sevastos. You were off in your piddlepot little town. You hadn't been my right arm all the way through the war with Genesios, and Rhegorios had. And ever since I gave him the post, he's done a first-rate job with it. We've been over this ground before, brother of mine. Why do you want to walk down the track again?"

"Because I didn't think you'd be stupid enough to commit in—" Parsmanios stopped, not quite soon enough.

"You are dismissed from our presence." Maniakes' voice went cold as a winter storm. "You have incurred our displeasure. We do not care to speak with you again until you have expiated your offense against us. Go." He hadn't used the imperial *we* half a dozen times since he had become Avtokrator, and now twice inside a few days. It seemed a better way to show his anger than shouting for the guards to fling Parsmanios in the gaol that lay under the government office building on Middle Street.

Parsmanios stalked away. Not two minutes later, Rhegorios rapped on the door jamb. "My cousin your brother looked imperfectly delighted with the world when he walked out of the residence here," he remarked.

"Your cousin my brother will look even less delighted if he tries to set foot in the residence any time soon," Maniakes answered, still fuming.

"Let me guess," Rhegorios said. "If it takes more than one, go get yourself someone with a working set of wits and put him in my place."

"You're in no danger there." Maniakes kicked at the floor. If he did it often enough, he might tear loose a couple of tiles from the mosaic there. That would give him the feeling he had accomplished something and vex Kameas when he noticed, which he would in a matter of hours. Kicking again, Maniakes went on, "When even my own brother shouts *incest* at me—"

"I wouldn't lose any sleep over it, my cousin your Majesty brother-in-law of mine." Rhegorios grinned at the clumsy collection of titles he had used to label Maniakes. "Forgive my bluntness, but I have trouble seeing Parsmanios leading rioters baying for your head."

"Now that you mention it, so do I." Maniakes came over to slap Rhegorios on the shoulder. "If you were leading the rioters, now—"

"They'd be laughing, not baying," Rhegorios said. "Most of the time, I just amuse people." Despite that claim, his face was serious. "But I might have been out there trying to make the mob howl, you know."

Maniakes gave him a pained look. "Not you, too? You never let on . . . and if you had, I don't see how Lysia and I could have gone on."

"I might have been out there, I said. Before I did anything, though, I went and talked with my sister. For some reason or other, marrying you was what she wanted to do, and I've come to have a great deal of respect for Lysia's good sense. If you have any sense of your own, you'll pay attention to her, too."

"I intend to," Maniakes answered. "If I didn't think I wanted to listen to her when she told me something, this would have happened differently."

"Yes, I can see how it might have." Rhegorios thought for a moment. "Better this way." He nodded judiciously. So did the Avtokrator.

Maniakes looked forward to Midwinter's Day with the same eager anticipation a little unwalled town in the westlands felt on the approach of Abivard's army. He could not hold back the passing days, though, and avoiding the Amphitheater would have been an unthinkable confession of weakness. When the festival came, he and Lysia went out across the plaza of Palamas to the great stone bowl where, he confidently expected, they would be mocked without mercy.

A few of the people in the plaza made a point of turning away from the Avtokrator and his new bride. More, though, treated them with the casual equality that was everyone's due on Midwinter's Day. The two of them leapt over a fire hand in hand, shouting, "Burn, ill-luck!"

Inside the Amphitheater, some catcalls and hisses greeted Maniakes and Lysia. He pretended not to hear them and squeezed Lysia's hand. She squeezed back, hard; she was not used to public abuse.

The elder Maniakes and her own father and brother greeted her warmly when she and the Avtokrator ascended to the spine of the Amphitheater. So did Tzikas, who looked splendid in a gilded chain-mail coat. Parsmanios tried to make his nods to her and Maniakes civil, but did not succeed well. The elder Maniakes scowled at him. Afterward, Parsmanios worked harder at acting friendly, but managed only to pour honey on top of vinegar.

Agathios the patriarch made no effort to be friendly. As far as he was concerned, Maniakes and Lysia might as well not have existed. He did recite the creed to begin the day's events, but even that felt perfunctory.

After the patriarch sat down once more, Maniakes took his place at the spot from which he could speak to the whole Amphitheater. "People of Videssos the city," he said, "people of the Empire of Videssos, we have all of us had another hard year. The lord with the great and good mind willing, when we gather here for the next Midwinter's Day, we shall have passed through sorrow into happiness. So may it be."

"So may it be," the people echoed, the acoustics of the Amphitheater making their voices din in his ears.

"Now let the revelry begin!" Maniakes shouted, and sat down to make as if he enjoyed the lampoons the mimes were going to aim at him. *Anything can happen on Midwinter's Day:* so the saying went. Usually that meant something like finding an unexpected love affair. But it could have other, more sinister meanings as well.

To the Avtokrator's relief, the first mime troupe mocked only his failure to regain the westlands. He had seen himself portrayed as running away from anything in Makuraner armor—even if it was an old man on a swaybacked mule—and as fouling his robes while he ran: mimes had been making those jokes about him since he took the throne. If he had managed to smile for them before, he could do it again without straining himself unduly.

When the troupe trooped off, he glanced over to Lysia. She smiled back and mouthed, "So far, so good." He nodded; he had been thinking the same thing.

It didn't stay good for long. The very next troupe of mimes had a fellow dressed in gaudy robes and wearing a crown of gilded parchment sniffing lasciviously after a band of pretty little girls played by pretty little boys in wigs and dresses. When he found one who wore a dress much like his robe and a scarf much like his crown, he slung her over his shoulder and carried her away with a lecherous smirk on his face.

The crowd roared laughter. It dinned in Maniakes' ears. He had to sit there and pretend to be amused. As he had warned her to do, Lysia also feigned a smile. But, through that false expression, she said, "What a filthy lie! I'm not that far from your own age, and anyone who knows anything about us knows it."

But most of the people in the city didn't really know anything about Maniakes and Lysia. That was the point. The city mob formed its opinions from things like mime shows and seventh-hand gossip.

Some people who did know Maniakes and Lysia were laughing, too. Parsmanios, for instance, was on the far side of a polite
show of mirth. So was Kourikos, who sat farther down the spine
among the high-ranking bureaucrats. Not far away from him,
Tzikas, glittering in that mail shirt, sat quiet, sedate, and discreet.
So did Agathios. The ecumenical patriarch continued to walk his
fine line, disapproving of the Avtokrator's conduct but not seeking
to inflame the city by his own.

Maybe I should have sent him as envoy to Sharbaraz, Maniakes
thought, wondering what had happened to poor Triphylles.

Another troupe came out. This one lampooned Niphone's funeral,
with people throwing up all along the route. It was in extremely
bad taste, which meant the crowd ate it up. Maniakes bared his
teeth, curled the corners of his mouth upward, and endured.

The next skit had Lysia chasing Maniakes rather than the other
way round. Lysia had no trouble bearing up under it, but it infuriated Maniakes. "I wish Genesios hadn't tried to put down the
mimes and failed," he said. "I don't want to imitate him at all,
but I could try suppressing the troupes myself if only he hadn't
had a go at them."

"It's all right," Lysia answered. "We pay one day a year to have
peace the rest of the time."

"That's usually a good bargain," Maniakes said, "but what the
people see here today will color the way they look at us for the
rest of the year, and for a long time after that, too."

The next troupe came out. What the people saw was another variation on the same theme: this one had Rhegorios pushing Lysia at
Maniakes. Rhegorios laughed at that one. It angered both Maniakes
and Lysia. Having to keep his face twisted into the semblance of a
smile was making Maniakes' cheeks hurt. He glanced over at his
guardsmen. Loosing them on the mimes would have turned his smile
broad and genuine. Instead of slaughtering the troupes, though, he
had to pay them for entertaining the people.

They certainly were entertaining Parsmanios. His brother
laughed long and hard until the elder Maniakes leaned over and
said something to him in a low voice. Parsmanios sobered after
that, but the sullen looks he sent his father said his mind had
not been changed. No one spoke to Kourikos. Maniakes' former
father-in-law showed more enjoyment of the mimes' crude jokes
than seemed quite fitting in such a normally humorless man.

One troupe's lampoon was of the patriarch Agathios, for being too spineless to do a proper job of condemning Maniakes and Lysia. The fellow playing him raised an angry hand, drew it back in fright, raised it, drew it back. Finally, a man dressed in an ordinary priest's robe gave him a kick in the fundament that sent him leaping high in the air.

Tzikas guffawed at that skit. Agathios assumed what was probably meant to be an expression of grave dignity, but looked more as if he had been sucking on a lemon.

At last, the ordeal ended. The crowd in the Amphitheater didn't hiss and scream curses at Maniakes when he rose to dismiss them. Not too many of them laughed at him. He considered that a major triumph.

When he and Lysia got back to the imperial residence, it was as still and quiet as it ever got: most of the servants and several members of his family were off reveling in Videssos the city. Lysia looked down the empty corridors and said, "Well, we got through it and we don't have to worry about it for another year. The good god willing, the mime troupes will have something besides us to give them ideas by then."

Maniakes caught her to him. "Have I told you anytime lately that I like the way you think?"

"Yes," she answered, "but I always like to hear it."

"A message from Abivard, you say?" Maniakes asked Kameas. "By all means, let's have it. If it's word Triphylles has been released, that'll be news good enough to warm this miserably cold day."

"True, your Majesty," the vestiarios said. "The servitors are stoking the furnace and the hot air is going through the hypocausts, but sometimes—" He shrugged. "—the weather defeats us in spite of all we can do."

"A lot of things lately have defeated us in spite of all we can do," Maniakes said wearily. "Sooner or later, the weather will get better. So will the rest—I hope. Send in the messenger."

After the fellow had prostrated himself, and while he was gratefully sipping at a steaming cup of wine spiced with cinnamon and myrrh, Maniakes opened the leather message tube he had given him. The Avtokrator was becoming all too familiar with the lion of Makuran on scarlet wax that Abivard used to seal his messages. He broke the wax, unrolled the parchment, and read the letter his foe had commanded some poor Videssian to write for him:

> Abivard general to Sharbaraz King of Kings, may his years be many and his realm increase, to Maniakes styling himself Avtokrator of the Videssians: Greetings. I regret to inform you that the man Triphylles, whom you sent as an envoy to the glorious court of Sharbaraz King of Kings, and who was subsequently imprisoned as just and fit punishment for undue and intolerable insolence before his majesty, has suffered the common ultimate fate of all mankind. I pray the God shall accept his spirit with compassion. In lieu of returning his corpse to you, Sharbaraz King of Kings ordered it cremated, which was of course accomplished before word of these events reached me so that I might transmit them to you.

Maniakes read through the missive twice. He still could not—and did not—believe Triphylles had acted insolently enough for any prince to find reason to cast him into prison. The noble had begged not to be sent to the Makuraner court at Mashiz, but Maniakes had overborne his objections. He had been confident Sharbaraz adhered to civilized standards of conduct. And now Triphylles was dead after a long spell in gaol, and who was to blame for that? Sharbaraz, certainly, but also Maniakes.

"Fetch me sealing wax and a lamp," he said to Kameas. As the eunuch hurried away, Maniakes inked a pen and wrote his answer. "Maniakes Avtokrator of the Videssians to Abivard slave to Sharbaraz Liar of Liars, Killer of Killers: Greetings. I have received your word of the mistreatment and tragic death of my emissary, the eminent Triphylles. Tell your master one thing from me, and one thing only: he shall be avenged."

When Kameas returned with the stick of wax and a lighted lamp, he took one look at Maniakes' face and said, "A misfortune has befallen the eminent Triphylles." He sketched the sun-sign above his plump breast.

"It has indeed: a mortal misfortune," Maniakes answered grimly. He tied his letter with ribbon and pressed his sunburst signet into hot wax. Then he popped it into the tube and gave it to the messenger. "Deliver this into Abivard's hands, or into those of his servants."

"I shall do as you say, of course, your Majesty." The messenger saluted with clenched right fist laid over his heart.

"Very well." Maniakes shook his head in sad bewilderment. "When I fought alongside them, Abivard and Sharbaraz seemed decent enough fellows." He plucked at his beard. "For that matter, Abivard still seems decent enough. War is a nasty business, no doubt of that, but he hasn't made it any filthier than it has to be—no great massacres in the towns he's taken, nothing of the sort. But Sharbaraz, now . . . Sitting on the throne of Mashiz has gone to his head, unless I'm sadly wrong."

The messenger stood mute. Quietly, Kameas said, "We have seen that in Videssos the city, too, your Majesty. Likinios came to think that anything could be so, simply because he ordered it; Genesios spilled an ocean of blood for the sport of it—and because he was afraid of his own shadow—"

"And the more blood he spilled, the more reason he had to be afraid," Maniakes broke in.

"That is nothing less than the truth, your Majesty," Kameas agreed. "We find ourselves fortunate with you."

The vestiarios did not lay flattery on with a trowel, as if it were cement—not with Maniakes, at any rate, no matter what he might have done for Genesios. He had seen the present wearer of the red boots did not care for such things. Now Maniakes had a disheartening thought: he imagined all his servants watching him, wondering if and how he would turn into a monster. So far, Kameas, at least, seemed satisfied he hadn't. That was something.

He waved to the messenger. The man nodded and hurried off to do his bidding. He would have been astonished and angry had the fellow done anything else. If you expected absolute obedience all the time, who would warn you when you started giving orders that did not deserve to be obeyed? If someone did warn you, what were you liable to do to him?

Would you do what Genesios had done to anyone upon whom his suspicions fell—had he had cloudbursts of suspicions? What Sharbaraz had done to Triphylles when the envoy said something wrong—or when the King of Kings imagined he had said something wrong?

How *did* you keep from becoming a monster? Maniakes didn't know, but hoped that over the years he would find out.

The broad lawns of the palace quarter, so inviting and green in spring and summer, were nothing but snowfields now. When the snow was fresh and the sun sparkled off it, it was pretty in a frigid way. Today, gray clouds filled the sky and the snow was gray, too, gray with the soot from the thousands of braziers and hearths and cook fires of Videssos the city. Looking out at it through the bare-branched trees surrounding the imperial residence, Maniakes screwed his mouth into a thin, tight line. The gloomy scene matched his mood.

A servant walking along a paved path slipped on a patch of ice and landed heavily on his backside. Maniakes faintly heard the angry curse the fellow shouted. He got to his feet and, limping a little, went on his way.

Maniakes' eyes went back down to the petition for clemency he was reading. A prosperous farmer named Bizoulinos had started pasturing his sheep on a field that belonged to a widow who lived nearby. When her son went to his house to protest, Bizoulinos and his own sons had set upon him with clubs and beaten him to death. The local governor had sentenced them to meet the executioner, but, as was their right, they had sent an appeal to the Avtokrator.

After reviewing the evidence, he did not find them in the least appealing. He inked a pen and wrote on the petition: "Let the sentence be carried out. Had they observed the law as carefully before their arrest as they did afterward, they and everyone else would have been better off." He signed the document and impressed his signet ring into hot wax below it. Bizoulinos and his sons would keep their appointments with the headsman.

Maniakes rose and stretched. Condemning men to death gave him no pleasure, even when they had earned it. Better by far if people lived at peace with one another. Better by far if nations lived at peace with one another, too, or so he thought. The Makuraners, perhaps understandably given their successes, seemed to feel otherwise.

A flash of color through the screen of cherry tree trunks drew his eye. A couple of men in the bright robes of the upper nobility were walking along not far from the Grand Courtroom. Even at that distance, he recognized one of them as Parsmanios. The set of his brother's wide shoulders, the way he gestured as he spoke, made him unmistakable for Maniakes.

The man with whom he was talking was smaller, slighter, older than he. Maniakes squinted, trying to make out more than that. Was it Kourikos? He couldn't be sure. His hands closed into angry fists just the same. His brother had no business associating with someone who so vehemently disapproved of his marriage to Lysia.

His scowl deepened. Parsmanios disapproved of that marriage, too, and hadn't been shy about saying so. He hadn't said so in an effort to change Maniakes' mind, either. He had just been out to wound—and wound he had, metaphorically anyhow.

Who was the fellow beside him? Maniakes could not make him out, though he brought his eyelids so close together that he was peering through a screen of his lashes. If that was Kourikos, he and Parsmanios could cook up a great deal of mischief together.

Whoever they were, the two men went into the Grand Courtroom together. "They're plotting something," Maniakes muttered. "By the good god, I'll put a stop to that."

He listened in his mind's ear to what he had just said and was appalled. He didn't know with whom Parsmanios had been talking, or what he had been talking about. This had to be how Genesios had started: seeing something innocent, assuming the worst, and acting on that assumption. Two men together? Obviously a plot! Stick their heads up on the Milestone to warn others not to be so foolish.

Acting without evidence led to monsterdom. Ignoring evidence, on the other hand, led to danger. But would his brother, *could* his brother, betray him? The clan had always been close-knit. Until he had evidence, he wouldn't believe it. He wished he and Parsmanios were boys again, so their father could solve their differences with a clout to the head. That wouldn't work now, even should Parsmanios deserve it. *Too bad*, Maniakes thought.

One thing Maniakes found: he was far happier wed to Lysia than he had been before they married. Had he not been so worried about the state of the Empire, he would have said he had never been so happy in his life. That came as a considerable relief to him, and something of a surprise, as well. He had done the honorable thing with her after they found themselves in each other's arms, but hadn't guessed the honorable would prove so enjoyable.

Lysia had always been a companion, a sounding board, someone who could laugh with him or, when he deserved it, at him. He still sometimes found himself bemused to be waking up in the same big bed with her. "I was afraid," he said one morning, "we wouldn't stay friends once we were lovers. Good to see I was wrong."

She nodded. "I had the same fear. But if we can't rely on each other, who's left?"

"No one," Maniakes said as they got out of bed. Then he backtracked. "That's not quite true. My father, and yours, and Rhegorios—" He started to name Parsmanios, but he couldn't. How sad, not to be able to count on your own brother.

In any case, Lysia shook her head, then brushed the shiny black curls back from her face. "It isn't the same," she said. After a moment, he had to nod. She frowned thoughtfully, looking for the right words with which to continue. At last, she found them: "What we have is . . . deeper somehow." She flushed beneath her swarthy skin. "And don't you dare make the joke I know you're thinking. That's not what I meant."

"I wasn't going to make the joke." Maniakes did not deny it had crossed his mind. "I think you're right."

"Good," Lysia said. She seemed happy, too, which eased Maniakes' mind. He reached for the bell pull that summoned Kameas, who slept in the room next to the imperial bedchamber. Lysia went on, "As well it's winter, and I'm in a woolen gown. I wouldn't want the vestiarios to come in after I'd got out of bed bare, the way I do when the weather is hot and sticky."

"Yes, Niphone was modest about him at first, too, but she got used to it," Maniakes said.

"I wasn't thinking of that," Lysia answered. "What would it do to him to see me naked? He's not a man in his body, poor fellow, but does he think a man's thoughts even if they do him no good?"

"I don't know," Maniakes admitted. "I wouldn't have the nerve to ask, either. I suspect you're right, though. That sort of consideration couldn't hurt, anyhow." He clicked his tongue between his teeth. If you did have a man's urges all those years, and were utterly unable to do anything about them—How could you go on living? He thought it would have driven him mad. For Kameas' sake, he hoped the eunuch was as sexless as his voice.

When he did summon Kameas, the vestiarios went through the robes in the closet with a critical eye. At last, he said, "Does the leek-green wool suit your Majesty this morning?"

"Yes, that should do." Maniakes felt of it. "Good thick cloth. This one would keep me warm in a blizzard."

He threw off his sleeping robe and was about to let Kameas vest him in the formal one for daily wear when he felt a warmth that had nothing to do with thick, soft wool. His hand went to the amulet Bagdasares had given him back in Opsikion, when he was still trying to overthrow Genesios. The gold-and-hematite charm was almost hot enough to burn his chest, almost hot enough to burn his palm and fingers as they closed on it.

For a moment, he simply stood there in surprise. Then he remembered the wizard's warning: if the amulet grew hot, that meant he was under magical attack. He also remembered Bagdasares warning him that it could not long withstand such an attack.

Clad only in drawers and the amulet, he ran out of the imperial bedchamber and down the halls of the residence. Behind him, Lysia and Kameas both cried out in surprise. He didn't take the time to answer them—at every step, the amulet felt hotter.

He pounded on the door to Bagdasares' room, then tried the latch. Bagdasares hadn't barred the door. He burst in. The wizard was sitting up in bed, looking bleary and astonished. Beside him, with the same mix of expressions, was one of Lysia's serving women. Neither of them seemed to wear even as much as the Avtokrator did.

"Magic!" Maniakes said, clutching the amulet.

Intelligence lit in Bagdasares' fleshy features. He bounded out of bed, making the sun-sign as he did so. He *was* nude. By the way she squeaked and clutched the bedclothes to herself, so was the maidservant.

Maniakes felt as if something was squeezing him, inside his skin. However much good the amulet was doing, it wasn't altogether keeping the hostile spell from having its way with him. He yawned, as if trying to clear his head while he had a cold.

That did nothing to relieve the oppressive sensation slowly building inside him.

Bagdasares kept his case of sorcerous supplies by his bedside. Reaching into it, he pulled out a ball of twine and a knife whose white bone handle had a golden sunburst set into it. He used the knife to cut off a good length of twine, then began tying the ends together in an elaborate knot.

"Whatever you're doing there, please hurry," Maniakes said. He felt something wet on his upper lip. Reaching up to touch it, he found his nose was bleeding. Worse was that he thought a nosebleed the least of what the magic would do to him when it fully defeated the power of the amulet.

"Your Majesty, this must be done *right*," Bagdasares answered. "If I make a mistake, I might as well not have done it at all." Easy for him to say—his head wasn't being turned to pulp from the inside out. Maniakes stood still and hoped he wouldn't die before Bagdasares got through doing things right.

The mage finished the knot at last. When Maniakes looked at it, his eyes didn't want to follow its convolutions. Bagdasares grunted in absentminded satisfaction and began to chant in the Vaspurakaner language, running his hands along the circle of twine as he did so.

It wasn't just pressure inside Maniakes' head now—it was pain. He tasted blood; it dropped onto the floor of Bagdasares' room. By the expression on the maidservant's face, he wasn't a pretty sight. And if Bagdasares didn't hurry up, he was going to find out that being a slow wizard was one way of being a bad one.

Bagdasares cried out to Phos and to Vaspur the Firstborn, then passed the circle of twine over Maniakes' head and slowly down to his feet. It began to glow, much as had the lines of power from his protective spell back in Opsikion. The wizard invoked the good god and the eponymous ancestor of his people once more when the circle of twine touched the ground. He was careful to make sure it surrounded the blood Maniakes had lost.

What color was the enchanted cord? Gold? Blue? Orange? Purple? Red? It flickered back and forth among them faster than Maniakes' eyes could follow. After a moment, he didn't care. The heat from the amulet began to fade against the skin of his chest, and his head no longer felt as if the walls of his skull were going to squeeze together, crushing everything between them.

"Better," Maniakes whispered. Still in her nightdress, Lysia appeared in the doorway, her eyes wide and frightened. Kameas was right behind her. Maybe Bagdasares' magic hadn't been so slow after all, if they were just now getting here. It certainly had seemed slow.

With his head no longer feeling as if it were about to cave in on itself, he was able to pay more attention to the shifting colors of the twine. They changed ever more slowly. Red ... gold ... blue ... and all at once, the twine was just twine again. "What does that mean?" Lysia asked, before Maniakes could.

"It means the assault against his Majesty is over," Bagdasares answered. "He may leave the circle now, if he so desires." Maniakes had wondered how long he would have to stay in there. Even so, he hesitated before stepping out beyond the confines of the cord. If by any chance Bagdasares was wrong—

Maniakes didn't let himself think about that. He stepped over the cord. If he had felt in the least peculiar, he would have jumped back into the circle. Nothing untoward happened. He glanced over at Kameas. "I'm glad I hadn't put on that leek-green robe, esteemed sir," he said. "I would have bled all over it, and that's very fine wool."

"To the ice with the wool," Kameas said, unwontedly emphatic. "I am glad your Majesty is safe."

"Safe?" Maniakes said. "An Avtokrator isn't safe from the day he dons the red boots to the one when he gets shoved into a niche under the temple dedicated to the holy Phravitas. Nobody's trying to kill me right now, though. A few minutes ago—" He shivered as he realized what a narrow escape he had had.

Lysia seemed to have understood that all along. Turning to Bagdasares, she said, "Can you find out who did this, sorcerous sir? No. Let me ask it another way: can you find out who was behind the attempt? If the mage escapes, that's one thing. But if whoever paid him to try to slay the Avtokrator stays free, he will surely try again."

Bagdasares' frown brought his heavy eyebrows together. "Finding out who did the deed or planned it will not be easy, not in the abstract. I think I could determine, on a yes-or-no basis, whether any particular individual was involved in the attack."

"That should do the job," Maniakes said. "I can think of most of the people who might want to be rid of me, I expect. What would you need from them for your sorcery? Whatever it is, I'll arrange it, I promise you that."

"I shouldn't require much, your Majesty," Bagdasares answered. "Something that belongs to one of the individuals you suspect would suffice. A sample of his writing, for instance, would be excellent."

"I'll have trouble taking care of that for Abivard, I fear—maybe I promised too readily." Maniakes paused. "Or maybe not. Would a fragment of the wax he used to seal a letter he dictated do the job?"

"It should, your Majesty. A man's seal is almost as much uniquely his own as his script." Bagdasares ran a hand through his tousled hair. "And whom else shall I examine?"

Lysia and Kameas both flicked a glance toward the serving maid who shared the wizard's bed. Maniakes didn't need that hint. He had thought of her, too. But, while he did aim to thwart gossip or warnings, he didn't want to hurt her feelings. He said, "Let's not think of that while we're all so disheveled." Kameas wasn't disheveled, but then Kameas, as best Maniakes could tell, was never disheveled. He finished, "After breakfast is time enough."

After breakfast, the four of them gathered in a small reception chamber and considered who was liable to want Maniakes off the throne. Kourikos' name quickly came up. So did that of Phevronia, his wife. "She is liable to resent your marriage to me even more than her husband does," Lysia said quietly.

"I might not have thought of that for myself," Maniakes said. "Thank you."

"I have good reasons—many good reasons—to want you on the throne for a very long time," Lysia answered.

"Speaking of reasons, Agathios has—or thinks he has—reasons to want you deposed, your Majesty," Bagdasares said.

"So he does," Maniakes agreed. "Well, the most holy ecumenical patriarch is prolix with his pen. We'll have no trouble getting a writing sample from him."

"The eminent Tzikas," Kameas said.

"We'll check him," Maniakes said, nodding. "I'd be surprised if he proves to have anything to do with this, though. He may want the throne, but I think he'd like to see it drop into his lap."

"He is not aboveboard in what he does," Kameas insisted. "Such men earn close scrutiny, and deserve it." Eunuchs had a reputation for deviousness. Maybe they got suspicious when they sensed it in others.

"The drungarios," Bagdasares said. "Thrax."

Maniakes had all he could do to keep from bursting out laughing. If ever there was a man who wasn't devious, Thrax was the one. But he nodded again even so. Straightforward men got ambitious, too.

"The eminent Triphylles will have kin who may resent his passing in a foreign land," Kameas said. Maniakes hardly knew Triphylles' kin, but that was a possibility.

"Genesios' widow, too," he observed thoughtfully. "She may be mured up in a convent, but nothing is ever sealed as tight as you wish it was. Messages can go in, messages can come out."

After that, a silence fell. "Have we no more candidates?" Bagdasares asked. "If not, let us be about the business of obtaining samples of these persons' writings or other articles closely associated with them."

"One more person comes to mind," Maniakes said, and then paused. He glanced over to Lysia. "Your brother would name the name if we failed to, and he would be right. Come to that, so would my father, I think."

"Parsmanios, do you mean?" she asked, naming Maniakes' brother to keep him from having to do it.

He sighed. "Aye. After we quarreled, I saw him—not so long ago—deep in conversation with someone who I think was Kourikos, though I would not take oath to that on Phos' holy scriptures. Bagdasares, we'll need to be extra careful in getting a sample from him, and you'll need to be discreet in and after your test of that sample. If he learns I suspected him, he may become willing to conspire against me even if he wasn't before."

"Your Majesty, a mage who gossips is soon a mage without clients," Bagdasares answered. "As you command, though, I shall exercise particular care here. That same care should be applied, as you say, in obtaining writings from him."

"We should have in the archives orders he wrote for the vanguard as we advanced toward Amorion," Maniakes said. "We can get some of those without his being any the wiser, I should think."

"That would be excellent, your Majesty," Bagdasares said with a nod. "As soon as you convey to me the necessary documents, I shall begin examining them to see if their owners were involved in this wicked effort against you."

"I'm sure I have here at the residence parchments written by Kourikos and Agathios," Maniakes said. "You can start on those right away. I also have the letters from Abivard here, so you'll be able to do whatever you aim to do with the bits of wax from his seal."

Kameas said, "It might be instructive to go out and ask the guards whether anyone came wandering by a little while ago, inquiring after your Majesty's well-being. You or I would not be so foolish, but few people find themselves at a disadvantage by underestimating the stupidity even of seemingly clever people."

No one who had held the imperial throne for a while would have presumed to disagree with that. Hoping the case would unravel like the sleeve of a cheap robe when the first thread pulled lose, Maniakes walked out to the entrance. No one, though, had come round to see if he was still intact. He sighed. Since the day he had donned the red boots, nothing had been easy. He didn't suppose he ought to expect anything different now.

When he turned back to deliver the negative news, he found his father coming up the hall toward him. "Are you all right, son?" the elder Maniakes asked. "The servants are telling all sorts of ghastly tales."

"I shouldn't be surprised, but yes, I'm fine." Maniakes explained what had happened.

His father's face darkened with anger. Sketching Phos' sun-sign above his left breast, he growled. "To the ice with whoever would try such a thing. Worse than hiring an assassin, if you ask me: a mage doesn't have to get close to try to slay you. Who's on your list?"

Maniakes named names. His father nodded at each one in turn. Then the Avtokrator named Parsmanios. The elder Maniakes' eyes closed in pain for a moment. At last, with a sign, he nodded again. "Aye, you'll have to look into that, won't you? He was away from us for a long time, and he hasn't been happy with his circumstances since he came to Videssos the city. But by the good god, how I hope you're wrong."

"So do I," Maniakes answered. "As you say, there's not been a lot of love lost between us, but he is my brother."

"If you don't remember that, you're a long step closer to the ice right there," the elder Maniakes said. "Bagdasares is finding out what you need to know, is he? How soon will he have any idea of what's toward?"

"Where we have specimens, he's already started work," Maniakes answered. "For some of the people who might have done it, we'll either have to pull samples out of the archives or else get them to give us new ones. We should have something from Parsmanios in the files."

The elder Maniakes sighed once more. "You have to do it, but this is a filthy business. I wonder if we wouldn't have been better off staying on Kalavria in spite of all the tears and speeches the nobles gave."

"I've thought the same thing," the Avtokrator said. Now he sighed in turn. "Going back wouldn't be easy, not what with everything that's happened since. But heading for a place where no one's plotting against you has its temptations."

"If we did go back, someone might start plotting against you," his father said. He named no names, but Rotrude sprang into the Avtokrator's mind. She hadn't married since he had left, she would be jealous of Lysia, and she would want to advance Atalarikhos' fortunes. The Haloga style in such matters was liable to include good old straightforward murder. Maniakes felt like jumping into the sea. Only the fish would bother him there.

Kameas stood in the doorway, waiting to be noticed. "Yes, esteemed sir?" Maniakes asked.

"The excellent Bagdasares has tested writings from the most holy Agathios and the fragments of Abivard's seal, your Majesty," the vestiarios replied. "He reports that neither man was involved in the attack on you. He is about to evaluate writings from the eminent Kourikos, and wonders if you might be interested in observing the process, as you expressed the belief that he may well be one of the guilty parties."

"Yes, I'll come," Maniakes said, glad not to have to gauge the odds of Rotrude's turning against him. "What about you, Father?"

"Thank you; I'll stay here," the elder Maniakes said. "What wizards do can be useful. How they do it never much interested me, because I have no hope of doing it myself."

The Avtokrator knew he would never make a wizard, either, but found what they did intriguing even so. When he walked into the chamber where Bagdasares was working, the mage showed him a piece of parchment with crabbed notations complaining about a lack of funds. "This is indeed written in the hand of the eminent Kourikos?" Bagdasares asked. Maniakes nodded.

Whistling softly between his teeth, Bagdasares set the parchment on a table. He poured wine from one jar and vinegar from another together into a cup. "They symbolize what is and what shall be," he said, "and this chunk of hematite—" He held it up. "—is by the law of similarity attuned to the piece of the same mineral in the amulet that protected you and allowed you to reach me. Now—"

He dipped a glass rod into the cup that held the mixed wine and vinegar, then dabbed several drops of the mixture onto the parchment. The letters and numbers there smeared as they got wet. Chanting, Bagdasares touched the wet places with the lump of hematite. "If the eminent Kourikos was involved with the magic, your Majesty, we should see those areas begin to glow as my sorcery exposes the connection."

Maniakes waited. Nothing happened. After a couple of minutes, he asked, "Has it done everything it's going to do?"

"Er—yes, your Majesty," Bagdasares answered. "It would appear that the eminent Kourikos was in fact not one of those who so wickedly plotted against you."

Pointing out to an Avtokrator that he was wrong could be a risky business. Maniakes, however, greeted the wizard's words with a shrug, and Bagdasares relaxed. Maniakes was just as well pleased not to have the logothete of the treasury under suspicion, for his innocence made Parsmanios' more likely. Maniakes wished he could have been positive it was Kourikos he had seen with his brother, but he couldn't, and no help for it.

Doing his best to make life difficult, Bagdasares said, "We do, of course, still have to test the script of the logothete's wife."

"I'm sure you'll attend to that in due course," Maniakes said. He supposed Kourikos could have been a go-between for Phevronia and Parsmanios without directly doing business with the mage who had tried to kill him, but it didn't strike him as probable. He rubbed his chin. "I don't think I have a handwriting specimen from the eminent Tzikas here. I'll send him a note and get one back in return."

As if on cue, Kameas stuck his head into Bagdasares' makeshift thaumaturgical laboratory and said, "Your Majesty, a clerk has fetched writings hither from the government offices." The

vestiarios had discretion and to spare; he never mentioned Parsmanios' name.

"Let him come in, eminent sir," Maniakes said. The clerk, a
weedy little man in a robe of wool homespun, prostrated himself
and then gave the Avtokrator a sheet of parchment tied into a
cylinder with a ribbon. When Maniakes slid off the ribbon, he
saw it was indeed one of Parsmanios' orders of the day for the
vanguard of an army now long defeated.

The clerk disappeared, presumably to return to the hordes of
pigeonholes where such documents slept against the unlikely
chance that they, like this one, might eventually need to be
revived. Maniakes forgot about him the moment he was gone.
His attention swung back to Bagdasares, who was preparing the
document for the same treatment he had given the one written
by Kourikos.

The mage sprinkled the marching order with his mix of wine
and vinegar. He began his chant once more and touched the piece
of hematite to the parchment. Immediately it was suffused in a
soft nimbus of blue-violet light. "The test has found an affirma-
tive, your Majesty," Bagdasares said. Like Kameas, he did not
speak Parsmanios' name.

A crushing weight of sorrow descended on Maniakes. "Are
you certain, sorcerous sir?" he asked. "No doubt or possible
misinterpretation?"

"No, your Majesty," Bagdasares said sadly but without hesitation. "I regret being the agent who—"

"It's not your fault," Maniakes said. "It's my brother's fault." He
walked down the hall to the room where he had left his father.
He looked in. "Parsmanios," he said. The elder Maniakes grimaced
but nodded. The Avtokrator walked out to the guards who stood
on the steps. He divided them in two and told one group, "Go
find Parsmanios. He'll probably be in one of the wings of the
Grand Courtroom at this time of day. Whatever he's doing, fetch
him here at once."

The guards asked no questions, but hurried off to do his bidding. When he went back into the imperial residence, he found
his father standing near the entrance. "What will you do with
him? To him, I should say?" the elder Maniakes asked.

"Hear him out," Maniakes answered wearily. "Then have him
tonsured and send him into exile in the monastery at Prista, up

on the northern shore of the Videssian Sea. It's either that or take his head."

"I know." The elder Maniakes clapped the younger on the back. "It's a good choice." He scowled. "No. It's the best choice you could make. I never dreamed I'd have to thank you for sparing your brother's life, but I do."

Maniakes did not feel magnanimous. He felt empty, betrayed. A messenger arrived with Tzikas' reply to his note. He didn't even look at it, but sent the fellow straight on to Bagdasares. Then he went out and stared east through the cherry trees toward the Grand Courtroom.

Before long, the guards headed back to the residence, Parsmanios in their midst. He was complaining volubly: "This is an outrage, I tell you! When the Avtokrator hears of how you high-handedly jerked me out of that meeting with the eminent Themistios, logothete of petitions, and how he stared as you did so, his Majesty will—"

"Commend his men for carrying out his orders," Maniakes interrupted. He spoke to the guards: "Make sure he has no weapons." Despite Parsmanios' protests, the soldiers removed his belt knife and, after some searching, a slim holdout dagger he wore in his left boot. That done, they escorted him to the chamber to which his father had returned.

"Why, son?" the elder Maniakes asked, beating the Avtokrator to the question.

"Why what?" Parsmanios began. Then he looked from his father to his brother and saw that wouldn't get him anywhere. From assumed innocence sprang fury. "Why do you think, the ice take you? You shut me away from everything you did, you gave Rhegorios the spot that should have been mine—"

"I didn't know you were alive when Rhegorios got the Sevastos' spot," Maniakes said. "How many times must I tell you?"

Parsmanios went on as if he hadn't spoken. "And as if that wasn't enough, you started swiving his sister. Why didn't you just take him to bed? Incest with one wouldn't be any worse than incest with the other."

"Son, you would be wiser to have a care in what you say," the elder Maniakes said. "You would have been wiser to have a care in what you did, too."

"Better you should tell that to *him*," Parsmanios said, pointing to his brother. "But no, you don't care what he does. You never cared what he did. He was your eldest, so it had to be right."

"My backside says you're a liar," Maniakes said, "not that you haven't shown that already."

"Say whatever you want," Parsmanios said. "It doesn't matter now. I failed, and you'll take my head, and that will be the end of it."

"I had in mind taking your hair, not your head," Maniakes said, "but listening to the swill you spew tempts me to give you what most traitors get." He shook his head. "Exile to Prista will do." He paused, wondering how best to put his next question. At last, he said, "Shall we send anyone into exile with you?"

Parsmanios stood mute. Maniakes thought of turning him over to the torturers to see what they could wring out of him, but couldn't make himself do it. He called the guards, saying "My brother is a proved traitor. I want him kept in a constantly guarded chamber here in the residence for the time being. Later, until he is sent off into exile, we'll move him to a cell under the government office building." Some of the guardsmen looked astonished, but they saluted to show they understood before leading Parsmanios away.

Maniakes looked up toward the ceiling. "Every time I think it can't possibly get any worse, can't possibly get any harder, it does."

"You did that as well as you could, son," the elder Maniakes told him. "Better than I would have managed it, and that's a fact."

"I never should have had to do it in the first place." Maniakes sat down and rested his chin on the knuckles of one hand. "My idiot brother—" He would have gone on, but Kameas paused in the doorway, waiting to be acknowledged. "Phos, what now?" Maniakes cried.

The vestiarios flinched, then gathered himself. "Your Majesty, the mage Alvinos requests your presence." He used Bagdasares' Videssian-sounding name more often than almost anyone else, perhaps because it fit in with his notions of what was proper. Vaspurakaners had played a major role in Videssian life for centuries, but Videssians seldom admitted or even noticed how large it was.

Bagdasares bowed when Maniakes came into the chamber where he labored. "I have here something I had not thought possible, your Majesty: an ambiguous result on my test of this writing from Tzikas. I do not know whether he was involved in the sorcerous attempt on your life or he was not." He wiped his forehead with the back of his hand. "It is a puzzlement."

"Show me what you mean by an ambiguous result," Maniakes said.

"Certainly." Bagdasares walked over to the parchment lying on the table. "As the ritual required, I sprinkled it with my mixture of wine and vinegar, then added the spiritual element of the spell and used the hematite. You see for yourself."

See Maniakes did. Most of the drops of the mixture had fallen on the writing, where they had had no effect save to blur it. But one or two had splashed down by the edge of the parchment. After Bagdasares touched his hematite to them, they had begun to glow like the entire document Parsmanios had written.

"It's almost as if Tzikas was in contact with the parchment without having written what purports to be his reply," Bagdasares said. "And yet the message is—or rather was, before it was smeared—addressed directly from him to you."

Suspicion flared in Maniakes. Tzikas was subtle, a master of defense. "I wonder if he took alarm at getting a message from me just after he tried to do me in and had someone else write a reply." He glanced at Bagdasares. "Will my looking at it or touching it do any harm?"

"No, your Majesty," the mage answered.

The Avtokrator stepped up to the makeshift worktable. As Bagdasares had said, the mixture of wine and vinegar had smeared much of the writing on the parchment. (It had also left the scraped sheepskin tangy to the nose.) Maniakes bent to examine those few words he could still make out.

"This isn't Tzikas' hand," he said after a moment. "I've seen his script often enough to recognize it, by the good god. I don't know who wrote this, but he didn't. If he took the note afterward, though—"

"That would account for the positive reaction at the edges of the sheet, where he would have touched it before returning it to your messenger," Bagdasares finished for him. "If that fellow didn't see with his own eyes Tzikas doing the writing, I think we can be confident enough in our evaluation to summon the eminent general to give an accounting of himself."

"We'll find out," Maniakes said. He called Kameas, who arranged to have the messenger return to the imperial residence.

"No, your Majesty, I didn't see him write it," the man said. "He stepped inside for a bit, then came back out. Nobody told me I was supposed to watch him do the writing." He looked anxious.

"It's all right," Maniakes said. "No blame for you." He went out to the guards. "I now require the immediate presence of the eminent Tzikas."

As they had when he had ordered them to fetch Parsmanios, they came to stiff attention. "Busy day around here," one of them observed as they went off to do his bidding. Maniakes let that go with a nod. Bringing in Parsmanios had been easy. If Tzikas didn't feel like coming, he had men loyal to him who might fight. Maniakes scowled and shook his head at the idea of a new round of civil war breaking out in Videssos the city.

He waited. The guardsmen were gone a long time. When they came back, they did not have Tzikas with them. Apprehension on his face, their leader said, "Your Majesty, we've searched everywhere the eminent Tzikas is likely to be, and we spoke with several men who know him. No one has seen him since shortly after he gave your messenger some sort of note."

"I don't fancy the sound of that," Maniakes said. "Go to the guard barracks, rout out the off-duty men, and make a proper search, crying his name through the streets and especially searching all the harbor districts."

"Aye, your Majesty," the guard captain said. "The harbor districts, eh? You fear he may try to flee to the Makuraners in Across?"

"No," Maniakes answered. "I fear he's already done it."

He went back into the imperial residence to report that dispiriting news to his father. The elder Maniakes made a sour face. "These things happen," he said. "He's no fool. The note must have put his wind up, and as soon as he gave it to you, he lit out for parts unknown—or parts known too well. What will you do now?"

"See how much Parsmanios will admit, then get him tonsured and send him into exile," the Avtokrator said. He again thought of giving his brother over to the torturers and again couldn't make himself do it. He doubted whether Parsmanios would have had the same compunctions about him.

Parsmanios scowled at him when he walked into the chamber

where his brother was being held under guard. "Come to gloat, have you?" the younger man said bitterly.

"No, just to let you know your comrade Tzikas has run off to the Makuraners," Maniakes answered. "I wonder if he'll get a better bargain from them than he would have from me. I wouldn't have sent him to the chopper, not when I was leaving you alive: no justice to that. You could have gone off to Prista together."

"How wonderful," Parsmanios said. "How generous."

Maniakes wondered if his brother was trying to provoke him to take his head instead of exiling him. He ignored that, asking "So he was your comrade?"

"If you already know, why bother asking?" Parsmanios replied.

"Who was the wizard?" Maniakes persisted. "Who hired him?"

"I don't know his name," Parsmanios answered. "Bring on the needles and the red-hot pincers if you like, but I never heard it. Tzikas and I met him in an old house not far from the Forum of the Ox. I don't think the house was his. I think he just—infested it. Tzikas got him. He'd known him, I guess, but said having me there would help make the magic stronger. Maybe it did, but it still wasn't strong enough, worse luck for me."

Even if true, none of that was very informative. No doubt that was deliberate on Parsmanios' part. Keeping his voice as light as he could, Maniakes asked, "What did the wizard look like?"

His brother said, "A man. Maybe your age, maybe a little older. Not fat, not thin. Kind of a long nose. He spoke like someone with an education, but a mage would, wouldn't he?"

"I suppose so," Maniakes answered absently. He knew considerable relief that the sorcerer Tzikas had found was not the horrible old man Genesios had employed. That old man had almost slain him across half the breadth of the Empire. Maniakes would have been happiest if he stayed lost forever. Against any ordinary mage, Bagdasares and the wizards of the Sorcerers' Collegium were protection aplenty.

Parsmanios said, "If you ever pluck my wife and son out of the provinces, don't blame them for anything I've done."

"You're in no position to ask favors, brother of mine," Maniakes said. Parsmanios stared at him, stared through him. He softened his words a little: "I wouldn't do anything to them because of you. As you say, they had nothing to do with your stupidity."

"I'm not the one who was stupid," Parsmanios answered—he had his own measure of the clan's stubbornness. "So many women all through the Empire would drop their drawers if you lifted a finger, and you had to go and wallow in filth instead. Even if I failed, Skotos waits for you."

Maniakes spat on the floor to avert the evil omen. "She's not my sister and she's not ten years old," he said in exasperation, but saw he might as well have been talking to the wall. He threw his hands in the air. "Fine, Parsmanios. Have the last word. Enjoy it all the way to Prista." He walked out of the chamber that confined his brother, and did not look back.

A blizzard blew in the next day. Maniakes had planned to send Parsmanios into exile on the instant, but realized that might well entail losing not only his brother, whom he would not have missed, but also a ship and its crew—the Videssian Sea was a bad risk in wintertime. He transferred Parsmanios to the prison under the government offices, with instructions to the gaoler to keep him apart from the other prisoners. When good weather arrived, Parsmanios would depart.

After the blizzard eased, a fellow with a message from Abivard came down to the shore at Across carrying a shield of truce. Upon his being conveyed to the palaces, Maniakes was less than delighted but also less than surprised to see him. The Avtokrator turned to Kameas, who had announced the messenger's arrival. "Would you care to place a small wager on the contents of that tube, esteemed sir?"

"Thank you, your Majesty, but no," the vestiarios replied. "I have a more pressing need for every goldpiece currently in my possession." He probably had a good many of them in his possession, too. Maniakes wondered how far confiscating his property would go toward making the Empire solvent. He shook his head, annoyed at himself. He wasn't that desperate—he hoped.

He popped the lid off the message tube, drew out the parchment inside, unrolled it, and began to read aloud: "Abivard general to Sharbaraz King of Kings, may his years be many and his realm increase, to Maniakes falsely styling himself Avtokrator of the Videssians: Greetings."

"He hasn't said '*falsely* styling himself Avtokrator' in a while," Kameas observed.

"So he hasn't," Maniakes said, and then, "Well, I insulted him and Sharbaraz in my last letter." He coughed. "I read on: 'Whereas the eminent general Tzikas, who in former days misguidedly gave allegiance to you, has now recognized his earlier errors, he bids me inform you that he acknowledges the sovereignty over the Empire of Videssos of Hosios Avtokrator son of Likinios Avtokrator, and rejects your regime as the vile, vain, illegitimate, and void usurpation it is universally known to be, and bids all Videssians to do likewise, seeing that only in this way shall peace be restored to your land.'"

Kameas pursed his lips as he considered the message. At last, he delivered his verdict: "The content, your Majesty, can hardly be reckoned surprising. As for the style, I must say I confess to a certain admiration; not everyone could have packed so much information into a single, grammatically proper, sentence."

"If I want literary criticism, esteemed sir, rest assured I shall ask for it," Maniakes said.

"Of course, your Majesty," the vestiarios said. "Are you then seeking advice as to your proper conduct in response?"

"Oh, no, not this time." Maniakes turned to the messenger, who looked miserably cold in a Makuraner caftan. "You speak Videssian?" When the fellow nodded, the Avtokrator went on, "I have no written reply for you. But tell Abivard he's welcome to keep Tzikas or kill him, however he pleases, but if he does decide to keep him, he'd better not turn his back. Have you got that?"

"Yes, your Majesty," the messenger answered, his accent strong but understandable. He repeated Maniakes' words back to him.

Maniakes spoke to Kameas: "Have him taken west over the Cattle Crossing. If Abivard doesn't worry about Tzikas more now than while he was holed up in Amorion, he's a fool." That would get back to Abivard, too. Maniakes couldn't do anything about his rebellious general's flight, not now. With a little luck, though, he could keep Abivard from taking full advantage of Tzikas. And if Abivard chose to ignore his warnings, which were, of course, hardly disinterested, the Makuraner general stood an excellent chance of falling victim to the refugee about whose presence he now boasted.

Kameas escorted the messenger out of Maniakes' presence. When he came back, he found the Avtokrator sitting with his elbows on his knees, his face buried in his hands. "Are you all right, your Majesty?" the vestiarios asked anxiously.

"To the ice with me if I know," Maniakes answered, weary beyond anything sleep could cure. "Phos! I didn't think Tzikas had the nerve to betray me, and he went and did it anyhow. Who knows what will come crashing down on me—and down on Videssos—next?"

"Your Majesty, that is as the author of our fate, the lord with the great and good mind, shall decree," Kameas said. "Whatever it may be, I am sure you will meet it with your customary resourcefulness."

"Resourcefulness is all very well, but without resources even resourcefulness struggles in vain," Maniakes said. "And Genesios, curse him, was right to ask if I'd do any better than he at holding back the Empire's foes. So far, the answer looks to be no."

"You've done far better at everything else, though," Kameas said, "Videssians no longer war with Videssians and, the present unpleasantness aside, we've not had a single pretender rise against you. The Empire stands united behind you, waiting for our luck to turn."

"Except for the people—my brother, for instance—who stand behind me so I won't see the knife till it goes into my back, and the ones who think I'm an incestuous sinner who ought to be cast into the outer darkness of excommunication and anathema."

Kameas bowed. "As your Majesty appears more inclined today to contemplate darkness than light, I shall make no further effort to inject with any undue optimism." He glided away.

Maniakes stared after him, then started to laugh. The vestiarios had a knack for puncturing his pretensions. This time, he had managed to pack a warning in with his jibe. A man who contemplated darkness rather than light was liable to end up contemplating Skotos rather than Phos. As he had when questioning Parsmanios, Maniakes spat on the floor in rejection of the evil god.

Someone tapped on the door: Lysia. "I have news, I think," she said. Maniakes raised an eyebrow, waiting for her to go on. She did, a little hesitantly: "I—I think I'm with child. I would have waited longer to say anything, because it's early to be quite sure, but—" Her words poured out in a rush. "—you could use good news today."

"Oh, by Phos, that is the truth!" Maniakes caught her in his arms. "May it be so." Likarios remained his heir, but another baby, especially one that was his and Lysia's, would be welcome. He resolved, as he had more than once before, to pay more attention to the children he had already fathered.

He studied Lysia with some concern. Niphone had been thin and frail, while his cousin whom he had wed was almost stocky and in full, vigorous health. Nevertheless . . .

"It will be all right," she said, as if plucking the alarm from his mind. "It will be fine."

"Of course it will," he said, knowing it was not *of course.* "Even so, you'll see Zoïle as soon as may be; no point waiting." Lysia might have started to say something. Whatever it was, she thought better of it and contented herself with a nod.

✦ XIII

Spring came. For Maniakes, it was not only a season of new leaf and new life. As soon as he was reasonably confident no storm would send a ship to the bottom, he took Parsmanios from the prison under the government offices and sent him off to exile in Prista, where watching the Khamorth travel back and forth with their flocks over the Pardrayan steppe was the most exciting sport the locals had.

Maniakes, on the other hand, watched Lysia. She was indeed pregnant, and proved it by vomiting once every morning, whereupon she would be fine ... till the next day. Any little thing could touch off the fit. One day, Kameas proudly fetched in a pair of poached eggs. Lysia started to eat them, but bolted for the basin before she took a bite.

"They were looking at me," she said darkly, after rinsing her mouth out with wine. Later, she broke her fast on plain bread.

Dromons continually patrolled the Cattle Crossing. Maniakes watched Abivard as well as Lysia. This spring, the Makuraner general gave no immediate sign of pulling back from Across. Maniakes worried over that, and pondered how to cut Abivard's long supply lines through the westlands to get him to withdraw.

But, when the blow fell, Abivard did not strike it. Etzilios did. A ship brought the unwelcome news to Videssos the city. "The Kubratoi came past Varna and they're heading south," the captain of the merchantman, a stocky, sunburned fellow named Spiridion, told Maniakes after rising from a clumsy proskynesis.

"Oh, a pestilence!" the Avtokrator burst out. He pointed a finger at Spiridion. "Have they come down in their *monoxyla* again? If they have, our war galleys will make them sorry."

But the ship captain shook his head. "No, your Majesty, this isn't like that last raid. I heard about that. But the beggars are on horseback this time, and looking to steal what's not spiked down and to burn what is."

"When I beat Etzilios, I'll pack his head in salt and send it round to every city in the Empire, so people can see I've done it," Maniakes growled, down deep in his throat. All at once, thinking of how fine he would feel to do that to the Kubrati khagan, he understood what must have gone through Genesios' vicious mind after disposing of an enemy—or of someone he imagined to be an enemy, at any rate. The comparison was sobering.

Spiridion seemed oblivious to his distress. "We'd be well rid of that khagan, yes we would. But you've got all these soldiers sitting around eating like there's no tomorrow and pinching the tavern girls. Isn't it time you got some use from 'em? Don't mean to speak too bold, but—"

"Oh, yes, we'll fight them," Maniakes said. "But if they're already down past Varna, we'll have a busy time pushing them back where they belong."

Where they really belonged was north of the Astris, not on any territory that had ever belonged to Videssos. Likinios had tried pushing them back onto the eastern edge of the steppe, and what had it got him? Mutiny and death, nothing better. And now the Kubratoi, like wolves that scented meat, were sharp-nosing their way down toward the suburbs of Videssos the city.

Maniakes rewarded Spiridion with gold he could not afford to spend and sent him on his way. That done, he knew he ought to have ordered a force out to meet Etzilios' raiders, but hadn't the will to do it on the instant. After Parsmanios and Tzikas had conspired against him, he had asked the lord with the great and good mind what could possibly go wrong next. By now, he told himself bitterly, he should have known better than to send forth such questions. All too often, they had answers.

A couple of minutes after Spiridion left, Lysia came into the chamber where Maniakes sat shrouded in gloom. "The servants say—" she began hesitantly.

He might have known that the servants *would* say. Trying to keep anything secret in the imperial residence was like trying to carry water in a sieve. Everything leaked. "It's true," he answered. "The Kubratoi are riding again. The good god only knows how we'll be able to stop them, too."

"Send out the troops," Lysia said, as if he had complained about a hole in his boot and she had suggested he take it to a cobbler.

"Oh, I will," he said with a long sigh. "And then I'll have the delight of seeing them flee back here to the city with their tails between their legs. I've seen that before, too many times." He sighed again. "I've seen everything before, too many times. It wouldn't take more than a couple of coppers to get me to sail off for Kalavria and never come back."

He had said that before when things looked bleak. Now, all at once, the idea caught fire within him. He could see the mansion up above Kastavala, could hear the gulls squealing as they whirled overhead—oh, gulls squealed above Videssos the city, too, but somehow in a much less pleasant tone of voice—could remember riding to the eastern edge of the island and looking out at the Sailors' Sea going on forever.

The idea of the sea's going on forever had a strong appeal for him now. If there was no land on the far side of the Sailor's Sea—for no one who had ever sailed across it had found any, no one, that is, who had ever come back—he would actually have found one direction from which enemies could not come at him. From his present perch in embattled Videssos the city, the concept struck him as miraculous.

He took Lysia's hands in his. "By the good god, let's go back to Kastavala. Things here will sort themselves out one way or another, and right now I don't much care which. All I want to do is get free of this place."

"Do you really think it's the best thing you could do?" Lysia said. "We've talked of this before, and—"

"I don't care what I said before," Maniakes broke in. "The more I think of leaving Videssos the city now, the better I like it. The fleet will hold Abivard away from the city come what may, and I can command it as well from Kastavala as I can right here where I stand now."

"What will your father say?" Lysia asked.

"He'll say 'Yes, your Majesty,'" Maniakes answered. His father would probably say several other things, too, most of them pungent.

He would certainly have something to say about Rotrude. *I'll have to deal with her,* Maniakes thought. He was surprised Lysia hadn't mentioned her, and mentally thanked her for her restraint. Aloud, he went on, "What's the point of being Avtokrator if you can't do what you think best?"

"Can you be Avtokrator if you don't hold Videssos the city?" Lysia said.

That had brought him up short the last time he had thought of removing to Kastavala. Now, though, he said, "Who says I wouldn't hold the city? An Avtokrator on campaign isn't here, but no one rebels against him because of that—well, not usually, anyhow. And the bureaucrats would stay right where they are." He laughed sardonically. "They don't think they need me to run the Empire, anyhow. They'll be glad for the chance to show they're right."

"Do you truly think this is best?" Lysia asked again.

"If you want to know the truth, dear, I just don't know," Maniakes said. "This much I'll tell you, though: I don't see how going to Kalavria could make things much worse than they are now. Do you?"

"Put that way, maybe not." Lysia made a wry face that, for once, had nothing to do with the uncertain stomach her pregnancy had given her. "It shows what a state we've come to, though, when we have to put things that way. It isn't your fault," she added hastily. "Genesios left the Empire with too many burdens and not enough of anything with which to lessen them."

"And I've made mistakes of my own," Maniakes said. "I trusted Etzilios—or didn't mistrust him enough, however you like. I tried to do too much too soon against the Makuraners. I've been hasty, that's what I've been. If I'm operating out of Kastavala, I won't be able to be hasty. News will get to me more slowly, and the orders I send will take their time moving, too. By all the signs, that would make things work better than they do now."

Lysia said, "Well, perhaps it will be all right." With that ringing endorsement, Maniakes got ready to announce his decision to the wider world.

Themistios, the logothete in charge of petitions to the Avtokrator, was a stout, placid fellow. Most of the time, his was a small bureaucratic domain, dealing with matters like disputed tax assessments and appeals such as the one the now probably late Bizoulinos had submitted. Now he presented Maniakes with an enormous leather sack full of sheets of parchment.

"Here's another load, your Majesty," he said. "They'll be coming into my offices by the dozens every hour, too, that they will."

"This is the third batch you've given me today, eminent sir," Maniakes said.

"So it is," Themistios agreed. "People are upset, your Majesty. That's something you need to know."

"I already had an inkling, thanks," Maniakes said dryly. What Themistios meant, at least in part, was that he was upset himself and making no effort to do anything about the flood of petitions begging Maniakes to stay in Videssos the city except passing them straight on to the Avtokrator.

Themistios coughed. "Forgive me for being so frank, your Majesty, but I fear civil unrest may erupt should you in fact implement your decision."

"Eminent sir, I have no intention of taking all my soldiers with me when I go," Maniakes answered. "If civil unrest does pop up, I think the garrison will be able to put it down again."

"Possibly so, your Majesty," the logothete said, "but then again, possibly not." He tapped the pile of petitions. "As is my duty, I have acquainted myself with these, and I tell you that a surprising number of them come from soldiers of the garrison. They feel your departure abandons them to the none too tender mercies of the men of Makuran."

"That's absurd," Maniakes said. "The boiler boys can no more get over the Cattle Crossing than they can fly."

"Your Majesty is a master of strategy," Themistios said. Maniakes looked sharply at him; given the number of defeats he had suffered, he suspected sarcasm. But the logothete seemed sincere. He went on, "Simple soldiers will not realize what is obvious to you. And, if their courage should fail them, what they fear may follow and become fact."

"I shall take that chance, eminent sir," Maniakes replied. "Thank you for presenting these petitions to me. My preparations for the return to Kastavala shall go forward nonetheless."

Themistios muttered something under his breath. Maniakes waited to see if he would say it out loud and force him to notice it. The logothete didn't. Shaking his head, he left the imperial residence.

The next day, Kourikos presented himself to the Avtokrator. After he had risen from his prostration and been granted leave to speak, he said, "Your Majesty, it has come to my attention that you are removing large sums of money in gold, silver, and precious stones from a treasury that, as you must be aware, is painfully low on all such riches."

"Yes, I am, eminent sir," Maniakes said. "If I'm going to center the administration at Kastavala, I'll need money to meet my ends."

"But, your Majesty, you'll leave too little for Videssos the city," Kourikos exclaimed in dismay.

"Why should I care about Videssos the city?" Maniakes demanded. The logothete of the treasury stared at him; that question had never entered Kourikos' mind. For him, Videssos the city was and always would be the center of the universe, as if Phos had so ordained in his holy scriptures. Maniakes went on, "What have I ever had here except grief and trouble?—from you not least, eminent sir. I shall be glad to see the last of the city, and of you. I tell you to your face, I thought the one who conspired with my brother was you, not Tzikas."

"N-not I, your Majesty," Kourikos stammered. He was suddenly seeing that having a family connection to the Avtokrator could bring danger as well as advantage. "I—I do not agree with what you have done, but I do not seek to harm you or plot against you. You are father to my grandchildren, after all."

"That's fair enough, eminent sir." Maniakes laughed ruefully. "It's better than I've had from almost anyone else, as a matter of fact."

Emboldened, Kourikos said, "Then you will abandon your unfortunate plan for taking yourself and so much of the Empire's wealth back to that provincial hinterland whence you came here?"

"Eh? No, I won't do anything of the sort, eminent sir," Maniakes said. "I've had more of Videssos the city than I want. Nothing anyone has told me has given me any reason to change my mind."

"It sounds to me, your Majesty, as if it would take a miracle vouchsafed by the lord with the great and good mind to accomplish that," Kourikos said.

"Yes, that might do it," Maniakes agreed. "I can't think of much less that would."

Kameas pursed his lips. "Your Majesty, this is the third time this past week that the most holy ecumenical patriarch Agathios has requested an audience with you. Do you not think you would be wise to confer with him? True, you are Phos' viceregent on earth, but he heads the holy hierarchy of the temples. His words are not to be despised."

"He won't sanction my marriage, and he wants to keep me from sailing off to Kalavria," Maniakes answered. "There. Now I've said what he'll have to say, and I've saved myself the time he'd take."

Kameas glowered at him. "There is a time for all things. This does not strike me as the time for uncouth levity."

Maniakes sighed. He had seen enough on the throne to know that, when the vestiarios was blunt enough to use a word like *uncouth*, he needed to be taken seriously. "Very well, esteemed sir, I'll see him. But he used to be a flexible man. If he's just going to repeat himself, he won't get far."

"I shall convey that warning to Skombros, his synkellos," Kameas answered. And Skombros, Maniakes had no doubt, would convey it to Agathios. The Avtokrator got the idea that Kameas and Skombros probably complemented one another well. Neither had much formal power; each had influence that made his formal insignificance irrelevant.

When Agathios came to the imperial residence a few days later, he did not wear the blue boots and pearl-encrusted cloth-of-gold vestments to which his rank entitled him. To take their place, he had on a black robe of mourning and left his feet bare. After he rose from his proskynesis, he cried, "Your Majesty, I beg of you, do not leave the imperial city, the queen of cities, a widow by withdrawing the light of your countenance from her!"

"That's very pretty, most holy sir, but you may bawl like a branded calf as much as your heart desires without convincing me I ought to stay," Maniakes said.

"Your Majesty!" Agathios gave him a hurt look. "I am utterly convinced that this move will prove disastrous not only for the city but also for the Empire. Never has an Avtokrator abandoned the capital in time of crisis. What necessity is there for such a move, when we shelter behind our impregnable walls, safe from any foe—"

"Any foe who has no siege engines," Maniakes interrupted. "If the Makuraners were on this side of the Cattle Crossing instead of the other one, we'd be fighting for our lives right now. About the only two peaceful stretches of the Empire I can think of are Prista on the one hand—which is not a place I want to go myself—and Kalavria on the other."

"Your Majesty, is this justice?" Agathios said. "You have borrowed from the temples large sums of gold for the sustenance and defense of the Empire, and now you seek to abandon Videssos' beating heart?" He sketched the sun-circle above his own heart. "What more concessions could we possibly offer you to persuade you to change your mind and return to the course dictated by prudence and reason?"

For a moment, Maniakes took that as nothing but more rhetoric of the kind the patriarch had already aimed at him. Then he wondered whether Agathios meant what he said. Only one way to find out: "I don't know, most holy sir. What do you offer?"

When he had first come into Videssos the city, he had watched Agathios go from thundering theologian to practical politician in the space of a couple of breaths. The shift had bemused him then and bemused him again now. Cautiously, the ecumenical patriarch said, "You have already taken so many of our treasures that I tremble to offer more, your Majesty, but, if our gold would make you remain in the city, I might reckon it well spent."

"I appreciate that," Maniakes said, on the whole sincerely. "It's not lack of gold that drives me out of Videssos the city, though."

"What then?" Agathios asked, spreading his hands. "Gold is the chief secular advantage I can confer upon you—"

They looked at each other. The patriarch started to raise an admonitory hand. Before he could, Maniakes said, "Not all advantages are secular, most holy sir. If they were, we'd have no temples."

"You swore to me when you took the throne that you would make no innovations in the faith," Agathios protested.

"I've never said a word about innovations," Maniakes answered. "A dispensation, though, is something else again."

"Your Majesty, we have been over this ground before," Agathios said. "I have explained to you why granting a dispensation for your conduct in regard to this marriage is impracticable."

"That's true, most holy sir, and I've explained to you why I'm leaving Videssos the city for Kalavria," Maniakes answered.

"But, your Majesty, the cases are not comparable," the ecumenical patriarch said. "I am in conformity with canon law and with long-standing custom, while you set established practice on its ear." Maniakes didn't say anything. Agathios coughed a couple of times. Hesitantly, he asked, "Are you telling me you might be willing to remain in Videssos the city and administer the Empire from here, following ancient usage, should you receive this dispensation?"

"I'm not suggesting anything." Maniakes stroked his chin. "It would give me ecclesiastical peace, though, wouldn't it? That's worth something. To the ice with me if I know whether it's worth staying here in Videssos the city, though. One more Midwinter's Day like the last couple I've had to endure and I'd be tempted to climb up to the top of the Milestone and jump off."

"I, too, have suffered the jibes of the falsely clever and the smilingly insolent on Midwinter's Day," Agathios said. "Perhaps you will forgive me for reminding you that, should your disagreement with the temples be resolved, one potential source of satire for the mime troupes would be eliminated, thus making Midwinter's Day shows less likely to distress you."

"Yes, that is possible," the Avtokrator admitted. "Since you've said no dispensation is possible, though, the discussion has little point—wouldn't you agree, most holy sir?"

Agathios drew himself up to his full if unimpressive height. "I have the authority to go outside normal forms and procedures if by so doing I can effect some greater good, as you know, your Majesty. Should I—and I speak hypothetically at the moment, you must understand—dispense you from the usual strictures pertaining to consanguinity, would you in turn swear a binding oath similar to the one you gave me at the outset of your reign, this one pledging never to abandon Videssos the city as the imperial capital?"

Maniakes thought, then shook his head. "Saying I'd never do something puts chains around me, chains I don't care to wear. I would swear never to abandon the city save as a last resort, but the definition of what constitutes a last resort would have to remain in my hands, no one else's."

Now the patriarch plucked at his bushy beard as he considered. "Let it be as you say," he replied in sudden decision. "You have proved yourself reliable, on the whole, in matters of your word. I do not think you will break it here."

"Most holy sir, we have a bargain." Maniakes stuck out his hand.

Agathios took it. His grip was hesitant, his palm cool. He sounded worried as he said, "Those of a rigorist cast of mind will judge me harshly for what I do here today, your Majesty, despite the benefits accruing to the Empire from my actions. The schism we have discussed on other occasions may well come to pass because of our agreement: The rigorists will maintain—will strongly maintain—I am yielding to secular pressure here."

"You will know more of ecclesiastical politics and the results of these schisms than I do, most holy sir," Maniakes replied, "but isn't it so that the side with secular support prevails in them more often than that without?"

"As a matter of fact, your Majesty, it is," Agathios said, brightening.

"You'll have that support, I assure you," Maniakes told him.

"Oh, splendid, splendid." Agathios risked a smile and discovered that it fit his face well. "You shall prepare the oath for me and I the dispensation for you, and all will be amicable, *and* you will remain in Videssos the city."

"So I will." Maniakes pointed at the patriarch as something else occurred to him. "The dispensation will need to have a clause rescinding any penalties you've set for the holy Philetos because he performed the marriage ceremony for Lysia and me."

"Your Majesty is loyal to those who serve him," Agathios observed, the smile fading. When he spoke again, after a moment's silence, it was as if he was reminding himself: "Such loyalty is a virtue. The clause shall appear as you request."

"I'll be as loyal to you, most holy sir," Maniakes promised, and the patriarch cheered up again.

Maniakes and Lysia peered through the grillwork that screened off the imperial niche in the High Temple. Maniakes had stored the parchment with the text of Agathios' dispensation with other vital state documents; he presumed the ecumenical patriarch had done something similar with his written pledge not to abandon Videssos the city save under the most dire of circumstances.

"The temple is packed today," Lysia said. Sure enough, nobles had trouble finding space in the pews because so many common people had come to hear the patriarch's promised proclamation.

"Better to let Agathios make the announcement than for me to do it," Maniakes answered. "If I did, it would seem as if I forced the agreement down his throat. Coming from him, it'll be a triumph of reason for both sides."

He started to say more, but the congregants below suddenly quieted, signaling that the patriarch was making his way to the altar. Sure enough, here came Agathios, with censer-swinging priests of lower rank accompanying him and filling the High Temple with sweet-smelling smoke.

When the patriarch reached the altar, he raised his hands to the great stern image of Phos in the dome of the High Temple. The worshipers sitting on all sides of the altar rose; behind the screening grillwork, so did Maniakes and Lysia. They intoned Phos' creed along with Agathios and the rest of the congregants: "We bless thee, Phos, lord with the great and good mind, by thy grace our protector, watchful beforehand that the great test of life may be decided in our favor."

Maniakes took less pleasure in the liturgy than he usually did. Instead of joining him to his fellow believers throughout the Empire, today it seemed to separate him from what he really waited for: Agathios' sermon. His prayers felt perfunctory, springing more from his mouth than from his heart.

Agathios led the worshipers in the creed again, then slowly lowered his hands to urge them back into their seats. Everyone stared intently at him. He stood silent, milking the moment, letting the tension build. "He should be a mime," Lysia whispered to Maniakes. He nodded but waved her to silence.

"Rejoice!" Agathios cried suddenly, his voice filling the High Temple and echoing back from the dome. "Rejoice!" he repeated in softer tones. "His Majesty the Avtokrator has sworn by the lord with the great and good mind to rule the Empire of Videssos from Videssos the city so long as hope remains with us."

Rumor had said as much, these past few days, but rumor was known to lie. For that matter, patriarchs were also known to lie, but less often. The High Temple rang with cheers. They, too, came rolling back from the dome, filling the huge open space below with sound.

"They love you," Lysia said.

"They approve of me because I'm staying," Maniakes answered, shaking his head. "They'd be howling for my blood if Agathios had just told them I'd be sailing day after tomorrow."

Before Lysia could respond to that, Agathios was continuing: "Surely Phos will bless the Avtokrator, his viceregent on earth, for this brave and wise choice, and will also pour his blessings down on the queen of cities here so that it remains our imperial capital forevermore. So may it be!"

"So may it be!" everyone echoed, Maniakes' voice loud among the rest. He tensed as he waited for Agathios to go on. The patriarch had set forth what he had got from Maniakes. How would he present what he had given up?

Agathios' hesitation this time wasn't to build tension. He was like most men: he had trouble admitting he had needed to concede anything. At last, he said, "His Majesty the Avtokrator bears a heavy burden and must struggle valiantly to restore Videssos' fortunes. Any aid he can find in that struggle is a boon to him. We all know of the tragic loss of his wife—his first wife—who died giving birth to Likarios, his son and heir."

Maniakes frowned. It wasn't really the patriarch's business to fix the succession, even though what he said agreed with what the Avtokrator had established. He glanced over at Lysia. She showed no signs of annoyance. Maniakes decided to let it go. In any case, Agathios was continuing: "All this being said, on reflection I have determined that a dispensation recognizing and declaring licit in all ways the marriage between his Majesty the Avtokrator and the Empress Lysia will serve the Empire of Videssos without compromising the long-established holy dogmas of the temples, and have accordingly granted them the aforesaid dispensation."

At his words, a priest near the altar set down his thurible and strode out of the High Temple, presumably in protest. Out went Kourikos and Phevronia, too. The logothete of the treasury was willing to go on working with Maniakes, but not to be seen approving of his marriage. Another priest left the High Temple, and a few more layfolk, too.

But the large majority of worshipers and clerics stayed where they were. Agathios had not presented his bargain with Maniakes as the this-for-that exchange it was at bottom. That probably helped reconcile some of the congregants to the arrangement. And others would be relieved enough to hear that Maniakes was staying in Videssos the city that they wouldn't care how Agathios had got him to do so.

The patriarch stood straighter when he saw his announcement was not going to set off riots under the temple's dome. "The liturgy is ended," he said, and Maniakes could almost hear him adding, *and I got away with it, too.* A buzz of talk rose from the congregants as they made their way out to the mundane world once more. Maniakes tried to make out what they were saying but had little luck.

He turned to Lysia. "How does it feel to be my proper wife in the eyes of all—" *Well, most,* he thought. "—the clerics in the Empire?"

"Except for morning sickness, it feels fine," she answered. "But then, it felt fine before, too."

"Good," Maniakes said.

If Maniakes stood on the seawall and looked west over the Cattle Crossing, he could see smoke rising from the Makuraner army's encampments in Across. And now, if he stood at the northern edge of the capital's land wall, he could look north and see smoke rising from the suburbs the Kubratoi were burning. Refugees streamed into Videssos the city from the north, some in wagons with most of their goods, others without even shoes on their feet. Monasteries and convents did what they could to feed and shelter the fugitives.

Maniakes sent the religious foundations a little gold and a little grain to help them bear the burden. That was all he could do. With the Makuraners holding the westlands and the Kubratoi swooping down toward the capital, the lands recognizing his authority were straitened indeed.

He visited a monastery common room. For one thing, he wanted to show the refugees he knew they were suffering. The fervent greetings he got made him uneasily aware of how much power his office held over the hearts and minds and spirits of the Videssian people. Had he sailed off to Kalavria, they might indeed have lost hope—though he had no intention of ever admitting that to Agathios.

He also wanted to get a feel for what the Kubratoi had in mind with their invasion. "I just saw maybe ten or twenty," one man said in a rustic accent. "Didn't wait for no more—not me, your Majesty. I hightailed it fast as I could go."

"Saw 'em out on some flat ground," another fellow said. "They weren't bunched up or nothin'—ridin' along all kind of higgledy-piggledy, like."

"They would have got me sure," a third man offered, his face breaking out in sweat as he recalled his escape, "only they stopped to kill my pigs and loot my house and so I was able to get away."

The stories confirmed what Maniakes had come to believe from other reports: unlike the Makuraners, the Kubratoi did not plan to make any permanent conquests. They had swarmed into Videssos for loot and rape and destruction, and spread themselves thin across the landscape.

He summoned his father and Rhegorios to a council of war. "If we can catch them before they're able to concentrate, we'll maul them," he said.

"I ask the question you would want me to ask," Rhegorios said: "Are you looking for us to do more than we can?"

"And here's another question along with that one," the elder Maniakes added. "So what if we do beat them? They'll just scoot back to Kubrat, faster than we can chase them. When they ride north, they'll torch whatever they missed burning on the way south. Even a win seems hardly worth it."

"No, that's not so, or at least I think I have a way to make it not so." The Avtokrator pointed to the map of the region north of Videssos the city that lay on the table in front of him. He talked for some time.

When he was through, the elder Maniakes and Rhegorios looked at each other. "If I'd been so sneaky when I was so young," the elder Maniakes rumbled, "I'd have had the red boots instead of Likinios, and you, lad—" He pointed at Maniakes. "—would be standing around waiting for me to die."

Before Maniakes could say anything to that, Rhegorios declared, "It all still depends on that first victory."

"What doesn't?" Maniakes said. "If we do go wrong, though,

we'll be able to retreat inside the walls of Videssos the city. We won't be caught in a place where we can be hunted down and slaughtered." He slammed his fist onto the tabletop. "I don't want to think about retreat, not now." He hit the table again. "No, that's not right—I know I need to think about it. But I don't want the men to know it's ever crossed my mind, or else it'll be in the back of theirs."

"Ah, there you come down to the rub," the elder Maniakes said. "But you're going to try this scheme of yours?"

Maniakes remembered the ambush Etzilios had set, remembered his failure in the campaign up the valley of the Arandos. As Rhegorios had said, he had tried to do too much in both of them. Was he making the same mistake now? He decided it didn't matter. "I will try it," he said. "We aren't strong enough to wrest the westlands away from Makuran. If we also aren't strong enough to keep the Kubratoi away from Videssos the city, I might as well have sailed to Kalavria, because it would be about the only place our foes couldn't come after me. That was one of the reasons I wanted to go there."

"Always Haloga pirates," Rhegorios said helpfully.

"Thank you so much, cousin and brother-in-law of mine," Maniakes said. "Does either of you think the risk isn't worth taking?" If anyone would tell him the truth, his father and cousin would. They both sat silent. Maniakes slammed his fist down on the table for a third time. "We'll try it."

Sunburst banners flapping in the breeze, Maniakes' army rode forth from the Silver Gate. The Avtokrator glanced south toward the practice field where his soldiers had spent so much time at drill. This was no drill. This was war. Now he would find out how much the men had learned.

Scouts galloped out ahead of the main body. Finding the foe would not be hard, not at the start of this campaign. All Maniakes had to do was lead his army toward the thickest smoke. He absently wondered why all warriors, regardless of their nation, so loved to set fires. But finding the foe was not the only reason to send out scouts. You also wanted to make sure the foe did not find you before you were ready.

"Haven't been on campaign in a goodish while," Symvatios said, riding up alongside Maniakes. "If you don't do this every year, you forget how heavy chainmail gets—and I'm not as young as I used to be, not quite." He chuckled. "I expect I'll still remember what needs doing, though."

"Uncle, I'm sorry to have to ask you to come along, but I'm short a couple of senior officers," Maniakes answered. "If Tzikas has a command these days, it's on the wrong side, and Parsmanios—" He didn't go on. That grief wouldn't leave him soon, if ever.

"I am a senior officer, by the good god," Symvatios agreed, laughing again. He had always been more easygoing than the elder Maniakes. "Not quite ready for the boneyard, though I hope to show you."

What Maniakes hoped was that his uncle would have the sense not to get mixed up in hand-to-hand fighting with barbarous warriors a third his age. He didn't say that, for fear of piquing Symvatios and making him rush into danger to prove he could still meet it bravely.

Towns and nobles' villas and estates clustered close to the imperial capital: rich pickings for raiders who managed to get so far south. The Kubratoi had managed. Maniakes' troopers ran into them on the afternoon of the day they had left Videssos the city.

When the scouts came pounding back with the news, the first question Maniakes asked was, "Are we riding into an ambush?"

"No, your Majesty," one of the horsemen assured him. "The barbarians—a couple of hundred of 'em, I'd guess—never spied us. They were busy plundering the little village they were at, and there's open country beyond it, so nobody's lurking there waiting to jump us."

"All right, we'll hit them." Maniakes slammed a fist down on the mailcoat that covered his thighs. He turned to Symvatios. "Hammer and anvil."

"Right you are," his uncle answered. "That's the way we'll be running this whole campaign, isn't it?" He called orders to the regiments he commanded: no horn signals now, for fear of alerting the foe. His detachment peeled off from the main force and rode away to the northeast on a long swing around the hamlet the nomads were looting.

Maniakes made the main force wait half an hour, then waved them forward. Following the scouts, he headed almost straight for the Kubrati-infested village: he swung his troopers slightly westward, to come on the Kubratoi from the southwest.

That worked out even better than he had expected, for an almond grove screened his approach from the Kubratoi. Only when the first ranks of Videssian horsemen rode out from the cover of the trees did the barbarians take alarm. Their frightened shouts were music to his ears. He shouted for music of his own. Now the trumpeters blared forth the charge.

A lot of the Kubratoi had dismounted. Several of them stood around waiting their turn with a luckless, screaming woman who hadn't been able to flee. The fellow who lay atop her at the moment sprang to his feet and tried to run for his steppe pony, but tripped over the leather breeches he hadn't fully raised. When the first arrow penetrated him, he screamed louder than the woman had. A couple of more hits and he sagged to the ground once more and lay still.

Arrows came back toward the Videssians, too, but not many. Most of the nomads who were on horseback or could get to their ponies rode away from the oncoming imperial force as fast as they could. "Push them!" Maniakes called to his men. "Don't let them think of anything but running."

Run the Kubratoi did. A lot of them outdistanced their pursuers, too, for the boiled leather they wore was lighter than the Videssians' ironmongery. And then, from straight ahead of them, more Videssian horn calls rang out. The nomads cried out in dismay: in running from Maniakes' horsemen, they had run right into the soldiers Symvatios commanded.

Trapped between the two Videssian forces, the Kubratoi fought as best they could, but were quickly overwhelmed. Maniakes hoped they had perished to the last man, but knew how unlikely that was. He had to assume a couple of them had escaped to warn their fellows he was in the field.

As fights went, it wasn't much, and Maniakes knew it. The Videssian army, though, had been without victories for so long that even a tiny one made the soldiers feel as if they had just sacked Mashiz. They sat around the campfires that evening, drinking rough wine from the supply wagons and talking in quick, excited voices about what they had done—even if a lot of them, in truth, had done very little.

"Hammer and anvil," Symvatios said, lifting a clay mug to Maniakes in salute.

Maniakes drank with his uncle. Kameas had wanted to pack

some fine vintages for him. This time, he hadn't let the vestiarios get away with it. Wine that snarled when it hit the palate was what you were supposed to drink when you took the field. If nothing else, it made you mean.

"We have to do this three more times, I think," the Avtokrator said. "If we manage that . . ." He let the sentence hang there. Fate had delivered too many blows to Videssos for him to risk tempting it now. He drained his mug and said, "You made a fine anvil, Uncle."

"Aye, well, my hard head suits me to the role," Symvatios replied, laughing. He quickly grew more serious. "We won't be able to work it the same way in every fight, you know. The ground will be different, the Kubratoi will be a little more alert than they were today. . . ."

"It'll get harder; I know that," Maniakes said. "I'm glad we had an easy first one, that's all. What we have to do is make sure that we don't do anything stupid and give the Kubratoi an edge they shouldn't have."

"You've got enough scouts and sentries out, and you've posted them far enough away from our camp," Symvatios said. "The only way Etzilios could surprise us would be to fall out of the sky."

"Good." Maniakes cast a wary eye heavenward. Symvatios laughed again. The Avtokrator didn't.

About noon the next day, the scouts came upon a good-sized band of Kubratoi. This time they were seen—and pursued. Some fought a rearguard action while others brought the news to Maniakes. He listened to them, then turned to Symvatios. "Move up with your detachment," he said. "Make as if you're at the head of the whole army. While they're engaging you, I'll swing wide and try to take them in flank."

His uncle saluted. "We'll see how it goes, your Majesty: a sideways hammer blow, but I think a good one. My guess is, the nomads don't yet know how many men we've put in the field."

"I think you're right," Maniakes said. "With luck, you'll fool them into believing you're at the head of the whole force. Once they're well engaged with you . . ."

Banners flapping and horns blaring, Symvatios led his detachment forward to support the Videssian scouts. Maniakes hung back and swung off to the east, using low, scrubbily wooded hills to screen his men from the notice of the nomads. Less than an hour passed before a rider galloped over to let him know the Kubratoi were locked in combat with Symvatios' troopers. "There's enough to give them a hard time, too, your Majesty," the fellow said.

Plenty of east-west tracks ran through the hills; this close to Videssos the city, roads crisscrossed the land like spiderwebs. Maniakes divided his force into three columns, to get all his men through as fast as he could. Again, he sent scouting parties ahead to make sure the Kubratoi weren't lying in wait in the woods. Even after the scouts went through safe, his head swiveled back and forth, watching the oaks and elms and ashes for concealed nomads.

All three columns came through the hill country unmolested. There on the flat farm country ahead, the Kubratoi were trading arrows and swordstrokes with Symvatios' detachment. The nomads were trying to wheel around to Symvatios' right; he was having trouble shifting enough men fast enough to defend against them. As the messenger had said, the Kubratoi were there in considerable force.

Their outflanking maneuver, though, left them between Symvatios' troopers and Maniakes' emerging army. The Avtokrator heard the shouts of dismay that went up from them when they realized as much. His own men shouted, too. Hearing his name burst as a war cry from thousands of throats made excitement surge through him, as if he had had too much of the rough camp wine.

The Kubratoi tried to break off their fight with Symvatios' men and flee, but the soldiers from the detachment pressed them hard. And then Maniakes' men were on them, shooting arrows, flinging javelins, and slashing with swords. The Videssians fought more ferociously than they had since the days of Likinios, now almost ten years gone. The Kubratoi scattered before them, madly galloping in all different directions trying to escape.

Maniakes called a halt to the pursuit only when darkness began to render it dangerous. "Like lions they fought," Symvatios exclaimed as they made camp. "Like lions. I remembered they could, but I hadn't seen it in so long, I'd started to have doubts."

"And I," Maniakes agreed. "Nothing like the sight of the enemy's back to make you think you're a hero, is there?"

"Aye, that's a sovereign remedy," Symvatios said. Not far away, a wounded man groaned and bit back a scream as a surgeon dug out an arrowhead. Symvatios' jubilation ebbed. "Heroing doesn't come free, worse luck."

"What does?" Maniakes said, to which his uncle spread his hands. The Avtokrator went on, "Etzilios will know we're out and after him: no way now he can help but know it. He's used to beating us, too. We may not have two fights ahead of us before we put our plan to the full test. We may have only one."

"Behooves us to win that one, too, so it does," Symvatios said.

"Now that you mention it, yes," Maniakes answered dryly. "If we lose, there's not much point to the rest, is there?"

The Videssian army pressed north unchallenged for the next day and a half. They overran a few small bands of Kubratoi, but most of the nomads seemed to have already fled before them. The relative tranquility did not ease Maniakes' mind. Somewhere ahead or off to one flank, Etzilios waited.

When the army moved, a cloud of scouts surrounded it to the front and rear and either side. If Etzilios wanted to strike, he could. He would not take Maniakes by surprise doing it. Whenever the army approached woods, the Avtokrator sent whole companies of troopers probing into them. He was beginning to believe his men would keep on fighting well, but he wanted them to do it on his terms, not those of the khagan of Kubrat.

A scout came riding back toward him. Alongside the cavalryman was a fellow in peasant homespun riding a donkey that had seen better days. The scout nudged the farmer, who said, "Your Majesty, uh—" and then couldn't go on, made modest or awestruck or perhaps just frightened at the prospect of addressing his sovereign.

The scout spoke for him: "Your Majesty, he's fleeing from the northwest. He told me all the Kubratoi in the world—that's what he said—were gathering close by his plot of land, and he didn't care to stay around to find out what they would do." The trooper chuckled. "Can't say as I blame him, either."

"Nor I." Maniakes turned to the peasant. "Where is your plot? How far had you come before the soldier found you?"

When the farmer still proved incapable of speech, the trooper once more answered for him: "He's well south of Varna, your Majesty. We can't be more than half a day's ride from the nomads."

"We'll halt here, then," Maniakes declared. Hearing his words, the trumpeters who rode close by him blared out the order to stop. Maniakes told the peasant, "A pound of gold for your news."

"Thank you, your Majesty," the fellow cried, money loosening his tongue where everything else had failed.

Maniakes and Symvatios huddled together. "Do you think your men can feign a retreat from the Kubratoi and then turn around and fight when the time comes?" the Avtokrator asked.

"I . . . think so," his uncle answered. "You want to make the fight here, do you? The ground is good—open enough so they can't try much in the way of trickery. And if things go wrong, we'll have a real line of retreat open."

"Aye, though I don't want to think about things going wrong," Maniakes said. "My notion was that, if I pick the ground here, I'll be able to set up the toys the engineers have along in their wagons. No chance for that if Etzilios is the one paying the flute player."

"There you're right," Symvatios said. "So what will you want me to do tomorrow? Ride ahead, find the Kubratoi, and then flee back to you as if I'd fouled my breeches like a mime-show actor?"

"That's the idea," Maniakes agreed. "My hope is, Etzilios will figure us for cowards at heart. My other hope is that he's wrong."

"Would be nice, wouldn't it?" Symvatios said. "If your boys see mine running and take off with them, the Kubratoi will chase us all back to Videssos the city, laughing their heads off and shooting arrows into us every mile of the way. It's happened before."

"Don't remind me," Maniakes said, remembering his own flight from Etzilios. "Tomorrow, though, the good god willing, they'll be the ones who run."

As he had every night since setting out from the capital, he strung sentries out all around the camp. He wouldn't have put a night attack past the Kubrati khagan. Come to that, he wouldn't have put anything past him.

Dew was still on the grass and the air was crisp and cool when Symvatios and his detachment rode north, as proudly and ostentatiously as if they were the whole of the Videssian army. Maniakes arranged the rest of the force in line of battle, with a gap in the center for Symvatios' men to fill. He had plenty of time to brief the troopers and explain what he thought would happen when Symvatios' men came back. While he spoke, engineers unloaded their wagons and assembled their machines with tackle they had brought up from the city. When they asked it of him, Maniakes detailed a cavalry company to help them.

Then there was nothing to do but wait, eat whatever iron rations they had stowed in their saddlebags, and drink bad wine from canteen or skin. The day turned hot and muggy, as Maniakes had known it would. Sweat ran into his eyes, burning like blood. Under his surcoat, under his gilded mailshirt, under the quilted padding he wore beneath it, he felt as if he had just gone into the hot room of the baths.

Scouts rode out of the forest ahead, spurring their horses toward him. Their shouts rang thin over the open ground: "They're coming!" Maniakes waved to the trumpeters, who blew *alert*. Up and down the line, men reached for their weapons. Maniakes drew his sword. Sunlight sparkled off the blade.

Here came Symvatios and his men. Maniakes' heart leapt into his throat when he spied his uncle, who had a bloodstained rag tied round his head. But Symvatios waved at him to show the wound was not serious. He shouldn't have been fighting at all, but Maniakes breathed easier.

Symvatios' rearguard turned in the saddle to shoot arrows at the Kubratoi behind them. The nomads seemed taken aback to discover more Videssians athwart their path, but kept on galloping after Symvatios' men. Their harsh, guttural shouts put Maniakes in mind of so many wild beasts, but they were more clever and deadly than any mere animals.

Maniakes waited till he spied Etzilios' standard and assured himself the khagan was not hanging back. Then he shouted "Videssos!" and waved his troopers into the fight. At the same instant, Symvatios and his hornplayers ordered a rally from his fleeing detachments.

For a dreadful moment, Maniakes feared they would not find it. Videssian armies had done so much real retreating, all through his reign and Genesios' before it—could the detachment, once heading away from the foe, remember its duty, or would it be doomed to repeat the disasters of the past?

He shouted with joy as, behind the screen of the rearguard, Symvatios' troopers reined in, turned their horses, and faced the Kubratoi once more. Fresh flights of arrows arced toward the nomads. Off on either wing, the catapults the engineers had assembled hurled great stones at the onrushing barbarians. One of them squashed a horse like a man kicking a rat with his boot. Another took the head from a Kubrati as neatly as an executioner's sword might have done. Still clutching his bow, he rode on for several strides of his horse before falling from the saddle.

Of themselves, the blows the stone-throwers struck were pinpricks, and only a few pinpricks at that. But the Kubratoi were used to facing death from javelins or swords: not so from flying boulders. Maniakes saw them waver, and also saw their discomfiture at Symvatios' rally.

"Videssos!" he shouted again, and then, "Charge!" The horns screamed out that command. His men shouted, too, as they spurred their horses toward the Kubratoi. Some, like Maniakes, shouted the name of their Empire. More, though, shouted his name. When he heard that, the sword in his hand quivered like a live thing.

The nomads' special skill was shifting from attack to retreat—or the other way round—at a moment's notice. But the Kubratoi at the rear were still pressing forward while the ones at the fore tried to wheel and go back. The Videssians, mounted on bigger, heavier horses and wearing stronger armor, got in among them and thrashed them as they had not been thrashed in years.

"See how it feels, Etzilios?" Maniakes shouted, slashing his way toward the khagan's horsetail standard. "See how it feels to be fooled and trapped and beaten?" He all but howled the last word.

A nomad cut at him. He turned the blow on his shield and gave one back. The Kubrati carried only a tiny leather target. He blocked that first stroke with it, but a second laid his shoulder open. Maniakes heard his cry of pain, but rode past and never knew how he fared after that.

All at once, the entire nomad host realized the snare into which they had rushed. Etzilios felt no shame at fleeing. The Kubratoi were remorselessly practical at war, and waged it for what they could get. If all they were getting was a drubbing, time enough to pull back and try again when chances looked better.

The usual Videssian practice was to let them go once the main engagement was won, the better to avoid sudden and unpleasant reversals. "Pursue!" Maniakes yelled now. "Dog them like hounds! Don't let them regroup, don't let them get away. Today we'll give them what they earned for invading us!"

The nomads' pursuit from Imbros down to Videssos the city had chewed his force to bits and swallowed most of the bits. That was what he wanted to emulate now. He soon saw it was too much to ask of his men. Because they were more heavily accoutered than the Kubratoi, they were also slower. And, unlike Etzilios' warriors, they were used to keeping to their formations rather than breaking up to fight as individuals: thus, the slower troopers held back those who might have been faster.

So they did not destroy the Kubrati host. They did hurt the invaders, running down wounded men, men on wounded horses, and those luckless enough to be riding nags that simply could not run fast. And, every so often, Etzilios' rearguard tried to gain some space between the rest of the Kubratoi and the Videssians. The imperial army rode over them like the tide rolling up the beach near Kastavala.

Maniakes hated to see the sun sink low in the west. "Shall we camp, your Majesty?" soldiers called, still seeking routine though they had broken it by beating the Kubratoi instead of shattering at the nomads' onslaught.

"We'll ride on a while after dark," the Avtokrator answered. "You can bet the Kubratoi won't be resting, not tonight, they won't. They'll want to get as far away from us as they can. And do you know what? We're not going to let them. We won't let them ambush us in the blackness, either. We'll have plenty of scouts and we'll go slower, but we'll keep going."

And keep going they did, sometimes dozing in the saddle, sometimes waking to fight short, savage clashes with foes they could scarcely see. Maniakes was glad when his horse splashed into a stream; the cold water on his legs helped revive him.

When dawn touched the eastern sky with gray, Symvatios looked around and said, "We've outrun the supply wagons."

"We won't starve in the next day or two," Maniakes answered. "Anyone who doesn't have some bread or cheese or sausage or olives with him is a fool, anyhow." He glanced over at his uncle. The bandage made Symvatios look something like a veteran, something like a derelict. "How did you pick that up?"

"By the time we get back to Videssos the city, I'll have a fine, heroic scar," Symvatios answered. "Right now, I just feel like a twit. One of my troopers was hacking away at a Kubrati in front of him, and when he drew back his sword for another stroke—well, my fool head got in the way. Laid me open as neat as if a cursed nomad had done it."

"I won't tell if you don't," Maniakes promised. "You ought to be able to bribe the trooper into keeping his mouth shut, too." They both laughed. Laughing, Maniakes discovered, came easy when you were moving forward

The pursuit went more slowly than it had the day before. Troopers had to go easy on their horses, for fear of foundering them. The Kubratoi gained ground on the imperials, for some of them, in nomad fashion, had remounts available. Etzilios kept on fleeing, though. Now he led the men who had been surprised and beaten and who wanted no more of their foes.

Then, toward late afternoon, a scout galloped back to Maniakes. The fellow urged on his mount as if it had left the stable not a quarter of an hour before. "Your Majesty!" he cried, and then again: "Your Majesty!" He delivered his news with a great shout: "The Kubratoi up ahead, they're fighting!"

"By the good god," Maniakes said softly. He glanced over to Symvatios. The bandage had slipped down so it almost covered one of his uncle's eyes, giving him a distinctly piratical air. Symvatios clenched his right hand into a fist and laid it over his heart in salute. Maniakes turned and spoke to the trumpeters: "Blow *pursuit* once more. Now we give all the effort we have in us. If we can get to the battlefield fast enough, the Kubratoi will take a blow they'll be a long time getting over."

Martial music rang out. Tired men spurred tired horses from walks up to trots. They checked their quivers. Few had many arrows left. The nomads would be in the same straits. Maniakes wished the supply wagons could have kept up with his host. If they had, he would have poured arrows into Etzilios' men till night made him stop.

To his initial startlement, a band of nomads charged straight back toward his forces. Symvatios figured out what that meant, shouting, "Etzilios knows he's in the smithy's shop. Are we going to let him keep the hammer from coming down on the anvil one last time?"

"No!" the Videssian soldiers roared. They were no more

enthusiastic about exposing their bodies to wounds than any men of sense would have been, but, since they had chosen that trade, they did not want their risks to be to no purpose. They surged forward against the Kubratoi, who, badly outnumbered, were soon overwhelmed.

Up ahead, Maniakes saw the rest of the nomads battling a force under sunburst banners deployed directly across their line of retreat. "Hammer and anvil!" he cried, echoing his uncle. "Now we come down."

The wail of despair that rose when the Kubratoi spied his force was music to his ears. He spurred his horse into a shambling gallop. The first Kubrati he met cut at him once, missed, then set spur to his own pony and did his best to escape. A Videssian who still had arrows brought him down as if he were a fleeing fox.

"Maniakes!" shouted the Videssians who kept the Kubratoi from escaping to the north.

"Rhegorios!" Maniakes shouted back, and his troopers took up the call. Now that Maniakes' men had reached the field, his cousin, instead of merely holding the nomads at bay, pressed hard against them. Rhegorios' soldiers were fresh and rested and mounted on horses that hadn't been going hard for a day and a night and most of another day. Their quivers were full. They struck with a force out of proportion to their numbers.

All at once, the Kubratoi opposing them made the fatal transition from army to frightened mob, each man looking no farther than toward what might keep his uniquely precious self alive another few minutes. In that moment of dissolution, Maniakes looked round the field for the horsetail that marked Etzilios' position. He wanted to serve the khagan as he had nearly been served south of Imbros. If he could kill or capture the leader of the Kubratoi, the nomads might fight among themselves for years over the succession.

He saw nothing to show Etzilios' place. As he himself had while fleeing from the Kubrati ambush, the khagan had abandoned the symbol of his station to give himself a better chance of keeping it. "Five pounds of gold to the man who brings me Etzilios, alive or dead!" the Avtokrator cried.

Though the battle was won, and won crushingly, a good many Kubratoi managed to squeeze out from between Maniakes' force and Rhegorios'. Then the light began to fail, which allowed more escapes. No one led Etzilios in bonds before Maniakes or rode up carrying the khagan's dripping head. Maniakes wondered whether he lay anonymously dead on the field or had succeeded in getting away. Time would tell. At the moment, in the midst of triumph, his fate seemed a small thing.

Here came Rhegorios, his handsome face wearing a smile as bright as the sun now setting. "We did it!" he cried, and embraced Maniakes. "By Phos, we did it. Hammer and anvil, and crushed them between us."

"I have two anvils—father and son." Maniakes waved to Symvatios, who sat his horse close by. "So much hope going into this campaign. I had to hope we'd win down south of here, win hard enough and often enough to make the nomads decide pulling back would be a good idea. And then I had to hope you'd put your men in the right spot after Thrax and the fleet carried you up the coast to Varna."

"I almost didn't," Rhegorios said. "The scouts I had out farthest ran up against the Kubratoi fleeing first and fastest. I had to hustle the lads along to get 'em where they'd do the most good in time for them to do it. But we managed." He waved to show the victory Videssian arms had won.

Like most triumphs, this one was better contemplated in song and chronicle than in person. Twilight started to veil the aftermath of battle, but did not completely cover it, not yet. Men and horses lay still and silent in death or twisting in the agony of wounds and screaming their pain to the unhearing sky. The stink of blood and sweat and shit filled Maniakes' nostrils. Hopeful crows hopped not far away, waiting to feast on the banquet of carrion spread before them.

Healer-priests and ordinary physicians and horseleeches strode across the battlefield, doing what they could for injured Videssians and animals. Other men, these still in armor, traveled the field, too, making sure all the Kubratoi on it would never rise from it again. Maniakes wondered if the scavengers could tell the difference between the men who gave them less to eat and those who gave them more.

"May I share your tent tonight?" he asked Rhegorios. "Mine is—back there somewhere," He waved vaguely southward, toward the outrun baggage train.

Rhegorios grinned at him again. "Any man would share with

his brother-in-law. Any man would share with his cousin. Any man would share with his sovereign. And since I can do all three at once and put only one extra man in my tent, how can I say no?"

"Can you spare some space in that crowd of people for your poor feeble father, as well?" Symvatios said. Despite the bandage, he didn't look feeble. He wasn't quite the cool calculator the elder Maniakes was, but he had led his troops bravely and done everything the Avtokrator asked of him. A lot of officers half his age couldn't approach his standard.

Rhegorios' cooks got fires going and stewpots bubbling above them. Hot stew went down wonderfully well after the two hard days just ended. Maniakes sat on the ground inside Rhegorios' tent—after some argument, he and Rhegorios had persuaded Symvatios to take the cot in there—and sipped at a mug of wine. He hoped it wouldn't put him to sleep, or at least not yet. Having won his victory, he wanted to hash it over, too.

"Most important is that the men stood and fought," Rhegorios said. "We couldn't know whether they would till we took 'em out and tried 'em. They didn't waste all that time on the practice field."

"That's so," Maniakes said, nodding. From the cot, Symvatios let out a snore. He hadn't wanted to fall asleep, any more than he had wanted to accept the cot, but however willing his spirit, his flesh was far from young. Maniakes glanced over at him affectionately, then went on, "The other important thing we did was land your men behind the Kubratoi. That turned what would have been a victory into a rout. I wonder if we got Etzilios."

"It was a fine idea," Rhegorios answered. "The nomads are nothing to speak of on the sea. I wish we had run up against some of those little pirate boats of theirs, those *monoxyla*. Thrax's dromons would have smashed 'em to kindling, and we wouldn't have landed an hour late."

Maniakes plucked at his beard. "The Makuraners haven't much in the way of ships, either," he remarked, and then paused to listen to what he had just said. Thoughtfully he went on, "We've taken advantage of that in small ways already, landing raiders in the westlands and so forth. But we could move along the coasts by sea faster than Abivard could shift his forces by land trying to keep up with us. We could . . ."

"Provided we have troops who won't piss their drawers the first time the boiler boys come thundering down on them," Rhegorios said. Then he too looked thoughtful. "We're on our way to getting troops like that, aren't we?"

"Either we're on our way or else we have them now," Maniakes said. "Going over the Cattle Crossing and ramming headlong into the Makuraners always struck me as the wrong way to go about clearing them from the westlands, and a good recipe for getting beat, to boot. Now maybe we have another choice."

"No guarantees," Rhegorios said.

Maniakes' laugh held a bitter edge. "What in life has any guarantees?" He remembered Niphone's face, pale and still, as she lay in her sarcophagus. "You do as well as you can for as long as you can. If we're not going to let the Makuraners keep the westlands, we'll have to drive them out. Making them move to respond to us would be a pleasant change, don't you think?"

"You get no arguments from me there," Rhegorios answered. "I'd love to see them scurrying about instead of us. Can we do it this summer, do you think?"

"I don't know," Maniakes said. "We'll have to go back to Videssos the city and see how long we'll need to refit, how many men we can pull together, how many ships we have. We'd have a surer chance of doing it if Etzilios hadn't jumped on us, curse him."

"You may end up thanking him one of these days," Rhegorios said. "You might never have come up with this idea if he hadn't invaded."

"There is that," the Avtokrator admitted. "Sooner or later, though, I think I would have. It's the best choice we've got. It may be the only choice we've got. Whether it's good enough—we'll find out."